LETHALLY
BLOND

Also by Kate White

LETHALLY BLOND

KATE WHITE

WARNER BOOKS

NEW YORK   BOSTON

Warner Books
Hachette Book Group USA
237 Park Avenue
New York, NY 10169

Visit our Web site at www.HachetteBookGroupUSA.com.

Printed in the United States of America

First Edition: May 2007
10 9 8 7 6 5 4 3 2 1

Warner Books and the "W" logo are trademarks of Time Warner Inc. or an affiliated company. Used under license by Hachette Book Group USA, which is not affiliated with Time Warner Inc.

Library of Congress Cataloging-in-Publication Data
White, Kate
    Lethally blond / Kate White. — 1st ed.
       p. cm.
    ISBN: 978-0-446-57795-3
    1. Women journalists—Fiction. I. Title.
    PS3623.H578L48 2007
    813'.6—dc22   2007000447

To Laura, wonderful
friend and fabulous blonde

ACKNOWLEDGMENTS

First and foremost I'd like to thank my wonderful editor Karen Kosztolnyik for her guidance and my fab, gutsy agent Sandy Dijkstra for her support, as well as her amazing team, including Taryn and Elise. And then there were the people who were so generous in helping me with my research, which is one of the best parts of writing: Kate Carcaterra; Barry Cunningham, television journalist; Barbara Butcher, director of forensic investigations, NYC Office of Chief Medical Examiner; Brad Holbrook, actor; Mark Howell, psychotherapist; Angela Jones, aerialist; Paul Paganelli, MD, chief of emergency medicine, Milton Hospital, Milton, MA; Trinka Porrata, drug consultant and retired LAPD detective; Richard Spencer, editor in chief, *In Touch*; Sheila Weller, author and journalist; Lt. Gene Whyte, DCPI, NYPD.

LETHALLY BLOND

CHAPTER 1

It all started with a coincidence. Not one of those totally creepy coincidences that make you feel as if someone has just walked across your grave. In fact, later I could see that the phone call I got that late summer night wasn't all that unexpected—but at the time it made me catch my breath. And, of course, it was the start of everything horrible that happened. . . .

I'd decided to stop by the office that day, something I rarely do on Tuesdays. It was crazy hot for the middle of September, and it would have been nice to just hang on the brick terrace of my apartment in Greenwich Village, chugging a few iced teas. But a new deputy editor had started recently—Valerie Crowe, a hyper, edgy chick who left you overwhelmed with an urge to shoot a tranquilizer dart into her ass—and I thought it would be smart to give her some face time. My copy goes through the executive editor, but it's one of the deputy editors who assigns me most of my stories and often suggests leads for me to follow up on. Since Tuesday is the day after closing, I knew she'd probably have a few minutes to spare. Most of the staff never even gets in before noon that day.

My name is Bailey Weggins, and I'm a reporter for *Buzz,* one of the weekly celebrity gossip magazines that have become like crack cocaine for women under thirty-five these days. Unlike most of the staff, I don't cover the botched marriages and bulimic ordeals of the stars. Instead, I report on celebrity crime—like when an A-lister hurls a phone at a hotel desk clerk or hires a hit man to shoot his wife.

It's not something I'd ever imagined myself doing. I was a straight crime writer for the ten years after college graduation, but when the job opened up early in the summer, curiosity and the need for a regular gig prodded me to take it.

"Celebrity crime reporter—are you saying it's some sort of specialized area of journalism?" my mother had asked at the time, as if it were on a par with becoming a pediatric neurosurgeon or astrophysicist.

Initially, I was at a disadvantage because I didn't know—excuse the expression—jackshit about celebrities. Oh, I'd picked up tidbits about the really major stars—you know, like Brad and Angelina and Gwyneth and TomKat—from listening to friends dish as well as perusing gossip magazines during pedicures. But I was clueless about most of the other stars in the celebrity universe. In fact, until two weeks into my job at *Buzz,* I'd thought Jake Gyllenhaal and Orlando Bloom were the *same person.* But I caught on pretty quickly, and to my surprise, I grew to really enjoy my two-to-three-day-a-week arrangement. Celebrities not only live large, they misbehave large, too. Covering their crimes, I discovered, could be awfully entertaining.

One more plus. In November, a small publishing house was releasing a collection of my crime pieces, *Bad Men and Wicked Women,* and the job would be leverage for PR.

The *Buzz* offices were practically tomblike when I stepped off the elevator, though it was mercifully cool, as if the low body count had prevented the air from rising above 65 degrees that day. I nodded to a few people as I walked through the huge cube farm/bullpen that constitutes a major chunk of our offices. I'm in a part of that area nicknamed the Pod, which abuts the art and production departments and houses many of the writers and junior editors. The senior editors are in glass-fronted offices that rim the area. My workstation is right next to that of a senior writer named Jessie Pendergrass and behind Leo Zern, a photo editor they couldn't find room for in the photo department.

"Hey," I said to Leo as I tossed my purse and tote bag onto my desk. He was the only one in the general vicinity. He tore his eyes off his computer screen and swiveled just his head in my direction.

"To what do we owe this honor?" he asked. "I thought you weren't coming in today."

"I had a few things I wanted to take care of. Jessie around?"

"She's not in yet. I heard her tell someone on the phone yesterday that her bikini line was a disaster, so maybe she's having it administered to."

"Anything going on here?"

"Not really. Oh, there was a little bit of a dustup this morning. You know how we said Britney Spears looked like a Smurf?"

"No. Okay, I'll take your word for it."

"Nash got a phone call today, and the fur was flying." He was talking about Nash Nolan, the editor in chief.

"From Britney's publicist?"

"No, it was from a *Smurf* representative. They don't want to be compared to her."

"Very funny. So what are you working on?" I sidled over to his desk and checked out the computer screen. There was a grainy shot of a blond starlet type I didn't recognize sitting at an outdoor restaurant, jamming half a dozen French fries into her mouth as if she were stuffing dirty clothes into an overfilled hamper. "God, the paparazzi don't let these chicks alone, do they," I said.

"The ones who take these shots don't consider themselves paparazzi," he said. "They're *snackarazzi.*"

"You're kidding, right?"

"Not at all. These are the real money shots these days. They're almost as good as one of a star scratching her ass."

"Remind me not to order a double bacon cheeseburger the next time I'm at a sidewalk café."

"I think *you're* safe, Bailey," he said, smirking.

I checked my e-mail and then a bunch of Web sites to see if any A-listers had landed themselves in hot water that day, but things seemed fairly quiet. After grabbing a cup of coffee, I wandered down to the office of the new deputy editor.

"Hi, Val," I said, poking my head in the door and forcing a smile. I've always wished I were good at office politics, but fawning and bullshitting just don't come easily to me, particularly if the person at the other end is a real jerk, which I suspected Valerie was. A guy I used to work with at the *Albany Times Union,* when I was a newspaper reporter right out of college, said that I butt-kissed about as well as a blowtorch.

"What can I do for you?" Valerie asked without enthusiasm. Her dark hair was slicked off her face today, accentuating the large sharp nose she sported between brown eyes. She reminded me of how our family dog used to look when he emerged sopping wet from a pond.

"Just thought I'd check in—see if you needed me for anything," I told her.

"What are you working on now?" she asked, a thin layer of impatience coating her question.

Gosh, I thought, you just don't like me, *do* you? But I couldn't tell why. She'd arrived at the magazine not long after the previous editor in chief, Mona Hodges, had been killed in her office by several blows to the head. It had been a tumultuous time, particularly for me, for not only had I found Mona that night, but I also had later figured out who had murdered her, nearly getting killed myself in the process. Nash, the number two at the time, had been named editor in chief shortly afterward; a deputy editor had taken over for Nash, and now Valerie had the deputy job. I sometimes wondered if she resented the fact that Nash and I were tight and that I had plenty of autonomy.

"Nothing major at the moment," I told her. "Just following a few leads. I probably won't come in again this week unless something breaks."

"Just let Aubrey know," she said, referring to the managing editor. Then she glanced over at her computer screen as if she were dying to get back to work.

"Sure," I said, and walked off. How nice that I'd bothered to take the subway up from the Village.

As long as I was at the office, I followed up with staffers on a few matters and polished off another cup of coffee. And then, with nothing more to do, I stood up to go.

"Oh, Bailey, I know what your favorite TV show is going to be this season," Leo said as I was shutting off my computer. "Have you seen the fall lineup?"

"No, but let me guess. *Survivor—The New York Singles Scene*?"

"Nope. A new show called *Morgue*. It's about investigators from the medical examiner's office. Sounds perfect for someone with your grisly interests."

"Aren't there a million shows like that already?" I asked.

"I guess the public can't get enough of them."

Just to humor Leo, I sauntered over to his desk and glanced down at his computer screen. Along with the description of the show, there were a few shots from episodes and a group photo of the ensemble cast, all perfectly coiffed and smileless, their eyes burning with desire to see justice done and have the show win its time slot in the ratings. Suddenly I felt my jaw drop. One of the actors I was staring at in the ensemble cast was Chris Wickersham. He was a model and actor I'd had a short fling with last winter.

"Oh, wow," I said.

"What—you think you're really gonna like it?"

"No, the guy on the far left. I know him."

"Really?" he said as he glanced back at the screen. "You mean—Chris Wickersham, who plays Jared Hanson, the sometimes moody but brilliantly intuitive investigator? Is he straight?"

"Very. It says it's about the New York City Morgue. Does that mean it's shooting here?"

"Not necessarily. Lemme see . . . Yes, shot entirely in New York City. Was this guy your boyfriend?"

"Sort of. For about four seconds. Is there anything else?"

"No, just that it premieres in two weeks."

"Look, I'd better fly. Tell Jessie hi for me, will you?"

I grabbed my purse and tote bag and headed out of the building. My mind was racing, thinking of what I'd just learned about Chris. The last time I had laid eyes on him was right before he'd struck out for L.A. last March, hoping like millions of other guys with dreamy eyes and perfect jawlines to be cast in a pilot for the fall. We hadn't promised each other anything about staying in touch (though early on he'd sent two e-mails and one goofy postcard of the Hollywood sign), and I'd just assumed he hadn't met with any real success yet. But he had. And based on the public love of carnage and corpses, there was every chance the show would be a success. I felt happy for Chris; he deserved fame and fortune. But at the same time, there was something vaguely disconcerting about the whole thing that I couldn't put my finger on. Maybe it was knowing that a guy I'd locked lips with was now poised to become the kind of hottie women across America drooled over and dished about the next day at the watercooler.

I took the subway to 8th and Broadway, hit the gym for thirty minutes, grabbed a few supplies at the deli, and then headed to my apartment at 9th and Broadway. Though I'd left home only a few hours earlier, my place was stifling hot. I turned on the AC, fixed an ice water, and flopped on the couch. As I took the first sip of my drink, I let memories of Chris Wickersham run roughshod around my brain. I had met him a year ago April, at a wedding, where he had worked as one of the bartenders, supplementing the money he made from modeling and small acting gigs. He was absolutely gorgeous, the kind of guy it almost hurt to look at.

Though he took my number and called me, I'd blown him off. He was ten years younger than me, and though that kind of age gap hadn't bothered Cameron Diaz or Demi Moore, I just couldn't imagine having a boyfriend I was old enough to have baby-sat for. Then, nine months later, we'd reconnected when I'd needed his help during a murder investigation. I was dating a guy named Jack steadily by then, and I tried not to send any of the wrong messages to Chris, but one night he had kissed me and I'd felt it all the way to my tippy toes. It was the beginning of my doubts about my relationship with Jack. Soon afterward I was single again. Chris and I had a few dates and some serious make-out sessions, but I'd been unable to take the relationship—sexually and otherwise—beyond that. One of the last things Chris had said to me was, "Jeez, Bailey, what *is* it with you—yes or no?" In the end, it had been no. In hindsight, I thought my doubts might have been due to guilt. I always associated Chris with my breakup.

If I met him today, would I still feel those doubts? I wondered. What would it be like to date a guy millions of people watched on TV? Christ, Bailey, I thought, you're starting to sound like a star fucker.

I drained the last of my water. I'd planned to stay in tonight to work on a freelance article. Plus, ever since I'd had my heart bruised during the summer by a guy named Beau Regan, I'd been lying low. But thanks to the heat wave, the idea now held nada appeal. I wondered who I might be able to drum up for companionship on short notice. My seventy-year-old next-door neighbor, Landon, who I sometimes palled around with, had said he was heading over to the Film Forum on West Houston Street to see a German flick. A college pal of mine from Brown had recently split with her husband, and she was game for anything that provided escape from her apartment, but an evening in her company could be exhausting. She tended to ask an endless series of borderline-hostile questions that were impossible for me to answer—like "Are all men dickheads or just the ones I meet?" "Who would *drink* a prickly pear martini, do you know?" and "Do *you* think I'm brimming with anger?"

Maybe I would just head out alone and eat a quiet dinner outdoors at one of the restaurants over on MacDougal. As I padded toward my bedroom to change, my cell phone buzzed from my purse, making me jump.

"Hello," I said after digging it out.

"Bailey?"

"Yes."

"Hi, it's Chris Wickersham."

For a moment, I thought it was Leo playing a practical joke. But he wouldn't have been familiar with that deep, smooth voice—so I knew for certain it had to be Chris. I caught my breath, stunned by the eeriness of the timing.

"Oh, my gosh," I said. "I—I was just reading about you two hours ago. Congratulations—I, er, heard about the show."

God, Bailey, this is why you *write* professionally, I thought. You shouldn't be allowed to open your mouth.

"Thanks," he said. "The opportunity kind of came out of nowhere. I've been planning to call you—I mean, just to say hello."

"So you're back in New York?"

"Yeah—I've got a studio in TriBeCa. I don't want to overextend myself until I know if the show is going to take off or not."

"Is the shooting schedule as brutal as you hear?"

"Fourteen-hour days, sometimes. But this is what I wanted, and I've got no complaints. The show kicks off in a couple of weeks, and then we play the ratings game."

"It sounds like a super idea for a show—I'm sure it will be a hit."

"Kind of your type of show, huh?"

"You're the second person who said that today."

"Well, look, the reason I called . . . I mean, I wanted to say hi, but—is there any chance you could meet me for a drink? There's something I need to talk to you about."

"Sure," I said. His tone didn't suggest a man who'd been pining for me for months and had decided to make one last stab at winning my heart, but I was still curious. "When were you thinking?"

"I know this is short notice, but I was wondering if you could do it now. It's really pretty urgent. You're the one person I can turn to on this."

"What is it? Are you in some kind of trouble?"

"No, no. But a friend of mine may be. I need your advice."

"Can you give me a hint?" I asked, though I figured that if a guy he knew was in trouble, it had to involve drugs or money or both.

"It— Look, would you mind talking about it in person? I hate the idea of starting to get into it on the phone and then having to cover the same ground again when we meet."

"Well, I *could* do it now, actually," I admitted. "I was planning to stay in and work tonight, but it can wait."

"That's terrific," he said. He suggested we meet in an hour and asked me to recommend a place near me. I threw out the name of a bar on Second Avenue between 9th and 10th. It would take me less than five minutes to walk there.

After signing off, I walked distractedly into the bathroom and splashed cool water on my face and in my armpits. I couldn't believe what had just happened. Maybe it was my destiny that Chris Wickersham would pop into my life every nine months or so. I wondered if there was any chance that he was using a so-called problem with a friend as an excuse to make contact with me. It had been hard to tell on the phone. And I wasn't at all sure how I'd feel when I saw him. I had never once stopped finding him staggeringly attractive. Perhaps now that I was no longer guilt stricken—and my love life was currently in the Dumpster with a capital D—I would feel the urge to go for it this time.

Covering my bets, I wore a pair of tight jeans and a flowy turquoise baby doll top with a V deep enough for me to flash some cleavage. I smoothed my blondish brown hair and applied just enough eye shadow, mascara, blush, and lip gloss to keep from looking as if I'd tried as hard as I had.

He wasn't in the bar when I arrived. I found a free table by the front window and ordered a Corona. Taking a sip of the icy cold beer from the bottle, I watched people stroll along the pavement in the September dusk. A couple of guys stared through the glass at me, and one even shot me a flirty smile. I realized suddenly how nice it was to be sitting in a slutty top, waiting for a hunk—even if it wasn't really a date. Along with my heart, Beau Regan had bruised my ego. This was the closest I'd felt in ages to being a bitch on wheels.

"Hey, Bailey, hi."

It was Chris's voice behind me. He must have entered the bar without my seeing him.

As I shifted in my chair, I caught two women gazing behind me, their mouths agape. As soon as I spun around, I could see why. Chris Wickersham had somehow managed to become even more gorgeous in the months since I'd last seen him. There were the dazzling green eyes and the intriguing cleft in his chin. But he'd gained a few pounds, filling out his face in the nicest of ways. His sandy brown hair was a little longer and tinged with blond highlights. The biceps were the same, though. They cockily stretched the sleeves of a gray T-shirt he wore over tan cargo shorts. Had I been the stupidest girl in America to reject him?

I stood up to greet Chris, and at the same moment he leaned forward to kiss me on the cheek. Because of the awkward angle of our bodies, the edge of his full, lovely mouth touched mine, and I felt the same rush I'd experienced the very first time he'd kissed me in Miami. Take it down, way down, Bailey, I told myself. I had no idea what Chris's intentions were—or mine, for that matter—and I didn't want to get ahead of myself.

"Hey there," was all I could muster.

"God, it's great to see those blue eyes again, Bailey. You look amazing."

"Well, I'm not the one with half the bar staring at me."

"I'll start describing what we do in the morgue with a Stryker saw and let's see how they like that," he said, grinning. He created a dead-on whiny saw noise that made me laugh out loud.

He ordered a beer for himself, and we talked for a few minutes about the series. It was being shot entirely in New York City, with all the interior morgue shots done on a soundstage at Chelsea Piers. He interrupted himself at one point to ask how my work was going, and I told him about losing my old arrangement at *Gloss* magazine and miraculously finding the gig at *Buzz*.

"Gosh, is it dangerous for me to be talking to you now that you work for a celebrity rag?" he asked, his eyes playful.

"Only if you hurl your cell phone at someone or try to bring a half kilo of cocaine through customs at JFK." I took a swig of beer, thinking of a zillion other questions I had about the series, but before I could ask one, Chris switched gears entirely.

"Like I said on the phone," he said, lowering his voice slightly, "I wanted to talk to you about this friend of mine. I really appreciate your meeting me."

Omigod, I suddenly thought, the "friend" is a girl. He's got chick trouble, and he wants my advice, like I'm some sort of big sister. I felt a flush of embarrassment begin to creep up my chest.

"Okay, tell me about it," I said awkwardly.

"It's about this actor I know—named Tom Fain. We met doing an off off Broadway show a year or two ago, and he ended up in *Morgue,* too. He's got just a small part, but he's generally in every episode."

"Is he in some kind of trouble?" I asked, feeling oddly relieved that it was a guy friend after all. I waited for a tale of woe that would probably include at least one long weekend in Vegas.

"I guess you'd call it that," Chris said. "He's missing."

"Missing?" I exclaimed.

"Yeah, he disappeared off the face of the earth a week and a half ago."

"Have you talked to the police—though they're usually not much help with young guys."

"The first person I called was this guy Tom had mentioned—Mr. Barish—who handles his money. He said he'd get hold of the cops. This detective called me a day later. He looked around Tom's apartment and said he'd make a couple of inquiries, but there was nothing more he could really do. He told me a lot of guys just take off. But I don't think that's what happened. This was Tom's first regular TV gig. He's a couple of years older than me, and he's been praying for this break even longer than I have. I just don't believe he would have walked away from it."

"Is there a girlfriend in the picture?" I asked. "Could he have had a blowup and gone off to lick his wounds?"

"There's a kind of girlfriend, a chick named Harper Aikins he's been seeing for about a month and a half. She's a former actress who does PR for the show. But it's not some major love affair, and she's just as clueless as I am about where he is."

"Parents?"

"Both dead. You ready for another?" he asked, cocking his chin toward my beer.

I'd noticed that he'd chugged down his own beer quickly, feeling churned up, perhaps, from talking about Tom. I was only halfway through mine.

"I'm set for now. So tell me the circumstances. When did you last see Tom? When did *anyone* last see him?"

"I talked to him the Thursday before he disappeared. We were on set together. He plays—or I should say *played,* because they've canned him now for being a no-show—this guy who mans the phones at the morgue, the one who's always handing someone a message or announcing that so-and-so is on line four. I'm not sure what he did the next day because they didn't need him on set, but apparently on Saturday morning he picked up his car from a lot downtown and took off. Harper was out of town that weekend, but she talked to Chris Friday night and he didn't mention anything about a trip. *Originally* he'd been planning to head out to the Hamptons to see this buddy of his, but the guy told me the plans got bagged late in the week. When Chris didn't show for work on Monday, I kept trying to reach his cell phone and finally went to his apartment. As far as I know, no one's heard from him since that weekend."

"Was he depressed—or in any kind of trouble that you know of?"

"Not that I know of. He's a helluva nice guy. He actually suggested I audition for the show."

"Aren't the producers worried about what happened to him?"

"Apparently not. One of the ADs—assistant directors—told me that Tom was apparently miffed about how small his part was. He'd also been having a little trouble on set. The rumor is he just bolted."

Chris drew his fist to his face and blew a stream of air into it. I waited, thinking he was going to say something else, but he only stared at me expectantly.

"How can I help?" I asked. I had no idea what I could possibly do, but I assumed that was the question Chris had been waiting for.

"I want you to tell me how I can find him. You solve mysteries, right? I just want some direction."

I sighed. "When I'm writing a story—or when I'm working on a case like the one I needed your help on last winter—I find that the best approach is to just methodically turn over every stone, one by one. It's not very sexy sounding, yet it's usually the best way. But I don't know anything about Tom's life, so I wouldn't know which stones to start with."

"I can help with that. I can tell you everything I know about him. Plus, I have a key to his apartment. He was nice enough to let me bunk there for a few weeks this summer before I got my own place, and I thought if you looked through it with me, we might find something—a lead."

"Uh, sure," I said. It would be more than providing a "little direction," but I was intrigued, and I liked the idea of being with Chris. "That would certainly be a start. When?"

"How about right now?"

"*Now?* Well, why not, I guess. Even though you've got a key to the place, is there anyone who could make trouble for you if they caught you in there?"

"No. Like I said, the parents are dead, he's got no siblings, and the super is used to me being around."

"Okay, then, let's do it."

He waved for the check, paid, and three minutes later we were out on the street. He said Tom lived on Mercer, so we headed there on foot. While we walked, Chris provided more details about Tom. He'd grown up in Manhattan, gone to private school, and then majored in theater at Skidmore College. Whereas Chris had used modeling as a potential springboard for acting and had eventually headed for L.A., Tom had plugged away mostly in the off off Broadway world, performing in many small "black box" theaters, once totally nude.

I was curious, I told Chris, about the guy Tom had said he was going to see in the Hamptons. Was there a chance Tom *had* headed out there and the guy was denying it? Perhaps he and Tom had ended up in an altercation, or at the very least this dude was covering up something. Chris didn't think so, based on his conversation with the guy. He was an old high school friend of Tom's.

His apartment was in an older, kind of grand-looking building that had obviously been renovated into living spaces. There was no doorman, but the lobby was nicely decorated with an original limestone fireplace mantel. Not exactly what I was expecting for an actor who until recently had done ten-dollar-a-ticket theaters and let his schlong dangle in front of an audience. Reading my mind, Chris explained that Tom had purchased his place with money from the sale of his parents' apartment on the Upper East Side.

We took the elevator to four, and I followed Chris down a long hallway, the walls painted tobacco color and hung with brass sconces. From the pocket of his shorts, he pulled out a set of keys and thumbed through several until he found the one to Chris's place. He turned the lower Medeco lock and, when that was unlocked, a top one. I was right behind him as he pushed open the door, and no sooner had he stepped into the vestibule than I felt his body tense.

I soon knew why: In a room at the very end of the hall, probably the bedroom, a light was glowing. Someone seemed to be home.

CHAPTER 2

Is it Tom?" I whispered.

"I—I don't know," Chris said, his voice as low as mine. "I don't think I left a light on."

I waited for him to make a move of some kind, and when he failed to, *I* did.

"Tom?" I called out. "Are you here? . . . *Tom?*"

There was no answer.

Chris patted the wall with his right hand and found a switch, flooding the vestibule with light. Side by side, we started down a long hall on the right toward the room where the light was burning. Once more I called Tom's name, and once more it was met with silence.

We reached the room, a bedroom, and stepped quietly through the doorway, Chris just ahead of me now. The room was empty. The lamp throwing off the light was on a wooden, antique-looking table by the window. I glanced instinctively toward the bed. There was a hunter green duvet across it, slightly askew and rumpled, as if the bed had been hastily made.

I jerked my head back toward Chris. "Has somebody . . . ?"

"No, it was that way when I came in before," Chris said, guessing my question.

"What about the light?" I asked. "Are you sure you didn't leave it on?"

"I thought I'd switched it off, but I guess I must have forgotten to. According to Tom, I'm the only person with a key besides him. He wanted me to keep the spare in case he lost his."

"Of course, *Tom* could have come back and turned the light on," I said.

"I know," he acknowledged. "But it doesn't make any sense. Why come back but not tell anyone—and not show for work?"

"I wonder if he's in some kind of trouble and feels the need to lay low for a while. Let's check the closet."

Chris slid open the closet door, which bounced on the tracks, making my heart skip. I waited silently as he made a mental inventory of the contents.

"It looks about the same as it did," he declared. "I'm just not familiar enough with his stuff to tell what's not here. The only thing I'm sure about is that there's still no sign of his duffel bag. He has an old leather one—the kind you use for short trips. I figured it meant that when he left that Saturday, he was planning on at least an overnight."

"His parents didn't leave him a condo in Florida along with the apartment, did they? I mean—"

"Not that I'm aware of. I know that they used to have some kind of weekend place in the country, but Tom sold it earlier in the summer. He said it wasn't the kind of place you'd go to if you were single."

"Let's look around the rest of the place," I said.

Chris led the way back down the hall toward the living room.

I noticed this time that the walls were lined with nicely framed architectural prints. The living room was even more of a surprise. It was spacious, with windows on two sides and an expensive-looking couch and two armchairs flanking a brick fireplace. There were several antiquey pieces in there as well. The one incongruous touch was the large empty pizza box strewn haphazardly on the coffee table with a pile of dried crusts in the center of it.

"Was . . . ?"

"Yeah, that was here when I checked this past weekend," Chris said. "So far, nothing looks different."

"I thought you said you were here over a whole week ago."

"I came back—just to double-check."

"This is quite the place for a struggling actor," I observed. "Were his parents well-off?"

"Apparently not as much at the end as they once were. His father played the market, and he was pretty good at it. But Tom told me that he made some bad investments a few years before he died and lost a lot of what he'd saved. His parents weren't destitute. They had their apartment in New York and some savings—and they had put a decent chunk of change in trust for Tom—but they didn't have the *big* bucks anymore. Tom said he thinks the stress contributed to his father's heart attack. His mother died of some kind of cancer about two years later—a year ago this summer."

We moved on to other areas in the apartment—the bathroom (toothbrush missing), the small eat-in kitchen (nothing in the fridge except a few bottles of beer and a quart of milk, which stank to high heaven when I beaked the top part to take a whiff), and then a room off the kitchen that must have once been a maid's room and now held a single bed, a desk, and several bookshelves mounted on the wall. Chris explained that this was the room he had crashed in before he'd rented his own place.

"What is it?" I asked. Chris had suddenly pursed his lips, perturbed.

"That copy of *Backstage*," he said, pointing to the newspaper on the far left side of the desk. "I know it sounds crazy, but I could swear it was in the middle of the desk when I was here before. But I'm probably wrong. Just like I'm wrong about the light. Because why would those be the only things that have changed?"

"Well, if he came back to pick up just a few things like clothes, he might not have disturbed much." I glanced instinctively behind me. If Tom—or someone else—had dropped by once, they could drop by again and catch us snooping around. I really didn't love being here.

I slid open the single drawer of his desk and glanced inside. There were pens, pencils, envelopes, odds and ends. I slid the drawer shut. On top of the desk were a few pieces of mail, which I thumbed through. Nothing more than bills and nothing dated later than right after Labor Day. There was one bill from a parking lot on Houston, and I jotted down the name and address.

"What kind of car does he have?" I asked.

"A black Audi."

"And what about a calendar? I don't see anything here."

"He uses a Sidekick—and I assume he took it with him."

"Computer?"

"There's a laptop over there in the corner," he said, pointing. "I tried a few passwords to see if I could get into his e-mail but nothing worked."

At the very back of the desk was a pile of papers, which I grabbed next. On top was another copy of *Back Stage* and underneath four or five head shots with the name *Tom Fain* printed on each of them.

"So this is what he looks like," I said, staring down at the shot.

If the picture was true to life, Tom was as great looking as Chris, but in a totally different way. He was brown-eyed and very blond, his hair long enough to be worn tucked behind his ears. His skin was incredibly smooth, almost embryonic looking, but his features were strong enough to prevent that from being a negative. If he'd passed me on the street while I was standing next to a girlfriend, I probably would have muttered something short and simple, like "Oh. My. God."

It wasn't simply his stunning looks. In the photo, he had that air of easy sophistication and casual disregard that New York private school kids always seem to possess, resulting perhaps from the strange convergence of growing up with all your needs provided for but also learning to rough it in the city, like riding the subway solo at fourteen.

"Yeah, that's a recent shot," Chris said.

"Did they make him cut his hair for the show?"

"No, they wanted it long. They thought that's what you'd see on a New York guy who worked the front desk at a morgue."

"Do you think it's okay if I keep one?" I asked. "Just for—"

"It's fine. He probably has a huge box of them somewhere."

I felt staples on the back of the photo and flipped it over. Attached to the back was a résumé. It listed not only stints on a few shows like *Law & Order*, but also lots of plays.

"That's where we met," Chris said, jabbing with his forefinger at the name of one of the plays. "Like I said, Tom did a lot more theater than me, but I did this one play with him at Stage Right Productions."

"*Julius Caesar?*"

"Yup. But mostly he worked at this small theater in the Village. Here it is," he said, pointing. "The Chaps Theatre. They put on over a dozen plays a year—some classics, some written by new playwrights. He was a member of the company."

I tucked one photo in my purse and let my eyes peruse the bookshelves. There were books on playwriting and acting and a few old college textbooks. On the top shelf was a big plastic tub.

"What's in there?" I asked Chris.

"Photos. I looked inside when I was here last but didn't go through them."

Assuming I'd want to investigate, Chris lifted down the plastic box and set it on the desk. There were some loose pictures, stacked sideways, others in wide envelopes with dates. Most seemed to be family photos, which Tom had probably taken possession of when his mother died. I leafed through them quickly. Many featured Tom with his parents in various locations around the world. There were Tom, at about twelve, and, I assumed, his attractive blond mother on the long green mall in front of the Eiffel Tower. On the back, in a woman's handwriting, was the date 1990 and, unnecessarily, "Paris." Another shot showed Tom and his father standing on a white-and-blue glacier, with "Alaska, 1991" on the back. And there was one shot of all three of them in long-sleeved shirts and jeans, a stacked stone wall behind them. On the back: "Andes, 1994."

"They clearly traveled a lot," I remarked.

"Yeah, Tom said his father loved seeing the world. That was one of the toughest parts about losing the money. His parents were going to have enough to live on, but not the extra to really travel well—and that had been something his parents had planned to do after he retired."

Without warning, I felt a swell of sadness. The family Fain looked happy, and you could sense the love they felt for one another—in one photo, Tom's mother hugged him in a gesture of pure adoration. How painful it must have been for Tom to lose both parents. My father had died when I was twelve, and I knew something about the ragged hole that the early death of a parent leaves in your heart.

I dropped the snapshots back in the box, and Chris returned it to the shelf. In unspoken agreement, we wandered back through the kitchen and out into the hallway.

"If you had to make a guess," I said, "do you think Tom has been back here?"

Chris let his eyes wander around the hall, as if the answer lay on the walls. "I don't know," he said finally, his brow furrowed. "I probably left the light on. And the magazine—it was probably there before, but I hadn't noticed. But why does it matter, anyway? Tom is still missing. He's AWOL at work."

"I know, but if he came back here, it means that he's basically okay. He just doesn't want anyone to find him. And that means we should probably just let sleeping dogs lie."

He shook his head. "Then if I had to guess, I'd say no. Tom's the kind of guy who tends to leave a trail. Like the pizza box."

"Okay, then, let's proceed from there. Tom went someplace a week and a half ago, and we need to figure out where."

"So what do we do?"

"For starters, I want to talk to the guy Tom was supposed to see in the Hamptons. I know you said he doesn't seem culpable in any way, but Tom might have said something relevant to him. I want to talk to his girlfriend, too. Is there anyone else at the show who might know something?"

"The show? That seems like a dead end to me. There's Harper, of course, and he was kind of friendly with some of the crew, but I'm pretty sure there was no one else he palled around with."

Simultaneously we both shifted our bodies, ready to leave. I was thrilled to be getting out of there. But just before we reached the doorway, I stopped dead in my tracks.

"Hold on for a second," I said. "Let's just check the clothes hamper. It's a tip a cop once gave me. If Tom did come back, he might have dumped clothes there."

It was an old wicker basket in the bedroom with one of the hinges missing from the lid. I flicked it open and we saw a pile of smushy-looking clothes reaching three-quarters of the way to the top. Chris reached his hand in, and as he rifled through the clothes, the smell of sweat wafted upward, but it was an old, stale smell like the kind that greets you in a locker room after the season is over.

"Nah," Chris said. "These are mostly running clothes that . . ."

"*What?*" I asked. I could tell by the expression on his face that his hand had touched something unexpected.

"There's a hard thing at the bottom." He tossed several T-shirts and pairs of running shorts onto the floor and then slowly lifted out a plastic storage container, this one the size of a shoebox. We could see through the transparent sides that there were envelopes inside. I felt a weird tingle go through my body.

We glanced at each other, both of us nearly bug-eyed.

"We better take a look," I announced. "Since he's hiding it, it could mean something."

As we carried the box across the hall to the living room, I felt dread gaining on me. Could the contents be tied to Tom's disappearance? Was I about to find records of cocaine deals carried out throughout Manhattan?

With the box on his lap, Chris lifted the lid and flicked through the envelopes.

"It's mostly from chicks," he said. "Jeez, we've found his love letter stash."

"Okay, we better put it back," I told him.

"Hold on," he said, lifting out one parcel of at least thirty cards bound by a fat rubber band. He tugged an envelope from the pack and drew a card from the envelope. "That's what I thought," he said, glancing at the few words scribbled at the bottom. "These are all from this actress he was seeing before Harper—Blythe. Blythe Hammell or Hamlin, I think. She used to call a ton when I was staying here, and it drove him nuts. After a while, he just started letting all her calls go to voice mail or his answering machine."

"So he just wasn't, as they say, into her?"

"He was *initially,* I think. Tom's a pretty private guy overall, so I don't know everything that went on between them, but I take it they had a fairly fun romp in the beginning. But she started getting real possessive after that. He tried to break it off, and she just kept hounding him. She sounded like a bit of a whack job to me. Of course, half the actresses you meet are—and besides, Tom has this way of seeing everybody's good side."

"Is that how they came into contact—through an acting job?"

"Yeah, she's part of that theater company he's involved with—the Chaps Theatre."

"Well, if she was a whack job, we'd better check her out," I said, sitting next to him on the couch and pulling a few of the cards out of their envelopes. Some of the ones from Blythe were greeting cards—silly ones with kitty cats and monkeys as well as sexy ones loaded with innuendo—all signed "Blythe" or "B." Others were just note cards with simple messages in a bold, dramatic script: "I'm missing you," for instance, and "Let me cook you something *delicious* tonight." According to the post-marks, a card had arrived every couple of days through the summer up until about six weeks ago, which meant about a month before Tom had disappeared. The last card had a picture of a pug on the front and was blank inside except for "Why don't you call anymore? B."

"July thirty-first," I said, pointing to the postmark. "Do you think she gave up the fight then?"

"Yeah, that sounds about right. I remember him saying something about finally having her out of his hair."

I took out my notebook and jotted down the return address on East 5th Street.

"By the way, where's his mail from the past two weeks?" I asked.

"Huh?" Chris asked distractedly. He was staring at something still in the box. "Oh, the post office has it because it was starting to pile up. Of course, they won't release it to anyone but Tom."

"What are you looking at?" I asked quietly, aware suddenly that something was up.

"This," he said, picking up a blue envelope. It was made of really heavy stock, the kind of stationery you buy at Cartier. He flicked up the flap and withdrew the note card inside.

There was just one sentence written in blue black fountain pen: "When you fuck me, it takes a week for my toes to uncurl." And then the name, "Locket."

"Obviously a woman who doesn't beat around the bush," I said.

"It's Locket Ford," Chris said soberly. "The star of *Morgue*."

"Oh, *really*. Locket? Is that some kind of nickname?"

"No. And it's not a stage name, either. She came from Appalachia or some other dirt-poor place, and apparently her mother gave her that name because she wanted her to grow up to be special. She was on soaps for twelve years, and this show is her big break into prime time."

"Could it be bad politically for her to be involved with Tom?" I wasn't sure how it worked on sets, but surely it wasn't the coolest thing for the star of the show to be bonking the actor whose part involved handing the morgue staff their paperwork.

"*Bad?* Well, her live-in boyfriend—Alex Ottoson—is the producer of the show, and he's the one who got her the part. *I'd* say that's pretty bad, wouldn't you?"

"Wow. Maybe this guy caught wind of it and that's why Tom split. He may be hiding out."

We took another few minutes to glance through the correspondence. At the very bottom were letters from Tom's mother in shaky handwriting, probably shortly before her death, but we didn't look through those. When we finally put the box back in the hamper, I felt ashamed for having been such a snoop—yet I was glad we had found the stash. The note from Locket could be significant. But now it was time to go.

The minute we stepped out onto the street, I felt a rush of pure relief. Mercer Street was crowded with people headed off to bars and parties and Starbucks, and we were jostled several times as we stood there decompressing from our foray into Tom's apartment.

"Why don't I walk you back to your place," Chris said.

I sensed by his tone that there was nothing loaded in his comment. There wouldn't be any expectation on his part to come up and wrestle with me on my couch for old times' sake. I suspected he was mentally fatigued from our search—just as I was—yet I felt a twinge of disappointment.

On the way over to 9th and Broadway, I told him my game plan for the next day. I would start making calls stat, but there were phone numbers I needed first—Tom's Hamptons friend, the cop, Harper, Blythe. He tugged the cop's business card out of his wallet and also scrawled down the name of Tom's friend, John Curry, as well as the number at the bank where he worked. He didn't think he could locate a number for Blythe but thought I might find it through 411. As for Harper, he'd arrange for me to talk to her.

"Do you think Locket has any idea where Tom is?" I asked.

"I haven't a clue," Chris said, "and there's no way for me to come right out and ask her. I want to find Tom, but I also don't want to shoot myself in the foot."

When we reached my building, Chris gave me a hug the way he had earlier in the evening, though this time the gesture felt more abrupt and awkward. He seemed distracted suddenly, as if thoughts were racing behind those beautiful green eyes. He might have once had the hots for me, but his blood seemed to be running lukewarm tonight. I wondered if a second search of the apartment had left him even more agitated about Tom than he had been before. Or maybe he was discombobulated by the fact that Tom had secretly bedded the star of the show.

I watched him as he hurried the short distance to the corner and then sprinted across Broadway. He may have been just catching the light, but it seemed almost as if he were in a hurry. I turned and entered my apartment. The doorman Bob was on duty tonight, and he gave me a pleasant, almost approving nod, as if he were happy to see that I was heading in alone again tonight. Bob never made me feel skanky, but I also sensed he kept tabs on the traffic coming in and out of 14B.

I popped open a beer as soon as I got in and carried it out to my terrace along with a bag of tortilla chips and a bowl of leftover, slightly tuckered-out salsa. I guess you'd have to call my apartment the spoils of my two-year starter marriage, and I never stop feeling . . . well, *spoiled* by it. Though it's just a moderately sized one-bedroom with an itsy-bitsy kitchen, it has two drop-dead features: the large brick terrace and what I behold from it. There's no glimpse of landmarks, but nonetheless it's a gorgeous, quintessentially Manhattan view. It looks to the west, toward a skyline of nondescript redbrick and limestone apartment buildings topped by nineteen wooden-shingled water towers. At night, when the sky is inky black and there are lights dabbled in different apartment buildings, it seems almost fake, like the backdrop of a Broadway musical.

I took a long swallow of cold beer and then leaned back in my chair, encouraging my mind to idle for moment. Though it was warm out and the red geraniums in my clay pots were still blazing with color, I could feel a touch of fall in the air. Just like cold spots in lake water, there were cool ribbons threaded through the breeze that hinted at the not-so-balmy October and November days ahead.

I should have been happy about the imminent arrival of fall. First and foremost I would be an author, with the arrival of *Bad Men and Wicked Women* late in the season. In addition, I'd just bought a pair of black suede boots that were so snug and gorgeous, my calves had nearly orgasmed when I'd tried them on. And last but hardly least, it had been a bitch of a summer, something worth distancing myself from.

Yet all of a sudden I felt overwhelmed by melancholy. Maybe it was because I'd had such high hopes for the summer, and it was tough to consider how pathetically they'd unraveled. My initial plan had been to write a few gripping articles, spend as many weekends as possible in the sun, take Rome by storm, and have a fling that would leave *my* friggin' toes curled. I know you aren't supposed to bank on anything in life, I know that "shit happens," but *nothing* had worked out as planned. What I'd anticipated as a Gorgonzola soufflé kind of summer had ended up resembling a grilled-cheese sandwich made with one of those individually wrapped singlets that taste like socks you've worn too many days in a row.

For starters, there was the humiliation of being bounced from the gig I'd had for several years at *Gloss* magazine. When the editor, Cat Jones, had confessed that her newsstand sales were plummeting and she was morphing the magazine from a sexy, edgy read for married women into *Take-a-Chill-Pill Monthly*,

I'd tried to be sympathetic to her plight. But that didn't make it any easier to know my crime pieces were going to be replaced by stories along the lines of "The Secret Power of Bath Salts" and "How to Cure Mild Depression by Organizing Your Shoes." Fortunately, I'd found my way to *Buzz*.

The worst thing about the summer was what had happened with Beau Regan, documentary filmmaker and documented heartbreaker. At first I'd thought he was the fun, sexy summer fling I'd been longing for, but I'd ended up falling hard—hard as in onto a car hood from a tenth-story window. I'd come right out and told him that I couldn't see him if he was sleeping with anyone else. I'd thought for a moment that he was going to give up the one chick he'd been seeing casually on the side. But then an assignment had come through out of the blue and he'd taken off for Turkey, saying that he felt he couldn't make a decision until he returned—in mid-September. There'd been one lousy postcard with the breathtaking message "Hope your summer's going well. I've been thinking about you."

My co-worker Jessie had suggested I read a book about the failed patterns of love and see if I could learn how to stop falling for the wrong guy. But I didn't think Beau had been the wrong guy. It had just been the wrong moment.

Something else was making me blue: Tom Fain. The fact that he'd lost two adored parents so young gnawed at me. And where the hell *was* he? Had he just hightailed it out of town on an adventure? Or was he staying below the radar as the result of a mess he'd made? And if so, what kind of mess? Money? Drugs? Or the kind you make for yourself when you fuck the producer's live-in girlfriend? And there was one other question to consider: Had something *terrible* happened to him?

I knew right then that I was going to do what I could to make sure Tom was okay. It was partly because I wanted to help

Chris, just as he'd once helped me, but also because of the lost parent connection I had with Tom.

Suddenly a scraping sound startled me out of my thoughts, and I glanced left. A dead leaf, broken off from one of my geraniums, scurried across the stone floor of my terrace, driven by a gust of wind. Fall *was* coming. That meant crinkly brown leaves, suede boots, and wool coats. But I could only wonder what my search for Tom would bring.

CHAPTER 3

I was at the desk in my home office before nine the next morning. Calling it an office may be slightly generous on my part. It's really just a large walk-in closet that I converted into a work area with a few bookshelves and a built-in desk where I set my laptop. The whole space is about the size of the crisper drawer in my fridge, but the upside is that there aren't any distractions. If I had to work in my bedroom, I'd be getting up constantly to defuzz my sweaters or trim the pad peeking out from under the area rug.

Fully caffeinated after two cups of coffee, I was nearly ready to focus my attention on Tom. First, though, I checked some Web sites—CNN, TMZ, Perez Hilton, the Smoking Gun, Gawker, and so on—to make sure nothing was brewing crimewise in the world of celebs. You never knew, for instance, when there'd be newly posted mug shots of someone like Nicole Richie, and I'd have to spring into action. Once I was sure that *Buzz* wasn't going to need me today, I wrote out a list of calls to make and started in.

The first one was to a cop I knew named Gina who had once worked in Missing Persons. I was hoping she still had buddies in that department and would call the cop Chris had talked to—Kevin O'Donnell was the name on the card—and grease the wheels for me, encouraging him to be forthcoming. I reached only her voice mail, and I asked her to call me.

I had better luck reaching John Curry, Tom's buddy with the Hamptons house. I called his line at the bank, and he answered himself.

"Curry," he said in a voice suggesting that though the day had barely begun, he was already bored to tears with it. I introduced myself, explained that I'd been enlisted to help look for Tom, and said that I was hoping I could meet with him as soon as possible.

"*Meet* with me?" he exclaimed with borderline irritation. "How's that supposed to help?"

"You were one of the last people to talk to Tom," I said, trying to submerge my own annoyance.

"Look, I've already talked to that friend of his and the cop. Besides, this week is a real bear for me. I'm up to my ass in about twenty different things here."

"Could you at least give me a few minutes on the phone?" I asked. "I'm sure you're as concerned about Tom as we are." I was hoping the last comment and the loaded way I'd delivered it would goad him into agreeing.

He sighed loudly, as if he were blowing out candles on a cake. "It's just that . . . Look, I've got five minutes now. Go ahead and ask what you want. And just so you know—I don't happen to be all that worried about Tom. He's been known to pick up and leave before."

"For what reason?"

"Tom's always been a little bit restless, even before his parents died. He's got a love for the open road."

"Did he say anything to you that suggested the open road was beckoning him right at this moment?"

There was a long pause.

"What?" I urged.

"Nothing really. You just put it in a slightly different way than the cop did. I mean, he asked if I knew where Tom might have gone. But I hadn't thought about it in a more general sense— about whether Tom was especially restless these days. I just don't know. Tom and I weren't in touch very much the last couple of years—I've been in Singapore, doing a stint for the bank there. We reconnected a few months ago, but I haven't seen a huge amount of him."

"Why didn't you two end up getting together on that weekend?"

He exhaled loudly again. "Totally my fault. I wanted him to come out and see our new house. But I hadn't let the wife know, and when I told her at the last minute, she got all pissy because she'd already invited her mental case sister and brother-in-law. I asked Tom if he'd mind taking a rain check."

"Go back to what you said about his parents' deaths. Was Tom pretty affected by that?"

"I was away when they both died, so I have no idea what it was like at the time. He didn't go all emo when he told me about it, but I could sense it was tough for him."

"You guys met in high school?"

"Yep. I was a year ahead of him, but we played baseball together. Then just by chance he ended up at Skidmore, too. He was in the theater department, which was a whole different world— but I saw a fair amount of him up there."

"What do you know about his love life?"

"He had this one chick he was seeing earlier this summer, but he wasn't that interested and she finally took the hint. Lately he's been seeing someone who works on the show—not an actress, but someone behind the scenes. I guess he likes her well enough, but the problem is, Tom isn't ready to settle down—despite how much these babes like to pressure him."

He let out another sigh. "Look, my boss has walked by twice and given me the evil death stare. I gotta get movin'."

"Just one more question, I promise. Can you think of anyone else who might have a lead on Tom? Someone he might turn to if he was in any kind of trouble?"

"There was a guy from Skidmore he was pretty close to—a professor named Alan Carr. Tom mentioned him lately, in fact. He had this big old house where a lot of the theater kids would hang. But like I said, I doubt Tom is in any kind of trouble."

"Okay, thanks. If you think of anything else—"

"Yeah, sure," he said, and hung up before I could give him my number.

I pulled up the White Pages online and found a B. Hammell at the return address on Blythe's cards. I left a message saying to call Bailey Weggins, that it was important. I *didn't* say it was about Tom.

Next I went on the Skidmore College Web site and found both an office phone number and e-mail address for Professor Carr. I left him a message on his voice mail and also shot him an e-mail. Thinking that the semester might not have even started yet, I tried directory assistance for Saratoga. There was an Alan Carr on Broadway. His answering machine picked up and a laid-back voice announced, "Hey, you've reached Alan Carr. Leave a message if you want, but I don't check this machine regularly, so if it's urgent, try my cell." But he didn't leave a cell number. I left a message on the machine just in case he *did* check it today.

No sooner had I ended the call than my phone rang. It was Gina. The clanging in the background suggested she was in a diner or coffee shop. Talking loudly to be heard over the din, I explained that I needed info from a detective in Missing Persons.

She said she knew O'Donnell and that she would speak to him on my behalf. "He's good people," she shouted. "I'll tell him to call you, okay?"

Moments later, my phone rang again. It was Chris—with an update on his end.

"Good news," he said. "Harper's on set with us. If you can get here quick, I can introduce you."

"Are you shooting at Chelsea Piers?"

"No, we're on location—in Tompkins Square Park."

I slipped on a pair of black leggings, a khaki-colored tunic, and black flats and headed toward my destination on foot. The park—an actual *square* oasis of green between 10th and 7th streets and Avenues A and B—is in a gentrified area of the East Village known as Alphabet City. In the 1980s, it had apparently been filled with homeless people and heroin dealers, but it had been refurbished recently and now held a dog run, handball courts, and a table designed with chessboards. Beneath the old elm trees you could find not only old women speaking Yiddish and men wheeling shopping carts filled with used soda cans but also hip young families with pound-rescued mutts and kids dressed in black instead of pink and powder blue.

Chris had told me to make my way to a long row of trucks and trailers on the eastern side of the park, to look for people with earpieces and then ask for Harper. The directions had sounded kind of vague, but as it turned out there was no way to miss the trucks. There were about eight of them in different sizes parked along Avenue A. Just inside the park was a large cluster of guys in jeans and T-shirts bustling about, setting up lights and other equipment. On the sidewalk outside the park were what appeared to be other crew members, drinking coffee out of cardboard cups. I informed one of them that I had an appointment with Harper Aikins. Speaking into a walkie-talkie, he delivered the message to someone and then told me she'd be right with me.

It was a good ten minutes before she walked up behind me and introduced herself. She wasn't at all what I'd expected. My imagination had conjured up an L.A. type—tiny, thin as a breadstick, with long, sleek hair—but Harper was about five nine or ten, with broad shoulders and wide-ish hips. Her dark blond, slightly wavy hair was cropped very short and brushed back hard from her face, drawing attention to coppery-colored eyes that were so round they looked like two pennies in her face. She was wearing a boatneck pink top with three-quarter sleeves, a tan skirt, and, despite the warm weather, a pair of cowboy boots. Though she lacked an L.A. aura, she exuded confidence. She was the kind of chick who you knew immediately had 1600 on her SATs and had probably gone to Princeton or Yale.

"Hi," she said, shaking my hand firmly, though it was one of those drawn-out hi's that never really sound happy to see you. "Shall I take you to Chris? He's in the honey wagon."

"Actually, Chris thought it would be helpful for us to talk. He told you, right, that I'm trying to help him look for Tom?"

"Yes, he told me. Though I'm not going to be much help. Tom didn't give me the slightest clue where he was going that day."

"Well, it would still help to talk."

She lifted her shoulders in a "whatever" shrug. "But let's get one thing straight," she said. "I know what you do for a living, and I need your guarantee that this is all strictly off the record. Our producer, Alex Ottoson, doesn't like outsiders. And Locket's been burned by *Buzz*."

"How so?" It was hard to imagine a soap actress like Locket even being on the radar at *Buzz*. The magazine, particularly the gossip section called "Juice Bar," focused on the hot young celebs everybody was, well, buzzing about. The sort-of-famous like Locket, as well as the used-to-be-famous and the never-gonna-be-famous-no-matter-how-they-try types made it into the pages only when they overdosed, had a boob break free from a dress on the red carpet, or went through a butt-ugly divorce, the kind that generated language like "Defendant repeatedly demanded that plaintiff engage in three-way sex with prostitute named Glamour."

"They make fun of her mouth. They once wrote that her lips had so much collagen, they should have a stamp on them that said 'Not to be used as a flotation device.'"

"You've got my word I won't feed any gossip to the magazine. I'm only here because of my friendship with Chris—to help find Tom."

She set her mouth in something between a pout and a grimace and glanced around. "Why don't we go over there," she said brusquely, indicating an empty bench just inside the park. As we sat down, she called someone on her walkie-talkie and told the person in a clipped, no-nonsense tone to let Chris know I was here and would stop by his trailer in about ten minutes.

"This must be pretty upsetting for you," I said as soon as she finished.

"I don't know *what* to feel," she said. A tear welled in each eye, but she hurriedly dabbed them away. "One minute I'm freaked that something has happened to Tom, and then the next minute I'm furious because I think maybe he just took off. I've only been dating Tom about two months, so I don't really know him *that* well. Maybe he *did* just blow town."

"Chris says he can't believe Tom would bag a job on a network show after working so hard to get here."

"Chris doesn't know as much as he thinks he does. Tom had *very* mixed feelings about being here."

"You're kidding?" I said, taken aback. "Why?"

"You can't say anything to Chris because I don't think he knows, but originally Tom was up for *Chris's* part. Tom's a nice guy—too nice, if you ask me—and as soon as he heard he was being considered for one of the main roles, he told the casting director about Chris for a smaller role. The next thing you know, everything ended up flipped. Tom never resented Chris—like I said, he's not that kind of guy—but he resented the outcome."

Her revelation threw a new light on the situation. So maybe Tom *had* just bagged it.

"And that's not all," she said. "Alex is *very* powerful—he created about twenty percent of what you see on TV—and he's exerting a lot of control over this show. A couple of days before Tom took off, Alex lit into him after a scene. Said he was 'working too hard.' That's something that actors with a lot of stage experience are sometimes guilty of—they tend to overact in front of the camera, when what you want to do for TV is keep it really small and natural. But from the cuts of the show I've seen, it wasn't true in Tom's case. It was almost as if Alex were just busting his chops for nothing."

So this must be the trouble on the set that Chris had mentioned. "Was Tom pretty upset?"

"It was hard to know because I was in L.A. most of that week and wasn't due back till Sunday. I talked to him on my cell whenever I could grab five minutes, and he did seem fairly bummed—though not I'm-going-to-drop-off-the-planet bummed."

"When was the last time you actually talked to him?"

"I called him on Friday night. He'd had weekend plans with this guy he knew at school, but the guy ended up bailing on him. We agreed to get together for dinner Sunday night after I landed. Then I never heard from him. At first I thought maybe he'd just forgotten about the dinner. It wasn't until he didn't show at work on Monday that I realized something might be the matter."

"He didn't say anything about what he was going to do instead that weekend?"

"No, he just said he'd be fine. There was one weird thing—just a little thing that at the time didn't seem odd, but I've wondered about it since."

"Yes?" I prodded.

"He said he had work to do."

"Work?"

"Right. When he said that his buddy had blown him off, I'd suggested half-jokingly that he fly out to L.A. There were some loose ends I had to tie up for work, but I had a nice room at the Mondrian and he could have chilled at the pool. He said no, he'd be okay. And then he said, 'I've got some work to do.' It's just an expression, and I didn't think anything of it at the time, but afterwards, after he just fell off the face of the earth, I wondered what he'd meant by it. We weren't shooting that weekend."

I didn't say anything, just tossed the words over in my mind. I didn't know Tom's life well enough to have any sense what he might have been talking about.

"Speaking of work, was there anyone besides Chris that Tom palled around with?" I asked.

She did that pouty thing again with her mouth while she reflected. "He was kind of friendly with these two grips named Danny and Deke, especially Deke. Since he had a fair amount of downtime, he'd play cards with them. Once, back in July, he and Deke even went to Atlantic City for a weekend. I told him it wasn't smartest thing in the world to be hanging with those dudes, but Tom has a hard time turning people down."

"And he got along with the other actors—Locket and people like that?" Clearly, she didn't know he was making Locket's toes curl up like Froot Loops, but I wondered if she'd had a hint of any flirtation.

"Yes, Tom is just one of those easygoing guys that everybody relates to. I . . ." She hesitated. "Why don't I bring you to Chris now. I've a reporter coming from *Time Out* in a little while, and I need to get myself in gear."

"What's your best guess about where he is?"

"Off licking his wounds. As soon as you find anything out, let me know, will you?—so I can ring his neck."

She rose abruptly then, making it clear that I could either follow her or sit by my lonesome and watch the ratty squirrels chase one another. I trailed behind her to the fourth truck, which behind the cab had a big silver trailer with several doors on the side, all in a row. She rapped efficiently on one, and Chris opened it almost immediately.

"So there you are," he said warmly. "Thanks, Harper."

She headed off with a backward wave and a brusque order into her walkie-talkie.

Chris took my elbow and pulled me gently into the truck. We were in a small room strewn with clothes, magazines, Styrofoam coffee cups, and cardboard food caddies.

"Welcome to my humble abode in the honey wagon."

"Is this room just yours?" I asked, glancing around.

"Yeah, though when you're a star like Locket, you get a whole damn Winnebago."

I pulled my gaze away from the interior and turned to him, smiling. "It must be thrilling, though—isn't it?" I said.

"Yeah, I keep thinking that maybe I won't have to pour another Scotch on the rocks for another asshole for the rest of my life. So how was your talk with Harper? A bit of a bulldozer, isn't she?"

"Seems so. Does Tom find that appealing?"

"Once she set her sights on him, I don't think he knew how to get out of her path."

"By the way, I talked to his pal John, and he isn't worried at all. He says Tom has a love for the open road. Do we have a whole head of steam up over nothing?"

"I don't know," he said, shaking his head. "One minute I'm worried, and the next minute I'm pissed, thinking that he just took off."

"That's exactly what Harper said." I wished I could share Harper's revelation, which gave Tom an even greater motivation to take off, but I'd given my word—and it would probably only upset Chris more.

I took a minute and a half to fill him in on my morning—the rest of my brief convo with John Curry, my discovery about Tom's friendship with Professor Carr. Chris said that they'd moved up the time for his next scene—it involved the discovery of a scantily clothed dead woman in her twenties (natch) in the park—and he would be pulled away at any moment.

"I might as well split now," I said. "I'll call you later if I learn anything."

As I descended the steps of the trailer, Chris, following behind me, squeezed my elbow.

"Check it out," he whispered. "There's the infamous Locket. She's talking to the first AD."

She was just inside the park in the area where I'd seen the crew setting up, an itty-bitty thing no more than five feet two, platinum hair in a bedheady kind of do, and gleaming, porcelain-like skin. Even from where I stood, I could see how big her lips were. They looked as though they'd burst if they came even near a pair of pincers.

Everyone behind her seemed frozen in place, waiting while she hashed something out with the AD. There were two guys with handheld cameras and two other guys with their hands on the lenses, as if to steady them. Also cooling their heels were two patrol cops who I assumed must be actors *and*—I suddenly realized—either a dummy or a person under a white sheet on the ground.

"Locket looks vaguely familiar," I whispered. "Did she once have longer hair?"

"Yeah. Apparently she fought like hell to keep it, but they told her that someone with her job as an investigator would never run around with Cher hair."

As Chris and I stood watching, a tall man in his forties strode toward Locket and the AD. He had tightly cropped gray blond hair, receding from a high, tanned forehead, a mustache, and a short beard, all very Nordic-looking. He was dressed in a black Armani-style jacket.

"That's Alex," Chris whispered. "Producer—and cuckolded boyfriend."

"He looks—how shall I say—stern?"

"Oh yeah. I wouldn't be surprised to see him in horned head-gear one day. A real Viking warrior."

Chris explained that he had to get back to his trailer, and we hugged good-bye. Before leaving, I joined a group of rubber-neckers near the park entrance and took a closer look at Locket. She was talking intently to both the AD and Alex now, looking slightly peeved but obviously trying to keep her cool. "If you think it's really, really necessary," she said at one point, the only thing I could make out. Since this was her big break into prime time, she seemed to be doing her best to be cooperative, but it was probably hard to keep her raging diva side at bay. How was a guy who found Harper appealing also drawn to Locket? They seemed so wildly different. Did Tom just have a hard time saying no to *any* woman? And what had Locket seen in Tom? She had Alex, after all—so why run the risk of blowing that arrangement?

As I hoofed it back west in the heat, I checked my voice mail. There was a call from Gina saying she'd talked to Detective O'Donnell and he'd be willing to speak to me. I found a stoop on a nearby building, plopped down, and phoned him. There was a tiny suggestion of an Irish accent in his voice, the subtle kind someone gets when he's raised here but his parents were born over there.

"I wish I could devote some more time to this one, but the

particulars don't warrant it," he admitted after I'd introduced myself and explained the reason for my interest.

"Because he's a twentysomething male and there's no reason to suspect foul play?" I asked.

"That's part of the reason," he said. "But there's something else. It turns out he withdrew seven thousand dollars in cash the day before he picked up his car. That sounds like a man with a plan."

CHAPTER 4

With that one statement, everything came into focus, and I felt a wave of both relief and irritation. Tom was probably perfectly fine, speeding his car along a highway at least ten states away, his blond hair whipped by the wind that blasted through the sunroof. Yet he hadn't cared a damn that there were people worrying about him. Or perhaps he'd convinced himself that no one cared all that much.

"So you're thinking he took off somewhere, then?" I said. "Any ideas?"

"Not a clue. He made one call from his cell phone about an hour after he picked up his car. Right near Newburgh Junction. We picked that up on the cell site record. It was to the second assistant director on the show. I checked with the guy, and the two never actually connected. Fain just left a message saying he'd call back later."

"Maybe to tell him he was quitting the show?"

"Could be. But Fain hadn't worked on Friday and so he didn't get the Monday call sheet. This guy said he assumed Fain was calling to check whether he had a scene to shoot on Monday. That part doesn't make sense. Why call for his schedule if he was bailing? But as you say, maybe he was calling to quit."

"I wonder what's in Newburgh Junction."

"He might have just been passing through."

"And that was the last call?"

"Yeah, I don't like that part, either. Maybe he lost his phone. The trouble is, there's nothing I can do. Gina said you're a friend of a friend?"

"Uh-huh—Chris Wickersham, the actor you spoke to. I'm a reporter, and he asked me to help follow any leads. But so far I haven't turned up anything."

"Well, look, would you call me if you hear anything? The money seems to point to him just splitting, but I don't have a good feeling about this one."

"Will do, and I'd appreciate being kept abreast of anything *you* hear. Can I ask why you've done as much as you have? Missing twentysomething guys usually *don't* warrant it—unless there's some evidence of foul play."

"The executor of the parents' will—a guy named Robert Barish—made a call to someone he knows higher up, pulled a few strings. They told me to follow up. But since the money seems to point to a split, there's really not much more I can do."

After hanging up, I flagged down a cab, my thoughts jostling around in complete confusion: Tom was okay—he'd withdrawn a large amount of cash so he could just take off and leave everything behind him. Tom *wasn't* okay—even if he'd decided to split, why wouldn't he have used his cell phone for nearly two weeks? Tom was okay—he wasn't playing the role he wanted on the show, plus the producer had chewed him out, so he'd obviously decided not to hang around. Tom *wasn't* okay—he'd been acting since college, so why burn bridges even if he hadn't been thrilled with his part?

Rather than go directly home, I took the cab to Tom's car lot on Houston—between Essex and Ludlow. There were two Guatemalan attendants on duty. They spoke broken English, but with the help of my rudimentary Spanish, I figured out that one of them had been on duty when Tom had driven off on Saturday. He said that Tom had left very early, at around eight o'clock. He had not mentioned where he was going or when he was coming back.

Five minutes after I returned home, my next-door neighbor, Landon, was knocking on my door. He was wearing a pair of khaki pants and a cerulean blue Ralph Lauren polo shirt. With his compact body, light brown eyes, and close-cropped silver hair, he's one of the best-looking seventy-year-old men I know.

"I heard you come in, darling. You're not at *Buzz Kill* today?" That was what Landon had taken to calling the magazine after the editor in chief had been murdered in July.

"There seems to be a moratorium on celebrity misdoings this week."

"Oh dear, is that going to pose a problem for you? If they stop misbehaving, you'll be out of a job. Maybe you should call Winona Ryder and casually mention that a new shipment of Marc Jacobs pieces has just arrived at Saks."

"Brilliant," I said, laughing. "What about you? How was your date the other night? Did you like the guy?"

"I did until he opened his mouth over dinner. Speaking of which, I stopped by to inquire if you wanted to come face-to-face tonight with the most delectable lamb chops you've ever seen in your life. I invited a client to dinner, but he's just canceled."

"I'd play second fiddle to score one of your lamb chops any day. I've actually got an interesting story to share, but I'll fill you in over dinner."

After throwing together a sandwich, I found a map of New York State online and looked for Newburgh Junction. It was, just as O'Donnell had said, about an hour north of New York City. But even more interesting, it was close to the New York State Thruway. I let my eyes run up the map. About two hours farther north was the town of Saratoga, home of Skidmore College. Bingo. What if *that's* where Tom had been headed? To hang with his old professor. To ask his advice on what the hell to do with his life.

I tried Professor Carr's office phone but once again ended up with voice mail. Next I tried the college switchboard, asking for the theater department and not Carr. A motherly-sounding woman answered.

"Is Professor Carr there?" I asked.

"No, dear, he left about twenty minutes ago. Would you like his voice mail?"

"I left a message earlier. Do you know if he picked up his messages?"

"I believe so. I'm sure he'll be in touch."

I'd indicated in both my voice mail and e-mail messages that people were concerned about Tom and asked for a reply right away. Carr hadn't obliged. Could that mean that Tom was there and Carr was protecting him? It seemed that the only way I would be able to learn if Tom Fain was now in residence in Saratoga was to get my little butt in my Jeep and head up there. I calculated the driving time—about three, three and a half hours each way. It meant investing a whole day and would also mean that I'd be a lot more invested than "making a few calls" for Chris's sake. But I didn't have a ton on my plate reportingwise this week, and besides, I felt a growing compulsion to find Tom, even if he had no regard for his friends. I called the garage and ordered my Jeep for nine the next day.

For the rest of the afternoon, I camped out on my terrace,

reading through clippings for a freelance article I needed to start sooner or later. Often my thoughts flew back to Tom.

At seven that night, I tapped on Landon's door. When I'd first moved into my apartment, not long after my wedding, I'd exchanged only neighborly pleasantries with Landon, but after my marriage had crashed and burned and my ex had fled his law firm job and the city, Landon had invited me in for a drink, and our friendship took off.

"Your cheeks are pink," he said as he ushered me into his apartment. Landon did not believe in gas grills, and from the open terrace door wafted the intoxicating aroma of burning charcoal briquettes.

"I caught a little sunshine late in the day. Here, some Pellegrino. I hear it's an excellent year."

The dinner was to die for: the aforementioned delectable lamb chops, haricots verts, roasted new potatoes sopping in olive oil and mint. Over dinner I shared the whole saga about Tom, beginning with Chris's phone call and ending with my decision to head to Saratoga tomorrow.

"Now that you've heard all the details, give me an objective opinion," I demanded. "Do you think something's terribly wrong?"

"Well, he may have just taken off, but there's something about it that doesn't feel right. You know what intrigues me even more? All this interest on *your* part."

"I've been wondering about the same thing, actually. Believe it or not, I've developed a soft spot for Tom. From everything I've heard, he seems like a really nice guy—and I feel bad that he's sort of alone in the world."

"What's up with you and Chris? Are sparks starting to fly again?"

"He's as hot as I remember him being, but I think he came to see me just as a friend."

"What about *you?*" he asked, his eyes twinkling in the amber light from the citronella candle.

"Well, things never got airborne the last time, so I suspect it's probably not meant to be. Plus, for all I know he's got a girlfriend now. But there's a part of me that thinks it would at least be a distraction from stewing about Beau Regan."

"Oh dear. Can't kick him out of your head?"

"It's getting better. Like today I've only thought about him forty or fifty times so far. He's due back soon, and it's torturing me. I keep wondering if he'll call as soon as he's home, and then realize that if he was interested in pursuing things romantically, he would have stayed in touch while he was away."

"You have the kind of problem that calls for more claret," he said, reaching for the bottle of Bordeaux.

"Nah, I'd better not," I said. "I need to get an early start tomorrow."

I was in my Jeep by exactly nine the next morning. As I pulled out of the garage, it struck me that this would be a good chance to swing by Blythe's apartment. It might be smarter to surprise her with a visit than leave a bunch of messages. The building on 5th Street turned out to be a brick tenement midway down the block. The kind of place that probably held a mix of artsy types and people down on their luck, typical for the neighborhood. Blythe's name was on the mailbox along with an apparent roommate, T. Hardwick. I rang the bell.

A female voice asked, "Who is it?" sounding both groggy and wary.

"Blythe?" I inquired.

Long pause.

"Who wants to know?"

"My name is Bailey Weggins, and I'm a friend of a friend, and something's come up that I think she'd want to know about."

"Blythe isn't here."

"Is this her roommate?"

"Yes, and I'm trying to sleep."

"When do you expect her?"

"I don't know. Maybe never."

The hairs on the back of my neck shot to attention, as if they'd heard a loud bang.

"Look, is it possible for me to come up? This is a fairly urgent matter."

There was another long pause. Finally, she announced that she would come down and I should wait in the foyer.

I was expecting another struggling actress, but the nebbishy, irritated-looking chick who pushed open the door into the vestibule was so lacking in charisma that it was pretty obvious the biggest part she'd ever played was a farm animal in a fifth-grade show. She was dressed in a pair of saggy jeans and an oversize mustard-colored T-shirt. Her blue eyes were nearly obscured by a pair of dark-framed glasses, and her hair, a reddish brown you see only on horses, was pulled back in a low ponytail under a baseball cap.

"What's so important?" she grumbled.

"You're T. Hardwick?" I said, smiling pleasantly.

"Terry Hardwick. What's this about?"

"Like I said, I'm Bailey Weggins and I'm looking for Blythe."

"You're the one who left the phone message."

"That's right. It's really important that I talk to Blythe."

"She owe you money? Good luck getting it."

"No, I just want to talk to her. Has she moved out?"

"That's one way to put it," she said scornfully. "I think the term they usually use is *skipped* out. She took off with a guy, saying they were doing a movie together. Not only does she owe me rent money, but she stole every tube of sunblock I had and this white eyelet bathing suit cover-up that cost me seventy-five bucks."

It sounded as if I might have just solved the mystery of Tom Fain.

"Was it about a week and a half ago?" I demanded. "With someone named Tom?"

"You a girlfriend of Tom's?" she asked, narrowing her eyes.

"No, but I'm a friend of a friend, and I'm trying to locate him. He's missing."

She scrunched up her mouth. "No, it wasn't with Tom—though he was here once or twice. This new guy had a foreign-sounding name. I think she met him in Williamsburg. And they took off longer than two weeks ago—around the first of August."

That was right around the time the cutesy Hallmark card campaign had come to an abrupt end. So she wasn't with Tom. She had obviously cooled on him once she'd found another dude to go apeshit over.

"Do you know where they went—and if there's any way I can reach her?"

"I don't know *where* she is," she answered with disgust. "She called a few weeks ago for her messages and said she was in the Miami area, but she's such a liar, it's hard to know. I can't believe I ever trusted her. She'd get all teary-eyed and ask if I could pleeeeease give her just one more week on the rent because she'd just done this commercial for Burger King and would be getting a big check. Between the rent and the food and all the clothes of mine she took or wrecked, she owes me a thousand dollars."

"That's a shame," I said, finding it hard to be all that sympathetic. Terry looked like the type of humorless chick one might relish torturing. Maybe Blythe had stolen her sunblock just for fun. "How did you two hook up as roommates, anyway?"

"I put a sign up. My mother said I was stupid sharing my place with an actress, and I should have listened to her. I may not work with people as thrillingly exciting as Blythe, but at least they wouldn't eat a whole bag of someone's miniature Snickers and leave all the wrappers in the bag—like you're not supposed to *notice* there aren't any candy bars in there anymore."

"What do you do, anyway?" I asked.

"I work in health insurance. So how you going to find this Tom guy?"

"I'm heading upstate today to follow up on a few leads. Do you think Blythe will call back?"

"Well, she left some of her shit here, so maybe she'll be back. If she doesn't, I'm seriously thinking of calling the police."

I offered her my business card, which she accepted with all the enthusiasm of someone being presented a dead eel, and asked her to have Blythe get in touch if she called again. Yet it didn't seem likely that Blythe would know Tom's whereabouts. She'd apparently found someone more receptive to her charms than Tom had been, someone willing to keep her in Snickers for the unforeseeable future. My best lead now was Skidmore, and it was time to haul ass and get up there.

I'd missed most of the commuter traffic, but there were still bumper-to-bumper patches on the Major Deegan, and by the time I reached the New York State Thruway, I'd been warming the seat of my Jeep for well over an hour. As I pulled away from the tollbooth, I experienced a moment of brain spritz—why in God's name was I spending an entire day in my car looking for a guy I'd never even *met*? Because I'd promised Chris I would help. Because I was moved by Tom's story. If the good professor couldn't help, though, I didn't know what else I could do.

The second half of the trip turned out to be relatively pain-less. I stuck in a CD of Maria Callas arias, and since there was nothing complicated about the route—New York State Thruway to Exit 24 and then the Adirondack Northway to Saratoga—I lis-tened to her haunting voice and kept my speed at around seventy-two most of the way. The suburbs fell behind me, and before long the Catskills rose in shades of blue and lavender off to my left. I passed stretches of woods and marshes, interrupted periodically by giant eyesores, like mini self-storage units that seemed to go on for miles. When I passed the first Albany exit, my tummy did a weird nostalgia flip, as I remembered my job as a beat reporter for the *Albany Times Union* my first two years out of Brown.

It was just after noon when I pulled off onto the main exit for Saratoga. Though my stomach was starting to rumble, I figured food could wait until after I'd located Carr. I'd visited Saratoga a few times when I was working for the paper—to take in the races, to hear concerts at the performing arts center—and I didn't need to ask directions. The road off the exit turned into Main Street, which I knew led through the town center, and then flowed right into Broadway. As I passed through the downtown area, I checked out the scene. Though Thoroughbred racing season was over, the town was bustling with people. They strolled along the street in shorts and tank tops and formed bunches in front of the shops and cafés in the five-story brick buildings, which dated back to the 1800s. Some of the buildings displayed American flags, which snapped in the end-of-summer breeze.

I decided I'd stop first at Carr's house, and if he wasn't there, I'd proceed down the road to Skidmore. Broadway was an amazing little street lined with glorious old houses that had once been owned by rich horse-loving families like the Vanderbilts. The owners would arrive in August for Thoroughbred season and then depart immediately afterward, leaving the servants to recover the furniture in big white sheets. Carr's house wasn't one of the near mansion-size places, but it was a nice big yellow one with a wraparound porch. Chances are he'd bought it run-down and had worked to restore it to its previous glory.

I was in luck, it seemed. An old Volvo sat in the driveway, and I could see that the front door was wide open to the day. I hopped out of the Jeep and scampered up the steps. Somewhere deep inside, classical music was playing, the perky sounds of Mozart, from what I guessed.

I peered through the screen door and, not seeing anyone, rapped on the frame. Nothing. But someone had to be here. There was the music, after all, and besides, there were cooking smells, something cuminy. I rapped again, louder this time.

"It's open!" a man yelled over the music. "I'm in the kitchen."

I stepped inside and adjusted my eyes now that they were out of the glare of the day. I was standing in a hallway with a parlor on either side, the one to the right set up as a study/library. Dark wood antiques filled the rooms, but they seemed mostly of the flea market variety, and the art on the wall was mainly framed museum posters. I followed the cooking smells and music to a kitchen in the back, a room that looked as if it hadn't been over-hauled since at least the 1970s. A tall, lean guy with a dark brown beard, who could have been anywhere from thirty-eight to fifty, stood at one of those rolling carts with butcher block on top, chopping away at a red pepper, with a pile of ten others await-ing execution. He glanced up when I entered, a look on his face of expectation that was immediately chased away by puzzlement. Clearly, I wasn't who he'd been waiting for.

"Can I help you?" he asked, pausing midwhack.

"Sorry to barge in like this. I did try to call you a couple of times. I'm Bailey Weggins. Are you Alan Carr?"

He scrunched his mouth over to one side and mentally tossed around what I'd just said. "Oh, you're the one with a question about Tom. Sorry not to get back to you—I'm serving chicken chili to twenty tonight, and I'm about an hour behind schedule. You're not a student, are you?"

"No, I live in New York City, and I drove up this morning. Why don't I get right to the point. Tom seems to have dropped off the face of the earth. A friend of his asked me to try to find him, and since I heard you stayed in touch with Tom, I was hoping you might be able to help."

"Dropped off the face of the earth?" he said soberly, wiping his hands on the red cook's apron he wore. "What do you mean by *that?*"

"There hasn't been any sign of him at his apartment for nearly two weeks, and he hasn't showed up for work on his TV show. He did withdraw a large sum of money, so it seems as if he may have wanted to take off for a while. I'm wondering if you've seen or talked to him lately."

There was a telling beat before he answered.

"No, I haven't."

"You hesitated."

"That's because I *did* talk to Tom fairly recently, but now that I think about it, it was probably more like a month or two ago. Not long after they starting shooting this show he's in. He called to give me an update." Pensively, he strode over to the CD player and killed the Mozart. "When was the last time someone actually saw him?"

"The last person who saw him that *I* talked to was a guy at his parking garage. Tom picked up his car early in the morning two weeks ago this Saturday. The last time he used his cell phone was that morning, and it was from a place downstate not far from the thruway. That's what made me think he might have been heading up to see you."

"No, there weren't any plans for him to come up here. Jesus, I don't like the sound of this at all."

"Is there any chance he could have just taken off for here, planning to show up unannounced?"

"You mean and then run into trouble. God, what if he's had an accident and gone off the road and no one has spotted the car?" With one hand he squeezed his cheeks together and shook his head. "Tom never showed up unannounced before, but who knows, maybe he *was* headed here. He wasn't thrilled with his part, that much I know. He was supposed to have had a much bigger role, and then all of sudden, bam, the rug got pulled out from under him. And yet, I can't see him just walking away from the job. It was a start in TV."

I massaged my temples, trying to think. I'd half convinced myself Tom was here or that I would at least walk away with a clue to his whereabouts. But I'd driven all this way simply to face another dead end.

"Is there anything, then, you can tell me that might help me find him?" I asked, looking up. "Anyone he knew in the Northeast that he might have decided to hole up with? Any secret problems in his life?"

"You want a cup of coffee?" Carr asked, yanking open a hulking old refrigerator that was the yellowed hue of old piano keys. He withdrew a carton of milk and set it down next to the peppers.

"Sure," I said, using the invitation as a sign it was okay for me to take a seat on one of the scattered stools in the room.

Carr took his time—filling the mugs slowly from the coffeemaker pot, pouring sugar from a yellow sack into a chipped bowl—and I sensed he was deliberating whether or not to make a disclosure. After he'd set everything on the butcher block, he wiped his hands again on his apron and looked me straight in the eye.

"Do you know or *not* know about Tom's stint in rehab?" he asked finally.

Oh wow, I thought. "When was this?"

"About a year ago."

"Are we talking coke?"

"Nope, antidepressants. He started taking them last year right after his mother died, along with sleeping pills, and he just got hooked. He did two weeks at a place in Massachusetts and then crashed here afterwards for another couple of weeks. It was actually great. He helped me on a project, and he worked in my garden every day. And he seemed in great shape when he left."

"Could he have relapsed?" I asked, reaching over and helping myself to a mug of coffee.

"I suppose it's a possibility, but Tom's not really the druggie type. I saw his situation as an isolated incident, all tied in with the depression he felt over losing two parents so close together." He shook his head hard in a gesture of frustration and worry. "No, that's not what concerns me. I keep seeing a car wreck in my mind. And we've got to do something."

"Okay, I'm going to explore that end next," I said. "I'll contact the state police. And I promise to keep you posted."

My stomach was churning when I left a few minutes later, a combo effect from downing an entire mug of coffee in two minutes and the new concerns I felt about Tom. What if he *had* had an accident? I was anxious to be on the road again, but I also needed to eat—and to think. I found a parking spot downtown, and before heading into a small restaurant, I picked up a New York State tourist map at the shop next door. After I'd ordered a Caesar salad, I spread out the map in front of me.

Tom's call to the assistant director had been made when he was less than an hour north of the city. If Tom had indeed had an accident in the hours after that, locating his car would be tough since we had no idea where he was actually headed. He might have been going to Saratoga, in which case he would have stayed on the New York State Thruway. But he could have gotten off onto a smaller road or picked up the Mass Turnpike in Albany to head to Boston or someplace else in New England. He could have even been on his way north to Canada for all I knew. I let my eyes roam the map. North of Newburgh Junction were Ulster and Greene counties. North and to the west was the Catskill

Mountain region, with old-fashioned-sounding towns like Margaretville and Loch Sheldrake.

And then I spotted it. I nearly gulped. A town called *Andes*. Like a flash, I saw in my mind the photo of Tom and his parents, with "Andes" written on the back. Because of their many travels, I'd instantly assumed Peru. But what if it was *this* Andes? According to Chris, the family had a weekend home, and Tom had been in the process of selling it this year. But what if he hadn't done so yet? The turnoff for Andes was right near Newburgh Junction.

My salad arrived, and I wolfed it down while I simultaneously phoned the intern ghetto at *Buzz*. I asked the chick who answered to pull up a Web site we used to check property records and told her to find anything belonging to Tom Fain. She promised to call me back in a few minutes.

"No, I'll hold," I told her, totally wired. I could hear the tap of her computer keys as she worked.

"There are a few Tom Fains," she said. "I'm not sure—"

I interrupted, giving her the address on Mercer.

"Okay, I see it," she said after an agonizing minute. "There's another place, too. Do you want it?"

"Yes!" I nearly screamed.

"Dabbet Road, Andes, New York." She pronounced "Andes" like "Ands," but I forgave her. I couldn't believe it. Mentally, I calculated how long it would take me to drive there. Just a couple of hours—south and west.

As I raced along in my Jeep minutes later, I considered the likelihood of Tom going there. Though earlier he had told Chris he was unloading the place, the sale might have fallen through, or he might have changed his mind. This could also explain why he hadn't made any more phone calls from his cell. Reception might be bad in the mountains, and he could be relying on a landline for any communication. I tried 411 and found a listing for Fain on Dabbet Road, but no one answered when I called it. *Why* would he have gone there? I wondered. Was it to chase the boredom because his weekend plans had fallen through? He'd told Harper that he had work to do. Was he working on the property? Getting it ready for a sale? Then why not return? Or let anyone know his whereabouts? Maybe his real goal had been to place himself far from the madding crowd for an indefinite period of time. Or maybe something had happened to him.

It was nearly six by the time I arrived in Andes, and the sun was sinking in the sky. Though it was still technically summer, the days seemed so much shorter now. I rolled down my window and felt a blast of cool mountain air. Figuring I'd probably be back in the city by this time, I hadn't brought along a sweater or jacket.

The town of Andes was small and charming without trying too hard. Along the main drag were a few little shops, a general store, and a little café where a few people still lounged at tables on the porch. I pulled into a parking spot, looking for someone to ask directions from. A tall older woman, her gray hair pinned up dramatically on top of her head, was sweeping the sidewalk in front of a red-painted antiques shop, with a sign that read NEST OF TREASURES.

"Excuse me," I said after climbing out of the Jeep. "Could you please tell me how to get to Dabbet Road?"

"You're looking for the Fain house?" she asked in a husky, cultured voice that suggested she might have packed up her life in Manhattan and moved here for a simpler existence.

"How did you know?"

"It's the only house on that road. Are you a potential buyer?"

"Buyer? No, I'm actually looking for Tom Fain. My name is Bailey Weggins. I'm a friend of a friend of Tom's."

"Oh, I didn't realize he was up here this week. Okay, then, you're going to have to head back the way you came and make a left on Harrow. Just before you reach the outskirts of town, you'll see Dabbet on your left. Tell him Beverly said hi, will you?"

"Sure thing."

My whole body was buzzing as I jumped back into the Jeep. I hadn't wanted to be too nosy with the woman, but it sounded as if the deal for the house, the one Tom had told Chris about, *had* fallen through and the house was once again for sale. Maybe that was why Tom had come to Andes—to goose the sales process.

It was no problem finding Dabbet. As Beverly had told me, it was only a short hike from the center of town, and I bet myself that as a boy Tom had probably walked it. Dabbet Road, a dirt one, was longer than I expected, maybe half a mile, and before long I was being jounced along the deep gouges under a dense canopy of maples and giant firs.

The first thing I spotted was a barn, a low, long gray one at the very end of the road. Then suddenly the house appeared, off to the right, a big old clapboard. Beyond that on the road was a small white cottage, probably a guesthouse, its back to the road. And right in front of it was a black Audi.

CHAPTER 5

I turned off the ignition and just sat in my Jeep for a minute, feeling my heart thump. I had found Tom. In the end, it hadn't taken all that long or been a particularly wearisome quest, but as of yesterday it had seemed it might be impossible. With the only clue being a single phone call from along the thruway, I had felt as if I were searching for someone lost on a catamaran in the Atlantic. But now here he was, just yards away from me.

I felt relief and an unexpected prickling of tears in my eyes. I also felt weird as hell. What was I supposed to do *now*? Wouldn't Tom be pissed that I'd just shown up out of the blue? What if he was holed up with some new chick, working his way through the *Kama Sutra*? But I couldn't turn around and just head back to Manhattan. Not without telling him that Chris and Harper were concerned about him. Not without making sure he was okay. Because there was still the chance that something wasn't right.

I slid out of the Jeep and slammed the door hard. Better, I

thought, to make noise and not catch him totally unaware. Because his car was pulled up tight to the cottage, I figured he must have been staying there. I wondered if the main house seemed too big to him or if it was too full of memories. I took a breath and started down a slate path that ran along the side of the cottage, its blue gray slabs almost obscured by yellowed tufts of grass.

Rounding the bend in the path, I saw that the front of the cottage faced the woods. It looked like something out of a storybook, with a narrow porch running along the width of the house and white curtains lining the windows on either side of a blue Dutch door. But as I stepped closer, I could see that the cottage was slightly worse for wear. The gray paint on the porch floorboards had mostly worn off, and the two wicker rockers were badly weathered and saggy in the seats. I glanced over toward the main house, whose front also faced the woods. It seemed even more forlorn than the cottage. The shutters had all been removed and lay stacked against the side of the house. Even from where I stood, I could see that it was in desperate need of a paint job.

I turned back to the cottage and mounted the steps, which creaked with each footfall. I rapped on the blue door. Once, twice, three times. No answer. Off in the woods, a bird screeched—a hawk, I thought—but no sound came from within the cottage.

"Tom," I called out. "Hey, Tom."

Still no answer, just a screech from the hawk again. I glanced behind me. The sun had begun to set, and the woods were becoming a smudge. It would be dark before long. I wondered if Tom was over in the big house—playing Mr. Fix-It.

Before heading over there, I gave the door one more rap, and then purely owing to my can't-keep-my-damn-nose-out-of-anything instinct, I tried the handle. It was unlocked. I gently pushed the cottage door open and stepped inside.

"Hey, Tom," I called out again. "Tom, are you around?" Nothing. Just the hum of a refrigerator off in another room.

The inside of the cottage had the same storybook quality as the outside. It was the kind of space that would be great to curl up in on a rainy fall day. I could see a small kitchen through a doorway on the far side, but most of the downstairs space was made up of a living room with a chunky gray stone fireplace. It was filled with an eclectic mix of dark wood tables and chintz-covered furniture begging to be flopped in. My eyes roamed the room and quickly fell on the coffee table. Several grease-stained pieces of sandwich wrapping paper lay on top, practically declaring, "Tom Fain ate here." I stepped closer and peered at the paper. In one of the folds was a small scrap of curled dried meat—it looked days old. An open newspaper next to it was dated the Saturday he disappeared. Dread swelled in me, and I found myself thinking of something an old reporter I once worked with used to say on such occasions: "I don't like the fuckin' looks of this."

"Tom," I called out almost frantically, but not even expecting an answer now. A partially enclosed staircase led up to the second floor, and I sprinted up the steps. There were two bedrooms on either side of the small hall at the top. The one to the right was empty; the one to the left, decorated all in white, showed signs of recent occupation—a pair of large hiking boots lying sideways on the floor and a man's shirt tossed on a chair. The white matelasse spread on the bed was rumpled, as if someone had made it hurriedly.

I glanced behind me and saw a brown leather duffel bag on the floor in back of the door. It was open but full, with a pair of jeans poking out from the top. Why, if Tom had been here for twelve days, had he worn so few of the clothes he'd brought? Just as with the sandwich paper on the coffee table, it was as if time had stopped days ago.

I flew back down the stairs and ducked into the kitchen, where the fridge hummed quietly, clueless to the fact that something was horribly wrong. On the counter I saw the plastic bag that must have once contained the sandwich and, incongruously next to it, an empty bottle of Veuve Clicquot champagne.

I hurried outside. As much as I dreaded it, I was going to have to check the main house now. When I stepped off the porch, I swept the woods with my eyes. Off to the left I could see a ruined stacked stone wall, the one, perhaps, that Tom had posed with his parents in front of. Behind it, through the dense trees, something glinted, and I realized that it was a sliver of silver pond. What if Tom had gone swimming and been stricken with cramps, incapacitated? What if he was lying at the bottom of that pond? Conjuring up that image made me want to hurl.

As I crossed the grass, I saw that the main house was even wearier looking than I'd realized earlier—peeled paint, flower beds long gone to weeds, drooping steps to an open porch along the width of the house. Please be alive, Tom, I pleaded to myself as I crossed the lawn. To my surprise, the front door, inside a screen door, was wide open. Maybe everything was all right after all. "Tom," I called out as I made my way to the steps.

But then the smell hit me like a bulldozer. I had smelled death on more than a few occasions—the first time as a reporter in Albany, watching as a body was hauled from the Hudson and being greeted by that ripe, nauseating whiff from twenty feet away. But this was more putrid than anything I'd ever experienced. It seemed to pour from the door like a force, and it was mixed, almost incongruously, with the awful stench of charred wood. I retched and covered my nose and mouth with my hand. Someone was dead inside the house.

I could see from the outside that the front hall was almost dark, illuminated only by the remains of daylight that seeped through the porch windows. Pulling up my shirt against my face, I stepped inside and fumbled for a light switch. I found one finally to the left, and as I flipped it, an overhead chandelier lit up, flooding the space with too bright light. I was in a large center hall, totally empty of furniture, and from what I could see, the rest of the house was empty, too, except for an odd piece of furniture here and there. The smell was nearly overpowering now. I retched again and forced myself to breathe through my mouth.

What I wanted to do was leave—no, let me rephrase that: I wanted to tear ass out of there so fast that I'd leave a trench in the lawn. But I had to know about Tom, no matter how horrible the truth was.

I did a fast sweep of the downstairs rooms, fighting the unrelenting urge to dry heave. Though the rooms were spacious, there weren't that many of them—to my right a big dining room, kitchen, and mud room; to the left a living room and screened-in porch; and behind the living room what must have once been the library, though the bookshelves were all empty now. Against a wall in the library was a large push broom, a mop, and a two-gallon plastic bucket of dirty water. Someone was housecleaning—or at least had been.

What I didn't find was the source of the smell. Which meant I was going to have to go upstairs.

I swung back to the hallway and began to mount the stairs. I knew I was breathing the scent of death, but what confused me was the burned notes of the smell. There'd been a fire of some kind, but *where*? At the top of the stairs, I discovered that two hallways led off from the landing. One led directly to the left. The other ran perpendicular to the stairs, toward the front of the house. The smell seemed to emanate from that direction, so that's where I headed. Frantically, I searched for a light switch, but when I found one and flipped it, nothing happened. I kept going, though, through the fading light of the afternoon and the upward glow from the chandelier. The first room I reached was huge, perhaps once the master bedroom. Enough daylight spilled into the space for me to see even into its corners. The only objects in the room were a small table lamp sitting forlornly on the dusty floor by a telephone and, near the window, several paint cans and a paint tray. And the smell. It was huge now. There was nothing in the room that could be producing it, but on the far left wall was an open door to what had to be a bathroom. The smell from hell had to be coming from there.

I glanced reflexively behind me and listened. Then I turned back and forced myself to walk to the bathroom. Despite the fabric against my face, the smell fought its way up my nostrils, making me retch again. I noticed the Knicks cap first, lying on the old white tile floor, the window on the right opened a crack, but then my eyes flew to the sink and the mirror above it. They were spattered with what looked like dried blood, as if someone had sprayed a canister of it. And then a movement caught my attention, yanking my eyes to the other side of the large bathroom—to the tub. I turned and gasped. It was the length of a body, partially charred and decayed into a toxic soup. But the face was moving. Terrified, I stepped closer and saw that the movement was coming not from the face itself but from a swirling mass of white maggots feeding on it.

On legs nearly limp, I backed out of the bathroom, my heart beating wildly with fear. It had to be Tom in the tub. Whatever had happened to him clearly had happened days ago, yet the whole house seemed ominous at the moment, as if someone were hiding in there, watching me. I grabbed a breath through my mouth and shot out of the bedroom. I took the stairs two at a time and practically threw myself onto the lawn.

The sun had set now, and I could barely find my way as I raced across the grass. Just as I reached the side of the cottage, a light came on over the porch. I jerked my head fearfully in that direction. It was obviously hooked to a light sensor. I scrambled to my Jeep and propelled myself inside.

Locked in the car, I breathed deeply and willed myself to calm down. I had to call 911, yet I couldn't bear the idea of waiting by the house for the cops. I decided to make the call from the place where Dabbet met the main road.

After I backed out of the driveway and began to make my way jerkily over the bumpy road, my fear gave way to grief. The body had been unrecognizable, but it had to be Tom. Had he *burned* to death? The tiles behind the tub had been singed gray and yet the tub had obviously managed to contain the fire—along with help from the slightly opened window. Was it some kind of freak accident—triggered by a combustible substance he was working with? But then why the blood near the sink? Someone must have murdered him. Bludgeoned or stabbed him and then set the body on fire with something nearby—like paint remover. Or had Tom killed *himself*? Slitting his wrists and then, when that didn't work, setting himself on fire? What if that was the whole reason he had come to Andes to begin with? Perhaps his parents' deaths had caught up with him again. Had the champagne been part of his suicide ritual—a toast to his life? A way to dull the pain? My stomach was sour, and I knew if I didn't stop picturing the body, I would puke all over my car.

The road seemed even longer on the way out, but finally I spotted the main road running in front of me. I hit the brake, put the Jeep in neutral, and dug my BlackBerry out of my bag. The 911 operator picked up after two rings.

"I need to report a dead body on Dabbet Road, in the town of Andes," I said. "It may be a homicide."

"Is there any chance the person is still alive?"

"N-no," I said, my voice nearly choked. She might as well have asked if there was any chance that Coldplay was about to do a concert on the lawn that night.

She asked for the exact address of the house, my name, and where I was calling from. Then she told me that she had dispatched a car from the county sheriff's office and that it should be there within ten minutes. She advised me to stay on the line.

"No, my battery's low," I lied. "I'll wait right here at the entrance of the road, okay? I'm in a black Jeep."

I didn't want to hold. I needed to call Chris right away and break the news to him. I had programmed in his number the other night, but my fingers fumbled like crazy just trying to bring it up. Part of me wanted desperately to hear his voice, to share my grief, and another part dreaded telling him.

He answered just as I thought his phone was about to go to voice mail, his "Hello?" barely climbing over the restaurant or bar sounds behind him.

"Can you go someplace quiet?" I shouted. "I need to talk to you."

"Gimme a second, okay?"

I could hear the noise diminish gradually as he walked, until finally it was totally muffled, as if he had found a spot in a back corridor or down a flight of stairs.

"There, that's better," he said finally.

"Where are you, anyway?"

"Just a bar with one of the guys in the cast. What's up?"

"Chris, I've got awful news. I think—I think Tom is dead."

"What? What do you mean, *think*?"

"I'm at his parents' old weekend home. Tom apparently hadn't sold it yet. There's a body here, in the main house. It's not recognizable, but I'm pretty sure it must be Tom."

"Jesus Christ, you're kidding."

"I'm so sorry, Chris," I said. "I—"

"Wait, where are you, exactly? Where is all this happening?"

"I'm in a town called Andes. It's in the Catskills, a few hours from New York."

"Oh God. What happened to him?"

"Chris, I hate doing this over the phone. The body was burned. I'm not sure how he died, but it's possible someone killed him. Like I said, I think it's Tom, but I'm not a hundred percent sure.

I'm waiting for the police to show up now, and maybe I'll know more in a little while."

"Oh God, this is awful," he said, his voice tight with anguish. "I need to tell Harper."

"Why don't you hold off for tonight, at least? There's no point in upsetting her if it turns out not to be Tom. In fact, it's probably better not to say anything to anyone yet. There's going to be a police investigation."

"Are you all alone there, Bailey? Are you okay?"

"Yes, I'm alone but I'm not in the house anymore," I said, touched by his concern. "It was just too awful. I'm down the road in my car, waiting for the cops."

"How did you end up there, anyway? I mean, I didn't even know where the house was."

"One thing just kind of led to another. I think I see the cops. I'll call you back as soon as I have a sense of what's going on."

What had caught my attention through the fir trees was a vehicle slowing down along the main road, just before the turn onto Dabbet. But it turned out to be a tow truck, headed to a breakdown somewhere. I waited in the car, restless and anxious, trying to banish the memory of the horrible ooze in the tub. It was another ten minutes before a Delaware County sheriff's car finally made the turn and pulled up beside me.

There was only one officer in the car, a woman probably in her mid-thirties. She rolled down her window.

"I'm Deputy Sheriff Sue Dannon. Are you the person who called 911?"

"Yes, I'm Bailey Weggins. I found a badly decomposed body in the house up the road. I think it's Tom Fain, who owns the house."

She eyed me warily. "Is there anyone else in the house at this time?"

"There doesn't appear to be. Tom's been missing for almost

two weeks, and it looks as if he might have been dead about that long. Do you want me to show you?"

"All right—I'll follow you."

She waited while I turned the Jeep around, which was no easy feat on the narrow rutted road. As we neared the property, my heart leapt. Light was now seeping out of one of the windows along the back of the main house. But then I realized it had to be the light from the chandelier spilling into the rest of the house.

Dannon pulled up her vehicle right behind me, and we both climbed out. As she approached me, I noticed that her hand instinctively touched her gun. She was about five six, probably just a few years older than me. If she was attractive, it was hard to tell because her hair was all under her big black hat and she had that tough-as-nails expression that cops are trained to wear.

"The body's in the big house?" she asked, cocking her head toward it.

"Yes, in a second-floor bathroom off one of the bedrooms. I don't think I can go in there again," I said.

She started to say something, and then I actually saw her nostrils flare. The breeze had shifted direction, and a hint of the putrid smell had found its way to us. The expression that suddenly crossed Dannon's face suggested that someone had just offered her a slice of grilled river rat.

"Jesus," she said.

"It's pretty bad. Do you have a mask?"

"Please stay right here," she said, ignoring my question and heading off across the lawn. I guess she didn't want to appear wimpy by taking me up on my suggestion, but as she walked I saw her yank a white handkerchief from her pocket and squash it against her face.

I jumped back into the Jeep and turned the AC on high. I knew she'd said to stay right where I was, but I wasn't going to take her literally. I couldn't stomach breathing in that smell and knowing it was probably Tom.

Less than ten minutes passed before I saw Dannon emerge like a specter from the darkness of the lawn. She was talking into a walkie-talkie, clearly calling in reinforcements. As soon as she'd attached the device to her belt, she dabbed at her mouth with the hankie. Something told me her last meal was somewhere back on the grass.

I jumped out of the Jeep again and discovered that the wind must have shifted because the smell wasn't as horrific now.

"Please get back into the car," she said. "I'd like to ask you a few questions."

She slid into the passenger seat next to me. Up close, I could see that her brow was damp with sweat. I knew from covering crimes that cops could work a lifetime without seeing body soup. This very well might have been the worst, most retch-worthy thing she'd ever laid eyes on.

"You think the body must be this fellow Tom Fain?" she asked after drawing a long, deep breath.

I told her yes and then offered a shorthand version of the story, leaving out details about the various players involved—like Tom shagging the star of the show. She listened thoughtfully, taking notes, but retained that wall of wariness she'd displayed from the first moment we'd spoken. To her, my tale probably sounded oddly far-fetched—I didn't even know Tom personally, yet I'd been out searching half the state for him. As far as she knew, I could have killed him myself and then returned to the scene of the crime.

She was still peppering me with questions when I heard the rumble of a vehicle above the AC and lights pierced the back window of my Jeep. We spun around in unison. Reinforcements had arrived.

"Please wait here," she told me. In my rearview mirror, I

watched her hurry toward the sheriff's car that had pulled up behind us, and then I lost her in the glare of the headlights. For ten
minutes I waited, wondering if she'd been beamed up, and then
suddenly someone killed the high beams and I could see her in
discussion near the car with two men in sheriff's hats. Soon, several other vehicles arrived, and people in uniform began tramp-
ing back and forth across the lawn, barking comments to one
another. Despite all the activity and how rattled I felt, I almost
nodded off a few times. I felt exhausted, achy, heartsick. Thirty
minutes later, I was still by myself in the car, and despite all the
excitement outside, things on my end seemed to be moving at the
speed of melting ice.

Finally, Dannon rapped on my window and asked me to follow her. There were more lights on in the big house now, illumi-
nating a huddle of several people in uniform outside, but she led
me instead to the porch of the cottage, where she introduced me
to a Sheriff Schmidt—a guy with a torso the size of a redwood
tree and a thick, wiry mustache that looked as if it would hurt as
much as a bitch slap if you tried to kiss him. He was probably fifty
and appeared far less shaken than Dannon.

"Thank you for waiting, Miss Weggins," he said. "Have a seat,
please."

With my butt perched on just the edge of one of the old
wicker rockers and my arms wrapped tightly around me against
the mountain chill, I went through a slightly more expansive version of my saga than I'd given earlier: who Tom was, why I was
looking for him, how I'd ended up in the town of Andes. He nodded politely, less stern looking than Dannon, but his next question proved I wasn't going to get an easy ride.

"Quite a bit of trouble to go through for someone you don't
even know," he said.

"True, but I do know *Chris* well—he's a good friend," I said.

"And since I'm a freelance writer, I had the time to check out a few leads."

Though he observed me expectantly, waiting for something *more*, I forced myself to stop. What I'd learned about cops—both as a crime reporter and having been interrogated by them myself—is that overexplaining makes them *real* suspicious. Plus the more you say, the greater the danger of becoming tangled in your own words and blurting out the wrong thing. All of a sudden, you're confessing to setting a string of warehouse fires or having helped Lee Harvey Oswald escape from the Texas School Book Depository.

"So you never met Mr. Fain personally?"

"Never, no, but I have a picture of him," I said, drawing the head shot out of my purse and handing it over to him. "Of course, it won't help with the identification, but you might want it for your inquiries."

After studying the photo, he flipped it over and read the résumé with furrowed brow, as if I'd just handed him a clue to the three secrets of Fatima. I took out a pen and paper from my purse and jotted down Tom's address and also Chris's phone number. They would want access to Tom's apartment to search for clues. It wouldn't be long before they'd be stumbling onto Locket's note.

"As you've been following up on your so-called leads, Miss Weggins," Schmidt said, looking up from the photo, "have you found any information that would be relevant to our investigation? Was Mr. Fain depressed, for instance?"

"Are you thinking suicide?" I asked. "The thought crossed my mind—but then how do you explain all that blood?"

"Just answer the question, please, Miss Weggins."

"Apparently, Tom was depressed at one point. After the death of his mother. But there wasn't any indication he'd been upset lately."

"Any enemies you're aware of?"

"No, not that I'm aware of. There is one thing you should know. Tom had apparently withdrawn seven thousand dollars in cash before he came up here. I don't know why or what for."

He considered the info wordlessly. I sensed he had something else to ask me, but suddenly he announced that I was free to go. He added that his office might be in touch with me over the next few days.

Dannon walked me out to my car, which gave me an opportunity to check directions back to the highway with her. As soon as I reached the end of the pitted road and turned onto the main drag, I rolled down all the car windows and let the wind blast away at the interior. The cool air whipped my hair around my face so hard that it stung, but at least I could breathe again.

The ride back to Manhattan was god-awful. My head had started to throb, along with my legs, and I could find only one Advil in my purse, a quantity that proved to be as useful as swatting at a fly with a rubber band.

Each time my mind found its way again to that horrible mess fermenting in the tub, I'd force myself to focus instead on the overall situation. During the next few days, forensic evidence would surely confirm that it was Tom lying dead in the house. I supposed there was a remote chance it could be someone else—a workman, for instance, who'd been painting the bathroom—but why would Tom's possessions and his car still be on site? It also seemed pretty obvious from the evidence that Tom had died the very day he'd arrived. His last phone call, after all, had been made that day, he'd barely unpacked his bag, and the one newspaper had been from that Saturday. I tried to re-create part of the day in my mind: He'd picked up a sandwich—perhaps at that little café in town—chowed down while reading the paper. Had he washed it down with champagne? That part was hard to explain. Had someone shared the bottle with him? Perhaps after lunch he'd taken a walk around the property (the muddy boots) and squeezed in a nap (the rumpled bed). Alone?

At some point before dark, he'd headed over to the main house, most likely to tackle the bathroom. This may have been the work he'd been referring to when he'd spoken to Harper. And then probably not long after he'd started, someone had shown up and killed him. Was it a burglar who had thought the house would be empty? But what had he been hoping to steal? Maybe Tom had an enemy in Andes, someone he'd enraged during one of the summers he'd spent there. Or maybe it was someone from the city who had known where he'd be or had followed him up there.

Of course, there was also the suicide theory. It had occurred to me and to Schmidt, too. But it didn't make a whole lot of sense. Stab yourself and then light yourself on fire? And there was no evidence that Tom had *recently* been depressed.

As I neared the city, I realized I'd been so roiled up, I'd never called Chris back. I punched in his number.

"You're not still there, are you?" he asked tensely as soon as he heard my voice.

"No—I'm about thirty minutes from home. How you doing?"

"Not good. But what about you? You're the one dealing with all this firsthand. I can't believe I got you into this." There was a note of real tenderness in his voice.

"I'll be okay. The police talked to me, and it's clear they don't know anything yet. I gave them your name and number because they need access to Tom's apartment."

"Um, okay," he said.

"Any chance we could get together first thing in the morning and I can go over everything?"

"Yeah, I really need to see you. I'm not shooting till ten, so I could come around eight," he said.

As soon as he hung up, I realized how quiet the car was. I hadn't played any CDs on the ride back because I'd thought the noise would drive me even crazier. The only sound now was my breathing and the whirring of cars outside. I was startled when my cell phone went off again. I figured it had to be Chris, calling back with a question.

"Hey," I said.

Nothing. And then the sound of someone—it was hard to tell whether it was male or female—crying with hard, anguished sobs.

"Who is this?" I asked, my voice catching.

Then there was only silence.

CHAPTER 6

W ho is this?" I asked again, my voice catching. Nothing. When I glanced at the phone to see the number, the words announced "Caller Unknown." A second later, I was disconnected.

Hesitantly, I rested the BlackBerry on the seat next to me, troubled by the sound that I'd heard, wondering if the person would call back. Had it simply been a wrong number—or perhaps an obnoxious prank? For a split second, I considered whether it might have been Chris. Had he broken down after he'd called me, phoned me back, and then hung up out of embarrassment?

My attention was yanked back to the highway. The traffic was picking up now that I was approaching the Tappan Zee, demanding my full attention. By eleven, I was finally back in the city, and the first thing I did after stepping into my apartment was strip off my clothes and stuff them into the hamper. Then I limped into the shower. I needed to get the smell off me—out of my hair, off my skin, out of my pores. I shampooed my hair twice and used a loofah to scrub my body so that it was flushed red by the time I was finished.

Wrapped in a towel and with my hair sopping wet, I traipsed to the kitchen in search of nourishment. I hadn't eaten since lunch, and I was ravenous, yet the thought of most food still made me gag. I settled for toast and tea. Just as the teakettle squealed, my intercom buzzer went off. I had no idea who would be stopping by out of the blue at nearly midnight on a Thursday night.

"Chris is here to see you," the doorman said as soon as I answered.

"Um, okay," I said, surprised. "Send him up."

I was anxious to talk to Chris, yearned, for that matter, to share the whole awful story with him, yet I hadn't prepared myself mentally to do it *tonight*. I threw on a pair of jeans, a tank top, and a pair of flip-flops and warned myself not to start blubbering. It would only make it worse for him.

Chris was in jeans, too, and a dusty green polo shirt, almost the color of his eyes. The look on his face said that the news about Tom was eating him up.

"Sorry to barge in like this," he said soberly. "I just couldn't wait until tomorrow to see you."

"No, I understand. Do you want a beer?"

"Definitely."

He was standing in the middle of the room, staring at the old kilim rug on my living room floor, when I returned a minute later with the bottle of beer and my mug of tea. There was only one lamp lit in the room, the one on the wooden end table by the couch, but it was enough to see his face by. He looked heartsick.

"Any developments since I talked to you?" he asked as I handed him the beer.

"No, and I'm sure the sheriff's department isn't going to want to share anything with me as things move forward. It's going to be tough to get news about the investigation."

"You said the body was badly decomposed. What makes you think it was really Tom's?"

"For one thing, his car was there, and his duffel bag was in the guest cottage."

I described the setup of the property, as well as some of the details of the scene, leaving out the most gruesome parts. He absorbed it all, his mouth clenched.

"Is there a chance that he died of some kind of freak accident?" Chris asked.

"I don't think so, though I wouldn't have any way of knowing from the brief glimpse I got of the scene. The sheriff who questioned me even suggested suicide, but—"

"*Suicide?*" he exclaimed.

"I just don't buy that, though. There was blood all around the sink and on the mirror above it. My guess—and it's just a guess—is that he was attacked with a knife or some heavy object and set on fire afterward." I didn't add, *Possibly while he was still alive.*

Chris shook his head in utter disgust. "Do you think—do you think someone from the show could have killed him?"

"It's a possibility." Alex Ottoson's name flashed across my brain suddenly. What if he'd learned of Locket's affair with Tom?

"I hate the fact that I got you involved, Bailey," he said. "But at the same time, who knows when Tom would have been found if you hadn't started looking."

I explained how I had made the connection to Andes and tracked down Tom's address through the Internet.

"He never mentioned to you that it was in the Catskills?" I asked.

"Uh, not that I recall. I mean, he might have, but if he did, it went in one ear and out the other. I do remember him saying that it had gone to seed after his father had died and that he was relieved to have finally sold it—this was in the beginning of the summer, when I was living with him."

"It seems like the deal fell through. I'll see what I can find out about it." I hesitated. "It's funny that he never told Harper about it, either. Or at least she never mentioned it as a possibility for where he might be."

"Speaking of Harper, do you still feel I should keep her out of this for now?" he asked.

"Actually, I've been rethinking that. Since it may be a few days before anything is confirmed about the identity, news is going to leak out. It's better for Harper to hear it from you than thirdhand. Why don't you tell her tomorrow?"

"I should probably tell the executive producer as well. Better he hear it from me, too."

I sipped my tea and thought a moment. "You know when we spoke earlier—while I was driving back?" I said. "You didn't call me right after that, did you?"

"No—why?" he asked.

"The phone rang, and someone was crying. It was a wrong number, obviously. At the time, though, I just wondered . . ."

"No, it wasn't me. But I've *felt* like crying."

"Gosh, Chris, I'm just so sorry."

I set my mug on the coffee table and squeezed his arms. Through the soft cotton fabric I could feel how hard his biceps were. Late last winter, those arms had wrapped around me on several occasions. I'd engaged in some pretty heavy make-out sessions with Chris on my couch, his jeans bulging and my bra bunched around my waist. But I had never gone to bed with him. It wasn't because that gorgeous face and awesome body of his had failed to make me crazy with lust. They *had*. But I could never stop associating my breakup with Jack—and *hurting* him—with my attraction to Chris, and every time I was about to urge us off the couch and into the bedroom, I would find this weird guilt dousing my desire. Tonight, though, Jack seemed like a long time ago.

"I just feel lucky to be with you tonight, Bailey," Chris said, and offered a grim smile. "This would be awful to handle alone."

He set down his drink then and pulled me into his arms. It was a friendly, caring hug, like the one he'd given me the other night. But as he held me, he sighed and his body relaxed into mine. He lifted his right hand and stroked my damp hair, softly at first and then with firmer, more urgent fingers. I felt something stir in me.

Chris pulled back slightly and stared into my eyes. Then his mouth found mine. I was instantly reminded of how good his soft, full lips could feel and taste. He kissed me hungrily, and I kissed him back with the same urgency. As I relaxed into his body even more, I couldn't help but notice the hardness between his legs.

"God, Bailey," he said. "I want to consume every inch of you."

"Okay," I whispered without any hesitation. I realized I was saying yes for a whole bunch of reasons—because what girl could resist a line like that one, because I *wanted* Chris and there was no guilt this time, and because I felt, as he probably did, that sex would chase away our sadness for a while.

"Why don't we just go to bed, then," I said.

I turned off the lamp and walked with him to my bedroom. I kicked off my flip-flops and found a stretchy to tie back my wet hair. When I turned around, Chris was pulling off his shirt. He was less tan than when I'd seen him before—perhaps from working all summer—but the color he did have accented his well-defined abs. He had two Chinese characters tattooed on his right arm, meaning good fortune, something I'd nearly forgotten about. I reached up and stroked his chest with my hands.

He leaned down and kissed me, his tongue in my mouth. He

laid both hands on my breasts and, through the fabric of my tank top, circled my nipples with his thumbs.

"You know what the first thing you ever said to me was?" I asked. "When you were tending bar at that wedding?"

He shook his head almost imperceptibly, his eyes squinted.

"You asked me if I wanted a buttery nipple."

He smirked. "I couldn't disguise my fascination with you even then."

With both hands, he pulled my tank over my head and took my breasts in his hands, stroking and massaging them while he kissed me again. My heart was racing now, and my legs felt all rubbery.

Still kissing me, he laid the heel of his hand against my groin and pressed, released, pressed, released. I let out a moan, not meaning to. He yanked apart the top snap of my jeans, pulled down the zipper, and then tugged off both my jeans and under-wear. I tried to reach for the button of *his* jeans, but he lifted me and laid me back on the white duvet that covered my bed. He took off his own jeans and stepped out of a pair of gray boxer briefs. His naked body was as gorgeous as his face. It seemed almost illegal that I was about to have sex with someone who looked like that.

For the next hour, he did what he had promised—consumed me. His fingers and mouth explored every inch of me, making me writhe with pleasure. I could see that he was being driven in large part by his despair over Tom's death. Was this what you'd call a grief fuck? I wondered. Maybe, but it felt too good to worry about. By the time he finally entered me, I was barely thinking straight anyway.

I fell asleep almost instantly in his hard, strong arms, totally spent. But an hour and a half later, I woke, needing to pee, and then there was no going back to sleep for me. After pouring my-self a glass of milk, I absorbed the view beyond my terrace. Even at this hour, buildings were dabbed with lights—suggesting party animals and floor pacers like me. For two years after my divorce, I'd been dogged by merciless, unrelenting insomnia, which had finally abated about seven or eight months ago. Any bout of sleeplessness put the fear of God in me. I hoped tonight was a fluke, a response to all the thoughts bubbling in my head—about Tom's ugly death, sleeping with Chris, thinking about Beau the moment Chris had thrust himself into me. From my coffee table, I picked up *The New York Times* that had been delivered the day before and skimmed through it. At about three, I dozed off on my couch and then at five crawled back into bed with Chris.

"Where'd you go last night?" Chris murmured when we both woke at about seven.

"Just a little floor pacing—due to everything that happened. Want a bagel? They're frozen, but if you slather them with raspberry jam, you can hardly tell."

"Sure," he said, slipping his hand between my thighs.

We made love again, quicker but just as urgent on his part as before. While he showered, I made coffee, dug the bagels from the freezer, and scraped ice crystals off them.

"So what do we do from here?" Chris asked, plopping down at the old pine dining table at the end of my living room. For a second, I thought he was referring to *us*—where did *we* go as a couple from here—but then in relief I realized he was referring to Tom's death. Because I wasn't at all sure where we should go from here.

"Well, as we said last night," I said, "you should tell Harper—and the executive producer. I'm going to break the news to this guy Barish. I'm not sure how close he and Tom were, but it will probably be upsetting."

"But how are we going to know if it's really Tom or not—like you said, the cops have no obligation to tell us. We're not family."

"I've got a few ideas on how to stay on top of this," I said. "Leave it to me."

Chris took a final slug of coffee and raked his hand through his hair. "Listen, Bailey," he said. "A bunch of us from the show usually get together on Friday nights at this pub in Chelsea—the Half King. It's mostly crew members and minor players, but everyone will be buzzing tonight about this. Do you want to come? Maybe we'll learn something about Tom we didn't know. Plus— I'd like to see you tonight. Every inch of you again, if it's okay with you."

"Sure, that would be great," I said, smiling—and meaning it.

"I'll call you when we finish up—it could be as late as eight tonight. If it's all right with you, I'll just meet you at the Half King."

After he'd left, kissing me gently good-bye, I grabbed my phone and called Detective O'Donnell.

"Goddamn," he muttered after I broke the news. "I said I didn't have a good feeling about this one."

I described the whole awful situation to him, and he pressed me for even more details. I sensed him silently calculating whether he could have done anything to prevent Tom's death.

"I'll touch base with the sheriff up there," he said, "and see what I can find out. The state troopers will probably get involved, too, and I've got contacts at their headquarters down here."

"I was thinking I'd better phone Mr. Barish as soon as I got off with you."

"Why don't you let me do that for you?"

"Great, thanks. But tell him he's welcome to call me if he'd like." I also asked if he'd call Professor Carr and break the news to him, since that was about the last thing in the world I wanted to do. He agreed and took down the info.

"May I call you in a day or two, just to see what you've learned from the sheriff's office?" I asked in closing.

"Sure. I'll tell you what I can."

After obtaining the number from directory assistance, I phoned Nest of Treasures, the antiques store I'd stopped in front of in Andes. I wasn't sure anyone would be in yet, but a woman answered and it was the same husky voice that had given me directions to Dabbet Road yesterday. I asked if it was Beverly.

"Yes, this is she." She sounded positively grim. Something told me the news had found its way to her.

"This is Bailey Weggins, the woman who asked directions to Dabbet Road yesterday. Have you heard about Tom Fain?"

"Good God, yes. Someone called me just a little while ago. You're the one who found him?"

"Yes, right after I left you. I wanted to call and let you know since you seemed to be a friend of his family."

"That was very kind of you. I'm devastated, of course—we all are. They were such a lovely family. You'd think there'd been a curse against them."

"In what sense?"

"The father dying, then Margo. And now poor Tom. They say they don't know how he died. That someone may have killed him. Or it may even have been suicide. What—what do you think happened?"

"I just don't know. Did Tom have any problems or issues with anyone up there?"

"Goodness, no. He'd actually spent very little time here after he started high school. Kids always feel there's nothing for them to do up here. Margo let the place go after her husband died, and once she became ill, she was rarely here, either. Tom only came back recently to sell the place."

"Tom told a mutual friend of ours that he'd actually sold the house earlier in the summer."

"Supposedly, yes, to some yuppie types—of course they don't call them that anymore. But in the end, the couple couldn't get a mortgage and had to pull out. There were no other bites this summer, apparently, and the real estate agent told Tom he'd have more luck if the house was in better shape."

"So he was trying to do it himself?"

"He was doing an odd job here and there from what he told me, but he'd hired Barry to do the bulk of it."

"Barry?"

"Barry's a kind of handyman/contractor up here. Tom had asked him to do some work on the house. Barry was waiting for the go-ahead two weeks ago but never heard from Tom."

I thought of the $7,000. "Would he have expected an advance?"

"I imagine so. That's how it usually works."

I asked her then if she would be willing to check with this Barry dude and let me know if he'd definitely been expecting a cash advance from Tom. She seemed hesitant, as if suddenly second-guessing her forthcomingness.

"Beverly, Tom apparently had a lot of cash on him, and I'm wondering if he may have been robbed. My goal is to find out who did this to him."

That seemed to reassure her. I promised to call back in a day or two. I had the feeling she was going to prove to be a good source for me.

Since the *Times* was predicting another day of warm weather, I threw on a tan-colored miniskirt, a sleeveless black top, and black slingbacks. Ten minutes later, I was on the train to *Buzz*. Tom Fain was no A-lister, but he was nonetheless an actor in a big new show, and Nash would probably want a small item about his death.

Fridays are always a pretty happening day at *Buzz*. Monday is the big closing day, when the cover story ships along with the other major "news" stories—about who dumped whom, who's shagging whom, and how many kids Angelina Jolie is thinking of adopting *this* week. It's also when the nasty gossip section "Juice Bar" gets written. (Never—let me repeat, *never*—get on their radar.) But many of these stories start coming to a head on Friday, and writers and editors start racing around out of their minds, as if we'd just landed a man on Mars.

I dumped my stuff on my desk and surveyed the scene. Leo was tapping away at his computer. Jessie's desk was empty, but there were corn muffin crumbs on the top of it.

"Jessie get her bikini line taken care of?"

"Yeah, but she's been in and out today. Something to do with Usher." Part of Jessie's job was to cover the music scene.

"You seem crazed."

"Yeah, well, I'm supposed to be doing a whole page on guys with back fat, and so far I've got only four. Any ideas?"

"No, but I'll keep my eyes peeled."

I glanced down toward the glass-fronted office of Nash Nolan. He'd be busier than hell today, but I needed to see him. Though the light was bouncing off the glass, making it hard to see, I discerned movement in there and headed off in that direction.

Nash *was* inside, talking to Mary Kay, the sixtyish former gossip columnist, West Coast based, whom the late and much-loathed Mona Hodges had brought on as a consultant. According to all reports, the last truly pertinent piece of celebrity news she'd broken was Liz Taylor's remarriage to Richard Burton. She seemed to rub Nash the wrong way, but since shows like *ET* loved her sound bites, and that was good for the magazine, her job seemed secure for now.

I tapped on the frame of the open door. Mary Kay glanced over and shot me the kind of look she probably reserved for times when someone came down hard on her instep.

"Got a minute?" I asked Nash. "I have some news I want to share."

"Yup. Why don't we finish up later, Mary Kay."

"All right, Nash, but we need to move quickly on this," she said, and bustled past me, glancing disapprovingly at my outfit. She was in a lightweight peach wool suit, her champagne-colored hair up in a French twist and her legs swathed in white hose that vaguely resembled mosquito netting. She probably considered it a style sin that I was sporting summer clothes in mid-September.

"What's up, Bailey?" Nash asked as soon as Mary Kay was out the door. "Tell me you've got something good, okay? I don't have jack for the cover this week."

I liked Nash. He was in his forties, with a handsome, rugged face and stocky build, barrel-chested. He wore his gray-tinged streaked hair slicked back on the sides, and there was always a pair of reading glasses perched on either the top of his head or the middle of his nose. Rumor had it that he'd had more than one fling at work—which once resulted in his wife dropping by and hurling her purse at his head—and now and then you caught him staring at your tits. But he was a great words editor and easy to get along with.

"It's not cover-worthy, but it's interesting. There's a new show being shot in New York called *Morgue,* and one of the young male actors with a small part on it has been killed, probably murdered."

I explained my own involvement and provided the Cliff Notes version of the situation.

"Jesus, what is it with you, Bailey? You give new meaning to the word *deadline.*"

"Do you want a short item?" I said.

"How'd he die?" he asked, peering at me over the reading glasses.

"Stabbed or bludgeoned. Then burned."

"All your favorite things. Tell me he also dated Lindsay Lohan at some point and then we're golden."

"Not that I know of," I said, ashamed suddenly of how I was bantering about Tom.

"I'll give you a column."

"Fine."

"And Bailey," he said as I moved out the door. "Try to keep your rear out of trouble this time, okay?"

Before talking to Photo about calling in a shot of Tom, I sauntered back to the kitchenette for coffee. Up ahead of me I saw Mary Kay, chin in the air, making her way toward one of the back offices that was reserved for L.A. staff when they came east. She was probably in town for a few days visiting contacts, something she did every month or so. Leo once told me it was so she could blow through the spa services at her hotel and let *Buzz* pick up the tab. I remembered something else he'd once told me about her. She used to write a column for *Soap Opera Digest* and loved that whole world. I grabbed a cup of coffee and poked my head in her office.

"Sorry to barge in on you back there, Mary Kay."

"Obviously it couldn't be helped," she declared in a tone that said she thought it certainly *could* have.

"I'd love to ask your advice if you've got a minute."

"All right, but please be quick about it, Bailey. I'm doing a TV segment in half an hour."

As I stepped into the office and closer to her, I could see that she was already made up for her appearance. Her face was covered in so many layers of Pan-Cake makeup, you'd half expect to find the fossilized remains of early life forms in there.

"What do you know about Locket Ford?" I asked.

"*Locket?*" she asked in surprise. "If *you're* interested, it means she's been up to no good. What did she do—test positive for Botox?"

"I'm simply curious," I replied. "A friend of mine is working on her new show. Has most of her career been in soaps?"

"Yes—and she had an enormous following. I believe she fancies herself as the next Demi—leaving the soaps behind for major stardom. And then there's the book."

"Book?"

"*Locket Ford's Guide to Beauty*. It's a fall book—and there's a party for it at Elaine's tomorrow night. Alex is giving it for her."

I filed away that info for later.

"What buzz do you hear about the show?" I asked. It was a selfish question—I was curious what was in store for Chris.

"Well, everything Alex Ottoson touches is a hit. Locket's always been known as a real fame digger, and hitching her star to Alex's wagon was a brilliant move on her part, professionally. But if you ask my opinion, nothing could be worth *that*."

"What do you mean?" I asked. I felt a tingle at the back of my neck.

"Oh, he's a nasty man. He's all debonair when you meet him, but he's got a cruel streak. And there's a rumor around that he likes to slap when he's mad."

CHAPTER 7

$\mathbf{D}$o you think it's true? Do you think he's abusive to her?"

"Don't tell me you want to run with this, Bailey. I was speaking off the record here."

I suppressed a sigh of exasperation. "Like I said, I'm just curious. I have a friend on the show."

"Well, for God's sake don't attribute anything to me when you're speaking to this friend of yours. And of course, if you pick up anything yourself, I hope you'll pass it on to me. Now, if you don't mind, I do need to freshen up for my segment."

As I walked back to my desk, I mulled over her revelation. Alex was nasty. Alex was possibly violent. What if he had gotten wind of Locket's toe-curling fling with Tom? Could he have followed Tom to Andes and killed him in a rage?

Tonight, there'd be a chance to chat with people from the show—though according to Chris, probably only minor players would be there. What I needed to do was crib an invitation to the party at Elaine's tomorrow night—for a firsthand look at both Locket and Alex. I certainly wasn't going to ask Mary Kay for help. She'd probably do her best to have me barred at the door. When I returned to my desk, I called the chick who oversaw the beauty coverage at *Buzz* and asked if she could get me into the event.

"You can have *my* invitation. There's a party for Jessica Simpson's beauty products I'd much rather go to anyway. Just let me know if anything good happens so I can file it."

Over the next hour, I drafted a brief write-up on Tom's death, knowing I'd have to flesh it out once I learned more. As promised, the beauty editor dropped off the invitation. Just as I was packing up my stuff to leave, Jessie strode in and plopped down at her desk.

"What's up?" she asked, her caramel eyes curious. "No offense, but you look like you haven't slept in four days."

I suggested we secure some coffee, and after grabbing two cups, we settled in an empty conference room, where I shared everything that had happened.

"Gosh, that's grisly," she said, frowning. "Any ideas about who did it?"

"Not so far. But you can help if you want. There's a book party for Locket Ford tomorrow night. It would be great if you could come with me. Having two sets of eyes and ears will be an advantage."

"Sure. I've got a date, but I've been looking for an excuse to bail. When this guy hits the dance floor, you worry the paramedics are going to show up looking for the person having the seizure."

After we finished talking, I headed home. As soon as I entered my apartment, I staggered toward my bedroom and fell on the bed, wasted. I craved a catnap, yet sleep eluded me. I kept seeing that horrible maggoty mess in the tub, and then my mind would ricochet to the lovely face of Tom Fain from his head shot. His family *did* seem cursed, just as Beverly had suggested. I also couldn't stop thinking about Chris. Had it been dumb to go to bed with him considering the circumstances? Would I soon regret the "we're both really sad so let's fuck" sex? But my interest in Chris had been rekindled *before* I'd found Tom's body, and there had to be more to our encounter than shared grief. I still missed Beau, ached for him, really, but it wasn't as if he were pounding at my door. For all I knew, he might even be back from Turkey by now. Stop thinking for one goddamn minute, will you, Bailey, I begged myself. Finally, from pure exhaustion, my mind shut the hell up. When I woke, the room was dim and the clock read 6:30.

At around seven-thirty, Chris called to say that they'd finally wrapped for the day and I could head over to the bar in about an hour. After speaking to him I left a message for Sheriff Schmidt, saying I'd like to touch base with him. Then I phoned Beverly, just to check in.

"I was just going to call you, dear," she said. "I hung up with Barry only a minute ago—it took me all day to get in touch with him. You were right. Tom asked Barry to do some work on the house, and he was supposed to give him a cash advance."

"What kind of work was Barry going to do?"

"Put in a new kitchen. It wasn't a total overhaul—just some new appliances and a new floor. He was also going to oversee the painting of the exterior. Apparently, Tom was trying to do a little bit of interior painting himself."

"Okay, thanks, Beverly. Let me know if you find out anything else, will you, please?" I wondered if she had really been planning to call me.

There was a long pause.

"They apparently found Tom's wallet in his pants," she said finally, her voice choking. "And there was a lot of cash."

"So I guess there's very little doubt now," I said quietly. "I'm sorry, Beverly. I'm sure this is hard for you."

After I hung up, I sat on my terrace for a while, watching the dusk turn to night. I was glad I was going out tonight. I was glad I would be having sex with Chris later and could push thoughts of Tom out of my head.

Just as I was heading out the door, my cell phone rang.

"Is this Bailey Wiggins?" a man asked in the no-nonsense, authoritative tone of someone used to getting his way.

"Weggins, actually."

"It's Robert Barish. Detective O'Donnell gave me your number. He said you found the body, but it's not a hundred percent clear that it's Tom," he said. "Please tell me everything you know."

Conscious of his need to know but also of the fact that I was now running late, I spelled out everything as concisely as possible—and shared the news about the wallet. He immediately began lobbing questions at me—how did I know Tom, why had I gone to Andes?

"Mr. Barish, I want to be of help to you, but I'm heading off to meet Tom's friend Chris right now. Actually, I'm going to be with some people from the show—and maybe I'll learn something. I could give you a ring tomorrow."

"Are you going to the set?" he asked agitatedly. "Is that what you're saying?"

"No, to a pub not far from there on Twenty-third Street. Do you want to talk tomorrow?"

He said he'd prefer to meet in person and suggested four o'clock at his office in midtown. I hesitated, not overly eager to drag myself up there on a Saturday, but I also knew that having him as a contact could prove useful. As soon as I'd agreed and signed off, I flew out the door, grabbing my jeans jacket as I left—it was supposed to be cooler tonight.

I'd heard of the Half King but had never been there. It turned out to be part neighborhood hangout/part Irish pub/part trendy night spot. And it was already packed. The bar in the main area, lit by several orange-coated hanging lights, was lined about three to four people deep, and the wooden booths across from it were all filled. Chris was nowhere in sight. I could see a back room from where I stood, as well as a brick-walled room on the side, filled with tables. That seemed the most likely spot for a large group to congregate. As I began to muscle my way into the side room, I spotted Chris edging through the crowd toward me. He held my eyes intently.

"Hi," he called over the din as he drew closer. His face looked freshly scrubbed of makeup, and he was wearing just jeans and a gray T-shirt. Wrapping one of his taut, muscular arms around my waist, he planted a soft kiss on my cheek. I felt myself stir from his touch.

"The gang all here?" I asked.

"About fifteen of them. Some crew, the second ADs, a few of the actors . . ."

"Locket, by any chance?"

"No, but there's a rumor she's stopping by. Let me get you a drink at the bar. It takes forever to flag down a waitress in there."

He grabbed my hand, and we snaked our way over to the bar. A spot opened up miraculously just as we got there. Chris ordered us two draft beers. As we waited side by side, I realized for the first time that there was music pounding underneath all the voices. U2, maybe. It was hard to tell. What wasn't hard was noticing all the chicks checking out Chris.

"How *are* you tonight?" I asked him as he passed me my beer. Since he wasn't budging from the bar area, I had the feeling he wanted to talk alone for a few minutes.

"Not great. My scenes today all called for me looking as grim as possible, so that made it a little easier."

"I've got a bit of news," I said. I told him about the wallet.

"So that pretty much confirms it, doesn't it?"

"I'd say so—though the final verdict will come with the DNA. What about Harper? I assume you've told her the news."

"I wanted to do it in person, and I certainly didn't want to do it on set, so I called her at her office and asked her to grab coffee with me during one of my breaks. She figured something was up, so she just kept demanding that I tell her why I was calling, right then and there. She was practically shrieking at me. And then when I told her about you finding the body, she just went totally silent—for like thirty seconds. I think she'd convinced herself that Tom had just taken off. And then she started to bawl. I felt really bad for her."

"Has word spread?"

"Oh yeah. I told one of the supervising producers, and Harper told people—and then the cops showed."

"From the sheriff's office?"

"No, these guys were state police. I guess the downstate part of the investigation has been turned over to them. They talked to me for about a half hour. I could tell from their questions that they'd been to his place—the super must have let them in—so the issue of me having to turn over my key never came up."

"Could you get any sense from their questions what they're thinking?"

"Not really. They asked if he'd been depressed—and whether he had any enemies."

"Be prepared for things to get ugly when they find Locket's note."

Chris pursed his lips and looked away.

"What?" I asked.

"I went over there after I left your place this morning and took the note."

"Chris, why would you do that?" I exclaimed. "That's evidence."

"Oh, come on, Bailey. We both know Locket didn't drive up there and set Tom on fire. I doubt she even knows there's an upstate. I just didn't want to cause trouble for her—and the show—unnecessarily."

"Maybe she didn't do it, but you can still end up in a lot of trouble for removing evidence. Promise me you'll think about it. You can still hand it over to them."

"Okay, I'll think about it," he said, flashing me one of his dazzling smiles meant to quell further protests from me.

"As long as we're confessing, I need to tell you that I filed a short story on Tom today—I would have been covering his death even if I'd never heard of him. But I included nothing the two of us discussed. That's between you and me."

"Wow, I never even thought of that. I guess I'm going to just have to trust you," he said somberly.

"You can," I assured him. "It's probably best not to tell anyone here what I do, but I also don't want to out-and-out lie. You could just say I'm a writer if anyone asks."

"Don't worry. People in show business *rarely* ask what other people do."

"Why don't we head into the other room?"

The group from *Morgue* was at the far end of the side room, at seven square tables they had apparently dragged together. Chris led me to the closest and pulled over a chair next to the one he'd obviously been sitting in. A few people farther down the table glanced in our direction. The mood seemed awfully somber, though there was enough conversation going on that Chris managed to introduce me only to the people right around us—a line producer named August who looked as if he were no more than twenty-one, a guy named Steve who Chris said played Brad on the show and had teeth as white as a new Sub-Zero freezer, and a gorgeous young black woman named Amy, wearing an off-the-shoulder rose-colored sweater and dangly gold earrings.

"Is Deke here?" I whispered into his ear.

"Deke? Why?"

"Harper said Tom palled around with him."

"Yeah, he's the beefy dude, the one in the T-shirt that says Mudfest 2004," he said into my ear, indicating with his eyes a guy way down the line. Deke was hoisting a glass mug of beer to his mouth and nodding to a fellow next to him, who looked as if he were crew, too.

Aware that several people at the table were watching us whisper, I turned my attention back to the group immediately around us and offered a smile that I hoped seemed friendly and inviting.

"You guys were smart to get drinks at the bar," Amy said. "I'm nursing my martini because it took about an hour for it to materialize."

"Amy works in PR—along with Harper," Chris said. I figured that was code for "She's in the loop on everything that's going on."

"How has response to the show been so far?" I asked.

"Great. We did our press party on the set—you know, in the morgue—and people went nuts."

"It must be an interesting show to publicize," I said.

"It has been—at least up until today. If you're a friend of Chris's, you must have heard the news about Tom Fain."

"Yes—have you already started to get calls about it?"

"A few—the word is just leaking out. What I'm waiting for is someone to start implying there's a jinx of some kind—you know, 'Work on *Morgue,* end up in one.'"

"Did you know Tom?" I asked.

"Not all that well. But Harper told me what a nice guy he was."

I was aware suddenly that Chris, who had been talking to Steve, had stood up and pulled a cell phone out of his pocket. He listened for a moment and then threaded his way toward the rear of the room, near a doorway to the outside garden area.

"That's what Chris told me—what a nice guy Tom was," I said. "It's so hard to imagine someone killing him." I let the remark just hang there, hoping she had an insight to share.

She shook her head, her dangly earrings flopping back and forth with each turn. "It's all just unbelievable—but you know, the weekend he disappeared, Harper had almost a sixth sense about it. I mean, she *felt* something was wrong."

So Amy *did* have an insight worth sharing.

"How do you mean?" I asked as nice and easy as I possibly could. I was afraid that if I got too pouncy, she'd drop the bulletproof shield PR types have practically trademarked.

"You know the stories about how people get a weird vibe before they get on a plane and end up changing their flight? It was kind of like that. We were out in L.A. meeting with folks from the network, and after Harper talked to Tom on Friday, she just got this really funny feeling something was the matter. She ended up taking the red-eye on Friday night instead of coming back Sunday."

I flashed back to my conversation with Harper. She might not have actually *said* she'd returned on Sunday, but she'd told me that was the plan and had *implied* she'd followed it. Liar, liar, pants on fire.

"Oh, so she got to see Tom before he left," I said, again all nice and easy. I felt like someone trying to pluck a dropped earring from the edge of an open drain.

"No, he was gone by then, I think."

As I offered a benign, bewildered-by-life's-injustices expression, my mind began to race. What if Tom had been less vague with Harper about his plans for Saturday and had told her exactly where he was going? She might have been aware of exactly what kind of "work" he had to do. She could have taken the red-eye home from L.A. and then hopped in a car and headed for Andes. Perhaps she'd learned about Locket. She may have exploded in jealous anger at Tom and hit him over the head with something— like a tool he'd been working with. Or stabbed him. Then set his body on fire. The info was too slim to take to the police—it might land Harper in trouble for nothing—but I needed to talk to her and determine why she'd misled me.

Chris returned just then and plopped back down in his chair.

"That was Harper," he said, sighing. "She says she's out just wandering the streets not far from here. She sounds totally wigged out."

"Is there anything we can do?" Amy asked.

"If there is, she doesn't seem to know how to articulate it. . . . Oh wow, Locket and Alex are here."

I looked up to see a couple standing at the farthest table— they'd obviously come in from the door closer to that end of the room. Locket looked hip and cool despite what a long day she must have had. She was wearing skintight black jeans, boots and a hot pink turtleneck (also skintight) and was carrying a pink Birkin bag. Alex took a seat, but Locket began working her way down the row of tables, saying hello to people one by one. If she was overcome with grief, she wasn't giving it away.

Her scent arrived at our end about four minutes before she did—an intoxicating blend of what I guessed to be patchouli and vanilla. When she finally reached us, Chris stood up and gave her a kiss on the cheek. I was closer to her than I'd been the day before, and I could see that though there were fine lines around her face, they did little to detract from her other attributes—the platinum hair, the large blue eyes, and skin as white and luminescent as the inside of a scallop shell. And then there were the lips. In some ways, they were like fake boobs—they might be absurdly larger than normal, but you couldn't peel your eyes off them.

"Bailey," she said after Chris introduced us. She let her eyes roam over my face, as if she'd been given permission to search it. "How does one end up with a name like that?" There was an edge to her words, and she looked intently into my eyes. The thought that bounded instantly through my mind was: Does she *know* me somehow?

"It's just one of those old family names that you end up with regardless of whether you're a girl or a boy. I believe it means the wall of the castle."

She wrinkled her nose in a manner that suggested my answer didn't smell right to her.

"Your name is quite unusual, too," I added, hoping to engage her a little in conversation. "Where does it come from?"

"You'll have to ask my mama that," she said, dismissing me, and then rounded the corner to greet Amy. When she moved past Chris, she gave his arm a squeeze.

As we sat down, she worked her way up the other side of the table, back toward Alex. I leaned toward Amy again, hoping to restart the conversation, but Chris's cell phone rang. All I heard him say was, "Okay, I'll meet you right in the front." That didn't sound good to me.

"That was Harper again," he said into my ear. "She's outside the bar. I'm going to meet her for a minute, maybe take her out in the garden and see if I can talk her off the ledge. Are you cool with that?"

"Uh, sure." I didn't like it, but what was I going to do? I had my own questions for Harper, but this wasn't the time or the place.

"Are you going to be all right hanging here for a while?"

"Actually, I'm done with my beer, and I think I'll just grab another at the bar."

Amy had ambled down to the middle section of the *Morgue* tables, and it didn't look as if she'd be missing me. As I stood up to make my way to the bar, I noticed Locket, now back with Alex, whisper something into his ear. He looked away from her and directly at me, his high forehead gleaming from the light. Was it just a coincidence? Again, I had that odd sensation that she knew me. Had I been marked as a *Buzz* reporter?

After fighting my way to the bar, I asked for another Guinness. Just as the bartender, a stocky redheaded guy, slid it toward me, a stool opened up. I decided to hop on and bide my time there. From that position, I could see into the side room and watch the goings-on.

Over the next ten minutes, I perched on the stool and nursed my mug of beer. Other than having to hose down two horn dogs who came on to me, I was left to my own devices in the orange glow from the bar lights.

It just happened that I glanced up at the moment Chris entered the pub with Harper. They stood at the front door, with her shaking her head vehemently and him clearly trying to soothe her. The whole scene bugged me. This was the guy I'd slept with last night, who'd announced he wanted to consume every inch of me. Though I knew he'd been called on to help Harper in her grief, it looked as if they were in the midst of a lovers' spat—he was mad, perhaps, that she'd been flirting with other guys, or she was pissed because he never called when he said he would. I felt that odd little sensation in the pit in my stomach, the kind you get when a guy you've gone to bed with for the first time unexpectedly starts putting on his pants at five the next morning with some story about a very early meeting, which if he doesn't haul butt to could lead to the collapse of not only the World Bank, but possibly even Western civilization. As I watched them surreptitiously, Harper suddenly looked all the way down the bar and made eye contact with me. Chris followed her gaze. His eyes seemed to plead for patience.

"Where'd your date go? He didn't abandon you, did he?"

Expecting to see another horn dog, I spun around to discover Deke's large head four inches from my own. He smelled like sweat, onions, and grease, and he eyed me up and down as if I'd just stripped to my panties. I would have liked to hose *him* down instantly, but it was a golden opportunity for me, my chance to finally learn what he knew about Tom.

"He's talking to Harper right now," I said. "She's pretty upset—about that actor Tom Fain." I figured I might as well jump right in and see what I turned up.

"Oh yeah, that's a real bummer. I'm Deke, by the way. Deke Jacobus. This is Danny De Mateo." He indicated his sidekick with a flick of his head.

"Bailey Weggins," I said, shaking Deke's hand, which felt as thick as a baseball mitt and as rough as plank wood. Danny shook my hand, too. He was tall and wiry, with frameless glasses that magnified his eyes so much, he looked like a bug.

"So you an actress?" Danny asked.

"God, no," I said. "The last time I was on stage I was playing a Pilgrim in a grade-school production. All they let me do was carry a squash." I flashed a little smile at the end, though trying to flirt with these two dudes was about as much fun as licking the inside of someone's shoes.

"So then how do you know Jared?"

"Pardon me?" I said.

"Chris, aka Jared. The guy who's supposed to give Dr. McDreamy a run for his money." He said the last part sarcastically, which was ironic considering Deke, with his thick, broken nose and greasy, dirty blond hair, was about as dreamy as a Spam sandwich.

"We're old friends," I said. "I know Harper, too. This is just awful for her—I mean, what happened to Tom."

Danny had turned away at this point, to shout an order to the bartender. Deke just let the remark hang there.

"You knew Tom, right?" I said.

"Yeah, about as well as you ever get to know any of the actors on a set."

"But I thought you guys played cards together. Harper said you even went to Atlantic City together."

He stared hard into me with slate-colored eyes. "Harper still has a real thorn in her claw about that Atlantic City trip, doesn't she."

"She didn't like Tom hanging at casinos?"

"That wasn't the prob. Tom had just started dating Harper, but on that trip he brought along this other chick—some actress."

Blythe? I wondered. In the days before she'd become a real pain.

"Was Tom much of a gambler? Do you think that could have anything to do with his death?"

"What are you anyway—a little Miss Marple?"

"Just curious."

"I really haven't a clue," he said, and moved past me, his thick thigh rubbing hard against mine. He and Danny claimed a spot halfway down the bar in the middle of the crowd.

Something was odd. It was clear Deke didn't like discussing Tom, and it wasn't because he was in mourning. I looked down the bar to the front door, hoping to catch Chris's eye again. I thought I spotted the edge of his shirt, but some other patrons were blocking him from complete view and there was no sign of Harper. This was starting to get *really* annoying. I turned and checked out the side room. A few chairs at the *Morgue* tables were empty now, and Locket and Alex were standing, clearly ready to be on the move. Locket glanced through the doorway in my direction and just for a second locked eyes with me, then looked away. Something caught my attention out of the corner of my eye, and when I turned my head, I spotted Amy standing by the door of the garden, gesturing for me to come over. After shrugging off my jeans jacket to save my stool, I headed over there, weaving my way through the crowd.

"What's up?" I asked.

"What's going on with Harper, anyway? I saw her at the end of the bar a few minutes ago."

"She's pretty upset, apparently. She showed up here and Chris is trying to talk her off the ledge."

"I know this sounds rude, but I hope she's going to be able to work next week. We're only two weeks from the premiere."

"I'm sure she'll pull it all together," I said, having no idea whether she could or not. Amy sighed, said good-bye, and wandered off. It took me a second to realize my cell phone was ringing.

"Hey, it's me," Chris said. "Harper's in the ladies' room right now, and when she comes out, I'm going to run her home in a cab. Are you cool with that?"

"Sure," I said, though I was actually sick of Chris playing baby-sitter.

"Do you want to wait here and I'll come back for you?"

"How long do you think it will be?" I asked.

"Not long—maybe fifteen, twenty minutes. She lives straight east of here—around Gramercy Park."

"Why don't you call me when you're done. If it's not too long, I'll stay; otherwise I'll head back to my place. You could come by—if you want."

"Great, I'd love that," he said.

The ladies' room was just around the corner, and before heading back to the bar, I slipped in there, curious. Harper was standing at the sink, staring at her reflection in the mirror.

"Harper, I'm so s—"

"Do you think he suffered?" she demanded, her penny eyes catching the reflection of my eyes in the mirror.

"I don't know—I hope not," was all I could muster. She stomped past me in her cowboy boots, as if my response had irritated her to death.

Two minutes later I threaded my way back to my stool. A pack of girls, all in low-slung pants or minis, shouted to one another nearby as they surveyed the room like falcons. Deke and Danny had slipped off to parts unknown. I continued to sip my beer, trying to decide whether to stay or leave. Was I right to be *this* annoyed? I asked myself. If Chris was just taking Harper home, why not let me ride along in the cab and then head to my place together? Finally deciding to blow the place, I slid off my stool. One of the girls next to me asked if she could have it.

"Sure," I said. But it came out "Sllur." Suddenly it was as if I were watching myself from far above me. And as I watched, the only thought in my mind was, God, you're drunk. Really, really drunk.

CHAPTER 8

The first thing I became conscious of was that it was cool, almost cold, out—and that I was shivering. I crossed my arms over my torso and rocked back and forth to generate heat. Just that small movement seemed exhausting, and I lowered my head, catching it in my hands. I could see my thighs, but my feet, I realized, were in darkness. And there was a taste of vomit in my mouth. I popped my head up. I was sitting on the stoop of a brick town house on a street lit only by the glow from streetlamps and the random lights on buildings. I glanced to the right and then the left, my heart pounding. I didn't have a clue where I was—or how I had gotten there. And from the emptiness of the street, I knew it had to be very, very late.

My first urge was to run, just tear down the street like a bat out of hell. But I was too tired even to move. My arms and legs felt as if they'd been poured with wet sand. I took a deep breath, trying to calm myself—and to think. What was this street, and what was I doing here? Even in the dark I could see that the street was pretty, tree lined, with mostly brick-fronted four-story or five-story buildings. I wasn't in the Village, I was pretty sure—the side streets there were much shorter. And the stoops here weren't high, like the ones on the Upper West Side.

I glanced to the left again. There were several more town houses and a big, white-brick apartment building and then the cross street, a few cars whizzing along it. It was an avenue, but I had no idea which one. Side streets this long might mean Chelsea. *Chelsea.* And then, like a wine stain spreading on a tablecloth, I began to see in my mind the Half King on 23rd Street. I had been there with Chris, and we had been talking to people, and then Chris was leaving and I was alone.

My arm jerked, and I felt clunkily for my purse. It was there, beside me on the cool stone steps. I dug through for my phone, flipped it open, and looked for the time: 3:47. God, I'd arrived at the pub just before nine. I didn't remember leaving. I remembered saying good-bye to Chris and being at the bar. But that was all.

A sound in the street—a scratching noise—startled me. I glanced up to see a rat the size of a tabby cat scoot from under a car and scurry across the road. My head had started to throb, and I fought off the urge to cry. I wanted to run, to get *out* of there. Though the strength was returning to my arms, my legs still felt leaden, and I couldn't imagine how I could get my body to move.

I forced my mind back to earlier. Why had Chris left me? *Harper.* That was it—he'd been taking her home. But he'd been coming back for me, hadn't he? And then I remembered. I'd decided to leave. And I was slurring my words. I'd felt woozy, plastered actually. But I'd had only two beers. And suddenly it hit me like a bloody hammer. Someone had put something into my drink—a roofie, maybe.

Fear overwhelmed me, squeezing my breath out. Had it been

a guy planning to date-rape me? I glanced at my clothes. They weren't disheveled. But where had I been for the past hours?

For an instant, I thought of calling 911. I realized, though, that it might take fifteen minutes for a patrol car to show, and I couldn't bear the thought of sitting alone in the dark here any longer. I flexed my feet several times. Miraculously, they felt much lighter now, and I was pretty sure I was going to be able to move. I shook out my arms and legs, trying to jump-start them.

And then my phone rang. I jerked my hand in surprise, as if the phone were electrified. I knew it had to be Chris. He had said he'd come back for me. He must be crazy wondering where I was.

"Hello," I said breathlessly.

The sound that came through from the other end was ugly and horrible. It was someone laughing, not a man or a woman, but something almost inhuman. Laughing demonically. And then it disconnected.

I sat there almost paralyzed again, staring at the phone. From down the street to the left, I heard a muffled sound from near the parked cars across from the apartment building. Was it the rat? Could someone be down there, crouching behind one of the cars?

I inhaled as well as I could, grabbed my purse, and lunged from the stoop. I began to run in the direction opposite from where the noise had originated. At first, lifting my legs seemed nearly impossible, like fighting an undertow, but after a dozen strides, they found their strength again. As I tore down the street, it seemed as if my heart were beating so hard, it would soon out-run the rest of my body.

Within a few seconds, I could see the traffic light at the end of the street, where it met the avenue. But which avenue was it? Would there be anything open? Would there be cabs? I slowed just enough so I could turn halfway around. There didn't seem to be anyone behind me, but the street was so dark and leafy, it was hard to know for certain.

I stumbled a little when I spun back around, and as I caught myself, a stitch popped in my left side. I slowed my pace, rubbing my side with my free hand, willing the cramp away. As the pain ebbed, I picked my speed back up again.

I was almost at the corner now, and there was a building on the near right side—a small hotel, its ground floor lit up and the front door open. I staggered into the lobby. An older guy, fifty or so, was sitting on a bench just inside the lobby, reading a rumpled newspaper, and his head jerked up in surprise when I stepped through the open doorway.

"I think someone is following me," I sputtered, figuring the "I was slipped a roofie six hours ago and have no idea where I've been since then" excuse wasn't going to make much of a dent with this guy. As it was, he looked as though he wanted me out of his lobby as fast as possible.

He craned his head so he could see behind me, a frown forming on his face.

"Look, miss, we can't help you here," he said in a gravelly voice. "We're just a hotel. You gotta call the police."

"Where am I, anyway?" I asked. "I mean—I know I'm in New York and everything, but what street is this?"

"Twenty-second Street," he replied almost reluctantly.

"That's Ninth Avenue, then?" I asked, tilting my head to the left."

"Yeah. Like I said, why don't you give the cops a call?"

"Sure," I told him. "Thanks for your help. It's nice to know that chivalry is alive and well in Chelsea."

Outside, I glanced up and down the street. There was no one in sight. I hurried the few steps to the corner and stepped onto the avenue. The entire block was empty of cars, the street pavement shimmering red from the traffic light, but several blocks farther down I could see cars bunched up at a light. Shivering, I glanced behind me. No one there. After what seemed an interminable wait, the traffic began to move again. I spotted a taxi with its top light on and threw up my arm. The second the cab stopped, I yanked open the door and jumped inside.

By the time I was back in my apartment, the fatigue had returned, but it was different now—not so much the leaden arm and leg thing, but an overall weariness. I stripped off my clothes and glanced over my body, checking for soreness or bruising. Then I popped two ibuprofen tablets and wolfed down a few stale saltines to help chase away the puke taste in my mouth. What I wanted more than anything was to sleep, but first I grabbed my BlackBerry and punched in the number for Dr. Paul Petrocelli, an ER doctor just outside of Boston whom I'd interviewed once for a story and now used frequently as a resource. I wasn't certain what his current work schedule was, but he favored the night shift. To my relief, he answered his phone. I asked if he had a few minutes to talk.

"Sure, no one's tried to drive through a tree tonight—yet," he said. "You don't sound so good."

"I don't feel so good, actually. I was out in a bar earlier, and I'm pretty sure someone slipped a drug in my drink."

"Were you assaulted?" he asked. His words were blunt, but I heard worry in his deep voice.

"No, I don't think so. I mean, I haven't got any bruises, and there's no sign whatever that I had sex." I had quizzed Paul easily about everything from poisoning to blunt trauma to the brain, but it was awkward to talk to him about my own body.

"So tell me what happened—though I take it you don't remember much."

"I don't remember *anything*. The last thing I know is that I was taking a swig of my beer at the bar, and then all of a sudden I felt completely woozy. A few minutes earlier, someone had called me over to talk, and I stupidly left my beer unattended. The drug could have been slipped in at—"

"Jeez, Bailey, if anyone should realize not to leave a drink on the bar, it should be you."

"I know, I know. Anyway, the next thing I realize, it's after three in the morning and I'm sitting on a stoop in pitch darkness. I had a headache, and I must have vomited somewhere because I could taste it in my mouth. Does it sound like I had a roofie?"

"How much were you drinking?"

"Why?"

"No offense, but it's not uncommon for women to think they've had a roofie when they've actually just overindulged. They assume they've been drugged because they can't remember anything, but what they've actually experienced is an alcoholic blackout."

"Honestly, I only had two beers. In fact, I didn't even finish the second."

"How many hours were you missing in action—give me a rough idea."

"Almost six."

"Did you come out of it pretty quickly—like you were popping awake?"

"Yeah, how'd you know?" I asked.

"I think what someone gave you was GHB. It's different from a lot of date-rape drugs in that the recovery time is shorter—and you just sort of come out of it with a jolt."

"Should I go to an ER and get my blood tested?"

"It only shows up in a urine test, and you have to do it within twelve hours. You still have time, but without any evidence of assault, most ERs won't administer the test for you."

I thanked him for the info and before signing off promised to provide an update later. Based on what he'd told me about my chances of getting tested, I decided that it was pointless to head to a hospital. My phone still in hand, I called up the log. The caller with the demonically evil laugh had rung me at three-fifty a.m. It had said "Caller Unknown," just as it had with the weeper's call on my way back from Andes. Were they the same person? I thought so. And was the caller the person who had drugged me? That laugh had been so knowing. It was as if the person on the other end had been fully aware that I was sitting alone in the dark, terrified, and had chosen to mock me. Even if the person wasn't close by, I sensed he or she knew I was alone and vulnerable. But why exactly was whoever it was doing this to me? Was the person Tom's killer? Did he or she know I was making inquiries?

While I sat there, bone tired with the phone in my hand, something else occurred to me. There were absolutely no calls in my log from Chris. If he had come back to the bar and not found me there, he should have been curious, even concerned—so why hadn't he attempted to track me down? I dragged myself off the couch and into my office to check the light on my phone. No messages. God, why hadn't Chris been worried about my where-abouts? He'd certainly been all fussy over Harper—was something going on with them?

On top of everything else that was happening, I now felt like giving myself a swift kick in the rear. On principle, I was in no way opposed to the occasional romp with a guy I'd never set eyes on again. But I couldn't bear the idea of going to bed with some-one who made it *seem* as though it meant something when it really didn't. And then the next day you felt like shit.

I returned to the living room and flopped on the couch, pull-ing a throw blanket over me. For some reason, the couch just seemed more appealing to me than my bed—more womblike, I guessed—and that's what I needed at the moment.

When I woke three hours later, it was to the light coming through the windows of my living room and my head was still throbbing. I popped another ibuprofen and swung open the door to my terrace so that the fresh air rushed in. Part of me longed to sink into the couch again and spend the day in a fetal position. The emotional hangover I was experiencing from being drugged was almost worse than the physical one. But I now had too many urgent things on my plate to wallow in misery.

After making coffee, I headed for my computer and Googled GHB—or what turned out to be the official name, gamma-hydroxybutyrate, sometimes called "GHB" or "grievous bodily harm." What a perfect term for it. The side effects were just as Paul had described. In low doses, the drug produced a high or euphoric feeling and a loosening of inhibitions. But if you upped the dose just a little, all sorts of bad things occurred: nausea, headache, drowsiness, dizziness, amnesia, and loss of muscle control. And with just the right amount, there was a loss of consciousness, respiratory arrest, and then last but hardly least, death. *Fun!*

Despite the fact that the drug was illegal in most states, it would have been easy enough for someone to get their hands on it. Apparently, the most frequent users were clubbers, rave party participants, date rapists, strippers, and bodybuilders—who believed it counteracted the negative effects of steroids. According to one site, all you had to do to score some was to walk in a gym and put the word out.

It also would have been simple for someone to slip it to me. It came in clear liquid form, and though it was salty, the taste was easily disguised by alcohol. Especially beer. I'd been drinking the perfect beverage for it. I cringed when I read that consuming GHB *with* alcohol increased the likelihood of death. It was lucky that I'd consumed less than two beers.

And just as Paul had pointed out, the effects of the drug lasted only about four to six hours, burning off quickly toward the end. There was one other fascinating tidbit buried on one of the sites: GHB could cause you to experience an out-of-body feeling. I suddenly remembered the sensation of slurring my words and simultaneously seeing myself from above as I did so.

That was enough research for the time being. Now I needed to get busy trying to find answers about what was going on. Not only was I on assignment for *Buzz* about Tom, but I also now had an urgent personal motive for trying to figure out who the murderer was: Someone was after me—and in all likelihood, it was the killer. I needed to know who it was before he or she did something worse than slipping a date-rape drug in my drink.

After plucking two eggs from my fridge, I scrambled them, made more coffee, and took my breakfast out to the terrace, along with a number two pencil and a black-and-white composition book. Whenever I'm working on a big reporting story, especially one with riddles and plenty of unanswered questions, I find it enormously helpful to jot down my musings in an old-fashioned composition book.

I spent the first few minutes creating a timeline of Tom's story and then fleshing it out with details I'd uncovered—about what Tom had been up to as well as the various players in his life. Then I started jotting down questions, beginning with the big fat obvious ones: Who had killed Tom—and why? Was it someone from Andes? Beverly had said it had been years since Tom had spent much time in the town, so the chances of anyone up there holding a grudge seemed next to nil. What about a stranger, though—someone who had showed up at the house thinking it was empty, only to discover Tom painting the bathroom. Would a burglar set a body on fire? It seemed unlikely.

Though the murder had taken place in Andes, it seemed far more logical to focus on Tom's circle of acquaintances in New York City—particularly people involved in the production of *Morgue*. There was the Nordic warrior and possibly abusive Alex Ottoson. Had Alex learned about Locket's fling with Tom and sought vengeance? He'd been snappish toward Tom during a recent taping, so he might have suspected the truth. But he would have had to know that Tom was traveling to Andes on Saturday, and if even Chris hadn't known, how would Alex have gotten wind of the plans?

And then there was the lusty-lipped Locket to consider. She'd been having a fling—or had *had* one—with a guy who was sleeping with someone else involved in the show. Certainly women *did* kill men in jealous rages, but how annoyed could Locket possibly have been over Tom's relationship with Harper? After all, she had Alex guaranteeing her fame and fortune. That was called having your cake and eating it, too. Plus, if Locket had minded Harper, and had verbalized that fact to Tom, it would have opened the door for Tom minding Locket's relationship with *Alex*. And there could be no way in the universe Locket would back out of *that*. She knew that without Alex's help, all the collagen and Botox in the world probably wouldn't catapult her into prime time.

Of course, she could be such a big diva that she wanted Tom to have the hots for her and her alone, despite her relationship with Alex. And that raised another point: What if Tom had fallen for Locket and had threatened to reveal his affair with her if she didn't dump Alex? Oh dear—Locket wouldn't have liked that at all.

Alex and Locket weren't the only people of interest. I had no good reason to suspect Deke, but I didn't like him. My encounter at the bar with him had seeped back into my consciousness, and the overwhelming sensation was of the nasty vibe he'd given off. And he hadn't seemed at all keen on discussing Tom. I tried to dredge up other elements of my brief conversation with him. I had mentioned the trip to Atlantic City, and he'd volunteered that Tom had brought an actress along—very possibly Blythe. Harper had learned about it, Deke said, and hadn't been happy. If I could reach Blythe, I might be able to discover more about that road trip.

Thinking of Harper nudged something else loose from my memory: what Amy had said about Harper returning to New York on Saturday, not Sunday. Of course, she was now supposedly in deep despair about Tom's death, desperate for Chris's shoulder to cry on, but that didn't necessarily undermine her likelihood as a suspect. In my days as a newspaper reporter, I had covered a case in which the most grief-stricken person on the scene was the killer. She had murdered her boyfriend because he'd been cheating, but she was still desperately in love with him and overwhelmed with a sense of loss.

All four people on my list of possible suspects had been at the pub last night. Any one of them could have slipped the drug in my drink after I'd followed Harper into the bathroom, including Harper herself, who'd departed before me. It seemed that whoever had done it must also be the killer. But why target *me*? Harper knew I was snooping around about Tom. Deke had called me a little Miss Marple. It seemed likely that whoever was harassing me believed I was playing detective.

But unless I wanted to assume the role of sitting duck, I was going to have to continue to play a little Miss Marple. At four p.m. I would be meeting Mr. Barish, which might provide more insight into Tom and his life. And at the book party at Elaine's, there would be more opportunity to study Locket. In the meantime, there were a few other things I could do.

The first was to try to piece together the missing hours of my life last night. At eleven I called the pub, figuring that they probably served lunch and there would be staff on the premises. I knew it wouldn't be wise to go on the offensive, proclaiming that I had been drugged. As a beat reporter, I'd learned that restaurant and bar people have a tendency to clam up and close ranks when they think you've got a gripe. I would have to try a different tack.

"You know the bartender with the red hair who was on last night?" I said after a youngish-sounding girl answered the phone.

"He wanted me to get him a phone number?" I lied. "Can I leave him a message?"

"You mean Rusty?" she asked after a moment's hesitation.

"Red hair? Kind of big?"

"Yeah, that sounds like Rusty."

"Would you mind taking down a message for him?"

I was pretty sure that she *would* mind.

"He'll be in at one today. Do you just want to call him back then?"

"Sure." But I wasn't going to call him. It would be smarter to just show up, let him see what I looked like, and watch his face and body language as he spoke to me. I checked my watch and decided I would set out for there shortly.

Next, a call to Harper. Again, I was going to have to proceed carefully and not box her into a corner about her travel plans the weekend Tom had gone to Andes. After all, she hadn't actually lied to me but had simply led me to believe she'd been in L.A. for the entire weekend. One strategy would be to cover that ground again with her, ask more specific questions, and see if she came right out and lied to me. If she did, *then* I would challenge her.

She answered her cell phone groggily, as if she were lying in twisted sheets, and I suddenly had this horrible image of Chris stretched out buck naked beside her. Had his grief counseling involved a long, sensuous shag, like what he'd offered me in my hour of need? Was that why he'd never called me last night and come back for me?

"Hi, Harper, it's Bailey Weggins," I said. My voice sounded unnaturally high, and I wondered if she could sense the rush of anxiety I'd just experienced. "How are you feeling today?"

"Just great," she answered sarcastically. "Can you call me back later? I didn't get much sleep last night, and I'm really trying to rest right now."

"Okay," I said. "In fact, would it be possible for us to get together at some point today?"

"What for?"

"I just wanted to talk about everything's that happened."

She sighed loudly. "I don't really care to talk about it—it just makes it worse."

"I understand. It's just that there are some details about Tom that I wanted to share with you." It was a cheap ploy, but I refused to allow her to dodge me. I could tell by the pause that it had worked.

"It will have to be tomorrow," she said finally. "There's a book party for Locket tonight and I'm coordinating it."

"The one at Elaine's."

"How do you know about that?"

"I'm actually going," I said. "A friend from work asked me to tag along." I wasn't going to give away that I'd hunted down an invite—from this point on it might be better not to reveal the extent of my snoopiness. "Why don't I look for you there."

"I'm not going to have any time to chitchat," she said almost sullenly. "What exactly do you mean by 'details about Tom'? You make it sound as if there were something bad going on with him."

"I didn't mean to imply that. Why don't I let you get back to bed and I'll see you later."

Harper might not be receptive to chitchat at the party tonight, but I would try to pull her aside for a minute. Tonight would also be a chance to really see Locket and Alex in action. But how was I going to learn more about Deke? Chris might be able to assist me on that one. Just thinking about him caused a pang. I had no idea what I wanted from him or exactly how I felt about him after our randy romp, but I hated how shabbily he'd treated me last night. At some point I was going to have to get in touch because I was dependent on his help in the case, but I felt awkward about phoning him right at the moment.

I nearly lurched to the shower and let the hottest water possible cascade over me. It seemed to wash away some of that slimy feeling that still clung to me from last night. While I toweled off afterward, a long-shot idea popped in my head. Maybe Blythe had phoned home again. She could provide info about the trip to Atlantic City—if she had, as I suspected, been the one with Tom. I decided to call Terry. At the very least, it seemed I should inform her about Tom's murder, which would give her extra incentive to have Blythe call me if she heard from her.

She answered the landline on the third ring, her voice sounding as irritated as when I'd talked to her in the vestibule. I started by breaking the news about Tom.

"Omigod," she said. I had the feeling that the excitement was going to make her weekend. "Blythe is going to die when she hears this."

"You haven't heard from her since I talked to you, have you?"

"No. God, I can't believe it. Do they know who did it?"

"Not that I'm aware of. But as you can see, it's important to have Blythe call me. I need to talk to her." I gave her my cell, home, and work numbers because I imagined the business card I'd handed her the other day had long since been tossed in the trash.

"If I hear from her, sure. What are they going to do about the show he's in?"

"I don't really know. Did Blythe ever mention going to Atlantic City with Tom?"

"Atlantic City? Yeah, she went with him—back in July, I think. She bought this little black dress that she thought would look like something a James Bond girl would wear at the craps tables in

Monte Carlo, but when she came back she said that all the other women were in track suits with fanny packs."

"There was another person on the trip, wasn't there? A guy named Deke?"

"I don't remember his name, but yeah, there was another guy. And he ruined the whole thing."

I caught my breath.

"How?" I demanded.

"He borrowed a huge amount of money from Tom. And then he wouldn't pay it back."

CHAPTER 9

How much money—do you know?" I asked her.

"Oh, it was a lot—like a couple thousand. They were at the blackjack table or the roulette table or whatever, and this guy— like I said, I don't remember his name—asked for a loan. He said he was on a streak and didn't want to lose it by having to go to an ATM. And then later he could only come up with, like, two hundred dollars. Tom and this guy had a big argument, and Tom and Blythe drove back early. The only reason I know about it is because Blythe was so pissed off that this guy ruined the weekend for her."

"Did Tom ever get the money back?"

"How would I know? Do you think that's the killer—the guy who borrowed the money?"

I told her I didn't know, but as I hung up I knew damn well that I now had a possible motive for Deke. If he had never repaid the loan, Tom might have been pressuring him to do so, possibly even making threats about taking the matter to a higher-up on the show. I was going to have to find out more.

For now I concentrated on the best way to extract info about my whereabouts last night. Because I wanted to convince the bartender Rusty that I wasn't a nutcase and troublemaker—and I would probably go directly from the pub to my meeting with Mr. Barish—I chose a blue-and-green Diane von Fürstenberg dress that I usually reserved for brunches at my mother's that involved shrimp salad and flan. As I reached for a jacket in my closet, I realized that my jeans jacket had never made it home with me last night.

As soon as the cab let me off in front of the Half King, I felt the muscles in my stomach tighten. I couldn't recall anything that had happened to me at the pub after around nine-thirty or ten, yet the sight of it made my tummy hurt.

Lunchtime was almost over, but there were still customers loafing at the tables outside, their elbows propped among empty bottles of Pinot Grigio and Saratoga water, their faces tilted to the sun. Once inside, I needed a minute for my eyes to adjust. There weren't many diners inside the pub—just one or two in the front room and, from what I could see, a few at the tables in the back garden. I scanned the bar area. A girl was working back there, a quizzical expression on her face as she surveyed a tab. No Rusty in sight. But just as I was about to inquire at the bar, he came around the corner, hoisting a case of Guinness on his shoulder. I shot a smile in his direction, hoping to start off on the right foot.

"You're Rusty, right?" I asked, stepping forward. He looked about ten years older in the half-light of day.

"Yup, what can I do for you?" he said, setting the case on the pockmarked wooden bar. It was not far from the spot where I'd sat the night before. As he looked up, I saw a flash of recognition in his eyes. He knew he'd seen me before.

"I was here last night with a bunch of people from that new show *Morgue*," I explained, figuring that mentioning the show would give me cred. "We were sitting in the other room, but then later I came out here with a few people and had a beer at the bar."

"Okaaay?" he said, dragging out the word in mock expectation of some kind of punch line from me. He didn't seem in the mood to gab.

"Something happened last night, and I could use your help. I promise it will only take a minute."

"Hey, if there's a problem, you really need to see the manager," he said. "He'll be in at three."

"I'd prefer to talk to you. I promise it will only take a minute."

A Hispanic busboy had emerged from the kitchen and began dragging a broom along the floor. Rusty glanced in his direction and back and then raised a large, freckled hand.

"So shoot."

"Do you remember me?" I asked. "I was down at this end of the bar, drinking a draft beer."

"Yeah, I remember."

"Someone put a drug in my drink, and I just want to know if you noticed anyone around who could have done it."

"Yeah, well, that really *is* something you should be talking to the manager about."

"I don't want to make any trouble. And there's no way the police could do anything, anyway. I think the person who did it might be someone I know, and I figured if you had worthwhile information, I could at least be on my guard with that person."

He sighed, flipped up a section of the bar that was on a hinge, and slid behind it. Effortlessly, he began sliding beer out of the case as if his arms were on pulleys and then dropped the bottles into a cooler under the bar.

"You were by yourself, right? But you talked to a couple of dudes at one point."

"Right. Could one of them have done it, do you think?"

"Don't know. It was pretty crazy here last night. What I do know is that you did seem kind of snockered all of a sudden."

"Did I say anything to you? Did I talk to anyone else?"

"Nothing to me. There were a bunch of girls nearby, trolling for guys, but I never saw you interact with them. You did talk to that black chick—after you made a trip to the head. By the way, you'd left your purse on the bar."

"But I talked to her over by the garden door," I said, lifting my chin in that direction.

"The one I'm talking about came right up to you by the bar—like I said, after you staggered back from the bathroom. Your hair was all wet around the edges then, like you'd dunked your face in the sink."

It must have been Amy. Perhaps something about my behavior had concerned her, and she had come up to see what was the matter. I closed my eyes and tried to conjure up a memory, *anything*. I recalled the sensation of water splashed on my face, but it may have been due solely to Rusty the bartender planting the seed.

"And then what happened?" I asked.

"You split, I guess. The next time I looked, there was someone else sitting on your stool. And no, you didn't leave a tip."

"Do you have any clue what time it—?"

My cell phone rang at that moment, and when I flipped it open I saw to my surprise that it was Chris. I asked Rusty to excuse me so I could take the call. He shrugged a shoulder as if he could have cared less what I did.

"Hey," I said, stepping away from the bar. Now that Chris had finally called, I wasn't exactly sure how to play it.

"Everything okay?" he asked, concern in his voice. Odd question from a guy who had ditched me at a bar the night before.

"Actually, no," I said. "Someone spiked my beer with a date-rape drug last night."

"*What?* Are you okay? Did—did anything happen to you?"

"Nothing bad happened from what I can tell. But there are still a lot of loose ends I'm trying to piece together. I'm at the Half King right now trying to get answers."

"Why didn't you call me?"

"*Call* you? You were supposed to come back for me. And then I never even heard from you."

"But you told me *not* to come back," he exclaimed.

"*What?* When we talked right before you left, you said you'd be back in fifteen minutes."

"But I got a text message from you when I was in the cab with Harper. It said you were splitting and not to come back. After dropping Harper off, I headed home."

My body went warm and liquidy, as if I'd been deboned.

"Read it to me, will you?" I demanded. "I need to know exactly what it says." I didn't use the option on my BlackBerry that saved text messages so I was going to have to take Chris's word for it.

"'Decided to leave, need sleep. Call you tomorrow.'"

I had no recollection of having sent it, which of course meant nothing because I couldn't remember anything past around nine-thirty or so. Yet I didn't think I *had* sent it. First, it didn't sound like me; and second, why would I have texted Chris instead of just calling him?

"I don't think I sent it. Someone may have gone in my purse. They could have overheard me talking to you and then would have seen yours was the last number on my log."

"God, I should have realized something was off. Who could have done it—some guy who was after you?"

I told him that I had to get back to my conversation with the bartender, but I would fill him in later.

"Tonight?" he asked.

"I'm going to Locket's book party. I want to see if I can engage her in a conversation about something other than the absurdity of my name."

"I wasn't planning on going, but since you're going to be there, I think I'll drop by—if that's okay with you. Maybe we could grab dinner after."

"Sure," I said. "I'm really relieved. I didn't understand why you hadn't gotten in touch."

"I never would have just left you there, Bailey. I feel terrible about what happened."

After signing off, I sauntered back over to the bar, where Rusty was wiping his hands on his tight gray T-shirt. He looked pleased as punch that I had returned for another round of Q&A.

"Just one more question," I reassured him. "Any idea what time I disappeared for good?"

"Nope, sorry. My best guess is that it was sometime around ten."

Amy might know, I thought. More than likely she would be at Elaine's tonight, and I'd be able to quiz her.

"Thanks for your help," I said, guessing from Rusty's expression that I'd used up his patience and it was time to leave.

"You know . . . ?" he said as I turned to go.

"What?" I asked, spinning around.

"Never mind."

"No, please tell me."

"Are you sure you didn't just get a little sauced? Sometimes girls get crazy thinking they were slipped a roofie when the truth is they were just pounding back one too many."

"Thanks for the insight," I said sarcastically, and hurried outside.

For the next hour, I combed the streets of Chelsea, starting with 22nd Street. In daylight, the street couldn't have been more charming. The block was lined with old brick buildings, and leafy plane trees ran along the outside of the sidewalk. Not far from Tenth Avenue, I was pretty certain I found the stoop I'd been sitting on the night before, but it could have just as easily been the one next door. A woman approached, pushing a stroller with a towheaded toddler, talking to him in a too loud, singsongy voice.

"That's a *very* smart answer," she said. "You are a *very*, *very* smart boy." I wondered how she'd respond if I suddenly asked: "By any chance did you happen to see me puking my guts out around here sometime last night?"

Systematically I made my way down every block from 25th to 21st between Eighth and Tenth avenues, hoping to jog my memory. Nothing seemed familiar to me. And there was no forsaken jeans jacket lying in a heap somewhere—that would have been scarfed up hours ago. At one point, moving north, I came to the block that Beau Regan lived on. There was no way I was going down there. I was pretty sure I'd never been on that block last night. I felt if I had, I would just know.

Though the skies were now a dazzling shade of blue and the day was as warm as yesterday, I felt overwhelmed with a forlorn feeling. Someone at the bar had not only drugged me, but riffled through my purse, used my BlackBerry to send a text message.

Or *had* they? What if, as Rusty had suggested, I'd simply overimbibed? The draft beer mugs at the pub had been hefty in size, and since I usually drank bottle beer, I *had* consumed a bit more than usual. If I'd been drunk, it was entirely possible that I'd decided to blow Chris off, since his coddling of Harper had started to work my last nerve. Man, it felt as though someone were fucking with my mind. The only thing that kept me from wanting to bawl my eyes out was the fact that Chris hadn't acted like a jerk after all.

At three-thirty, I threw in the towel. It was time to meet Robert Barish. After hiking through Chelsea, I had no energy for the train, so I hailed a cab and headed for East 43rd Street.

The building turned out to be on one of those short, cavernous blocks between Madison and Vanderbilt, just to the west of Grand Central Terminal. It was nearly deserted on the street and in the lobby, too. A security guard in white shirtsleeves sat in the crisp artificial coolness, staring desultorily at the *Daily News*. After motioning for me to sign the visitors log, he told me to take the elevator to the twelfth floor. The building looked like something out of a 1940s film noir—the marble lobby, the brass pointer above the elevator indicating the floors that were being passed. It was 1940s style on the twelfth floor, too, as if the area hadn't been touched in over sixty years. I walked down the wide, empty corridor, half expecting Sam Spade or Philip Marlowe to step out from behind one of the office doors with a frosted window.

Suite 1236 turned out to be all the way down one corridor and then another. It was so quiet on the floor, it seemed as if no one could possibly be here, that Barish had forgotten our appointment, but after I knocked on the door, I could hear the dull sound of footsteps from deep within. A man dressed in gray slacks and a gleaming blue dress shirt swung open the door and introduced himself soberly as Robert Barish. He was about six feet one and formidable looking, but his face was doughy, and there was a gut hanging over his pants, as if he'd stuffed his shirt with a small ham. He looked like the kind of guy who might suddenly turn purple one day on the squash court and be pronounced DOA while he was still in the ambulance

"Hello, Bailey—may I call you that?"

"Of course."

"I appreciate your coming to midtown," he said, leading me

through a small mauve-colored foyer. "I have a conference call with a client today, and I need to have all his paperwork in front of me."

"Are you a lawyer?" I asked. We were now in an open area of about four or five nondescript workstations, making our way to a doorway at the end that opened onto a spacious office filled with blond furniture and photographs of Barish shaking hands with husky men I didn't recognize.

"No, I'm a financial manager. I guide clients on everything from investments to estate planning."

"Was Tom Fain a client?"

"His parents were—not Tom himself. But I'm the executor of the Fains' will, so I had to spend some time with Tom for that reason. We weren't in contact all that much recently, but he was a fine young man, and as you can imagine, I'm devastated by what happened. Why don't you take a seat."

Though there was a sofa and two armchairs at one end of his office, he motioned to a chair on the opposite side of his desk and then skirted behind to his own chair. I felt as if I were on a freakin' job interview and that any minute he was going to start discussing the company's 401(k) plan.

"I finally managed to get hold of the sheriff's office," he said. "I know a bit more than when I spoke to you last night, but not much. You found the body in the main house?"

"Yes, in what I think must have been the master bathroom."

"What can you tell me about how Tom was killed?"

"It was pretty horrible. It appears he was stabbed or bludgeoned—there was a fair amount of blood—and then he was set on fire in the tub."

"Good God!" he exclaimed. "What kind of *animals* live in this world?" He turned right to gaze out the window—a view of nothing but windows of other buildings—and pulled on his chin. There was an oddly monochromatic quality to him: sandy blond hair with a hint of red, yellow brown eyes, a slightly ruddy face. I sensed I would forget what he looked like ten minutes after I left.

"Because the crime occurred upstate, I don't know how much time the police will devote to checking out matters down here," I told him. "I worry this case may fall between the cracks."

"Matters down here?" he said, narrowing his eyes. "What do you mean by that?"

"Well, unless Tom pissed off somebody in a town he rarely went to anymore, his killer had to come from his sphere of acquaintances down here."

"Are you saying that the motive wasn't robbery?"

"If it was, his murder is the biggest case of overkill I've ever seen—if you'll excuse the expression. Why would a burglar need to go to that much trouble?"

He raised his eyes and leaned back in his chair, one of those aerodynamic models that allowed him to put his whole weight on the back.

"Okay, I see what you're driving at," he said. "Any ideas who?"

"No, not at the moment." I certainly didn't feel comfortable sharing my suspect list with him.

"How is it that you ended up in Andes anyway?" he asked.

I explained how I had pieced it together after Chris had requested my help. He listened intently, watching me, it seemed, with a hint of skepticism, as if there were an element of my story that struck him as odd. He could prove to be a valuable resource, and I didn't want to alienate him. I decided to try a little stroking.

"Of course, you're a big part of the reason I found Tom," I said.

"How do you mean?"

"If you hadn't put a fire under the missing persons department, we might not have learned that Tom had headed north."

"Fortunately I was able to pull a few strings. After I learned from this kid Chris that Tom was AWOL and that the cops don't generally take action for missing young males—*despite* what we see on TV—I phoned one of my clients in media, and he made the call to the right person. It didn't get us more than a cursory effort—but at least you took the initiative to follow up on it. I want to thank you for what you did. As horrible as the outcome was, you must feel relieved to have all this behind you."

"Well, I'm not done yet," I said. "I'm still poking around."

"Is that really wise?" he asked. "It sounds like we're dealing with a real monster."

"Well, like I said, I don't know how much time and effort the sheriff's office will give the case down here. Besides, I plan to be careful."

I didn't point out to him that the night before, I'd spent six hours upchucking along the streets of Chelsea with no memory of having done so.

"Well, I hope so," Barish said. He studied me for a few seconds before rising. I'd just been signaled that we were through.

"Actually, I have a question for *you*, if you don't mind," I said hurriedly.

"All right, but I do have that conference call coming up—so if you could kindly make it quick."

"You dealt with Tom about money matters. Did he ever mention that someone from the crew of the show, a grip named Deke, had borrowed several thousand dollars from him and not repaid it?"

"You mean *recently*?" he exclaimed, sounding taken aback.

"No, earlier in the summer."

"Yes, I was aware of that incident. Tom was quite upset about it and called me to discuss whether he had any recourse. I told him that unfortunately he had no legal leg to stand on. Now that I think of it, that must have been one of the last conversations

I had with Tom. It was in July I believe. Do you know if he ever got the money back?"

"Not that I'm aware of."

"That's actually a nice little motive, isn't it?" he said, cocking his head.

"Possibly," I said. Suddenly another question rammed itself against my brain, something I should have thought of earlier.

"There's one other thing," I said as Barish moved toward the door.

"Of course. Why don't we talk on the way out." He led me back through the empty workstations. As I glanced to the right, I saw that there were several offices along the wall, and a young woman, her pale blond hair in a bob, sat in one of them, staring at a computer screen. She glanced up as we walked by. Must be fun to be holed up in an office on Saturdays.

"When you were talking to Missing Persons, why didn't you mention the fact that Tom might be in Andes?" I asked to Barish's back.

He stopped in his tracks and swung around to me. "That's easy to explain," he said, crisply. "Tom had told me he'd *sold* the house. The closing was supposed to be in July. I only found out when I spoke to the sheriff that the sale had fallen through."

"That wasn't something Tom would discuss with you? Or the fact that he was withdrawing money for work on the house?"

"As I said previously, Tom wasn't my client, and he handled his own bank account. As a courtesy, I would occasionally answer a financial question for him—like when he'd foolishly loaned someone money who wouldn't repay it—but that was really the extent of it. Of course, as executor, I keep an eye on the trusts."

"Who gets the money now that Tom is dead?" I asked.

Barish looked at me with what almost amounted to pity, as if he felt sorry for the fact that I was capable of asking such a crude question.

"As you might imagine, I can't discuss such things."

"My interest isn't prurient. I'm looking into Tom's murder."

"Understood," he said, and then offered a tight smile. "Between the two of us, the bulk goes to charity—his parents arranged the trusts that way. And please do understand that I appreciate all your efforts. I hope you will keep me informed." Of course, as executor, some money would go to him.

In turn, I asked to be informed of any funeral plans.

I had thought I'd just hop on the Lex at Grand Central, but as I rode down in the empty elevator, I felt overwhelmed by both fatigue and a weird malaise, as though the hangover from my experience in Chelsea had resurrected itself. I took a cab instead, and as soon as I was home, I poured a hot bath with a huge glob of bath gel and nearly fell into it. I laid a warm wet washcloth over my eyes and tried to clear my brain for a few minutes, but thoughts kept shoving their way in there. Who had killed Tom, and why? And was that person now after *me*? I hadn't learned very much from Barish, but his confirmation of Deke's debt had been important. That and the fact that Tom, a guy known for his live-and-let-live attitude, had been extremely agitated about it. As an old reporter I used to work with once said, money burns a hole in the gut no matter *who* you are.

My guess was that Tom hadn't let the issue die. It might have been uncomfortable for Deke to see Tom on the set, and the situation would have really heated up if Tom had threatened to go to management. Deke looked like a guy with a short fuse and a big temper—I remembered the hostile way he'd rubbed his hard thigh against me in the Half King after I'd tried to pump him about Tom—and I suspected that rather than allowing himself to be guilted out by Tom, he would have felt cornered. And mad. Had he turned violent when Tom had refused to back off? If he was the one who had driven to Andes and killed Tom, there may have been a nice bonus in it for him—the $7,000 Tom had brought with him. I wondered if the sheriff had found it or if it was missing. Maybe Deke had even gotten wind of the fact that Tom had the cash on him, and that had been part of the motive for killing him.

I was nearly positive Deke wouldn't be at the party tonight—I couldn't see him making Locket's list of power players—so I would have to find another way to check him out further. Tonight, instead, my plan would be to speak to Harper, observe Locket and Alex, and also grill Amy, who hopefully had answers about my lost hours. I stared down at my naked body, which had started to go all pruny around the edges. Where *were* you last night? was all I could think. Every time I considered my amnesia, I felt positively morose. Maybe a night with Chris would help chase away my gloom.

As soon as I was dried off from my bath, I called Jessie and asked if she'd be willing to meet about half an hour before the party started so I could fill her in on everything that had transpired. If she was going to be a second pair of eyes for me tonight, she needed to be in the loop. She was game and suggested a wine bar on a side street in the East 80s just a few blocks from Elaine's. The forecast promised cooler night weather again, and I ended up wearing a miniskirt, leggings, and a boxy short jacket over a low-cut top—I figured it said summer and fall at the same time.

Jessie had also opted for a mini and leggings, which made us both snort with laughter as she strutted over to greet me in the small wine bar. I saw that she'd really glammed herself up—coral lips and lots of black mascara. Pieces of her thick brown hair fell with perfect dishabille from a sloppy bun on top of her head.

"You look pretty darn gorgeous for a *book* party," I said. "Are you going to try to help me and get lucky at the same time?"

"I admit it—I'm in the mood for a new man. Though don't ask me *why*. Have you heard the age theory about New York men? They have their chronological age and then they have their New

York age, which is about four to five years younger. You meet a guy who's thirty, but the age he acts is *twenty-five*—and his idea of a good time is telling his buddies about the time some chick gave him road head while he was driving eighty miles an hour."

"Gosh, Chris is only in his early twenties, so that makes him, like, seventeen. Does that mean I could get arrested for sleeping with him?"

"So what's the latest?" she demanded.

I told her everything that had happened since we'd spoken the day before, including the drugging. A couple of times she opened her mouth to ask a question, then shook her head, as if she were too spellbound to break the flow.

"Oh, my God," she said when I'd finished, ending with my futile search for my memory along the streets of Chelsea. "It's like one of those awful good news/bad news jokes. The good news is that you're knocking boots with a total hottie who's starring in a major TV show. The bad news is that you're being stalked, drugged, and possibly marked for death."

"Yeah, and that's why I need your help," I told her. "Flirt your butt off tonight, but I want you to keep your eyes open and your ears perked. I want to know if you see anything weird going on between Locket and Alex. I'll keep my eye on them, but I won't be able to hover for too long."

We strolled into Elaine's at seven-thirty, about half an hour after the party had officially started. There were at least fifteen paparazzi out front, and though a couple of them snapped our picture just in case we might be *somebody*, most lowered their cameras as we walked past, the boredom registering on their faces. I wondered if within weeks Chris would be making his way into events with flashbulbs popping in his face and photographers screaming his name.

Inside, the place was already mobbed. Elaine's, one of those old-style New York restaurants referred to sometimes as a watering hole, is a favorite haunt of both celebs and literary types. The dark walls are crowded with old posters, black-and-white photos, and framed covers of books written by regular patrons. Which, along with the amber glow from the wall sconces, gives a clubby feeling to the place. I squeezed through a group of people bunched up at the door (including Mary Kay!) and cast my eyes around the main room. There was no sign of Chris, but Alex and Locket were stationed farther along to the left by the bar with a dozen fawning sorts ringed around them.

"That's them up there, holding court," I said, leaning into Jessie.

"Yeah, I know," she replied. "I actually used to watch her soap—until her character got kidnapped by terrorists and then decided to become a doctor."

I told her that she was free to patrol if she wanted because I'd take the first watch. We broke apart, and after grabbing a glass of wine from a passing waiter, I headed toward the end of the bar, making sure I didn't catch Locket's eye. She was busy regaling her admirers with a story, and I found a spot not far behind her and Alex, buffered by several other guests but close enough to hear snippets of their conversation.

"I'm doing a luncheon for beauty editors, but Alex thought this would be fun, too. A real old-fashioned book party."

Someone asked her a question I couldn't make out.

"The most important?" she said, rolling one shoulder forward coquettishly. "No sun *whatsoever*. This summer I practically wore a burka in East Hampton, even when I went to the farmer's market."

Alex scanned the crowd, looking bored with the bonus beauty tips, and cupped Locket's elbow as if anxious to change locations. "Ready for another drink?" he asked, almost like a demand.

"Please, darling, yes," she said.

A waiter passed by him with a tray of white wine and

champagne, but Alex shook his head and turned instead to the bartender.

"A glass of Veuve Clicquot," he demanded.

There was a good two-second beat before the connection caught up with me, but when it did, I felt my blood go icy. Veuve Clicquot was the brand I'd spotted in Tom Fain's cottage.

As Locket accepted the champagne glass, Alex grasped her elbow more tightly and began to maneuver her away from this particular thicket of people. I spun around, not wanting them to see me.

Only inches away, and nearly face-to-face with me, stood Beau Regan.

CHAPTER 10

As if I were seeing Beau for the first time all over again, the words that flashed instantly through my mind were the same ones that had formed that day last summer when I'd met his intense brown-eyed gaze across a hushed reception area: *I'm going to marry that guy.* They were now quickly chased away and replaced, however, with the words *Fuck-face scumbag.* Beau had arrived back in town and never called me. I clearly meant nada to him.

"Bailey," he said, obviously as taken aback as I was. "I— What brings you here?"

"Just trying to pick up a few beauty tricks from Locket Ford," I said. "I hear she has a recipe for an oatmeal-and-apricot scrub that takes about five years off your face." Ha, ha, Bailey, you are so freakin' funny! I felt like screaming. But I couldn't totally fault myself. I was so nervous right then that my tongue felt as heavy as a U-Haul trailer parked in my mouth, and I was lucky I could say anything at all.

"You aren't covering this for the magazine, are you?"

"No, I'm still on the fun and fabulous crime beat for *Buzz*." That didn't really answer his question, but who the hell cared.

Well, I cared, clearly. My heart was beating wildly just from the sight of him. He was wearing black pants and a cobalt blue long-sleeved shirt open at the collar, which looked awesome with his smooth, tanned face. His dark hair seemed a little lighter, perhaps bleached out from weeks in the Turkish sun, and it was longer, brushed behind his ears.

I figured it was my turn to ask how he had ended up at the Locket Ford book bash, but I couldn't summon the energy for any phony cocktail banter. If he wanted to make a stab at it, let him. And he did.

"Her book agent's a pal of mine. I just got back yesterday, and he said he thought this would be good reemersion therapy. I'm not so sure, though."

"Yeah, well, any party where the paparazzi almost outnumber the guests probably isn't going to be good therapy." Oh great, now I was playing Dr. Phil. But I felt incapable of saying anything witty, paralyzed by conflicting emotions. There was the longing to dazzle him blind, making him realize that he really wanted me desperately after all, but also a fierce desire to be my own angel of mercy and extricate myself from the bloody situation.

"Well, it's great to see you, Bailey," he said, his voice low and soft. "I was planning to call you this week. I'd really like to—"

He stopped suddenly, his attention caught by something just over my right shoulder. Before I had a chance to turn to see what it was, I felt a strong, muscular arm enclose me. Biceps like that could belong to only one man. There *is* a God, I thought as the arm pulled me close to the body it was attached to so brilliantly.

"So here you are," Chris said. "I've been looking for you."

"I just got here a minute ago."

I glanced back at Beau. I may have been mistaken, but I

thought I saw a hint of discombobulation in his eyes, a chink in the unflappable manner that he was such a master at presenting to the world.

"Oh, sorry. This is Beau Regan. Chris Wickersham. Chris is working with Locket."

"Are you with the publishing house?" Beau asked. That was funny. I could just imagine Chris calling Locket and announcing, "I've got page proofs for you, Miss Ford. Would you like me to drop by and review them with you?"

"No, we're on *Morgue* together. Do you know her?"

"I don't, actually. I'm just a hanger-on tonight." Beau sounded breezy enough as he spoke, but I could see his eyes scrutinizing Chris, taking in everything about him. "What's *Morgue,* anyway, a new soap?"

"Actually, a new nighttime drama. Listen, would you mind if I steal Bailey away? I've got something important I need to discuss with her." He lifted his arm from my shoulder and combed his fingers in one languorous stroke through the back of my hair. It was the kind of cock-blocking gesture that announced he'd been to bed with me or at least damn well *intended* to be there tonight. One of Beau's eyebrows lifted just a little, involuntarily, I guessed.

"Of course," was all he said. "Nice to see you, Bailey." He turned and melted into the crowd. Chris took my hand and led me to the side room, which wasn't nearly as mobbed as the rest of place. We claimed a corner to talk in.

"Sorry to do that to you," Chris said. "That wasn't the most important conversation of your life or anything, was it?"

"Hardly," I said with the kind of disdain I'd normally reserve for people guilty of cell yell.

"I've just been really worried about you. When you first told me about getting drugged, I naturally assumed some guy did it. But later this afternoon, I started to wonder if it might have something to do with Tom's murder."

"I'm wondering the same thing," I admitted. I filled him in on the details of last night—both what I'd recalled and what Rusty had shared—as well as what I'd learned about GHB. He winced as I described my terrifying experience on the street in Chelsea.

"Jesus, Bailey, this is getting really scary," he exclaimed. "I think it's time for you to back off—I don't want to put you in any more danger."

"It's too late now. If it's the murderer who drugged me and has been calling me, he—or she—knows I'm snooping around. I'm better off trying to figure out who it is before the person tries anything else."

"And from the phone call you couldn't tell whether it was a man or a woman?"

"No, that's the odd thing. Both the laughing and the crying sounded as if they came from some bizarre androgynous creature. Chris, you may be able to help," I added. "It's more than likely that my beer was messed with while you were still in the bar. I drank more than half of it, and I was just fine. Then I went over to talk to Amy, and after that I dropped into the ladies' room to find Harper. Do you remember seeing anyone over by my stool around that time? Because that's when someone must have slipped the drug in."

He scrunched his mouth and thought for a moment, then shook his head back and forth methodically. "I didn't see anything—it was just so crowded in there."

"Amy is my only other hope, then. Is she here tonight, do you know?"

"Yeah, she's here. The last I saw her, she was toward the back of the other room—with Harper."

"Why don't we meet up later. I want to talk to Amy and Harper—and maybe Locket as well. Oh, I nearly forgot the big news." I told him about Alex ordering the Veuve Clicquot for Locket.

"That doesn't necessarily mean she was there—at Tom's place," he said, frowning. "Other people drink that champagne."

"I know—it's just an odd coincidence, and I never like coincidences."

"Well, it might be connected—but not in the way you think. Since Tom had his little fling with Locket, he could have started drinking it himself—because he thought it would impress her."

"Possibly," I said. "But it's worth keeping in mind. One more question. Were you aware that Deke had borrowed several thousand dollars from Tom and never paid him back?"

"You're kidding—are you sure about that?"

"Yes, two people told me."

"What an asshole. I— You know, now that I think of it, I got the sense that things had cooled between the two of them, but I figured it was because Harper kept advising Tom to spend less time with the crew. But there was one night—about a week or two before Tom disappeared—when a bunch of us were going out and at the last minute Deke decided to come. The next thing I knew, Tom bailed with some flimsy excuse. I never connected it to Deke until now."

"I talked to Deke briefly last night, and he seemed hostile."

"Do you think *he* could have killed Tom?"

"It's a possibility. If Tom was threatening to get him canned, he may have decided to shut him up. Maybe he never intended to kill him but things escalated. And Deke was right near my drink last night."

"And guess what? You know how you said gyms are a good source for GHB? Well, Deke is a big bodybuilder."

"I've got to find a way to have more face time with Deke, as unpleasant as that may be. Can you make that happen, Chris?"

"I'll try. You've just got to promise me to be careful."

I smiled, gave his elbow a squeeze, and told him I'd connect with him in about an hour. I made my way toward a corridor in the back that led to another door to the front room. People were really jammed in there now, rich and successful-looking New Yorkers with their heads bobbing in conversation or muscling their way through the crowd in search of someone better to schmooze with. I spotted both Amy and Harper in the back, just as Chris had predicted, but before heading over there, I glanced toward the front. Jessie was standing at the bar with none other than Alex himself and another man. And Beau was in the same vicinity, in a cluster that included a man, perhaps his buddy, and two hot-looking chicks. But his eyes were scanning the room. Was he looking for me? What words had he been about to say before Chris had interrupted our conversation? "I'd really like to . . ." *What? Talk* to me? *Get together* with me? *Explain things* to me? I could feel an ache beginning to form in my heart, but I was too wired for it to take over. I had work to do.

Amy had a look of concern in her eyes as soon as she saw me approach her, and I figured she probably thought I was still recovering from a *Guinness Book of World Records*–caliber hangover.

"Got a minute?" I shouted to her above the din.

"Sure. You okay today?"

"Not so much."

"I know, I know. I probably should have made sure you got home okay. But it was so early, I figured—"

"Look, you probably think I was drunk, but I wasn't. Someone slipped a drug of some kind in my beer."

She raised both eyebrows. *"What?"*

"I can tell you about it later, but right now I need answers since I remember practically nothing. The bartender told me you came back over and spoke to me again—after we'd talked by the garden. What was I doing then?"

"Just sitting there. I realized that Harper had left, and I asked you if there was some new development. As soon as you started to speak, I could tell you were . . . well, I thought you must have had a pretty good buzz on. Your hair was kind of wet, and you were slurring your words."

"What did I say?"

"You told me that Harper and Chris had left."

"And then?"

"Nothing, really. I asked if you wanted me to find you a cab, and you said you were going to walk for a while, get some air. Then you left. It was still early, and I figured you'd be fine. No one *attacked* you, did they?"

"No, I'm okay. But if you think of anything else, will you let me know?"

"Of course," she said emphatically. She looked sheepish, and I suspected she had a case of the guilts. Maybe that gave me a chit I could use to my advantage down the road. As for my missing night, it seemed as if I'd never be able to fill in the pieces. I'd apparently gone to the ladies' room to try and revive myself and then later headed outside, where I'd wandered aimlessly, searching for my bearings.

My next target was Harper, but I could tell by the expression on her face as I approached that I was the last person she wanted to chat with tonight.

"How are you doing?" I asked. She was standing next to a woman with a clipboard, and they both appeared to be "on duty."

"This isn't a good time," she said. She was pretty dolled up, in a slinky black cocktail dress and dangly silver earrings, but her face looked fatigued, smudged with bluish circles under her copper eyes, verifying the fact that she *had* tossed and turned last night. If she'd killed Tom, why get all churned up now and not two weeks ago? It might be that the discovery of the body made it finally real. Or she could be wigged out now that the police were on the case.

"When, then?" I asked.

"Tomorrow. Call me tomorrow." She turned back to the woman with the clipboard, offering me a view of her bare back.

I summoned the energy to edge my way through the crowd again, and when I'd progressed about two feet, I felt someone grab my arm. I thought it must be Chris, but when I twisted around, Jessie was wedged behind me with an impish expression on her face.

"Have you *seen* him? Beau Regan's here."

"Yeah, I almost had to call for a defibrillator."

"It took me a minute to realize who he was—I'd just seen him once at that party in the Hamptons. If it's any consolation, I gave him the evil eye for about ten minutes. I think it worked because someone sloshed a glass of red wine on his shirt."

"Thank you. Could you try for a vat of rancid cooking oil next time? That would *really* make my night."

"Don't look, but he's staring at you. That's funny—he has no idea that I know him, and he's just gawking away like an idiot. Do you think the two of you will hook up again?"

"Not likely. Anything interesting going on between Locket and Alex?"

"They seem perfectly pleasant to each other. But if he squeezes her elbow any tighter, it's gonna pop like an egg."

For the next half hour we inched our way around, checking out the scene, with me biding my time for just the right opportunity to approach Locket. It was interesting to play total observer at a party, not worried about meeting anyone or having someone to talk to, but just happy to be the proverbial fly on the wall. I watched people air-kiss, fawn, flirt, fake interest, slug down drinks, and shove their way through the crowd. One woman got her large silver bracelet caught in the zipper of a man's pants, and she went nearly frantic trying to get it off, like a muskrat with its leg in a trap. At one point I figured out that Beau must have left, because there was no sign of him. Chris, on the other hand, seemed to be at the throbbing center, having clearly been dubbed the new It boy. An ever changing group of people ringed him—mostly superslick guys who might have been producers or agents hoping to poach him as a client, and babes—tons of babes. There were both hot young chicks with flat shiny hair, Chloé tops, and $3,000 handbags and so-called cougars—too-smooth-faced, over-forty glamazons who looked hungry for a no-strings-attached romp in the sack with him. Chris remained rooted in one spot, and women were sucked in his direction from every which way, like birds into the engines of a jet on takeoff. If my twinges of jealousy were any indication, I was starting to feel more than lust for Chris.

Unfortunately, Locket also remained surrounded most of the night, and Alex's large pale hand was usually holding her elbow or pressed to her like a Post-it note. At about a quarter to ten, just before the party was due to end, I left the main area and ducked into the bathroom, considering what I should do. Perhaps I needed to enlist Chris to work his way into the phalanx around Locket—with me in tow. But it turned out not to be necessary. As I was rummaging through my purse for a tube of lip gloss, I heard the door open, and before I had a chance to glance up, I recognized the overwhelming scent of patchouli and vanilla. Miss Ford, *Morgue* star and beauty guru, had entered the bathroom. Her eyes went instantly to her reflection in the mirror, so it was a few moments before she realized who was standing alongside her.

"Lovely party," I said. "Congratulations."

"Thank you," she said haughtily, her eyes making contact with mine in the mirror. "My, my—you and Chris are getting to be quite the item."

"Actually, I came with a friend," I told her. I swiped on my lip gloss, buying time while I quickly considered how to maximize the few short moments I would have alone with her. I decided to go for broke.

"It must be hard for you tonight, though," I said, offering a newly glistening but sympathetic smile.

"What do you mean?" she asked bluntly. She was the kind of woman who didn't appreciate people other than herself defining anything about her.

"Well, you have this wonderful celebration for your book, but at the same time you must be grieving over Tom's death. I happen to know that you two were extremely"—I paused for emphasis—"*close*."

She was a damn good actress, I had to hand that to her, because her face registered no emotion whatsoever, but I saw her eyes quickly skirt the floor, making certain no feet were visible below the doors of any of the stalls.

"Who told you *that*?" she asked as her eyes found mine again in the mirror.

"Someone with real information."

At that moment, two postpubescent actressy types burst into the ladies' room, gawking at a photo on one of their cell phones and giggling like idiots. For the first time, I saw alarm on Locket's face. She wanted to know what I knew, and she wasn't going to be able to find out right now. She swung open the ladies' room door and motioned with her head for me to go first into the small, dark corridor. It appeared that she wanted to resume our conversation there.

But Alex was standing outside, rigid and waiting.

"What's going on?" he asked when it registered with him that we'd obviously been talking.

"Have you met Chris's girlfriend, darling?" she asked brightly, rolling her shoulder forward coyly. "Her name is Bailey, of all things."

"No, I haven't had the pleasure," he said coolly, though I

could see recognition in his eyes as he met my gaze. He snapped his head in greeting rather than shake my hand. I nodded back. I didn't have Locket's acting chops, and I wondered if he could tell by looking at me that we hadn't exactly been chatting about the new Jimmy Choo shoes while we powdered our noses.

"People are waiting for us, Locket," he said. "It's time to go."

He took her elbow yet again, guiding her away. Neither of them said another word to me.

Damn, I thought. It had seemed as if I'd been about to get *something* from Locket—an admission, perhaps, or a *hint* of admission—but thanks to the two Lindsay Lohan wannabes, I'd come away empty-handed.

Eager to reconnect with Jessie, I decided to call her cell rather than try to search for her. As I was punching in her number, I caught a movement in my peripheral vision. I glanced to my right, and there was Beau again. So he hadn't left after all.

"Calling in an exclusive on that apricot scrub?" he asked.

"Yeah, they're bumping a Kevin Federline item for it. Now we'll never know what books are on his night table." Still at the top of my game with the witty comeback. Gosh, I was surprised I hadn't been tapped to do an HBO comedy special.

"How did your summer end up, anyway?" he asked, his eyes quizzical—as if he really *were* curious. Those brown eyes still had the power to blow me away, and I could feel my pulse starting to race again, as if I'd just mainlined a Red Bull. But I felt something else as well: the first swells of anger. Beau had come back and never made contact, subjected me to a DWE—dumping without explanation. And now he was insisting on torturing me with tedious small talk.

"Pretty good, I guess," I said flatly. "I went up to Cape Cod—my mother has a place there. Ate a lot of clams."

"I'm sorry I never sent more than a couple of postcards, Bailey. It was pretty crazy in Turkey. We sometimes worked fourteen-hour days."

"One."

"Sorry?"

"One. You sent one postcard. But that's okay. The thing about getting *one* postcard is that it really lets you know where you stand."

I'd caught him off guard with my sarcasm, and he opened his mouth ever so slightly in surprise. He pulled up the left side of his mouth in a rueful smile.

"Well, you obviously didn't waste any time fretting over it," he said, matching my sarcastic tone.

The two gigglers spilled out of the bathroom suddenly, squealing now, as if they'd just done a few lines of coke in a stall. Before things got any worse between Beau and me, I decided to beat a retreat.

"Well, I'd better go," I said. "Have a nice night."

"You too," he said dryly as I turned from him.

Walking away, I smirked. It was fun to imagine him thinking of just *how* nice a night I would probably have with the star of the show. But as I emerged from the corridor into the main room of the restaurant, my heart sank. Until tonight I'd harbored fantasies that there was still a chance for me and Beau, that he would return from his journey, blow off the Turkish dust from his belongings, and realize that he had missed me horribly. Now I had to face the truth: It was really over.

The crowd had thinned out in just the short time I'd been absent. Obviously, as the first wave of A-listers had moved to the door, others had taken it as a signal that the fun was about to come crashing to an end. To my despair, Chris was at the bar talking to two Bottega Veneta bag bimbos, but as soon as he spotted me, he broke free and made his way to me. Simultaneously, Jessie headed toward me from another direction. I introduced her to

Chris, and I could tell from Jessie's expression that she liked what she saw.

"I ran into some friends from *People*, and we thought we'd head downtown and hear some music," she announced. "Want to come?"

Chris glanced at me with uncertainty on his face. "Are you up for that, Bailey? You've had a pretty rough twenty-four hours."

"Probably not," I told him. "We could grab a bite some-where—or I could just make you something at my place."

"Really? That sounds pretty appealing."

We said good-bye to Jessie and hailed a cab outside. As we hurtled down Second Avenue, Chris pulled me into the crook of his arm.

"How you doing, anyway?" he asked softly. "Do you really feel up to standing over a hot stove?"

"I think it'll be therapeutic—though I can't make any prom-ises about the quality of the food."

I had learned to cook in just the past few years. During my marriage, I'd been more than game to wrestle with a chicken breast or two in the kitchen, but my ex had been almost rabid about eating out. We were always in a different bistro, brasserie, or sushi bar, and it was only later that I understood why. He'd already begun to accrue his mondo gambling debts, and being on the move made him feel safer, less in the line of sight of guys who wanted to break his legs in two. After the divorce, I'd bought a few cookbooks, and though I was no Giada De Laurentiis, I could whip up a dozen or so dishes pretty well.

My cupboards were nearly bare at the moment, but I had bacon in the freezer, so after we arrived at my place, I cooked a few pieces in the microwave and made spaghetti carbonara. All you need are bacon, eggs, white wine, and Parmesan cheese, but the sauce is dreamy, especially when accompanied, as Hannibal Lecter would say, by a nice Chianti. I served it indoors, with the

terrace door open a crack because the night was indeed cool, finally more fall than summer. I was grateful for the temperature
change, because pasta on my terrace would have reminded me
too much of Beau—and I was having a hard time chasing him
from my thoughts.

"You were really holding out on me last winter," Chris said. "I
had no idea you could cook like this."

"I like to keep a few aces up my sleeve," I said, smiling.

"Oh, is that what you were doing?" he said, leaning toward
me and stroking my hair. "I thought you were just torturing me."

"Not intentionally."

"Speaking of torture, anything else from the party?"

I shared my conversation with Locket outside the bathroom.
"She's definitely hiding something," I said.

"Well, we know she's hiding her fling with Tom," Chris exclaimed, almost in exasperation. "But that doesn't mean there's
more. Just because Tom was drinking her brand of champagne
doesn't mean she drove up there—or—or killed him."

"What makes you so sure?" I said, surprised by his stance.

"I just don't see her doing it. What would be the reason?"

I was about to make the case for Locket as a definite suspect
but decided to back off. Chris didn't seem at all happy with that
as a possibility, and I wasn't interested in any contentiousness. I
moved on to Deke.

"Do you think you can get me in his presence again soon—
like on set?" I asked.

"We're shooting at Chelsea Piers on Monday," Chris said. "I
may be able to sneak you in."

He helped me with the dishes after that, and then we didn't
even bother to sit on the couch and play the seduction game—we
went straight to my bed. The sex was different this time, not the
fierce, bittersweet variety we'd engaged in the other night, but still
amazing. Later, his arm around me, Chris made me laugh with

a story about sharing a bed one summer with his little brother, nicknamed Kicker.

I nodded off right after, with him spooning me, but just after one, my eyes popped open. It had started to rain suddenly, and I could hear the drum of it on the metal railing around my terrace. I closed my eyes again, willing sleep to return, but it was clear within a few minutes that it had no intention whatsoever of doing so.

After slipping out of Chris's grasp, I padded naked out to my kitchen, where I tried milk therapy, night two. Yet even as I swallowed the milk, I knew it probably wasn't going to do the trick. Seeing Beau again was bugging the hell out of me, and the afterglow of sex with a gorgeous guy I really dug wasn't going to ameliorate the situation. What had he been about to say when he'd uttered the words *I'd really like to . . .* ? Thanks to that sarcastic missile I'd lobbed, I'd blown my chance of ever knowing.

As I set the glass in the sink, my home phone rang, startling me. I wondered if it might be the infamous night caller, now with access to my home number, too. I picked it up as quickly as possible, not wanting to wake Chris.

"Is this Bailey Weggins?" demanded the voice on the other end.

"It is." I glanced at the clock: 1:14.

"This is Locket Ford."

I caught my breath in surprise.

"Hello," was all I said. Clearly she was the one with an agenda now, and I was not going to say anything that would short-circuit it.

"We should talk," she said coolly.

"Now?"

"Now isn't good. Tomorrow."

"Okay, when?"

"At four. Meet me at my apartment." She gave me a number on Central Park West.

"Is that in the Seventies?"

But she'd already hung up.

I slipped back into bed a few minutes later, and Chris stirred.

"More insomnia?" he murmured.

"Unfortunately."

"I have a way to help."

"I'd love to try."

"I heard the phone ring," he said as he pulled me toward his naked body, ready for sex again.

I opened my mouth to tell him about Locket's call—and then, for some reason I couldn't define, I thought better of it.

"Wrong number," I said.

CHAPTER 11

This time I slept straight through till morning and woke to the light seeping through the shades on my windows. I felt Chris stir beside me. I turned my head toward the middle of the bed and saw him lying on his stomach, his bare arms folded on the pillow under his head. It felt really good to have him next to me, and I couldn't help thinking of the contrast between last night and the horrible night before.

"Hey, good morning," Chris said. His eyes were still closed, but he offered me a sleepy smile.

"Good morning to you. Are you hungry?"

There was a pause, as if he were deliberating.

"Actually, yes," he said, opening his eyes. "I'm ravenous." By the mischievous look he gave me, I could see that he didn't mean for breakfast. We had sex in the soft, almost autumnal light. I felt a growing connection between us, but I didn't know what the heck we were supposed to do about it. As we lay in each other's arms Chris announced that it was his turn to cook, that if I had more eggs, he would make me an omelet to end all omelets.

After starting coffee, I turned my tiny kitchen over to him. Before long, I could hear him rummaging through the drawers of my fridge.

"There's some cheddar in there somewhere," I called out.

"Found it. I've also located some scallions that have clearly been here since the Clinton administration—but they don't cause botulism, do they?"

"Only heartburn, I think."

As I set the table, I watched him out of the corner of my eye. He had slipped into his pants but not bothered with a shirt yet and had tucked a yellow dish towel into his waistband as an apron. He hummed as he worked, at least when he wasn't exclaiming a triumphant "Yes!" at each successful step in the omelet-making process. There was a totally boyish quality to his effort, as if he were a kid working with a chemistry kit that he secretly hoped would blow up the kitchen. I realized for the first time that the boyishness wasn't because he was barely over twenty-one; it was just the way Chris *was*. Chris would be eternally open and easy and fun—what you saw was what you got. Unlike with Beau, there was nothing that felt elusive about him or maddeningly mysterious.

That's not to say I felt I totally knew Chris. As he set the plates on the table, announcing, "I'm Brent and I'll be your waiter today. We used only eggs from free-range chickens and aged California cheddar," I couldn't help wondering how many other chicks would love to be treated to one of his après amour omelets. That swarm around him last night had been awful. When Chris and I had dated briefly in the winter, I'd been conscious of how good-looking he was and that other women were often devouring him with their eyes, but I'd never felt very discomfited by it. His success, however, was going to ratchet up everything. How would I fit into the picture? Wouldn't Chris want to sample all the bounty before him, especially all the lithe twenty-two-year-olds? Did I really want to get involved with a hot young actor who was ten years my junior to boot?

"You okay?" he asked. "You look kind of perplexed."

"Oh, I was just contemplating the feast I'm about to devour." I took my first bite. "Oh wow, this is awesome," I said. "You're a real soup-to-nuts kind of overnight date, aren't you?"

"In a manner of speaking," he said, laughing. "I do like cooking, though, and I want to get better at it—preparing great food for friends. What I don't want to ever do again is put on a black tie and serve a meal to people I don't know."

"I think your waitering and bartending days are over. Maybe the next time you put on a black tie will be for an event like the Golden Globes."

"You just can't ever count your chickens in this business," he said. "Guys like Patrick Dempsey and George Clooney did a billion pilots before things took off for them. Think of how many times they must have thought, Okay, this is it. And then it wasn't. And even worse is when you consider the people who did a billion pilots and *still* didn't make it."

"Are you worried that the show won't take off and you'll be back making the rounds in L.A.?"

"Oh yeah. I lucked out and got a show right away. But instead of relishing it, I worry that it came too easily."

I asked him then about the couple of months he'd spent in L.A., because other than during those brief moments in the bar last Tuesday night, we really hadn't had a chance to talk about it. He described the craziness of pilot season, the nonstop auditioning, meetings, and drinks, and the occasional trips to the beach just to stay tanned through the whole thing. He made me laugh out loud as he imitated the *Entourage*-style way agents and casting directors talked. It was one of the first times since he'd been back that we'd been discussing a topic other than Tom. His disappearance and death had colored so much of our interactions, and it was nice not to be burdened with that for a brief while.

It wasn't long, though, before Tom was rushing my thoughts. As Chris reached the part about auditioning for *Morgue* and his screen test with Locket, I flashed back on what Harper had revealed to me: Tom had nearly nailed the role originally, but after providing the tip about the show to Chris, he had promptly lost the part to him. If Chris ever found out, it would probably be devastating for him.

"Speaking of *Morgue*, I'd better tackle these dishes and high-tail it out of here," Chris announced. "I've got a lot of lines to learn today. Alex has a shit fit if you mess up."

"So he's around a lot during shooting?"

"In the beginning, apparently. I hear his MO is to microman-age like crazy, make sure the show's a hit, then finally step back a little."

"Has he ever been really tough on you? Harper said he came down pretty hard on Tom a few times."

"No, thank God. He lit into Tom in front of people, and it was pretty awful. Even the director seemed taken aback."

"Maybe he sensed something was up with Tom and Locket."

"Or maybe *Tom* felt totally awkward because he was banging Locket, and that affected how he delivered his lines."

"That's a legitimate explanation. But in my mind, both Locket and Alex are still suspects. There's motive for both of them."

"To be honest, I just don't see either one of them going to the effort," he said.

This would have been the moment to mention the call from Locket and her insistence that she needed to speak with me, but once again I decided not to go there. For some reason, Chris didn't seem to want to entertain the idea of Locket as a murderer.

"For the show's sake, let's hope they're innocent, then."

"I thought Deke was at the top of your list right now," Chris said, rising from the table. He picked up both our plates and headed toward the kitchen. "Tom had a long fuse, but he wouldn't let you just roll over him. I bet he was furious at Deke about the money. I could definitely see a confrontation happening."

"Yes, Deke is still high on my list. I need to get in Deke's face a little bit and see what his reaction is. I hope you can really get me on set tomorrow."

I heard the sound of running water and dishes being slid into the dishwasher. Chris stepped back into the living room, his eyes lowered as he thought.

"They let people sneak in a friend or relative as long as they don't get in the way. I think I could pull it off. But I'd have to call you later and let you know. I need to enlist one of the production assistants to help me."

"Great. Leave the rest of the dishes. I don't want Alex taking off that gorgeous head of yours."

As he leaned down to kiss me good-bye, a memory surged through my mind: Chris admitting Friday night that he'd snatched the note from Locket to Tom so the cops wouldn't find it. I had urged him to turn it over. I needed to follow up on that, but this wasn't the moment.

"So I'll call you later about the set visit," he said. "I'd love to see you tonight, but I try to hit the sack pretty early on Sundays. Are you open Monday night? If I can get out in time?"

"Yup," I said, experiencing a twinge of disappointment. I was enjoying the sex, the comfort, and everything else that came from being with Chris. "Why don't we talk tomorrow."

"I was thinking of more than talk," he said, grinning, and kissed me again, long and tenderly.

It was just nine-thirty when he left, too early to call Harper without irritating her any more than I already had. I grabbed my tote bag of exercise clothes and headed over to the gym. Thirty minutes on the StairMaster seemed more miserable than usual, but when I was done and showered, I realized that for the first time since Friday, I actually felt completely like myself again. Maybe I'd sweated the last of the drug out of my system.

Before returning to my place, I headed off in search of a cappuccino. On University Avenue, I ran smack into Landon, walking down the street in a navy blazer and lemony yellow tie.

"Are you doing the walk of shame—preppy style?" I asked.

"If *only*," he said. "No, I have a very nasty client who insisted we meet for breakfast early Sunday morning. I was actually going to knock on your door when I got back. What's the latest?"

"Could you handle more coffee? You wouldn't believe everything that's going on—and I could really use your advice."

He agreed eagerly, and we slipped into a small café halfway up the block. I ran through all the developments on the case with him, including my Friday night saga.

"Goodness, Bailey. Oil riggers have safer jobs than you do. You worry me sick."

"I admit that I'm a little bit freaked this time. I feel I've been able to defend myself pretty well in a bunch of situations in the past. But getting drugged is a whole other story. You're completely helpless. That's why I have to figure out who killed Tom. Whoever it is—man or woman—is toying with me. Right now the plan seems just to scare me, but it could get uglier."

"Any ideas who it is?"

"A few. But that's not all I need to talk to you about. Guess who was at the party last night? None other than Beau Regan— back from the sacking of Constantinople."

"Oh dear. How did it feel to see him?"

"Not bad, really. About the same as if someone had just backed over me with their SUV. Honestly, it was this god-awful mix of unrequited love and raw humiliation over the fact that he hadn't called me. If they could only harvest that feeling, it would make a perfect weapon of mass destruction."

"How long has he been back in town?"

"A day or two, I guess."

"Well, that's not so bad. He may have intended to call when—"

"He started to say something about it. He said, 'I'd been planning to call you. I'd really like to . . .'"

"Like to what?"

"I don't *know*. Chris came by at that moment and grabbed me like the Jaws of Life. I'll never know what he was going to say."

"You could call and ask him."

I told him then about the final conversation and Beau's sarcastic barb about my not wasting any time.

"That kind of seals the deal, doesn't it?" I said. "There's no place to go from there."

"Well, what do you want to happen? I thought you had the hots for Chris these days."

"I *do* like him—very much. But I can't seem to get Beau out of my system."

"Then I'd call him," he said, swirling his spoon around in his coffee. "Ask him what he was going to say."

"Isn't that groveling?"

"Yes, but as you know, I do think it has its place in love. Besides, you really have nothing to lose. If he's hoping to connect with you, you'll be giving him a second chance. If he was just blowing smoke up your you-know-what, you're no worse off than if you didn't approach him—except for the dent in your pride, that is."

Later, after our walk home, I mulled over what he'd recommended. It was the kind of advice (permission to call him) that I'd secretly been hoping for, the kind of advice that friends often give because they know it's what you want them to say, but in the end all it does is leave you feeling like an idiot for making contact with a guy who probably couldn't even remember what state you were from. I pushed it out of my mind and settled down to work.

First I tried Harper—yet again—but got only voice mail. I left a message, saying it was urgent that I speak with her. I also tried Sheriff Schmidt's cell and, when he didn't pick up, the office. The woman who answered told me he was unavailable but she would take a message. Last, I called Beverly's antiques store again. She answered the phone grimly. Clearly, Tom's death was still weighing on her.

"The sheriff's department has been around talking to people," she told me. "I know they've spoken to Barry and also the Realtor, but based on the questions they're asking, they're not very far along in their investigation."

"What will happen to the house, do you think, considering there are no heirs?" she inquired.

"I learned that the money in Tom's trust will probably revert back to the Fain estate and go to charity. But I don't know what will happen to anything that was outright Tom's. At his age he may not have had a will."

There was a moment before she said anything else, and I could sense her ruminating.

"It's a shame there couldn't be a way for the play to still be staged, though," she said finally.

"The play?" I asked, curious.

"Tom had written a play, and he was hoping to mount and direct it at a small theater somewhere. He was going to use part of the proceeds from the house to do it."

"Why not just use money he already had? I mean, he was able to come up with plenty of cash to advance Barry."

"Oh, Tom needed more than that to put on a play. Originally he was hoping to get it from his trust, but there turned out to be complications from that."

A question for Mr. Barish, it seemed.

I thanked her for her help and asked her to call me if she heard anything at all—even if it was only rumor.

There was an empty chunk of the day ahead of me before my planned assignation with Locket. I scribbled notes in my composition book—recaps of my meeting with Barish and the party. For the next two hours, I worked on my freelance piece, writing a rough draft on my laptop.

When it finally came time to dress for my trip uptown, I spent more energy than I would have liked selecting an outfit. That's because Locket, I knew, would be checking me out, running her eyes up and down me and then widening them slightly in that way of hers, suggesting that I had a skanky wet stain on the front of my pants. I didn't want to award her any more power than she already possessed. I finally settled on a pair of black slacks, a long-sleeved black sweater, and killer red slingbacks. And the diamond studs my mother had given me after my divorce to make up for the jewelry my husband had pawned for his gambling debts.

As I'd expected, the apartment building she lived in on Central Park West was one of those big, imposing stone edifices that look as though they could survive a massive meteor attack. Her apartment, on the other hand, was far *more* than I'd expected. I'd assumed, of course, that she and Alex lived in something spacious and classy—why wouldn't they? But after she'd ushered me into her gallery-size foyer, I saw that the apartment behind her was beyond sumptuous and seemed to go on forever. The ceilings were easily fifteen feet high.

"A slight change of plans," she announced before I even had a chance to say hello. "Alex just called, and his golf game is over earlier than expected. I certainly don't want him to find you here."

"What if we run out for coffee?" I asked. I was *not* going to let her out of confessing whatever dirty little secret she had planned to spill to me.

"Actually, I thought we could go over to the Central Park Boathouse for a drink. I can give the dog a walk."

She turned and headed down a hallway to the right of the gallery, where it seemed the bedrooms must be. Halfway down, she gently slapped her thigh several times and called out the name Muchi. Why wasn't I surprised by the name of the dog?

As she entered a bedroom in search of what I knew for certain would be a dog no bigger than a head of Bibb lettuce, I edged my way to the back of the gallery and peeked into the living room. It was gigundo, with three different seating areas, fabrics splashed with oranges and gold and pale, minty green, killer views of Central Park, and a floor-to-ceiling limestone fireplace that you could roast a pig in. Through a doorway at the end of the living room, I could see a huge dining room, also looking onto the park, with not one but two huge round tables. This would be tough to have to relinquish.

At the pitter-patter of little feet, I spun back around. The dog was indeed a teacup pup, a fluffy little white thing with coal black eyes that I knew was neither a pug nor a Chihuahua, but I had no clue to the breed and didn't care enough to ask. Locket had tied a Hermès scarf around her head and donned a pair of big round black sunglasses. In her slim yellow pants and crisp white blouse with three-quarter sleeves, she looked as if she were attempting to channel Jackie-O.

After crossing Central Park West and entering the park, we walked about another twenty minutes before reaching our destination—and she didn't say a word to me the entire way. I took her silence to mean that we would wait until we were sitting down—and she didn't have to concentrate on yanking Muchi's nose out of every dog turd that she encountered—to talk. Heads turned as we walked, people either recognizing Locket even behind the headgear or guessing that with so much camouflage going on, she had to be *somebody*.

When we reached the Boathouse restaurant, nearly on the East Side, she steered me to the outdoor café part along the side and then toward a table by the water. There were still a few people rowing boats on the lake, many of them clunkily, as if they'd never used oars before. The lake was that mossy green color of hip waders and almost thick looking, though you could see flecks of orange from the koi. Though the willows and maples bordering the lake drooped from the lack of much rain late this summer, they were still vivid green. The trees in my mother's backyard were probably already tinged with yellow, but there wouldn't be a sign of autumn in Central Park for weeks.

"So what did you want to see me about?" I asked after we'd each ordered a glass of wine and she'd positioned Muchi on her lap—as if she were holding a large powder puff. I'd spent the walk through the park waiting and wondering exactly what she had up her sleeve, and I didn't have any patience left.

"I'd like to know what you were insinuating last night—about me and Tom?"

For all her haughtiness, she couldn't prevent the catch in her voice when she said his name.

"I wasn't insinuating anything," I replied.

She let out a breath, clearly confused by my comment. "Well, it certainly sounded like you were. I have a reputation to maintain, and I can't have people going around making careless remarks."

"Actually, I was calling a spade a spade. I *know* you were involved with Tom sexually."

She still had her sunglasses on, a disadvantage for me, but I could spy her eyes just enough through the lenses to spot the alarm that registered in them.

"How dare you," she said in an angry whisper. A young guy at the next table shot a look in our direction, probably not because he'd overheard her words, but because her whole body had stiffened and her mouth was tight in anger. Muchi seemed to sense her discomfort, too, and raised her itty-bitty snout. I hoped she wasn't contemplating leaping across the table and taking a bite out of my face.

"Locket, let's not play any games," I said. "I know, and you know I know. That's why you wanted to meet with me."

"What is this—some kind of extortion?"

"No, all I want are facts. I know you were in Andes the day Tom died. I want you to tell me what happened that day." I was playing a hunch, based totally on the empty bottle of Veuve Clicquot and the rumpled bed.

"Did you *date* Tom or something? I thought you were *Chris's* girlfriend."

"I'm a *friend* of Chris's—and I was looking into Tom's disappearance for him. Now I'm trying to find out who killed him."

"Just for sport?" she asked sarcastically.

"No, because I'm worried that the local sheriff's office may have a hard time investigating a case that took place up there but has so many ties to New York. Now, tell me about your trip to Andes."

She started to open her mouth, and all I could think was, Bingo. But then a young woman dressed in tennis whites and a visor and carrying a tennis bag barged over to our table.

"Do you mind my asking what kind of dog that is?" she asked. "I want one like that." There was something about her manner that suggested she'd recognized Locket, and I guessed that the dog inquiry was a ruse just to get up close to a legendary soap star.

"It's a Maltese—and they're very ferocious," Locket said in exasperation. The girl looked irritated and plopped down at the table that had just emptied behind us. I hoped I hadn't lost momentum.

"Should I repeat the question?" I asked.

"Why should I have to tell you?" she asked.

"If the answer is satisfactory, I may be able to keep it between the two of us. Otherwise I may have to take action."

She thought for a moment, the fingers of her right hand pressed against those inner-tube lips. They were so ripe, they looked almost edible.

"First you have to tell me how you developed this little theory of yours," she demanded. "If you have information, regardless of whether it's true or not, someone else may have it, too."

"No one else has access to the info I have," I lied. "Of course, that's not to say someone else hasn't learned about you and Tom in some other way. Tom arrived at Andes on Saturday morning, and my guess is that you met him there sometime that afternoon."

Locket exhaled loudly. "All right, I *did* go see Tom that afternoon," she confessed. "That weekend I was staying with some friends of mine about an hour south of Andes, and I drove to Tom's house for the afternoon. But he was very much alive when I left, I can assure you."

"Is there any chance Alex knew about your affair with Tom?"

"Absolutely not," she declared with indignation. But I could tell by the way she stiffened again that the same thought had crossed her mind recently.

"How can you be so sure?"

"He was working that day—in New York. Things are fine with us—he had no idea."

"What about Harper?" I asked. "Could she have figured it out, that you and Tom were lovers?"

She lifted her hand from its spot on Muchi's back and took a sip of her wine, which until now had gone mostly untouched.

"It's possible," she said, setting down the glass. "Harper had started to put more pressure on Tom lately. I could tell from her behavior that she wanted to take the relationship up a notch. But

Tom wasn't ready for a long-term relationship with anyone, let alone her."

"Was that a problem for you—did *you* want to take things with him up a notch?"

She snorted. "You *can't* be serious. I worked my fanny off to get from some no-name town in West Virginia to where I am today, and I'd hardly throw it away for a boy toy, no matter how hot he was between the sheets. Tom was a wonderful diversion for me—and I for him. We provided a certain—*comfort* to each other."

"What about Deke—did you know about Tom's problem with Deke?"

"Deke? I have no idea what you're talking about. Believe it or not, our relationship didn't involve a lot of *talking*. I'm not the kind of woman who needs chitchat."

"So—"

"Look, I wish I knew who killed Tom, but I don't. You asked me to tell you about that afternoon, and I have. I've kept my end of the bargain, and I expect you to as well."

"What time did you leave that afternoon?"

"At around four. I needed to get back to where I was staying."

"What were the last words Tom said to you?"

"Pardon me?"

It was kind of a wacky question, but I wanted to hear how authentic she sounded. It would give me a sense of whether he was really alive when she left.

"You heard me."

"He walked me to my car and said good-bye, and then he kissed me."

"And that was it? Nothing about his plans for the rest of the day?"

"No," she said, but she'd hesitated for a second before responding.

"What?" I demanded.

She glanced around the area. The girl with the tennis visor was reading a magazine. There was just one last boat on the lake, and the people in it were rowing toward shore. Out of the corner of my eye, I saw a turtle surface and poke its head above water.

"I talked to Tom later on the phone," she admitted. "He wanted to be sure I arrived back okay to my friends' house, so I called him. It was about five-thirty."

"There wasn't a record of it on his cell phone."

"I called the house phone. He'd given me the number since his cell phone got such bad reception up there."

"And he said something about his plans then?"

"No, he said he had to get off the phone. Somebody had just driven up."

CHAPTER 12

An editor I used to work with once cut the word *thunderstruck* from a lead I wrote, saying it was not only hyperbolic but antiquated. Yet I don't know what word could have better described how I felt at that moment with Locket. *You stupid, silly, Botoxed, blubber-lipped ninny!* I wanted to scream. She possessed information of crucial importance to the police, and she was just sitting on it to protect her bony ass.

But I didn't scream. I didn't want to do anything to freak her out and thus derail the revelation that was in the process of unfolding.

"Driven up?" I said. "He used those exact words?"

"Yes. He said someone had just driven up."

"He didn't say who it was?"

"No, and I didn't ask. I didn't butt into Tom's business."

"And when you called him, where was he?"

"I don't know. He just said he was working—painting."

"Did he say anything else? Anything at all?"

She paused, foraging through her memory. "He made a strange comment that I thought might be a quote—like from a play or a poem. He said he had to—let me think—'arm himself against some unhappy words.'"

"Sounds Shakespearean," I said, puzzled. Chris had tossed out a line from *Merchant of Venice* when we'd first met, so it would be worth asking him if he recognized it. Alan Carr, however, might be an even better resource.

"Had you ever heard him use that phrase before?"

"No, never."

"Locket," I said as calmly as I could, "Tom may not have offered up a name to you, but this is still a critical piece of information for the police to know. It's evidence that Tom knew the person who killed him—that it wasn't a stranger."

"But the person who stopped by didn't necessarily kill him," she said defensively, almost petulantly. "I heard that the police aren't sure when he died. It could have happened the next day for all they know."

"Aren't we dealing with an awfully big coincidence, then? Tom's holed up for the weekend in a town where he barely knows anyone anymore, and as far as I can tell, you're one of the few people he's informed that he's there. All of a sudden someone drives up, and he tells you that he's about to come face-to-face with someone's unhappiness. That *has* to be just before he was murdered—it's essential that you go to the police with this information."

"I *can't* do that," she exclaimed in a loud whisper, a hint of her Southern roots suddenly creeping into her voice. "There's no way in the world I can let Alex find out I was up there."

"This is a murder investigation, Locket."

The sun was beginning to sink in the sky somewhere behind the buildings that rimmed the park; Locket slipped her sunglasses off her face and dropped them on the table. Her eyes betrayed both worry and anger.

"I bet the next thing you're going to tell me," she said, "is that if *I* don't do it, *you* will."

"No, I'm not going to say that. I don't have to. Because the police are going to have a record of that call, and it's only a matter of time before they contact you about it. I just think it would be a lot smarter for you to take control and reach out to them first."

She caught her breath, started to say something, and then bit her tongue. She took a sip of wine as if she were fortifying herself.

"All right, I'll do it," she announced as she set the glass down firmly. "But I have to pick the right moment. I can't do it when Alex is hovering around me. I'm not shooting any scenes on Tuesday, and that's going to be the best time. I'll call that detective I spoke to—he gave me his card."

Something was cooking in that little brain of hers—something that had eased her worry. I couldn't figure out what it might be.

"And you know what—I don't have to say I was involved with Tom," she added. "I can just tell them I was calling him about something to do with the show—a scene we were shooting."

Oh, so that was it. Well, let her lie about that, I thought. What mattered was that she was going to tell them about the phone call—and the cops were surely smart enough to fill in the blanks.

Locket signaled for the check, and I decided to let her pay since she was Miss Moneybags. After she'd slid several bills from her wallet and laid them on the plate, she looked directly in my eyes.

"You probably think I'm so cold, don't you. But I cared about Tom, I really did. After they decided to cast me as the lead, they tested me with him—for the part that went to Chris in the end. We had a special connection from that moment on."

"I heard Tom came pretty close to landing the part. Do you know why they went with Chris instead?"

"Yes—but you can't say anything to *anyone* about this. They thought Tom was terrific, and they were all set to go with him, but they found out that he'd been in rehab—for an addiction to antidepressants. They just weren't going to take a chance with someone like that. I don't think he ever realized the reason why—*I* certainly never brought it up with him."

"Was Tom going to stick with the show? I heard things hadn't been going so well for him."

"I don't know. He wasn't all that invested in it after he lost the big part of Jared. He wanted to be able to try out for other things."

She glanced at her watch, a white ceramic Chanel rimmed around the face with a couple of rows of dazzling little diamonds, worth many thousands. "Look, I have to get moving," she announced irritatedly. Her tone indicated she'd just managed to reconnect with her inner diva. "I don't want Alex wondering why I took the dog out long enough to circumvent the reservoir twice. Are you weady, Muchi?"

It was pretty clear she didn't want me moseying on back to Central Park West with her, so after she departed with a curt good-bye, I sat for a while at the table, sipping my wine and thinking.

There was a chance, I knew, that parts of her story were a bunch of malarkey. Just as she'd thought nothing about twisting the truth for the cops, it would have been easy as pie for her to lie to me to protect herself. Maybe she really *had* killed Tom, and the whole bit about talking to him on the phone was just a fabrication calculated to add a layer of authenticity to her story. Of course, the phone records, which she'd seemed to have lost sight of, would either back her up or sink her.

I was inclined to believe her. It was one thing to cover her ass by making up a story, but the part about the Shakespearean quote seemed like such an odd element to throw in.

So if Locket didn't do it, who did? Who had pulled up in a car late that afternoon and caused Tom to predict an eruption of unhappy words? Harper could certainly fill the slot. Let's say she came back early from the West Coast, knew about the Andes house, and headed up there. She may even have seen Locket's car and waited for her to depart (God, maybe she'd simply smelled her trail of patchouli), and that could have led to the fight from hell.

Deke was another strong possibility. If Tom had made noises about exposing Deke's dishonesty to management, Deke could have decided to confront him about it. His intent may not have been to kill Tom, just to make him back off, but the situation could have escalated into violence.

And then there was Alex. The fact that he'd been down on Tom lately suggested that he'd picked up a whiff of the affair, or at least of an attraction between his star and the boy toy, and he could have decided to follow Locket when she went out of town that day. But if it had been Alex pulling up in the car, wouldn't Tom have announced that to Locket? Maybe not. He may have not wanted to alarm her until he knew what it was all about.

As I drained the last of my wine, I glanced around me. The outdoor café had nearly emptied, and the last of the boats had been tied up on the shore of the lake. I picked up my bag and headed out of the park, past joggers and bikers on their final lap. I caught the subway at Lex and 68th Street and rode it to Astor Place.

I stopped at the grocery near my apartment and scarfed up a couple of chicken breasts, arugula, and cherry tomatoes in order to make chicken Milanese. Before I let myself into my apartment,

I scribbled a note to Landon on an old envelope I dug out of my purse and slid it under his door. I could feel the early twinges of the Sunday night blues, and sharing a meal with him would help ameliorate things, especially if he provided a bottle of a super Tuscan, something he almost always did when I cooked Italian.

Chris had called when I'd switched off my phone during drinks with Locket, saying that he'd arranged for me to meet him at nine-thirty at Chelsea Piers. He gave me all the info I needed and said he'd see me the next day. Jessie had checked in, too, and I returned the call as soon as I'd dumped my supplies in the kitchen. She wanted to be filled in on anything that had happened at the party after she'd left and, as she put it, the latest developments in the sordid love triangle I now found myself in the middle of.

"I was no whiz at geometry," I said, "but if I remember correctly, by definition you need three sides to make up a triangle. Since Beau has no interest in me, that only leaves two."

"I told you he was gawking at you. These two girls kept trying to chat him up, and he would do this thing of looking off as if he were contemplating some brilliant answer, but he was always looking in your direction, checking you out."

"Well, if there was any chance of ever seeing him again, I blew it." I told her what had happened outside of the bathroom.

"Ouch. But I like what you said about the one postcard. Very funny."

"Do you think there's anything I can do? Landon told me I should just call him and ask him what he was going to say earlier. That I have nothing to lose by doing that."

"*God, no,*" she exclaimed. "Landon is such a wienie to say that. If you go crawling on your belly like a reptile, you look desperate. You need to be a challenge to him, make him want you bad."

"Well, the star of the show wrapped himself around me as tight as a python. Doesn't that make me a challenge?"

"Too *much* of one. Guys don't like challenges they can't surmount."

I sighed. "So are you saying there's really nothing I can do?"

"No, I didn't say that. You have to try what I call the sugar-and-spice strategy—and I suggest it only because Beau appears to have the hots for you—otherwise it would be pointless."

"Okay, so tell me," I demanded.

"Pick a time you don't think he'll be around and call his cell phone. Do *not* talk to him in person. Tell him there's no need for him to call you back, you just wanted to apologize for being a little snippy. Make it light and say something funny. But not directed at *him*, Bailey, okay? Tell him good luck on his project—that you'd love to see it when it comes out."

"How is that sugar and spice?" I asked.

"The sugar part is you being nice, not bitchy like you were last night. The spice part is you being kind of elusive. Not needing him to call back and saying you'd love to see the project when it's finished, which is probably going to be a whole fucking year from now. You've opened the door just enough to let him kick it down if he wants to."

"Okay, okay, thanks," I said, doubtful.

"Just one condition. If you end up with Beau, you have to give me Tad Hamilton. He's to die for."

After I hung up, I didn't give myself time to digest her comments and advice. I tried Harper again but struck out just as I had earlier in the day. I left another message on her voice mail saying I *really* had to talk to her. Then I made the call I was dreading—to Professor Alan Carr.

"Who did this to Tom?" he asked before I could get more than a couple of words out. "Do you know?" It was pretty clear he'd been drinking; he wasn't slurring his words, but there was a sloppiness to them that suggested a few glasses of booze.

"No, but I am going to do everything possible to find out."

"How could someone kill him? He was the world's nicest guy. Tom wouldn't hurt a fly."

"I'm so sorry for your loss."

"Maybe that was his problem. Too nice of a guy."

"How do you mean?"

"He didn't know how to say no to people. Damn, I can't believe it."

"I have a question for you, Professor Carr. Like I said, I'm doing what I can to investigate Tom's death. Shortly before he was killed, he apparently told someone he was arming himself against some unhappy words. Do you know if that's a line from a play—and what it might mean?"

The phone went quiet as he thought, but after a moment I almost wondered if I'd lost reception.

"Profess—"

"'Be thou armed for some unhappy words.' Baptista says it in *The Taming of the Shrew*."

"What are the circumstances?" I asked. That was one play of Shakespeare's I probably hadn't read since high school.

"Petruchio is sure he won't have a problem wooing Katherina because he's as obstinate as she's supposed to be. Baptista wishes him luck but predicts he's in for trouble. He tells Petruchio, 'Be thou armed for some unhappy words.'"

"Would that line or the play itself have had any kind of special meaning for Tom?"

"He did a scene from it here for a class. Not that particular scene, but he played Petruchio. I remember because he was so goddamn good. And later he told me he did the play in New York. At some off off Broadway place. Or maybe it was just in a workshop."

"But why would he quote that particular line?"

"I dunno. Tom loved Shakespeare. He loved to toss out lines from the plays."

"Speaking of plays, did Tom mention he'd written a play?"

"Yes, it was a great little play he hoped to stage. Do the police have any leads? We're all sick about this."

I revealed that the police weren't sharing much with me, but before I hung up I promised him I would pass on what I knew when I knew it.

Washing the arugula, I considered what I'd learned about the line. If Tom were in the habit of quoting the Bard, he might have used that phrase whenever he was faced with unhappy words in life. But there was a chance it could have a more particular significance. What I needed to do was find out when and where Tom had been in the play. I had turned over his résumé to the sheriff in Andes, but Chris might know about Tom's stint as Petruchio.

As it turned out, Landon never knocked on my door—perhaps he'd gone out early for the entire evening. I tossed one of the chicken breasts in the freezer for another night. I pounded the other one until very thin, coated it in egg and bread crumbs, and began sautéing it in olive oil. I dried the arugula, added the cherry tomatoes, and made a lemon vinaigrette. My kitchen smelled heavenly, and I sipped a glass of cold Pinot Grigio as I worked, humming to another Maria Callas CD. What more could anyone *want*? In fact, I decided, I could have been in a freakin' documentary about single chicks who cook feasts for themselves, buy their own crystalware, and live their lives to the fullest—knowing all the while that they may want a man at some point but don't *need* one. The problem was, I could feel myself falling into a big ugly slump.

It only got worse as I ate alone on my terrace. It was crisp enough for me to need a jacket, but gloriously clear, the kind of night that would have been nice to share. My aloneness was exaggerated by the sounds of frivolity—some of it probably naked—that wafted over from the open windows of the NYU dorm one block north; apparently, these particular students had not been informed that Sunday night was a time to buckle down, get into their jammies, and prepare for the week ahead.

Consuming my meal, with a wine-to-food ratio that was definitely more on the side of the vino, I thought of how Beau had rescued me two months earlier from the Sunday night blues. I'd been making *spaghetti alle vongole* at the time, and he'd dropped by, sucked down a bowl of it, and then seduced me in my tiny kitchen.

I wondered if Jessie's plan would work if I tried it. There was nothing to lose by calling Beau's voice mail—Landon had been right on that account. If he wasn't interested and didn't respond to my phone call, I'd be in the same exact place I was now. Except why should I bother leaving a coy little message with someone who had treated me so shabbily? That, speaking of the Bard, was the rub. No matter how much I wanted to know what Beau had been about to say, I couldn't bring myself to suck up to him.

Jessie. I loved her, but as I poured myself another glass of Pinot Grigio, I thought of how much I'd hated what she'd said about wanting dibs on "Tad Hamilton." I might still be pining for Beau, but I really, really liked Chris and didn't want to consider him with another chick.

My head was pounding at nine o'clock the next morning as I hailed a cab for Chelsea Piers. In an attempt to stave off any insomnia, I'd polished off most of the bottle of wine and woke with a vein throbbing so hard in my forehead that I could see the movement in the mirror above my bathroom sink.

I'd been to Chelsea Piers a few times over the years. It's a series of buildings constructed on four adjoining piers where the West 20s meet the Hudson River. Back in the early part of the twentieth century, it had been a thriving part of the riverfront, where some of the great ships docked in between their transatlantic crossings. In fact, according to a sign posted there, the *Titanic* had been destined to dock at Pier 59, and hundreds of people gathered there after the sinking, waiting for word of their loved ones. Eventually, the docks fell into disrepair and spent decades just sagging in the Hudson until they were finally rescued and renovated. Now there was everything from a netted-in driving range to a bowling alley to photo studios to restaurants with river views. One large warehouse-looking blue building housed the sets of several television shows that filmed in Manhattan.

Chris had told me the unmarked entranceway was at the corner of the building, and the cab had just overshot it when I yelled, "Stop here!" Slipping inside, I found myself in an empty, grungy area with a carpet that appeared to be stained with everything from gum to diesel fuel. The walls, however, were lined with posters for the shows being shot there, proving I was in the right spot. There was even a poster for *Morgue*. Locket stood boldly in the middle of a small group of people, her brow furrowed in the name of justice. Chris was just to her right, looking hunky but weirdly airbrushed. Following Chris's instructions, I took the stairs one flight up.

On the second floor, I found a seating area with a receptionist engrossed in a Nora Roberts novel. Whereas the entranceway downstairs had been oddly quiet, up here I could hear the sounds of bustling activity emanating from the corridors that shot off in different directions. As I was about to give my name to the receptionist, someone came up behind me and asked, "Bailey?"

I spun around to find a spunky-looking girl with spiky black hair, dressed in cargo pants and a clear earpiece plugged in her ear, stepping toward me.

"I'm Cara," she said once I'd acknowledged that I was indeed Bailey Weggins. "Chris asked me to keep an eye out for you. I can take you to him now."

After securing me a visitor's pass from the receptionist, she led me down one of the long corridors, nodding as she walked to various people we encountered along the way. There were lots of doorways along the hall, which I assumed must be dressing rooms, but based on the spacing between them, they couldn't be very big. A door to one opened, and as a man emerged dressed in a cop uniform, I saw that a fake leather reclining chair ate up most of the narrow room.

"These are the dressing rooms for day players, who have just a few lines," Cara said, seeing me check out the room. "Chris is around this way, with the regulars."

He wasn't in his dressing room, however. After knocking once, Cara entered, and when she saw the room was empty, she motioned me in with her shoulder.

"He said that if he was in makeup, you should just have a seat. Why don't you make yourself comfortable. I doubt he'll be that long."

His dressing room here was larger than the one in the honey wagon, and though one chair was strewn with clothes, the rest of it was orderly—neat stacks of books and magazines, a brand-new looking Bose CD player, and a row of water bottles. There was a Rubik's Cube on a tabletop, and I picked it up, turning it over a few times in my hands.

"Please, take that," I heard Chris say behind me. "It's driving me insane."

"I didn't picture you as a Rubik's Cube man."

"My mother sent it to me when I told her the TV business is all about hurry up and wait."

He was dressed in jeans and a button-down Oxford shirt, and he was wearing a touch of makeup, just as he'd been when I'd visited him on location last week. He leaned down and kissed me hello. "How you doing this morning, anyway?"

"I finally feel as if that drug is out of my system—except I've got this killer headache. I overdid the vino last night."

"Do tell," he said, looking at me quizzically.

"Oh, just me alone on the terrace," I said quickly, "losing track of how much I was imbibing as I watched all the city lights come on." I felt oddly guilty, perhaps because so many of my thoughts had been focused on Beau. And also because I was planning to withhold Locket's revelation. I'd given my word to her.

"Well, maybe I can get out early enough tonight so you won't have to drink alone," he said. He was grinning, but he seemed slightly preoccupied. I knew he must feel wired up about shooting, and the last thing he needed was me on the premises.

"I like the sound of that," I said. "Now, tell me what's happening this morning."

"I'm doing a scene with Locket—in our offices. Cara is going to be your escort. She'll make sure you don't trip over any wires—or accidentally get placed in one of the morgue drawers."

"*What?*" I exclaimed.

Chris laughed. "When the drawers are pulled out during a scene, there are real people on them—they use extras. They just look a lot more realistic as dead people than dummies do. . . . Look, though it's fine for me to have visitors, you should try to be as inconspicuous as possible this morning. Alex is around, and we don't want him to wonder what you're doing here."

"Will do. Though I'm dying to watch you shoot a scene, my main goal is to ask Deke about the loan—to see how he reacts. Where will *he* be?"

"He'll be around, mostly on the periphery. He's a grip, in charge of scenery. Everything's already set up, but if they decide to change anything, he's got to be standing by, ready to do it."

"I'm not looking forward to chatting with him, but it has to be done."

"Just try to keep it low-key. If Alex gets wind of—"

"I know, I know."

There was a light tapping on the door. After Chris called, "Come in," Cara poked her head inside the room.

"They're ready for you, Chris."

"Okay, be right there." He waited for her to close the door. "Get this—shows *insist* on escorting the stars from their dressing rooms to the set. It makes you wonder if a few actors have panicked over the years and bolted out a side door."

"Have *you* ever had the urge?"

He glanced to the left wistfully and then returned his gaze to me, smiling. "Nah. I mean, there are moments these days, now that success seems within my grasp, that the pressure feels freaking intense, and I wonder if I'll look back with any regrets. But there's no urge to bolt. That's why I couldn't believe Tom had just taken off."

"So do I come with you now?"

"No, Cara will bring me down and get me settled and come back for you in a few minutes."

"Well, break a leg. Just one thing before you go. Do you know when and where Tom performed *Taming of the Shrew*?"

"What makes you ask that?" he asked, his eyes squinted in puzzlement.

"Just a funny little lead I'm pursuing."

"He did so many plays—some at that little theater company I mentioned, but others all over the place." Absentmindedly, he glanced in the mirror along one wall and smoothed down his shirt.

"Does he have an agent I could talk to?"

Chris froze. "An agent?" he asked. "Why would you need to talk to an agent?"

"To find out about the play."

"He didn't have a regular agent—just used a few people free-lance. Look, I better go, okay?"

He left the dressing room seeming even more distracted than when he'd first come in. I realized I probably shouldn't have bothered him about the case right before he'd been about to shoot a scene.

For the next few minutes, I cooled my heels in the dressing room, and then, out of boredom, I stepped just outside the door. A few crew types dressed in jeans and grungy T-shirts ambled up and down the corridor, and then a woman who appeared to be a makeup artist—with a large fanny pack around her waist—sprinted down the hall as if she were answering a code blue. Maybe one of Locket's lips had exploded. I watched her run and as I turned back, I spotted none other than Deke, making his way down the corridor. I saw a flash of recognition in his eyes, but he completely ignored me. As he passed in front of me, he hoisted a can of Diet Coke to his mouth and took a swig.

"Hey, Deke," I called out after him, knowing this might be my only chance. "Have you got a sec?"

"Not really," he said, turning in his tracks and eyeing me surlily.

"It's really important. Really."

"You got exactly thirty seconds. What is it?" He stepped closer to me and let his slate-colored eyes bore into me. I noticed, to my disgust, that he had a bunch of coarse hairs hanging from his nostrils.

"Remember how we were talking about Tom? I found out you borrowed a huge chunk of money from him and then didn't pay it back." I was stirring things up big-time, yet if Deke were the one who'd poisoned my drink, he already had plenty of suspicions about me, and I wasn't going to be any worse off than before.

He kept his hard eyes steady, but the edge of his tongue escaped involuntarily, flicking at the corner of his mouth like an ugly red lizard.

"You really are a little Miss Marple, aren't you?"

"Just trying to help," I said.

"Well, to put it politely, it's none of your f-ing business. But if you *must* know, I paid Tom back the week before he died. Everything was nicey-nice with us."

"Is that right?" I asked incredulously. "So it would be indicated by a deposit to his bank account?"

"He didn't ask me to manage his finances," he said, smirking.

I tried to figure out where to go next, but before I had a chance, Cara called out my name from the end of the corridor and motioned me to hurry with her. I wanted to keep poking at Deke, but it wasn't going to be possible now.

Cara and I double-timed it down the corridor, made another turn, and then descended a staircase. Once on the lower level, she led me to a door with a red alarm light to the right.

"Your cell phone off?" Cara said, stopping.

"Good point," I said, and fumbled for it in my purse. After I'd switched it off, she pushed open the door and we entered a dim, cavernous space bustling with at least thirty people. There were plenty of crew, dressed in the standard uniform of jeans and T-shirts and some with tool belts about their waists, but there were also a few businessy types hovering around the edges.

To my left was a huge three-sided morgue, with gleaming stainless-steel tables, sinks, hanging scales descending from the ceiling, and even, oddly, the smell of disinfectant. Maybe they added that for true verisimilitude, to make the actors really believe they were in the world of death. The only thing not totally real were the windows. Behind each one was a fake backdrop of brick city buildings, though I assumed they would look real enough when you saw them on TV.

With me two inches behind her, Cara proceeded to the next section on the floor, which featured a stage—this one brightly lit—with a shabby-looking bullpen area of a dozen work desks. Chris was sitting on one of the desks, staring into space. Locket stood right in front of him, studying a small white script packet, while a hairstylist used his palm to flatten her flyaway hairs. A few crew members fussed on the set, apparently following the orders of a fortysomething guy standing among them. While the scene in the park had been shot with handheld cameras, this one involved two cameras on dollies.

Cara parked me on the sidelines in a small cluster of crew who at the moment seemed to be just waiting around. There was a large group of people farther down, all sitting on director chairs in front of several monitors. I caught a glimpse of Alex in the mix, but he was involved in a discussion with someone I assumed must be the director. And suddenly there was Deke, too. He must have come from a different direction. Trying to be less conspicuous, I stepped back a couple of feet, deeper into the shadow created by a wall on wheels beside me.

There was a palpable tension in the room, as if everyone were on pins and needles awaiting news of some kind. "Last looks," someone called. The makeup artist I'd seen earlier stepped quickly from the shadow, brushed something onto Locket's lips, and scurried off.

"Rolling," the same person called next. Then, "And action."

Cara tapped a finger to her lips, indicating I should be quiet, and then, concentrating on someone's words into her earpiece, wandered off.

Locket spoke first. "But death occurred before midnight, Jared. The autopsy's going to show that."

Chris shook his head. "But consider how hot the room was," he said. "That changes everything." He seemed so at ease, so comfortable, with all these people around him. I forgot about

Tom and Deke and everything else and allowed myself to be mesmerized by the exchange of lines between the two stars.

Then, without warning, I felt the oddest sensation across the rise of my foot. I glanced down and peered into the shadows. A huge black snake, endlessly long, was slithering over my foot. My breath seemed to freeze in my chest. I fought a scream, I did everything possible *not* to scream, but I couldn't help it. I let out a wail like a banshee and leapt backward.

CHAPTER 13

The snake shot forward, hugging the wall, and then I couldn't see it anymore. I became aware that the low-level hum in the room had ceased in a split second and that the two actors had stopped speaking their lines. I looked up and around. Cara was rushing toward me, and everyone else was just staring at me or craning their necks, trying to pinpoint where the scream had emanated from.

"What the hell's going on?" the director yelled.

I didn't say anything, feeling paralyzed and also hoping that maybe it was just a rhetorical question and that in a few seconds the director would call out, "Rolling" again, or *something*. Then I could simply whisper into Cara's ear about what had happened and slink off, letting her deal with it all.

But the director shouted again—"I *said*, 'What the hell is going on?'"—and that surely meant I was supposed to volunteer an answer. The shock and repulsion I'd felt at the sight of the snake were snatched away and replaced by a feeling of total and complete humiliation. I hadn't felt this embarrassed since fourth grade, when my underpants had slipped to the ground while I was jumping around in my best pink party dress. The feeling got even worse when I finally made eye contact with Chris and saw that he looked completely chagrined—and that the blood had drained from his face, leaving it as colorless as a latex glove.

"I—I'm so sorry," I sputtered. "But there was a huge black snake on the floor next to me. It—it slithered off toward the back there."

At the sound of the word *snake,* people all over the set let out cries of alarm and began sweeping the floor anxiously with their eyes.

"A snake?" the director snapped, slipping off his chair. "There aren't any *snakes* in here." He began walking in my direction, followed, to my dismay, by Alex.

"Well, there was one today," I declared. "I think you should try to find it. It might be dangerous."

"I am absolutely petrified of snakes," Locket announced loudly. "We have to find it—or I can't work."

The director reached the spot where I stood. "What kind of snake?" he demanded. "You mean like a garter snake?" Alex, I noticed, was standing silently behind him, his top lip curled. He had a look on his face that suggested he wouldn't mind seeing a python crush every bone in my body and then swallow me whole.

"No, not like that," I said, trying to sound as calm and sane as possible. "It was at least four feet long, black—with some white markings."

"You're *sure?* And you say it went toward the rear of the set?" He swung his shaven head in that direction, then looked back and posed the question I'd been dreading: "Who *are* you, anyway?"

Oh God, I thought. I didn't want to get Chris in any kind of trouble. "My name is Bailey Weg—"

"*That's* what she saw," a man's voice exclaimed, interrupting. Simultaneously, the director, Alex, and I all turned. Squatting behind me, arms resting on his beefy thighs, was my good buddy Deke. He jabbed his finger at a partially coiled length of black cable on the ground to my left. "That's her snake right there."

"Oh, for chrissake," the director said. He sighed in annoyance and strode back toward his chair.

"That *isn't* what I saw," I called after him, feeling totally sandbagged. "I definitely saw a real snake—with white markings."

"You need to leave," Alex snarled, his voice low but frighteningly firm, like someone squeezing your arm really hard with his thumb. "Right now."

I wasn't going to argue. Nothing I said was going to convince them, and nothing would make me happier than to just get out of there. As for the snake, I didn't care if they all ended up with fang puncture wounds in their asses—except for Chris, of course. At the moment I didn't dare look him in the eye. I lowered my head and walked quickly down the hall, with Cara nipping at my heels. I suspected she was trying to make it appear as if she were taking action like a good PA but didn't know me from Adam. Once we were back near the dressing rooms, though, she gave me a piece of her mind in a loud, rapid whisper.

"I leave you alone for two seconds and you disrupt the whole set. I could get fired."

"And what would *you* have done if some huge snake had slithered over *your* foot? Grin and bear it?"

"*If* you even saw a snake. What would a snake like that be doing in here, anyway?"

"You tell me. Is there any chance it's being used in an upcoming scene?"

"In *CSI* they'd think nothing of having one crawl out of a corpse during an autopsy. But we're a much more realistic show."

"Look," I said, realizing that there was no convincing her,

either, "I'm sorry for creating any problems for you. Will you please tell Chris I'm really sorry, too? I'll give him a call later."

Luckily, a cab was dropping off a passenger right outside the building, and I hailed it. As I leaned back against the leather seat, I realized I could barely think straight.

"You gonna give me the address?" the driver grumbled as he was pulling out onto the West Side Highway. What I felt like doing was telling him to drop me in a bar in the Village where I could pound down a margarita, but I had to show at *Buzz* and finish my story on Tom.

As the cab shot uptown, I replayed the scene in the studio again and again in my head. Was there any possibility my imagination had gotten the better of me? Maybe what I'd seen *had* been the cable, yanked at that precise moment by one of the crew members so that it slid across my foot—and in the dim light just *looked* reptilian. Deke might have even been the yanker himself, eager to scare the bejesus out of me. Originally, I'd noticed him standing far off to the right, but then I'd become spellbound by Chris's performance and had momentarily lost track of Deke's whereabouts.

No, I was almost positive—what I'd seen was a live, butt-ugly snake. There'd been those whitish markings on its back—which the cable didn't have—and I'd observed its head, too, with the snoutlike shape that could trigger primordial fear in just about everyone.

But what was a snake doing on a soundstage? Was it possible that it belonged to Deke and he'd set it loose when he saw me arrive on the set? He looked like the type of guy who would enjoy having a pet that slithered. Or perhaps the snake belonged in the building for a reason unbeknownst to me. Chris would clearly learn more as the day went on and would clue me in later. Thinking of Chris, though, made my stomach knot. Shouldn't he have come to my rescue back then? It would have been such a relief if he'd acknowledged me as his friend and assured the director that I wasn't prone to hallucinations. But everything had happened so fast, I couldn't totally blame him for hanging back, unsure of what to do.

When I arrived at *Buzz*, the place was *literally* buzzing, as if someone had dropped a thousand cicadas on the floor. Monday was always at least a nine on the nutty scale, but it could reach a ten when something really big was happening—for instance, when a star couple split or an A-lister ended up caught with his pants down. This seemed like one of those days.

"What's going on?" I asked Jessie as I parked myself in my workstation. "It seems like all hell is breaking loose." Just as I spoke, I caught a glimpse of Nash in his glass-walled office shaking his head hard as he spoke to Valerie and one of the other deputy editors.

"Apparently Nash is changing the cover story, so people are scrambling," Jessie said. "What's up with *you*? Your face looks kind of pinched, like you slipped a disk as you were walking into the building."

I described my nightmare at Chelsea Piers. Leo, who started off half listening, rolled his chair closer as the tale got juicier.

"A *snake*?" Jessie said after I'd reached the climax of the story. "You've got to be fucking kidding me."

"They say if you dream about snakes, it means you're really horny," Leo said. "Or wait—that you're *afraid* of sex. I forget which."

"I didn't *dream* I saw a snake, Leo," I said, aggravated. "I really did see one." He shrugged and returned to his computer. Jessie, on the other hand, pumped me for more details.

"And what about Chris?" she asked. "Was he there through this whole thing?"

"Oh yeah. And from the look on his face, you would have

thought I was flashing my boobs for a *Girls Gone Wild* video. He looked positively mortified."

"Did you talk to him afterwards?"

"No, because he was shooting. I'll catch up with him later—I'm sure everything will all be okay." But a part of me remained worried.

I needed to tackle my work, but first and foremost I was going on a snake hunt. I Googled big black snakes and found several Web sites devoted to the delightful creatures. It didn't take long to find a species that matched what I'd seen: *Lampropeltis getulus,* better known as the common king snake. It was found in most parts of the southern United States (which, of course, didn't explain what the hell it was doing at Chelsea Piers) and grew anywhere from just over two feet long to almost seven. It was black or dark brown with white or yellowish markings—that often took the form of crossbands or stripes. The good news for the actors prancing around the set was that it was nonvenomous. The king snake's claim to fame: It liked to feed on other snakes, even poisonous ones. Yummy.

After grabbing coffee, I checked in with the art department to review the final layout for the item on Tom. They were using his head shot as the photo along with an inset of a shot that the network must have provided, because he was sitting at his morgue desk, holding out a slip of paper. The entire piece was just a few paragraphs long, short by even *Buzz* standards. Sad, I told myself, to think that a change in hairstyle by Jessica Simpson garnered more ink than Tom's death. But then maybe Tom would have never wanted to possess any real estate in a magazine like *Buzz*.

Back at my desk, I reviewed the text I'd submitted Friday. What I needed was an update on the investigator, and this gave me the excuse to hound Sheriff Schmidt again. I got right through to him this time and explained that I was now calling as a journalist.

"Why didn't you tell me that from the beginning?" he demanded, sounding Miffed with a capital M.

"I'm sorry about that," I said, not wanting to burn any bridges. "But I didn't know that I was going to be writing the story then. I'd been searching for Tom as a favor to a friend, not in any journalistic capacity."

"Well, I don't have much to tell you. We've confirmed that the body is that of Tom Fain, and that death was the result of repeated blows by a sharp object. We are questioning people in the Andes area and, with the assistance of the New York office of the state police, people in New York City as well. At this time, we do not have a suspect."

Something about the tone of his voice made me assume that there hadn't been much progress on the case, though that was a point he would neither confirm nor deny.

"Do you think that Tom could have been killed by someone who worked on the show with him?" I asked, knowing he wasn't going to share but curious as to how he'd respond.

"I'm not at liberty to discuss any of our theories at this point."

I couldn't help feeling guilty as I considered the info I was sitting on—Locket's visit to Tom and her revelation about the unnamed visitor. But I had given my word to Locket that I would let her break the news to the cops. If she didn't do it tomorrow, as promised, then I would have to take matters into my own hands.

There was a piece of information I *could* share with Schmidt, though, and I decided this was the moment. I told him that in the course of doing my research for my article (*slight* distortion), I had discovered that Tom had loaned a crew member several thousand dollars and then had run into difficulty getting it repaid. I'd been reluctant to throw Deke under the bus until I learned more about the situation, but it was clear to me now that the dude was a real creep.

Schmidt didn't comment for a few seconds, though I could discern him breathing.

"We're aware of this matter, yes," he said at last.

I wondered how he'd stumbled onto it. "Oh, Mr. Barish must have told you," I said. He didn't say anything back, making me suspect my guess had been right.

"You don't have anything else you want to share with me, do you?" he asked.

"No, I don't," I said, convinced that my voice had jumped an octave as I'd spoken. He was gonna be mad if come Wednesday I was the one breaking the news about Locket's little sojourn to the Catskills.

"Well, I want to hear from you if you learn anything of significance."

"Of course," I told him.

My item in *Buzz* also gave me an excuse to call Harper again. She could play hard to get with me on a personal level, but as the PR rep for *Morgue*, she would have to respond to the message I was about to leave on her cell.

"Harper, it's Bailey Weggins. We're going to bed at *Buzz* with a short item on Tom's death, and I'm calling to get an official response from the producers and cast of *Morgue*." On the one hand she might not have much interest in crafting the perfect "We are deeply saddened" message for *Buzz*, but as a publicist she wouldn't want an item going to press without her knowing what it said and how it might impact on her—and without her having had a chance to mold it to her liking.

For the next half hour I fiddled with my little piece, incorporating what I'd learned from the sheriff's department and leaving room for whatever Harper coughed up. I called Tom a promising young actor, and my heart ached as I reread those words on my computer screen.

After I routed the piece to Valerie, with a few TKs indicating I was still waiting for more pieces of info, I refilled my coffee cup in the kitchenette. On my stroll back I considered what my next move should be. I'd reported on Tom's death, but I still had to figure out who had brutally murdered him. Deke and Alex were definite contenders, and so, too, was Harper, but right now I didn't have a reason to suspect one more than another.

There was only one possible clue left for me to work with—the line Tom had spoken from *Taming of the Shrew*. I needed to find out more about when and where he'd performed the play and what meaning it held for him. Chris didn't know who Tom used as a freelance agent, but Barish might. I phoned him.

"Actually, I do have a name in my file," he said after I was put through. I could hear a drawer slide open. "Okay, here it is—Buddy Hess." He ran off the number.

"Thanks, I'll follow up. I spoke to the sheriff's office today. I hear you passed on the information about the unpaid loan."

"Yes, I'm glad you reminded me of it. It's definitely a motive, and I want them looking into this Deke fellow."

"I saw him today on set, and he told me that he repaid the loan the week before Tom died. Could you check and see if there's any record of Tom depositing that money in his bank account?"

"Let me see what I can find out, but he may have just decided to use it as a cash reserve."

I also realized that Tom could have used the cash as part of the fund he was pulling together for Barry, the guy doing work on the house in Andes—though I highly doubted the loan had ever actually been repaid.

"Well, thank you for keeping me in the loop," Barish added. "I have a client waiting, so I need to sign off."

"Just out of curiosity," I said before he cut me off, "was Tom trying to mount a play he'd written?"

"Who told you that?"

"A few people mentioned it to me."

"Yes, as a matter of fact, he was. We're not talking Broadway, of course. He would have gone the off off Broadway route."

"I hear part of his motivation in selling the house was to obtain money to finance the play."

"I believe that was his intention, yes."

"But it seems like he already had money at his disposal. Why couldn't he have simply withdrawn money from his bank account for the play?"

"Because it was going to cost more than he had in his day-to-day reserves. Putting on even a minor production is fairly expensive."

"Could he have taken money from his trust fund?"

Barish sighed as if I'd just suggested the earth was flat. "The house was a white elephant, and Tom wanted to unload it anyway. And besides, I'd be derelict in my duty letting Tom dip into his capital. His parents' intentions were for the trust to last Tom for a lifetime. Now, if you'll excuse me . . ."

I looked up Buddy Hess's number and phoned his office. Rather than identify myself as a reporter from *Buzz*, which would guarantee that Hess *wouldn't* pick up, I told the arrogant-sounding woman who answered that I was calling with important information about the murder of Tom Fain. Hess picked up a minute later.

"Who is this, anyway?" he said curtly.

I explained my involvement in looking for Tom and how I was now trying to figure out who had killed him.

"What a damn shame this all is," he said, softening. "Tom was a real sweetheart, and you don't find many of those in this business. So what's this news you want to share with me?"

"Actually," I said, "I was hoping to get a bit of info from *you*. I'm following a few leads related to Tom's death, and I really need your help."

"Isn't that a job for the cops?" he said.

"Yes, but they're upstate and they may not have the resources to devote to this. As you say, Tom was a real sweetheart, and I hate the idea that his killer might not be apprehended."

"Okay, so what can I do for you?"

"Tom was in a production of *Taming of the Shrew* here in New York. Do you know when and where?"

"*Taming of the Shrew*? Sounds vaguely familiar. Maddy, get me a copy of Tom Fain's résumé, will you? You have to understand that I only represented Tom on a freelance basis, so I can't tell you off the top of my head."

"How does that differ from having him as an actual client?"

"A client is under contract. But you don't sign anyone until you're reasonably sure it's going to be good for both of you. There's a big pool of actors I keep head shots on, and when I hear of something they might be right for, I submit their shots to casting agents on a freelance basis. I sent Tom out for a small part on *Morgue,* and they liked him so much they tested him for the bigger role, too. He was *this* close to nailing it, but they pulled out at the last minute, and ironically he ended up with the part he'd first auditioned for."

"I hear he was pretty bummed."

"Yeah, but like I told him, it was still a nice break. He's—he *was* a good actor and a great-looking guy, and I think it was only a matter of time before something else turned up for him. I offered to sign him at that point, but he was suddenly gun-shy. I think he suspected I was partly responsible for him not getting the bigger role. . . . Okay, here we go. He did *Shrew* last February. It was at the Chaps Theatre on West Thirteeenth Street."

"That's the theater where he was a member of the company?"

"Yeah, it's an off off Broadway theater, small, but I do some scouting there. It's a pretty decent group."

"Thanks. By the way, is it true that Tom didn't get the part of Jared because the producers found out he'd been in rehab?"

"How'd you hear that?"

"It turned up in my inquiries."

"Yeah, that was lousy. I tried to make the producer see that it was extenuating circumstances—his parents dying and all that. I could see absolutely no reason for it to become a problem for him again. But they didn't want to take the chance of getting burned."

"Did they do an investigation—is that how they found out?"

"They do conduct background checks, but I had the feeling in this case that someone tipped them off."

I felt goose bumps rise on my arms. "You mean squealed on him?"

"Yup. No one said this was a pretty business. You ever see *Rosemary's Baby*? Her husband makes a pact with the devil so he can land a part. That's tame compared to some of the stuff I've experienced."

After I signed off, I headed for the kitchenette in search of more coffee and then, with my Styrofoam cup in hand, stole into one of the small conference rooms at the far end of the floor. I closed the door and fell into a chair, finally removed from the cacophony of closing day. I felt really weird, but I wasn't sure why. Maybe the events of the past few days were finally catching up with me. Maybe, too, I realized, the more I learned about Tom, the more heartbreaking his whole story became. It seemed as if the poor guy really *had* been cursed: First he loses his parents, then the role of his dreams, and finally his life. Yet his own personality may have contributed in part to his death. Tom was a good guy, kind and generous, yet also somewhat of a pushover—and that trait had on certain occasions conspired against him. He had a tough time saying no to guys like Deke who wanted cash and to chicks who wanted to bed him—from what I'd discovered, Blythe, Harper, and Locket had all been the aggressors.

After chilling for a while, I went back out to the zoo. People were charging around the cube farm, barking into phones, and shouting to one another across workstations. As far as I knew, Tom Cruise had just run off with Paris Hilton, and that was the new cover story Nash was crashing. But I couldn't have cared less.

Just after the first proof of my piece surfaced, Harper called.

"So now you're Miss *Buzz* Reporter, is that it?" she said. Her tone was as testy as her words.

"I've always been a reporter for *Buzz*—you knew that."

"But I didn't know you were covering this story. You were just helping Chris."

"Look, Harper," I said, trying to keep any edge out of my own voice, "I swear I never misrepresented the situation. We're doing a very small story on Tom. Can you give me a quote I can use—just something nice about Tom from the cast and producers."

" 'We are deeply saddened by the death of Tom Fain. He was a wonderful actor and a terrific asset to the show, and we will all miss him.' There—is that it?"

"Actually, no. I want to talk to you about your relationship with Tom—totally off the record. I was trying to do that all weekend."

"I really have nothing to say to you. What went on between me and Tom is private."

"Well, my question isn't about the private aspects of your relationship. I'm curious why you implied to me that you returned Sunday night of the weekend Tom disappeared when you actually took the red-eye back on Friday night."

"What the hell difference does it make? We finished up early, and I just felt— You're not trying to imply that *I* killed Tom, are you?"

"Did you know he had a home in Andes?"

"No, though it's none of your business whether I did or didn't. I can't believe what you're hinting at. What possible motive do you think I had? Tom and I were dating. We cared about each other."

"And what if you found out Tom was seeing someone else?"

"What are you talking about?"

"Let's just say you found out Tom was involved with someone else. Like someone on the show. That could make you angry."

It was like throwing a stink bomb. But goading her might be the only way to trigger a reaction.

"Who the fuck are you talking about?"

"No one in particular. I'm just tossing out a theory."

"Look, I gave you the quote, now leave me alone. And I don't want you coming by the set—ever again. Do you hear me?"

"That's not for you to say, is it?"

"No, you're right—it's not for me to say. But Alex doesn't want to see your face again. And I bet Chris doesn't, either. You totally humiliated him."

"I—"

But she had hung up.

Oh jeez, what did she mean by that? I wondered. I had not phoned Chris yet, expecting that I'd be hearing from him, but maybe I needed to do damage control. I called his cell and left a short message, asking him to ring me.

For the next few hours, I hung at my desk sullenly, waiting for my story to clear. I made a call to the Chaps Theatre phone number, but discovered it was only a central box office service. I'd clearly have to stop by. Finally, at seven, I was good to go. Almost everyone else, except for the fashion and beauty writers, was still at their desks, held hostage by Hollywood.

It was dark when I arrived home. After changing out of my work clothes into jeans and a short-sleeved sweater, I headed out for a walk. I wanted to check out the Chaps Theatre, which wasn't far from me, but mostly I just wanted to give my brain a respite from murder and mayhem. I picked up a slice of pizza on University Place and then zigzagged my way north and west. I could tell half a block from the theater that it was closed—no light fell onto the sidewalk in front of it. When I reached the building, I peered through the glass doors into the small, weary-looking lobby. One light remained on and lit rows of framed memorabilia of old productions. A sign announced that performances for the current production, a new play called *Coeds from Hell,* ran from Wednesday through Sunday.

I continued to ramble, stopping at one point for a double chocolate ice-cream cone—because I damn well felt like it—and when I left the shop I headed north. I had walked for about ten more minutes, thinking about trips I'd taken and stories I'd written, anything to keep my mind temporarily off Chris and Tom and Locket and Harper, before it hit me: I was making a beeline for Beau Regan's building.

CHAPTER 14

Don't be an idiot, a little voice in me commanded. I felt as if I were watching a horror movie in which the heroine is spending the night in a sagging old house about six miles from the main road and has decided to investigate a tapping sound she's heard in the attic or basement, despite the fact that it's thundering and lightning and the power is promising to go out at any second.

But I couldn't stop myself. What I realized, however, was that I wasn't heading to Beau's in order to try out Landon's or Jessie's tactics for winning him back. He wasn't interested, and nothing I did would change that. The reason for my trip was that I had unfinished business with Beau. On Saturday night, I'd relished delivering my zinger about the postcard, but that hadn't really conveyed how disappointed I was by his behavior. So I would ring his bell, and if he was home, I would apologize for being snippy. And then I would use up five minutes of his precious time to tell him how I really felt. Weren't articles in magazines like *Gloss* always suggesting the importance of closure?

It was eight-thirty when I reached his neighborhood. There was only a decent chance that he was home. For instance, he might have stopped by his apartment for a shower or change of clothes or to pick up a jumbo box of Trojans before heading out for the night. *Or* he might even be there with a chick. Oh God, was it really smart to be doing this? But I just couldn't stop my little legs in their quest. They were like a pair of Disney movie dogs that had been separated from their owner and were crossing the Rockies in order to make it home.

I reached his building and opened the door into the empty foyer. Taking a breath, I pushed the buzzer. Excruciating seconds passed without a response, and I tried again, just for the sheer torture of it. Still no response. With a surprising surge of relief, I turned to go. And then, just as I reached the door, Beau's voice came over the intercom, jerking my body like I'd just stuck a fork down a toaster.

"Yes?" he asked. He sounded sleepy.

"Um, hi, Beau, it's Bailey. I'm down here in your foyer"—*obviously*—"and I was wondering if you might want to grab some coffee—or like a glass of wine."

There was the longest pause, and then it hit me. He *was* with a woman. He'd probably just finished having a *predinner* sack session and had padded down the hall to the intercom, leaving her flushed beneath his pale gray comforter while he determined who had rudely interrupted their carnal bliss.

"Oh, hi. Sure. But why don't you come up first. I need to put some clothes on."

Fucking great, I thought. He's going to *introduce* me to her.

"I don't want to interrupt anything. I was nearby and—"

"It's not a problem. I was taking a nap, but I'm up now."

He hit the buzzer, and I pushed open the door. My legs felt

wobbly suddenly, not the brave doggies they'd been only minutes before.

Beau had thrown on some clothes by the time I got up there—a pair of blue jeans and a blue-and-white-striped dress shirt, with just one side tucked in. His hair was tousled, and his eyes had that dreamy quality I'd noticed in the few mornings I'd awoken next to him.

"Sorry to wake you," I said, staving off the awkward shift my body was dying to make.

"I'm glad you did," he said. "I've had a little jet lag since I got back. Come on in. Would you just like to have a drink here?"

"No, I don't want to put you to any trouble." I would have liked to stay, to be in that serene space again, *his* space, but it didn't seem like the smartest idea. "I was thinking we could just go in the neighborhood someplace—you know, like a coffee place."

"Okay. Just let me get my shoes."

He wandered off to the bedroom, and I let my eyes dart around his living room like bumblebees. There were piles of papers on the ottoman, as if he'd been going through the mail that had accumulated when he'd been in Turkey. An exotic, musky scent hung in the room, just a slight undertone, and I panicked until I remembered that it was *Beau* who smelled that way.

He came back in less than a minute, wearing a pair of flip-flops. I knew he had to be curious about why I was here, but in that Zen way of his, he gave nothing away.

We walked up toward the avenue, him leading. As we maneuvered around pedestrians and baby strollers, we didn't talk much. I asked if he generally suffered from jet lag.

"No, not usually," he said.

He asked why, since Monday was closing day, I was out of work reasonably early, and I explained that I'd had only a short crime piece to do tonight. Gosh, at the rate our zippy banter was going, people were going to accuse us of trying to top Bogey and Bacall.

When we reached the avenue, I thought he was going to steer me to the little café/bakery where we'd eaten breakfast together once, but instead he nodded toward a storefront restaurant with a dark wood bar and dozens of little votive lights twinkling on every surface.

"We can sit at the bar," he said. "They'll even let you have a cappuccino if you want."

I was dying for a glass of wine, just to take the freakin' edge off, but I thought it would seem as though I'd duped him into a quasi-date—so I went for the cappuccino. As he asked for a draft beer and shifted his body on the stool, I felt his leg brush up against mine. Those slim but muscular legs underneath had on several occasions been wrapped around me brilliantly in bed.

"So how was Turkey, anyway?" I asked, stalling just a moment before plunging into what I really wanted to say. "How did the film go?"

"I'm just starting the editing now, but I think the shooting went well. Aphrodisius's pretty awesome. It wasn't looted by the Europeans the way places like Ephesus were. The days were hot and dusty, so the work was tough, but it was all pretty fascinating."

And there was a girl, undoubtedly. Some archaeology student working on a master's degree, brown as a nut from the sun and absolutely gaga, no doubt, when the hunky documentary film-maker blew onto the site.

"I'm glad it worked out," I said as the bartender set down his beer. Beau stared at the glass for a second and then looked back at me, his eyes expectant.

"So what can I do for you?" he asked.

Stalling opportunity over.

"First of all, I wanted to apologize for the nasty comment I made at the party. It wasn't really what I intended to say."

"It's nice to know you don't actually harbor any evil thoughts about me."

"I didn't say *that*," I corrected, half-joking.

He raised one eyebrow. "Ahhh."

"Don't worry—I'm not going to bite your head off. I want to be honest, though. I shouldn't have been rude the other night, but there's a reason I acted bitchy. It really bothered me that you just went incommunicado. I would have accepted it if you'd told me before you left that you flat-out couldn't commit. You'd already been candid about your situation. But you left saying that things were still open for discussion. And then I didn't hear from you."

He rubbed at his chin, clearly choosing his words. "I don't have any excuse you'll like, Bailey. Like I told you before, you blew me away when I met you. But I was at a weird place in my life, not really feeling ready for anything serious relationshipwise. I thought Turkey would be a time to think it through. But once I got there, New York seemed like another planet, and I just didn't feel like I was in a spot or a position to make a decision. The longer I waited to try to write you those words, the harder it was to do. I'm sorry that I handled it that way."

"Okay, well, at least now you've explained it, so thanks." My voice sounded squeaky suddenly, and I realized that I was stinging a little inside, as if I'd been snapped by a big fat rubber band. I'd already accepted the rejection by him, but this was the first time I was hearing it verbalized.

"I hope you're not always going to view me as some giant rat," he said.

"No, I don't think I implied that." My cappuccino arrived, and I took a sip, then licked the foam off my lips. "I just feel it was unfair of you to make me sit around waiting rather than letting me know where I stood. End of lecture."

He cocked his right eyebrow again. "Actually, the other night it didn't look as if you'd waited all that long."

"Just because I spent time with another man doesn't mean it hurt any less not to hear from you."

"What's his show about again? Hard bodies finding dead bodies?"

"Sort of," I said, smiling. "It's about the New York City Morgue."

"Where does one meet an actor if you're not in the business? At the gym?"

My, my. He seemed hot and bothered. Was the unflappable Beau Regan actually flapped?

"We met over a year ago," I said, ignoring the little dig. "And then recently he asked for my help with a friend of his." I gave him a brief overview of the Tom situation, of finding the body and trying to figure out what in the world had happened.

"That sounds horrible," he said. "Any leads?"

"A few that I'm checking out."

I glanced surreptitiously at my watch. It seemed time to high-tail it out of there. I'd said what I needed to, and now the last thing I wanted was for the night to dissolve into idle chitchat between us.

"Well, I should go," I said. "I'm sure you've got things to do, too."

"Ready if you are," he said, reaching for his wallet.

"No, no, I asked you," I insisted, riffling through my purse.

"I'll tell you what," he said. "We'll have a drink one day, and you can pick up the tab that time."

"Oh, is this the 'Let's try to be friends at least' part of the conversation? Why don't we aim for 'Let's be *friendly*' instead—in case we bump into each other at another Locket Ford party? That seems like a more realistic goal."

"Okay, if that's how you'd like it," he said, and offered what seemed like a rueful smile.

Suddenly we were out on the street. I felt a weird sinking sensation as I realized that it was definitely over, that *this* was the last time I'd ever be with Beau.

"I don't know what good it will do for me to say this, but I hope you'll be careful on this story," Beau said. "It sounds pretty scary." He didn't know the half of it—I hadn't told him about the drugging or the phone calls.

"Of course, yes. I'll be careful. Well, good-bye. Take care."

"Good-bye, Bailey." He leaned forward and kissed me lightly on the cheek. I caught the full force of the musky scent he wore. I turned quickly and strode off, wondering if he stood on the sidewalk watching me or if he was already hurrying home, glad to have his closure-over-cocktails experience with me behind him.

By the time I was two blocks away, I felt close to blubbering. But I didn't let myself. If Beau couldn't recognize the brilliant connection he had with me, then I couldn't help him. And I had Chris—Chris, who made me laugh and seemed so caring and protective and wasn't some freakin' mystery man.

I fished my cell phone out of my purse, wondering if I'd missed a call from him. There wasn't any word. "Chris," I said, leaving another message, "I'd love to catch up with you. Please give me a call."

Back at my place, I poured a glass of wine and took it over to the couch, where I leafed through a stack of magazines and newspapers that had accumulated on my coffee table over the past couple of days. There was a hurricane watch along the coast of Florida that I'd been completely oblivious to.

At ten-thirty, when I was on my second glass of red wine and gnawing at a block of cheddar like a rodent, Chris finally phoned. I felt a rush of relief when I heard his voice.

"Sorry not to call earlier," he said, sounding less than his usual delighted-to-talk-to-me self. "I worked a lot later than I expected. I don't think we can get together."

"Okay," I said, wondering still why he hadn't let me know, at least. "About this morning. I really feel awful about that whole incident. I hope it didn't embarrass you—or throw you off your game with the scene you were doing."

"God, what was that all about, Bailey?" he asked, his voice rife with irritation. "I told you that you needed to keep a low profile."

"What was that all *about*?" I said. "A huge snake shot across my foot, and as far as I knew, it was poisonous."

"Deke said what you saw was a cable."

"Deke is an asshole, and I'm surprised you'd believe anything he said." I took a breath, telling myself to take my annoyance down a notch. "I looked the snake up, and it was a common king snake. I'm wondering if they might be planning to use it in an episode."

"No, there aren't any episodes that involve a snake."

"Well, there's got to be an explanation. I am absolutely positive it wasn't a cable."

"Sorry to sound so testy. Locket was jittery to begin with this morning, but once you yelled that thing about the snake, she could barely focus—and then Alex turned into a real tyrant after you left."

"Okay, well, I just wanted to check in. Try to explain what had happened."

"Did you accomplish anything while you were there? I mean, I know it wasn't long, but—"

"I spoke to Deke again. He claims he repaid Tom the money the week before he died, but I seriously doubt it. Anything new on your end?"

"Not really. Everything just felt kind of off today." There was a pause, as if he were taking a slug of a beer. "Look, I better hit the sack. I've got a six a.m. call tomorrow."

God, this was amazing. At the rate I was going, there was a

chance I'd set a land record for being rejected by the most hunky guys in one twenty-four-hour period.

"Good night, then," I said.

"It's gonna be a pretty crazy week for me, but maybe we could get together Wednesday or Thursday. How's your schedule look?"

"I'm fairly open this week."

"Okay, I'll give you a ring tomorrow."

He had sounded more like his normal self toward the end of the conversation, but not a hundred percent. Was his coolness all due to what had happened this morning?

Feeling glum, I crawled into bed and plotted out the next day. I would check up on Locket to make sure she'd made contact with the police. I'd try to determine if there was any way that Deke had indeed repaid the loan and that Tom had planned to use it in his down payment to Barry, the contractor. The Chaps Theatre wouldn't be open until Wednesday, so I would have to wait until then to pursue the *Taming of the Shrew* lead. I still had several suspects, glaring brightly, but no way to learn if one of them really *was* the killer. I'd done my best to provoke them, but the only one that had coughed up anything worthwhile was Locket—and I wasn't a hundred percent sure she'd spoken the truth about every aspect of her visit to Tom. If I were a cop, I'd be able to check on key info—Harper's whereabouts on Saturday, for instance, after she'd taken the red-eye back from L.A.; Deke's bank account, to see if there was any record of him withdrawing cash to repay the loan. But I didn't have those options. I was running out of stones to overturn, and I had no idea what to do next.

I fell asleep in just a wife beater and panties, a book on my chest, and was jarred awake by the sound of my cell phone ringing on my bedside table. I peered at the clock as I reached for it clumsily: 12:02.

There was only silence. I felt a pinch of fear, remembering how the caller from hell liked to use silences.

"Hello," I said again hoarsely.

And then there it was, that awful laughter I'd been subjected to before.

"Who is this?" I asked stupidly, knowing there wouldn't be an answer. And then the caller was gone.

I scooted up in bed, my back against the headboard, feeling freaked. There'd been that same undertone of evil to the laugh. And also that same asexuality. For the life of me, I couldn't tell whether the voice belonged to a man or a woman.

After climbing out of bed, I paced my living room. On the two previous occasions, it had seemed as if the caller had had an uncanny sense of where I was and what a vulnerable state I'd been in, almost as if the person had been following me. And each call had come at such a consequential time. What did the call tonight mean? I wondered.

Just as I tucked myself back into bed, my cell rang again. Grabbing a breath, I answered the call. It took a second to recognize the voice: It was a Manhattan cop named Caleb Hossey, who used to give me tips regularly when I was covering crime for *Get* magazine.

"You still covering the celeb crime stuff?" he asked, chomping on food as he spoke.

"Yeah, what have you got?" I said, scooting up in bed again.

"Got a DOA in Central Park. Celebrity. I don't know her from Adam, but a bunch of the guys here do—Locket Ford. Soap star."

My hand flew to my mouth in shock. "Omigod. Do they have a suspect? What were the circumstances?"

"Don't know. Might be a sexual assault or a mugging gone bad. The report just came in around eleven-thirty, and I thought of you."

"Where was it, exactly?"

"Near the boat pond, closer to the East Side. Enter the park at Seventy-second Street and just look for the camera crews."

I thanked him profusely for the tip. By the time I hung up, I was almost shaking. I hadn't liked Locket one bit, but the fact that she'd been murdered was horrifying. There was a chance, this being New York, that a stranger had assaulted her as she'd walked that little powder puff pooch of hers through Central Park. But my mind immediately leapt to a more likely scenario: that someone she knew had followed her into the park and murdered her, someone who had gotten wind of the fact that she was planning to share a pivotal piece of information with the police tomorrow. I felt a surge of worry, wondering if I'd made a huge mistake in not forcing her to go to the cops immediately. The delay might have cost Locket her life.

And surely it was the *killer* who had called me. The timing was just too perfect to think otherwise. Something else gnawed at my mind, but each time I tried to grab hold, it slipped away.

I called Nash immediately on his cell phone and told him the news, as well as my suspicion that Locket's death could be related to Tom's.

"This is big. How soon can you get up there?"

"I'm five minutes from hailing a cab. What are the chances of getting anything in the issue?"

"I'm here now, and there's still time to have the art department tear up the cover and put Locket's picture on the roof. Lemme think—we can drop some of the fashion, so you've got at least one spread to play with, and we'll want to move the stuff about the actor into this story. As long as we ship everything by eight in the morning, we're okay. And of course we're going to want to break this on the Web site."

I threw on a pair of pants, sweater, and jacket. As I dashed from my apartment building, I glanced up and down 9th Street.

Was there a chance the killer was watching me, just as I'd sensed Friday night? The street appeared nearly empty, though.

There were plenty of cabs tearing down lower Broadway, so I hailed one and had the driver turn down 8th Street and head back uptown. Chugging a Red Bull with one hand, I called Chris on my cell with the other. Not surprisingly, his voice mail picked up. There was a slim chance he knew already, that someone from the show had phoned him, but more than likely he was fast asleep and wouldn't learn the grim news until morning. My stomach sank as I considered what a wrench Locket's death would throw into the production of *Morgue* and how that might impact Chris's career. Would they write her death into the show and try to salvage it? Or would they just scrap the whole show? I wanted to offer as much support as possible to Chris. I also, selfishly, wanted to find out what he knew about Locket's last day on the face of the earth.

I had the cab let me off at East 72nd Street, near two or three TV vans with satellite dishes on their roofs. There were fewer vans than you'd expect, but the murder had gone down at an awkward time for the TV stations, when they would have already sent their crews home for the night. The ones who usually showed up at late night crime scenes were freelance camera guys who a reporter friend of mine liked to call "the ghoul squad." Some of them even kept traffic cones and yellow police tape in the trunks of their cars so that if the cops had cleared out before they arrived, they could re-create the scene for their camera.

I entered the park and headed west. I wasn't far from the Boathouse café where Locket and I had stopped on Sunday. Seeing the vans made me think that there'd be lots of activity in the park, but as I hurried along the rambling sidewalk scattered with leaves, I suddenly found myself alone. Ordinarily, I'd never be so stupid as to go into Central Park by myself this late, but here I was. I paused and looked around me anxiously. Get a grip, Bailey, I told myself. Far off through the trees to the left, I saw flashes of white, which I assumed were the police lights. I broke into a jog and made my way in that direction.

The scene I emerged onto had that eerie quality that crime scenes always have—the overly bright lights like a movie set and the hum of the generator overpowering the quiet of the night. Yellow police tape had been strung around a wide area, and there were a bunch of cops congregated inside—forming almost a human shield around the body. I spotted only the tiniest sliver of a white sheet up against a cluster of large bushes, yards away from the path. I winced as I thought of Locket lying there dead, that lovely white skin possibly bruised and battered. Why had she gone off the path? I wondered. Had she let the damn dog wander in the darkness? Had she been lured there by someone she knew and then strangled or bludgeoned?

The crowd rimming the yellow tape wasn't huge—a few dog walkers, a handful of reporters, several camera crews—but it pulsed with a nervous energy. Standing on the periphery was a reporter from Channel 5, nearly sixty, who I used to bump into regularly when I was covering the crime beat for *Get*. He had once dispatched reports from the Middle East in tan safari jackets, but after losing his hair and his stamina ten or so years ago, he'd ended up as a local reporter, covering murders, water main breaks, and elderly women found dead in their apartments from heat exhaustion.

"Hey, Stan," I called out, strolling toward him. He greeted me with his typical warm but weary smile.

"What took you so long?" he asked. Though he'd kicked the two-and-a-half-pack-a-day habit a few years back, he still had a hoarse smoker's voice. "You don't have access to up-to-the-minute police info at that slick little rag you work for these days?"

"No, but I can tell you what kind of shoes Nicole Richie had on tonight. So give me a fill-in, will you?"

"Well, as I guess you heard or you wouldn't be here, it's Locket

Ford lying over there. She was apparently out walking her dog—on the late side, I'd guess—and someone nailed her. Not sure if we're talking rape or not—the ME's people have been in there for a while, but no one's saying anything yet."

"Who found her?"

"Another dog walker. Heard Locket's dog whimpering over by the bushes and went to investigate."

"Has her boyfriend shown up yet?"

"Alex Ottoson?" He shook his head. "My news desk says that they haven't been able to locate him yet. That's usually a bad sign. You know about the other death, don't you? I wouldn't be telling you this if you were with Channel Four, but someone else on the show got knocked off lately. Just a small-time actor, but still . . ."

"Yeah, thanks, I did hear about that," I said vaguely. "Are the police saying they might be linked?"

"No, but our assignment editor mentioned it to me. Ironic, isn't it—the show's called *Morgue*?"

"Yeah, I'll say. I'm gonna wander around a little. I'll check back with you later, Stan."

I pulled my reporter's pad from my purse and moved along the border of the police tape, trying to manage a better glimpse of the body, jotting notes about the scene. I found one of the freelance photographers *Buzz* uses and arranged for him to contact the photo department about selling shots of the scene. I also approached each of the six people with dogs, thinking one of them may have been the first on the scene, but they all admitted they'd arrived only later. Suddenly, the cops reconfigured their positions inside the cordoned-off area, and I caught a full view of the body, Locket's tiny frame draped in the death sheet, a chunk of her blond hair sticking out at the end. Seeing her body that way made me feel like puking into the bushes.

Had she died because of what she knew? If only I'd pressured her to go to the police *sooner*. I wondered if *Alex* had killed her. Locket may have decided to 'fess up to him, knowing that he might learn the truth anyway once she spoke to the police. He would have been furious to find out about Tom. But if he hadn't known about Tom until tonight, that would mean he wasn't *Tom's* killer. Could there be two separate murderers? It just seemed too far-fetched.

Once again, a vague thought gnawed at my brain, but this time I finally grabbed it. When I had talked to Harper on the phone earlier, I had goaded her, implying that Tom had been involved with someone else, someone on the show. Perhaps she had known Tom had cheated, had killed him in a fight about it, but had never been exactly sure who his other lover was. I'd given her the hint she needed. And then she might have gone looking for Locket.

CHAPTER 15

For the next fifteen minutes nothing much happened, though more reporters arrived, as well as several additional camera crews, unshaven guys with rumpled hair who looked as if they'd been called out of bed by their news desks. The crime scene people shuffled about looking for evidence, the ME investigators poked around alongside them, and in terms of excitement, the whole thing ended up being one notch above waiting in a line at the DMV. Of course, if I was a good citizen, I would have called over one of the cops and announced that I had important information to share. But if I did that, I'd be spending the next two hours talking to the cops instead of doing my job.

Since there was a lull in the action, I called Harper. She answered on the second ring. Was that because she'd been up dealing with the horrible mess for a while now—or because she was the creator of the horrible mess?

"Yes," she demanded, sounding wired.

"It's Bailey. I take it you know about Locket."

"God, don't you ever go away?"

"I'm covering the story for *Buzz*. Can I get a statement from you?"

"It's horrifying and sickening. There's nothing more I can say." Though she was wide awake, clearly she hadn't had time yet to cook up the perfect canned statement with the people at the top, and she wasn't seasoned enough to do a great job just winging it. Harper was probably in over her head on this one.

"What about Alex?" I asked. "I've heard that the police can't find him."

"That's absolutely not true. He was out with friends tonight. And now he's talking to the police in his apartment."

"What will they do with the show? Will they have to scrap everything they've shot so far, or will they write Locket's death into an upcoming episode?"

"That will all be determined over the next few days. I've got to go."

"Some people are saying there's a *Morgue* curse. What comment do you have on that?"

It was a cheap shot, but Nash might want something on the curse angle, and I didn't want to return empty-handed.

"That's fucking ridiculous," she said. "There is absolutely *no* curse. This show is going to be a huge hit." Then she disconnected. She had sounded extremely wigged out, but it was impossible for me to tell whether that was due to guilt or stress over everything that was going down.

"Who you talking to?" It was Stan behind me. I liked the guy, and he'd given me the fill-in, but I was hardly going to offer up Harper's name and number to him.

"Just my boss. I have to file something before too long. Do you think they'll make a statement?"

"From what I hear, not tonight. I'm probably going to pack

it in myself before long. At this point there's not much to run with, is there? Unless you know something from your end about Locket's personal life? You get all that kind of dirt at *Buzz*, don't you? How were things between her and this Alex Ottoson guy?"

"Locket wasn't exactly the kind of A-lister they keep tabs on at *Buzz*. Now, if she'd been living with Jude Law, that would have been a whole different story."

I made another sweep around the periphery, watching the cops work, eavesdropping on conversations among crews, taking a few more notes on the scene. Eventually one of the cops from the press office gave us some info "on background only." The victim was Locket Ford. EMS pronounced her dead at 23:14. They would await the medical examiner's cause of death at the postmort. I phoned Nash and told him I'd be coming in soon. I would have preferred to stay at the scene, just in case the cops did make a statement, but it was almost two a.m. and I needed to start writing.

As I was planning my exit, I spotted Stan with his camera crew starting to make their way from the scene, and I scurried over in that direction. I hated feeling like a scaredy-cat, but I had no interest in walking through the park alone. I followed about twenty yards behind, not so close to be obvious but close enough to feel safe. One stretch we traveled was absolutely desolate—nothing but black trees and bushes and the intermittent puddles of light from the streetlamps along the path.

When I tore into *Buzz* fifteen minutes later, there were more than a dozen people hanging around the bullpen—a deputy editor, a couple of production guys, the art director and a designer, a copyeditor/fact checker, and a few reporters. Nash spotted me immediately through his glass door and jumped from his desk.

"Bailey, get in here," he called from his doorway. "And everyone else, too."

We all crowded into his office, congregating near the round

conference table. People seemed tense but also giddily excited. Though they were used to breaking stories that required pulling all-nighters, they generally involved celebrity breakups or DWI arrests, not homicide.

"Tell us what you've got, Bailey," Nash said, shoving his reading glasses on top of his head, "and then we'll put it all in play."

I filled everyone in on the fairly meager details I'd learned about Locket's death.

"That's enough to work with," Nash said. "We've got shots of the scene and plenty of pix of her." He nodded toward one of the staff reporters. "Bethany's done all the background on Locket. She's writing the sidebar—and she'll help you fill in any blanks you have about her brilliant career in soaps. I'd write long, and that's what we'll post on the Web site. Then we'll trim it back for the magazine. Try to get me something in thirty or forty minutes, okay? I'm gonna work on the cover."

I nodded, but as people hustled out of the office, I hung back.

"Why do I smell a Bailey Weggins bombshell?" Nash asked, staring me straight in the eye as I stood planted in the middle of his office.

"It's pretty big—and it's going to ruffle some feathers," I told him. "On Sunday, Locket admitted to me that she had been having a fling with that young actor who was murdered, Tom Fain. She was at the house in the Catskills several hours before he was murdered."

"Holy shit. Bethany told me Ford was living with Alex Ottoson. Do you think he found out about the affair?"

"I don't know. If he found out, it makes him a suspect in both deaths. If he didn't know, learning the truth in *Buzz* is going to piss him off. That's what I mean about ruffling feathers."

"Why would Locket Ford tell *you* what was going on?"

"Because I stumbled on some information, and I told her

I'd figured it out. She was afraid that if I went around looking for proof, it would cause more problems for her than if she just 'fessed up."

"Okay, I better get the lawyers on the phone and run all this by them. How do you see working your personal conversation with her into the piece?"

"I'll just be very up front about it. 'In an exclusive interview, Ford told this reporter'—that kind of thing."

"Okay, get going. And I hope you're ready for your close-up—because you're going to be doing a hell of a lot of press this week."

I grabbed a cup of coffee first, though I was pretty sure I could have survived without it: I was being powered by a high-octane mix that could have given crack cocaine a run for its money—it was a blend of agitation, grief, a fierce desire to make a mark with my story, and a big splash of fear. I'd mentally outlined my story during the cab ride to *Buzz*, so as I soon as I sat at my computer, I started writing. Though questions about the murder kept dragging at my brain—Had Alex murdered Locket because she'd confessed about Tom? Had I inadvertently goaded Harper into killing Locket?—I knew I couldn't include them in the story, and I had to shove them aside so they didn't slow me down.

I spent just over a half hour pounding out the article. I broke the news about Locket's relationship with Tom right at the end of the opening paragraph and then, after offering the few known details about her death, circled back to her revelation and how it might mean the two deaths were linked.

I'd told Nash my piece was going to ruffle Alex Ottoson's feathers. But the police were going to be bent out of shape, too. I was sharing info in my story that I hadn't yet offered up to them. Not everything, though: I was *not* going to spill the news about Locket's phone call to Tom and his comment about the person heading up the driveway. It would have been great to be able to include that stuff, but those details would be critical to the official investigation, and just because Locket hadn't had the chance to go to the police with them didn't mean I could run with the info. As soon as I had a chance today, I needed to share what I knew with them.

There were other feathers that might get ruffled, too: Chris's. He'd brought me into this whole business as a friend, and he'd confessed his discomfort when I'd morphed into reporter. Now I was taking things one step further: I was exposing the affair, something Chris had obviously wanted to keep under wraps. That's why he'd snatched Locket's note to Tom. Of course, with Locket dead, there was no reason now to safeguard her privacy. I knew I'd done the right thing for my story. But I was worried Chris would feel I'd betrayed his trust. We'd literally clung to each other after Tom's death, and I'd liked that clinging. After Chris learned what was in my piece, however, he might be pissed enough to blow me off. Maybe I should have realized that his job and my job were never going to be simpatico.

Though we had until eight to get the piece out the door, we ended up finishing before four—with the exception of the production guys, who stayed behind just in case I called in an update. Nash walked out with me, hammering out press details on his cell with someone in the PR department.

"Great news," he said to me as he snapped his phone shut, "you're on the seven o'clock hour of the *Today Show*."

"The *Today Show today*?" I exclaimed, trying to keep my eyes from bugging out of my head.

"Yeah, a car will pick you up at six, so it's probably best just to stay up. Our PR people are suggesting what they call an even-break strategy—giving the story exclusively to a few places—the *Today Show*, CNN, a few radio stations. You can crash later this morning."

Thank God I was too wired to feel sleepy or freaked about

the TV appearance. I'd done both television and radio for previous articles, and though I didn't relish the day ahead, I knew I could handle it without breaking into a cold sweat.

Back at my place I showered, dug out a little purple suit I hadn't worn in a year, and used about a quart of volumizer when I styled my hair. Then I plopped down on the couch with a cup of tea.

I must have dozed off because the next thing I knew I was being roused from my sleep. I'd had a dream, an ugly one. There'd been a snake in it, the size of an anaconda, and then later an interminable train ride in the darkness. I rode in a near empty car that rocked back and forth. I was filled with anxiety because I wasn't sure where I was supposed to disembark. When a noise jarred me awake, it felt as if I were surfacing from the bottom of a lake. With a damp hand I slapped at what I thought was my alarm clock buzzing until I remembered I was on the couch, and that it was my cell phone that was going off. I fumbled for the phone and flicked it open. Chris's number was on the screen.

"Oh, Chris, there you are," I said hoarsely as I checked the time: 5:15. "Are you okay? I've been so worried about you." What I didn't add was that I was feeling guilty, too.

"You've heard, then?" he said.

"I'm covering it for *Buzz,* so I was up in the park late last night after word leaked out. This must be awful for you."

"One of the producers just woke me and told me the news. I've got to see you, Bailey. This is awful. Can I come over? Needless to say, we're not shooting today."

"Believe it or not, I've got to leave here at six. But why don't we meet in the coffee shop in my building. They're open all night."

"Okay, see you in ten minutes."

After gulping down a glass of OJ, I went online and skimmed through the reports on Locket. I hadn't missed much while I was sleeping. The police had released a sheet saying Locket had been stabbed numerous times. And that was it. A few of the news sites mentioned my report. Some had a more polished statement from Harper than the one she'd given me, and there was also a comment from a network suit, declaring that they were determining what to do with the show but that for now their thoughts were focused on Alex Ottoson and Locket's family. Alex was reportedly sequestered in his apartment and not making any statement. Last, I checked the *Buzz* site. Already people all over America were sipping coffee and discovering the bomb I'd dropped.

Chris was already in the near-empty coffee shop when I arrived, staring gloomily into a coffee cup, his long legs stretched out sideways from the table. I felt a terrible stab when I saw how dejected he looked. He rose from the table at the sight of me, and we hugged each other tightly. It was a relief to have those arms around me. But I dreaded having to disclose to him that I'd busted the Locket-Tom affair. From his tone on the phone, I was pretty certain he hadn't heard yet.

"I was desperate to talk to you last night, but you didn't pick up your cell phone," I explained as I sat down. "I wanted to tell you the news myself."

"I had my cell phone near my bed, but I guess I didn't hear it when you phoned last night. After I hung up with the producer, three different reporters called. God knows how they managed to get my cell phone number. There was no press outside my building this morning, but I bet it's only a matter of time before the vultures descend in force."

Oh boy. I was technically one of those vultures.

"This has got to be such a nightmare for you," I said, stroking his hand.

"Yeah, I feel sick about Locket," he said, laying his hand over mine. "*And*, I'm ashamed to admit, I'm worried about what all of this means for me and the show."

"Don't be ashamed, Chris. Your world got turned upside

down today, and that's a totally legitimate concern. Any inside word about what the network might do?"

"I've talked to a few people already, and according to the rumor mill, at least, they're going to write Locket's death into the show and find a new female lead."

"That makes a lot of sense," I said after ordering a cappuccino. "It would be crazy to bail after all they've invested."

"Yeah, but that could very well happen. With two actors on the show murdered, the network's got to feel the show is tainted, and they may want to bag the whole thing."

"Well, it's awful to say, but they may feel this actually works to their advantage. There's going to be a hell of a lot of morbid curiosity."

"You said you're covering the story—do you know anything yet about how Locket died?"

I explained how little info I *did* have and asked if he'd managed to glean any details from his end.

"Nobody seems to know anything. I got through to Harper once, but she was like a maniac and had nothing to offer. The papers are saying it might be a botched robbery, but of course everybody at the show is wondering if Locket's death is connected to Tom's."

"I'm pretty sure it has to be," I said. "Right before I found out she'd been killed, I got one of those awful phone calls again—the person laughing like someone gone mad. And I still couldn't tell if it was a man or a woman. It's as if they had called to announce what they'd done—to brag about it."

"Have you told the police?" Chris asked.

"Not yet—but I will today. There's something else I need to share with them, too. On Sunday, Locket *admitted* to me that she'd been having a fling with Tom—and also that she'd been with him in Andes the Saturday he disappeared. What's even more amazing is that after she left, she called Tom to check in and he mentioned that a car was just pulling up in the driveway." I quoted the line of Baptista's that Tom had used.

"So that's why you asked me about *Taming of the Shrew* yesterday."

"Yeah, exactly."

"But why not tell me about this before?" Chris said, his voice hardening. He stared at me so intensely that his green eyes seemed to penetrate mine. "I thought we were being completely open with each other."

"I couldn't tell you because I gave Locket my word I wouldn't say anything until she'd had a chance to go to the police," I said, feeling my cheeks redden. Chris had never seemed this miffed at me about anything—and he didn't know the half of it. "I planned to fill you in as soon as I could. Locket said she had Tuesday off and was going to call the cops then."

His shoulders relaxed as he seemed to accept my explanation. "Are you thinking that someone found out she had info and killed her before she could go to the cops?" he asked.

"That's one possibility. Another is that she spilled to Alex— knowing he was probably going to find out anyway."

"That's a piece of news he wouldn't have been pleased to hear."

"Did you see any interaction between the two of them yesterday?"

"He was curt with her through most of the day, but like I told you last night, he was a real tyrant yesterday, and *nobody* was spared. Something was definitely eating at him. At first I thought it was because of the whole snake incident, but it lasted too long for that.

"And hey, by the way," he added. "You were right. There really *was* a snake."

"Do tell," I said.

"One of the ADs told me they found out that a snake had

escaped from a cage on some kind of vet show that's also shot in the building. Sorry I didn't just take your word for it, Bailey. I—"

"Don't worry about it," I said, relieved that things seemed back to normal with us. "Talk to me more about yesterday. Did you see Locket interacting with anyone else in a way that might be significant? Like with Deke, for instance."

"No, not Deke, though something weird was going on with him. He seemed to be on his cell most of the day, and one of the ADs finally complained to him. But Locket had a tiff with Harper. I couldn't tell what the problem was, but they were barking at each other in a corner."

"What time was this?"

"Late afternoon. Why?"

"She avoided my calls all weekend, but I finally got her on the phone yesterday to ask her why she let me think she'd returned to New York on that Sunday night rather than Saturday. She was all pissy and defensive, so I goaded her a little. I said something about the possibility of Tom having an affair with someone on the show. I'm wondering if she may have confronted Locket about it."

"Well, they weren't clawing each other's eyes out, but their voices were raised."

"So what this all means is that there's still no clear suspect. I've got one or two small leads to follow up on—like the *Taming of the Shrew* stuff—but if they don't lead anywhere, I'm at a dead end."

I took a long sip of my cappuccino. It was time to break the news about my story, and I needed fortification.

"There's something you need to know, Chris," I said. "I had to include the information about Tom's affair with Locket in my piece."

"*What?*" he demanded, his face pinched in agitation.

"I know you wanted to keep it private, but it's a critical part of the story."

"But why does the world have to know about it? All it does is sully Tom's name and Locket's, too."

"The affair explains why the two deaths are probably linked. And like I told you, I'm going to be filling the police in on this today—I *have* to—so the news on this will come out anyway."

"And so what does this mean for me? Are you going to tell the cops I took Locket's note from Tom's apartment?"

"You haven't told them about it yet?"

"No—no, I haven't. I just haven't wanted to open that can of worms."

"They're going to wonder exactly how I learned the truth about those two, but I won't say anything about the note. I'll—I'll tell them that I heard rumors about the affair and that I bluffed with Locket, hinting to her that I had evidence when I really didn't. But I still think it's essential for you to turn in that note. Chris, it was one thing to be protective when the affair didn't seem to have anything to do with Tom's death, but now it looks like it may have—and Locket's, too—and you have to be forthcoming. It might help catch Tom's killer."

Chris stared at the table, massaging his forehead with his hand.

"Chris, talk to me."

"Okay, I'll go to the police. You've got a point. But I just hate all this *Buzz* stuff. One minute you're helping me, and the next thing you're turning it all into a story."

"I see what you're saying. But I never knew the situation would blow up this way. There's one thing you've got to know. I may be covering this story, but first and foremost my goal is still to find out what happened to Tom."

"Am I going to end up in a *Buzz* story?"

"God, Chris, of course not," I insisted. "I'd never do anything to hurt you."

He sighed. "Okay, I guess I'm just going to have to trust you."

My cell phone buzzed in my purse. It was Nash on the line.

"You up with your hair combed?" he asked.

"Yup."

"Then you need to call the PR folks. They've got a pretty big plan for you."

I promised I would and signed off.

"Look, unfortunately I need to get moving," I told Chris. "But let's stay in touch today, okay? I promise to do a better job of keeping you in the loop."

"I'd appreciate that."

Outside the coffee shop, Chris and I lingered awkwardly on the sidewalk. Please kiss me good-bye, I thought. I don't want any more friction between us.

"Promise me you'll be careful," he said. "This is all really scary."

"Promise. And let me know if you hear anything about the show."

As if he'd heard my mental pleading, he leaned down and kissed me tenderly on the mouth.

"When this is all over, I'm going to whisk you off to Jamaica for a long weekend," he said. "We'll listen to Bob Marley songs and drink lots of rum."

I beamed at him, happy that things were straight between us. "That sounds divine."

But as I watched him cross Broadway, I saw from his profile that his face was scrunched in consternation. He had a lot on his mind right now, of course, but I wondered how much of his agitation had to do with my breaking the news about Tom and Locket.

From that point on, the day moved like a bullet train.

I felt jittery as I sat on the *Today Show* couch in my purple suit with my hot pink lips, compliments of the makeup artist, but once I was talking and just describing what I knew about the case, my fears slipped away.

Later, while I waited for the car to take my PR escorts and me to CNN, I called the Central Park police precinct and told the desk cop that I had information that was pertinent to the investigation of Locket Ford's death. I was transferred to a detective who urged me to come in immediately. I said I had work obligations, and though he pressured me, I stuck to my guns. Nash would strangle me if I blew the press bonanza.

After a blitzkrieg two hours, I was dropped off at home, told I could rest, but that I needed to begin round two in the early afternoon. I slept for two hours and then bolted awake, knowing how much I still had to do. I checked with my contacts in the police and ME's office for more info on Locket (she definitely hadn't been sexually assaulted; there were no suspects yet). My cell phone was clogged with calls from reporters I knew (including Stan, who chided me for holding out on him). When I checked in at *Buzz*, I was told my phone had been ringing off the hook.

I was back on the press bus by one for *Court TV* and a couple of live radio shows. By three-thirty I was finally done for the day.

Still in my suit and slingbacks, I headed north in a cab for the Central Park precinct on the 86th Street transverse, rehearsing my remarks in my head. I'd decided not to raise the idea of Harper as a suspect until I had more facts. I would, however, share what I knew about the loan to Deke.

I waited only a couple of minutes on a folding chair in a small entrance area before being summoned by a detective named Mark Windgate, a good-looking African American, mid-thirties, who was dressed neatly in a khaki blazer and blue-and-tan tie.

"You've been a busy lady today," he said as I took a seat, in a tone that indicated he knew all about my *Buzz* story and the press I'd been doing—and he was none too pleased. "The next thing you know, Greta Van Susteren's gonna be out of a job."

"I'm sorry I wasn't able to stop by before now," I said as apologetically as possible. I'd learned with cops that it's always best not to become defensive.

"*Sorry?*" he nearly shouted. "And are you also sorry that you released critical information to the world at large before giving it to us, possibly screwing up our investigation?"

I fought the urge to squirm like an earthworm tugged from the ground.

"My boss insisted that I do the press as part of my job," I explained lamely. "I got here as soon as my last interview was completed."

"And why not inform us on Sunday, after Ms. Ford reportedly told you about the affair?" he asked, arms folded tight against his chest.

"Because I felt that it was *her* obligation, and she swore to me she was going to contact you on Tuesday."

He eyed me warily as he used four fingers to smooth his thin mustache again and again. Finally, he let his hand drop. "Have you asked yourself how things might have turned out differently if you *had* come to us immediately?" he asked.

Ouch.

"Look, I promise to cooperate every step of the way going forward," I told him. "And I have something very important to share, something I didn't think was appropriate to put in my story."

"Let's hear it."

I told him then about Locket's call to Tom, the arrival of the visitor to Dabbet Road, and Tom's line from *Shrew*.

He took notes as I spoke, his face blank. I knew he must find the revelation about the visitor crucial, but it was impossible to tell how meaningful he thought the line from Shakespeare was.

Then the questions started. He came at my conversation with Locket from several different angles, clearly hoping to extract info I might have forgotten to mention or didn't realize was significant—about the affair, about the mystery visitor—but there was nothing to add. Sure enough, he asked why Locket would have been so candid with me, and I told the fib I'd promised Chris I would. When we'd exhausted that subject, he had me backtrack, describing my trip to Andes. That gave me the chance to raise the phone calls I'd begun receiving on my return and the incident at the Half King.

"And why not contact us about *that*?" he asked.

"I had no proof I'd been drugged, and it may have been unrelated. As for the phone calls, I thought they could be pranks. It wasn't until the call last night—timed so perfectly to Locket Ford's death—that I was sure they were really connected."

He jotted down my cell phone number, saying they would make an attempt to trace the calls.

By the time we were done, I felt wiped, and the back of my cute little suit was damp with sweat. As he walked me to the front of the precinct house, his manner softened.

"So, we've got an open line of communication now?" he asked, holding open the door for me.

"Absolutely. Any update on the case, by the way?" It didn't hurt to try.

He smirked, mildly amused at my chutzpah. "Not that I can share with you. And I don't want to read a *word* about the phone call we discussed. It's essential that it be kept under wraps for now."

"Fine."

"And last but not least, you need to be careful, Miss Weggins. The killer knows now that Ms. Ford spoke to you. If she was murdered because of information she was privy to, the killer may suspect you have that information in your possession now."

Not that I'd taken my situation lightly up until then, but hearing him put words to the danger made my fear harden like a boulder in my gut.

Out on the 86th Street transverse, I checked my voice mail. Two requests from the relentless PR department for me to do additional shows tomorrow, a call from Nash asking if I had updated info for the Web site. Just as I was about to return calls, my phone rang.

"Is this Bailey Weggins?" asked a pompous, vaguely familiar voice.

"Yes, who's calling?"

"Alex Ottoson. I want to see you."

I probably shouldn't have been surprised.

"Okay. Where—and when?"

"My apartment. Now. Central Park West at Seventy-fourth Street. How long will it take you to get here?"

"I'm actually only fifteen minutes away."

"There's a horde of paparazzi out front, so you need to use the service entrance around the corner. A few of the jackals will probably be positioned there as well, but my assistant will be waiting."

Alex had of course read the *Buzz* Web site or been told about it and wanted to grill me on the subject of Locket's fling with Tom. This would be the perfect chance for me to take a measure of him, yet it wasn't going to be a pleasant situation. As I picked up my pace along the park, my eyes roamed the large dusty bushes off to the left, not unlike the one Locket had been killed near. It would have been so easy for Alex to follow her as she walked the dog—or catch up with her at a spot he knew she'd be. She would have been surprised to see him, but not necessarily alarmed. And he could have bashed in her head before she even knew her life was in danger.

There *were* paparazzi by the service entrance, as it turned out, about five of them, but the assistant, a slim Asian woman dressed in a black tunic, leggings, and pointy black ankle boots, was waiting just outside the door and whisked me by them. She led me up a flight of back stairs and then around to the front lobby. She said nothing at all to me as we rode the elevator and then only, "Please follow me," after she'd unlocked the apartment door. I trailed behind her through the gigundo living room and down a long corridor lined with closed doors, a different route from the one Locket had taken when I'd visited her. The place was totally silent, tomblike, like a space belowground. At the very end of the hall, the assistant rapped on a door, and through it we heard Alex's muffled voice announce, "Enter." As I stepped into the large spare study, the assistant faded back into the recesses of the apartment.

Alex was sitting at a sleek black desk, with absolutely nothing on it but a phone. He wore a crisp white cotton shirt, long-sleeved, and a camel-colored cashmere sweater was knotted around his neck. Kind of spiffy for someone in deep mourning. He didn't rise, and he didn't offer me a seat.

"I'm very sorry for your loss," I said.

"Let me cut right to the chase," he said bluntly. "I want to know everything Locket told you about her relationship with Tom Fain."

"I'm under no obligation to share with you what Locket revealed to me."

"But you didn't hesitate to reveal to the world that she was having an affair with Tom Fain."

"She was about to go to the police with that information. It wasn't going to be a secret any longer."

"Was she in love with him?" His voice cracked slightly when he spoke, releasing a soupçon of pity in me.

"I don't think so," I admitted. "She said she never wanted to jeopardize her relationship with you."

"Lovely," he said, his voice thick with sarcasm. "And why, might I ask, would she share all this information with you?"

"I'd been looking into Tom's death—not as a reporter, but because I'd found the body and wanted to know what had happened to him. I heard a rumor about her and Tom, so I confronted her. Were you aware of what was going on?"

"I had my suspicions, but no proof. Locket was quite the master of deception, and she could cover her tracks brilliantly. She visited some old friends the weekend Fain apparently died, and when I called they told me she'd gone antiquing. She even returned with several eighteenth-century silver serving spoons just to drive home the point."

"Where were *you* that day?" I asked. If he was going to cut to the chase, so would I.

"Off the record—with a young lady. As I was last night."

Oh, nice. Mr. Pot calling the kettle black.

"Have the police given you any indication of what they think happened to Locket?" I asked.

"All I know is from the doorman. She left to walk the dog about nine. I assumed she'd stopped by a friend's. Now if you'll excuse me . . ."

I wondered if I was supposed to see myself out, but when I turned toward the doorway, I saw that the assistant was back, hovering. Had a bell under the desk summoned her?

"Just one question," I said to Alex as he reached for the phone. "How did you find out that Tom Fain had been in rehab?"

"If you must know," he said, "Chris Wickersham's agent in L.A. told us, though of course we had it verified."

The news almost knocked the wind out of me. It had been *Chris* who had sabotaged Tom. The thought sickened me.

On the other hand, was it such a surprise? Perhaps I should have guessed the truth when Locket had told me what happened. I knew Chris was driven. He wanted fame and glory—what actor who heads for L.A. doesn't? I'd even understood why he hadn't come to my rescue on the set—because it might hurt his standing with the director. But betraying Tom was in a whole other league.

By the time the cab pulled up in front of my building, I felt miserable. I hobbled to the door in my wrinkled suit and scuffed slingbacks and offered Bob, the doorman, a pathetic hello.

"You just missed her," he said.

"Who?" I asked, confused.

"Your sister-in-law. I let her into your apartment like you asked."

"Like I *asked?*" I exclaimed, feeling a charge of adrenaline. "What do you mean?"

Bob stared at me, his eyes widening in alarm beneath the brim of his brown cap.

"You called me an hour ago. And told me to let her in."

CHAPTER 16

I paused for a split second to gather my wits, then charged across the lobby and around the corner to the elevator bank.

"Is everything all right, Ms. Weggins?" Bob called out behind me.

"I don't think so," I yelled back. "I never called you today."

My heart was thumping hard as I rode the elevator to the fourteenth floor. I *hadn't* called Bob, and for all I knew, one sister-in-law was in the Caribbean with my brother and the other was in Boston coping with her addiction to the Crate & Barrel catalog. That meant someone had phoned the lobby impersonating me. And that person apparently had shown up and spent time alone in my apartment.

I'd no sooner stepped onto the floor than the door of the other elevator slid open and Bob darted out.

"I got the porter to watch the door. Are you saying you weren't the one who phoned here this afternoon?"

"No—and my sisters-in-law aren't in New York now. What exactly did this person say when she called?"

"Just hi, that it was you, Bailey, and that you wanted me to let your sister-in-law use your apartment while she was between planes. We're supposed to get written notes on stuff like that, but it was so clearly you who was calling. I wanted to do you the favor."

He pushed back the brim of his cap, and I could see that his forehead was glistening with sweat. Poor Bob—he probably suspected he was going to get canned before the day was through.

"The woman who showed up here—what did she look like?" I asked. "And how long did she stay?"

"To be honest, I didn't get a great look. She was on the tall side, maybe five eight or nine, though she may have been wearing heels. She had on big sunglasses and some kind of hat—like a fedora. And oh, her hair was peeking out a little from the top—it was blond. She stayed about thirty minutes. Like I said earlier, she left about fifteen minutes before you got here."

"And you're sure it was a woman?"

"Huh? You mean could it have been a guy dressed up like a woman? I—I don't think so."

"Okay, we better check my place now," I said, glad Bob was with me. I had no idea what I was going to find there. Had it been trashed? Booby-trapped?

"You better be prepared for the fact that you may have been robbed," Bob advised. "She certainly didn't take your TV out of here, but she might have stolen cash or jewelry."

But when I stepped into my entranceway with Bob at my heels and glanced around, nothing at all seemed amiss. We moved with trepidation from the living room to the kitchen and then back through the living room to the bedroom, the bathroom, and my tiny office. There were no rifled drawers, no cabinet doors flung open. And my small cache of jewelry, the pieces my ex-husband hadn't managed to pawn, was still tucked in a nest of my thongs.

"Is anything missing?" Bob asked nervously.

"No, not that I can see."

"Then what did she want?"

"I don't know, Bob. I don't know."

"Do you want me to call the super?"

"That may not be necessary. Let me get settled in and I'll take a closer look around. If I find anything wrong, I'll let you know."

Bob departed looking totally chagrined, his collar wet from flop sweat. I didn't fault him for what had happened. But that didn't mean I wasn't freaked.

After I'd stripped off my suit and kicked my heels into the closet, I searched through my bedroom again, mostly through drawers, and I did the same in my office. My papers seemed in order. My laptop was in the exact spot I'd left it. Why had she come to my apartment? Who *was* she? She had to be a good actress or mimic—after all, she had managed to imitate my voice well enough that my doorman had assumed it was I.

There was an even more chilling question to consider. Was the mystery visitor related to the murders? If yes, it narrowed the field. It certainly couldn't have been Deke disguised in a hat and sunglasses. Or Alex. But it might have been Harper. Or possibly someone in league with the murderer. Or maybe it didn't have anything to do with the killings at all. But then why would someone go through the whole ruse and spend a half hour in my apartment the day after Locket's murder?

I pulled on a pair of tan capris and a black jersey top and returned to my office. I called Detective Windgate and described on his voice mail what had happened. I asked him to call me the first chance he got, and I also left a message for Nash saying that there were a few new developments, but nothing that couldn't wait, and

I'd fill him in tomorrow at the office. Then I made calls to some of my contacts, coming up with nothing new.

By this point, my stomach was grumbling and my whole body ached from fatigue. I phoned Landon, hoping he was up for company because the thought of spending the next hours alone in my apartment gave me the willies. Ever so faintly, I heard his phone ring through the wall in my office, again and again until his machine picked up. It looked as though I were going to be on my own with whatever sorry provisions I could locate in my fridge.

On my way to the kitchen, I checked my terrace door, making certain it and the windows were still bolted. I started to relax just a little, realizing that no one was going to be able to gain entry.

Practically limp from hunger and exhaustion, I foraged through my freezer for a pork cutlet I had vague recollections of having tossed in there and finally discovered it, lying rock hard beneath a sleeve of frozen bagels. As I turned with it toward the microwave, my eye caught a flash of silver in the sink. Lying in the otherwise empty basin was a steak knife with a wooden handle. It was from a fancy set I'd received as a wedding gift, from some relative who had wrongly envisioned my ex and me savoring thick sirloins together for the rest of our lives on earth. I hadn't noticed it earlier when Bob and I had done our sweep, but then I hadn't looked there. I was sure I hadn't put the knife in the sink. I hadn't, in fact, used those knives in ages. The blade looked cold and menacing lying there by itself.

In all likelihood, the intruder had left the knife there. Had she used it to open something? I didn't think so. I thought instead that the knife was a message: *I can hurt you if I want to, just like the others.* Perhaps it was even a promise.

I backed out of the kitchen, leaving the knife where it was, and left another message for Windgate, this one even more urgent. Though I no longer had the same appetite, I ordered a deep-dish pizza over the phone. While I waited for it to arrive—and for

Windgate to make contact—I sat at my dining table with my composition book and began to write. Having a pencil in my hand gave me a small feeling of control.

I started by jotting down Bob's description of the woman, and then I wrote a single name: "Harper." *She* was about five nine, maybe five ten, the height Bob had assigned to the intruder. Her hair was short, but there were definitely pieces long enough to peek out from under a hat. And, I suddenly remembered, she had planned to be an actress once. Chris had told me that when he'd first come to me about Tom.

I certainly had every right to consider Harper a prime suspect. She'd led me to believe she'd been in L.A. that weekend, but she had actually rushed back, presumably because she had a bad feeling about Tom. She could have begun to suspect he was cheating on her—and she may have killed Tom without ever learning who the other woman actually was. When I'd hinted yesterday that it might be someone on the show, Harper might have convinced herself that it was Locket and confronted her in the park.

I'd become so preoccupied about my intruder that Alex's revelation had escaped my mind temporarily—but now it popped into my brain like a sunken object finally shooting to the surface of a pond. Chris had cost Tom the part in the show, all because of his own fierce ambition. I imagined how it had probably happened: Tom had called Chris and told him about being cast in the show and suggested to Chris he get in to see the casting director. Chris had auditioned, had inferred somehow that everything wasn't totally nailed down yet with Tom, and told his agent to leak the info about rehab.

The revelation made me both angry and sad. Angry because Chris had derailed Tom's career. Was that why he'd wanted me to find Tom—out of wretched guilt? And sad because I really cared about Chris. I'd liked going to bed with him, I liked the way he made me laugh, I even liked his freakin' omelet with aged cheddar. And now I could see he wasn't the guy I thought he was. It would have been nice to call Chris for comfort tonight, to possibly spend the night at his place away from the nasty steak knife, but there was no way I'd do that after what I'd learned about him. I realized, in fact, that I had never heard from Chris this evening, despite the fact that when we'd had breakfast together, he'd implied we'd talk later. Tomorrow I was going to force him to tell me the truth.

As I sat staring at a blank page of my notebook, my pizza arrived, and no sooner had I paid for it than Windgate returned my call. I explained the whole situation about the intruder. When I was done, there was only silence on his part.

"Are you—" I started to say.

"Could it be a woman you know personally—someone from your own life?" he interrupted, his voice neutral. "A woman who's trying to get back at you for some reason? Maybe she thinks you stole her boyfriend, for instance."

"You mean a stalker?" I asked, trying not to sound as exasperated as I felt. "God, no, I don't think so. There's been no indication that anyone's obsessed with me. And I've never stolen anyone's boyfriend."

"Okay, okay, just sit tight, then. I'm going to send an evidence collection team over to lift fingerprints. And I want you to be extremely careful, is that understood?"

As relieved as I felt that the police were taking the intrusion seriously, I was ready to crawl into bed and pass out. Now I was going to have to hang around my living room while guys brushed the surfaces of my apartment with fingerprint powder.

The smartest move, I decided, was to try to grab a catnap before the cops arrived. I took two bites of pizza and staggered over to the couch. Cell phone in hand, I sprawled out on the length of it. As soon as I'd closed my eyes, my cell rang again.

"Did I catch you at a bad time?" a voice asked. It was Beau Regan.

Yeah, I'm in the reverse cowgirl position with a dude, and it's kind of hard to talk right now was what I was tempted to say, but instead I just muttered something about eating take-out. I couldn't even muster the gumption to lie and imply I was having a fabulous time.

"I heard about Locket Ford. You said she'd worked with that actor who died—whose death you were looking into. I wanted to make sure everything was okay with you."

"Uh, that's nice of you to call. To tell you the truth, I'm pretty sure the two deaths are related."

"That's what I wondered. Are you doing all right? You're not in one of those hot spots you love to gravitate toward, are you?"

"Actually, I—" My voice caught, much to my chagrin. "Someone got into my apartment—and I think it might be the killer. The police are supposedly on their way to look for prints."

"What do you mean, it might be the killer? What happened, exactly?"

I ran through it quickly for him. My voice caught again during part of my story, and I felt ridiculously wimpy. The last thing I wanted to do was make Beau think I was a "boo-hoo" kind of girl in need of rescue.

"Bailey, you can't stay there tonight," he said, my efforts apparently a failure. "I hope you're not planning to."

"I'm sure I'll be okay," I insisted. "It's not like this person has a key. I don't want to put out a friend on such late notice." I wondered if he was curious why I wouldn't bunk down with my "hard body."

"Why don't you stay at my place," he said, his voice gentle.

My breath froze in my chest, like a paralyzed nerve.

"You could have the couch," he added. "Or I could. I just

don't like the idea of you staying alone there. Remember, I was the guy who put the ice pack on your bruises last July."

I was about to say no, *really* I was, because from the moment I'd left Beau on the sidewalk in Chelsea the night before, I had felt as if I were finally moving away from him mentally and no longer wondering if there was a snowball's chance in hell for us. Staying at his place, even if only on the couch, would surely set me back.

But I also knew how freaked I felt and how much I didn't want to be in my apartment contemplating 101 things someone could do with a steak knife. So I said yes.

While I waited for the evidence collection team to arrive, I zipped my laptop into its case and packed an overnight bag with the only other suit I owned. The cops finally showed at around eight-thirty. After explaining the situation to them and giving them the lay of the land—as well as letting them take my fingerprints—I beat it out of there. When they departed later, the door would lock behind them automatically. In the lobby, I arranged for the night doorman to go up to the floor after the police left and make sure the dead bolt was on with the key they kept to my place. Though I'd felt wasted earlier, my body had been totally recharged by adrenaline.

Only a day had passed since I'd seen Beau last, but now he looked far more rested. He was wearing tan cords and a yellow crewneck sweater, and his feet were bare. My tummy started to go all weird at the sight of him.

"I opened a bottle of red wine, thinking you might need it," he said after walking me into the living room. "And I have a huge chunk of Stilton cheese my mother sent home with me."

"Just what the doctor ordered."

While he put things together in the kitchen, I sank into his sofa and took the chance to study the living room. The pile of papers that had been strewn about yesterday was now cleared away, and everything else was pretty much as it had been earlier in the summer: the sleek black leather furniture; the primitive-style rug in blue, black, and orange; the striking black-and-white photos of the Far East lining the white walls. There were several new photos, though, of what I assumed must be ancient streets in Istanbul, propped against the base of a wall. It made me nervous to prowl every inch of the room with my eyes—I'd once found a pink Daisy razor in the shower of a guy I was gaga for, squashing any hopes for eternal love, and I hated the thought of discovering bread crumbs from some chick here—but I couldn't help myself.

"So your mother sent you home with a wedge of *cheese*?" I said as Beau carried in a wine bottle, two glasses by their stems, and a plate with crackers and the blue-veined Stilton.

"Wedge isn't quite the right word," he said, pouring a glass of wine and handing it to me. "Wheel, I'd say. I went up there for dinner the other night—they wanted to check me out after I got back, perhaps hoping two months in the Turkish heat had convinced me to stop making documentary films and start a hedge fund. And as I'm leaving, my mother has the housekeeper hand me a shopping bag of food. I could win a bloody Oscar for a film someday, and my mother would still be asking me if I had enough clean clothes for the week."

"You seem to take it in stride," I said.

"Years of practice. So tell me more about the intruder. What makes you think she could be the murderer?"

I took a long drink of the wine first. It was an excellent-tasting Bordeaux that was probably noted for being redolent of things like plums and tobacco and saddlebags. Interesting, I thought, that he'd opened such a great bottle.

"I suppose there's a chance it's unrelated," I said. "The detective I've been dealing with even posed the idea I could have a stalker unrelated to the killings—someone who's convinced I'm after her man, for instance. But I just don't see it. It would make everything that's happened so coincidental."

I described the calls I'd received and also the incident at the Half King.

"Bailey, it's clear you're really in danger," he said. "I'm glad you came to your senses and decided not to stay at your place."

"Well, I appreciate your offer. It's horrible how something like this can leave you feeling so miserable in your own home."

He took a sip of wine and leaned back into the sofa, one leg crossed over the knee of the other, and just stared at me with those intense brown eyes. He had an uncanny ability to be *still*, to sit in one position without shifting or flexing or sweeping his hand through his hair. And he could hold your gaze until it became unbearable and you were forced to look anywhere but his eyes. I met his gaze awkwardly for a second and then glanced away, taking another long sip of my wine. I realized suddenly that my cheeks were hot—and not just from a combo of the Bordeaux and my own distress. It was due to lust, pure and simple. I'd kept it at bay yesterday, but now that I was all alone with Beau in his apartment, it felt unstoppable, like trying to contain an oil spill in the Atlantic.

"Why not stay with your actor friend?" he asked finally. His voice was even, as if he were simply curious, asking, perhaps, why I'd chosen Verizon over T-Mobile.

There was no way in hell I was going to describe what I'd learned from Alex Ottoson, the revelation that would create an irreparable rift between Chris and me.

"It's not like he's my steady boyfriend or anything," I said. "I just figured he had plans tonight."

"Sounds like a kind of casual thing." Again, perfectly even.

"Well, yeah, I guess. I mean, it's not some big exclusive deal."

"I thought you preferred exclusive," he said. An eyebrow went up this time.

"I wanted things to be exclusive with you and me. But that had to do with how I felt about you. I— Look, why are you asking this stuff, anyway?"

"*Why?*" he said, setting down his glass. He straightened up and looked me dead in the eye again. "To be perfectly honest, I don't really like thinking of you with that actor."

"Oh yeah," I said, unable to resist smiling. This was really very funny. "Why? You think I'll go all Hollywood?"

"Yeah, maybe," he said, smiling back. "You'll buy one of those yappy little dogs and carry it in your purse."

"And have Paris Hilton as my bff?"

"I think you know where I'm headed, Bailey," he said, serious now.

"No, honestly, I don't," I said.

"I don't like the idea of you in bed with another guy."

I couldn't believe how this conversation was unfolding.

"Well, what is it that I'm supposed to do about that?" I asked.

"Don't go to bed with him."

"Isn't that pretty unfair on your part? I believe they call that having your cake and eating it, too. Because you want to go to bed with other women."

"I know I told you that I didn't feel ready for any kind of steady relationship. But I realize I was wrong about that."

"So what are you saying, then?"

"I'd like to give it a shot," he said, his voice soft and smooth. "You and me. I want a relationship with you."

I nearly gulped. Here was the declaration I'd been yearning for and had given up on ever hearing. It was coming totally out of the blue, like the wheel of a plane that snaps off midflight and plunges to earth.

"Gosh," I said. "I'm just—I just wasn't expecting this."

"I know I didn't stay in touch, because things were kind of

crazy in Turkey and I didn't know what I wanted and didn't know how to say that. But as soon as I was in New York and had my head on straight, I realized how much I'd missed you and that I did want to be with you. I had every intention of calling you, but after I saw you at Elaine's, I figured you weren't interested anymore."

"Nothing's changed about my feelings," I said. And I knew for certain nothing had.

I'd let my eyes wander because I felt so flustered that I could barely even *meet* his gaze this time, and after a moment my eyes fell on the large ottoman. I flashed on the night he had laid me down on it, pulled off my dress and underwear, and covered every inch of me with his mouth. I blushed, a rush of blood to my cheeks so fast that it felt like a firecracker going off—and when I turned back, I could tell he knew what I'd just harkened back to.

He grinned. Then he leaned toward me and laid his right hand on my left thigh. Underneath, through the fabric of my capris, I felt my skin turn hot. He slid his hand up the length of my thigh and then moved it to the space between my legs. With his thumb he began tracing the seam of my pants, back and forth, back and forth, until I could feel myself trembling.

"Well, since we're both on the same page, why don't we go to bed and remind ourselves of how good it is between us," he said, grinning.

My tongue felt so numb, I could barely talk. So I didn't. I just let things unfold. He reached for my right arm and pulled me toward him, kissing me softly on the mouth and then, after a moment, more urgently. I closed my eyes and let myself just savor the taste of him. His tongue slipped into my mouth, and he began to run his thumb more firmly back and forth between my legs. It was almost unbearable.

I leaned into him, kissing him back deeply. His hand moved from my groin to the buttons on my cardigan. With one hand he unbuttoned the entire sweater and pulled the sides apart. He took my breasts in both his hands, and then reached behind me, unhooked my bra and pulled it down. Now his hands were on my bare breasts, kneading them, caressing them, using his thumbs to circle my nipples in that same deliberate, intoxicating motion he'd used between my legs.

"So what do you say?" he said, pulling back but with his face just inches from mine. "Shall we go to bed?"

"Yes. Though I thought you were partial to ottomans."

He laughed. "Oh, did you like that? Well, why don't we try again—with a variation this time."

As he said the word *variation*, I felt a shot of red hot lust run through me. He worked off my sweater and bra and tugged my pants down. Then he laid me on the ottoman, facedown this time.

"I promise this will take your mind off everything—and you don't have to do a thing."

"Seems awfully selfish," I muttered.

"You'll have a chance later to return the favor."

He began to rub my back with sensuous, hypnotic strokes. One hand worked its way up my neck, and his strong fingers kneaded my scalp over and over again. Then slowly his hands made their my way down my back and my butt, massaging, caressing. It was pure bliss just to surrender, to think of nothing but the pleasure of what was being done to me—and by whom. Slowly he eased off my thong, and I heard it almost silently touch the rug. By the time he slipped two fingers inside me and began to move them rhythmically in and out, I had lost track of my own name.

It took me only seconds to climax once he entered me, and then I just let myself concentrate on Beau's quickening breath, him filling me as he thrust powerfully inside me, and the sounds of his groans as he came and relaxed his weight into me.

Afterward, he poured us each more wine, and we took it

with us to the bedroom, where we had sex again, and finally I could hear his gentle breathing beside me. I was totally, utterly exhausted, but I knew within minutes that sleep had decided to elude me yet again.

I lay still for a while, as still as Beau was, trying to just let go, to ignore that prickly feeling of awakeness, but eventually it overwhelmed me. I couldn't believe I was going to be dogged by insomnia again. I tried gradually relaxing all my major muscle groups, but it was as futile as blowing on a burn.

"You okay?" Beau whispered. He'd been lying on his stomach, but now he turned on his side and spooned me.

"I guess I'm too wound up to sleep. Would you mind if I rummaged through your fridge?"

"Be my guest. There's a quart of milk in there. Isn't that supposed to be good for insomnia?"

"Yeah—or chopping one's head off."

I made my way to the kitchen, a sleek, smallish space with lots of stainless steel, brightened by a large abstract painting of red and gold. As I opened the fridge, I let my eyes explore the few things tacked on the door—a take-out menu from a sushi restaurant, a photo of a small girl splashing in the ocean who I assumed might be a niece. Next to the fridge on the counter was a white ceramic bowl with two oranges and papers that appeared to have been thrown there during a cleanup mission. Another take-out menu, this one from a Mexican restaurant. A Con Ed bill. And one of those small cards that accompany a floral arrangement: "Welcome home, Beau. I missed you."

CHAPTER 17

Oh fuck, I thought. Was this the Daisy razor moment I'd been dreading? Please let it be from his mother, I pleaded in my mind. After all, the kind of mother who forces a wheel of cheese on you is also the kind of mother who would send flowers upon your return home from a long trip. But, of course, it *could* be from a chick.

I wondered if Beau had been honest with me earlier, if he was really ready to forsake seeing other women and date me alone. I worried that a surge of testosterone had prompted him to bullshit me into bed with him. Guys were brilliant at deceiving chicks when they wanted to pants them. But I had no reason right now *not* to believe Beau.

For the first time all night, I thought of Chris—and experienced an accompanying twinge of guilt. It's not as though we'd pledged to have an exclusive arrangement, yet there had been this implied sense of getting into something special. But what did it

matter now, anyway? As far as I knew, he'd totally misrepresented
himself to me as a person, allowing me to believe that he was
Tom's friend and had never had anything but Tom's best interest
at heart. That was totally affecting how I felt.

I took my milk into the living room, where I unzipped my
laptop and set it up. I assumed, rightly, that Beau had wire-
less service, and I went online, checking Web sites for updates
on Locket—nothing yet but endless speculation—and e-mails.
There was a message from Nash, which he'd assumed I'd read on
my BlackBerry—saying he'd heard I was continuing to handle the
press well and that there'd be plenty more tomorrow. There were
also e-mails from the PR team, detailing my responsibilities for
tomorrow. Oh, goody. I had my suit with me, of course, and I'd
do what was required—but I also needed to find the time to talk
to both Chris and Harper as soon as possible. There were loose
ends to tie up as well: I still wanted, for instance, to determine if
Deke had actually repaid (fat chance) the loan to Tom. Certainly
Deke wasn't the person who had prowled around my apartment,
but he may have convinced some chick to do it for him. And I
needed to get to the Chaps Theatre.

After dashing off a few replies, I felt suddenly ragged, almost
shaky with tiredness, as if the day were finally catching up with
me. It seemed as if the sheer power of my fatigue was going
to be able to defeat my insomnia. Before staggering back to the
bedroom, though, I Googled "stalker." Detective Windgate had
piqued my curiosity with his question. I couldn't imagine who
from my own universe might have suddenly decided to stalk me,
but I wanted to at least consider what Windgate had suggested.
Though I'd recently investigated the subject for a piece on a celeb
with an obsessed fan, I wanted to look at the information again
and see if it sparked an idea.

Experts broke stalking down into categories. The types that
showed up most often in films and pop literature were love ob-

sessional—what some experts called "intimacy seekers"—and erotomania stalkers. Intimacy seekers are obsessively in love with their victims, a person they may have once been involved with or just know casually (think Alex Forrest in *Fatal Attraction*). They know their love isn't reciprocated, so they begin a campaign to win over the person—e-mails, letters, gifts. Erotomanic stalkers, on the other hand, are completely delusional. They believe the object of desire loves them back, though in many cases the two have never even met. Everything the victim says and does is interpreted in some way to support the delusion.

The harassment I'd experienced—the nasty calls, the knife in the sink, possibly (but not necessarily) the drugging—didn't bear any resemblance to these types of stalking. But it did fit under the umbrella of predatory or resentful stalking. That was stalking done to cause distress to the victim or frighten her silly, possibly out of a desire for revenge. Was there someone out there who was mad as hell at me over a perceived injustice on my part? I *hadn't* stolen anyone's boyfriend, at least not that I knew of. But could this be someone I'd covered in a story once—a criminal now at large or the girlfriend of a criminal? Or even an individual I'd written about in a human interest story? It was possible that some woman who had eagerly agreed to an interview had experienced negative ramifications from her moment in the limelight and now resented me for exposing her.

But surely if either of those scenarios was what was going on, there would have been an initial tip-off—an angry letter or call, for instance, or a warning from a source of mine that the person wanted to make trouble.

Totally wiped by this point, I snapped my computer closed. With my last reserve of energy, I checked my voice mail. There were a ton of calls—everyone from Landon, to reporter pals looking for info, to my mother congratulating me on my press blitz but chiding me for not letting her know what I was up to.

And there were two calls from Chris. "Where are you?" he asked almost plaintively in one. "I'm going nuts here, and I need to talk to you," he said in the other message. I felt such a weird mix of guilt and anger hearing his voice.

This time when I hit the pillow, sleep overtook me almost instantly. The next thing I knew, Beau was sitting right next to me, touching his hand to my shoulder. The room was filled with a sooty light that meant it was still very early or raining outside.

"I believe your public awaits you," he said, grinning.

"What time is it, anyway?"

"Ten of seven."

"Shit. I set my internal alarm clock, but I guess I was so zonked I never heard it."

"I figured I'd better wake you—I can hear your cell phone buzzing like crazy in your purse."

"Oh God, I better get going."

He ran his hand up just behind my ear, his open fingers firmly stroking my scalp. "I had to resist jumping your bones. I figured you needed the sleep."

I smiled groggily. "Rain check, then. Do you have an iron? I never took my suit out of my bag."

"I'll dig it out for you. I think it still works."

I checked my voice mail—the PR chicks wanting to make sure I was on schedule—and hopped into the shower. It was my first shower at Beau's, and as I dried off with a huge bath sheet, I glanced around the lovely white-tiled bathroom, with its clean, sparely covered surfaces, and tried to imagine myself here on a regular basis. How many nights a week would I sleep over at Beau's? Was it really going to happen? On the one hand, it felt like my destiny to be with him, yet at the same time it seemed like such an elusive concept.

While Beau took his turn in the shower, I chugged coffee and ironed my suit, using the kitchen counter as a makeshift ironing board. I allowed my eyes to be tugged back to the "welcome home" note again. Give it *up*, for God's sake, Bailey, I told myself. The man redefined the phrase *Ottoman Empire* for you last night, so you have every right to believe he's smitten. But as I chased my doubts away, I realized that something else was gnawing at me, some elusive thought that I couldn't snatch. It was not unlike what had happened to me the other night after I'd learned about Locket's death. Only later in the park did I realize that it had been my subconscious jostling me, trying to suggest that I may have goaded Harper into realizing Locket was the other woman. I wasn't sure if my brain was trying to tell me something about Beau or the murders. Hopefully if I were patient and bided my time, I would eventually learn what was nudging me.

Beau walked me to the elevator and suggested, to my relief, that I spend tonight there, too. He was going to be editing late into the day in his studio but we agreed that I'd call him around seven-thirty and we could grab a bite after that. I figured it would be smart to let a day or two pass before seeing him, but I craved being with him again. And I had about as much desire to be in my own apartment tonight as I did to be riding the Lex at four in the morning.

On my way to my first interview I called Windgate, and this time I reached him, not his voice mail.

"Did the crime scene people turn up anything at my place?" I asked.

"It's too early to know anything about the prints we found around the kitchen. But smudging on the knife in your sink indicates that the last person who used it wore gloves. Which means we probably won't turn up anything from any other surface."

"I gave some more consideration to your stalker question," I said. "But I can't think of anyone who might be holding a grudge. This has to be related to the murders."

"I tend to agree. I've put surveillance on your place in case this person shows up again. I want you to let me know if anything out of the ordinary happens."

"Absolutely," I said. His comments had sent a jolt of fear through me, though I felt a soupçon of comfort knowing that the police would be keeping an eye on my building. Oddly, I also experienced that nudging sensation in my brain again. I made a hard grab for the thought, but it escaped my grasp once more.

"And I want you to be extremely careful," he added. "You should talk to your super about security in the building and watch your back when you're out. This person is extremely dangerous."

I wondered if I should volunteer Harper's name. But I didn't want to create trouble for her and taint her reputation if she wasn't the killer.

"I hear you. By the way, is there anything you can share with me about the case in general? There's got to be some kind of up-date." I was hoping he might be inspired to cough up a tidbit in light of how cooperative I was being.

"There is one thing I'll share," he said after a pause. "There was no sexual assault. And Miss Ford's purse was still on her, with three hundred dollars in it."

"What about Alex Ottoson? Is he still a person of interest to you?"

"I can't comment on that."

After signing off, I immediately phoned *Buzz* and dictated a rough update on Locket to one of the deputy editors so it could be posted on the Web site. Then, with a lump in my throat, I phoned Chris.

"Bailey, where've you been?" he said, his voice thick with concern. "It's like you've been off the grid for the past twelve hours."

"I'm sorry," I told him. "I—I've been juggling so many balls. I've had to cover the story and also do a ton of press."

"Did you go to bed last night and just turn off your phone or something? I tried your home phone about twenty times."

"I only managed about an hour of sleep the night before, and I was zonked," I said, skirting the need to tell the lie. "How are you, anyway?"

"Okay, I guess. I mean, I feel sick about Locket—we all do. But it's sounding, at least, as if the show is safe. They had a big meeting with all of us, and though they were vague about details, they told us to be prepared to start shooting Monday—and that they'll somehow write Locket's death into the show. My agent told me that they're auditioning every actress over thirty in Hollywood for the new part. For all I know, I could end up starring with Meg Ryan."

I forced a laugh at his Meg Ryan line, but just hearing him mention his agent had made my stomach knot.

"So as grim as things are, my part seems relatively secure," he added. "At least by Hollywood standards. And I have the rest of the week off, thank God. Do the police know anything more—about Locket *or* Tom?"

"All I know is that Locket wasn't assaulted sexually and she apparently wasn't robbed. By the way, have you seen Harper since we talked yesterday?"

"She was in the meeting we had, offering tips on how to blow off the press, which by the way were staked out around my apartment this morning. Are you still thinking Harper may have done it?"

"Things just keep pointing to her. Didn't you tell me that she once wanted to be an actress?"

"Yeah, but what does that have to do with it?"

"I'll tell you more later. Look, Chris, there are some other things I need to talk to you about. Is there a time when the two of us could meet up later?"

"Is something the matter?"

"I just want to talk face-to-face."

"Sounds pretty ominous." He sighed heavily. "Like I said, I'm off this week, so you name the time."

I suggested six-thirty, figuring that would give me time to finish my press rounds and also swing by *Buzz*. He proposed we meet at his apartment in TriBeCa.

"I can't believe you haven't seen it yet," he said. "It's just been so crazy."

I finished the call just as my cab pulled up in front of the Fox News building. Two members of the PR team were waiting outside for me, both looking as brisk as a spring breeze. This kind of press coverage was a big deal for them, proving that *Buzz* could break hard news rather than simply offer up exclusives on which celebs were sneaking into the trailers of their costars.

Shortly after we were shown to the green room, I was led to makeup. As a solemn woman dabbed at my face with one of those little white wedges, I deliberated on what my strategy should be with Harper. The chances of her taking a call from me or returning a message were next to nil—she'd already indicated just how *unfun* she found talking to me and that I was persona non grata as far as folks at *Morgue* were concerned. I decided I had no choice but to flush her out. Once my face had been painted and my hair sprayed from a can the size of a subway car, I slipped into the corridor and tried Harper's number. "Harper, it's Bailey, and I need to talk to you ASAP," I said. "I *know*—so let's talk."

Maybe *that* would get a rise out of her.

For the rest of the morning, I zipped around in a town car with the PR twins, going to several TV and radio stations. Some of the interviewers tried to drag me into the speculation game—one guy, I swear, would have asked me who I thought killed Natalee Holloway if we'd had the time in the segment—but I stayed with the facts I'd presented in my article and didn't proffer any theories. The older of the PR chicks told me she thought I was doing great, but it would be super if I could smile a bit more. *At which point?* I wanted to ask. *Like when I describe the blood-spattered bathroom I found Tom's charred body in?*

We were done by one o'clock, and the girls told me to keep the car for the rest of the afternoon. I directed the driver to *Buzz* and told him I'd be several hours.

Nash was chomping at the bit for an update.

"At this point, I don't have anything more than I gave to the Web site," I told him. "It's a high-profile case, and everybody's being pretty tight-lipped."

"Who do you think did it?" he asked, peering over his black reading glasses at me.

"Someone who knew her, that's for sure."

"But *who*?"

"I'm not sure."

"Like hell you're not. Tell me what you're thinking."

"Let me dig just a little deeper."

He shook his head in mock disgust. "Bailey," he called as I was walking toward the door.

"Yeah."

"You look damn cute in a suit. When this is over, I'm buying you a celebratory dinner."

Oh great, that's all I needed.

Back at my desk, I brought Jessie up to speed on everything that was going on, leaving out my night with Beau. I wasn't sure why exactly, because I liked her and trusted her and had shared lots about Beau with her. Was it, I asked myself, because I didn't want her to go all pouncy on "Tad Hamilton"?

For the next few hours, I trolled for info about Locket's death, did several more radio interviews from my desk, and kept checking my BlackBerry to see if Harper had responded to my goosing—but there was nothing from her. When I had a spare moment, I called Beverly, something I'd never gotten around to doing yesterday, and asked her to call Barry and determine the exact amount that Tom was due to advance him.

At around five, I finally headed home, almost cross-eyed with fatigue. I still had the town car at my disposal, and I took full advantage, telling the driver to drop me right in front of my apartment building. It was nice to play Cat Jones, my former divalike boss at *Gloss*, but there was an additional advantage to sitting behind those tinted windows: I felt safe, something I doubted I was going to experience at home. I had called Bob from the office and made certain he had warned the other doormen to be extra cautious. I probably should have involved the super, too, but I was loath to throw poor Bob under the bus for failing to follow all the rules earlier.

My door was still double-locked, a relief, and I pushed it open slowly, letting my eyes search through the foyer into the living room. They fell finally to the floor, and I jumped. Just inside the door near my feet was a plain white envelope marked "Bailey." But on closer inspection, I saw that the handwriting was Landon's. There was a note inside, saying he was home and to drop by no matter what time I returned or who I'd "dragged home" with me.

After checking through my apartment and cleaning off surfaces smudged with fingerprint dust, I knocked on Landon's door.

"Dear Lord, Bailey, how could you go totally incommunicado at a time like this?"

"Sorry, sorry," I said as he ushered me into his apartment. "It's been absolutely insane, and I've had to do all these interviews. You didn't catch any of them, did you?"

"Yes, last night. It was on a news show, but they were showing a clip with you from earlier in the day. It took me about sixty seconds to realize it was you because I've never seen you in a *suit* before. You looked stunning, by the way. Do you want an espresso?"

"No, I've got to split in a minute to meet up with Chris. So you know all about Locket's murder, then?"

"As much as I can know from being forced to buy the *New York Post* rather than talk to *you*. I hadn't realized when you first told me about her that she was a former soap star. She wasn't on one of those shows with a title like *One Life to Live*, was she? That would be ironic."

I shot him a mock withering look. "That was not her show, no."

"Well, who do you think did it? Was it a simple mugging that escalated?"

"No way. I'm almost certain that she was killed by a non-stranger who followed her into the park—and that it somehow ties into Tom's death. But there's so much more to tell you. And one thing that's pretty serious."

I described the intruder's visit to my apartment. Landon had gone almost ashen by the time I reached the part about the steak knife in the sink.

"That's absolutely horrifying," he said soberly. "Weren't you nervous staying there last night? You should have called me."

"Well, I was on the verge of doing that, but then lo and behold, Beau Regan phoned and basically announced he wanted to go steady with me."

"*What?* That's—but—but what about Chris now?"

"That's a whole other story, and I need to have about two hours with you to take you up to speed on everything. But let's get back to my intruder. The police are going to be watching the building, and the doormen know to be careful, but can you keep an eye out, too? She was about five nine, average weight, blond hair."

"What time did this all happen, anyway?"

"About six-thirty."

His jaw slackened. "Good God, I was here then. I *heard* her."

"What do you mean, exactly?"

"I was sitting at the desk in my bedroom, and then I heard you—or what I *thought* was you—going through your closet. Your closet, you know, backs up against mine. There was a fair amount of activity in there, so I just assumed you were reorganizing. I was dying to talk to you, so after the noise quieted down I called your home phone, but there was no answer. I assumed I'd just missed you."

I could feel goose bumps on my arms and neck.

"Oh boy," I said. "I wonder what the hell she was doing in there. Look, I better check it out before I meet up with Chris. But I promise to call later."

I opened the door of my apartment, feeling even more wigged out than I'd been earlier. Using a flashlight in addition to the overhead light in my closet, I pawed through my clothes, half expecting another nasty leave-behind, but I didn't find anything. I made another discovery, though. Two of my tops were missing. Though there was a chance they were hanging in a plastic bag at the dry cleaner's, I didn't think so.

It was now almost time to meet Chris. I scrubbed off the layers of makeup I'd worn for my interviews and changed into jeans. The renewed dread I felt about the intruder blended into my dread about meeting with Chris like two water spills converging on a glass tabletop, and it was hard to know which one was worse. As I was swiping on lip gloss, Beverly called me back.

"I have the information you requested," she said. "Tom was going to advance Barry exactly seven thousand dollars."

"Ummm. Okay, thanks."

"Do you mind my asking why it's significant?"

"I was just trying to piece some information together. Someone who borrowed money from Tom claims he paid it back, and

I thought if he had, Tom might have included the cash in his payment to Barry. But he took out exactly seven thousand from the bank."

"I'm sorry I couldn't be more helpful. I wonder what will happen to the house now."

"The parents' financial manager, Mr. Barish, will most likely get involved."

"Mr. Barish? Ugh!"

I froze. "Why do you say that?"

"Tom was upset with him. He wouldn't let Tom handle his money the way he *wanted* to. When Tom wanted to mount the play, for instance, he told this Barish fellow that it was something his parents would have wanted for him, but Barish wouldn't advance him the money. I almost mentioned this when I was telling you about the play, but I hate to tell tales out of school."

That would explain why Barish hadn't had much contact with Tom in recent weeks. Interesting that Barish had not given even a hint of the tiff. I had only his work number, and when I tried him after signing off with Beverly, no one picked up. I left a message asking him to call me immediately. As I broke the connection, I realized that there'd been no word from Harper. Clearly my message hadn't flushed her out as planned.

Leaving my building, I glanced up and down the street. There was no one skulking about, at least from what I could tell. Up the block, two men sat in the front seat of a dark blue car, and I wondered if they might be the police—but they seemed deep in conversation, oblivious to my presence.

By the time I was headed in a cab toward TriBeCa, it was six-forty-five, and by the time I reached Chris's place I was nearly thirty minutes late.

"Hey," he said as he swung open the door. "I was worried— considering everything that's happened."

"Sorry, I should have called," I told him. He leaned down and kissed me on the mouth, and I instinctively jerked my head away ever so slightly.

"Are you about to blow me off, Bailey?" he asked, eyes quizzical after he'd pulled back to look at me.

"No, no, I—I just need to talk to you." I was suddenly a jumble of emotions, the dominant one being anxiety. I was going to demand the truth from Chris, but I wasn't looking forward to hearing it.

He turned and walked into the apartment, expecting me to follow. It was a large loft-style studio apartment, really nice, with high ceilings, exposed water pipes, big windows, and pumpkin-colored wood floors. The kitchen, dining, and living areas were all one room, and a small staircase led to a sleeping area. The only furniture was four bar stools by the kitchen counter and a large cranberry-colored sofa—and there wasn't a lick of art on the walls.

"Great place," I said.

"Yeah," he replied, smirking. "If you love the really, really *spare* look. I just need to spend a day at Pottery Barn. Maybe this is finally the week to do it."

"Well, it takes time to pull things together," I said, a hopelessly dull observation that reflected how freaking awkward I felt.

"I've got a great white wine," Chris said, striding toward the counter. "Why don't we go up to the roof. There's a kind of terrace-garden thing up there."

That wasn't at all what I was up for considering the topic of conversation we were about to embark on—plus, I was supposed to talk to Beau at seven-thirty—but I didn't know how to refuse. After Chris pulled a white Burgundy from the fridge and filled two glasses, I trailed him back through the apartment and up a flight of stairs from the hallway to the roof garden. It was simple but well done, with several boxed trees and weatherproof teak tables and chairs. The lights had come on in the buildings all around us, and in some of the windows I could see people moving about, but we were the only ones on the roof. A light wind lifted my hair from the back, making me shiver.

"So what's on your mind, Bailey?" Chris asked. "Something's clearly eating at you."

I wandered over to one of the tables, and Chris followed behind me. We both took seats. As I stared across the table at him in the waning light, I felt a swell of sadness. Up until now, I'd allowed myself to be mostly angry about what he'd done, but it was more complicated than that. I cared about Chris, we'd had sex together, we'd forged a bond because of Tom—but I'd discovered that he'd done something morally reprehensible. It meant that he wasn't the guy I'd thought he was. And there didn't seem to be any way I could forgive him.

"There *is* something bothering me," I said after taking a sip of wine for fortification. "I found out that it was your agent who leaked it to the show that Tom had been in rehab."

"Who told you that?" he demanded, sounding shocked that I knew—but not surprised at what I'd said.

Suddenly something clattered behind me, and instinctively I spun around.

"It's just the wind rattling one of the planters," Chris said.

"Someone in the know told me," I said, turning back. "So please don't try to deny it."

"I won't deny it," he said, his voice hard. "My agent told Alex Ottoson—and that's how Tom got knocked out of the running for the role I ended up with."

"I can't believe it," I said. "Part of me was hoping that you *would* deny it, that it hadn't happened that way."

I rose from the table, just wanting to get the hell out of there. Chris reached out and grabbed my wrist.

"No," he said. "You're not leaving."

CHAPTER 18

"What?" I said sharply. "I'll leave if I damn well please."

"You can't, Bailey. You have to let me tell you the whole story."

He relaxed his grip, and I tugged my hand away.

"You mean, you had a good reason for what you did," I said sarcastically. "That your success was more important than Tom's?"

"No, it didn't happen like you think it did. I swear."

To my utter amazement, tears began to well in his eyes.

"Okay, shoot," I said, sitting down again.

"When I tried out for the part of the morgue desk assistant, Tom supposedly already had the part of Jared, the one I have now. I hadn't tried out for that myself because it looked like I'd been cast in another pilot for the season. When that pilot fell through, it seemed I'd be *lucky* to get the assistant part and so I agreed to read for it. Plus, my agent kept saying maybe they'd expand the part once they saw my test. He asked me about Tom at the time—like, why he hadn't heard much about him. It seemed purely out of curiosity—a 'Who *is* this guy?' kind of thing. I told him about Tom doing mostly theater and how he went off the radar for a while after losing both parents. I mentioned the rehab just in terms of explaining the low profile.

"Later, when they ended up giving *me* the big role, my agent told me that it was because they'd rethought the part a little, and I was more the physical type they now had in mind. I felt like shit, but Tom seemed to take it in stride. Then late this summer, this lackey who works for my agent spilled the story to me. My agent had apparently told one of the producers under Alex about the rehab. I couldn't believe it. I told my agent to try to fix it, but it was too late."

He heaved out a long, sad sigh and let his head drop into his hands.

"Is that the truth, Chris?" It *sounded* real, but how could I be sure? He was a goddamned actor, after all.

"Yes," he said, looking back up. "I'm as ambitious as the next dude in this business, but there's no way I would have hurt Tom."

"Why didn't you tell Tom the truth once you found out?"

"I couldn't bear to. Plus, I was afraid if he learned what had really happened, it would send him into a tailspin and he might even start using drugs again. This is partly why I was so crazy to find him. I thought maybe he'd heard what had happened from someone else and just bolted because of it."

In the dim light of the terrace, I saw Chris clench his fists on the table.

"Now, of course, I could kick myself for *not* telling him. If Tom had known what had really happened, maybe he would have just bailed on the show. And he and Locket wouldn't be dead."

I felt an emotional jab as I watched his face, faintly illuminated by the two wall-mounted lights. I'd accepted Alex Ottoson's words as the truth. I'd allowed my anger to bloom without ever first asking for Chris's side of the story—and I'd used the info as a reason to sleep with Beau with a clear conscience.

"Chris, I think you probably made the right judgment call at the time. Tom *could* have gone into a tailspin, and he might have bagged the part—which would have been a lost opportunity for him."

"I was looking out for myself, too. I didn't want to rock the boat. It's the same reason I took Locket's note. I didn't want to make any waves that would affect the show."

"Have you called the police yet about the note?"

"No. But I will. I swear."

I took a long sip of wine as I gathered my thoughts.

"Why don't we grab some dinner?" Chris suggested. "We could do take-out here if you want."

"Um, gee, I'd like to, but I still have a few leads to follow on the case." I wasn't lying. I needed to swing by the Chaps Theatre before I met up with Beau. "Maybe we can get together tomorrow sometime."

"What kinds of leads? Are you still thinking Harper might have done it?"

"Yes, she's a definite suspect, but I'm just trying to turn over every stone regardless of whether they seem directly connected to her or not. What I'm hoping to find out tonight is whether that line Tom used from *Taming of the Shrew* meant anything."

"Just be careful tonight, okay? Promise me."

I opened my mouth to tell him about the intruder but decided against it. He seemed pretty shaken up by our discussion, and I didn't want to make things any worse.

"Promise. Look, I better fly now."

Downstairs, by the elevator, Chris hugged me and kissed my

forehead. It was a relief, knowing the truth now, but I also felt like a heel.

"Tomorrow, then?" he asked.

"Absolutely," I said.

As soon as I was on the street, I tried Beau. To my chagrin and annoyance, I reached only his voice mail. True, I was phoning later than I was supposed to be, but why wouldn't he be available?

I gave the cabbie the address to the Chaps Theatre. As I sank into the saggy leather seat, my thoughts raced back to Chris. He hadn't betrayed Tom after all. He *was* the same person I'd always thought he was. Though we certainly hadn't gone to bed with any promise of exclusivity, there'd been an undeniable connection between us, and if he knew what I'd been up to last night, he'd see it as a real breach of trust. I felt the flames of ho hell licking at my ankles. Speaking of which, what the hell was I going to do? Beau was the guy I'd been pining for, and now, finally, I had him, and the thought of that made my heart pound like crazy. But I also felt an attraction to—and bond with—Chris. I had tried chasing him from my brain after the revelation from Alex, but he was there again, after our talk tonight.

The theater was all lit up, and I felt hopeful of finally picking up what I needed. But as I tugged at the door, I found that it wouldn't budge. I glanced at my watch: 8:25. The lobby was empty, and from this angle, at least, I couldn't spot anyone in the box office. I leaned my head toward the door and pressed my ear against the glass. I was pretty sure I heard the rustling sound of muffled laughter from an audience. My guess was that the door had been locked after the last stragglers had arrived, perhaps so the box office person could hit the restroom or take care of another duty in the theater. I would just have to wait until signs of life appeared. There was a small café diagonally across the street, and I headed for it. While I was stepping off the curb, my cell phone rang. Beau, I figured.

But my guess was wrong. The number was unrecognizable. I answered and discovered Harper on the other end. The pheasant had finally been flushed from the woods.

"Do you want to explain that cryptic message you left me?" she demanded.

"I think you know what I was referring to," I said.

I'd wondered if my message might infuriate her, regardless of whether she was guilty, but what I'd never imagined was what happened next. Her voice caught in her throat as if she were about to cry.

"Do you have something *against* me?" she asked quietly. "You keep hounding me, and I don't know why."

"I don't have anything against you. I just want to know the real story."

It sounded as if she choked back a sob. Was it all a damn *act?* I wondered.

"Let's talk, then," she said. "Do you want to come to my place? I don't feel like traveling far. It's supposed to rain tonight."

Not on your freaking life, I was tempted to say. There was no way in hell I was going to be alone in an apartment with her.

"You're in the Gramercy Park area, right?" I asked. "Why don't we meet at the bar at the Gramercy Park Hotel. Twenty minutes from now."

She sighed as a way of agreeing to the location, and I flagged down a cab. I wanted to be sure I was there ahead of her, safely in my seat in the bar.

The Gramercy Park Hotel is on Lexington Avenue, just where it meets the legendary park. The hotel had been totally refurbished into an extravagant, enchanting place with two bars, each opening onto the other. I went to the larger one in the back, a cross—with its velvet armchairs, high, wood-beamed ceiling, sawtooth chandelier, and massive stone fireplace—between Barcelona, a medieval gallery, and *Citizen Kane.*

I found a chair by the fireplace and plunked down, scooting it slightly so I could see the door. Was this going to be it, I wondered, the moment I learned the truth? Was Harper unraveling enough to finally spill everything? Or was this a trap set by a woman so wily that she'd been able to hoodwink my doorman?

Harper was late, and as the minutes ticked by, it occurred to me that she might not be coming, that this was indeed a trap of some kind. But at nine-ten she finally stepped through the doorway dressed in jeans, black boots, and a black turtleneck sweater. She looked spent, like someone who'd been trying to rescue people from rising floodwaters for several days. Her skin was splotchy and broken out, suggesting she was a major stress mess, and there were deep blue and yellow circles under her eyes, like old bruises. Either her grief was getting the better of her, or she was being eaten alive by guilt.

"Would you like a glass of wine?" I asked, pulling over a chair for her. I had ordered a glass of wine myself but was taking baby sips so my head would be clear.

"I'll take care of it," she said, and after flagging down the waiter with a quick whip of her hand, she asked for a single-malt Scotch on the rocks. She wasn't messing around.

I didn't say a word, just waited. She'd indicated earlier that she wanted to talk, and I sensed that the best strategy was to just bide my time—and create a vacuum of silence that she would feel overwhelmed to fill. After her drink arrived, she opened her mouth.

"This is off the record, okay? I agreed to talk to you, but I have no intention of finding myself in that Web post of yours."

"Okay," I said.

She took a deep breath. "Believe it or not," she said, "I really don't respect myself for what I did. I wish I could take it all back."

Oh boy. Was she about to confess to me that she was the murderer?

"Why don't you start from the beginning," I said softly.

Elbows tight against her body, she pressed the tips of her fingers to her mouth, as if trying to prevent the words from escaping. Her penny eyes began to gleam with water. Gosh, I was bringing half of New York to tears tonight.

"Okay," she said, dropping her hands to the table. "I know I was the pursuer in the relationship, but from what I could tell, Tom came along willingly. Right before he disappeared, however, he suddenly seemed to cool down toward me—he was vague about plans, just sort of wishy-washy. I suspected there might be someone else, but I didn't have any proof. Of course, now, thanks to your blog or whatever it is, I know *exactly* what he was up to. I have to hand it to Locket—I never thought she was much of an actress, but she disguised her fling with Tom brilliantly."

The last line was delivered with total scorn, and she took a slug of her drink afterward, as if it would cool down her anger.

"The weekend he disappeared, I'd planned to stay in L.A.," she continued, "but when Tom said his trip to the Hamptons got scrapped, I decided to take the red-eye back. I told him I could now see him earlier than Sunday, but when I arrived home there was a message on my machine saying he'd made other plans for the weekend. I was furious at him for taking off. And that's why I did it."

What? I wanted to scream. But I sat there nearly motionless, an expression (I hoped) of knowingness on my face, as if I knew the truth but was giving her the chance to put it into words.

She took another sip of Scotch and straightened her back.

"I called Alex and used the excuse that we should have lunch that day to review the sweeps PR strategy. But Alex knew what it was all about. He'd been giving me these looks for weeks. So after lunch we went back to his place—Locket was away for the weekend—and fucked each other's brains out."

Oy. So *this* was the info she thought I was privy to. I hadn't seen it coming at all.

"So you're saying the last time you ever spoke to Tom was that Friday night phone call?" I said, pretending not to be nonplussed by her revelation.

"That's right. Up until yesterday, I felt eaten up by guilt. I kept thinking that if I'd convinced Tom to be with me that weekend—and I hadn't ended up with Alex—he might still be alive. Of course, then it turns out Tom had been with *Locket* that weekend. But I'm still disgusted with myself for sleeping with Alex."

"Were you also with Alex Monday night?" I asked, remembering Alex's alibi.

"Yes," she said sullenly. "He came back to my apartment with me after a meeting. I kept thinking that maybe if I *felt* something for the man, I could excuse myself for what I'd done, but it's just not possible. I can't imagine what Locket saw in him."

"Do the police know?"

"They do *now*. Alex gave me as his alibi. I bet it took about two seconds for him to decide to offer me up."

"Was he unhappy in his relationship with Locket? Is that why he cheated?"

"Do you think he lay in bed with me sharing all his deepest feelings? Alex's idea of being self-revelatory is to tell you he once had arthroscopic surgery on his knee."

"What time did he leave your place on Monday?" I asked.

"Around eight-thirty."

"And what time did the two of you split up that Saturday?"

"Midafternoon. *Why*? You're not suggesting Alex killed Tom and Locket, are you?" She straightened her back again. "Or that *I* did?"

It was still a possibility. Locket hadn't gone out until nine, which meant either one of them could have spotted her going into the park—and followed or joined her. The trip to Andes took two and a half hours. If they'd split in the afternoon, either would have had time to drive there that Saturday.

"I'm not suggesting anything," I told her. "I'm just trying to learn the truth. I hear you had a heated discussion with Locket on the set the other day—after I'd hinted Tom had been seeing someone besides you. Did you confront Locket about that?"

"Hardly. Like I told you, I had no clue about their relationship. If you *must* know, Locket was miffed because I wasn't helping more with her book PR. I told her it wasn't in my job description. You really think I might have killed her, don't you?"

"No, I'm not saying that, Harper. But I do have reason to believe the killer might be a blond woman who has acting skills. Someone who can impersonate people and even make her voice sound like a man's. Any ideas?"

"Oh, great. So now you're implying Tom was seeing someone *else*?"

"It's possible the killer is a man, and this woman is simply in cahoots with him. Does Deke ever have anyone like that around? Or even Alex?"

She looked as me as if her wheels were spinning but shook her head. "No one comes to mind."

Surreptitiously, I glanced at my watch. I needed to make my way back to the theater. I thanked Harper for her help and signaled for the check.

"I need to know," she demanded. "How'd you find out about me and Alex? Does everyone else know?"

"The police let it slip," I lied. "I'm not aware of who else knows at this point, but you better be prepared for the fact that news may leak out on the set."

It had started to drizzle when I left the hotel, and it took me forever to hail a cab. My clothes were damp and spongy by the time I collapsed in the back of one. I checked my phone and saw that Beau had finally called—I had turned off my cell phone before entering the hotel so there'd be no interruptions. I wanted to call him back and firm up our plans for tonight, but first I needed time to think.

I hadn't suspected anything between Harper and Alex, but it wasn't tough to accept it. What I couldn't be sure about, though, were her claims of innocence. She was a former actress and now a professional spin doctor, and that meant she was probably a damn good liar. Maybe the whole point of her confessing to me about the booty calls with Alex was to deflect my attention from the bigger crime she was guilty of.

But if she wasn't the murderer, who *was?* There was still Deke hovering in the wings. I wondered if he had a chick in his life, someone who would be willing to play havoc with my mental state by making scary phone calls and going through my steak knives. Maybe Chris would know.

As the cab pulled up in front of the theater, I could see movement in there. An overweight woman with long, lank red hair and thick black-framed glasses (the "I'm hip and live downtown" style) was screwing the cap back on a Pepsi bottle on a small table, left over obviously from intermission. I tried the door and this time it opened.

"May I help you?" she asked gruffly. "The box office is closed."

"I just wanted to see if I could get some information. My name is Bailey Weggins, and I'm curious about a play you did a year or so ago."

"I'm a member of the company—I can probably help you. My name's Natalie."

"*Taming of the Shrew*," I said. "I want to check who was in the cast."

She crinkled her eyes curiously but then cocked her head in

the direction over my left shoulder. "We did it at the end of the winter. The program's up there on the wall someplace."

As she resumed her cleanup, sliding cookies from a paper plate into a plastic tub, I crossed to the other side of the small lobby. It was a shabby space, stuffed with a few worn armchairs and scarred café tables.

From the cheaply framed programs on the wall, I could see that the theater had done an eclectic mix of productions: some of the classics like *Julius Caesar*, *All's Well That End's Well*, Anouilh's *Antigone*, *Six Characters in Search of an Author*, and then a range of contemporary stuff by playwrights unknown, with kooky titles like *Hearts Too* and *Black as Day*.

It took only a second to find *Shrew*. While some of the other programs featured illustrations or photos, this one was fairly simple, with just a border and the words set in a kind of Elizabethan-style type. My eye went instantly to Petruchio and then followed the line to the opposite side of the page: Tom Fain. In that split second, Tom seemed alive, and I felt a gigantic stab of remorse. I dragged my eye down to Katharina and then followed that line. When I saw the actress's name, I gasped. Suddenly it felt as if someone had grabbed me hard by the back of the neck. It was *Blythe* who had played the role. The play had run last February— ten performances. That may have been when Tom had first met Blythe. Was *she* the mystery visitor in Andes? Had Tom quoted Baptista to Locket because it was Katharina herself who had driven up that day?

"Everything okay?" the woman behind me asked.

"Did you know Tom Fain?" I said.

"Of course," she said soberly. "We all did. He was part of this company."

"I'm a friend of a friend, and I'm looking into his death. Is there anything you could tell me about him that might be significant?" I wanted to know about Blythe, of course, but I sensed it was smart not to tip my hand with someone in the theater group.

"No—other than the fact that the guy was a real sweetheart. He was the only actor I ever met who asked questions about *you*. Why so interested in *Taming of the Shrew*? What would that have to do with anything?"

"I'm just following up every lead possible. Was he friends with anyone in the company?"

She pulled off her glasses and turned them around, examining the lenses—for *what*, a smudge? Her eyes seemed much smaller without the lenses in front of them.

"He had a few buddies," she said, sliding the glasses back on. "And he used to date Blythe Hammell, the girl who played Katharina. She's just sick about what happened—as you can imagine."

Every muscle in my body froze.

"Oh, Blythe's around?" I asked as casually as possible, but my voice seemed muffled to me, like the dampened sounds of laughter emanating from inside the theater. My mind was reeling. "I thought she'd gone to Miami."

"She went somewhere south for a while—she had a part in an independent movie down there. But she came back when she heard about Tom."

"And you had a chance to talk to her."

"She dropped by yesterday. She wants to do another play. She thinks it will help take her mind off things."

"Is she a good actress?" I said.

"Blythe? Oh, she's brilliant. The problem with Blythe is that she's a bit of a maniac. The reason she isn't any further along in her career isn't because of lack of talent—she just doesn't realize that you're only entitled to be a *diva* after you've made it."

"Will she be around again?"

"Yeah, but I don't know when."

"She looks like she's on the tall side," I said, thinking of the visitor to my apartment.

"*Tall?*" she said, her tone indicating that her patience was now wearing thin. "I *guess*. She's probably five eight or nine."

She glanced at her watch and gathered up a batch of empty soda liters in her arms. "I need to finish up here. Is there anything else?"

"A cell phone number for Blythe," I blurted out almost desperately. I forced a smile. "I'd love to touch base with her—she might know something."

"You'll have to talk to the manager. He should be around the office tomorrow." She rattled off a number that I hurriedly entered into my BlackBerry.

"I know you're busy, but just one more thing," I nearly pleaded. "Is there a cast shot somewhere—from *Taming of the Shrew?*"

"Over there," she said, indicating another wall.

I hurried over there. Tom was dead center in the shot, his hair very short at the time. Standing next to him was a woman with thick black hair.

"Is this Blythe?" I asked. "With the black hair?"

"Yes, but she doesn't actually look like that," she said. "Blythe's really a blonde, but she's a master with wigs."

Oh, I bet.

When I stepped outside a minute later, I discovered that it was teeming now. Ducking under an awning, I hit Beau's number.

"There you are," he said. "I was worried about you."

"There's a new development," I blurted out. "I'll fill you in when I see you."

"Can you come over now? I want to hear everything."

"It's raining absolute buckets out here. I have to find a cab home first and then one to your place. It may take me forever to get there."

"Why don't I meet you at your place. That means only one trip for you—and it's usually easy to find a cab around here."

I thanked him for the offer and sloshed my way toward Fifth Avenue. A taxi came hurtling down the street, spraying water with its wheels, but as soon as I stepped into the street, a cab poacher leapt out a few yards ahead of me and shot up his hand. It was fifteen minutes before I managed to hail one successfully. I was soaked to the bone by the time I finally threw myself into the back of it.

As soggy as I was and as shivery as I felt, there was only one thought on my mind: Blythe. She was an actress, reputedly a brilliant one. Now I knew why I'd felt that jostling sensation in my brain: The stuff I'd read online about stalker behavior had clearly lined up in my subconscious with the memory of all those cards and notes Blythe had sent to Tom. Although theoretically her behavior was within the realm of what your average red-blooded girl might resort to in the desperate days after being kicked to the curb, it also hinted at a possible obsession. Perhaps Blythe had never gone to Miami at all. She may have been aware of the house in Andes and shown up there that Saturday afternoon. Tom, not knowing how dangerous she was, would have seen her arrival as more of a nuisance. He may have called to her from the window when she emerged from her car, told her to come up to the bathroom. At the time, her intention may not have been to kill him, just make him see reason. When he hadn't, she could have attacked in a frenzy.

Why kill Locket, then? Perhaps she'd actually seen Locket leave Tom's place in Andes and had decided she had to die, too, once an opportunity presented itself. Or maybe she suspected Locket knew something about Tom's murder. But how would she have gotten wind of that?

As I climbed out of the cab in the rain, I glanced anxiously around the area in front of my apartment building. You'd have to be crazy to be out on a night like tonight, but whoever had talked their way into my apartment—Blythe or not—might very well *be* crazy, and I was worried that she'd be back at some point.

Even before stripping off my sopping wet clothes, I did a full under-bed-and-in-closet inspection of my pad—slightly overboard, perhaps, but I knew if I didn't, I wouldn't feel totally safe. The place looked exactly as I'd left it—no daggers lying about tonight. Once I was in dry jeans and a sweater, with water heating for tea, I grabbed my composition book and furiously jotted down notes and questions to myself. Should I go to the police immediately? It was hard to imagine them wanting to investigate Blythe simply on my hunch. A whole bunch of cutesy Hallmark cards spelled heartsick chick, not necessarily dangerous stalker. And the line to Petruchio was hardly a definitive link. Since Tom liked quoting the Bard, you could argue that he might have used that line to refer to *anyone* he was about to have an unpleasant conversation with, not simply someone who was in the play with him. I needed to gather more info before I approached Windgate with my theory.

If Blythe was planning to spend more time hanging around the Chaps Theatre, that could provide me with the perfect opportunity to come face-to-face with her and initiate a discussion. But in order to find out when she'd be there, I was going to have to proceed delicately, or someone might tip her off that I'd been making inquiries. If she were indeed the killer, she would be easily spooked.

The hapless roommate, Terry: That was another avenue to pursue. If Blythe was back in town, she may have made contact and revealed her whereabouts. I tried the number, and Terry picked up on the third ring, sounding as if she'd long since crawled under the covers for the night.

"I'm so sorry to bother you," I told her. "It's Bailey Weggins again."

"I *just* got to sleep. And I've got a presentation on rolling benefits to do tomorrow."

"I'm sorry, but it's really important."

"Yeah, well, actually I was going to call *you*, but I lost that slip of paper with your number. Blythe is back in New York."

"You *talked* to her?" I exclaimed.

"Yeah, she called me. She swears—and I mean *really, really* swears—that she's going to pay me back everything she owes me. According to her, she made a nice chunk of change from the movie she did."

"Is she planning to move back in with you?"

"No, and she won't tell me where she's staying. She won't even give me her cell phone number."

Damn, I thought. "Does she know about Tom?"

"Yes, I told her, and she said she'd already heard. And it was weird—all she said was that she felt sorry but that he wasn't really all that nice of a guy."

"Have you any idea what she's up to?"

"Now that her movie is done, she says she wants to get back into *theater*." She said the word *theater* in a fluttery, mock highfulutin way. "She practically told me to expect to see her as a presenter at the Tonys next year."

"But did she say anything *specific* about her plans, about what she's going to be doing over the next few weeks? Any auditions, for instance?"

"Well, I think she's doing stuff with this theater company she's a member of. It's in the Village. I know she's going there tomorrow afternoon because she said that afterwards she was going to drop by the apartment here and pick up some stuff she left behind. I told her she'd better have a check with her—for the *full* amount she owes me."

"Did—did you mention me, by any chance?"

"I gave her your message—I mean, that's what you *told* me to do. I thought maybe you'd have already talked to her."

"Why?" I asked. There was a stirring of the hairs on the back of my neck.

"Because she seemed to know who you were."

CHAPTER 19

Did she *say* she knew me?" I asked.

"Not in so many words. I could just tell that she did. What's going on now? Is she in some kind of trouble?" She asked the last question eagerly, as if nothing would please her more than learning that Blythe was under suspicion for something like running a giant Ponzi scheme.

"She may be. But you can't let on to her about it."

"I *knew* it. My mother was *so* right about her."

"What time is she supposed to come by your place tomorrow night?"

"Around six or seven. You aren't going to send the cops here, are you? If the super sees them, he could decide to evict me."

"No, no. I might drop by the theater, though, just to ask her a few questions. I know the theater. Did she say what time she's going to be there?"

"I think around four. She's meeting a few people to talk

about a play. You know, maybe I should show up there, too. Then I'm guaranteed to see her."

"But you don't have any leverage if you go by the theater," I said hurriedly. "You've got her things at your place, and you can ask for the check before you hand them over to her." I was scrambling to talk her out of it because Terry would be a major fly in the ointment if she tried to lobby for money from Blythe at the precise time I was attempting to extract info.

"I guess," she said.

"Just do me one favor, Terry. When you *do* see Blythe, it's best not to get into any kind of confrontation with her tomorrow, okay?"

"Okay, okay. Now let me get back to sleep."

I hung up and leaned back into my sofa. So tomorrow, if everything went as planned, I would have the chance to meet Blythe. Would asking her a few questions really give me any sense of whether or not she had killed Tom and Locket in a frenzy of sexual jealousy, of whether or not she was the one who had left a steak knife calling card at my apartment? I didn't know, but that was all I had to start with. My strategy, I decided, would be to tell her that I wanted to interview her for my story for *Buzz* since she and Tom had once dated. I would watch her, listen to her. And see if she gave anything away.

About fifteen minutes later, after I'd wolfed down a grilled-cheese sandwich and tried to decompress, Beau arrived. He was wearing this amazingly sexy black trench coat, damp on the shoulders as if he'd had a hard time finding a cab after all. His hair was wet, too, and his skin was glowing. I had this one totally Harlequin romance moment in which I thought, God, he's here, he *chose* me. I had been convinced that would never happen.

As soon as he'd peeled off his trench and hung it over a dining table chair to dry, we both collapsed on the couch. He said he was dying to know what the new development was. I carefully laid out my theory about Blythe.

"If you're right, it's absolutely chilling," he said. "There's something totally film noir about it. You half expect Blythe to be played by a young Barbara Stanwyck."

"But do you think I could be right? I have no proof whatsoever."

"Let me play devil's advocate. What if Blythe actually *was* making a movie in Miami during this time? Is there some way you can check on that?"

"The roommate didn't have any details. I could certainly find out from *Buzz* if a major studio was shooting a film in Miami recently, but there's no way to know about minor indie films—or grad student projects."

"So where's she been living all this time? And how's she been getting around? She'd need a car to get up to Andes, and according to the roommate, she's always broke."

"We know she's a conniver and extremely manipulative. I'm sure she's managed to mooch off other people—even borrow a car from someone."

"It's pretty clear why she might kill Tom. But why Locket? Just because she'd been sleeping with Tom?"

"That's what I'm assuming for now."

"Why not Harper, then, too?"

"Well, Harper *could* be in danger. Or maybe Harper never struck Blythe as much of a threat on a romantic level. Or maybe Locket was killed because Blythe thought she might know something about the murder."

Beau pushed himself off the couch and paced the room for a few moments, thinking.

"You got the first phone call on the way back from Andes. How would she have known you went there?"

"I've thought about that," I said. "I'm wondering if she may have been hanging around the property and saw me drive up. In fact, she could have been staying up in Andes for a good chunk of this time. You know, it's true that killers often revisit the scene. She may have wanted to know exactly when the body was finally found, so she was keeping an eye out for any activity."

"That's really scary to imagine," he said, plopping back onto the sofa and slipping an arm around my shoulder. "That she was there and may have been watching you."

"But you know, you just made me think of something," I said. "How in hell did she get my cell phone number?"

"Would they give it out at *Buzz* if she called there?"

"Not to just some stranger calling. But she's such a damn good actress—for all I know, she called pretending to be my mother and said she'd lost it. But—but that would mean that on the Thursday I drove up there, only *one day* after I started looking into Tom's disappearance, she'd already gotten wind of the fact that I was, as they say, on the case. How could she have possibly known so quickly?"

"Here's another scary thought," Beau said. "What if she's ingratiated herself with a friend of yours, pretending to be someone else?"

"That's a possibility," I said. "But—you know, as I'm talking about it, the whole theory is starting to sound a bit far-fetched. Maybe I'm completely off base here."

At that same moment, though, I felt something tug yet again maddeningly at my subconscious. I would just have to give it time to surface.

"Have you talked to the police about her?" Beau asked.

"I haven't yet because I felt I needed more proof. And now that I've discussed it with you, I see that I've really got to sort more of it out before I go to them."

"Promise me you won't do anything that's potentially dangerous. If Blythe did commit the murders, she's obviously a real psycho."

Sharing my plan to drop by the theater tomorrow afternoon suddenly seemed like a bad idea.

"Okay, I promise not to hotdog it," I said. "Look, do you feel like a drink or anything? I haven't even offered you one."

"You know what I feel like on such a rainy night? Sharing a bath. Any interest?"

"That sounds like a perfect idea."

While the tub filled up, I lit some candles in the bathroom and poured us each a few splashes of brandy. We set the glasses on the floor by the tub as we slid in. Beau positioned me between his legs, and he spent a good ten minutes massaging my shoulders and neck, working his thumbs into all the tight knots there. It felt delicious, and for a little while, at least, all my thoughts about murderous machinations slipped away.

Before Beau and I went to bed, I ducked into the kitchen and called Harper. I hadn't ruled her out as a suspect, but at the same time I didn't want it on my conscience if anything happened to her. Her voice was low and tight when she answered, suggesting she'd been crying.

"Are you okay?" I asked.

"What do you need *now*?" she asked, not bothering to answer.

"Remember how I mentioned that Tom may have been killed by a blond woman? I now think it might be a girl he was dating before you. There's a possibility she became obsessed with him."

"*Who?*"

"An actress named Blythe Hammell. Did you ever hear of her?"

There were several seconds of silence.

"There *was* an actress," she said finally, "but I never knew her name. He apparently took her to Atlantic City with him just after he and I started dating. Deke derived some pleasure in spreading that around. I was furious, but Tom told me that he'd booked the trip with her weeks before and wanted to honor the commitment. He swore that was the last time he was ever with her."

"Well, like I said, I think she became obsessed with him—and she was convinced that he was in love with her, too. It's what they call erotomania. She may have killed him in a frenzy once she confronted him and realized he didn't care at all. And then she may have been so consumed with sexual jealousy that she killed Locket, too."

"Do the police know?"

"I need to gather a bit more evidence before I present this idea to the police," I said, my voice low. "I'm going to drop by the Chaps Theatre late tomorrow afternoon because Blythe is reportedly going to be there. But I wanted to let you know so you'll take precautions. If Blythe really is the killer, she may be crazy. You could possibly be a target, too, because of your relationship with Tom."

"I can't bear any more of this. I went into PR because it seemed more *sane* than acting."

After I'd signed off, I went back into the bedroom. Beau was propped up on a pillow, the sheet pulled up just to his waist.

"Getting a little glass of milk to help you sleep?" he asked.

"Hopefully, I'm tired enough that I'm not going to need it tonight. I had insomnia really bad a year or so ago, and I dread it coming back again."

"Were you going to bed thinking about your work? That could keep *anyone* awake."

"Actually, it was just after I got divorced. I wasn't sorry it was over, but it's the sort of thing that weighs on you no matter how much you swear you won't let it. I love how all these actresses today rebound so quickly. Two weeks after they announce they're separated, they're dating someone like George Clooney and claiming they've never been happier. We mere mortals require a longer rebound phase."

"I don't know anything about that part of your life."

"Bailey Weggins, the Dark Years. I'll save it for a day when there is absolutely nothing else in the world to do."

"What did your ex do for a living, anyway?" Beau asked.

"His day job or night job?" I said, smirking. "He was a lawyer—criminal cases. I met him on a story I was doing. But it turned out he was also a compulsive gambler who had loan sharks pursuing him with tire irons, and it took me way too long to figure that out. At first I thought he must be having an affair, and then I even wondered if he might be gay. I should have been asked to turn in my press credentials for being such a lousy reporter when it came to my own life. But look, let's save the gory details for another time. You told me last night that I'd have my turn to focus attention on you. Why don't we try that tonight?"

"As long as I can leave the light on," he said, laughing. "This is something I'd like to watch."

We made love in the light and then again in the darkness. It was a little different from the other times we'd been together—slower, more languorous, but just as intoxicating. As relaxed as I felt, my mind went crazy as soon as my head hit the pillow, with thoughts about the murders ricocheting from one side of my brain to the other. I kept replaying everything I'd heard about Blythe, wondering if she was indeed the stalker-killer. I also contemplated how I should handle her if I *did* get the chance to talk to her.

For a few minutes, I thought of Chris, too. I'd believed the worst of him and had told myself that I never wanted to be with him again romantically. I'd gone to bed with Beau assuming that it was over with Chris. But Chris wasn't guilty of the crime I'd thought, just of being as ambitious as the next person in his business. I was thrilled that Beau had decided he wanted to make a go of it with me, but that meant I was going to have to break off my relationship with Chris, and the odd thing was, that made me sad. As I'd realized last night, I still felt an attraction to Chris. What a mess.

Overwhelmed by that mess, I fell asleep after only about thirty minutes of brain burn. I awoke the next morning to the distant ringing of my cell phone in my purse. It was one of the PR twins, rattling off the drive-time radio shows I needed to do. While I conducted one interview over the phone in my office, Beau showered. We ended up with only a few minutes together, chugging coffee at my dining table.

"You're great on radio," Beau said. "I overheard it."

"I'd much rather be *asking* the questions, but of course these days if you're press, you have to *do* press, too. Nash told me that he actually looks for staffers who are *mediagenic*. I should be writing off my highlights on my income tax."

"Ah, another secret I've managed to procure before leaving. It's only a matter of time before I figure you out, Bailey."

I laughed, but his remark gave me pause. I probably *did* hold back with him. But it was in part because *he* was a mystery of sorts. He didn't seem closed off, but his quietness at times, the way he had of studying me without saying anything, left me with the sense that I just didn't know what was really going on behind his eyes at all times.

"When do you plan to speak to the police today?" he asked.

"Soon," I said. "I'll probably call them right after you go." My legs were crossed beneath the table, easing my guilt slightly.

While he slipped into his trench coat, Beau mentioned that a friend from out of town had called a few days before and asked if he could crash at his place for the night.

"It's the last thing I need since I'm just catching up after Turkey—plus I'd really like to be with *you*—but he's too good a friend to say no to. Can we skip tonight and spend the weekend together?"

"That sounds nice. I just have to stay a bit flexible because of doing press, that sort of thing."

"Call me today and let me know what's happening. I want to be sure you're safe and sound."

The kiss he gave me was long and intense, and my heart was pounding as I shut the door. A week ago, I had given up hope of ever being with Beau again, but now everything had changed. I had no choice but to let Chris know things were over with us. Yet I couldn't stand the thought of doing that.

After pouring another cup of coffee, I made several calls to contacts I had in the police department to see if there had been any break in the case, but I heard the same word from each source: No definite suspects, no arrests. Though Alex Ottoson initially had been a person of interest, one source acknowledged that he'd produced an alibi that had checked out. I wondered if the news about Harper had started to leak out.

I really wanted to see a good photo of Blythe before I showed up at the theater, but I didn't want to tip off the theater manager that I was coming by—in case he told her. It suddenly occurred to me that she might have a Web site. I found it under her exact name, but the words *Under Construction* were all that came up on-screen.

Going over my notes, I realized that this would be a good time to try Barish again, since I hadn't heard back yet. A young woman answered. When I said my name, she hesitated, as if she'd been told to be on the alert for a call from me. She asked me to hold and then came back a minute later announcing that Mr. Barish would be with me shortly. I wondered if she was the same woman I'd seen in the office on Saturday.

The man who picked up the phone a minute later was the

nice and friendly Barish, his first comment an apology for not returning my call.

"September is a very busy time for us. We're coming up on the final, final deadlines for filing all tax returns. What's going on with the case? I heard the news about Tom and the Ford woman."

"I have one piece of news. The amount Tom was going to advance the handyman was exactly the amount he withdrew from the bank. So if Deke gave him a few thousand dollars that week, Tom did something else with it."

"This Deke fellow seems very suspicious to me. I hope the police are taking him seriously as a suspect."

"I wouldn't know. Any word on when Tom's body will be released—so that a funeral can be arranged?"

"They keep promising any day. Was that your urgent question?"

"Well, I was interested in learning when the funeral will be. But I had another question for you. Were you and Tom on speaking terms during the last weeks of his life?"

"I beg your pardon?" he demanded testily.

"I've been told that things were strained between the two of you—that Tom didn't like the way you were dealing with him on money matters."

"What in the world would make you say that?"

"Tom said as much to people."

"I was very fond of Tom, but as I told you, he was not my client—his parents were. And it's—correction, it *was*—my fiduciary duty to make certain, as his parents desired, that Tom's financial future was protected. That meant saying no to the occasional whim on his part."

"But—"

"I'm not at liberty to say any more. The Fain family finances are a confidential matter. And they don't involve you at all. Now, I must get back to my work. Good day."

As I listened to dead air, I realized that I'd hit a nerve of some kind with Barish. Why was he being so defensive? I wondered. Had Tom stopped speaking to him simply because of the play, or was something else going on? What if Tom had discovered that Barish was guilty of an impropriety with his money? My fingertips suddenly felt icy. I had never once considered Barish a suspect, but maybe I'd been stupid not to look at him that way. Barish had certainly known about the house in Andes.

I would have to find a way to look into the matter, but today there was Blythe to contend with. I glanced at my watch; it was just before noon. Based on the facts that Terry had shared, I figured my best bet was to show up at around four-fifteen. If I was too early, I might arouse suspicions. If I was too late, I might miss her.

So that meant cooling my heels for the next few hours. I made more calls to my sources, perused online sites, drank coffee, left a message for my mother saying I was alive and well, paced around my apartment, and pushed aside thoughts about the freaky state of my love life.

At three-thirty, I finally threw on a trench, grabbed an umbrella, and departed for the Chaps Theatre, figuring that if I saw a cab, I'd grab it, but otherwise I would walk. There was only one word worth using to describe the day, weatherwise: raw. The sky was low and bruised looking with clouds, though at the moment it was spritzing rather than raining, which in some ways was even more annoying. No matter how I positioned my umbrella, water sprayed at my face.

I could tell even before I reached the theater that I was out of luck. No light fell from the windows onto the sidewalk. I tried the door anyway. It was locked. I rapped several times on the glass just in case, but it was totally dark inside, and it was clear no one was there. Damn.

But that didn't mean Blythe wouldn't eventually show—it was still relatively early. I jumped a large puddle just off the curb and dashed diagonally across the street toward the café I'd noticed the other night. After ordering a cappuccino, I positioned myself at a table by a window in the nearly empty room. From this far down the street, I had no view of the door of the theater, but if someone turned on the lobby lights, I'd be able to see the reflected glow on the slick sidewalk.

For the next fifteen minutes, I sipped my drink distractedly and peered outside. Nothing happened. Once I got up and checked outside, just to make sure I hadn't missed anything. The waiter shot me an aggravated look when I returned, as if he thought I'd been attempting to skip on the $3 tab or was waiting to do a coke deal in the street. I paid the bill and waited some more.

Minutes later, I glanced up and saw that the sidewalk directly in front of the theater was now gleaming with light. I willed myself to stay calm, but as I punched my arms frenetically through the twisted sleeves of my trench coat, I could tell how anxious I was.

It had started to really rain, and I dashed down the street, not bothering to open my umbrella. When I peered in the glass door of the theater, I saw that the lobby was empty, but I heard the faint sounds of music. I knocked on the glass a few times. No response. I tugged at the door, and to my surprise it opened. Inside, I could hear the music better now—it was some kind of rock, playing from around the back of the theater to the left.

I decided not to announce myself by calling out a hello. That would likely bring someone to the lobby, who would then go back and explain my presence to anyone else who was there. It just seemed smarter to catch Blythe unawares. I snuck over to the double black doors to the actual theater and quietly opened one a crack. The lights were down, except for one floor lamp with a bare bulb standing forlornly on the stage toward the front. A friend had once explained to me that in the theater world there used to be a superstition that if the theater was left totally dark at night, it might become haunted, so a "ghost light" was always left burning on stage to discourage any spirits from taking up residence. It's a practice that's followed even now.

Though the bare bulb created only one circle of light, I could see some of the pieces that made up the spare set: two twin beds with pink bedspreads, two desks, a shag area rug. It must be, I realized, where the coeds from hell spent their nights.

I eased the door closed again and decided to follow the music. To the left of the box office was a corridor that seemed to lead to where it was coming from. I made my way past two doors, each marked RESTROOM, and a small kitchen with a light burning. On the countertop were several liters of soda and a few Tupperware tubs with cookies inside, obviously the refreshments for tonight's intermission. Next door was an office, darkened, and then the corridor veered to the right. This seemed to be the official backstage area. The music was growing louder.

I heard a creak behind me suddenly and spun around.

"Hello?" I called out. The hallway, up to the bend, at least, was empty. "Is there anybody here?"

There was no reply. I waited a moment but heard nothing. I proceeded on.

The first room on my right was a narrow, shabby makeup room. Mirrors lined one of the long walls, and on the counter sat five identical white plastic wig heads. No humans, though. I kept going. I passed a messy storage room filled with props, a vacuum cleaner, period furniture, and large plastic tubs stuffed with what I assumed were costumes and more props, and then finally the room where the music was coming from. It appeared to be a dressing room. More mirrors, odd chairs strewn about, two stained, beige Victorian-style clothing forms without a stitch on, and a radio/CD player. Snow Patrol was singing "Chasing Cars." But there wasn't a soul in sight.

As I turned away from the doorway, I heard another noise. Above me. It seemed to be the sound of a chair scraping—and then footsteps—on the second floor. That, apparently, was where people had gathered. I hurriedly retraced my steps along the corridor toward the front of the theater. As I stepped into the lobby, a woman with reddish-brown hair and dressed in a baggy beige sweater and black pants emerged from the doorway on the far side. I started to open my mouth to explain my presence, then realized it was Terry. Crap, I thought.

"So you decided to come after all," I said, barely able to contain how less than thrilled I was with this development. Terry offered a self-satisfied smile, as if she were the brightest bulb in the box. She didn't have a hat on today, so I had a closer look at her reddish brown horsehair. It was about the weirdest color I'd ever seen.

"After I talked to you, I decided I was stupid to wait around for Blythe to bring the money to me," she announced. "I knew she might never show. So I decided to come here, just like you. And guess what? I got the check." She tapped her big brown shoulder bag for emphasis.

"So Blythe is here now?" I exclaimed.

"She's upstairs. But she's not staying long, so if you want to see her, I'd hurry."

"Where exactly is she?" I asked, starting to move.

"In the office on the second floor. You just follow the hallway and take the first set of stairs up, and there's a door at the top. You go through into a little hallway, and then there's another door to the office."

"You didn't tell her I called, did you?"

"No, I *said* I wouldn't, didn't I?" she proclaimed petulantly. She turned away and crossed the lobby, heading toward the exit.

"Is Blythe alone?" I called out to her back.

"No, one of the other theater geeks is with her."

Good. I certainly didn't relish the idea of being alone with her in the theater.

I made my way through the door Terry had come through and followed the hallway. This passageway was narrower than the one on the other side of the theater, though it eventually widened nearer the stage. I peeked through a curtain to the stage, lit eerily by the bare bulb. That was where Tom had performed, I realized, dreaming of one day being a star.

To my right was a set of stairs—just one flight with a landing at the top—that was clearly the one Terry had referred to. There was no light at the top, but there was enough light from the hallway for me to see my way up. I climbed the stairs, my ears pricked. From where I was now, I could no longer hear the music, and the theater was totally hushed.

The door to the left at the top was black metal, scuffed and dirty, with a bolt beneath the handle that had been drawn. Odd to have a bolt on this side, I thought. What were they keeping up here, anyway—Mr. Rochester's first wife? I put my ear to the door and listened. There were no sounds of conversation or activity, but then Terry had said I needed to go down a hallway before I reached the office. I paused for a moment, thinking. Something was gnawing at my mind again, but it felt totally unformed.

I reached for the handle and yanked, and after pulling open the door, I automatically lifted my foot to take a step forward. As I peered ahead, I saw that rather than a hallway, I was looking at a wall of cottony grayness, lit from below. In a second that seemed to last forever, I realized that the space I was stepping into was only air.

My mind yelled for me to pull back, but it was too late. I pitched forward, scrabbling with my hands for something to grab hold of. As my left leg slipped off into nothingness, my right hand found something hard and metallic above me to grasp. A half second later, my right leg followed the left into the abyss below. And then I was dangling.

My brain seemed to split in two. Part of it thrashed in complete terror and confusion over what was happening to me. The other observed it all calmly, as if I were watching a documentary called *Girl Falling off Edge*. I realized that I had stepped through a doorway that opened onto a space high above the stage. I had grabbed a metal chain across the doorway and was now hanging by my right hand. If I let go, I would fall and possibly die. At the very least, I would break my neck.

Straining, I reached with my left arm upward as high as I could and managed to grasp the metal chain with that hand, too. I was suspended now like someone holding on to a trapeze, facing the doorway, with a grid of black stage lights just off to my left. The chain, I could see, had been strung across the door as a final but pathetic barrier. The real protection against someone falling, the bolt on the door, should never have been undone.

"Help!" I screamed. "Help me!" I tried to maneuver my right leg back up onto the landing, but I was hanging so low that it was impossible. I steeled myself to take a look below. My stomach turned over at the sight of the stage floor and the ghost light below. The drop was easily fifteen feet.

"Help, help!" I screamed again. As my body dragged on the chain, the links cut painfully into my palms, and my arms started to ache. I didn't know how much longer I could hold on. Suddenly, I heard the sound of footsteps. Someone was coming up the stairs to the landing. The person was moving slowly, like someone old and tired—or someone deliberately taking her time. Please, I begged in my mind, don't let it be her.

But it was. As the footsteps reached the landing, I craned my neck back and saw Terry looming above me, a snicker on her face. But it wasn't Terry, of course, under that hideous wig. It was Blythe.

"Oh dear," she said. "I should have told you to watch that first step. It's a killer, isn't it?"

CHAPTER 20

"Help me up, will you?" I pleaded. "Don't make things any worse for yourself."

"You know what?" Blythe said. "You are *absolutely* right. What was I thinking?"

And then she hoisted her big purse above her head and brought it down as hard as she could on my hands.

My knuckles stung from the blow, but I didn't open my hands. From sheer terror, they remained glued to the metal. But I knew Blythe wasn't going to stop at one measly swipe from her handbag.

I glanced down to the stage floor again. There was a chance, if I let myself drop straight down, feet first, like someone jumping from a diving board, that I might only break an ankle or a leg, but the thought of just letting go was terrifying. As Blythe brought up her purse again, ready for another strike, I glanced to the left. Hanging from the light grid was a long, thick rope, some kind of pulley, it seemed, connected to the lights. I mentally measured the distance to it. If I could scoot across the chain, I might be able to swing my legs out and grab hold of the rope with them. But I couldn't let on to Blythe what I was up to.

The second blow was even more forceful, and I had to fight the urge to both scream and unclench my hands from the chain. As Blythe stepped back, plotting her next move, I inched my hands quickly down the chain. There was a groan from the door frame as the screw on the right side protested the strain. Blythe might not even *need* a next move. There was a chance that the chain would just be ripped from the door, and I would end up hurtling to the stage below.

"Now, now, be careful," Blythe admonished as she heard the sound. She couldn't keep the delight off her face.

I was within reach of the rope finally—or at least my legs were. There was no way I would be able to use my arms in the process, so I was going to have to grip as tightly as possible with my thighs. But first I needed to find momentum. I looked up toward Blythe, my neck aching from the angle I was holding my head.

"The cops are coming," I told her, trying to shift her attention. "They're going to meet me here."

"That's not true, and you know it, Bailey," she said in an exaggerated chiding tone. "You're trying to tell me a *really* big lie—and I don't like that."

"Do you think I'd come here alone? Of course I called the cops. I told them to meet me at the theater because you were going to be here. They know all about you."

She made a *tsk-tsk* sound. "Do you think any woman who has her apartment decorated in shabby chic style like you do—that is *soooo* nineties, Bailey—would be smart enough to call the police? I know you didn't. I've seen you—and you like doing things all by your little self."

She straightened up and flicked her head back and forth in a maniacal gesture of disagreement. The door frame groaned again, louder this time. My arms were starting to quiver. If I was going to move, I was going to have to do it now.

I slung my eyes to the left. In one swift move, I thrust my left leg and then my right one over and coiled them around the rope, and then as I did so, I drew the rope closer to my body. Out of the corner of my eye, I saw Blythe pull back, startled, unsure of what was going on. Reaching as far as I could, I grabbed the rope with my left hand and pulled myself over there. As I let go of the chain, I heard it snap from the door frame. Two seconds later it reached the stage floor with a loud thwack.

I was now hanging perilously from the rope by just my left side, like some Cirque du Soleil performer. "You little bitch!" Blythe screamed at me. With the help of some muscle memory from a gym class fifteen years ago, I managed to lift my torso fully toward the rope, clenching it with my other hand.

For a few short seconds, I just hugged the rope. My body was nearly trembling with fatigue, and my legs stung from rope burn. I needed to keep moving, though. I'd outsmarted Blythe for one brief moment, but if she reached the stage before me, it wouldn't do me any good.

Loosening my grip slightly, I began to slide down the rope, trying to ignore the burning sensation on the insides of my arms. I craned my head to the right to see what Blythe was up to. She was on the landing, watching me, but as soon as our eyes met, she spun around, and I could hear her clattering down the stairs I'd come up earlier. I loosened my grip to increase my speed downward toward the stage floor.

Without warning, the light grid, which was attached to the rope, rammed against the ceiling. I hadn't realized that the rope was a pulley to raise and lower the grid. The rope jerked in my hands, and before I knew what was happening, I had lost my grip.

I hit the floor hard, collapsing in a heap, and in the same instant, my right ankle made a popping sound. Pain shot through my foot like a loud scream.

I lay on the ground long enough to gather my strength and then struggled up to a standing position. I wasn't sure if I'd broken or sprained my ankle, but it hurt like hell. I looked all around me. At any second, Blythe was going to come charging through the door at stage left. The best escape route for me would be stage right, but even then she could easily catch up to me. I swept the stage with my eyes, looking for a makeshift weapon. Leaning against the dresser by the fake wall at the back was a field hockey stick. I limped across the scuffed stage floor and grabbed it.

Something was weird, though. Blythe should have been down the stairs by now. Was she going to try to ambush me somewhere else in the theater as I tried to escape? All I knew was that I had to get out of there.

I staggered across the small stage, toward the door that I knew led to the corridor lined with makeup and dressing rooms. Suddenly Blythe appeared in the doorway, ten feet ahead of me, her hands behind her back as if she were about to present me with a fun birthday surprise. She'd obviously gone down the stairs and circled around to the other side of the theater.

"Ahh, I should have known you played field hockey, Bailey," she said, her eyes wide in mock fascination. "Even with all those hip little clothes of yours, I could sense you were a preppy at heart. By the way, I hope you don't mind—I took a few of your tops when I was over at your place the other day."

"Blythe," I said, trying to sound calm, "why don't you stop this now and make it better for yourself."

"Oh, you want me to believe that not killing you will make it *better* for me? Bailey, I keep getting the feeling you don't think I'm very smart."

"Oh, I think you're *very* smart. And very talented. You totally fooled my doorman, you know."

"Please, that hardly deserves an Oscar. Sure, I imitated your voice, but that doorman of yours has a brain the size of a lichee nut."

"How'd you nail my voice?"

She smiled coyly. "I heard you at the Half King. I was standing right by you at the bar the whole time."

The pack of girls next to me. There had been one hanging off to the side, and that must have been Blythe.

"So you put the drug in my beer—and texted Chris?"

"If you say so."

"What have you got against me, anyway?"

"You got all snoopy, Bailey. Coming around my apartment, leaving me all those messages, bugging poor Terry."

"Where's the real Terry, anyway?"

"She said she was going away on a long trip. You know, the health insurance business is *hopelessly* boring."

I wondered if Blythe had killed her, too—weeks ago.

"Tell me about Tom, will you?"

"Bailey, if I'm not mistaken, you're doing that stalling-for-time thing. I really don't have the patience for that."

"I want to hear your side of the story—really. You drove up to Andes to see him?"

"Do you know, Tom never told me he had a place there? Maybe he secretly wanted to surprise me when he got it all fixed up. But I'd been doing a little research on Tom, and I found out about the house. Needless to say, I was very, *very* disappointed to see he was there with another woman, someone who was not only beneath him, but a very bad actress as well. And did you *see* that woman's lips? She looked like a hippo."

"So you killed Tom out of jealousy?"

She snickered. "No, Bailey," she said firmly. "I broke *up* with

Tom that day. And I could see by his reaction that if he couldn't be with me, he didn't want to live. He pleaded with me to put him out of his misery. Thank God I'd found that axe out by the barn."

"Why the fire? Was Tom dead by then?"

"I'm not *cruel,* Bailey. Of course he was dead. I just couldn't look at his face anymore. FYI, paint thinner is an excellent accelerant."

"And then you went back to your place—not Miami?"

"If you say so. If you must know, one night I even stayed at Tom's for old time's sake. I promised him I would." That explained the light left burning.

"What—"

"Who do you think you are—Oprah? I'm getting really tired of answering all your questions."

"Just tell me about Locket," I said. I was trying to keep my voice easy, casual, despite my fear and the blinding pain in my ankle. "Why her? She wasn't a threat anymore now that Tom was dead."

"Locket was another snoopy dog, just like you. I could tell she knew something—she was talking to you about it."

"You—you were the girl in the visor?" I said, stammering. "The one who asked about Locket's dog at the Boathouse?" It had to be, I suddenly realized. The girl had seemed so intrusive.

"Oh, Bailey, you think you know all my tricks, but you don't."

With that, she pulled her right hand out from behind her. It clutched a black-handled butcher knife with a glistening blade about eight inches long. My body felt leaden with fear.

"Don't you know the police will figure this out?" I told her. "They'll know you were here today."

She laughed too loudly. "But you see, Bailey, I have my own private key to the place, and no one knew I was coming except you." She laughed again. "And Terry, of course. But like I said, she's not available for comment these days."

I tightened my grip on the hockey stick, sensing that she was done talking and was going to take some kind of action now. Turning my head slightly, I calculated how long it would take her to catch up with me if I made a mad dash toward the door on stage left. Only seconds because of my ankle. As I turned my head back in Blythe's direction, she made her move, lunging toward me with the knife.

I raised the hockey stick and whipped it across her body as hard as I could. I had hoped to dislodge the knife from her hand, which didn't happen, but she reeled back in pain from the blow.

"You little bitch!" she screamed. "How dare you do that to me?"

She shifted her grasp on the knife and raised it above her head in a stabbing position. And then she lunged once more.

I swung the hockey stick at her again. But just before contact, Blythe raised her free arm and managed to grab the stick. She jerked her arm to the right, and the stick went sailing out into the theater. It bounced and clanged over the backs of several seats.

"Oops," Blythe said, and formed her face into an expression of grossly exaggerated glee.

I shot a glance to the set on my right. There was nothing else there that could help me, just the beds and dressers and pink shag rug. I started to back up, careful not to edge too close to the end of the stage, my ankle hurting so much that I could barely think over the pain. On my fourth step back, I bumped into the ghost light, just behind me and to my left. It rocked slightly and then steadied itself.

Blythe puffed up her chest, ready for another strike. And then she charged. Taking one more step backward, I grabbed the lamp with both hands. It was sturdy but lighter than it looked, probably made of hollow metal. Like a little kid holding a light saber,

I swung it as hard as I possibly could. Suddenly the lightbulb went out as the cord was yanked from the socket; a moment later, in total darkness, I felt the lamp make full contact with Blythe's body.

There was a thud and a burst of air from her lungs. I could hear the scuffing sound of her shoes as she staggered on the stage. Then, suddenly, I realized she was airborne. A second later, I heard her crash hard into the seats below the stage.

I squinted, trying to see. A little bit of light was coming from the corridor off stage left, the one with the stairs I'd taken. I dropped the lamp, and with my hands out in front of me, I staggered off the stage in that direction.

Once I was in the corridor, I could finally see again—there were wall sconces burning along the way. Dragging my right leg, I made my way as fast as I could down the corridor, retracing the steps I'd taken earlier. Approaching the lobby, I heard movement out there. My heart stopped as I wondered if Blythe had quickly managed to right herself and hurry up the main aisle of the theater.

But as I peered out into the lobby, I could barely believe my eyes. Detective Windgate was standing out there, along with a small man of Asian descent.

I limped into the lobby, and Windgate pulled his head back in surprise.

"What in God's name is going on?" he demanded. Both men glanced down at my bum leg, searching for the injury.

"Blythe Hammell is in there," I blurted out. "She tried to kill me with a knife, and I knocked her over, into the seats. She must be hurt—but I don't know how badly."

Windgate shot his partner a look of exasperation and turned back to me.

"You stay right here, do you hear me? If I find out you moved a muscle, I'm going to arrest you."

"Okay," I said meekly.

"Which is the best way to get there?" he asked brusquely.

"I'd go right through there," I said, pointing to the double doors that opened into the theater.

As I collapsed into one of the saggy old armchairs, they stepped across the lobby and with guns raised swung open the doors cautiously. The light from the lobby poured into the theater. It was still fairly dim in there, but they would be able to see where they were going,

"She's probably in one of the front two rows," I called out in a loud whisper. I watched as they made their way down the aisle.

It didn't take long for them to find her. I heard one of the cops talking, and then Blythe began ranting, though I couldn't make out anything she was saying. At least I hadn't killed her. That would have been a real mess.

I kept my word and didn't move a muscle, which would have been difficult to do anyhow considering the sorry state of my ankle. Now that I had a chance to look, I could see that it was swollen up as if I had a tennis ball under my skin.

About five minutes later, Windgate came sprinting back up the aisle into the lobby. Just as he arrived, two cops in uniform rapped on the glass door to the lobby. Windgate motioned them in and told one of them to assist "Detective Kwong" and the other to search the premises.

"Do you know if there is anyone else on-site?" he asked me.

"No, but they've got a show tonight, so people should be arriving before long to set up. What made you come here, anyway?"

"You can thank the PR director for the show—Harper Aikins. She got a phone call from someone who claimed to be you but didn't seem familiar with a conversation that the two of you had engaged in. She thought it might be this woman Blythe since you'd worked her into a frenzy on the subject. Miss Aikins called me and said you planned to come here to meet Blythe. You know, I made it very clear to you that you needed to watch your back."

"But until tonight I just wasn't really sure that Blythe was the killer."

"How bad are you hurt?"

"It's just my ankle. Hopefully it's only a sprain."

"I've got two ambulances coming. Until they arrive, we need to find a place to talk."

I told him about the dressing rooms, and after I'd reassured him I could make it back there, he helped me hop to the closest one. I took a seat on a small bench while Windgate went into the kitchen for ice. He returned two minutes later with a chunk of cubes in an old dish towel, which I laid carefully against the swelling. Windgate dragged over a chair and sat next to me.

"I'm going to hold off on the questions for a minute," he told me, his voice firm. "Why don't you start with your version of events."

"*My* version?" I said. "That sounds like you're entertaining another one."

"Miss Hammell claims you lured her here and tried to kill her."

"You can't possibly believe that," I exclaimed. "She's the one who lured *me* here and tried to kill *me*. And she's the one who murdered Tom and Locket. She *admitted* it to me."

Windgate eyed me skeptically, stroking his mustache methodically. I couldn't tell if he was really suspicious of what I was saying or was just acting that way to scare the pants off me—and make sure I coughed up the entire story.

"Blythe also happens to be a very good actress who's going to tell you a pack of lies," I continued. "She's the one who talked her way into my apartment after pretending to be me on the phone. She's also been impersonating her roommate, Terry. For all I know, she killed Terry, too."

I was talking too fast and sounding way too defensive, but I was suddenly overwhelmed by the idea that Blythe could manipulate this whole situation and possibly land me in trouble.

"Okay, relax," Windgate said. "I want to know exactly what you've been up to since the last time we talked—when you promised me you'd be careful and behave yourself."

Figuring he didn't mean *everything,* I skipped any mention of ottoman sex and related how I'd come to the Chaps Theatre to follow up on the clue from *Taming of the Shrew,* how Blythe had tricked me into going through the doorway after obviously undoing the bolt beforehand, and how I had been forced to defend myself with the lamp like a Jedi warrior after she'd tried to attack me with a knife.

"So you're saying that you came to this brilliant conclusion about Blythe Hammell as the killer because of a line from Shakespeare?" Windgate asked doubtfully. He folded his arms against his brown tweed jacket and leaned back in his chair.

"It wasn't any kind of brilliant instant conclusion," I said. "I'd just always wondered if the quote from *Taming of the Shrew* meant anything, and I decided to check it out. When I saw Blythe's name on the cast list for the play, I realized there was a chance that *she* had been the visitor in Andes that day. You'd prompted me to think about stalkers, and I suddenly saw that maybe Blythe had done more when Tom dumped her than send a bunch of silly cards. Maybe she'd become obsessed with him. But I really wasn't sure of any of it. I thought if I talked to Blythe, I'd get a feel for what she was like. If something seemed off, I was going to call you immediately."

"What do you mean, she's been impersonating her roommate?"

"She showed up here pretending to be her roommate, Terry, just as she had when I first went by her apartment. You've got to try to figure out where Terry is. Blythe may have killed her."

"At what point did you realize 'Terry' was actually Blythe?"

I thought for a second.

"Unfortunately, not until I slipped off the ledge. But on a subconscious level, I think my brain had been figuring it out over the past few days."

"You gonna tell me how?"

The cold from the makeshift ice bag was beginning to sting, so I lifted it off and set it onto the counter next to me. My ankle was not only obscenely huge, it now had turned several ugly shades of green and purple.

"One thing that kept nagging at me was how the person who was making the crank calls to me had managed to get hold of my cell phone number—and how he or she knew to call me so soon after I found Tom's body last week. Once I started focusing on Blythe, I didn't think she could have my number. But I'd given my cell phone number to *Terry* that day, after telling her I was going upstate to look for Tom. She told me she had no way to reach Blythe, so theoretically Blythe didn't have it. But *Terry* did.

"And then there was Terry's hair. It was this really weird color, and on some level I guess I realized it was a wig."

He flicked at his mustache.

"How is she, anyway?" I asked.

"She may have a concussion and a broken bone or two. I'm not really sure at this point. But speaking of that, I'd better check on things. If I leave you here, are you going to be okay?"

"Yes, but while you're gone, can you look for my purse? It came off my shoulder as I fell."

He didn't return with my purse, but a patrol cop did a few minutes later, and then shortly after that, before I had a chance to dig out my cell phone, two EMS workers arrived. The guy who examined me said he thought it was a sprain, not a break.

"Then I don't really need to go to the ER, right? I could just nurse this at home."

"Yes, you have to go to the ER," said Windgate, sticking his head through the doorway. "It's protocol. I will call you tomorrow morning at nine o'clock. Understood?"

"Yes, absolutely."

I felt foolish being carried out on a stretcher. By now there was a crowd outside, rubbernecking. As the EMS workers loaded me into the back of the ambulance, I saw another stretcher being carried out of the theater. Blythe lay on it, motionless in her baggy Terry clothes. The wig had fallen off her head, and her long blond hair was matted tightly to her scalp. Just having her that close to me made my pulse race again.

After a short ride with no siren, the ambulance deposited me at St. Vincent's, a hospital in the Village a few blocks west of my apartment. The last time I'd been in the ER had been to remove a pebble lodged in the corner of my eye, and I'd waited four hours to be put out of my misery. But catastrophes seemed on the light side tonight, and it wasn't long before I was ushered into the examining room. A doctor ordered an X-ray of my ankle, and after that I found myself sitting on a bed in a curtained-off area, listening to a man on the other side of the droopy green fabric deal with a world-class phlegm problem. Nearby, a baby began to cry, and its mother gently tried to shush it. Even I, who had yet to experience any maternal yearnings, knew that repeating "Shhh" over and over again to a wailing baby was about as effective as reading it Dante's *Inferno*.

Despite the noise, I needed to call Beau. I had resisted phoning him from the theater because I hadn't wanted to make Windgate wonder what I was up to, but I was dying to share tonight's awful saga with him. I yearned for a shoulder to cry on. Though I had come out of the confrontation with Blythe with just a sprained ankle, I felt badly shaken. When he didn't pick up his cell phone, I tried his home number.

To my shock, a woman answered. I'd had Beau's number on speed dial, so I knew there was no mistake.

"Is Beau there?" I asked hesitantly. I wondered if it could be a cleaning lady, except she sounded far too arrogant to wield a Swiffer.

"He's not home yet," she said. "May I take a message?" There was a trace of amusement in her voice, as if she'd detected my awkwardness and damn well liked it.

CHAPTER 21

Great. The night was going quickly from sucky and nightmarish to *Texas Chain Saw Massacre* caliber. I took a breath and reassured myself that there had to be a reasonable explanation for why a smug little chick was answering Beau's phone. We'd been going steady for forty-eight hours, so he'd hardly be cheating already.

After torturing myself for a minute, I sat back up and called Nash. I dictated an update on the murder investigation for the Web site and told him I would report back when I knew more.

"Where are you, anyway?" he asked. "It sounds like a bus station."

"Sort of," I said. He'd know soon enough about my ankle when he saw me struggling with crutches tomorrow.

As I started to put my BlackBerry away, it rang in my hands.

"Bailey, are you okay?" It was Chris, rushing his words out before I'd barely said hello. "Harper called me all worried."

"I'm okay, but I almost wasn't. It was *Blythe* who killed Tom—

and Locket. She tried to kill me, too, tonight—at the Chaps Theatre. I'm over at St. Vincent's with a sprained ankle."

"I'm coming there right now."

"Chris, you don't have to."

"Look, I may not be a doctor, but I practically play one on TV. I'll be there in ten minutes, fifteen tops."

I didn't fight him. It was going to be awkward with Chris and me, but he was entitled to know everything that had transpired with Blythe. And I felt so lousy, it would be great to have someone for support right now.

There wasn't much time to think about it, anyway, because a few minutes later a different doctor parted the curtain and walked in. He was dressed in corduroy pants and a navy wool sports jacket—tall, sandy haired, and good-looking. A resident, I guessed.

"The good news? It's only a second ligament sprain," he said briskly. "That's not super serious. The bad news is that you're going to have to stay off it for about three weeks."

He wrapped my ankle in an Ace bandage, gave me prescription ibuprofen for the swelling, and told me that I needed to follow the RICE strategy: rest, ice, compression, and elevation. The hospital would supply me with crutches.

Chris arrived just as I was trying out the crutches—and doing a pathetic job at it. He placed his hand on the back of my head and kissed my forehead.

"Are you ever going to forgive me for getting you into this?" he asked, his eyes worried.

"My book tour isn't until November, and my volleyball career ended with college, so there's no harm done."

"Thank God for small favors."

"Chris," I said over the sound of the still-wailing baby, "in all honesty, I don't regret any of this. Though I never met Tom, I *cared* about him. And I'm glad I found his killer."

While I waited near the door of the hospital, Chris hunted down a cab. When we arrived at my apartment, there seemed to be no question that he was going to help me upstairs.

"Do you want a cup of tea or something?" he asked after he settled me on the couch with my leg elevated.

"Brandy," I said. "Make it a double."

"Is that going to mix okay with your pain medication?"

"I don't care. I just want to pass out."

Chris clearly decided to ignore that request because I heard him fill the teakettle. While he worked in the kitchen, I called the manager's number at the Chaps Theatre on my cell. A woman answered who I thought might be the redhead I'd seen the night before in the lobby stuffing cookies into Tupperware containers.

"This is Bailey Weggins," I told her. "I'm the woman who was attacked in the theater today. Do you have a minute?"

"Well, when we arrived at six, the cops told us they wouldn't let us put on the play tonight, so basically I have all the time in the world."

"There's something I need to know. I fell through a door fifteen feet above the stage. Why in the world is that there?"

"Oh God, I heard," she lamented. "I don't know how that happened—we always keep it bolted."

"But why is it there?" I repeated. "Does it have something to do with sets you use?"

"No, that's not it. This was once an apartment building, years and years ago. That was a flight of stairs that went to the second floor—long before the stage was there."

After I hung up, I leaned my head back against the couch, suddenly feeling close to tears. Chris emerged from the kitchen carrying two mugs of tea.

"To you, Bailey," he said, raising his mug after handing me the other.

"Gosh, Chris, it was just last Tuesday that you called me. I can't believe all that's happened since then."

"Thanks for what you said earlier. About not being sorry you did this."

"I meant it."

"So tell me what happened tonight from beginning to end, okay, including how you finally figured it all out."

I'd provided highlights in the cab, but now I went through the whole awful saga in detail.

"How did you manage to think straight during all of it?" he asked. "If you hadn't, you might be dead now."

"From pure adrenaline, I guess. And the sheer desire not to want to go splat on the stage. Thank God I used to be decent on ropes during PE."

"Is Blythe *sick*—I mean, crazy?" he asked.

"Screwed up, certainly. Crazy, maybe. In hindsight, did Tom ever say anything that pointed to the fact that her feelings for him had morphed into an obsession?"

"Well, like I told you in the beginning, I thought Blythe was a bit of a whack job, but Tom seemed to view her as more of a nuisance—he wasn't the type to get all hot and bothered by it. And then all of a sudden she went off the grid. The calls stopped—and as we saw, the cards and letters stopped, too. She didn't seem to be an issue anymore."

I took a sip of the hot tea and thought for a moment.

"You know, I told the police that Blythe may have killed Terry, but now I'm not so sure. I'm wondering if Blythe actually *is* Terry."

"What do you mean?"

"That maybe they're one and the same person. Blythe could have created this alter ego for herself—to help her out of sticky situations. When people came looking for her because she owed them money or whatever, she could just trot out Terry. Or maybe she created her after she killed Tom—so that she could lay low but keep an eye on things at the same time."

"God, that's insane. What about Harper? And Deke? They're in the clear?"

"Well, I'm pretty sure Deke never repaid the money he borrowed from Tom, but that may be the worst of his crimes. And Harper? She actually helped save my butt tonight. She told the cops where I was. The one guy I'm not fine with is Barish. It seems Tom had a falling-out with him, and I wonder if he could be up to something funny about the trust. I may call my family lawyer tomorrow and just see if there's any way to check him out."

The ice pack the hospital had given me was warm and Chris went off to the kitchen to empty an ice tray. After he'd positioned a plastic freezer bag of cubes on my ankle, he straightened up in front of me.

"Well, look, probably the best thing for you right now is to get to bed. Are you going to be okay on your own here?"

I didn't want him asking to stay because that would be awkward as hell, but it also felt weird that he didn't *want* to. My mixed emotions clearly registered on my face.

"I don't know what's going on with us, Bailey," he said. "I thought you had a pretty good sense of me, yet you somehow thought I'd been a total dickhead to Tom."

"I don't think that anymore. I'm sorry I thought that."

"Well, there's still something off between us."

"It's nothing you did, Chris." I said. I dreaded where the conversation was going, but I didn't have any choice. "There was someone I was seeing before I reconnected with you, and I honestly thought it was over between him and me. But he came back to New York, and now I'm not so sure."

He shook his head in frustration. "Is it the guy who was at Elaine's?" he asked.

"Yes."

"Christ."

"I'm sorry, Chris," I said plaintively. "I've really felt so good about the time we've spent together—despite how it came about. But I—"

"You don't have to explain it. I'm going to get out of here."

"Chris—"

"There's nothing more to say, Bailey." His face set. "I appreciate all you did. I'm just sorry how it's ending. I would have really liked to be with you."

I couldn't believe how sad it was to see him go out the door.

I laid my head back on the couch again. I was really close to blubbering, and I almost didn't hear my cell phone go off. If my purse hadn't been on the coffee table, I wouldn't have caught it in time.

It was Beau on the other end—with restaurant sounds all around him.

"What's going on?" he asked. "I thought you were going to give me an update."

"I did try to call," I said, sounding as pissy as I felt by this point. "Some girl answered your phone, so I didn't bother with a message."

"A girl? Oh damn, it was my friend Jason's girlfriend."

"What?"

"Remember I mentioned I had a friend from out of town visiting? He's staying at my place with his girlfriend."

"Why would she feel she had to answer your phone?" God, we'd been together two days, and I was turning into a nag and a shrew.

"Because she's a troublemaker. I really like Jason, but I'd be thrilled if he dumped her. Tell me what's going on. Have you talked to the cops about Blythe?"

I sighed, feeling weary. The explanation made sense, but even with Beau's promise of commitment, I kept wondering about him.

"They arrested her."

"Do they think she definitely did it?"

"Yes, she's admitted as much."

"Are you okay, Bailey?"

"Yeah, just tired."

"I wish I didn't have these plans tonight. Can we get together tomorrow?"

"Sure," I said. "Let's talk tomorrow."

I couldn't believe I hadn't told him about the attack and my ankle and everything else. But the combination of pain in my ankle and his friend's bitch of a girlfriend had left me too annoyed to want to talk.

I hobbled to the bathroom, wriggled out of my clothes, and splashed warm water on myself, just to feel cleansed of the whole experience tonight. As I raised my head from the basin, I flashed myself a little smile in the mirror. In spite of my sorry state, I felt pretty pleased with how I'd coped tonight. I'd rescued myself from a precipice and fought off a killer. Granted, I'd probably looked a little ridiculous swinging that lamp like Obi-Wan Kenobi, but what mattered was that I was alive—and that I'd found Tom's killer.

Tom. The thought of him still made my heart swell with sadness. His easygoing nature, his willingness to trust, his susceptibility to any girl who wanted to mount his hot bod, had conspired against him, but in no way had he deserved his fate. I thought suddenly about his play. Maybe I could try to locate a copy and see if it could still be produced.

I pulled down an extra pillow from the closet and wedged it under my comforter toward the end of the bed. Bone tired, I crawled into bed, turned off the light, and elevated my ankle as best I could on the pillow.

It seemed like a joke that I was sleeping alone. If I'd swallowed my annoyance at Beau and confessed what had happened, he would have surely left his friends at his place and flown over here.

Yet for some reason I'd held back. Something about my encounter with Chris had made me hesitate.

What it came down to, I realized, was that I didn't really know what I wanted. I was crazy about Beau. Yet I had hated seeing Chris walk out of my apartment tonight. I dug him, I really did. Okay, he was ten years younger and involved in a business in which guys not only were horribly self-absorbed but routinely fell in love with their fake-titted costars, and yet he seemed to love my company and making me laugh. Beau, who I'd pined for, had finally come round, but he always seemed so damn mysterious, so hard to read.

As I laid my head on my pillow, I realized I had no idea what I was going to do.

But there was one thing I could be grateful for. I was so freakin' tired, nothing would keep me awake tonight.

Whi

White, Kate

Lethally blond

DUE DATE		E798 24.99	

BLOOD
GAMES

ALSO BY JERRY BLEDSOE

Bitter Blood

JERRY BLEDSOE

BLOOD GAMES

A TRUE ACCOUNT
OF FAMILY MURDER

A DUTTON BOOK

DUTTON

Published by the Penguin Group
Penguin Books USA Inc., 375 Hudson Street,
New York, New York 10014, U.S.A.
Penguin Books Ltd, 27 Wrights Lane,
London W8 5TZ, England
Penguin Books Australia Ltd, Ringwood,
Victoria, Australia
Penguin Books Canada Ltd, 10 Alcorn Avenue,
Toronto, Ontario M4V 3B2
Penguin Books (N.Z.) Ltd, 182–190 Wairau Road,
Auckland 10, New Zealand

Penguin Books Ltd, Registered Offices:
Harmondsworth, Middlesex, England

First published by Dutton, an imprint of New American Library, a
division of Penguin Books USA Inc.
Distributed in Canada by McClelland & Stewart Inc.

First Printing, November, 1991
10 9 8 7 6 5 4 3 2 1

FOR
GRETA

CONTENTS

Names of some minor characters have been changed and some identifying characteristics slightly altered to protect privacy. Names changed are indicated with an asterisk on first use.

I SEEK A FATHER WHO MOST NEEDS A SON.
—JOHN MALCOLM BRINNIN

PREFACE

THE HOGS NEVER SHOWED
alarm, no sense of their awful and imminent fate. If they had,
Noel Lee wasn't sure that he would have been able to raise
them. He had been a hog farmer for just two years, a small-
time operator raising only five hundred at a time, a sideline to
the nine hundred acres of tobacco, peanuts, corn, and soybeans
that supplied his main income.

The hogs actually weren't his. They belonged to a contractor, W. L. Murphy, who ran the biggest hog operation on
the East Coast. Murphy supplied pigs, feed, and medicine to
Noel Lee, and he simply provided a place and care for the
pigs to grow. They came to him ten weeks old, weighing about
forty pounds each. Sixteen weeks later, they weighed six times
that much and were ready for market.

Lee had mixed feelings when that time came. He looked
forward to being paid for his work, but felt a sadness about it,
too. Hogs were friendly and intelligent, he had discovered,
and despite his best intentions to the contrary, he grew close
to them in the four months that he tended them. They
recognized him and sometimes came up to him seeking affec-
tion, not unlike a dog, making it harder to send them off to
the packing house when the time came.

That always took place in the middle of the night. Hogs
were easier to handle when they were still drowsy with sleep.
What's more, in the hot Carolina summer, moving hogs at
night was imperative. Hogs can't survive long in heat. Even in
the coolness of night they had to be sprayed with water while
being moved to keep them from overheating and dying.

That was the primary reason that loading times ranged
from midnight to 6:00 A.M., the coolest hours of the day, and
on the twenty-fifth of July, 1988, Lee drew a four o'clock
loadout, as the operation was called. He was up after only a
few hours' sleep, and at three-fifteen, he climbed into his gray
Chevrolet pickup and headed for his hog house, just a short
distance up Grimesland Bridge Road from his large brick
house on the eastern edge of Pitt County. Situated on a sandy

1

lane well back from the road, the hog house was long and low, with a corrugated metal roof and canvas sides that remained open in summer to provide air circulation. When Lee arrived, he was surprised to see the lights on, the big truck with its railed, double-decker trailer already backed up to the wooden loading chute at the rear.

Newton Carter, head of the three-man loadout crew, was already in the pens, marking the backs of the biggest hogs with a fat orange crayon. Only the biggest, most aggressive hogs would be taken. The others, more timid at the feeding troughs, would be left to fatten for another week or so.

"I'm glad to see y'all early," Lee said. "Might get some sleep tonight."

Loading hogs was hard and smelly work. The stench permeated clothing after only a few minutes and was powerful enough to set sensitive stomachs aboil, but loadout crews were accustomed to it.

After the biggest hogs were marked, Lee and the two crew members went into the pens carrying heavy plywood boards with handholds cut into the top. These cutting boards, as they are called, were used to isolate and direct the selected hogs to the gates of the pens and into the aisle, where Newton Carter encouraged the reluctant toward the chute and into the trailer with a battery-operated electric prod. The hogs were disgruntled and confused at being rousted from sleep, and the loadout always proceeded with much recalcitrance and squealing on their part and much scrambling and yelling from the men. This night, however, it went more smoothly than usual, and by four, the job was done, the men sweat-drenched and dung-besmeared, the hogs snorting and squirming in the close confines of the trailer, cooled by automatic sprinklers. By mid-morning, the hogs would be hanging by their rear legs, eviscerated, soon to be rendered into bacon, pork chops, ham, and sausage.

The truck driver, taking no chances on losing any of his crowded passengers to the heat, left immediately with his load, but the crew lingered for a while, chatting with Lee, discussing the next loadout.

"Well, see you next week," Lee said, as the crew made ready to depart. After they left, he returned to check the automatic feeders, to make sure the pens were secure and to shut off the lights.

Ten minutes later, he was back in his truck heading home, eager for a shower. But as he neared the road, he saw an orange glow against the trees to the north, perhaps half a mile away. His first thought was that a neighbor's trailer home might be ablaze, but then he saw that the fire was too near the road to be the trailer. A wreck, he thought. There'd been wrecks in that curve before. Perhaps somebody was trapped in a burning vehicle.

Lee had been a volunteer fireman and rescue squad member for more than twenty years, and he turned instinctively toward the blaze, his foot pressing hard on the gas pedal. Up closer, he saw that the fire was not from a wreck either. It was about eight feet off the road, beside a path that led through the trees to an old black cemetery, overgrown and never visited anymore. A small pile of something was burning, the flames blue at the base and leaping straight into the air, four feet or more. Lee taught fire science at the community college, and he recognized immediately that the fire was fueled by an accelerant, probably gasoline or kerosene. Clearly, it had been set only minutes earlier. What was burning? And who would set such a fire alongside a lonely country road in the middle of the night? Something odd was going on here.

Lee slowed the truck, but the thought struck him that whoever had set the fire might still be lurking nearby and might not want anybody to know what was burning. That sent a shiver up his spine. He crept on past, seeing no sign of anybody, and started to turn around in the first driveway that he came to, only a few hundred feet beyond the fire. But the driveway angled back sharply from the road so that he couldn't see if a vehicle might be parked there, and he continued on a few hundred yards to the intersection of U.S. 264, a four-lane highway with a grass median. There he turned around and drove back to the fire, which was still burning vigorously. This time he paused without getting out of his truck so he could make sure that the fire had no chance of spreading. The surrounding area was naturally swampy, and the roadside was still wet from a thunderstorm that had passed earlier in the night. Satisfied that the fire would be contained, Lee headed for home and his much needed shower, but he couldn't stop thinking about the fire and how strange it was. Surely whoever had set it had been up to no good.

PART ONE

TERROR IN SMALLWOOD

WHO DOESN'T DESIRE HIS FATHER'S DEATH?
—DOSTOEVSKI

1

APPROACHED FROM THE
south on U.S. 17, the Coastal Highway, the town appears
suddenly beyond a tree line at the drawbridge that marks the
end of the Tar River and the beginning of the murky and
quickly broadening Pamlico. Hunkered on the north bank, its
back to the river, the town has a low profile broken only by
the spires of the Methodist and Presbyterian churches and the
skeletal tower that identifies the telephone office.

Little Washington, the town is called throughout the rest
of North Carolina, that to distinguish it from the seat of
national government three hundred miles to the north. But
the townspeople prefer to call it "the original Washington." It
was, after all, the first town to be named for George Washington. Originally called The Forks of the Tar, the town named
itself for General Washington in 1776, the year of indepen-
dence, thus gaining the distinction of being the first town in
the new nation to bestow such an honor on the man who would
become the country's first President.

Situated just twelve miles upriver from Bath, North Carolina's first town, Washington is proud of its history but has
few historic structures. Most succumbed to two fires that swept
the town, the first set by retreating Union forces in 1864,
leaving the townspeople with a lingering resentment of north-
erners and the federal government. The town was rebuilt, only
to be devastated again by a fire started by a faulty flue in 1900.
But a few antebellum homes, including one dating to 1780,
survived, most near the riverfront, proudly maintained and
decorated with historic markers so that passing tourists might
find them easily.

A town of twenty-five lawyers countered by twice that
many churches, Washington is the civic center of Beaufort
County, a county of farming and fishing and ever dwindling
expanses of wooded and boggy wilderness; the county's forty-
five thousand residents depend more and more on the indus-
tries that have settled in Washington and other nearby towns.
For much of its history, Washington was a trading town,

dependent on river traffic, but river commerce had gradually died in the twentieth century, leaving the town with a waterfront eyesore of decaying wharves and abandoned warehouses, all swept away by urban renewal in the '60s and replaced by a broad waterfront parkway lined with flowering cherry trees, park benches, and tall streetlights that double as flagpoles.

With a population of about ten thousand, Washington prides itself on its waterway location, its relative isolation, its friendliness, its quiet and slow-paced lifestyle. A good place to raise a family, most townspeople agree. "A sleepy little town," the town manager called it.

And in the predawn hours of Monday, July 25, 1988, the town was largely asleep. It was a sullen, sultry night, as most midsummer nights are in coastal Carolina, the temperature still in the seventies, the humidity nearly unbearable after showers earlier. Only an occasional vehicle passed along the strip of fast-food restaurants, convenience marts, and motels on Highway 17, almost all of them closed. On military pay weekends, the traffic at this hour on Monday morning usually would be heavier, with marines rushing back to their bases farther south from weekend passes in Norfolk and other points north, easy targets for speeding tickets from police officers with little to do, but payday was still a week away.

Four police officers were watching the town this night, three patrol officers assigned to separate zones and a patrol sergeant who backed up all calls and to whom decisions of any magnitude were left. As four-thirty approached, only one of those officers, Danny Edwards, actually was on patrol. He was assigned to Zone B, which included the downtown area, now deserted as he slowly eased his car east on Main Street, one block north of the river.

The other three officers were only a couple of blocks away. David Sparrow, a plump and friendly man of twenty-two, had just settled into a chair in the county jail in the basement of the courthouse to eat the country ham biscuit he'd picked up at Hardee's, which operated the only all-night drive-through in town. Sparrow usually took his thirty-minute break at the jail so that he could bring food to the two jailers, who were as confined as the sleeping prisoners they watched over.

Sergeant Bradford Tetterton and Patrolman Ed Cherry were across the alley from the jail at the communications center in the back of the Beaufort County Law Enforcement Center,

8

chatting with the dispatcher, Michelle Sparrow, David's wife. Cherry, a close friend of the Sparrows, had followed David through the Hardee's drive-through to pick up a country ham-and-egg biscuit and Tater Tots for Michelle's breakfast.

It had been one of the slowest nights in recent memory. Central Communications received calls for seven rescue squads, sixteen fire departments, the Beaufort County Sheriff's Department, and the Washington City Police, but only a few calls had come this night, none of any consequence, and Michelle, an avid reader, had passed much of the night so far with a Stephen King novel, *Misery*.

Normally, Michelle didn't work the radio. She had been promoted to communications supervisor and worked regular daytime hours. But one of the regular dispatchers was on vacation this week and the other scheduled for duty Sunday night had called in sick. Michelle had no choice but to come in and work the late shift, 10:00 P.M. to 6:00 A.M. She really didn't mind. After all, her husband was working the same shift. In another week they would have been married for three months, and Tetterton was teasing her about it when the telephone rang at four-twenty-four.

"Beaufort County Central Communications," Michelle answered.

"This is an emergency," said a soft female voice, so low that Michelle couldn't understand it.

"Can I help you?" Michelle said.

"Yes," came the whisper again. "This is an emergency."

"Well, what do you need, ma'am?"

"I need the police and . . . and an ambulance."

"Where do you need 'em?"

"One-ten Lawson Road."

The voice was barely audible, and Michelle strained to hear it.

"One-ten, what road?"

"Lawson."

"One-ten Lawson Road?"

"L-A-W-S-O-N."

"I can't hear you, ma'am. Could you speak up?"

"I'm sorry. The intruder may still be in the house."

Michelle's senses quickened. "Okay, why do you need an ambulance?"

"My husband may be dying and I think I may be, too."

9

"You husband did what?"

"My husband may be dying, and I may be dying, too."

Was this one of the regulars? A mentally disturbed woman frequently called the dispatchers, usually late on full-moon nights, to report that awful acts were being committed upon her. Indeed, she had called just the week before, claiming her husband had tied her up in her bathing suit and was killing her. But this voice was so faint that Michelle couldn't tell if it might be the same person.

"Okay, what is your name, please?" she asked.

"I am bleeding."

"Okay, what is your name, please?"

"Bonnie Von Stein."

"Bonnie what?"

"Von Stein."

No, this was not the regular.

"Okay, Bonnie, hold on just a minute and I'm getting an officer on the way. Okay? Don't hang up on me, all right?"

Tetterton had started back outside to his patrol car, carrying a handful of forms he'd come to pick up, but he stopped when Michelle called anxiously to him.

"Sergeant, I don't know what we've got here, but there's a woman on the phone says she's got an intruder in the house and she and her husband may be dying. I don't know whether she's crazy or for real, but it's one-ten Lawson Road."

Tetterton left the building at a run, calling to Ed Cherry, who headed to his own patrol car. Michelle returned to the telephone.

"Bonnie?"

"Yes, I'm here," said the weak voice.

"Okay, is someone in your house?"

"I don't know if they are still here or not."

"Okay, did someone—where are you bleeding?"

"In the chest. I've been beaten and stabbed, I think."

"Okay, is your husband, has he been beaten and stabbed also?"

"Yes."

"Okay, I have an officer on the way . . ."

"C-thirty-three is ten-seventeen Lawson Road," Michelle heard Cherry say over the radio, giving his code number and reporting that he was en route.

"And I want you to stay right with me," Michelle was telling Bonnie. "Don't hang up until the police get there."

"I don't know where my daughter is," the woman said.

"Ten-four," Michelle said into the control board microphone, acknowledging Cherry. "She advised she and her husband have been beaten and stabbed. She advised her daughter is also in the house and she doesn't know where she's at."

Danny Edwards heard the call on his radio just as he was reaching Market Street on Main.

"What's the address, Central?" he called.

"One-ten Lawson. One-ten Lawson."

Market Street was a straight shot to Lawson. He turned left onto it, switched on his blue light and siren and floored the accelerator, his car leaping forward with a roar in the quiet downtown streets.

David Sparrow heard the radio talk on his handset in the jail. Lawson Road was in his patrol zone, C, on the northern edge of town, away from the river. He knew that it ran through the town's plushest subdivision, Smallwood. People in Smallwood did not have intruders who beat and stabbed them in the night. Such a thing was almost inconceivable. He abandoned his coffee and ham biscuits and yelled to the jailers to slide open the heavy, electronically operated doors and free him.

Michelle had never heard patrol cars leaving in such a rush. Now she heard the squealing tires of her own husband's car as he sped from behind the courthouse. At Fifth Street, in front of the fire department, where sleeping rescue squad members were about to receive a call from his wife, he saw the blue lights of three other police cars streaking ahead of him blocks away. In the communications room, Michelle Sparrow heard Bonnie Von Stein whisper into the telephone: "Please hurry."

"Okay," Michelle told her. "They're getting there just as fast as they can and I am going to stay with you, okay? I hear the sirens going out right now. You just hold on."

"I'll try," Bonnie said.

2

THE WEEKEND AT 110 LAW-
son Road wouldn't have been out of the ordinary if Chris
hadn't come home Friday night, unexpected. He hadn't been
home much at all during the summer, so his mother was
pleased when he called after dinner to say he was driving in
from Raleigh for no special reason.

She always had felt a special closeness to Chris, her
firstborn. He was shy and sensitive and gentle, although she
knew that some might not realize that about him, and she had
always tried to fill his special need for love and attention
without pampering him. He'd been away at college for nearly
a year now, and she worried constantly about him, calling him
frequently to make sure that everything was all right. She was
a worrier when it came to her children, and she worried
especially when Chris was on the road. She knew that he drove
too fast.

She realized that she probably wouldn't see much of Chris
on his visit. On the weekends that he'd come home during the
past year, he either brought some new college friends with
him, or he wanted to spend time with old high school buddies
who were still in town. This weekend likely would prove no
exception, but she was comforted just knowing that he would
be at home.

He arrived late, and after giving his mother a hug and
chatting briefly, he hurried out to visit friends and cruise the
mall and the waterfront to see what was happening. He stayed
out late, but his mother was relieved that he was in good spirits,
that everything had seemed all right, that apparently there was
no ulterior motive for this visit. He'd caused her a lot of concern
recently. After a rocky first year at N.C. State University, he'd
changed his major, got a part-time job, enrolled for both
sessions of summer school. Although he'd had a problem with
his class in the first summer session, a misunderstanding that
had kept him from receiving any credit, she was hopeful that
he was getting on a more even keel now.

She didn't have much chance to see him Saturday either.

He didn't get up until about nine, and after breakfast he announced that he was going to "check out the town" and left. She had to run errands that morning, and afterward, she and Lieth drove twenty miles west to Greenville to have a late breakfast at the Waffle House, their weekend ritual. They stayed a while in Greenville to look at mobile homes. They were planning to buy one and put it in a nice, wooded trailer park, Maryanna Mobile Estates, on the western edge of Washington, so that Lieth could put an office in it and they would have someplace for Bonnie's many relatives to stay when they came to visit.

When they got back home early Saturday afternoon, Chris was still out, and his sister, Angela, who'd graduated from high school only a few weeks earlier, had gone off to the beach for the day with her friend Donna Brady.

The unusual phone call came later that day. A stranger was on the line, the mother of a high school student who lived in a town near Raleigh. She wanted to know why Chris had written a check to her son for thirty-five dollars the previous afternoon. Her son had tried to get her to cash it, but she was suspicious. He had told several stories about the check: that it was for yard work, which was what Chris had written on the check; that he'd helped Chris move some stuff into a dorm; that he'd given Chris money to get home on because Chris was broke and couldn't get a check cashed. She suspected instead that it might have something to do with drugs.

The call upset Lieth, and they confronted Chris about it after he came in late in the afternoon, but he maintained that the boy had helped him with some work at school. Lieth didn't believe that, just as he had not believed the cockamamy tale Chris had told about how he had spent the three days when he had disappeared earlier that month, prompting his worried mother to report him missing to the campus police.

"If you're getting involved with drugs, I'm going to kick your ass," Lieth had told Chris angrily, but Chris had known that he didn't mean it, for although Lieth had a temper, he was not a violent man.

Later, after further questioning from his mother, Chris admitted that he had given the boy thirty-five dollars in cash and a check for another thirty-five for half an ounce of marijuana that the boy was supposed to bring back to him. But the boy had ripped him off, left him waiting for hours in a shopping center parking lot Friday before he came home. Chris acknowledged that he had been smoking a little pot at school, but at State, he maintained, it was almost impossible not to smoke it. As he told it, the dorms were virtual dope dens, and almost everybody, except for him, of course, was dealing drugs of some sort.

His mother and Lieth had thought that this might be the case. Chris's actions in recent weeks had caused them to wonder if he might be using drugs. They were perturbed to learn that their fears were justified, but eventually, his mother recalled later, they settled down and talked reasonably about it. After all, it was only marijuana. It could be much worse. And Lieth, a student in the '60s, had smoked pot in college himself without any ill effects. To condemn his stepson for doing it would make him a hypocrite. Finally, as Chris recalled it later, they had told him that if he was going to smoke pot, he should do it in his own room, not get caught, not overdo it, and never do it and drive. And they didn't want him spending a lot of money on it, especially any of the fifty-dollar allowance they gave him each week. He should buy it with the money he was making from his clothing store job. And he'd better not sell it, either. That could get him in deep trouble.

That evening, Chris suggested he grill hamburgers for supper, and dinner had been pleasant, the family all together, along with Angela's friend Donna. Right after dinner, Chris said that he had to return to N.C. State to work on an important paper that was due Monday morning. His mother tried to talk him into staying until Sunday, but he insisted on going back.

She walked him to his car, a classic '65 Ford Mustang fastback that Lieth had bought him for his sixteenth birthday, and as she was bidding him good-bye, she spotted the gaping hole with dangling wires in the car's dashboard.

"What happened to your radio?" she asked. She and Lieth had bought him the expensive JVC stereo radio and cassette player for Christmas the year before.

Somebody had broken into his car at school and stolen it a few weeks earlier, he explained, along with all of his tapes. He hadn't told them because he didn't want them to be disturbed about it.

One more thing to upset Lieth. With Chris there always seemed to be something. Later Bonnie mentioned the loss of the radio to Angela and Donna, but she decided to keep it from Lieth, at least for now.

Bonnie and Lieth were up earlier than usual Sunday morning, and again they drove to Greenville for breakfast at the Waffle House, as Bonnie recalled the day later. They came straight back home and spent most of the day going through back issues of *The Wall Street Journal* and recording stock prices in their computer. Both had once worked as computer programmers (indeed, that was how they had met), and they had developed a program to help Lieth keep up with stock trends, now that he was playing the market.

In the past year, Lieth had come into a large inheritance, and he was certain that he could make it even larger. A meticulous record keeper and planner, he did not develop his investment strategy in a haphazard way. He studied and plotted and made careful moves, and that required a lot of tedious time at the keyboard, but both he and Bonnie were enjoying it.

They worked until late afternoon, then Lieth opened a Budweiser and went upstairs for a shower while Bonnie tended to her cats. There were thirteen cats now, counting the four abandoned kittens she recently had rescued and was keeping until the Humane Society could place them in good homes. When she came upstairs, she found Lieth in an amorous mood. They had the house to themselves—Angela was off indulging her passion for horseback riding—and they made love in their bedroom. Afterward, they decided to drive back to Greenville for a nice dinner.

They went first to the King and Queen, the most expensive restaurant in town, but found it closed on Sundays. They chose instead Sweet Caroline's, which occupied a white stuccoed building with a blue-and-gold awning and a wood-shingled roof near the campus of East Carolina University. Sweet Caroline's had a dark dining room with colorful quilts draped from the ceiling, and advertised a New Orleans-style French cuisine. Bonnie and Lieth both ordered the $11.95 Sunday special, Lieth choosing *suprême du poulet*, Bonnie the beef bordelaise.

Lieth was in a good mood, and they talked about his success with the investments he'd been making and their future now that the children both soon would be in college. Lieth finished most of a carafe of wine as they talked. Perhaps it was the wine, combined with the food and the setting, but something brought out the sweetness in Lieth. He told her something she would cling to later. He would have no life if not for her, he said, as she remembered it later, and no reason to live without her.

They left for home a little before nine. *The Deliberate Stranger*, a two-part TV movie about Ted Bundy, the serial killer, was beginning that night and she wanted to see it. It was already on when they got there. Lieth went straight to bed, but she settled on the cushions of the heavy wood couch in the den to watch it, thumbing through the Sunday newspapers during commercials.

Angela came in just before eleven. She had been home until about nine after returning from horseback riding, then she and Donna had gone out to cruise the mall and the waterfront. She had sort of promised to go out that night with a new boy she had met, but she really didn't like him much and when he called she had made excuses and called Donna to come over.

"You didn't leave a note," she chided her mother, who was now sipping a cup of tea and working on a poster for the Humane Society to display at the Washington Summer Festival on the waterfront the coming weekend.

Her mother laughed and acknowledged her slipup. She had a firm rule about leaving notes on the bulletin board next to the wall telephone in the kitchen so that family members could keep up with one another's whereabouts. She was always getting onto Angela and Chris about it.

"How was your day?" she asked.

"Boring," said Angela, who went on upstairs to bed.

Her mother stayed downstairs to watch the beginning of the news before switching off the TV and putting her pocketbook away in the cabinet under the built-in microwave, where she kept her "junk," as she called it, extra pocketbooks, snapshots, doodads, recipes, and whatnot. She looked in on the cats on the back porch, made sure the pet rooster, a by-product of one of Angela's school science projects, was all right in his covered cage in the utility room off the back porch, then checked the front door to make sure it was locked (she'd

16

checked the back porch door when she came in from dinner) before going to bed.

She could hear music coming from Angela's room when she got upstairs, and she opened the door to tell Angela good night and to ask her about the whereabouts of some cassette tapes that Angela had borrowed and was supposed to return.

In her own bedroom, she turned on the brass extension lamp on the typewriter table by her side of the bed, and woke her husband, who always slept on the side of the bed nearest the door, to ask if he'd like to have a glass of iced tea or something. He mumbled no, turned over, and went back to sleep.

A dressing table with cosmetics on it stood by the door. She removed her jewelry and put it in a heart-shaped bowl, took a twenty-dollar bill and some change from her pocket, and placed it on the tabletop. Then she undressed, put on a gown, climbed into bed, and reached for a book from the stack of paperback historical romances on the floor beside the bed. She read for a few minutes, but she'd left the bedroom door open, and she still could hear music coming from Angela's room. She got up, closed the door, returned to bed, and read for another twenty or twenty-five minutes without musical intrusion, before drowsiness overtook her. Sometime about midnight, she put down the book, turned off the lamp, and went to sleep.

3

LATER, SHE COULD NOT be certain whether it was the thud of the first blow striking her husband or his first scream that startled her from sleep.

She only knew that she awoke confused in the darkness, and that her husband's screams were short and piercing, so loud that they seemed to fill her head. He was trying to sit up, but he couldn't, and she reached out her left hand to help him, only to feel it deflect a blow. Only then did she see the figure that she later would come to think of as "the shadow." It stood near the foot of the bed, silhouetted in the wisp of light that filtered through the open bedroom door. A man. She was sure of that, although she could see no distinctive features. He was tall and broad-shouldered, strong, and with no neck at all, or maybe he had a hood on. She couldn't tell. All was darkness, and without her glasses everything from more than a few feet away was blurred. She could tell that his arms were raised, though, and in his hands he held an object that appeared to be cylindrical, maybe three feet long. He swung it methodically, his aim precise. And he made no sound other than the whoosh of the flailing weapon and the thud when it struck. Each blow brought more screams of terror from her husband. She couldn't be sure how many times he screamed, ten, fifteen? Nor could she be certain how many blows were struck.

Two blows caught her, then another, sending her reeling from the bed onto the floor. And as she lay there, she heard her husband taking more blows, these different, lighter and followed by sucking, gushing sounds. No longer did he scream.

She made no sounds herself, at least none that she could remember later. Shock, she later decided, was the reason for that, the utter surprise and horror of it all. The force of the blows had stunned her, and as she lay on the floor, she slipped briefly into unconsciousness, only to revive and see the shadow again, this time standing at her feet, arms upraised in the same menacing position. Again she heard the whoosh and remembered no more. Until she heard footsteps, the soft closing of her bedroom door. And she knew that the shadow had gone. She was sure that she heard whoosh sounds again and more thuds, three this time, and she was struck by the awful knowledge that her daughter, sleeping in her room just down the hall, was being attacked and there was nothing that she could do to protect her. Blessedly, unconsciousness again intervened to deliver her from her agony.

She did not know how long she was out, but when she came to again, she realized that she was on the floor. At first she thought she'd had a bad dream and fallen out of bed. But when she reached to get back into bed, she grabbed her husband's hand, hanging from the side of the mattress, and

18

found it limp and sticky. She recoiled, and a sensation came to her that she later described as "this gushy, yucky, warm feeling that came up on my neck." She brought her hand to her head and felt a big hole there, and the horror of her situation returned in a rush.

For a few moments she lay still, listening, fearful that the intruder might still be in the house. She was reassured to hear her husband breathing, although it seemed to be growing fainter and fainter. Her own breathing was difficult, and when she tried to get up, she couldn't. She felt no pain, but she knew that she was gravely injured. Somehow, she realized, she had to get help. The telephone was the obvious answer. Even in the darkness she could tell that her head was at the typewriter stand beside the bed. The telephone was on a filing cabinet to her right, not far away. She angled her head toward it and began to push herself across the carpet with her heels, scooting on her rump.

When she finally got to the filing cabinet, she couldn't pull herself up to reach the phone. The cord, she thought. She edged herself onto a briefcase, reached between the filing cabinet and the adjoining desk, found the cord, and yanked on it. The heavy phone plopped onto her chest, but again she felt no pain, only gratitude. She grasped it to her and began trying to punch 911, not knowing that there was no 911 emergency line in her county. Her attempts to seek out the right buttons met only with failure, however, and with frustration growing, she lapsed again into unconsciousness.

When she awoke once more, the telephone still on her chest, she told herself to think logically. One button at a time eventually would give her the operator. She began pushing buttons and hanging up when she got a busy signal or some strange noise. Finally, a button produced a ring and the welcome voice of a long-distance operator.

"This is an emergency," she told the operator. "I need the police and an ambulance."

Later, she wouldn't remember the operator's response, but she would remember the voice of Michelle Sparrow a few moments later, saying, "Beaufort County Central Communications."

4

As EVERY POLICE CAR IN service in Washington sped northward on Market Street, Michelle Sparrow dialed the number of the Washington Fire Department.

Captain Jerry Lewis answered.

"Captain Lewis, this is Michelle in communications. We have a possible stabbing and beating, one-ten Lawson Road. We have three officers on the way at this time. I can't give you any more than that right now because the lady can hardly talk."

"One-ten Lawson Road," said Lewis.

"One-ten Lawson Road. There may be more than one person injured."

"Okay, we're rolling."

"Okay, Bonnie, the rescue's on the way, too. Okay?" Michelle said into the receiver.

"Yes."

"But I am not going to hang up until you hear 'em there with you."

"I don't hear my husband breathing as fast."

"Where is your husband, Bonnie?"

"In bed."

"Can you wake him?"

"I can't reach him. I'm on the floor."

"Okay, can you call him?"

"No."

"Okay, and you don't know about your daughter?"

"No."

"Is there anybody else that lives there with you?"

"They're not at home."

The voice seemed to be fading again.

"Okay, Bonnie?"

"Huh?"

"You still with me?"

"Yes."

"Now, look, you hang in there. Don't, don't pass out on me, okay?"

"I'll try."

Officer Danny Edwards, in the lead car, was going so fast that he almost missed Lawson Road, but he hit his brakes in time to swerve right onto the street when he saw the sign. Tetterton cut beneath him and was the first to arrive at the house, Edwards and Cherry right behind him.

"Okay, 'cause you stay calm and cool like you're doing," Michelle was telling Bonnie. "You're going to help everybody. Where are you in the house?"

The three cars screeched to halts, one behind the other, in front of the two-story house with its steeply pitched roof and narrow, railed front porch.

"Thirty-one, thirty-two, and thirty, ten-twenty-three," Danny Edwards called to Michelle, reporting their arrival.

"I'm in the bedroom on the right," Michelle heard from the telephone.

"Ten-four," she responded to the officers, then spoke again into the phone, asking, "You're in the what bedroom on the right?"

"Upstairs. The bedrooms are upstairs."

"She advised she is upstairs," Michelle relayed to the officers as they bolted from their cars, unsnapping their holstered weapons, and ran toward the darkened house, carrying heavy flashlights and hand radios.

"You take the front, I'll take the back," Tetterton called to Edwards.

A short, freckled man with a reddish crewcut that now was graying, Tetterton had been with the police department for twenty-six years, the only veteran among the four officers on duty that night. He thought the intruder might still be in the house, and so did the other officers.

As Edwards went to the front door, Tetterton threaded his way between the four cars parked in the driveway toward a gate in a six-foot-high wooden fence that enclosed the backyard.

"My daughter in bedroom on the left," the woman told Michelle.

"Your daughter is what, dear?"

"In the bedroom on the left."

21

"She advises she's in the bedroom on the right, her daughter's in on the left," Michelle radioed the officers.

"God, I hope this is a bad dream," Bonnie said.

Tetterton pushed open the backyard gate and shined his heavy Mag-Lite at a recently enclosed back porch lined with windows. The light revealed that the porch door was slightly open, the window beside it broken.

"I've got an open door," he radioed to Edwards, who had just tried the front door and found it locked.

Edwards came off the front porch and told Cherry, who'd been a police officer for only four months, to station himself at the western end of the house where he could see the fence around the backyard as well as the front door.

"Don't let him get out either way," he said.

Michelle was asking Bonnie if she could hear the officers.

"Think so."

"Okay, how can they get in?"

"I don't know."

"You don't know how they can get in?"

"No."

"Can you give . . ."

"I don't know how somebody got in."

"You advise which door was unlocked?" Edwards called.

"She says she doesn't know how they got in," Michelle told him. "Stand by. I'm trying to get you more."

"Okay, I got the back door open," Tetterton radioed. "The back door's been forced open, I believe."

"The back door is open . . ." Michelle told the other officers, and Bonnie heard her over the phone.

"Oh, my god," Bonnie said.

David Sparrow had arrived at the house and jumped from the car carrying a twelve-gauge Ithaca shotgun.

"The front door, David," Edwards called to him as he unholstered the .45 on his hip and hurried to the back to meet Tetterton.

"You just lay right there," Michelle was saying into the telephone. "Don't get excited, okay, Bonnie?"

"The front door," Edwards again called to Sparrow. "Don't let him out."

"You calm down," Michelle was telling Bonnie. "Calm down, okay?"

Tetterton and Edwards entered the back porch cautiously,

Tetterton carrying his .357 Magnum, both shining their Mag-Lites into dark corners. Cats cowered and skittered before the beams. Through a window the officers could see a light inside the house, apparently in the kitchen. Both were tense as they opened the door that led from the porch into the house, not knowing if a crazed person might be lurking inside, waiting for the right moment to attack.

"I have cats," Bonnie was saying into the telephone. "Please, I don't want my cats hurt."

In the kitchen, a fluorescent light was on over the sink, and Tetterton and Edwards saw cabinet doors open under the microwave oven to the right of the sink. A woman's white pocketbook lay on a stovetop built into an island in front of the sink, the contents strewn.

"Somebody's dead," Edwards said in a near whisper. "I can smell it. Smell the blood?"

Rooms led off from the kitchen in two different directions. "You take the right," said Tetterton. "I'll go left."

"Okay, Bonnie, you just calm down and think good thoughts," Michelle was saying. "I'm not going to hang up with you until Officer Sparrow comes in and talks with me. Okay?"

"Okay."

"Officer Sparrow is my husband. Okay? So you ask for him . . ."

"Okay."

". . . And tell him I'm on the phone and let me talk to him."

Tetterton and Edwards had made quick sweeps through the darkened downstairs, Tetterton taking the dining room-den, Edwards the living room. They met at the foot of the stairs that led to the second floor from an alcove at the front door.

"All clear down here," said Tetterton.

If the intruder wasn't downstairs, there were only two other possibilities: he'd already fled, or he was waiting upstairs. Tetterton took a deep breath. "We gotta go for broke," he said. "You ready?"

"Ready," said Edwards.

"I'll go right, you go left," said Tetterton.

He flicked on a light switch at the base of the stairs and both officers charged up, to be greeted at the top of the steps by five closed doors leading off a hallway. One door was immediately to the right at the top of the stairs, and Tetterton stopped and rapped on it lightly.

"Please come in. Please come in," Bonnie called to him from inside the room, but he couldn't hear her.

He rapped again.

"Please come in!" she called louder.

"This door?"

"Yes, please," Bonnie pleaded as Tetterton opened the door to see only darkness.

"Okay, I'm with you," Tetterton said, although he couldn't see her yet.

"Turn the light on," she said.

Tetterton swept the room with his flashlight, the beam jolting to a halt on the most horrible sight of his twenty-six years of police work. The whole room seemed red with blood. Lying diagonally across a bed, face-down, was the body of a burly man wearing only cotton briefs that once had been white but now were blood-red.

Several stab wounds were visible in the man's upper back and shoulder on his left side, and there was such a huge, ragged tear in the back of his head that Tetterton at first thought that he could peer inside his skull.

Tetterton had grown up on a farm near Washington, each fall participating in the ritual of hog killing that provided the winter's meat for his family, and the first image that came into his head on seeing the man's body was that of a hog, eviscerated, and laid out on the carving table for rendering.

"Oh, my god in this world," he said, falling back instinctively from the sight, back out of the room, pulling the door closed as he went.

"Officer," Bonnie called from the floor beyond the bed. "Officer. Officer Sparrow."

Tetterton was on his radio, calling communications.

From the floor, Bonnie had seen her husband on the bed in the ray of Tetterton's flashlight. "Oh, it's not a dream," she said into the telephone.

"Dispatch rescue ten-thirty-three," Tetterton was excitedly calling to Michelle Sparrow. "Call the rescue!"

"Ten-four. I hear. I got 'em on the way."

"Advise them it's ten-thirty-three traffic," Tetterton said.

"Four-thirty-one," Michelle called to the ambulance that

was now streaking toward Lawson Road. "Ten-thirty-three! Four-thirty-one, ten-thirty-three!"

5

LIETH VON STEIN LIKED to joke about the reason his parents never had more children. "They only had one," he said, "because they were afraid to risk having another one like me."

Born in Queens, in New York City, where both of his parents came from prosperous families of German descent, Lieth was brought to North Carolina as a baby. His father, Howard, a philosophy graduate of Brown University, had been a professional musician, playing saxophone in several big bands, before going off to fight in World War II. After the war, he returned to find the big band era gone and work as a saxophonist hard to get. With a wife and a new baby to support, he had to have a job and he took one offered by his brother-in-law.

Richard Hensel, who was married to the sister of Howard's wife, Marie, had come to North Carolina as a salesman of laundry equipment in the '20s and stayed to buy a Winston-Salem laundry called Camel City. He was getting ready to expand, and he hired his brother-in-law as general manager.

Howard and Marie settled happily in Winston-Salem in a modest frame house on Konnoak Drive on the city's south side. They became faithful members of St. John's Lutheran Church, and Howard, quiet and gentlemanly, began playing with a small dance band on weekends, an activity he would continue into old age.

Marie, who was lively and outgoing, doted on her only child. "She had him a little bit spoiled," recalled a family friend. "She was always waiting on him. He kind of had his way."

By the time Lieth was in high school, Camel City Laundry

25

and Cleaners had become one of the most successful laundries in the country, with several branches and more than 130 employees, and Howard had become part-owner. Lieth had no interest in the laundry business, however, and never even took a part-time job at one of the plants.

He had decided on another field, and before his graduation from James Gray High School in 1964, he was accepted into the School of Engineering at N.C. State University. He did okay there his first two years, but his junior year brought difficulties.

"I think he got burned out," said a fellow engineering student. "He was a numbers guy, but not to the engineering standpoint. He just got very tired of engineering school, and he got into the party routine. We used to party strong."

His grades fell precipitously, and by the end of his junior year, he had flunked out and was invited not to return to N.C. State. That was in 1967. The Vietnam War was raging and Lieth had just turned twenty-one. He was drafted before the year was out. His years at State got him assigned to clerical work, and instead of going off to war in Southeast Asia, he was sent to his family's homeland, Germany.

After his discharge in 1970, Lieth returned home and enrolled at Guilford College in Greensboro, this time as a business major. Guilford was a small Quaker college with a liberal bent. Some faculty and students held a weekly silent vigil against the Vietnam War on the federal courthouse lawn. Although basically conservative ("He was the most Republican guy you ever met," one friend later said of him), Lieth had come to share the views of many of his fellow students about the war. "He kept asking, 'Why are we there? What are we doing? We ought to get out of there,' " recalled his friend Rob Lorber.

While he was at Guilford, Lieth let his hair grow to shoulder length, wore a headband, blue jeans, and the tiny, round, wire-rimmed glasses made popular by John Lennon. He often went for a week or two without shaving. And he frequently smoked marijuana in late-night bull sessions. Friends teased him by calling him "the weird hippie."

Lieth's parents took his changes in appearance in stride. "Whatever he wanted to do was all right with Marie," one friend later remembered. "But he knew how to act around his mother. She was somewhat sheltered from the real world."

Lieth always took his friends, both male and female, home to meet his mother and father, and his friends all were impressed with their warmth and openness. But more than that, all later would remark about the obvious depth of love and respect between Lieth and his parents. "They were just devoted to one another," one said.

Lieth's friends all thought of him as offbeat, just eccentric enough to be charming. They admired his intellect, his outspokenness, his quick, wry sense of humor. "He liked to look at life in the absurd," Rob Lorber recalled later. "He was a structured person, but he was also a very creative person, had a tremendous imagination."

Most of his friends, at one time or another, had undergone Lieth's intense examination of their views. He relished playing devil's advocate, even to the point of strongly defending positions he didn't actually believe, especially if he came upon an unwary innocent who didn't know him and fell into his trap.

"He would absolutely take it to the hilt," recalled one friend from his days at N.C. State. "Make you prove your point."

Lieth and Rob Lorber spent many nights in grungy bars drinking beer, proving points, solving the world's problems, making sarcastic comments about the other customers, usually ending up sometime after midnight arguing about which one was going to marry the waitress.

During one of their late-night drinking sessions, Lieth and Lorber decided that Lorber should run for president of the Guilford student body on the Apathy ticket. Lieth would be his campaign manager. Lieth devised a series of satiric posters for the campaign. In Lorber's favorite, Lieth photographed three jockstraps that had been hung by thread in front of straight-backed chairs. In a fourth chair sat Lorber, in animated conversation, wearing an aviator cap. "Even after a hectic day on the campaign trail, Rob Lorber still has time to talk to some of his supporters," said the poster.

Computers were beginning to make heavy inroads into American life at that time, and Lieth became fascinated with them during his two years at Guilford. He was always going to the computer lab to play with them. After his graduation in December of 1972, he got a job working with computers at Integon, an insurance company in downtown Winston-Salem.

He cut his long hair, forsook his John Lennon glasses, traded his blue jeans for business suits, and began trying to make his mark in corporate America.

At Integon, Lieth met another person who had taken a strong interest in computers. Her name was Bonnie Lou Bates Pritchard. She was two years older than Lieth, recently separated from her husband, and she had two small children.

Bonnie had grown up in the lush and rolling red-dirt farmland of northern Davidson County about ten miles south of Winston-Salem. Her father was a brick mason, and she grew up with three sisters and a brother in a spacious brick house on Hoover Road surrounded by piney woods, grain and tobacco farms, and family, enjoying the welcome attentions of many aunts, uncles, and cousins who lived nearby. She and her family regularly attended Central Methodist Church in Welcome.

Slim, shy, and quiet, Bonnie wore glasses and was not as pretty as her sisters. She liked reading and loved animals. At North Davidson High School in Welcome, she worked on the school newspaper staff and was a member of the Library Club and Dramatics Club. Two years after her graduation in 1962, she went to work for Integon, then called Security Life and Trust Company.

Bonnie was married on August 5, 1967, three weeks after her twenty-third birthday. The wedding took place with her big family in full attendance at Central Methodist Church. Bonnie wore an embroidered wedding gown that she designed and made herself. Her sister Ramona was her maid of honor. Bonnie's new husband was David Stephen Pritchard, who was working that summer at Miller Tool and Plating Company. He was five years younger than Bonnie. After a brief honeymoon Bonnie went back to work at the insurance company. Her new husband returned to West Davidson High School to finish his senior year as a special student.

With the help of Bonnie's family, the newlyweds bought a new ranch-style brick-and-frame house on a cul-de-sac in a rural subdivision called Winchester Downs, just two miles from her parents' house. Their first child, Christopher Wayne, was born on November 25, 1968, in Lexington, the county seat. A second child, Angela Christine, followed in 1970.

Bonnie's marriage had been shaky from the beginning, but children made it unworkable. Later, Bonnie complained that her husband was immature, irresponsible, and wouldn't keep a job. They separated four days before Bonnie's twenty-eighth birthday, four and a half months shy of their son's fourth birthday. Bonnie later maintained that she and her children had been abandoned. With her family's help, she remained in the house on Winchester Court and struggled to pay the bills she and her husband had accumulated. Her children often stayed with their grandparents and other nearby relatives while she worked. On November 9, 1973, Bonnie and Stephen Pritchard were divorced, the judge ordering that Stephen pay Bonnie $750 for debts they had incurred, plus $160 a month in child support.

Although Lieth Von Stein had several close female friends, he had no girlfriends that his friends knew about, nor did he date much.

"He was very unusual, very humorous, very bright," recalled one of his female friends, "but he wasn't handsome. I always thought he would have liked to have had dates, but he was uncertain about asking."

One of his closest male friends, with whom Lieth spent much time talking about women, thought that Lieth may have had more dates than friends realized. "He was so secretive about his relationships," he said. "He didn't let people know if he was seeing somebody."

That was brought home to him in an embarrassing fashion. Lieth spent nearly three years at Integon designing forms on computers, but he found the work boring and unchallenging. He quit in September 1975 to take a traveling job as an internal auditor for Federated Stores, a conglomeration of department store chains, with headquarters in Cincinnati. He moved into an apartment across the Ohio River in Kentucky.

One weekend when Lieth was home for a visit, his friend who thought him secretive about his relationships got a call from Lieth's mother, Marie.

"Is Lieth there?" she asked.

"Is he supposed to be?" Lieth's friend asked warily.

"He told me he was spending the weekend with you," Lieth's mother said, and his friend began trying to cover for him.

"Okay, what are you up to?" Lieth's friend demanded when he saw him later.

That was when he learned about Bonnie.

When he met her later, he was surprised. She and Lieth were so unalike and had so little in common, except for their work with computers, that he wondered what the attraction was. He was not alone. Other of Lieth's friends, after meeting Bonnie, asked one another, "What in the world is he doing with her?"

"She never really made any impression at all," said one of his friends from his days at Guilford. "She could blend into the wall."

Lieth left Federated Stores in May 1977 and moved to South Bend, Indiana, to become a traveling auditor for The Associates, a financial services company with loan offices throughout the country. During his two years in Cincinnati, Lieth was seeing less and less of his old college friends, but he kept in touch with Bonnie. He had not yet been in Indiana two years when he came home for a visit and called Rob Lorber. He was thinking about marrying Bonnie, he said.

"Are you sure you want to do this?" Lorber asked.

He thought so, Lieth said, but he was worried because of her two children. He'd never been around children, he said. He didn't know whether they would accept him or if he would be a good father.

Lorber thought the concerns were normal. He chose to listen and not advise. He felt that Lieth had already decided that marriage was what he wanted, and he was right. When next he heard from Lieth, it was to be told that he and Bonnie were getting married.

The wedding took place on August 17, 1979. She gave up the job that she had held at Integon for fifteen years, and she and her two children moved into a house with Lieth at 1842 Acorn Court in Mishawaka, a suburb of South Bend. Chris was three months shy of eleven; Angela was nine. Lieth continued traveling after the marriage and was home mostly on weekends, making the transition for him and the children less traumatic.

The company for which Lieth was working was in the process of moving its headquarters to Dallas, but when it decided to leave its computer operations in South Bend, Lieth began looking for a new job, preferably in North Carolina. He did not like the fierce winters that blew in off Lake Michigan. He also was concerned about his parents getting older and being far away from them. In the spring of 1981 he was hired as head of internal auditing at National Spinning Company in Washington, N.C.

Bonnie and Lieth and the two children he had taken as his own moved to Washington in July of 1981 and settled in the modern, two-story frame house at 110 Lawson Road in Smallwood. Lieth later got a loan from his father to pay off the mortgage, allowing the monthly interest to be kept in the family. Lieth had to travel during his first two years in Washington, but after that he began spending most of his working hours in the big plant on the western edge of town. In the fall of 1983, Bonnie took a job teaching data processing at a community college in adjoining Martin County. In late summer of 1984, she went to work as a programmer analyst at the big Hamilton Beach appliance factory only a few miles from her house, a job she would keep for the next two years.

In 1982, with his health beginning to fail, Richard Hensel retired from the laundry he had operated for more than half a century in Winston-Salem, turning the company over to his brother-in-law, Howard Von Stein. By then Camel City had seven outlets in Winston-Salem and other nearby towns. Howard's reign at the top was short. Two years later, he and his partners received an offer from a Texas company that was hoping to create a nationwide chain of laundry and dry cleaning plants by buying out regional companies. "It was one of those offers they couldn't refuse," said one person who had some knowledge of the deal. The partners sold the laundry, and Howard joined his brother-in-law in retirement. His share of the proceeds from the sale and his investments over the years had made him a wealthy man, but few people realized it. He and Marie still lived frugally and without ostentation in the same small, modest house they had moved into in 1950. They felt no need to change the habits of a lifetime, but Howard did splurge and buy a new Buick Century.

Howard's retirement was to last only three years. He died suddenly of an aortic aneurism on a Saturday morning in February 1987 at the age of seventy-nine, leaving an estate valued at more than $1.2 million, most of it in two trusts he had established for his wife and son. He had named his only child to be his executor.

Lieth had little spirit for dealing with his father's estate.

He was too worried about his mother. A heavy smoker, she had suffered for years from emphysema and heart problems. Her grief for her husband was more than she could bear. She began deteriorating, and Lieth and Bonnie frequently made the eight-hour round trip from Washington to Winston-Salem to attend to her. In July she died in the same hospital in which her husband had died four and a half months earlier.

The loss of both of his beloved parents in so short a period—soon to be followed by the death of his Uncle Richard—hit Lieth hard and settling his parents' estates occupied much of his time in late 1987 and early 1988. It also brought him a considerable amount of frustration and irritation.

"I'm so relieved. I've just settled this thing," he told an old friend. "Don't ever get involved with the trust department of a bank. It's just so unbelievable."

With his father's wealth now at his disposal, Lieth had the opportunity to do something that he had been thinking about for several years: change his life.

He had settled into a boring routine. On weekdays, he got up at seven, showered, had coffee with Bonnie until about eight-fifteen, left for work. Because he had gained so much weight (he was only 5'6", but he had ballooned up to nearly 170 pounds), he rarely ate lunch anymore, often settling only for a piece of fruit. He was home in late afternoon, always had a few beers before supper, which was always at six-thirty. After supper, he watched *Wheel of Fortune* and *Jeopardy* on TV, and was in bed by eight-thirty or nine. On weekends, when he and Bonnie were not visiting with her relatives, they went to Greenville for breakfast, always to the same restaurant.

Lieth had fallen into a rut. He was aware of it, and it worried him. He thought that he wouldn't live long. He was overweight. He drank too much. He didn't exercise. Shortly after his mother's death, he took out another life insurance policy, this one for $350,000.

In the spring of 1988, Rob Lorber heard that Lieth was in Winston-Salem, staying at his parents' house, which he did not plan to sell. They rarely saw each other anymore, but Rob decided to drop by.

"I yelled at him for not getting in touch with me more," Rob recalled later. Rob's and Lieth's senses of humor had always meshed and fed off one another. "We were really silly together," Rob recalled. No matter how infrequent or short their visits, they always fell back into the old routines, joking and laughing.

That happened on this visit, too, but Rob thought that he detected an underlying sadness in Lieth, a sense of fatalism about his situation.

Rob knew that Lieth didn't really like his work and never had. His new wealth, though, could change that. Indeed, Lieth already was thinking of quitting his job at the end of the year, of using the money his father had made to make more of his own. So work alone could not account for the sorrow Rob sensed in Lieth. Other factors, no doubt, prevailed. Family factors, perhaps.

Lieth rarely talked with friends about his relationship with Bonnie, and as far as they knew, it was fine. But all of his friends knew that his relationship with Bonnie's children wasn't so fine. They knew that had to be especially distressing to Lieth, because he had wanted so desperately for them to accept him and love him as a father.

Some of his friends thought that Lieth had made a mistake all too common to stepparents: he had tried to buy their love. He bought Chris and Angela whatever they wanted, and although he tried to attach responsibility to the gifts, that never quite worked. In Indiana, he had bought both children expensive bicycles, paying nearly six hundred dollars each for them. When Chris went out and wrecked his, Lieth got him another one. Later, when Chris wanted a classic Mustang for his sixteenth birthday, he got it. When he wanted an expensive stereo for his car, he got it. When he asked for a computer, that, too, was quick in coming. Yet there was always an underlying tension between Lieth and the children, especially between Lieth and his stepson after Chris got into his teens.

"It's hell trying to raise teenagers," Lieth told one friend. "We just don't know what to do with Chris. He won't do anything. He's not interested in anything."

"Respect for his parents and the work ethic were so deeply ingrained in Lieth that it was hard for him to relate to someone who didn't have those values," Lieth's friend said. "I think that was what he was struggling with with Chris. He had the feeling that Chris was a total fuckoff and didn't care about anything."

Even to coworkers and casual acquaintances Lieth frequently had remarked that he would be happy when both of Bonnie's children were grown and gone. And as the summer of 1988 approached, that time seemed imminent.

By fall, Angela would be in college in Greensboro. And if Chris didn't flunk out, which seemed highly possible, he would be back at N.C. State for his sophomore year. Lieth and Bonnie would be alone, and Lieth soon would be quitting the job he never had liked.

Lieth should have been excited by the prospect, but to his old friend Rob Lorber he seemed resigned, as if he sensed that life had passed him by.

6

WHILE BRADFORD TETTER-ton was calling frantically for the rescue squad, Danny Edwards began trying the other upstairs doors, still uncertain whether an intruder was hiding behind one of them.

He opened one door, shined his flashlight inside, and saw a form lying in bed. He switched on the light to a scene of teenage disorder. Clothes were strewn. The walls were covered with posters of rock stars, horses, a frosty mug of beer, a string of Budweiser long-necks. Shoes, socks, a hair dryer lay on the floor by a rug that had "Horse Country" on it. A big square fan hummed, blowing directly on a young woman with short light brown hair and freckles, sleeping soundly in a T-shirt.

"Ma'am . . . ma'am," Edwards called.

The young woman stirred and sat up abruptly, frightened. "What is it?"

Edwards recognized her, although he didn't remember her name. Before he'd joined the police department, he'd been security chief at the mall, and he remembered seeing her many times with the other teenagers who regularly gathered there.

"Something has happened," he said. "You need to get up and get dressed."

He stepped out of the room to leave her alone and began checking the other doors: a closet, a bathroom, another bedroom, this one with posters of cars on the walls, Ford Cobras, obviously a boy's room. Nobody in any of them.

The young woman emerged from her room as Edwards completed the quick search. She had pulled on shorts and sneakers.

"Is there any way to get into the attic up here?" Edwards asked her.

"There's an opening in my room," she said. "In the closet."

Edwards went into her room and opened the closet, but it was so jammed with stuff that he knew nobody could have gone through it to hide in the attic.

"I think I heard my daughter talk," Bonnie Von Stein said over the phone to Michelle Sparrow in communications.

"C-thirty-two, please advise me if that subject's daughter is all right so I can calm her down," Michelle said over the radio.

"Ten-four," Edwards responded. "She's okay."

"Okay, Bonnie, your daughter is fine. Okay?"

Tetterton had reentered the blood-splattered bedroom where Bonnie Von Stein lay on the floor and was checking the body on the bed.

"My husband must be bad, oh god," Bonnie said.

"I think he's gone," Tetterton said.

"I see him," Bonnie said into the telephone.

"Okay, don't look at him, Bonnie," Michelle told her. "Bonnie, don't look at him."

"He was trying . . . he was trying to help me."

"Okay, do you remember seeing anybody?" Michelle asked, trying to divert her attention.

"Oh, it was dark, I don't know."

"Okay."

"I know he had a big club or a baseball bat . . ."

The phone rang and Michelle answered it. Captain Lewis at the fire station, a meticulous record keeper, wanted additional information.

". . . And a knife," Bonnie said.

For a few moments Michelle tried to talk to Bonnie and Lewis at the same time. "Captain Lewis, I've still got ten-thirty-three traffic," she finally said. "I'll call you as soon as I get some more, buddy. Bye-bye."

"Bonnie?" she said into the other phone.

"Yes."

"Okay, now you hang in there with me."

"Don't let my daughter in here," Bonnie said.

"Okay, tell her not to come in here," Tetterton called to Edwards in the hall.

"She advised not to let her daughter in there," Michelle radioed.

"Ten-four," said Tetterton.

"Bonnie," Michelle said.

"Yes."

"The rescue's coming, okay?"

"Yes."

"Okay, don't look at your husband."

She looked up instead to see Tetterton looming over her.

"Officer Sparrow," she said.

"This is the policeman, hey," said Tetterton, reaching for the phone.

"Tetterton?" Michelle said into the phone.

"Yo."

"God . . ." Michelle said with a sigh of relief. ". . . I'm glad to hear you."

"We got to have a uh . . . uh . . . a rescue right quick," he said.

"They're on the way."

"Okay, I'm going to hang up, then."

David Sparrow had heard Tetterton's frantic calls for rescue over his car radio. He had been an emergency medical technician before becoming a police officer. Still carrying his shotgun, he got a portable oxygen tank and mask from his car and sprinted to the house. Edwards opened the front door for him. Sparrow hurried up the stairs and entered the bedroom to see Tetterton taking the telephone receiver from a woman lying on the floor in a bloodied nightgown. He quickly checked the man on the bed, searching for a pulse, but realized that he was dead. He took the oxygen tank to the woman, and saw that she had been stabbed in the chest and was having trouble breathing.

"Okay, we're going to take care of you," he said, preparing the mask.

"Don't let my daughter in here," the woman repeated.

Sparrow had seen the young woman in the hallway outside

the door, and he went out and asked her to go downstairs and wait.

"Don't touch or move anything," he said as she descended the steps.

The ambulance turned onto Lawson Road, its siren further rending the shattered silence of the morning. It came to a halt, and the two men inside, David Hall and Mike Harrell, both firefighters and emergency medical technicians, jumped from the vehicle. Hall was carrying the trauma bag, and Harrell, who had been driving, followed him to the front porch at a trot.

Through the glass storm door they saw a young woman sitting on a step near the bottom of a staircase, chin in hand. She stood when she saw them and opened the door.

"Upstairs," she said.

At the top of the stairs they encountered Edwards and Tetterton.

"You got one on the bed and one on the floor," Tetterton said. "I think one of 'em's gone and the other one's fading fast."

Hall and Harrell were expecting some blood, but they were startled when they entered the room and saw blood everywhere. Both men pulled on rubber gloves and went first to the man on the bed. They rolled him over and saw a big stab wound in the center of his chest, right above his heart. Blood already had begun to gel on the man's chest, and he had no pulse.

Both men turned their attention to the woman on the floor.

"How're you doing?" Hall asked, kneeling beside her in a small puddle of blood.

"Not too good," she said.

He began wrapping a blood pressure gauge around her arm.

"Is he dead?" the woman asked.

"Yes."

"Well, at least he's not suffering," she said.

She had cuts on her head and a sucking chest wound that no longer was bleeding. But she had lost a lot of blood, and her blood pressure was dangerously low. A call had to be made to the hospital emergency room to alert the staff to the situation and to get a physician's permission to start an IV and wrap the patient in Military Anti-shock Trousers, an inflatable suit used to stabilize injured patients. Not wanting to report the woman's condition in her presence, Harrell went downstairs to find another telephone. The young woman directed him to one on a kitchen wall, but the receiver was disconnected and missing. He found it on the table. David Sparrow held his flashlight on the phone while Harrell reconnected the receiver and made the call.

He had two patients, he told Dr. Elizabeth Cook, the young emergency room physician. One was DOA, and a hospital vehicle would have to be sent for the body. The other was conscious, but appeared to be gravely injured and declining rapidly. Dr. Cook approved the IV and the application of M.As.T. trousers, and began to prepare for the patient's arrival.

Upstairs, Hall was ripping open a dressing to put on Bonnie's chest wound.

"I'm going to have to cut your gown, is that all right?" he asked, and she nodded her approval.

Harrell returned to help him get her into the stabilizing trousers, then he went to the ambulance, and, with the help of officer Ed Cherry, carried the stretcher into the house.

At communications, Michelle Sparrow was still busy. She called Captain Danny Boyd, chief investigator for the Washington Police, and he told her to call Melvin Hope and John Taylor, two of the department's four detectives. She called Captain Zane Osnoe, second-in-command at the police department, and asked him if she should call the chief. No, Osnoe said; he would call him. She returned Captain Lewis's call at the fire department. When she found a spare moment, she stopped the device that recorded all calls, removed the big tape reel, marked it, and put it in a special place. She knew that investigators would want it for evidence.

While the technicians worked on the injured woman, Tetterton went downstairs and found her daughter sitting calmly in the den. He needed some basic information for his preliminary report, and he wanted to get it before she found out just how bad things were upstairs and perhaps lost control. He told her that her mother had been stabbed, but that she was conscious and talking and he didn't know how seriously she was hurt.

38

Her father, he said, also had been beaten and stabbed and was seriously injured. He was surprised that she showed no reaction to what he was telling her and calmly agreed to answer his questions. Her name, she told him, was Angela Pritchard. She was seventeen. Her mother was Bonnie Von Stein. She was forty-four. The man upstairs was her stepfather, Lieth Von Stein, two years younger than her mother. He worked at National Spinning Company, a yarn plant, the biggest employer in Beaufort County, and was an executive there.

Only then did Tetterton realize that he had met the bloodied man upstairs before. He had seen this young woman before, too. More than a year earlier, while off duty, he had been witness to a minor car wreck in which Angela had been involved near the high school. He had waited at the scene to tell the investigating officer what had happened. Liability for the accident later fell into dispute, and Von Stein complained to Police Chief Harry Stokes about Tetterton's version of events. Tetterton had been summoned to accompany the chief to Von Stein's office at National Spinning to talk about the matter. Tetterton felt that Von Stein implied that he had lied and wanted him to change the truth to benefit his stepdaughter, and he had left the meeting in a huff.

Now the young woman was telling him that she also had a brother, Chris Pritchard, who was away at N.C. State University. Should she call and tell him what had happened? Tetterton told her to go ahead and call, and if she wanted to call somebody to come and be with her, that would be all right, too, but she should stay at the house. Detectives would be wanting to talk with her later.

7

THE CALL CAME AT 5:17 A.M. from emergency call box EO8 next to Burgaw dormitory on the campus of N.C. State University. Such call boxes were spread strategically around the campus, mounted on poles topped by blue lights so that they could be easily spotted. None was more than a minute or two away from a patrolling campus police officer. A male, apparently young, was on the line, and dispatcher Barbara Dew had trouble understanding him. He sounded hysterical and he kept saying something about losing his keys and his parents being stabbed, and he needed to get to Washington, North Carolina. Dew asked his name, but all that she could understand was "Christopher." She tried to calm him to learn more, but he grew even more hysterical.

"Just hold on," she told him. "I'm sending an officer out."

When call box EO8 came into sight, Lieutenant Teresa Crocker saw a young man dressed in shorts and T-shirt. His back rested against the pole on which the phone was mounted, his knees pulled up, his head on his knees. When she brought her red-and-gray campus security car to a stop beside the box, the young man leaped up and came to her car yelling. He was thin and of medium height, with a shock of dark hair and a wild look in his eyes, so agitated that she couldn't make out what he was trying to tell her. "I couldn't find my fucking car keys," he kept saying. He also kept repeating something about his parents being beaten and stabbed. As he was flinging his arms and stalking back and forth, "ranting and raving," as Lieutenant Crocker later described it, a second campus security car arrived, and Patrolman Michael Allen got out.

"What's the trouble?" he asked.

"I don't know," Crocker said in exasperation. "I can't make it out. See if you can talk to him."

Allen couldn't get much more out of him, and he suggested that they take the young man to the Public Safety Office. Both officers were certain that the young man was either drunk or on drugs and thought that he might be hallucinating.

Melvin Hope always claimed that he was a bear to wake up, but he had no trouble stirring himself when the phone rang shortly before five and Michelle Sparrow told him there had been a murder in Smallwood. He pulled on blue jeans and moccasins and hurried out.

At forty-four, Hope no longer cut the same trim figure that he had when he first joined the marines at eighteen. His waistline had been creeping up on him, and his hairline had done something that marines didn't do: retreat. Hope had served fifteen years in the marines, including two tours in Vietnam, before he left the Corps as a staff sergeant, due to problems with his first wife. He had joined the reserves to complete his military retirement and had become a police officer in Jacksonville, a town sixty miles to the south, on the edge of the sprawling marine base, Camp Lejeune. Eventually, he had grown weary of wrestling drunk marines and followed a friend to the Washington Police Department at the end of 1981. He had been made an investigator the following July and now was the department's detective sergeant. A gruff man with a bushy mustache, seldom without a cigar between his teeth, Hope was filled with macho bluster and war stories, and others in the police department sometimes referred to him as their John Wayne.

Hope arrived at 110 Lawson Road to find his captain, Danny Boyd, had arrived before him and had already been upstairs to see the body.

"What happened?" Hope asked.

"We got a mess," Boyd said, going on to explain the situation briefly. Hope went on up to see how big a mess for himself.

Whoever had set out to kill Lieth Von Stein had done a thorough and vicious job, Hope saw. The savagery of the attack was impressive.

Von Stein now lay on his back, his eyes swollen and closed, his neatly trimmed beard matted with blood. His pale legs, which looked almost too thin to support his thick, hairy body, were spread. His left hand was clenched, and his entire body was bathed in its own blood. He had five gaping wounds on his head: three across his balding forehead, one just above and slightly to the side of his left eyebrow, and the biggest above and to the back of his left ear. Hope counted six stab wounds from a large-bladed knife in Von Stein's upper back, near his left shoulder. Another, in the center of his chest, had gone straight to his heart. The carpet was bloodied on both sides of the double bed for more than three feet out. Blood was splattered on the ceiling and on three walls of the sixteen-by-twenty-foot room.

John Taylor's real first name was Haskell, but nobody ever called him by it. The song "Big Bad John" had been popular when he was a bruising toddler, and his daddy had started

41

calling him that. The nickname soon got shortened to plain John and nobody had called him anything else since. At twenty-seven, he was the youngest detective in the Washington Police Department and one of its most promising officers. One of his fields of training was photography, and he took most crime scene photographs for his department. After Michelle Sparrow called him, he drove his pickup truck to the police department, loaded his photo equipment into the police evidence van, and went to 110 Lawson Road. He arrived as Melvin Hope was looking over Lieth Von Stein's body.

David Sparrow and Ed Cherry were on the porch, and Taylor told them to seal off the yard with the yellow crime-scene tape he had brought in the van. Nobody was to pass beyond the tape without an official reason for being there.

Taylor joined his sergeant and captain in the bloody bedroom and got a brief rundown on what had happened before the three detectives took a quick walk-through of the house to begin scouting for evidence.

It was apparent that the intruder had entered and departed the house by the back porch door, but the broken window by the door was a mystery. It had been broken from the outside, because the glass shards were scattered on the beige linoleum of the porch floor. But why had the window been broken when the wooden door itself had nine panes of glass? A person would need long arms and have to stand on tiptoes to reach through the broken window and unlock the door. Also the cuts on the screen didn't seem to match the breaks in the glass. Could somebody have entered with a key and broken the window as an afterthought to try to make it seem like a break-in?

Another odd thing on the back porch was a faded, torn military knapsack lying on the floor by a plastic garbage can. It was obviously out of place. Had it been abandoned by the intruder?

Two cabinets in the kitchen stood open, along with two drawers. Two purses lay on a countertop, and the contents of another purse, this one white, had been spilled across the range top in the kitchen island. A wallet, a fat folder of credit cards, and a small aspirin bottle were spread over stove eye covers decorated with fox hunt scenes. The wallet and purses appeared to have been rifled, but the detectives weren't convinced that robbery had been the motive for this crime.

Too many things that a robber might take had been left behind: televisions, stereos, tape players, a VCR, computers. A twenty-dollar bill and a handful of change lay in clear view on a dressing table in the Von Stein bedroom. Lieth Von Stein's wallet and watch lay untouched in a letter box. His wife's wedding rings were in a small bowl. Other valuable jewelry was in an unlocked box atop a chest.

Could Lieth have awakened and startled a burglar before the thief had a chance to find all these things? If so, why didn't the burglar just flee? And why would a burglar creep into an occupied bedroom in the middle of the night carrying a baseball bat or club and a large knife unless he had come with an intention to murder?

While the detectives were doing their walk-through, others had been arriving at the house: Chief Harry Stokes, Captain Zane Osnoe, two technicians dispatched from the hospital to remove Lieth Von Stein's body, a news crew from the local TV station.

"Take a number and get in line," David Sparrow told the news crew, who were not allowed inside the crime scene tape. No one would be talking to them for a while yet, not until things had been sorted out.

One young man was allowed behind the tape. Andrew Arnold once had dated Angela briefly, and they had remained close friends. She had called him after telephoning her brother. He identified himself to Sergeant Tetterton, and Tetterton told him that Angela was inside and it was okay to go on in. Bonnie, Tetterton told him, was still alive, but Lieth was dead, although Angela didn't know it yet. Angela was sitting in the living room when he came in. She had little to say, and Arnold didn't know what to say to her. The two sat quietly until Tetterton came to tell Angela that her stepfather was dead. When he did, Tetterton said later, he saw what he thought was a tear beginning to well in the corner of one eye. Shortly afterward, Sergeant Hope came to suggest that Angela ride downtown to the police department with him so that he could take a statement from her. Her friend, Hope said, could follow in his own car.

In the emergency room at Beaufort County Hospital, only a half-mile from the swarming scene on Lawson Road, Dr. Elizabeth Cook was determining the extent of Bonnie Von

Stein's injuries. Her patient was alert but acting "bizarre," as Dr. Cook later described it.

"Is he dead?" Bonnie asked as the doctor worked over her. "I'm glad he's dead. He's not suffering. He's out of his misery."

Dr. Cook had found that her patient had three ragged lacerations on her head: two near the hairline at the center of her forehead, each about an inch long; another over her right eyebrow, this one larger, C-shaped. Bonnie's left thumb was swollen and bruised, perhaps broken, although she still could move it.

Her most serious injury was to her chest. Above her right breast was a bruise the size of a grapefruit. Just to the right of her sternum was a two-inch stab wound, deeper on the right than on the left. The blade had apparently glanced off the bone and cut into the chest wall. The lung had not been penetrated, but it had partially collapsed.

Dr. Cook ordered a transfusion, started an IV, and began inserting a catheter into the chest to allow the wound to drain and the lung to re-inflate.

"Can't you put me to sleep?" Bonnie asked as the doctor worked.

"No, darling, I'm sorry, I can't."

Bonnie's breathing improved almost immediately, and Dr. Cook went on to suture all her wounds and order a second unit of blood before admitting her to the hospital's intensive care facility.

At the Public Safety Building at North Carolina State University, Patrolman Michael Allen and Lieutenant Theresa Crocker had managed to get the agitated young man they'd picked up at emergency call box EO8 calmed enough to learn that his name was Christopher Pritchard. His sister had called him in his dorm room a little before five to tell him that their parents had been beaten and stabbed and that he'd "better get his butt home." He couldn't find his car keys. And he had been so upset that he had left his dorm not knowing what to do until he saw the call box and asked for help.

Allen and Crocker told him that they would try to find out for certain what had happened and asked if he would like something to eat or drink while they did it. He declined and perched in a chair hugging his knees.

Melvin Hope had just radioed Michelle Sparrow that he was leaving 110 Lawson Road to bring Angela Pritchard to the police station when Michelle got a call from Patrolman Allen at N.C. State. She gave him the number for the direct line to the Washington Police Department and told him to wait five minutes and call Sergeant Hope for details.

Lieutenant Crocker notified her supervisor of the situation, and after she called Hope and confirmed the young man's story, he authorized two officers to drive him to Washington in a public safety car. Crocker and Allen were about to go off duty, but they volunteered to take him.

"How long does it take to get to Washington?" Allen asked him.

"An hour and a half if I drive," Chris Pritchard said.

Traveling at the speed limit, the trip normally took about two and a quarter hours.

The three left Raleigh about six. Allen was driving, Chris Pritchard riding in the front seat with him.

Chris said little as they began the trip, and after fifteen minutes, Allen asked him if he'd like to get into the backseat and try to sleep. Chris said yes, and Allen pulled off the road so that Chris and Crocker could exchange places. Soon after Allen pulled back onto the highway, his backseat passenger was curled up, fast asleep.

Melvin Hope did not understand how the young woman before him could be so unemotional. Angela Pritchard answered his questions as if she had been not at all distressed by the terrible events of the morning.

She had just graduated from Washington High and would be going to Greensboro College, a prestigious private school, in the fall, she said. She told Hope about going out riding with her friend Donna Brady the night before. Donna had let her out in front of the house a little before eleven. Her stepfather had been in bed but her mother had been up watching TV. They'd talked briefly and she'd gone on up to her room. She went to sleep about twelve-thirty, and the next thing she knew, Danny Edwards was waking her. She hadn't seen or heard anything. Melvin was incredulous that she'd heard nothing, but he tried not to show it when he pressed her on it. Well, she explained, she was a heavy sleeper. And her door was closed, and her fan was blowing on her. She'd slept with a fan blowing on her since she was a baby.

The young woman seemed so detached that Melvin finally said, "Look, do you realize what's happened here?"

"Yes," she said. "My mother and stepfather have been stabbed and my stepfather's dead."

Only when she mentioned that her stepfather was dead did her voice crack and she display the first sign of distress to Hope.

A little before six, Francis Brady, an executive with an area TV station, answered his doorbell in Smallwood to find Angela Pritchard and Andrew Arnold at his door.

"Is Donna up?" Angela asked.

"Should she be?" Brady asked, thinking perhaps his daughter had made plans that she had forgotten.

"My stepfather's been stabbed and Mother's in the hospital," Angela told him.

Shocked, Brady invited the young pair into his den, and when his wife, Lillian, came to see who was calling, Brady told her what had happened and she went immediately to wake Donna.

Donna came into the den shortly and went straight to hug Angela. Later, she said that she thought Angela was almost about to cry.

Melvin Hope returned to 110 Lawson Road, and he and Captain Danny Boyd decided to go to the hospital to see if they might be able to talk to Bonnie Von Stein. The detectives hoped to get some description of her attacker so that they could put out an alert.

Dr. Cook gave permission for them to ask a few questions, but they found Bonnie "befuddled and kind of whacked out," unable even to tell them whether the intruder was black or white.

"It was dark," she kept saying.

Chris Pritchard did not stir in the backseat of the N.C. State Safety Patrol car until Allen and Crocker had found their way to the Beaufort County Law Enforcement Center, only to discover that they had come to the wrong place. Chris directed them instead to the Washington Police Department a few blocks away. They arrived about eight-thirty, and Sergeant Hope was not there. He had gone home to shower and change clothes. While they awaited his return, Chris nervously paced.

Hope arrived shortly, shaved and wearing a suit. He told Chris that he had left the hospital only a short time earlier and his mother was going to be all right. But he was sorry to report that his stepfather was dead. All the while, he watched Chris closely for a reaction, and later he described it this way: "Chris was really trying to appear grief-stricken, but he wasn't quite making it. It was almost like he was going for an Emmy."

"Look, I'm going to need to talk to you," Hope said. "Do you want to talk now, or would you rather go to the hospital first and see your mother?"

"I want to go to the hospital," Chris said, his voice cracking.

"It was almost like he had one eye on the exit and the other on me when he left," Hope recalled later.

At the hospital, Chris was allowed into the intensive care section for a short visit. He stood holding his mother's hand and crying as she told him what had happened.

8

NELSON SHEPPARD, A TALL, amiable man, had been in law enforcement for twenty-six years. During that time he had become as skilled a politician as he was a law enforcement officer, a combination of abilities that had allowed him to serve for seven years so far as sheriff of Beaufort County, a job he hoped to hold for some time to come. He was Michelle Sparrow's boss, and he made sure that she kept him fully informed. Early on the morning of July 25, she called to tell him about the murder in Smallwood. The case was not in his jurisdiction, but he liked to keep up with what was going on in the county. On his way to work, he stopped by the house at 110 Lawson Road.

He spotted John Taylor and went over to talk to him.

Taylor had worked for Sheppard as a deputy before joining the police department, and Sheppard liked him and respected him. Taylor showed his former boss through the house and told him what little was known about the situation.

"Something stinks about this one, John," said Sheppard, who had been a detective himself for five years.

Sheppard noticed that Lewis Young was not at the scene and was not surprised. Young was the resident agent of the State Bureau of Investigation in Beaufort County. His primary duty was to assist local law enforcement agencies with difficult cases, but local officials had to first request his help. Sheppard knew that there were problems in the Washington Police Department, and that in recent years an unspoken animosity had grown between the department and the SBI.

Young was perhaps the best educated and most widely trained law enforcement officer in the county. A native of Louisburg, in the central part of the state, he was a graduate of the University of North Carolina, and had been a teacher and parole officer before joining the SBI more than twelve years earlier. He had been the first full-time SBI agent assigned to Beaufort County, his first and only duty station. A soft-spoken man with an easygoing disposition, Young had quickly earned a reputation as an honest, dedicated, and thorough officer. He and Sheppard had become close friends, and had made many cases together.

Young's office at the Beaufort County Law Enforcement Center was just a couple of doors from Sheppard's, and when Sheppard arrived at work, he went straight to Young's office and found him doing paperwork.

"Why aren't you out in Smallwood?" Sheppard asked.

"What's going on in Smallwood?"

Sheppard told him about the grisly events of the morning.

"Well," said Young, "I sort of like to be asked."

Sheppard intended to make sure that he was. He went straight to his office and called Mitchell Norton, the district attorney for the Second Judicial District, a five-county area. Norton's office was only a short walk away, and he came straight to the law enforcement building after receiving Sheppard's call.

"I want you on this," he told Young.

"I have to be asked," Young said.

"I'll see that you are," said Norton.

Soon after Norton and Stokes spoke by telephone, Stokes and Young rode to 110 Lawson Road together. By the time they got there, Lieth Von Stein's body was at Beaufort County Memorial Hospital, where Medical Examiner A. L. Potts had already examined it and authorized its removal to the medical examiner's office at East Carolina University School of Medicine in Greenville. John Taylor had photographed the body from every angle before it was removed, and had photographed the rest of the house as well, knowing that the photographs would be needed as evidence. Taylor also had directed the patrol officers in a grid search of the Von Stein yard, which had turned up nothing significant. Other officers had been dispatched to talk with neighbors to see if any had seen or heard anything unusual in the night, but nothing had turned up there either. Captain Danny Boyd and John Taylor filled in Young and Stokes on what was known so far, and Young attempted to get an SBI mobile crime lab to the scene, only to discover that none was available, because crime lab operators were attending a conference. Left with no other choice, he decided to conduct the meticulous evidence search himself, with the help of Taylor and Detective Arnold Cox.

Meanwhile, Melvin Hope was trying to learn more about Lieth Von Stein. He called National Spinning Company, where word of Von Stein's death was just beginning to circulate. He was referred to several people before he talked with Brad Hughes, the company's vice president for finances. Hughes invited him to the plant and offered him access to Von Stein's office.

At the plant, Hughes told Hope that Von Stein was in charge of internal auditing for the company, overseeing two other auditors. He also did special projects for Phil Wander, the company's third-highest executive, in New York. Von Stein used to make frequent trips to New York, but not so often anymore. Wander was about to retire, and Hughes was gradually assuming his duties.

An auditor's job is not one designed to win friends, Hughes acknowledged, but Von Stein was well regarded by his fellow employees nevertheless. Hughes had become perturbed with him once, he said, when he learned that Von Stein recorded their telephone conversations. But he thought there was no sinister motive behind it, that Von Stein simply used the tapes to refresh his memory. Hughes knew of no especially sensitive or unusual audits that Von Stein had been involved in, certainly none that might cause somebody to kill him.

But as he talked with Hughes, Hope learned two things that might offer a motive for Von Stein's murder. First, Hughes told him that Von Stein had been shopping for a mobile home, for what purpose he did not know. Could Von Stein have been having an affair and contemplating setting up a little love nest? If that was the case, perhaps a jealous husband or boyfriend had discovered the affair and taken out his anger in a middle-of-the-night sneak attack with a baseball bat and a knife. That might also explain the brutality of the assault.

The second revelation that Hughes offered was even more intriguing. Von Stein had recently inherited a lot of money, Hughes said. A million dollars or more, he'd heard. That had caused company officials to wonder how much longer he would continue working at National Spinning.

Hope's pulse rate quickened at the revelation of Von Stein's worth. He knew that the man was upper-middle-class, but neither his house and its furnishings nor his cars had indicated that he might be a millionaire. A million dollars, Hope well knew, was more than ample motive for murder.

Hughes allowed Hope to poke around in Von Stein's office, gave him four cassette tapes thought to contain some of Von Stein's recorded telephone conversations, and left him to talk with the two auditors who worked for Von Stein, Robin Reid and Earlene Rhodes.

Both women had been stunned by the news of their boss's death, and neither could think of any reason anybody would want to harm him. He was strongly opinionated, they noted, but he usually offered his views in such a way that nobody took offense. They described Von Stein as an easy person to be around, a person who liked to joke and kid.

Both knew that Von Stein had been looking for a mobile home. When he got calls about it, they said, he would close his office door. But neither could believe that Von Stein had a girlfriend. They just didn't see him as that type.

Once when they were teasing him, they said, Von Stein had said, "I'm more interested in beer than sex."

By the time the Washington *Daily News* began hitting the streets shortly after noon on Monday, July 25, news of the murder in Smallwood had already spread through the town by word of

50

mouth, and people were hungry for details. The paper offered little.

WASHINGTON MAN
KILLED, WIFE HURT

From the headline, a reader who hadn't already known about the murder might have been led to think it had been no more than an accident. Only a photograph of the Von Stein house with a close-up of the crime-scene tape hinted to the casual reader that something far more sinister had occurred in the town's wealthiest neighborhood.

The news story was brief, quoting only Sergeant Joe Stringer, the police department spokesman. It said that the Von Steins apparently had been attacked by burglars, leaving Lieth dead and Bonnie in guarded condition in the hospital. Stringer was quoted as saying that their teenage daughter, Angela, was not injured and apparently slept through the attack. The house was not ransacked, the story noted, and it was unclear whether anything was missing.

As the newspapers were first hitting the streets, Detective John Taylor was setting up a video camera in the autopsy room at the medical school at East Carolina University in Greenville. At twelve-thirty, he began taping the autopsy of Lieth Von Stein. The operation was being performed by one of the country's leading pathologists, Dr. Page Hudson. Until a year and a half earlier, Dr. Hudson had been North Carolina's chief medical examiner, a job he'd held for eighteen years. He had stepped down to teach, write, research, and garden, but he still liked to take up the scapel, the bone saw, and the other tools of his trade now and then, especially in intriguing cases. Although he had been an effective administrator, creating the state's system of medical examiners and establishing data bases to help law enforcement agencies investigate homicides, suicides, and different types of accidents, he relished the role of medical sleuth above all others. He had conducted more than four thousand autopsies, many of murder victims, and he was a noted authority on arsenic poisonings. He even had discovered a new technique for detecting arsenic in the body. Despite all that he had seen, he never ceased to marvel at the horrible things that humans do to themselves and to one another, and the body of Lieth Von Stein was a prime example.

Von Stein, Dr. Hudson discovered, had died from a stab wound to the heart. He had bled to death within minutes of receiving it. He likely was unconscious when he was stabbed. His skull had been fractured under the biggest laceration on the back of his head, and his brain had suffered a contusion and hemorrhaged. That blow to the head alone might have killed him if he hadn't been stabbed.

In addition to Von Stein's major wounds, his right wrist was broken, and he had numerous scrapes and bruises on his hands and arms, typical defensive wounds. But he also had fresh scrapes on his shins, particularly on the right leg and ankle. These wounds were more common in cases where the person attacked had been standing rather than lying in bed.

Other than having a mildly fatty liver, the result of drinking too much alcohol, Von Stein had been in good health and could have expected to live a long life.

Dr. Hudson found no alcohol in his blood, but he did find one thing that was curious indeed. When he cut into Von Stein's stomach, he found it full, as if he had just consumed a large meal. Among the foods that could be identified were chicken and rice. Normally, those foods were easily digested and should have passed from the stomach within an hour or two of being eaten.

If Von Stein had been attacked shortly before 4:00 a.m., that would have meant that he had eaten a large meal around two or three, which seemed unlikely. If this was his Sunday night supper, then he might have been attacked much earlier than the police believed, although severe stress, Hudson noted, might delay digestion by a few hours.

Earlier that day, the detectives at the house on Lawson Road had decided that Bonnie could still be in danger. When word got out that she had survived the attack, the killer might return to finish the job. They didn't have to point out that it would be terribly embarrassing if she were murdered in her hospital room. The merest thought of such a thing was enough to convince the chief that he should immediately assign officers to protect her around the clock.

———

By mid-afternoon, the Washington Police Department had already received numerous calls about the murder. Some callers were merely curious and wanted information. Others were provoked by fear. Was a mad killer loose? Had an arrest been made? Would one be made soon? Still others were trying to be helpful. They had information that they thought the police should know. Some of these calls were deemed important enough to check out.

Lewis Young and Melvin Hope went to talk to a man who was the local sales supervisor for a large bakery. The man had driven down Lawson Road shortly before four o'clock that morning on his way to work. As he was leaving Smallwood, he said, he had seen a car turning into the development. A Japanese car. Not old, not new. Baby blue. Had a luggage rack on top. He was sure of that. And he was almost certain that it was a station wagon. Anyway, there were two "scroungy look-ing" young white men with long hair inside. The one on the passenger side was slouched in his seat, his knees on the dashboard. The man knew that, because his headlights had shined directly into the car when it turned in front of him. But he couldn't tell how the young men were dressed. He was suspicious of the car, because he drove through Smallwood every morning on his way to work, and that was the first time in ages that he could remember seeing a car out in the area at that early hour. He just wished he'd gotten a license number.

The man also told the officers that a coworker who didn't want to get involved thought that they should check out a fellow who had been living in a tent in some woods near Smallwood. The fellow, who was thought to be feeble-minded or emotionally disturbed, had been spotted early that morning riding a bicycle near Smallwood. And he had a bandage on his arm.

Hope and Young dutifully added one more item to the scores of things they had to check out.

Before the detectives could go chasing after half the crackpots in the county, however, they first had to know more about the people most directly involved in the crime: the Von Steins.

And shortly after four-thirty that afternoon, they returned to the Washington Police Department to meet Angela Pritchard and begin prying into the family's life.

53

The officers began by asking Angela to recount her activities of the day before, and she did, telling everything right up to the time she went to bed. The next thing she knew, she was being awakened by a police officer. She reiterated that she hadn't even been aware that the attack was going on. She had since seen her mother at the hospital, however, and her mother had told her about it. Her mother was certain that if she hadn't fallen off the bed, she would have been killed, too, Angela said. Whoever had done it, her mother had told her, had to be young and strong.

Hope asked if she knew anything about a mobile home that her father might have been thinking of buying. Yes, her parents were looking at house trailers so that her grandparents would have a place to stay when they came to visit. So much for the love nest theory.

The officers asked about her natural father. His name, she said, was Steve Pritchard. He was a long-distance trucker who lived in South Dakota, but he was thinking of moving back to North Carolina and going into the real estate business. He was supposed to come to see her and her brother sometime soon.

Did her natural father have any feelings about Lieth Von Stein?

"He thought he was the best thing for me and Chris," she said.

Angela offered only sketchy information about her stepfather. His father, mother, and uncle had died recently and he had inherited some money. But she didn't know how much.

Her brother was in summer school at N.C. State and would be a sophomore in the fall, she said. He lived in Lee dorm, room 611-B, and she had called him there about five that morning to tell him what had happened.

How did she and Chris get along with their stepfather? Lewis Young asked.

Fine, she said. Just fine.

Did she have any idea who might have wanted to kill her stepfather?

The only thing she could think of was that it might be somebody he had fired at work. But she didn't know whether he had fired anybody or not.

At least the detectives came out of the interview with one bit of pleasing information. Angela had never seen the faded army knapsack that had been found on the back porch, and

54

she was certain that nobody in the family owned it. Chances seemed good that the killer had left it behind. Perhaps it could help lead them to him.

This was one of the busiest and most critical times of the year for Noel Lee. Priming time, time for harvesting tobacco, his primary cash crop. Temporary workers were prowling his fields in the hot sun, stripping the heavy leaves from the stalks. Others were packing the crop into bulk barns—long, trailerlike containers—where it would be cured golden with gas heat. Lee had little time for thinking as he oversaw his field hands, going from one field to another. But he couldn't get out of his mind the strange fire he had seen early that morning after he had sent his hogs off to market.

Lee told his mother about the fire when he went to her house for lunch. Later, she told his brother, Edward, with whom he farmed, about it, and his brother stopped by the fire site out of curiosity.

When Noel Lee got home after finishing work that Monday, his phone was ringing. His mother was on the line. Did he think the fire he'd seen that morning might have had something to do with that murder in Washington?

What murder? Lee hadn't heard about any murder.

It was right there on the front page of the Washington *Daily News*, his mother said. On the TV news, too. A big executive had been killed in Smallwood. And it had happened just about the time that Noel had seen that fire. Could it be connected? Edward had stopped by the fire site, she told him, and he said it looked as if some kind of clothing might have been burned.

It seemed a strange coincidence, Noel agreed. And after talking with his mother, he got his newspaper and read about the attack on the Von Steins. It did seem possible that the fire could be connected, he thought. He considered calling the police, then thought better of it. He didn't want to look foolish. But the suspicious fire wouldn't leave his mind, and an hour and a half later he picked up the telephone and called the Washington Police Department.

Lee finally was switched to a detective who didn't seem especially interested in what he had to tell him. The detective took the information and thanked him, but Lee had the distinct impression that that would be the last he'd hear of it. He thought the detective figured that he was just another kook trying to get in on a big event. He almost wished he hadn't called, but he had done his civic duty. If the fire had anything to do with the murder—and the thought caused another shiver to course up his spine—at least he'd told the police about it.

The police were discovering that most of the Von Steins' neighbors considered them private and standoffish. Visitors to the Von Steins' house tended to be teenage friends of their children more than adults. The only adult neighbors who knew them well were David and Peggy Smith, who lived across the street. David had his own business, and he and Lieth occasionally got together to shoot pool or talk sports. Peggy, like Bonnie, didn't work outside the house, and she and Bonnie visited frequently. Peggy had gone to the hospital to visit Bonnie that morning, and that afternoon David had organized a group of neighbors to clean up the Von Steins' bloody bedroom. Peggy couldn't understand why the police had cut large chunks out of the walls and carpet in the room.

At nine-forty-five Monday night, Lewis Young and Melvin Hope went to the Smiths' house to talk with them and learned some things that proved to be of great interest.

Lieth had a million dollars in life insurance, David told the officers. Only that morning, Hope had learned that Lieth recently had inherited a million dollars. A second million in life insurance would make his death a lucrative venture indeed. Did the Smiths know who might be beneficiaries? They were certain that Bonnie was, and David thought that her children might be co-beneficiaries. Furthermore, David was highly suspicious of both Angela and Chris. It simply isn't normal to go on as if nothing had happened after something like this, he said, and both Angela and Chris were doing just that. Beyond that, Angela said she had slept through the entire attack, and he just didn't see how that was possible, she being only a room away.

Peggy admitted that Chris and Angela seemed to be acting strangely, but she couldn't conceive that they might have had something to do with attacking their mother and killing their stepfather. Bonnie loved them and they loved her. Why, Bonnie was "everyone's mother," a second mother to all of Chris's and Angela's friends as well as to other neighborhood teenagers. They would go to her to talk about their problems when they wouldn't go to anybody else. Peggy wasn't troubled by Angela's lack of emotion. Angela was just like her mother, Peggy said. Neither showed emotion. At least not publicly.

The Smiths agreed that Angela and Chris seemed to get along well with their parents, but David said that Lieth had told him that he would be glad when the children finally were gone off to college.

The Smiths also offered some other possibilities for the officers to check. One neighborhood young man was fascinated with guns and other weapons and into "blood and gore," they said. They called him "weird" and said he had once been a frequent visitor at the Von Stein house. And this young man had a friend who used to walk Lawson Road a lot. They went on to tell about a neighbor who had noticed suspicious traffic on the road the night before the murder. And somebody had rattled another neighbor's door late Sunday night, they said. All things for the detectives to check out.

Asked if they could think of anybody who might have held a grudge against the Von Steins, Peggy remembered that Bonnie had been involved in an unpleasant incident a year or so earlier. Bonnie and Chris were at the dentist's office when a man struck Lieth's car with his truck. The man got angry when the police came to investigate and tried to attack the officers with a knife. They pulled their weapons, subdued him, and took him to jail. Bonnie later was called to testify against him, and the man was sent to prison.

The Von Steins were good, kind people, Peggy said, and that was the only person she could think of who might have held something against them.

The detectives left the house realizing more than ever that their work was just beginning.

It had been a long day for Young, and an even longer one for Hope, but there was one more person they wanted to talk with before they quit for the night. They had been having trouble meeting up with Chris all day. Apparently, he had gone off to Greenville with a high school buddy, they discovered. But at ten-forty that night, after leaving the Smiths' house, the detectives stopped by Donna Brady's house and found Chris there.

He seemed nervous. He sat on a sofa with the officers and smoked one cigarette after another as they questioned him.

He'd come home for a visit that weekend, he said. He'd

stayed Friday night but he had to go back Saturday night to work on a school paper that was due. On Sunday night, he said, he'd gone out with friends, then stayed up playing cards and drinking beer with them until three or three-thirty. He'd only been in bed a short time when his sister called to tell him about the attack. Public safety officers from N.C. State had brought him to Washington, he said, because he was distraught and couldn't find his car keys.

Were his parents having any problems? Young asked.

No, Chris said, none that he knew about. They were getting along fine with one another. And he couldn't imagine them having trouble with anybody. He didn't even know anybody who disliked them. He had no idea why anybody would want to do this.

David Smith's suspicions caused Hope to watch Chris closely as he talked, taking note of the fluttery hand gestures, the nervous glances. He disliked Chris instinctively and distrusted him. Yet he tried not to show it. This, after all, was a friendly interview. The detectives were just looking for background information, a direction in which to set the path of their investigation. At this point nobody and everybody was a suspect.

Did he and Lieth get along okay? Chris was asked.

Oh, yes, very well.

How about his real father? Did his father and stepfather know each other?

Yes, and they got along very well, too.

Did Chris know anything about his stepfather dealing in stocks?

Well, he knew that Lieth had inherited some stocks, and maybe some cash, too, but he didn't know how much, or anything about it. He just didn't keep up with that kind of stuff.

One possibility the detectives were considering was that somebody in the crew that recently had painted the Von Stein house its muted aquamarine color might have come back and tried to rob them. Chris said that he wasn't at home while the house was being painted but he knew that the job had been done by a man who worked as custodian at the high school, and the detectives probably wouldn't have any trouble finding him.

As Young and Hope were getting ready to leave, they asked if Chris had ever owned a green canvas knapsack.

No, he said, and he'd never known of one being in his parents' house.

On the way back to the police station, Hope and Young talked about the case, which both now knew was going to be a tough one.

They had a dead man with a million-dollar inheritance and another million in life insurance. In murder cases, detectives always ask themselves one basic question that guides their investigations: Who stands to gain from this death? In this case, that seemed to be Bonnie Von Stein and her children. But Bonnie had been viciously attacked, too. Was she meant to be killed or not? Could she be involved? They thought it unlikely. She almost had died. Would anybody run that risk for money? Had the whole thing been set up by her children? Could Angela actually have slept through the attack on her parents? Was Chris's presence in Raleigh during the murder all too convenient? Was there somebody else who would gain from Lieth Von Stein's death that the detectives didn't yet know about? Were the Von Steins simply the victims of a random, maniacal killer?

As tired as they were, the detectives could hardly wait for the next day, when they could talk with Bonnie and begin trying to ferret out answers to some of these questions.

9

BONNIE WAS WEARING A fresh pink gown when Young, Hope, and Chief Stokes arrived at her room in the intensive care section of Beaufort County Memorial Hospital shortly after ten Tuesday morning. Her head was swathed in bandages, her eyes purpled from the blows she had received. The bed had been cranked up so that she could be in a sitting position to talk more comfortably. The detectives introduced themselves and Bonnie received them cordially. Stokes, who had talked with her briefly the day before, explained that the detectives needed to question her in more depth, and they began by asking her to recall the events of the previous weekend.

She told about Chris arriving home on Friday night and recited all the family activities right on through Sunday. When she told about going to Caroline's in Greenville for dinner Sunday night, the detectives asked if she remembered what she and her husband had ordered. Yes, the Sunday night specials. She'd had the beef. Lieth had chicken with rice. That fit with the autopsy results, the detectives knew, and they were careful to ask about the time of the meal. They'd arrived at the restaurant about seven-thirty, Bonnie said. They left no later than nine. That would have put six or seven hours between the meal and the attack, and the detectives knew from the medical examiner that such a meal should have been gone from Lieth's stomach within a couple of hours unless his digestive system was severely distressed.

Wincing with pain whenever she moved, Bonnie went on to tell about the attack, and again the detectives were careful to question her about one aspect of it: Lieth's screams. Was he screaming loud? "At the top of his lungs," Bonnie said. How many times did he scream? She couldn't be sure, but at least fifteen, maybe twenty or more.

The detectives had already been wondering how Angela could have slept through the attack on her parents. This only made them more suspicious.

Bonnie went through the details of the attack matter-of-factly, her story interrupted only by the questions of the detectives. She still was unable to give any better description of the attacker, or whether more than one intruder had been in the room.

Had Lieth done anything to provoke such an attack? Did he have problems with anybody? Was he prone to violence?

"He was a gentle soul," Bonnie said. "He wouldn't hurt anything. He was a very nonviolent person. He wouldn't even allow a gun in the house."

She knew of no problems he'd had with anybody, of nothing he or she had done to cause somebody to do such a vicious thing.

Questioned about Angela's theory that the attack might have been revenge from somebody Lieth had fired at work, Bonnie could recall only one person Lieth had to let go. That had been a few years ago, and it really wasn't his doing. Another employee had written an anonymous letter to top officials about the man's work habits and Lieth had been instructed to fire him. Bonnie could think of nothing from Lieth's work that might have prompted the attack.

The detectives turned the conversation to a touchier subject: the Von Steins' finances. Bonnie showed no reluctance to talk about it.

She acknowledged that Lieth had inherited a little more than a million dollars from the deaths of his parents the year before. Most of the inheritance was in a trust fund at a large bank in Winston-Salem, but Lieth thought that the bank was getting a poor return on the investments. He was sure he could do better himself, she said, and he recently had taken about $150,000 out of the account to play the stock market. They had been dealing in "dividend captures," buying stocks that were about to pay dividends, then selling them after the dividend was paid. Lieth had made about $20,000 in recent weeks doing that, she said. They'd done so well, she said, that Lieth was planning to take all of the money out of the trust and invest it himself, putting the bulk of it in treasury notes. Indeed, they'd talked about it at dinner at Caroline's the night he was killed.

Did anybody in Washington know about their financial status? Lewis Young asked.

Nobody, she said. Not even their children.

After getting the names of the bank trust officer and the family attorney who had handled Lieth's parents' estates, the officers asked about the trailer Lieth had been planning to buy.

He was going to put computers in it and use it as an office for trading stocks and managing his money, she said. He was planning to quit his job after Christmas, and he wanted a place to go to every day. He didn't want to work at home. Also it would be a place for her family to stay when they came to visit.

The officers wanted to know about service people who came regularly to the Von Stein house, and Bonnie told them about the housekeeper who came every Monday, two high school boys who mowed the grass every Thursday, a pet-sitter who had a key to the house and came when they were out of town. She gave the name of the school maintenance man who had painted the house recently with a couple of helpers. They had painted it on weekends over a two-month period.

Had any of the painters been inside the house? Only one, the man in charge, and he'd come in only once, about a week earlier. He stepped into the kitchen to pick up some shrimp she had offered him to take home.

Young now brought up another delicate matter. Life insurance. Had Lieth bought any recently? Not recently, she said, but she volunteered without hesitation that he was heavily insured and she was the sole beneficiary. How heavily insured? the detectives inquired.

Probably between $800,000 and $1 million, she said.

Why did he have so much insurance?

Well, he was a fairly heavy drinker, about a six-pack every night, plus occasional vodka and wine. He also had a job that entailed a lot of stress. He thought it inevitable that his health would fail before he got old. It was a sound investment in his view. "He just had a feeling that he wouldn't live very long," she said.

Bonnie could think of no reason why she and her husband had been attacked. She only knew that the shadow who had done it had seemed big and strong and had been methodical in his work.

Asked about the man she had testified against in court for attacking police officers after he had struck Lieth's car at the dentist's office, Bonnie's voice broke and rose and she appeared to become excited as she related the frightening and violent incident. But Lieth had not been present, was not a witness, and didn't even go to court when she had to testify, she said. If that man were seeking revenge, wouldn't it be only against her. Why kill Lieth?

The officers ended their interview with no more idea of who the killer might be than when they had arrived. But Chief Stokes had come to one conclusion. He didn't think that Bonnie was in any danger of further attack, and he was going to remove the around-the-clock guard at the door of her hospital room.

Young and Hope spent much of the afternoon talking with neighbors of the Von Steins. They asked more questions of Peggy and David Smith, talked with other neighbors who had

62

seen suspicious cars or strangers in the area over the weekend. They also went to the junior high school and questioned the school maintenance man, Louis Moore, who had painted the Von Stein house. He described the Von Steins as "kinda quiet" and said he couldn't imagine why anybody would want to hurt them. "No nicer people in the world to work for," he said.

Tuesday night, Young and Hope gathered with other detectives in the small, cluttered detective squad room at the Washington Police Department. They wanted to assess what they had learned so far about the case and as they bandied theories and talked about leads, one detective mentioned a call he'd received the night before. A farmer in Pitt County had called about a fire he'd discovered alongside a country road early Monday morning. Thought it might have something to do with the murder. The call had come just as the detective was getting ready to leave for the day, and it had slipped his mind until now. But he had taken the farmer's name and number and he still had it. The farmer's name was Noel Lee.

"We need to check that," Young said, trying not to show his irritation that he and Hope hadn't heard about this earlier. "We can't afford not to follow any leads."

Young called Lee's number, but discovered that he was at a rescue squad meeting. Probably wouldn't be home until after eleven. Shortly after eleven, Young called back. Lee told him what he had seen the morning before and how he had thought it very strange, even before he had heard about the murder in Smallwood. He didn't know whether it might be connected or not, he said, but he thought he ought to let somebody know. Young asked if he would mind going tonight to point out the spot where he'd seen the fire.

"Not at all," said Lee.

"We're on our way," said Young.

Lee's farm was just across the Pitt County line from Beaufort County, a nine-mile drive from the Washington Police Department. Young and Hope arrived about eleven-thirty and talked briefly to Lee in his front yard. He told them about loading out hogs the previous morning, about spotting the fire as he was heading home. All three climbed into Young's SBI Ford and drove back out Grimesland Bridge Road toward U.S. 264.

Lee pointed out the spot where the fire had been, and Young pulled his cruiser across the opposite lane and onto the narrow shoulder, his headlights shining onto the blackened circle left by the fire. A tree-trimming and brush-cutting crew had been along the road earlier that day clearing power-line right-of-way and had run a heavy mower called a bushhog over the fire debris, scattering some of it for several feet around. A few pieces had been thrown onto the pavement and struck by passing vehicles.

"Smells like they used kerosene or diesel fuel," Hope noted.

Young took a pen from his pocket and used it to sort through what was left of the debris in the burned circle.

"What have we got here?" he said, coming up with a socket for an extension wrench. "A blunt object."

"Could that tie into it?" Hope said, taking the cigar from his mouth.

"We don't have anything else. If I could only find a knife," Young said, squatting again to stir the ashes. "Well, looky here."

Lee and Hope came closer, being careful not to block the light from the headlights. There in the debris was a large hunting knife, the handle melted, the six-inch blade blackened.

"Well, I'll be goddamned," said Hope.

"Is your crime lab operable?" Young asked.

"I could call," said Hope.

"Use my radio," Young said.

The three men waited on the roadside for Detective Arnold Cox to get there with the crime scene van. After Cox arrived, the officers set up floodlights, collected all the fire debris, and scoured the roadside for hundreds of feet with flashlights, searching for any other possible evidence. When they finally called off the hunt about 2:00 A.M., they had gathered what appeared to be the burned remnants of blue jeans, melded hunks of a sweater of some sort, the charred bottom of a black Reebok sneaker, the wrench socket and knife, and a couple of wadded sheets of paper, one of them partially burned, that had been lying only a couple of feet from the fire.

Young and Hope were exhausted from a second extraordinarily long day, but they were excited about the night's find. They were almost certain that they had the knife that had been used to kill Lieth Von Stein, and if that proved to be the case, they knew that this evidence would be invaluable. After dropping Noel Lee off at his house, they returned to the Washington

Police Department and parted for a few hours' sleep before they would meet again and try to determine if they could indeed link these charred remnants to the murder.

10

Early Wednesday morning, July 27, the second day after the murder of Lieth Von Stein, a group of detectives drove to the fire site on Grimesland Bridge Road to photograph it and to search it more thoroughly in daylight. They prowled the roadsides for half a mile in each direction, turning up nothing more of significance.

Afterward, Melvin Hope left for Greenville with the knife that had been found in the fire debris the night before. He wanted to show it to Page Hudson, the medical examiner who had performed the autopsy on Lieth, to find out if it was consistent in length and shape to the stab wounds Lieth had suffered.

Lewis Young returned to the Washington Police Department with the other detectives to sort, catalog, and bag the rest of the material that had been picked up along the roadside. It was messy and tedious work, the material fragile and charred, and the detectives' hands were black with oily soot.

In that material were two wadded sheets of paper, one singed by flames and partially burned. Young unfolded the one free of burns and discovered it to be a blank worksheet from the company that had done the brush clearing and tree trimming along the road the day before. The second sheet was white with blue rules, and Young was especially careful with it because of the burns. When he finally got it spread out, he stared at it with disbelief.

"Look at this," he said.

"What is it?" asked John Taylor, who had photographed the fire site that morning.

"It's a damn map of Smallwood," Young said incredulously.

"Are you kidding?" asked Taylor as the other detectives huddled around the sheet.

"No, it's a map of Smallwood."

Clearly it was, crudely drawn in ballpoint pen. One word had been handprinted on the sheet: "Lawson." Clearly Lawson Road. Several blocks were drawn in, obviously to represent dwellings, but one house was clearly marked: number 110. The Von Stein house.

Melvin Hope was jubilant. Dr. Hudson had told him that the charred knife that had been found in the roadside fire debris was consistent with Lieth's stab wounds. Hope couldn't wait to get back to Washington and tell the other detectives that they might indeed have the murder weapon. He walked into the detective squad room and found the detectives smiling impishly.

Something was afoot, he knew. A practical joke?

"You won't believe this, Melvin," Young said.

"What?" Hope asked warily.

"Guess what," said Taylor.

Hope wasn't about to try.

Instead somebody handed him the burned sheet of paper. Hope stared at it for a few moments before realizing what it was. Then the word "Lawson" hit him.

"Well, what the fuck," he said. "Goddamn, this shit is just getting weirder and weirder."

The map told the detectives several things. Clearly, the murder was no random burglary gone wrong. It had been planned. And the murderer they were seeking probably wouldn't be found in Washington. He apparently hadn't been to the Von Stein house before, and may not have been familiar with Washington at all. Could it be a professional hit man? It seemed improbable. A pro would have been unlikely to kill in such a fashion and probably wouldn't have been so careless as to dispose of the murder weapon in a way that might attract attention and cause it to be found.

Noel Lee had spotted the fire a little after four, no more than twenty minutes before Bonnie called the dispatcher's office. The trip from the Von Stein house to the fire site was only about a fifteen-minute drive, so the attack on the Von Steins probably had occurred sometime between three-thirty and three-forty-five. Whoever killed Lieth and set the fire probably was headed west on U.S. 264, and had turned onto

Grimesland Bridge Road looking for an isolated spot to get rid of incriminating evidence. That he hadn't made sure that the map burned and that he put the knife into the fire indicated that he was in a hurry and not thinking clearly. After setting the fire, the killer, or killers, probably had turned around, gone back to U.S. 264, and continued west. That road led to Raleigh and N.C. State University, two hours away. There, less than an hour after the fire was spotted, Chris Pritchard supposedly was awakened by a telephone call from his sister, telling him that his mother and stepfather had been beaten and stabbed.

Nothing that the detectives had discovered so far proved that Chris was involved, but the map and the location of the fire fueled the suspicions they already harbored about him and his sister. They wanted to make sure that neither he nor anybody else knew that they had found the map and the murder weapon, and they vowed one another to secrecy. Nobody outside of the investigative team and the district attorney's office was to know anything about the fire, the map or the knife.

One item that the detectives had searched for in vain at the fire site was the baseball bat or club that had been used to beat the Von Steins. Surely, if the killer had abandoned the knife in the fire, he also would have gotten rid of the club. But if it had been put in the fire, portions of it surely would have been found in the debris, for as Bonnie described it, it was too long to fit in the small circle of the blaze. If it had been tossed into the woods or a ditch near the fire site, their search should have turned it up.

Perhaps the bat had been abandoned earlier, closer to the murder scene. A person carrying a bloodied bat in an upper-class subdivision at three-forty-five in the morning would have risked suspicion and detection if spotted. Maybe he had tossed it somewhere near the house.

So Wednesday afternoon a group of officers descended again on Smallwood. They prowled through backyards and empty lots, waded drainage ditches, poked into hedgerows, looked into storm drains, but they saw no sign of a baseball bat, a club, a steel pipe, or anything else that might have been used to split open Lieth's head.

Some of Bonnie's relatives were at the Von Stein house

that afternoon. Her only brother, George Bates, and his wife, Peggy, spotted Hope and Young searching near the house and called them over.

Earlier that day, George had taken Chris to Raleigh to pick up his car, the '65 Ford Mustang fastback.

"I don't know if you've noticed," George told the officers, "but Chris and Angela aren't acting right. They're going on just like nothing's happened."

He went on to tell some things that had been bothering him about Chris particularly, about his problems with grades at school, about his disappearance earlier that month, and the outrageous tale he'd told to explain it. Something just wasn't right with Chris, George said.

"I don't know if Chris is involved or not," said his wife, "but if he is involved and you need a family member to run interference, just let us know."

11

THURSDAY'S WASHINGTON *Daily News* reported that a ten-thousand-dollar reward was being offered for information leading to the conviction of Lieth Von Stein's killer. Police Chief Harry Stokes and SBI Supervisor R. P. Hawley had requested that Governor Jim Martin approve a five-thousand-dollar reward, and he had done so. National Spinning Company had agreed to match the state's reward. The story quoted Chief Stokes, who said that the investigation of the murder "is definitely still a priority," and that he was confident the case would be solved. "I have a very positive outlook on it," he said.

Just as every other newspaper story about the murder had done, this one also mentioned that Angela Pritchard had "apparently slept through the attack in another upstairs bedroom" and that her brother, Chris, was away at N.C. State when the attack occurred.

Angela and Chris were much on the minds of Detective Hope and Agent Young. And on Thursday afternoon, they went to a local company to talk to a young man who knew both teenagers. The young man, who was a couple of years older than Chris but had been in the marching band with him at Washington High School, described Chris as a "wussy."

"Not the most masculine individual I ever saw," he said with obvious contempt.

Chris wasn't lucky with girls, he said, but he tried desperately to pretend otherwise. After Chris graduated from high school, he started spending a lot of time in Greenville, the young man said, and word on the street was that he had started using drugs, both marijuana and cocaine.

As for Angela, the young man said that if she didn't like her stepfather, she didn't make it known. She sometimes complained about her mother, he said, but usually only when her mother wouldn't let her do something that she wanted to do.

The young man supplied the officers with the names of Chris's closest friends, who, he said, should be able to tell them a lot more.

A funeral service for Lieth Von Stein was held at four o'clock at Paul Funeral Home in Washington while a thunderstorm raged outside. The chapel was packed with Bonnie's relatives, Lieth's coworkers, neighbors, and friends of the family. Lieth's body was not present. It had been cremated, the ashes to be buried in Winston-Salem later, following a second service. Bonnie, wearing a black bedroom gown, was brought to the service from the hospital in a dark blue Lincoln Continental sent by the funeral home. Angela and Chris rode with her. She walked into the chapel helped by her son and a mortuary employee.

The service was conducted by the Reverend Charles Pollock, pastor of Washington's First United Methodist Church. He had never heard of the Von Steins before he was called by a representative of the funeral home, but Bonnie had requested a Methodist minister, and he was the most prominent in town. He had gone to the hospital earlier to talk with Bonnie, but he hadn't been certain what to say or ask. He had difficulty preparing a eulogy, not only because he did not know Lieth and had found it difficult to ask Bonnie questions about a husband who had been murdered beside her, but also because he had heard that Lieth considered himself an atheist. In the end, he kept the service short, saying only a few words about Lieth and being careful not to emphasize the awful tragedy that had occurred. Instead, he spoke of how all people have needs, especially when faced with the mystery of death. And from the Bible he read Philippians 4:19: "But my God shall supply all your need according to his riches in glory by Christ Jesus."

No police officer attended the funeral. As the service was beginning, the two detectives investigating the murder were at the office of Bonnie's attending physician, Zack Waters, Jr., questioning him about the seriousness of her wounds. The stab wound was serious, Dr. Waters assured them, but he could not determine the depth of it without opening the chest again and measuring it, and he was not about to do that. Bonnie was responding well to treatment, and he planned to release her from the hospital on Monday, just a week after she had been attacked. It was his understanding that she intended to move to Winston-Salem but would remain in Washington for a few days after her release. He had recommended that she not return to her house on Lawson Road for emotional reasons. She had told him that she would be staying at the Holiday Inn with her family. It was clear that Dr. Waters considered his patient to be a victim, and the possibility that she might have submitted willingly to such injuries probably never crossed his mind.

Asked if he objected to the police taking a blood sample from Bonnie, Dr. Waters said that he didn't object, but he would not order it. It would have to be voluntary on her part.

On the day following the funeral, Hope and Young returned to Beaufort County Hospital to talk again with Bonnie. She had been moved from intensive care to room 268, and she was doing well enough that she was able to sit up for the interview.

The detectives questioned Bonnie closely about the locks on the doors at her house and who had keys. Both front and back doors had dead-bolt locks which had been installed a few years earlier, she said, although they were used only when the family went out of town. Those locks had not been set on the night of the attack.

People who had keys to both the regular locks as well as the dead-bolt locks were herself, her husband, her two children, and the pet-sitter who came when they were away. Lieth never carried his dead-bolt key and left it somewhere in the house. Chris had a dead-bolt key, but it didn't work, because it was a copy that she'd had made cheaply.

The detectives took her again through the attack to see if she remembered anything new, or told anything differently, but she repeated the same story as she had over and over, and she was no more help in describing her attacker than she had been earlier.

Young turned the questioning to her son. Had Chris ever been in trouble with the police? Once, she said, a couple of years earlier. He and a friend had been at a football game at Chocowinity High School and Chris's friend had pointed a BB gun out the car window at a black man, who took the license number and called police. Law enforcement officers stopped the car and searched it, finding wine coolers in the trunk and ninja weapons such as throwing stars and nunchakus in addition to the BB gun. Both Chris and his friend were charged with possession of alcohol by under-aged persons and possession of weapons on school grounds, both misdemeanors. Both were taken to the county jail, and she and Lieth had to go down and bail Chris out. Lieth had not been happy about it and was less trusting of Chris afterward.

Asked about Lieth's relationship with Chris and Angela, Bonnie said that he'd always been very good to them and treated them as his own children. One of the main purposes of his life was to see that they both got good educations, she said. Indeed, he had remained at his job after coming into his inheritance just to make sure that he would have enough money to get them both through college. Lieth and the children got along well, she assured the officers. Whenever Lieth had discipline problems with them, he always went through her. They were, after all, her children. He expected her to handle the discipline problems, and she did.

The officers had been told by several people of a rumor that had been making its way around town that Lieth had had a fight with one of Angela's boyfriends on the day before the murder and ordered him to keep away from the house. Did Bonnie know about any trouble between Lieth and any of

Angela's boyfriends or any of Chris's friends? None that she was aware of, she said.

How much did the children know about the family's financial situation, Bonnie was asked. They knew that Lieth had inherited a large sum, but they didn't know how much, she said. Neither did they know what was in her will or Lieth's, nor who was beneficiary on any insurance policies. She and Lieth had set up their wills so that if both died, their estates would go into trust funds for Chris and Angela that neither could touch until age thirty-five, except to draw money for basic needs and education, she said. But only she, Lieth, and their attorney in Winston-Salem knew the terms of the wills and trusts, she said.

This interview lasted longer than any that the officers had conducted so far, nearly two hours. And as it drew to a close, Young asked Bonnie if she would mind giving them a blood sample to compare to the blood that had been collected at her house. Not at all, she said, and a technician was summoned to take it as the detectives watched.

As they left the hospital, the two detectives had to agree that Bonnie was a highly cooperative witness, a sweet woman who seemed unlikely to be even peripherally involved in committing so atrocious a crime. But neither was yet willing to dismiss the idea completely.

12

THE MURDER OF LIETH VON Stein affected Washington as no other crime ever had.

On the morning of the murder, as Smallwood was aswarm with police officers, a neighbor whom the Von Steins did not know, Hiram Grady, sat down to write a letter to the editor of the newspaper.

"I sit here at my desk this morning feeling frustrated,

confused, and saddened," he wrote. "I am too numb at this point to feel much else.

"I do not know the family in Smallwood whose world has been shattered this morning. I have never spoken to them although they live only a few houses down from my backyard. I do not know them, but I share their grief. It overwhelms me. How can such a crime happen in our own backyards?

"How can anyone commit such a violent, unfeeling act upon anyone? . . .

"This terrible act of violence does not affect just the family and friends of the victims. It affects us all. We are all victims. Let us pray to God we will never feel the pain of such a terrible crime in our backyards again."

Many in Smallwood were thinking the same thoughts and asking themselves the same questions. And they were fearful of just the thing that Hiram Grady suggested: that they might indeed again feel the pain of such a terrible crime, and next time not just in their backyards but in their own houses.

If the Von Stein murder was not the ultimate suburban horror story, it was close to it. Here were Bonnie and Lieth, decent, respectable people to all appearances, hardworking, successful, healthy, well-off, involved in no wrongdoing, thinking themselves safe in their comfortable home in their manicured subdivision far removed from the fears and dangers of big-city life. Yet they had been invaded by a fearsome shadow in the night, attacked in their sleep, and Lieth Von Stein had died a terrifying death, screaming and helpless.

And then the shadowy killer had slipped back into the night from whence he had come, and even now he might be walking among the people of Smallwood, of Washington, stalking still, with new victims in mind. Just the thought of this fearsome possibility sent a collective shudder through all of Beaufort County.

Nowhere was that awful possibility felt more intensely than in Smallwood. Nobody knew whether or not a maniacal killer might be loose in the area, and as days passed with no arrests and no news to relieve worried minds, the subdivision's frightened residents grew tense, jittery, and extremely suspicious. Locksmiths and installers of alarm systems couldn't keep up with the demand from Smallwood. Unknown cars or strangers passing through the area brought immediate calls to the police. Outside and inside lights were left on at night, and although police patrols were stepped up in the area, some residents kept all-night watches. Others began locking their bedroom doors when they went to bed.

Detectives found themselves going back to Smallwood time and again to talk to fearful residents who had things to report. One woman, the wife of another National Spinning Company executive, thought that perhaps she and her husband were supposed to be the victims, that the murderer might have mistaken the Von Steins for them. Her husband had left for an extended business trip to England on Sunday, the day before the murder. On the Friday before, he had received a substantial check for expenses. Many people knew about that check, she said. Perhaps the murderer had wanted that money, but had confused the two houses. Both Von Stein and her husband drove similar company cars, the same color, she pointed out, and their house numbers would be the same if only a single digit were transposed.

Another Smallwood resident called the detectives to his house to tell them that he'd been awakened by a mysterious noise almost every morning about four for more than a year. He didn't think he needed to point out that the murder had occurred at about that time. He just thought the two things might be connected. The detectives thanked him for the information and left shaking their heads. For all they knew, the guy might be being startled awake by the sound of his own gas passing.

It was not only in Smallwood that people were uneasy and losing sleep over the Von Stein murder, however. Michelle Sparrow, the dispatcher who had kept Bonnie on the line until officers could get to her, was so disturbed by the murder that she had trouble sleeping for days. Danny Edwards, the second officer into Bonnie's bedroom, began locking his own bedroom door when he went to bed, and for several nights he was awakened by dreams of Lieth Von Stein's bloodied body. In Pitt County, Noel Lee, who had come upon the fire that contained the murder weapon, was looking at his neighbors with suspicion, wondering if one of them might have been the murderer and if he had put himself and his family in danger by reporting the fire to police.

Not since another killing fourteen years earlier had murder been such a topic of conversation in Washington and Beaufort

County. At 3:55 A.M. on August 27, 1974, a sixty-two-year-old white jailer had been found stabbed to death in a cell at the Beaufort County Jail. He was nude from the waist down and had semen on his left leg. The cell in which he was found had been occupied by a twenty-year-old black woman named Joan (pronounced Jo Ann) Little, who had been serving time for larceny and burglary and was alone in the female wing of the jail. She was missing, as were the dead jailer's keys. Tracked down and arrested for murder and escape, Joan Little claimed that the jailer had forced her to perform oral sex and she had killed him and fled. Her cause was taken up by women's and civil rights groups, and Washington found itself the unwilling focus of national and international attention. Reporters flocked to Washington, and many townspeople felt themselves unfairly portrayed as ignorant, redneck, and racist. In an eight-week trial in Raleigh a year after the killing, Joan Little was defended by a flamboyant, liberal attorney named Jerry Paul, a native of Beaufort County. A jury of six whites and six blacks took just over an hour to acquit her of the murder charge.

Although that case had caused a lot of talk and resentment in Washington, it had not been the source of nearly as many rumors as the Von Stein murder. And it had produced none of the fear that now had the entire town on edge.

As each day passed, more calls came to the police department, the newspaper, the town manager's office, wanting to know if certain rumors were true, asking when an arrest was going to be made. And each day, the pressure grew greater on Lewis Young and Melvin Hope, the detectives who had primary responsibility for the case. And they still had nothing conclusive to connect anybody to the murder.

To make matters worse, shortly after four on Friday morning, July 29, four days after the murder, a series of telephone calls sent new waves of fear through Washington.

Three times that morning, telephones rang in or near Smallwood. When sleepy residents answered, a male voice whispered, "You are next," and quickly hung up.

One of those calls was made to the home of Angela Pritchard's best friend, Donna Brady.

Young and Hope thought that these calls probably came from somebody with a warped mind, exciting himself by exploiting the community's fears. But they couldn't ignore the possibility that there might be a crazed killer in their midsts, preparing to strike again.

Bruce Radford, a gangling, gregarious man, had been in Washington two months, barely time enough to acquaint himself with the problems he was facing, when he found himself deeply and unexpectedly entangled in the murder of Lieth Von Stein. Radford was thirty-three, and he had just been named the town manager of Washington, his second such job in what he expected to be a long career in municipal government.

Nobody had to brief him about the fear that the murder had engendered in his town. His telephone was ringing constantly. Citizens kept demanding to know what the police were going to do to protect them. Radford thought that the reaction bordered on hysteria, and he realized that he had a serious problem in quelling it, for part of that fear, he knew, lay in the town's lack of confidence in the Washington Police Department.

"The police department was in shambles," he recalled later. "High turnover, low conviction rates, low morale. I had been told when I came here, 'Your biggest problem is the police department.' I could see that it was my Achilles heel."

The main problem, Radford thought, lay at the top. Chief Harry Stokes, Radford thought, was "from the old school," not attuned enough to current management techniques to run a modern police department of twenty-eight officers. Stokes had been born in Pitt County, the son of a farmer who moved his family to Washington when Harry was thirteen. After high school, Harry joined the army and saw combat in Korea. He returned home to Washington and went to work at a service station until a job opened up at the police department in June 1953. He had been in law enforcement ever since, leaving the police department for only one six-year break in the early '60s when he served as the county's Alcoholic Beverage Control officer. After returning to the police department in 1966, he began climbing through the ranks. He had commanded both the patrol and detective divisions before being appointed chief in 1986, when the former chief took a job in another town.

Radford had met many times with Stokes and several times with the entire police department about the problems, which included carelessness, damaging property, and verbally abusing citizens. He already had begun cracking down and instituting changes, suspending some officers, reprimanding others. He was considering personnel changes to control the problems when the murder of Lieth Von Stein threw everything into turmoil.

Stokes had called Radford at five-thirty on the morning of the murder to tell him about it, and at eight Radford had gone to the house on Lawson Road to look into the situation himself. He talked to the detectives and realized that this case would produce problems. The type of murder that it was, the location of it, the prominence of the victim, would create a great public outcry to solve the case quickly. He also knew that a solution was not apt to be forthcoming any time soon.

"At the end of the first day, Harry came to me," he recalled later. "He said, 'We just don't have any clues, not a lot of leads.' He seemed perplexed by the whole thing."

Radford decided then that he would have to take a strong hand in the investigation himself. He instructed the chief to present him with a daily written report on the progress of the investigation and other major activities in the police department.

Stokes resented that order and considered Radford to be meddling in his department. "That was nonsense," he said later. "I didn't have time to do all that mess. He wanted to keep his hands on everything going on. He wanted to run everything, make the decisions and call the shots. I didn't like that. When a city manager tries to tell the chief of police what to do, that just don't cut it."

Radford made no excuses for pressuring Stokes and the detectives working the case. He was feeling pressure himself, and not just from fearful citizens who were calling to ask if an arrest was forthcoming.

On Friday, July 29, Radford got a call from Ashley Futrell. Futrell had been in Washington for forty years. He had been editor and publisher of the Washington *Daily News* for most of that time, and he kept close touch with all the town's power brokers. Now seventy-seven, he had moved to emeritus status at the newspaper, but he still came to work every day, still wrote a regular column and occasional editorials, still kept his fingers on the pulse of the community, and he was a force to be reckoned with. He asked Radford to come to his office for a chat, and Radford went immediately. Futrell took him for a ride in his car to talk.

"He said he had received dozens and dozens of calls," Radford said later. "He said this thing had gone on for four days, and the police department just wasn't doing its job. We had to bring somebody to justice. He felt like it was just that simple."

Later, Futrell would recall the conversation a little differently: "I told him this was a case that ought to be solved quickly. People were restless. It ought to be solved quickly to allay public fears."

Radford's response was ironic in one aspect: "I said it was a very serious case and it would take a long time for somebody to be brought to justice." That was almost exactly the same response Radford was getting from the chief of police.

"People expect you to solve a case like they do on TV," Chief Stokes said later. "But you don't do it. Everybody wanted an arrest made, but you don't make an arrest until you get the evidence, and the city manager didn't understand that."

Stokes was well aware that his officers had no evidence to connect anybody to the murder yet, but he felt that it was just a matter of time. His own suspicions were strong, and they had begun to be formed when he sat through that first long interview with Bonnie Von Stein.

"I had a weird feeling," he recalled later. "I just felt like there was something more than what I heard. I just knew there was no serial killer running loose in the neighborhood. My feelings were she was not intended to be killed, and Angela was not intended to be killed. It made me realize that there was no outsider who went in to kill anyone. There was somebody inside. Then we found that map. We knew there was no doubt about it. It had to be somebody on the inside. I knew it would be resolved. I didn't lose no sleep over it at all."

13

WASHINGTON'S SUMMER
Festival began as scheduled on Friday evening, July 29, on the
town's waterfront. Bruce Radford, the town manager, blew a
deep note on a conch-shell horn to mark its opening.

The festival drew record crowds Friday night and Saturday, an estimated 24,000 on Friday and 28,000 on Saturday.
Maurice Williams and the Zodiacs, a popular southern beach
music group, played. Stewart Parkway was lined with food
stands and exhibits of arts and crafts. The river was alive with
boats, more than anybody could ever remember seeing.

Although the Von Stein murder had disappeared from
the front page of the newspaper on Friday, and Saturday's
paper had carried only a brief and nearly hidden mention that
the investigation was "progressing," according to the police
chief, the specter of the murder hovered over the festival, and
the murder remained a chief topic of conversation. Nearly
everybody seemed to have a theory about it, or had heard
some "inside" information. Rumors had swept through the
town in waves, so many that Bonnie's friend and neighbor,
Peggy Smith, began keeping a list of them.

Some of the rumors were outrageously farfetched. In one,
Lieth was an undercover FBI agent who had discovered that
National Spinning was controlled by the Mafia and was a front
for a major drug distribution ring. The "Mob" had sent a hit
man from New York to kill him. In another, the murderer
had turned loose dozens of chickens in the house to distract
Bonnie's forty cats while he went about his nefarious work.
Other rumors offered gruesome details: Lieth had been stabbed
fifty-two times; his eyes had been plucked out; his stomach had
been ripped from his body; a message had been carved into
his chest.

But most of the rumors on Peggy Smith's list had to do
with Bonnie and her two children. Bonnie was having an affair
and her boyfriend did it. Lieth had ordered Angela's boyfriend
to leave the house and never come back. Chris had been kicked
out of the house after a heated argument with Lieth. Chris

and Angela hated Lieth and the family fought constantly. Angela was secretly married and her husband did it. Angela, her boyfriend, and Chris did it to collect a million dollars in insurance. Chris and Angela were on drugs and belonged to an occult group. Bonnie's injuries were self-inflicted and weren't serious.

While many in Washington remained fearful that the town harbored a crazed killer who might strike again, it was clear that many others had already come to the same conclusion that the police chief had reached: no serial killer was loose in Washington; the murder of Lieth Von Stein was an inside job.

Chris and Angela attended the summer festival with friends that weekend. Wherever they were recognized, whispers followed.

Detective Melvin Hope and SBI agent Lewis Young had no time for merrymaking at the Summer Festival. They were working that weekend, trying to learn more about Chris and Angela.

On Saturday afternoon, they went to a downtown store to talk to a young woman who had dated Chris. She said that she hadn't had any contact with Chris since the previous fall when he came up to her at Burger King after a Friday night high school football game and "hugged my neck." She had met Chris a couple of years earlier on a blind date, she said, and she once had gone as his date on a group trip to King's Dominion, an amusement park in northern Virginia. She described the King's Dominion trip as a "mistake."

Why? the detectives asked.

"Chris was no gentleman," she said.

How so?

"When I tell a boy no, I mean *no*," she explained. "He wouldn't keep his hands to himself."

She had quit dating him after that trip, she said.

The young woman said she had been once to the Von Stein house with Chris and some of his friends. Angela was also there. She knew Angela but didn't like her. She didn't know of any particular ill feelings that Chris and Angela might have held for their stepfather, but she'd heard that they didn't care for him.

The young woman did tell the detectives several things of interest, though. Chris was "strange," she said. He talked all the time about a game called Dungeons and Dragons that he played regularly with his friends Jonathan Wagner and Eric Smith. She didn't know much about the game. No girls ever played with them, but Chris was so deeply into it that he would dress up in costumes and act out his parts. She also had been told that Chris was "heavy into drugs," marijuana and cocaine, although she had no firsthand knowledge of it.

She'd heard one other thing, too, that she couldn't confirm: that Chris and Angela had murdered Lieth. Her boyfriend had told her that, she said.

The detectives also talked that day to another young woman who was a friend of both Chris and Angela. She'd heard that Chris had "really flipped out" when leaving another friend's house on Wednesday night, two days after the murder. Chris had told this other friend, another young woman, that he needed to talk to her in private. He'd given her some notebooks containing material he'd written.

This piqued the detectives' interest. Could Chris have written something about the murder that he wanted to keep but didn't want to be found in his possession?

This young woman also had heard something about the murder: Angela had a boyfriend who was an ex-convict and Lieth had kicked him out of the house the night before the murder.

How did she know this?

A friend's mother had told her.

Bonnie Von Stein was released from Beaufort County Hospital on Monday, August 1, one week after she was attacked and her husband killed. That afternoon, she came voluntarily to the Washington Police Department to be fingerprinted so that police would be able to eliminate the fingerprints of family members from others that were recovered at the house.

After washing her hands, Bonnie was interviewed again by Lewis Young, who questioned her about friends of Chris and Angela. Police had heard that Angela had a boyfriend from Belhaven who could have been involved, but Bonnie knew of no such boyfriend. She named Chris's roommates at the university, but she also made it clear that she had no concerns about any of Chris's friends.

Young also went over a list of the contents of Bonnie's pocketbooks to see if she noticed anything missing, and for the first time she realized that something had been taken on the night of the murder. On Friday, she'd gone to a bank machine and withdrawn one hundred dollars in twenty-dollar bills, she said. She'd had one of those bills in a pocket and had put it on a table in her bedroom Sunday night. But at least another eighty dollars should have been in the purse in the kitchen, the one that had its contents strewn across the stove top.

Angela and Chris also came to be fingerprinted that afternoon, Chris following his mother by an hour. After Chris was finished, Young and Hope took him aside to question him again about his activities on the weekend of the murder.

He'd come to Washington that Friday night because he hadn't been home much during the summer and he just wanted to visit, he said. After he returned to Raleigh Saturday night to work on a paper, he actually went off with a friend to look for a party, he said. When they didn't find one, they returned to his friend's room and drank beer.

He'd worked on his paper for a little while Sunday but didn't finish it, and Sunday night he'd drunk beer and played cards with other friends until about three-thirty in the morning. The paper wasn't due until nine-fifty that morning and he'd planned to get up at seven and finish it. But Angela had called about five, not long after he'd gone to sleep. His roommate took the call and woke him, but his roommate went back to sleep. Chris said that he couldn't find his car keys and had left the room and called the campus police, who picked him up and later brought him to Washington. His roommate found the car keys under a chair cushion later, Chris said.

Chris gave the detectives the names of the three roommates he'd had at college. But none of them, and none of his other friends, had ever had any problems with Lieth, he said. He didn't know of any boyfriends of Angela who'd ever had problems with him either.

"I don't know of any problems Lieth had with anybody," he said.

By Tuesday, August 2, all the evidence that had been taken from 110 Lawson Road and the fire site in Pitt County had been tagged, packaged, and catalogued. Detectives John Taylor and Melvin Hope loaded it into an unmarked cruiser and, in an unprecedented move, headed for Washington, D.C., to deliver it to the forensics labs of the Federal Bureau of Investigation. Normally, evidence was routinely sent to the SBI labs in Raleigh, but this case was special, and the police chief, the city manager, the district attorney, and other officials wanted it to go to the more sophisticated labs of the FBI, where it likely would get a quicker and better analysis. A lot of hope was being placed in this evidence, and they wanted it to reveal all that it could in as short a time as possible. The local newspaper carried a story the following day about the evidence being sent to Washington. Detective Captain Danny Boyd was quoted. "It will answer a lot of questions," he said.

After Melvin Hope returned from Washington, he and Lewis Young continued chasing rumors and tracking leads that led nowhere. Although their suspicions were focused on Chris and Angela, they couldn't risk passing up any possibilities. And several people who had the misfortune of having their license tag numbers jotted down by suspicious residents of Smallwood soon found the two detectives at their doorsteps.

Hope's and Young's attempts to trace rumors to their sources proved frustratingly unending, particularly when they tried to find out if Angela indeed had an ex-convict boyfriend. Their efforts to delve more deeply into the lives of the Von Stein family were more fruitful.

They returned to National Spinning Company and talked with more of Lieth's coworkers. One told them that he had talked with Lieth on the Thursday or Friday before he was killed, and that Lieth was upset with Chris about his studies at N.C. State.

"If he doesn't make it this semester, that's it," the coworker recalled Lieth saying. "I won't pay for Chris to flunk out."

The detectives also talked to two of the company's top executives, Phil Wander, the chief financial officer for whom Lieth had done special jobs, and Don Barham, the vice president for human resources, both of whom had been in New York when Lieth was murdered. Other than Wander's information that he was certain Lieth never had extramarital affairs while he was in New York, because he stayed at Wander's apartment while he was there, nothing new was turned up.

Hope and Young also interviewed the two emergency medical technicians who had come to Bonnie's aid, as well as the two hospital workers who had come to pick up Lieth's body later. All of them made note of one thing they had found curious at the Von Stein house that morning: the teenage daughter had acted differently than anybody they had ever seen in a situation like that. She had seemed utterly unattached, emotionless.

"You have to know Angela," Andrew Arnold told the two detectives.

Arnold was the young man whom Angela had called on the morning of the murder. He had accompanied her to the police department and stayed at her side much of the day. Angela actually was upset, he said. She just didn't show it.

"If you knew her good enough, you could tell it was hurting her," he said.

Angela and Lieth got along fine, Arnold said. When he first met Angela, she always referred to her stepfather as Lieth. Recently, she had started calling him her father. Arnold didn't know of any boyfriend of Angela who might have been kicked out of the house. She had broken up with her last boyfriend, Steve Prettyman, a few months before the murder. Since that time, she had spent most of her time with Donna Brady.

Arnold knew Chris, too. They had graduated in the same class, but he and Chris never hung out together, he said. Chris was really into Dungeons and Dragons, he said, but it was "no big deal." He had seen Chris on the morning of the murder, when Chris came to Donna Brady's house after visiting his mother at the hospital. Chris, he said, was "pretty shaken up."

Arnold knew of no problems in the Von Stein family, and no enemies that they might have. He did know one interesting tidbit of information: He'd heard that Lieth had inherited a million dollars, but he couldn't recall where he had heard it. Bonnie was aware that he knew about it, though. He and Bonnie were very close, he said, and she had told him that Angela and Chris couldn't touch the money until they were thirty-five. The detectives found this information interesting. Bonnie had told them that nobody in Washington knew about the family's financial circumstances, not even Chris and Angela. Now they had discovered that one of Angela's friends knew about it. How many others might also?

After talking with Arnold, Lewis and Hope drove to Pamlico Plantation, another subdivision near Washington, to talk with William Lang, Chris's roommate at N.C. State during his freshman year. Although they had roomed together, Lang said, he and Chris didn't hang out together. Their habits were different. Chris didn't study, he said, and barely made it through his first year. Chris announced that he was going to be one of the school's mascots, Lang said, one of several who wear the heavy wolf suits and prance around at football and basketball games drumming up enthusiasm for the Wolfpack, as N.C. State's teams were called, but he'd missed the practice and didn't pursue it any further. Chris drank "a little bit," Lang said, and was "a little into pot," but didn't use cocaine because it was so expensive. He liked Canadian Mist and would get drunk and type furiously on the computer his parents had bought for him. Chris never played Dungeons and Dragons in their room, Lang said, although he did read books about it. Lots of Chris's friends from Washington came to visit him at State, Lang said. His sister Angela also came with her friend Donna to go to concerts with Chris.

Did Chris have girlfriends? Lang thought he might be dating a girl in Winston-Salem. And he went to South Carolina once to see a girl he had dated who was a friend of one of his cousins.

Asked about Chris's feelings toward his stepfather, Lang said that Chris seemed to like him. He never even mentioned his real father, Lang said.

The hope that Chris might have written something about the murder faded when Young and Hope talked to the mother of the young woman to whom Chris supposedly had given his journals. The woman told the detectives that Chris had called her house several times during the week after the murder looking for her daughter, but her daughter was staying with her father in Greenville. The woman knew that her daughter had some journals Chris had written, but she thought that they were assignments he had written for his English classes in college, short stories or essays about incidents that had happened in his life. He'd given them to her before the murder. The woman had no idea where the journals might be now.

The woman said she'd heard that Chris was a problem child, but she had found him to be reserved, quiet, and shy.

Bonnie Von Stein and her children did not plan to live again in the house at 110 Lawson Road. They were going to move to Winston-Salem to live in the modest house that had been the home of her husband's parents, but Bonnie did not want to move in until she could have an alarm system installed. Until then, she, Chris and Angela were keeping their whereabouts private.

On August 10, Bonnie called Lewis Young to tell him that she had talked with her family attorney and he thought that she and her children were still in danger and needed protection, especially if they came back to Washington. She had to return soon for a doctor's appointment, and she had talked to a private detective agency about hiring bodyguards.

"Can you confirm whether I'm in any danger or not?" she said.

"I can't confirm or deny that," Young told her.

The August 11 edition of the Washington *Daily News* contained an editorial page column that appeared every Thursday. It was called "Puttering Around the Pamlico," and it was written by Ashley B. Futrell. In the column was this brief item:

"Tragedy: When there is a murder and people are shaken and scared, there are demands for quick law enforcement solutions. Sometimes answers are not so easy to come by. The tragedy out in Smallwood recently has upset people. In recent days we are having people call or come in to ask about progress. Now this week we have had perhaps six or eight people to give us full accounts of what has happened, and they talk about having inside information and they vow that they know what they are saying. We have even been taken to task here at this newspaper for not publishing the full story since 'everybody on the street is now informed.' Well, when we are informed officially, we shall carry the full story. False information is dangerous. Half truths are damaging. Let not wild rumors be the order of the day. They can hurt tremendously. And let's get this case solved without delay."

There had been no mention of the Von Stein murder in the paper for more than a week until the Futrell column appeared, but everybody knew that Futrell spoke for those who held the power in Washington. The following day's paper carried a news story with a headline that said, "Investigators Work '24 Hours A Day' on Murder Probe." The article quoted Police Chief Harry Stokes, who said that officers were still interviewing and "following up every lead."

14

As WEEKS PASSED WITH-
out any new murders, the fear that the death of Lieth Von
Stein had fomented in Washington began to subside. But talk
about the murder was as widespread as ever, and rumors
continued to mushroom.

One thing that was upsetting to the officers investigating
the case was that many of the rumors were true, or contained
germs of truth. Clearly, information was leaking from the
police department.

One of the rumors that fit into this category was that Lieth
might have died earlier than Bonnie had said because his
supper had not been digested. Another was correct in one
aspect: that Lieth had a million dollars' worth of life insurance.

Yet another rumor was that Angela was not asleep when
the police officer entered her room to find her in bed, and that
the officer saw a glass of tea by her bedside with ice in it. This
was true to the extent that Danny Edwards, the officer who
awoke Angela, had seen a glass by her bedside with conden-
sation on the outside.

The rumor that angered the detectives most, however, was
that an area farmer had seen a car stop on a rural road on the
morning of the murder and watched as somebody got out and
set a fire. He reported it to the police, the rumor had it, and
they found bloody clothes and a knife in the fire. All the
officers who knew about the fire had been sworn to secrecy,
but word got out about it anyway.

Ashley Futrell later said he knew about the fire on the
morning after Hope and Young first went to inspect the site.
A man called and told him about it but wouldn't reveal his
identity. Futrell said his newspaper didn't publish anything
about it because he was unable to confirm it.

Although the initial rumor about the fire placed it in the
wrong location, word eventually got around not only of the
correct location but of the identity of the person who had
found it. Noel Lee was startled when, a few weeks after the
murder, he got a call from his banker asking him what he'd

found on the roadside. Soon others were mentioning it to him or questioning him about it. Lee had thought that his identity would be kept secret, at least until an arrest was made, and now that it was out, he worried that the murderer might seek retribution against him and his family.

The rumor about the fire even reached Bonnie Von Stein, and she called Melvin Hope to ask him about it. Hope, remembering his vow not to reveal anything about the fire to anybody, was put on the spot. "I didn't tell her the truth, but I didn't lie to her either," he said later, although Bonnie later would tell another officer that she thought he had indeed lied to her.

One rumor made the rounds so often that even Hope began to wonder if it might have some validity. It was that Chris belonged to a satanic cult (in other variations, Angela and Bonnie also practiced the occult) and that Lieth had been killed to raise money to perpetuate the cult. Hope recently had attended a special training session on occult groups with Detective John Taylor, and Taylor got out some of the material from the classes and discovered that July 25, the day of Lieth's murder, was a voodoo holiday in honor of Papa Ogou, calling for blood sacrifices, particularly of sheep and goats.

"The damn thing just kept getting weirder and weirder," Hope recalled later.

Bonnie spent another long session with the detectives when she returned to Washington for a checkup on August 15. She offered a possibility that Hope and Young thought absurd: perhaps somebody at the bank where Lieth's trusts were held had instigated the murder out of concern that he might be planning to remove all of his money.

The detectives were interested in Lieth's financial affairs, however. Having learned that others knew about his inheritance, they wanted to know just how much Chris and Angela knew about these matters.

They were aware that Lieth's father had more than a million dollars from the sale of his share of the laundries in Winston-Salem, Bonnie said, and they probably would have known that Lieth inherited it. But the only other people who would have known about it, she maintained, were his banker, a couple of his bosses at work, and a cousin who was a stockbroker, from whom Lieth occasionally sought investment advice.

Without any prodding from the detectives, Bonnie began talking about an incident involving her son, Chris, that had happened on the weekend of the murder.

She told about receiving a call from the mother of a young man near Raleigh to whom Chris had given a check for thirty-five dollars. Although both the young man and Chris had lied about it, Chris later admitted that he'd given the check to the young man for marijuana. The young man was supposed to pick up the pot and deliver it to him, but he didn't come back. Chris also had bought marijuana from this young man earlier, she said. The young man, only sixteen, was a friend of Tim Parker*, a friend of Chris's at N.C. State. Chris had told her that Parker also was a drug dealer and kept a gun in his room. Chris was very scared of Parker, she said, and fearful that his life could be in danger because of what he knew about the drug dealings. Although other friends of Chris's had come home with him, Bonnie said, Parker never had been to their house.

If Chris was indeed so afraid, that could be an indication that he had been involved in drug dealing himself, the detectives reasoned, and the attack on his parents might well have something to do with it. If Chris owed a drug dealer money and the dealer thought his parents to be wealthy, the dealer might also reason that if his parents died, Chris might receive their money and be able to pay his debt. And even if Chris weren't involved in drug dealing himself and had only been looking for somebody to kill his parents so that he could claim his inheritance early, a former roommate who sold drugs and kept a gun might be a good place to begin looking for an accomplice. Especially one who never had been to the Von Stein house and would need a map.

While Bonnie was talking about her son, the detectives remembered Bonnie's brother telling them about Chris turning up missing earlier in the summer, and they asked her about it.

That happened about the first of July, she said. She and Lieth were planning to go to Winston-Salem for several days, and Angela and her friend, Donna Brady, decided that they wanted to stop off to spend the night with Chris at N.C. State before going on to Winston-Salem the following day. They had called and arranged to stay with Chris, but when they arrived that night, Chris was not to be found, and none of his friends knew where he might be. Angela and Donna spent the night in Angela's car, she said, and drove on to Winston-Salem as planned the next day. Bonnie was worried when she learned what had happened. She began a search for Chris that produced no results. He hadn't even shown up at the clothing store where he worked, she discovered, and his boss also was concerned. Bonnie worried and searched for a day and a half before she finally called the campus police and filed a formal missing persons report. Later that night, Chris called her from N.C. State. He had just arrived back on campus, only to be met by the police, who instructed him to call his mother. Chris said that he had gone on what was intended to be a short trip to the mountains with a friend called Moog. They were going to visit Moog's uncle. On the way, the fan belt broke on Chris's car, and they had to go to an old lady's house to call for help. She offered them a baloney sandwich and a glass of goat's milk. After they got the car repaired and got to Moog's uncle's house, they both became deathly ill with food poisoning and stayed in bed for three days. Moog's uncle lived back in the hills and didn't have a telephone and they didn't have any way of getting word to anybody.

Later, Bonnie had learned that Chris and his friend actually had been at her sister's house in South Carolina the whole time. Bonnie said that her sister's daughter had a friend whom Chris had dated, and he had gone there to see her. He'd asked his aunt not to reveal that he was there if his mother called. When Bonnie called her sister to ask if she'd heard anything from Chris, her sister had covered for him. Bonnie said that she didn't hold it against her, because her sister had had a lot of problems lately.

Bonnie said that she had been concerned at that time that Chris might be getting involved with drugs, and she wondered if that trip might have had something to do with drugs.

Lieth hadn't believed Chris's story from the beginning, Bonnie said. He knew that Chris was very intelligent, and he always had strongly supported and encouraged Chris in every way. But he had been very disappointed in Chris when he got in trouble with the BB gun and wine coolers in high school, and he had been more questioning and suspicious of him after that. The wild tale about his disappearance, and the later incident with the check, when he revealed that he had indeed been using marijuana, had caused Lieth to be even less trusting of Chris, she said.

After Chris's graduation from high school the year before, Lieth got Chris a summer job at National Spinning Company, and he had been very proud of how Chris handled it. Lieth had been proud, too, that Chris wanted to study engineering, but he got upset at Chris's low grades.

The only serious argument between her husband and her son that Bonnie could remember had been about Chris's study habits and grades at college. It happened at the dinner table one night, she said, and she had never seen Lieth so angry. His face grew red and he doubled his fists. She was afraid that he might hit Chris. Chris was shocked by his reaction, she said. He got up from the table, stepped back and said, "Look, I'm not going to do this with you."

The incident lasted only a few minutes, Bonnie said. After Lieth calmed down, she told him in private that he had been wrong in the way he handled the situation, and that Chris had conducted himself in a more adult fashion than he had. He told her that from then on, she could handle the problems of the children, whatever they might be, Bonnie said.

Young questioned Bonnie about Chris's involvement in Dungeons and Dragons. He and some of his friends had been playing the game since he was about eleven, she said. In fact, this summer, he'd taken his Dungeons and Dragons materials to college with him. It was just a tabletop game, she said. Nothing else. Neither she nor Lieth had any concerns about him playing it. They thought that it was a game that required high intelligence, and they considered it to be innocent. She had never heard of Chris dressing up in costumes and acting out the game in anybody's backyard.

The detectives also had learned that Chris showed up at a local pawnshop four days after the murder and hocked his saxophone. Why did he need money? Could it have been for drugs? Bonnie was surprised. It was the first she had heard about it.

On August 23, Young and Hope went to Raleigh, hoping to talk with some of Chris's college friends. They stopped first in a town called Garner on the outskirts of Raleigh and found the sixteen-year-old high school student who had ripped off

Chris in the marijuana deal on the weekend of the murder. He was slim, with a bushy, helmetlike hairdo, and he seemed nervous and wary. The detectives interviewed him in the presence of his stern-faced father. He admitted knowing Chris, but not well. He'd just met him that summer, he said, and only had seen him two or three times, never for more than fifteen or twenty minutes. He'd been to Chris's dorm room, he said, but never alone with Chris. Others always were there. Chris bragged a lot about how rich he was, the young man said. More than once he'd heard Chris say, "Yeah, my mom gave me some more money." He had a nice car, too, a hot Mustang.

Questioned about the thirty-five-dollar check, the young man admitted taking it from Chris because Chris couldn't get it cashed anywhere. The young man said he'd first taken the check to Tim Parker, Chris's friend, but Parker "didn't want to mess with it." The young man then took it to his father, who questioned him about it. He'd given his father several reasons for having the check, and his mother eventually had called Chris's parents to ask about it.

With careful questioning, Young finally got the young man to admit that Chris had given him the check for marijuana, which he hadn't delivered.

Asked about Parker, the young man said that he'd known him only for a couple of months. He described him as "just a normal person."

Was he into drugs? Young asked.

"He might drink a beer," the young man said, "but I never heard him say anything about drugs."

Before Hope and Young left, the frightened young man offered to give them thirty-five dollars to return to Chris, but the detective declined and left him to deal with his father.

After talking to the young man, Hope and Young drove to N.C. State and interviewed the campus police dispatcher who had taken the call from Chris on the morning of the murder. They also talked with the two officers who picked up Chris and later drove him to Washington.

Hope and Young found Tim Parker at his mother's house in a Raleigh suburb. Parker said he hadn't seen Chris since the end of June, when the first summer session ended, but he'd heard about the attack on Chris's parents. Chris never said much to him about his parents, Parker said. He didn't know that Lieth wasn't Chris's real father.

He had mentioned that his family was rich, though, Parker said, and he was aware that Chris got a weekly allowance from his parents. Chris was always throwing money around, he said, spending a lot particularly on alcohol and drugs. At one point, Parker remembered, Chris had gotten in a bad financial bind and had to borrow money to get out of it.

What kind of drugs was he using, the detectives wanted to know.

Well, he'd seen him with pot, Parker said. But there was LSD, too. Chris had first tried that hallucinogenic drug on a Friday night about the middle of the first summer session, some time in early June. He'd used it two or three other times since. Parker said he'd tried to warn him about that stuff, but Chris wouldn't listen.

A long-haired dude named Hank* got Chris started on LSD, Parker said. Chris had met Hank only that summer, but Hank, who was not a student, came around frequently, and Chris often went off to do things with him. "Hank was always trashed in one way or another," Parker said.

Chris was easily influenced by his friends, said Parker, which was one reason he did so poorly in school. He'd do whatever his friends wanted him to do, whether or not he had classes to attend or homework to do. He spent a lot of time playing Dungeons and Dragons.

Asked about the group Chris played with, Parker could only recall a couple of names, a first name, a nickname, no last names at all. Hank played sometimes. And another long-haired guy called Moog. A black dude. A skinny white guy who was a resident adviser in Lee dorm. A guy called Brew.* A short, overweight guy. Usually, they played in one of the dorm rooms, Sometimes they'd get trashed and go down into the labyrinth of steam tunnels beneath the campus.

Asked if any of them had weapons, Parker said he thought that some had Buck knives and darts. "I don't know of any guns or anything like that," he said.

When asked about girlfriends Chris might have had, Parker only laughed.

"He's a wimp," he said. "He couldn't get a piece of ass."

Parker admitted knowing the high school student the detectives had talked with earlier that day. And he knew about the marijuana deal that went bad. After the incident Parker said, the young man told him, "I ripped off your roommate."

Did Parker think the young man could know something about the murder of Lieth Von Stein?

"Wouldn't surprise me," Parker said. "He would do something stupid. He's always working some kind of hustle."

Bonnie had returned to Washington with a bodyguard to visit her doctor, and on the day after their Raleigh trip, Young and Hope interviewed her yet again at the Washington Police Department.

Questioned about the reason for installing dead-bolt locks at the house, Bonnie said that Lieth's car had been broken into while it was parked in the driveway and they were away from home. A radar detector was stolen. That was during the time of the illness of Lieth's parents when they had to be away from home a lot to look after them. They just thought that the dead-bolt locks would make it more difficult to get into the house and to carry things out. The locks were never used when they were at home, she said.

The detectives asked her about names that they had come upon from tips, rumors, and interviews, but Bonnie recognized none of them. Then Bonnie brought up the name of a woman that Young had asked her about earlier. She'd been thinking about it, she said, and she thought she had heard Lieth mention the name before. She thought the woman had something to do with business matters at National Spinning.

One thing she felt confident about: that Lieth had not been involved in any love affairs. At least not in the past four years or so. During the first four years of their marriage, she said, they had lived largely apart because Lieth's work demanded that he be gone all week and they were together only on weekends. What he did then, she couldn't be sure about, she said, but she doubted that he'd had affairs even then.

"He was a one-woman man," she said.

During more recent years, his life had been so structured that there simply wasn't room or time for any other women, she said.

The detectives used this moment to bring up another difficult subject. The possibility of homosexuality. One of Lieth's coworkers had told the detectives that she and Lieth had a long-running but good-natured argument about homosexuality. Lieth contended that there was nothing wrong with homosexuality and defended the rights of anybody to practice consensual sex of his or her choice privately without the interference of government or self-appointed moralists. His coworker argued that homosexuality was morally wrong and went to the trouble of giving Lieth several pages of hand-written biblical quotations to prove it.

Bonnie said that Lieth had several homosexual friends with whom he was open and receptive, but she didn't think he'd ever had any sexual involvements with them. After one of Lieth's friends died of AIDS a few years earlier, she said, she had become concerned about the possibility that he might have had sexual liaisons with some of his friends, and questioned him about it. He denied it. (Lieth had met this friend, an architect who grew up in a small town near Greensboro and later moved to San Francisco, while in college. He had been surprised to learn of his friend's homosexuality, other friends said, but had not allowed it to affect their friendship.) And she was almost certain that he never had done any such thing. She had no doubt that if he'd been sexually involved with anybody else, male or female, in the past three or four years, she would have known about it.

There was a woman at work with whom Lieth had to make a few business trips, Bonnie said. She was certain that nothing had happened between them, but she'd heard that the woman's husband was very jealous. She hadn't heard of any trouble he'd caused, however. It was just a thought.

In trying to think of suspects, Bonnie also had come up with the name of her former husband, the father of Chris and Angela. The detectives knew from earlier interviews that she held a low opinion of Steve Pritchard. He had stayed in the Von Stein house several times while visiting the children, and he and Lieth got along fine, she said. But recently she'd heard that he had a setback of some sort with his trucking business and was badly in need of money. She didn't know how much he might have known about the money Lieth had inherited, but if he'd found out about it, he might have figured that if Angela and Chris inherited it, he could manipulate them to get some of it. She didn't think he could commit murder himself, but he might be capable of plotting it, she said.

The detectives were still unclear about several aspects of

Lieth's financial affairs, and they questioned Bonnie more closely about them. Hope also brought up Lieth's life insurance again. Bonnie said that she had gone over the policies with her attorney recently, and she thought that the face value of the life insurance was only about $770,000, not $1 million. The order of beneficiaries, she said, was first, herself; second, Chris and Angela; third, her parents; four, Lieth's mother, who, of course, was dead. It was just that order that was bothering the detectives.

On August 31, Young and Hope drove to Williamston, twenty-three miles north of Washington, to talk to Stephen Prettyman. He'd dated Angela for three months that spring before she caught him with another girl. They had broken up after that, he said, but they still talked.

Prettyman said that he got along okay with Lieth, but that Lieth was rough on Angela's male friends. He was strict with Angela, and any time Angela wanted to do anything, she and her mother had to scheme to get around Lieth so that she could do it. He thought Lieth's strictness had made Angela rebellious. Lieth seemed to get along better with Chris than with Angela, Prettyman said, but both of them used the same nickname for Lieth: Asshole.

Prettyman said he'd been told that Lieth was worth $3 million. Angela had told him that Lieth's parents were rich and that when they died their money went to Lieth. Prettyman said he thought that whoever killed Lieth knew the family, because he had gone straight to Lieth's and Bonnie's bedroom and hadn't disturbed Angela.

Prettyman also fed more fuel to one of the rumors that had made its way through Washington: that Angela had a boyfriend who was an ex-convict. Prettyman said he'd seen Angela with a guy on a couple of occasions in recent months, once at the mall, again at the beach. He was pretty certain that the guy had recently been released from the Williamston prison unit. He thought he'd seen him on a road gang. "I knew it was bad news," he said of seeing the guy with Angela.

Prettyman said he thought the guy he'd seen with Angela had been in a class a couple of years ahead of his at Washington High School, but later he was unable to pick out his picture in a school year book. He gave the officers a description and said that Angela's friend, Donna Brady, should be able to identify him.

By the time September arrived, Bonnie bore only scars from her wounds. She was living alone in Winston-Salem. Chris had returned to N.C. State to start his sophomore year. Angela had begun freshman classes at Greensboro College, only twenty-five miles away. Bonnie told friends that she was angry at the police because they wouldn't tell her anything. But she was all too keenly aware that the detectives were highly suspicious of her children. She knew from the questions they had asked her, and from the questions they had asked others with whom she had talked, that they seemed to be focusing their investigation on Chris. She thought that the detectives were wasting their time, while the real killer slipped further and further from their grasp. She knew that her children could never be involved in something so heinous. Sure, Chris had been in trouble, had experimented with drugs, had told lies and given his parents reason to mistrust him, but so had lots of other teenagers. Murder was another matter altogether.

She *knew* Chris. He simply was too sweet and gentle and nonviolent to have had any part in killing Lieth, much less in hurting her, or trying to have her killed. And she had no doubt that the killer had intended for her to die. Chris was like her. He wouldn't hurt a fly. Moreover, Chris loved her. She had no doubt about that. It was apparent in his every act. He also had been very upset by Lieth's death, and continued to be. He was worried about his mother, and even had offered to drop out of college and get a job to help out and look after her. But she thought it would be better for him to be back in classes and among his friends so that the awful events of the summer wouldn't prey so heavily on his mind. She could cope alone. She always managed to cope.

15

SUMMER TURNED INTO
fall without major developments in the Von Stein murder case.
Melvin Hope and Lewis Young had continued chasing rumors,
checking out false leads, and talking with friends of Chris and
Angela.

Donna Brady, who had spent much of the weekend of the
murder with Angela, told the detectives about her activities
with the Von Steins that weekend, all of it meshing with what
the detectives already knew from talking with Bonnie, Chris,
and Angela. Donna said that the rumor that Lieth had had a
fight with one of Angela's boyfriends and ordered him from
the house had no foundation. She knew of no friends of Angela
or Chris who ever had had problems with Lieth. Angela hadn't
had a boyfriend since she broke up with Stephen Prettyman,
Donna said. And the young man that Prettyman had seen
Angela and Donna with at the beach was just a friend and not
an ex-convict. She gave the detectives his name.

Donna also was confident that Angela had slept through
the attack, and not just because Angela had told her so. "She's
hard to wake up," Donna said. Besides, Angela had a fan
blowing on her and her door was closed.

About Angela's seeming lack of emotion following the
murder, Donna said she thought that Angela was in shock.
But even if Angela wasn't in shock, Donna wouldn't have
expected any great show of emotion from her. Angela was like
her mother. Neither talked about her feelings nor displayed
them.

Donna knew that Angela and Chris sometimes called Lieth
an asshole, but she pointed out that lots of teenagers occasionally call their parents that, or something similar. "She wasn't
being hateful," Donna said.

Angela and Lieth had been getting closer, she said, and
Angela had begun calling him Dad instead of Lieth. Angela
knew that Lieth had received a substantial inheritance, but she
didn't know how much, Donna said, because Angela just wasn't

concerned with money. She felt certain, however, that Chris knew how much Lieth had inherited.

Steve Outlaw told the detectives that he had been Chris's closest friend all through high school, but they had drifted apart after Chris went off to college. He'd seen Chris about six weeks before the murder, he said, and hadn't seen him again until the day of the murder, when he went looking for him at Donna Brady's house. He described Chris's actions that day as "odd." He seemed nervous and jittery, Outlaw said, talked incessantly to everybody, chain-smoked, and rocked back and forth in his chair. But he did not seem to be grief-stricken. He appeared to be a little more normal at the funeral, Outlaw said.

Outlaw said he'd heard that Chris had gotten deeply involved in drugs—marijuana, cocaine, and acid. He said he'd also heard that Lieth had been killed by a drug dealer to whom Chris owed money, but when Young and Hope pressed him on that, he couldn't recall where he'd heard it.

As far as he knew, Outlaw said, Chris and Lieth got along great, especially after Chris graduated from high school.

Melvin Hope was frustrated with his inability to produce anything decisive in the case, and he lost a lot of sleep worrying about it.

"I beat my brains out with it," he recalled later. "It got to be almost an obsession with me. We were looking at Chris, and Captain Boyd and I agreed that Chris was in it up to his eyeballs, but we couldn't prove it. It was just a mess. I would find myself out there at 110 Lawson Road at three o'clock in the morning almost willing myself to be a fly on the wall back on the morning of July twenty-fifth. It was one I wanted to solve bad."

By the end of September, the investigation had slowed. Both Young and Hope found themselves having to deal with other matters, with previous cases coming to court, with new and less flashy crimes that had to be dealt with. In October, Hope came to work one day to be told by his captain, Danny Boyd, "You're left holding the bag now. Lewis has been kicked upstairs." Young had been promoted to a special unit that worked on sensitive cases out of SBI headquarters in Raleigh, but he planned to continue living in Washington and to keep an office at the sheriff's department. He wasn't going to give up the Von Stein case, however. He still would be available to work it on a limited basis.

Hope wasn't the only one feeling frustrated about the progress on the case. Washington City Manager Bruce Radford was seeing less and less hope for a solution in the brief written reports that he still was requiring Police Chief Harry Stokes to submit to him daily. And although the public outcry about the murder had waned, people had begun saying that they knew the case would never be solved, not with the Washington Police Department looking into it. After all, two other recent murders in the town remained unsolved, one of a convenience store clerk killed in a robbery, another of a suspected drug dealer assassinated while he slept. Radford was feeling pressure from the mayor, the town council, and others.

"Nothing seemed to be happening," he recalled later. "We had sent all of this stuff to the FBI for the quicker turn-around time, and we still hadn't got anything back."

Radford had involved himself in the case to the point of reading Hope's reports, personally inspecting the evidence and making suggestions to the chief, and he wasn't about to let it go unsolved for what he saw as a lack of leadership and initiative within the police department. "This was the biggest thing in the town of Washington," he said, "and I was putting on the pressure on a lot of fronts."

By mid-October, Radford had decided that the case would not be brought to a successful conclusion until he had solved the major problem at the police department, which he saw as a failure of leadership. The only way to do that, he decided, was to start at the top and work down. He first had to rid the department of its chief, Harry Stokes. He called the town's personnel director and asked her to tabulate how much money the chief would draw each month should he choose to retire. She soon came back with a figure that gave hope to Radford.

"I called Harry and said, 'Come over and let me talk with you,'" Radford recalled later. "When he got here, I said, 'I just found out that you can make the same amount retired as you're making working. I wanted to see if you might be interested in retiring.' He said, 'Well, I don't know. Let me take that home to the wife.' Next morning, he was back all teeth and smiles, said he'd decided he was going to retire."

Later, Stokes said that the Von Stein case had no direct

bearing on his decision to retire, and that he reached that decision on his own. "He was trying to put pressure on me and trying to control everything," he said of Radford. "I didn't feel like I wanted to work under somebody who put pressure on me. I didn't have to put up with that. I said, 'I'm fifty-eight years old and I don't need it.' And I was beginning to lose money working."

Stokes submitted his resignation, effective November 30, and Bruce Radford began advertising nationally for a new police chief. One requirement the new chief would have to possess was an advanced degree in police science. That effectively eliminated any candidates from within the department.

On October 18, Bonnie called Lewis Young to tell him about a rumor she'd heard about Chris. Chris supposedly had talked to a minister in the South Carolina town where her sister lived, and the minister had told her family that Chris had some problems as a result of playing Dungeons and Dragons in the steam tunnels at N.C. State and was in fear of his life because of them. Chris supposedly had overheard other players laughing about Lieth's death and calling it punishment for Chris's wrongdoing in the game. Chris had told her nothing about this, she said. It was only a rumor. But she planned to ask him about it, and would let Young know if there was any truth to it.

Bonnie also had some news about her son. Chris had not been doing well at N.C. State, and she had taken him out of college for the time being. He'd been seeing a university psychologist who had determined that he had serious emotional problems stemming from his senior year in high school, she said. The psychologist hadn't been able to get to the root of the problems but recommended that Chris drop out of school until he could control them. She thought it significant that the psychologist had been able to trace Chris's problems back to his last year in high school. That was just after Chris took a cross-country trucking trip with his father, Steve Pritchard. Chris was going to move in with her, Bonnie said, and would begin seeing a psychiatrist in Winston-Salem.

Bonnie also called Melvin Hope from time to time, and he knew that she was aware of his suspicions of Chris. "She remarked to me one time, 'If Chris is involved, I want to see that he gets the full measure of what's coming to him,'" Hope recalled later. "She said, 'If either one of my children had anything to do with this, I'm not going to try to protect them.'" But Hope was convinced that nothing short of Chris confessing to her would ever get her to believe that her son had anything to do with it. And even then, he thought, knowing that Chris had tried to have her killed, her maternal instincts probably would take over and lead her to protect him still.

Lewis Young's new assignment and the impending changes in the police department distracted him from the Von Stein investigation. Hope greatly admired Young, especially his extraordinary gifts as an interviewer, and he had let Young, with his greater education and training, take the lead in the investigation. Hope knew that Young wanted to resolve the case, despite his new duties, and he didn't want to plan moves without Young's approval and participation. Hope himself had problems attending to the case. He had tried to get approval to continue working it full-time, he said later, but had been told that was not possible. He still had three other detectives to oversee, other cases that had to be worked, paperwork that had to be done, court appearances that couldn't be put off. Arranging interviews on the Von Stein case to fit both detectives' schedules became extremely difficult.

Still, they managed to get together early in November for another trip to Raleigh to try to find some of Chris's friends and acquaintances at N.C. State.

They found Chuck Jackson* at the frozen yogurt place where he worked near campus. Jackson had met Chris soon after they both arrived at N.C. State the year before, and he had roomed with him during the second session of summer school when the murder occurred. He had gone home with Chris on several weekend visits.

Jackson remembered answering the phone on the morning of the murder, handing it to Chris and going back to sleep. He also remembered Chris waking him before he left and saying something about his parents being attacked by a burglar. But his other memories of that weekend were vague. He didn't remember Chris going home at all that weekend and thought they might have just sat around watching TV. They could have been playing spades the night before the murder, he just couldn't recall. There were a couple of girls, Sandra* and

Sybil,* who came to the room a lot to play spades. They could have been there.

He did remember that when Chris returned after the murder he said that his stepfather had died, the police didn't know who had done it, and he didn't want to talk about it.

Jackson described Chris as the kind of person who never looked to the future and lived one day at a time, his activities mostly spur-of-the-moment. He was easily influenced, Jackson said, and did a lot of things out of a need for approval and attention from his friends. Using drugs, for one thing. Jackson, who kept up his own grades and often could be found in his room studying, said he'd been concerned because Chris was smoking so much pot, skipping class, and never studying. He'd got onto him about it, but it did no good.

Chris had renounced drugs on several occasions, Jackson said, but he always went right back to them. And it wasn't just marijuana. He tried cocaine but didn't like it. And during the summer he'd been using acid. Jackson said that a guy named Hank probably was Chris's drug connection.

Questioned about Dungeons and Dragons, Jackson said he had played in some of the games that summer but had been too busy with his studies to play since. In the summer they'd had a campaign going in the game. A female cavalier had been wronged by an evil baron and had asked for help, he said. He identified several others who had played in that campaign.

Did they play in the steam tunnels?

They didn't play D&D there, but they had gone exploring in the tunnels, he said. A large group had gone, including the two girls, Sandra and Sybil, and they had carried some large Japanese swords, just to be carrying them. They had spray-painted their names on the walls of a big room under the central campus, he said. Jackson said that Chris and his friend Moog went into the tunnels more than the others.

Did he know about anybody having a gun or a knife in the dorm?

No.

Did Chris talk about his stepfather's wealth?

Jackson recalled a conversation instigated by another friend, Brewster Simpson*, called Brew by his friends, about how financially well off their families were, and Chris had boasted that his had a lot of money. Jackson said Chris told of opening Lieth's financial portfolio once and seeing stock of the R. J. Reynolds Tobacco Company.

But Jackson thought that Chris and his stepfather got along fine. He'd spent the night with them, he said, and Chris and Lieth talked and laughed and seemed to enjoy one another.

The detectives did not think Jackson the type to be involved in murder, and they went looking for other acquaintances of Chris's. They tracked Hank, whom Vince had said was Chris's drug connection, to an apartment building on Hillsborough Street but got no answer. They tried to find Sandra and Sybil, but couldn't locate either one. Neither did they have any luck in searching for the friend called Moog. Several students knew him, but they said that Moog had dropped out of school, and nobody seemed to know his whereabouts.

Bonnie had waived attorney-client privilege to allow Attorney John Surratt to discuss Lieth's financial affairs with the detectives. And after spending a fruitless evening in Raleigh searching for Chris's friends, Hope and Lewis drove to Winston-Salem the next morning to interview him. Surratt had known Lieth's parents for years, but did not even know they had a son until he wrote their wills and set up the trusts that Howard Von Stein established. Surratt noted that if Lieth had died before his mother, Bonnie and her children would have been out of luck in getting any of the million dollars that Howard Von Stein had received for his share of the laundries. When Lieth's mother died in 1987, leaving everything to Lieth, Lieth came to him and said, "I've got to have a will," Surratt said, and he had written the will, setting up trusts just as he had done for Lieth's father.

The way the trusts worked, Lieth could have taken out any of the money at any time, Surratt said. But when Lieth died, $200,000 went into a trust for Bonnie, any amount of which she could withdraw at any time. The remainder went into a separate trust for Bonnie's lifetime that eventually would pass to the children. Bonnie would receive the income from it until she died. If she died before the children reached age thirty-five, the children received the income. The children could not touch any of the money until their mother died, and not even then if they were not yet thirty-five. If Bonnie died without having removed the money from the marital trust, that money would revert to the irrevocable trust for the children, available to them only at age thirty-five.

Lieth had been concerned about the children, Surratt said, and was worried that because he had not adopted them, they might not be able to inherit from him unless he spelled out his desires. He set the age limit because he did not think Chris and Angela were responsible enough to handle large sums of money. He wanted them to have the money, but didn't want them to be spoiled by it, Surratt said.

Surratt estimated that Lieth's estate was worth between $1.75 million and $2 million, including life insurance. Surratt said he did not know whether the children were secondary beneficiaries on Lieth's insurance policies (they were), but if Bonnie had died with Lieth and the children were not secondary beneficiaries, the insurance money also would have gone into the irrevocable trust that the children couldn't touch until thirty-five.

As far as he knew, Surratt said, only Bonnie knew the provisions of Lieth's will. The children did not. That being the case, the detectives knew, either might have assumed that with Lieth and Bonnie dead, all of the money would come to them immediately.

At the end of November, the long-awaited evidence report finally came back from the FBI, and nobody was very happy about it. The Washington *Daily News* made it a front-page news story.

"City Manager Bruce Radford, who has maintained contact with police investigators, said the FBI report on fingerprints and fibers gathered at the scene was inconclusive," wrote reporter Michael Adams.

"Radford became involved in the matter because of a transition of power in the police department. Chief Harry J. Stokes will retire Thursday. Capt. Zane Osnoe will act as interim chief until a replacement is named."

Only one thing in the evidence report gave any new clues. In the burned remnant of a Reebok sneaker that had been found on the side of Grimesland Bridge Road two days after the murder were two hairs. One was from a Caucasian, the other from a black person. Hope and Young remembered that one of the players in Chris's Dungeons and Dragons group at

N.C. State was black. It wasn't much to go on, but at the moment it was all they had, and as soon as they could get their schedules together, they intended to look into it.

After the return of the evidence report, Bruce Radford had given up hope that anything would develop in the case until he found a new police chief. He realized that Lewis Young was in command of the investigation and had little time to work on it. He could tell from the reports he had been getting from Stokes that Young was telling him little, if anything, about developments in the case. He thought that probably was due to the unspoken resentments between the SBI and the police department, but he knew that it might also have to do with his own involvement, which was greatly resented by Young. Hope, Radford knew, would defer to Young and make no moves on his own. And with Young unable to do much because of other duties, the case would be dormant until a strong leader could be installed at the police department to get things moving again.

Hope and Young were not leaving the case completely at rest, however. When they learned that Bonnie would be visiting in Washington early in December, they arranged to meet her at the police department for yet another interview.

Chris was doing a little better since he had left college, Bonnie told them. He was living with her and had a job at a tire store in Winston-Salem, working every day but Tuesday and Sunday. Every other Tuesday he was seeing a psychiatrist. He would continue working until he felt ready to return to N.C. State.

Angela would finish her first semester at Greensboro College soon, Bonnie said, but she had hardly studied and was seeing a psychologist who felt that it might have been a mistake to put her in college so soon after Lieth's death. Angela would drop out after this semester, Bonnie said, and next fall she would be going to a small college in Virginia that had a strong equestrian program.

Bonnie spent an hour and a half with the detectives, and just as the interview was about to come to a close, Young asked the question that both officers had been wanting to ask for a long time.

How would she, Chris, and Angela feel about taking polygraph tests?

Bonnie answered without hesitation. She'd be happy to do it, she said, and she was certain that Chris and Angela would too. She told Young to go ahead and set up a date for the tests.

The polygraph examinations were set for January 17, 1989, one week short of the sixth-month anniversary of Lieth Von Stein's murder. The detectives had put off any further investigation pending the outcome of the tests.

But when Bonnie met them at the SBI office in Greenville that day, only Angela was with her.

Chris couldn't come, Bonnie said, because he had an appointment with his psychiatrist. Pressed about when Chris would be available, Bonnie finally said, "I don't know, and it will be his decision whether or not he takes it."

Later, the detectives learned that after agreeing to the tests, Bonnie had consulted with John Surratt, who said that she needed to see a criminal attorney. She had sought out one of the best-known, and most expensive, in the state, Wade Smith of Raleigh, who had helped to defend Green Beret Dr. Jeffrey McDonald against charges of killing his wife and children, and he had advised that Chris not submit to the test.

SBI polygraph examiner William Thompson administered the tests to Bonnie and Angela. He asked three key questions of each.

Of Bonnie, he asked:

"Did you plan your husband's death?"

"Did you help plan your husband's death?"

"Do you know who stabbed your husband?"

Bonnie answered no to each question.

Of Angela, Thompson asked:

"Did you help someone stab Lieth?"

"Were you involved in stabbing Lieth?"

"Do you know who stabbed Lieth?"

Angela also answered no each time.

After studying the results of the tests, Thompson determined that both Bonnie and Angela were telling the truth. Bonnie's results were well on the side of truthfulness, Angela's less so. Under former standards of grading, Angela's results were close enough to the line separating truthfulness from deception to be called inconclusive. But more recent standards called for determining any results above the line to be deemed truthful, anything below the line deceptive.

Regardless of the finer points of Angela's examination, the results were enough to convince the detectives that neither Bonnie nor Angela had played a role in Lieth's death.

But Chris's reluctance to take the test only reaffirmed what they already believed: that he knew exactly who had killed Lieth. And as soon as they could arrange their schedules, they intended to begin questioning his friends and others to find out who that was.

PART TWO

COMING OF AGE

MY MOTHER GROANED! MY FATHER WEPT.
INTO THE DANGEROUS WORLD I LEAPT;
HELPLESS, NAKED, PIPING LOUD,
LIKE A FIEND HID IN A CLOUD.

—WILLIAM BLAKE

16

Even today Caswell County remains the image of what North Carolina once was: a bucolic vision of verdant land, old, two-story white farmhouses at the end of tree-lined lanes, slanting, unpainted sharecropper houses by the edges of farm fields, and rows of ancient log tobacco barns, mud-chinked, rusty-roofed, and vine-entwined. Few other counties in North Carolina have remained so unchanged by the sweep of "progress" that has so radically altered the character of the once rural and small-town state in the last half of the twentieth century.

Although the county lies in the teeming Piedmont, North Carolina's center of population and industry, less than an hour's leisurely drive north from burgeoning cities such as Durham and Greensboro, no four-lane highway penetrates it. Indeed, the county boasts only a single stoplight, and that of recent vintage.

Situated on the Virginia line, Caswell County is hilly and lushly forested, a haven for deer, wild turkey, bobcats and other wildlife, even an occasional black bear. The state-maintained fifteen-thousand-acre wildlife preserve in the heart of the county attracts hunters from all over the state. In hunting season, pickup trucks and four-wheel-drive vehicles carrying the carcasses of deer are common sights on county roads. Most males in Caswell County are hunters. Boys are taught to shoot and stalk and kill at an early age. Camouflage clothing is common year-around. And venison roasts, squirrel stews, fried rabbit, baked quail, and wild turkey are regular dishes on many local tables.

The land is Caswell County's primary sustenance. Its soil is a sandy loam, underlaid by a thick, rich layer of red clay, ideal for growing tobacco, the county's primary crop and the base of its economy for two centuries. Tradition is important in this county steeped in history, and that history is inextricably bound with tobacco. Caswell's soil attracted planters who established big plantations early in the nineteenth century. Using slave labor, they cleared and planted hundreds of acres in tobacco. The county prospered and produced an aristocracy of planters, manufacturers, and merchants who lived in stately columned houses attended by hosts of servants. Prior to the Civil War, Caswell was one of only sixteen of North Carolina's one hundred counties in which slaves outnumbered free people. But Caswell was an anomaly among those counties, the rest of which lay in the low country to the east, where the plantations depended primarily on cotton.

A happy accident in 1839 brought more fortune, even fame to Caswell County. Until that time, cured tobacco was dark brown, heavy, and splotchy. But that fall one barn of tobacco on the farm of Abisha Slade cured to a fine texture, with bright, unblemished yellow-gold leaves that proved to be of immensely superior quality.

In attempting to find out what had caused this, Slade learned that a slave named Stephen who was tending the fires in the barn went to sleep and let the flames die. When he awoke and discovered what he had done, in panic he dragged some charred log ends from a blacksmith's fire and threw them on the dying embers. The sudden rush of heat from the charcoal came at just the right moment in the curing process and produced the bright golden leaves. Slade and his brothers began experimenting with techniques using charcoal until they could produce the same leaves every time. Their crops brought higher prices than ever before had been paid for tobacco and created a sensation.

The tobacco that Slade developed was first called Bright Leaf, later flue-cured, and it brought a revolution to the tobacco business, making possible the big tobacco conglomerates such as R. J. Reynolds and American Tobacco that came many years later.

Although no battles were fought there, Caswell County was devastated by the Civil War. The economy was destroyed and the county never completely recovered. Without slaves, the plantations could not produce, and the land grew wild. The tobacco factories closed, never to reopen. Merchants moved away. Commerce withered. Towns shriveled and died. The families of planters who did not lose their land continued on proudly in their big houses under greatly reduced circumstances. Some slaves fled, but many had no place to go and remained, eking out meager livings as sharecroppers. But never again did the county experience the prosperity to which it had been accustomed before the war.

Isolated by geography and circumstances, Caswell County became a place with little to offer its most promising young people. The offspring of its educated, aristocratic families continued to become leaders in business, politics, education, religion, but most had to go somewhere else to do it. By the turn of the century, Caswell was a place to leave, not to go to, the sustaining land offering little opportunity.

Yet Ernest Frederick Upchurch saw it differently. Upchurch was an ambitious young lawyer from Wake County with political aspirations, and in 1909, he, his wife, Mary, and their four-year-old son, Norman, set out in a buggy for their new home in Yanceyville, the county seat of Caswell County, where Fred Upchurch set up a practice. Caswell had a reputation for being wary of strangers and newcomers, but the young family found a hospitable reception. Within six years, Fred Upchurch was returning regularly to Raleigh as the state senator from Caswell County. Later, he became the county's prosecuting attorney, a job he held for many years.

Fred and Mary Upchurch had three more children after moving to Caswell County: two sons, Fred Jr., born in 1910, and James, called Jimmy, born two years later, were followed by a daughter, Emmy Lou, born in 1919. The Upchurch sons all followed their father to Wake Forest College, a Baptist institution, and all of the Upchurch children were reared with the strong sense of right and wrong and the fear of hellfire that came from regular attendance at Yanceyville's First Baptist Church, where their parents were staunch members.

Jimmy, the youngest son, always his mother's baby, had the shortest and perhaps most tragic life of the four Upchurch children. He contracted tuberculosis, apparently from his mother. Although the disease went into remission, allowing him to resume a normal life, he seemed to some family members to be without drive or direction. He married and drifted from job to job before his disease flared anew. He died at thirty-five, leaving two young sons as his legacy to the county that had taken in his family and become their home.

The town of Milton, hard by the Virginia line in northeastern Caswell County, has been described as "a museum without

113

walls," a picture-perfect image of a nineteenth-century American town. The town's beginnings date to 1796, when a station to inspect tobacco and flour was built near the Dan River by act of the state's general assembly. A warehouse was constructed. A few houses grew around it. A store opened, then a tavern. By the early 1800s, the town was thriving and lots were selling for high prices. In the decade preceding the Civil War, Milton was the home of five tobacco factories and one of the most modern cotton mills in the South. But Milton, like the rest of Caswell County, deteriorated after the war. By the time Carolyn Moore was born there in 1915, Milton was practically a ghost town.

Carolyn Moore's ancestors were among Caswell County's earliest settlers, and she grew up in Milton in a two-story brick antebellum hilltop house just up the street from the old tavern-turned-residence in which she was born. She was a sensitive child with an interest in history and a fancy for art and reading.

At age fifteen, Carolyn was at the house of a friend, Mary Motz, when an acquaintance of the Motz family stopped by for a visit. He was a slim young man with short, curly red hair and sharp good looks. Although he was quiet and reserved, Carolyn was impressed by his obvious intelligence and quick wit. He was eighteen, she learned, a student at Wake Forest College, and his father was one of Caswell County's most prominent men. The young man's name was James Bartlett Upchurch, but everybody called him Jimmy. His father had given him his middle name in honor of one of Caswell County's most famous figures, Bartlett Yancey, a U.S. congressman elected in 1815 who sometimes presided over the House in the absence of his close friend, Speaker Henry Clay. When next Jimmy Upchurch drove his father's cumbersome Packard to Milton, he was coming to call on Carolyn Moore.

Carolyn went on to graduate from Caswell County's only high school, then attended Appalachian State Teachers College at Boone in the mountains of western North Carolina. During that time she saw little of Jimmy Upchurch. In her first year at Appalachian, he fell ill with tuberculosis, and his worried family was seeing that he got the best treatment available.

Soon after Carolyn returned to Caswell County with her degree in 1936, she and Jimmy began seeing one another again. His disease was in remission and he had regained his strength and his spirit while working as a bookkeeper in the mountains of Virginia, where the pure air was thought to be a help to his condition. They were wed two years later.

Carolyn gave up teaching at the local elementary school when her first child, a son named William Nanning, was born on March 28, 1943. Wanting a bathroom of their own, the family moved out of their apartment over Fred Upchurch's law office into a one-bedroom apartment in an old, two-story house, the Johnson House, next to the Methodist church. A second son, this one named James Bartlett Upchurch, Jr., was born on October 2, 1945. By the time James Jr. was born, his father's tuberculosis was reactivated.

Jimmy was working then at a clothing store in Burlington, twenty-five miles away, but he had to give up his job as his condition worsened, and with Carolyn not working, Fred Upchurch had to help out with expenses. Jimmy deteriorated quickly and soon had to be committed to a sanitorium in Danville, Virginia, just north of the Caswell County line. Carolyn, whose father had died when William was eight months old, took her two young sons and moved back in with her mother in Milton to be closer to her husband. She went weekly to visit him, taking the children and holding them up outside so that he could see them through a window. But after Jimmy had to be moved to a state sanitorium in eastern North Carolina where the most contagious tuberculosis patients were confined, she had to make a long trip by bus to visit him. She only got to see him a few more times before his death on January 27, 1947. Jimmy Upchurch's eldest son was not yet four when his father died, and later he had only the faintest memory of him. His youngest son, and namesake, was not yet sixteen months old, and later had no memory of his father at all.

In 1952, five years after her husband's death, Carolyn, now thirty-seven, remarried. Her new husband, Charles Thomas, a widower of only six months, father of three grown children, was almost twenty years her senior. She had known him all her life. A busy man, always on the go, he now owned what was called The Big Store, a general store in downtown Danville. It filled a huge brick building that had been used as a prison during the Civil War. He had used his store profits to buy land in Caswell County when it was very inexpensive during the Depression, and his holdings were among the largest in the county. He owned twenty-two tracts, ranging from eighty to several hundred acres, all of them farmed by tenants who

115

made the crops and paid him a share of the income. His health had begun to fail, and he had turned his store over to a manager and retired to indulge his passion for bridge. That was how Carolyn had become reacquainted with him.

Thomas had a house in Danville, but after their marriage, he moved into Carolyn's small brick house in Yanceyville so that she could complete her teaching contract. She soon learned that he tended to be impatient with children. Both of her sons were having problems, and the situation only irritated her new husband. Bill, the elder son, pitched terrible, uncontrollable tantrums. Jim began having crying spells after his new step-father moved in. They became so bad that Carolyn finally took him to a doctor in Danville who told her that the problem likely would take care of itself, and after a period of months it did.

Carolyn quit teaching again, and she and Charles played bridge as often as they could. Two years after their marriage, Carolyn discovered that she was pregnant again. Soon after-ward, Charles Thomas suffered a devastating stroke. Her third son, John Thomas, was born seven months later, on September 21, 1955, and Carolyn found herself in the unenviable position of having to care for a new baby and an invalid husband at the same time.

As his son grew, Charles Thomas gradually deteriorated. In his last years, he was mostly bedridden, although with help from Carolyn he sometimes could sit in a wheelchair. His condition eventually became so bad that Carolyn had to put him in a local nursing home. "I just needed a rest," she said later. "I was about to fall apart."

Charles Thomas died on November 27, 1960, leaving most of his estate to Carolyn. Carolyn returned to teaching for a while, then toured Europe and came back to Caswell County to restore old houses and fill them with the antiques that she loved collecting. Her three sons all finished high school at the same school from which their mother had graduated, then went off to college. Carolyn had great expectations of all three. She had reared them in the small Episcopal church that her family had helped to found, and she had tried to instill in all a sense of history, family, and a deep respect for education. Her dream was that Bill, like his grandfather, would become a lawyer, and later, possibly, John, too. She wanted Jim, with his deep and thoughtful silences, to be a priest. And if they should choose to live in Caswell County, she would be very proud. All three sons eventually did return to Caswell County to make their lives and rear their families near their mother, all on farms that Charles Thomas once owned. Carolyn had become a well-known figure in the county by that time, and with her wealth of land, she reigned over her family as a respected matriarch.

"They're just solid old Caswell cornbread aristocracy," one prominent Caswell County resident said years later of Carolyn and her sons. "They've been around here for generations." This person had been in Caswell County for only twenty-eight years and recognized that she was still considered a "newcomer." "There are a lot of things acceptable for those families that aren't acceptable to newcomers," she went on, "a tolerance of idiosyncrasies that doesn't exist for others."

In coming years, there would be idiosyncrasies in Carolyn Moore Upchurch Thomas's family that would stir much talk in the county and even be tolerated. But there also would come a time when idiosyncrasies would step beyond the line of tolerance: when they led to charges of murder.

17

CAROLYN THOMAS'S TWO older sons showed no indications of living up to her dreams for them.

Bill, the eldest, went off to the University of North Carolina at Chapel Hill, but stayed only a semester before dropping out and joining the Air Force.

His younger brother, Jim, followed him to UNC but with no intentions of becoming the priest his mother hoped that he would be. Although he had been briefly an acolyte in Yanceyville's Episcopal church, he had no genuine religious leanings of any type. His major was history, but his major interests were

117

drinking, partying, and chasing girls, and his grades showed it.

By the end of his sophomore year, Jim's attentions had fastened on a single girl. Her name was Joanne Ensley, and she was from Gastonia, a textile town west of Charlotte, a three-hour drive from Chapel Hill. But Jim didn't have to drive that far to see her, for she was a student at Greensboro College, less than an hour away.

Joanne had grown up in a family of military men, the second of three children. Her father was in the Air Force, her uncles were all marines. "It was 'yes sir,' 'yes ma'am,' 'no sir,' and a great deal of respect for your parents as well as your elders," she later recalled. Respect was sometimes difficult. She came to despise her father, who was abusive to her mother. Her parents went through a bitter divorce when she was in the fourth grade. Afterward her strong-willed mother supported her three children by working as a secretary to a textile mill executive. The children grew up in the First Methodist Church and regularly attended gatherings of their mother's big family, most of whom lived nearby.

Joanne was an honor student in high school, and her major interest and favorite activity was serving as a Candy Striper volunteer at Gaston Memorial Hospital. She dreamed of being a nurse, but that was not to be.

In her senior year of high school, Joanne won a full four-year scholarship given through the textile industry, and in the fall of 1966, she began classes at Greensboro College. By this time she had developed into a striking young woman with a slim, voluptuous figure, light brown hair, and intense, blue-green eyes. As a teenager, she was very close to her mother. So close, indeed, that later she would come to think that her mother tried to live out her own dreams through her. "I went to GC because that's where my mother wanted me to go," she said later. "I wasn't really given a choice."

Her roommate, Gloria Myers, was a brilliant student from Caswell County. Gloria was dating a young man from Caswell County, Ricky Frederick, a close friend of Jim Upchurch. It was on a weekend visit to Gloria's house that Joanne first met Jim. Not long after, Jim and Ricky were driving from Chapel Hill to Greensboro almost every weekend to see Gloria and Joanne.

One classmate of Joanne's, the novelist Candace Flynt,

later remembered thinking of Joanne and Jim as being glamorous and sophisticated. "They both were gorgeous people," she recalled. "Everybody thought they should get married just for their gorgeousness."

By December 1967, marriage was on both their minds. "I think I'm pregnant," Joanne told Jim shortly before Christmas. She hadn't yet been to a doctor, but she knew somehow that it was so.

"Find out for sure," he told her.

She did.

Abortion was illegal in North Carolina at the time and never was considered. For Joanne and Jim, there was only one alternative.

The wedding was set for February 3, 1968. It was to be a small affair, just for family and a few close friends, at St. Luke's Episcopal Church in Yanceyville, Jim's family church. Joanne's mother, Margaret, was distressed when she learned about it. She didn't think that Jim, quiet and reserved, was a proper match for her smart and outgoing daughter. She had other dreams for Joanne. "My mother always planned for a huge wedding at First Methodist Church," Joanne recalled later, "but it was *her* wedding, not mine."

The wedding was Joanne's first independent stand against her mother, and although her mother was upset, she still attended the ceremony and paid for a catered champagne reception, but she passed out drunk in retribution.

The young couple settled on one of Carolyn's many farms, near Leasburg in eastern Caswell County. The farm was called Cedar Hill for the ancient and gnarled cedars that lined the rocky lane leading to it. The story-and-a-half red farmhouse, built in the nineteenth century, had a huge stone fireplace and an airy sunroom and sleeping porch on the back. Carolyn had just finished refurbishing it. The old house was isolated, far off the paved highway, with no neighbors in sight.

Faced with the impending responsibility of fatherhood, Jim dropped out of college and got a job at a textile plant in Roxboro in an adjoining county. Joanne, to her mother's great dismay, gave up her scholarship to be a farm wife and mother.

"That was a real change for me," she recalled later, "but I did like it. I was very happy there."

Joanne deeply loved her maternal grandparents, whom she called Mama and Papa Jenks. Papa Jenks always grew a large garden, and Mama Jenks canned, froze, and otherwise preserved its produce. Joanne always admired them for that. Now she began emulating them. Jim planted a garden. Joanne froze, canned, and dried the vegetables. Joanne surrounded the old house with great banks of flowers, just as her grandmother did her own house.

Carolyn, who lived only a couple of miles away in the village of Leasburg in another antebellum house she had preserved, came to visit occasionally, but mostly it was just the two young lovers on the isolated farm until James Bartlett Upchurch III was born August 16, 1968, at Danville Memorial Hospital, the same hospital in which his father had been born. He weighed six pounds, eleven ounces, and had pale blue eyes. His father was twenty-two, his mother twenty, and neither was sure that they were prepared for parenthood.

"Dr. Spock was the reference book," Jim later recalled. "That was our Bible. We kept that thing well-thumbed."

Fortunately, Bart, as his parents called him, was not a fretful baby. Caring for him presented no special strains. Bart began walking at seven months without ever crawling, convincing his parents of what they already had suspected: that they had a precocious child.

By this time, Jim had decided that he needed to return to the university, and his mother was happy to pay for it. He got his degree in history in 1970 and took a job with the Caswell County Department of Social Services in Yanceyville. The following November, his second son, Emory, was born, expenses paid by Carolyn.

In the spring of 1974, four years later, Carolyn suggested that Jim and Joanne move into the house in which she had been living in Leasburg. She had bought another historic house just across the street from her childhood home in Milton, which she was restoring and planning to move into.

Historic houses in Caswell County all have names, usually those of the families who built them or first lived in them. The house in which Carolyn had been living in Leasburg was called the Thompson House. Jacob Thompson, a congressman, U.S. secretary of the interior from 1857 until 1861, and a Confederate secret agent in Canada during the Civil War, was born in the house. It sat in an island of greenery cut off by roads on three sides, its back to the major highway that passes through Caswell County, U.S. 158. A huge, two-story white house with dark shutters and monstrous chimneys, it offered much more room than Jim and Joanne had in the cramped farmhouse at Cedar Hill. With the boys growing quickly, they needed more space, and they moved in June. Joanne loved the house but worried about its location on the highway, fearing for her children's safety, even though the yard was fenced and cut off by a barrier of trees and wild growth.

Bart, who was two months shy of turning six and beginning first grade, was particularly taken with his new surroundings. He loved the grounds and garden, the huge, woodpecker-riddled pecan tree that yielded tasty treasures, the giant oaks, and the nearly tame squirrels that lived in them. "It was like living in a park," he recalled years later. The collection of outbuildings offered new prospects for adventure, and prowling there one day he discovered a big boxful of old comic books and immersed himself in them, the beginning of a fascination that would endure.

Bart had proved himself to be not only precocious but independent and willful as well. Joanne read regularly to her sons, and Bart had begun to read well before he was old enough to go to school. Later that summer, when he began school at High Rock Elementary, more than five miles from his home, his mother wanted to pick him up at the end of the first day. He would not allow it. He insisted on riding the bus with the other children. Joanne would never forget the image of him arriving home that day. He was wearing red shorts, a red-and-white striped polo shirt, white socks, and navy blue Keds. "I remember him getting off that bus," she recalled. "He had the biggest smile on his face. He felt like he had accomplished something on his own and he was so proud."

Bart tested well above most of his fellow students in first and second grade, but halfway through the second grade, his parents were concerned. He was losing interest in school, didn't want to complete assignments, seemed frustrated. "Bart was bored," his mother said. "He was not challenged."

That could not be allowed. And although it troubled their liberal instincts, Joanne and Jim removed Bart from public school and placed him in the only private school in the county, all-white Piedmont Academy. They felt better when his grades and interests began to improve, and the following year, when Bart was starting third grade and Emory was to begin first grade, they put Emory in Piedmont Academy, too.

121

Many things had changed by that time. Strains had crept into Jim's and Joanne's relationship. Later, they would disagree about the main cause. But three factors were primary.

First, Jim disliked village life. He longed for fields and woods and isolation. He had acquired another farm from his mother, this one eighty acres, several miles from Leasburg, near Hyco Reservoir, a huge lake that has its beginnings in Caswell County. The farm had an ancient two-story farmhouse on it, with big chimneys on two sides, but it was not in good condition and lacked any modern conveniences. Jim loved spending weekends there, puttering around, taking long walks, roughing it in the old house, activities that were not quite as appealing to Joanne and the children.

There was an additional attraction. The farm adjoined another of Carolyn's farms, Hickory Hill, where Jim's brother, Bill, was now living with his family. After getting out of the Air Force, Bill had married and eventually returned to the University of North Carolina to finish his degree. Both Bill and his wife Lydia had taught briefly in Caswell County schools, then quit to drop out of mainstream American life and tour the country in a Volkswagen van. They had returned to Carolyn's farm to live off the land, hunting and fishing and growing vegetables and other necessaries. "They were . . ." says Carolyn, pausing as if she has trouble even saying the next word, ". . . hippies."

Long-haired friends regularly came and went in great numbers from the wooded farm where Bill and Lydia lived, and the county was abuzz with rumors of the scandalous activity that was believed to go on there. It was even whispered that people danced naked on car tops. Nobody said anything directly to Carolyn about this, of course, but she was well aware of the talk and was horrified about it.

"My parents were hippies when it was cool," their daughter Kenyatta said years later. She was named for Jomo Kenyatta, the champion of African nationalism and revolutionary first president of Kenya whom her parents greatly admired. Kenyatta was the same age as Emory, Jim and Joanne's younger son. "I thought it was great when I was little," Kenyatta said. "I used to lead stoned people around in the woods giggling. I was a tour guide."

Joanne disapproved of Bill's and Lydia's lifestyle and didn't want her children around them. She had a strong aversion to drugs and once had walked out of Bill's and Lydia's rented house in Chapel Hill when she realized that other guests were smoking marijuana. Jim enjoyed visiting at his brother's house, though, and Joanne was certain that he used marijuana there. She was willing to tolerate that, but she laid down one rule: He was not to bring any into her house.

Later, Joanne would blame her differences with Jim about Bill and Lydia for much of the strain that had come into their marriage. He blamed something else: her mother.

Soon after Emory was born, Joanne's mother had remarried. Margaret and her new husband came frequently to visit, and soon they were coming every other weekend. After Jim and Joanne moved into the Thompson house in 1974, Joanne's mother persuaded her husband to move to Caswell County into the old house at Cedar Hill Farm from which Joanne and Jim just had moved. Carolyn rented it to them.

Joanne didn't encourage her mother to move so close, but neither did she protest, much to her later regret. "My mother always ran my life, and I guess she wanted to continue to do so," she said years later.

As Jim saw it, that was exactly what began to happen. Joanne had gone to work in the drug store in Yanceyville after Bart started to school, and when she wasn't working, her mother usually was at the house. Often Margaret would come to the house before Joanne got home from work, cook dinner, and have it ready when her daughter arrived. Even Joanne began to feel a lack of family privacy. Also Margaret, unaccustomed to the isolation of Caswell County, constantly wanted Joanne to go places with her. "Mother depended on me for her entertainment," Joanne said.

Once Joanne and Jim had done everything together. Joanne had even taken up hunting to please Jim. Now it seemed to Jim that he and Joanne never did anything together anymore. And her mother was always there, setting the agenda.

"I guess what he was wanting and what I was wanting wasn't the same," Joanne said years later. "I was working, out in the world for the first time in six or seven years. Jim was a homebody. He didn't want to go anywhere, didn't care to have people over, and I did. I needed more than what was just there in the house, and he didn't. He wanted to be on the farm, free and loose and in earth shoes. He admired Bill and Lydia. They were able to do something he couldn't do."

They didn't bicker and argue about these differences. They became two people living together who had not grown together, rarely reaching out or communicating. One night in April 1977, as they sat quietly apart, Joanne broke the silence.

"I think you need to move to the farm," she said.

"I do, too," he replied.

Next day, before the boys got home from school, she helped him pack up his stuff and load it into his old, dented Ford pickup. The truck was light blue—Carolina blue it was called in North Carolina, the school color of his alma mater.

Bart was eight then, soon to finish the third grade. Emory was six, just nearing the end of his first year in school. When they got off the school bus that afternoon, their parents were waiting. Joanne sat them on the back steps of the house and took a seat between them. Jim stood nearby.

"Your dad's going to go live at the farm for a while," Joanne told her sons. "You kids and I will be staying here. He won't be far away. He'll be coming over. You'll still see him."

That was it. Jim got into his truck, and Joanne and the boys stood at the back of the house and watched him drive away. Joanne was fighting back tears, but for the boys' sake, she tried not to show it.

18

BART UPCHURCH, FOUR months shy of being nine years old, watched with an air of detachment as his father drove away that spring day in 1977. Later, he remembered the moment clearly but attached no emotional significance to it.

"They explained it to me. I thought, okay. I didn't really understand it. There was some sort of trouble going on, but I didn't know what. There wasn't any commotion. At that time, there wasn't really anything traumatic."

Later, Jim thought that his leaving had no special effect on either of his sons. "I never detected any emotional problem from either one of the kids because of it," he said. "If it was there, it was something I didn't see."

His mother, Carolyn, whom Bart called Nanny-ma, did see a change in her grandson. Bart never showed his emotions. In that way, he was like Carolyn and his father. He wouldn't allow anybody to see him cry. If he were about to cry, he would duck his head or run away. But when he came to visit his grandmother after his father left home, he would cry when the time came to leave. It caused her to recall the crying jags Jim had had as a child soon after she married Charles Thomas. She was certain that the separation was the reason for Bart's crying.

"It had a devastating effect on him," she said. "It was a turning point in his personality. He was without his father."

Bart's crying, she thought, was a symptom of a security breakdown, a weakness sensed by bullies among his classmates, who began taking lunch money from him on the school bus. Bart also developed another problem soon after his father left, one Carolyn didn't know about until later. He began wetting his pants.

Joanne wasn't concerned about the wetting at first. She saw that Bart could control it if he wanted to. He never did it at school. He didn't wet the bed at night. He only did it after school at home. She thought he did it for attention and didn't really associate it with Jim's leaving.

Like Jim, she thought that the boys were not greatly affected by the separation. For one thing, there already was an emotional distance between Jim and his sons, she said later.

"Jim was not close to the children. Jim is a very private, very individual person, very quiet, passive, reserved, a very inward person. He's a good father, but he didn't really do things with the children. He didn't take them to school, to plays, to Scouts. He would not sit on the sofa and read to them. I read to them. I took them up to bed, tucked them in, and gave them hugs. Jim never gave them hugs. He didn't know how to do that."

With Bart, Jim thought, the separation between father and son was not just one-way. "Bart maintained a certain distance all the time," Jim said later. "Even as a little boy he was not one for showing his feelings. Bart was difficult to communicate with. He would not open up. He didn't want you cuddling him."

As Joanne remembered it later, the boys never even asked about their father after he left.

"It wasn't as if Jim left and they never saw him. We began seeing each other again almost immediately."

The farm was only a few miles away, and only a couple of weeks after he left, Jim was coming over regularly. He sometimes ate dinner with Joanne and the boys, sometimes even spent the night. Occasionally, he would take the boys to the farm for the weekend. Later, Bart remembered feeling resentment about only one aspect of his parents' separation: having to spend weekends at the farm with his father. "Dad didn't have a color TV," he said.

Jim had gotten fed up with his job at the social services department and quit before he and Joanne split up. He went to work as a salesman at a lumber company in an adjoining county, but the job was no more satisfying and not much better paying than the one he had left, and in the fall of 1977, he returned to work for the Caswell County Department of Social Services.

If he was not finding his professional life satisfying, Jim was at least enjoying the isolation and primitive lifestyle of the farm. He spent a lot of time hunting and walking alone in the woods. Fortunately, he also devoted a lot of time to cutting and chopping wood for heating and cooking. That winter proved to be one of the harshest in years, and he felt good about surviving it in the drafty, uninsulated house, his only warmth provided by his own labor. "I'd get up in the morning and have to break the ice on a bucket of water to make coffee," he recalled.

By winter, he and Joanne were again finding warmth in one another, and before the season was out, she discovered that she was pregnant again. Pregnant. And their relationship still unresolved.

Jim did not want to return to live again in the house in Leasburg. He had grown too attached to the farm. And the problem of Joanne's mother remained. She was still at the house regularly, constantly reminding Joanne of what a mistake she'd made in marrying Jim and getting stuck in the wilds of Caswell County. At one point, at her mother's urging, Joanne even had considered taking a job in a distant town and leaving Caswell County forever, but something held her back.

On her birthday late in January, Joanne came home from work to find her mother had cooked dinner and made a cake for her. That was to be her birthday, she and her mother, dinner and a cake. She could see an endless string of similar birthdays in her future and she suddenly knew it wasn't what she wanted. But Joanne couldn't bring herself to admit that to her mother just yet. Within a few months, though, the explosion would finally come.

One day that spring, Joanne came home to find her mother and stepfather at the house again, sitting at the kitchen table. It had been a frustrating day, but later she didn't remember what touched off the bitter confrontation that followed.

"It was not planned," she said later. "It was just one of those things where you get out of your car and words just come out of your mouth. I blew up. I guess I said things I wanted to say all my life. My mother is a very strong-willed person. She had to be a strong person. But if my mother says the sky is purple, that's right. You don't argue with her. I said, 'There is no compromising with you, Mother, it's either your way or nothing. Since there can be no compromise, that's it.' "

She ordered her mother out of her house, and told her she never wanted to see her again. She had cut her mother out of her life for good.

But she was not willing to do that with Jim. She was more than three months pregnant, and now that she had resolved the problem with her mother, she wanted to resolve the problem with her marriage, too.

"She told me, 'You're going to have to make a decision,' " Jim recalled later. " 'Either I'm going to have an abortion, or we go back together.' I said, 'Well, let's try it again.' "

Joanne was even willing to make a major concession. She was ready finally to move to the farm. She and the children moved in with Jim in April 1978, in time to plant a big garden.

The house into which they moved was in splendid isolation at the end of a narrow lane that wound through deep woods to an open ridge crest with a sweeping view to the southwest of distant ridges. The house had been built in the 1830s, a solid two-story structure on a stone foundation with a dark and dank cellar underneath. Never painted, its board walls had cured a dark gray. The tin roof had rusted to a deep

127

maroonish-orange. A dilapidated front porch stretched the full width of the house. Inside were two high-ceilinged, plastered rooms downstairs, both with fireplaces. One served as a living room, the other as a dining room and den. Upstairs were two bedrooms. The boys shared one. Jim and Joanne took the other. A kitchen had been built onto the back of the house, standing high on the sloping ground. In it was an old wood-burning range that was used not only for cooking but for warming water and for supplemental heating of the house. There was no kitchen sink, for there was no running water.

Water came from a stone-lined well outside the kitchen, brought up by hand in a bucket attached to a rope on a rusted pulley. The outhouse was down the hill. Baths were taken in the kitchen in a huge galvanized tub.

The house was shaded by big trees—hackberry, wild cherry, black walnut, cedar. Jim set out fruit trees, apple and cherry, to go with the big pear tree beside the house. Two log tobacco barns stood at the edge of the woods in front of the house, and a third was out of sight, just down the hill. Behind the house, a corncrib slanted precariously on its stone foundation. A hundred feet beyond it was a small livestock barn. Nearly ten acres had been fenced for pasture, plenty of room for horses and cows. But goats came first.

Emory was allergic to cow milk, and Jim and Joanne had been buying goat milk for him. Now that they had room for goats, why should they buy milk? They ended up with a herd of six—and more milk than they knew what to do with. Some they sold, some they gave away. Joanne began making cheese with the rest.

Goats led to sheep. They began raising lambs for slaughter and a calf each year for beef, eating only meat they had raised. If they ran short, Jim always could supplement the supply in the freezer by hunting. Some mornings he would rise early and see more than a dozen deer grazing in the mists of his pasture.

Years later, Jim would think of these days on the farm after he and Joanne were reunited as his "Walton Family days," perhaps the happiest period of his life. "It was just something I wanted to do," he said. "It was almost like I was driven to do it. To me it was fun."

Certainly, Joanne had never seen him happier. "The farm was always his passion," she said. "He loved the farm dearly.

128

Jim was happy there. We were very, very happy there. It was the first time I'd seen Jim really come into the picture of family life. He was more open. We were doing things as a family."

Everybody had specific chores, including Bart and Emory. Bart always did his, but without enthusiasm. One of their chores was tending to the goats and milking them. They joined a 4-H dairy goat group and began taking their goats to shows and fairs. Emory's goat, Diva, won a blue ribbon at the Greensboro Agricultural Fair, and both boys took goats to the N.C. State Fair in Raleigh. The *Caswell Messenger* featured the boys and their goats in a front-page story.

Although the family was closer together, working as a unit, Jim realized that the life he enjoyed so much was from an earlier era, when life was simpler and harder, and that it was not easy on his wife and children.

"I probably imposed it on the family," he said later. "I used to tell the kids, 'No matter what happens after this, you can always say you had it worse.' I don't think the children appreciated it at all. They wanted to be just like every other kid, have the things that other kids had, and do the things that other kids did. I think sometimes I was real selfish when I look back on it. But I don't think it hurt any of them."

A daughter, Carrie, was born in September 1978, followed by a second daughter, Alex, in September 1980. All along, the plan had been to remodel the old farmhouse someday, add plumbing, a bathroom, a modern kitchen, a better system for heating, but the arrival of Carrie and Alex made it almost imperative. Jim and Joanne wanted to do as much of the work as they could themselves, but living in the house and working on it, they realized, would be difficult. They would need another place to live for a while. As it happened, an ideal place was available. It was less than half a mile away, close enough to make tending to the livestock on the farm no problem.

The Judge Long House, as it was called, was a green-shuttered, white-columned, nineteenth-century mansion set on a spacious lawn shaded by two-hundred-year-old oak trees. An immense magnolia sheltered one side of the house. The family moved in December 1981. The house had twelve rooms, enough so that every child—Bart, thirteen, Emory eleven, Carrie, three, and the baby, Alex, one—could have a private room. To everybody's great relief, there were two full and functioning bathrooms. Joanne was thrilled to have a dishwasher, a washing machine, and dryer. The Upchurches had returned to civilization, leaving their Walton Family days behind. But they were leaving behind the innocence of those days in more ways than they realized.

19

SHEEP FARMING HAD BEEN a prosperous enterprise in North Carolina in the days before synthetic yarns. At the turn of the century, the state counted more than half a million sheep within its borders, but by 1980 sheep farming had become little more than a hobby. It soon enjoyed a resurgence in Caswell County.

One of the county's most famous plantations, Melrose, built in 1770 by James Williamson, had been turned into a sheep ranch by a young Duke University graduate named James Coman, who moved to Caswell County from Durham with dreams of reviving the sheep industry in North Carolina. Several other families in the county also were raising a few sheep, enough that a Caswell Sheep Producers Association was formed.

Jim and Joanne Upchurch had been gradually increasing the size of the herd of ewes that they kept on their farm, primarily for the lambs they slaughtered to fill their freezer. A by-product of their herd, of course, was wool, for which they had little use. That was the reason they joined the newly formed association. At one of the meetings they met James Coman and got swept up in his dream.

By July 1982, seven months after they moved out of their farmhouse to begin remodeling it, Jim and Joanne joined Coman and another couple, Bill and Pat Bush, teachers who also had a small flock of sheep, to start a new venture in the sheep business.

They would raise lambs for meat, but their primary business would be selling fine-quality finished wool yarn to hobbyists. Joanne was a talented knitter who had spent many cold winter hours in her farmhouse making items of apparel for her family, and she knew that fine wool yarn was difficult to come by.

The venture was begun with a ton of wool that the group already had on hand at their farms. They found a processor in Virginia that would produce their yarn on a rare, nineteenth-century device called a spinning mule. The mule-spun yarn, as it was called, was as light and fluffy as if it had been hand-spun. After the wool was spun, it had to be trucked back to Caswell County, where it was hand-dyed. That was done in an old tenant house at Melrose in a row of huge stainless-steel pots heated by portable gasoline stoves. It seemed fun at first, although it was hard, back-bending work, a regular weekend project for the two couples and Coman, accompanied at first by much beer drinking and laughter.

After the yarn was hung out and dried, it was packaged and placed in a few outlets to see how it would go. It sold so quickly and at such good prices that the group bought four more tons of wool from other sheep farmers and began producing their yarn on a bigger but no less primitive scale.

By December 1982, they were so encouraged that Coman sold off some of his flock to raise capital, and he and the two couples incorporated their partnership as the Caswell Sheep and Wool Company.

Joanne had given up outside work when she moved to the farm, pregnant with Carrie, three and a half years earlier. As the only one in the group without a full-time outside job, she was chosen to keep the company's books and be its marketing director, although she would receive no salary for the extra work. She went at the job with great enthusiasm.

The idea in the beginning was to sell the yarn at craft shows, but Joanne had a grander vision. She not only got several major retail outlets around the state to carry their yarn, but she wanted to distribute it nationally as well. She began flying off to trade shows in Chicago, New York, Atlanta, and St. Louis, setting up booths and trying to interest dealers. "She got really obsessed with this thing," Jim recalled later.

The company began to get attention. A reporter for the Greensboro *News & Record* wrote a story about it that nearly filled the entire feature page, including three color photographs: one of Joanne holding a baby lamb, another of her knitting, and a third modeling a jacket and cap that she had designed and made from the yarn.

The business was expanding rapidly, but more money seemed to be going out than coming in. Soon the company had gone through James Coman's original investment, and the partners had to sign a note for a loan from a Durham bank to keep going. When that was gone, the partners had a falling-out. Coman demanded to see the books. "Joanne just turned a deaf ear to everything," Jim recalled later. "She was real sluggish in getting those books to him."

Not long after Joanne turned over the books, Jim got a call from a lawyer who represented the company, a friend and neighbor, who asked him to drop by his office. James Coman was there with a cardboard box full of records for the Caswell Sheep and Wool Company. The lawyer told Jim that it seemed as if Joanne had not accounted for some of the company's money.

"I said, 'Maybe she made some mistakes,'" Jim recalled later. "They chuckled and said, 'It's more than that.'"

Coman was claiming that a lot of company money was missing and Joanne had embezzled it. Jim had a hard time accepting that. "If she had any money, it didn't show up anywhere," he said later. He knew that Joanne had mishandled the books. It was a job she never should have taken in the first place, he thought; she couldn't even keep her own checkbook straight. But he also thought that most of the money that was unaccounted for had been legitimately spent, although Joanne didn't have the receipts or records to prove it.

Jim consulted a lawyer friend, George Daniel. Daniel learned that Coman had talked with the county district attorney, Phil Allen, Jim's old buddy from high school and college. Allen let Daniel know that if Coman chose to press the matter, an indictment might be forthcoming.

"George said, 'Well, they've got a case,'" Jim recalled. "We didn't have any choice but to deal with it. I said, 'Let's do what we can to keep it out of court.' The kids would have been devastated by it. I just didn't want it to be publicized."

The alternative was to come to a settlement with Coman so that he wouldn't press charges. He wanted the bank loan repaid and his original investment returned.

"Hell, he had us over a barrel," Jim said. "What could we

do? Either go to court on a felony charge or pay him what he wanted."

Jim went to his mother, who had paid off some bills Joanne had accumulated while they were separated, and told her about the situation.

"Well, what do you want me to do?" Carolyn asked.

"We need thirty thousand dollars," Jim said.

She arranged a loan, and the lawyers took care of the matter. But the situation opened a new rift in Jim's and Joanne's marriage.

"I was really upset about it," Jim said. "It really caused us some terrible hardships at the time. We had this terrible debt. We had to struggle along after that. It really hurt our relationship."

Soon Joanne would be hurt in turn, and the source of her anguish would stem, ironically, from their churchgoing. After the girls were born, Joanne had decided that the family should start going to church. Although Jim was not particularly religious, he went along for the sake of the children and family unity. They joined St. Luke's Episcopal Church, which Jim's family had helped to found. It was a small church that shared a priest with another church in an adjoining county. On a good Sunday, maybe twenty-five people attended services. The Upchurches added measurably to the congregation. Bart and Emory were confirmed and became acolytes. Joanne was elected president of Episcopal Women. Jim became a churchwarden.

Not long after Jim and Joanne joined the church, they became acquainted with another couple, Ted and Judy Gold*, who had three children. The two families soon were attending social functions together. Joanne didn't like Judy from the beginning. She thought that Judy was flirtatious and had an eye for Jim.

"She's after you," Joanne told her husband. "She's chasing you."

Jim laughed it off. But he soon found himself involved in volunteer work with Judy. "One thing led to another," Jim recalled later. "We started having an affair. I didn't plan it. I didn't go looking for anybody. I had not had any affairs. But I was so disillusioned with my marriage."

Late in June, Joanne found a letter from Judy in Jim's billfold and confronted him about it, but he denied that anything was going on between them. Judy called and invited Jim, Joanne, and the children to their house for a cookout on July 4. They went. Joanne was friendly but also wary and watchful.

Not long afterward, Joanne saw a blanket in the back of Jim's four-wheel-drive Japanese pickup truck and became even more suspicious. One day, she was driving to Person County with Bart and Emory to help with a church cleaning project, and she spotted Jim's truck parked at Hyco Lake with nobody around. She might have stopped and searched for Jim if the boys hadn't been along, but she already had a picture of what she likely would have found.

After more than a year and a half, Jim and Joanne finally were finishing work on their old farm house. They had torn off the front porch, removed one chimney, replaced rotted boards, and painted the old house blue. Inside, they had added a large bathroom, a modern kitchen, plumbing, and new wiring and lighting. They had redone the floors, and Joanne had painted and wallpapered and added new moldings. They moved back into the house in early August.

A time that should have been joyous, returning to the redecorated house on the farm that Jim loved so dearly, was instead sullen and strained. Jim seemed preoccupied and even more remote than usual, as if embroiled in some inner conflict. Suspicions about her husband's fidelity were gnawing at Joanne. The air in the house was nearly palpable with tension.

On Bart's birthday, August 17, Joanne was driving him and Emory and some of their friends to the Pizza Hut in Danville for a party. Joanne drove past the business where Judy worked and saw Jim's truck parked outside, rekindling her turmoil and anger.

"I was falling apart," she recalled later. "I was miserable."

Although Joanne had a volatile nature, she knew it would do no good to confront Jim and scream at him. He would just clam up and walk away. Besides, she had no proof that he was actually having an affair. A few days after Bart's birthday, Joanne noticed a change in Jim.

"I knew something was wrong," she recalled later. "He was like a cat, slipping around, getting his stuff together."

The next morning, Jim broke the news.

"I'm going to move in with Carolyn for a while," he said.

He offered no explanation. He just loaded his things in the truck and once again was gone. Joanne was left to explain to the children that their father would be staying with Carolyn for a while. This time, Joanne felt, it did affect the children. Emory, a sensitive boy just entering his teens, showed his pain. Bart, as usual, displayed no emotion and seemed less bothered by it.

"Somewhere subconsciously I was aware they were having trouble," he said years later, "but it was not something I focused on. I just went on with my day-to-day routine. Go-with-the-flow type thing. Mainly, it was inconvenient."

"That was the time Bart told me that he loved his dad but he didn't respect him," Joanne said later.

Not until after Jim left did Joanne get confirmation that he was having an affair. But it was something more than just a fling, she discovered. He was in love, he said, with Judy Gold. She planned to leave Ted, and they already were looking for a house together in Milton.

"It tore me up," Joanne recalled later. "I'm a very faithful dog. I couldn't accept that he would do that. I said, 'The hell with this. I can't live with this.' "

She was furious and determined to get back at her rival. She called Ted Gold to make sure that he knew what was going on. When Judy arrived at a meeting Joanne was attending, Joanne quickly departed, proclaiming loud enough for others to hear that the facility was "not big enough for me and a whore."

When Carrie and Alex came home from a visit to Carolyn with presents they said Judy had given them, she called Carolyn and made it clear that the woman was never to be allowed anywhere near her children and she would do whatever was necessary to prevent it.

Her spleen vented, Joanne decided to get on with her life. She would do what she had wanted to since high school: work in medical care. She went to Danville and got a job as a supervisor in the support department at Danville Memorial Hospital, where all four of her children had been born.

Once the consequences of their actions became clear, the ardor began to cool between Jim and Judy. They broke off their relationship only weeks after Jim left home. Judy remained with her husband and children. Jim stayed on with his mother for a while. Then, less than three months after he had driven away from his family for the second time, Jim drove back to the farm and asked Joanne to allow him to return.

"He could not live without the farm and without the children," she said later. "I knew that."

She allowed him to come back, but her unforgiving nature could not allow her to erase what he had done from her mind.

"I never did get over it," she said years later.

20

IF THERE IS A CENTER OF community life in Caswell County, it is Bartlett Yancey High School in Yanceyville, the county's largest town with some thirteen hundred people. Indeed, the auditorium of the county's only high school doubles as the civic center, a place for community gatherings and entertainment.

The school has an enrollment of about one thousand, half of whom, like the population of the county, are black. Those students who don't come to school in big orangish-yellow buses usually drive their own cars, and the student parking lot is always jammed during school hours.

In its athletic conference, Bartlett Yancey is known as "the hick school." Future Farmers of America is one of the school's major extracurricular clubs. Vocational training programs are popular courses of study.

Teachers who come to Bartlett Yancey from outside Caswell County often are surprised by the behavior of the students. The school has no big drug problem, no real trouble with violence. On the whole, the students are attentive, well-mannered, and respectful. A veteran staff member could not recall a single incident of a student confronting a teacher in a violent way.

On the other hand, Bartlett Yancey is not known as a bastion of academic excellence. The Caswell County school

136

system hires only the state-allocated teachers. It employs no extra or special teachers on its own and offers no salary supplements to attract better teachers, as many school systems do in wealthier areas of the state. Despite this, a sizable number of Bartlett Yancey students go to college and do well, although many feel deprived when they meet students from the cities and realize the differences in academic opportunities.

The best students at Bartlett Yancey all bear a single identity. They are proudly known as Slayton's Kids. Weldon Slayton started the program for gifted and talented students in Caswell County in 1975, and he still directs it. At any given time, the number of gifted and talented students, or GT students, as they also are known, numbers about fifteen at each grade level. They begin studying together in junior high school, and by the time they reach high school, they are a unit. Before they leave, they all look upon Weldon Slayton as a guru of sorts, not just a teacher but a friend, confidant, and advisor.

"I have a tendency to invest a lot of my emotional self into my students," says Slayton, who never married. "I get attached to them. I get very possessive of them in a sense. I work hard to keep professional so I don't adopt them."

Even in high school, Slayton, who grew up in Caswell County, realized that he had a gift for teaching, and after working his way through college, he returned home to follow his calling. "I really did want to give something back to the county," he said.

While teaching, he enrolled at the University of North Carolina at Greensboro, got a master's degree in teaching the gifted and talented, and became one of the first GT teachers in the state. So effective did he become with the best students in Caswell County that people often ask why he hasn't left to pursue greater opportunities elsewhere. His answer is simple. "I keep thinking if I were to leave, they wouldn't get anybody who would care about my kids like I do."

Among those kids he came to care about were Bart and Emory Upchurch. After Bart had completed the fifth grade and Emory the third, Joanne and Jim took them out of faltering Piedmont Academy and allowed them to return to the public schools, which were improving. Later, the school system classified Emory as a gifted and talented student. Bart was not accepted in the program.

Joanne was incensed. Although Bart's grades were above

average, they rarely were exceptional. Bart applied himself to that which interested him and got along without great effort in those subjects that didn't. Joanne knew that Bart was smart, however. His IQ was 135, in the highest percentile in the county school system. He always did well on achievement tests and she thought he deserved the best the school system had to offer.

Joanne demanded that he be retested and reconsidered for the gifted and talented classes, and he finally was accepted in the program, beginning in the ninth grade at Dillard Junior High in Yanceyville, not far from Bartlett Yancey High. Weldon Slayton, who then taught English and social studies to gifted and talented students from the ninth through the twelfth grades, thought that the classload that GT students had to bear was a shock to Bart, who, to his mind, had just been cruising through school to this point. Bart, who insisted on being called James outside his family, failed both history and English in the first nine weeks of GT classes. His mother came to the school to meet with Slayton and Bart about the problem.

"He's lazy," Slayton recalled Joanne telling him.

"I think he's going to be fine," Slayton replied. "He's understanding what we're doing."

Joanne said that she and Jim had discussed taking him out of the GT classes.

"Bart said, 'You'll take me out over my dead body,'" she told Slayton. "We've never known him to care before."

"Give him some time," Slayton said.

And time was all it took. Before the year was over, Bart had brought his failing grades up to Bs, although he was capable of even better. But Slayton was troubled by one thing his mother said in that first meeting.

"She said, 'I told him when he gets to be eighteen, he goes out the door. He's going to have to fend for himself.' I think it bothered James for me to hear that."

Slayton saw that Bart kept an emotional distance from everybody, and Joanne's remark caused him to wonder if there hadn't been pain at home that caused Bart to shut himself off and deny things that were distressing.

By the time Bart found himself under Slayton's influence, something other than schoolwork had caught his imagination, an escape that was taking a bigger and bigger hold of his time and energy.

An avid reader since early childhood, Bart had gravitated to science fiction and fantasy. In his reading, he'd come across mention of a game called Dungeons and Dragons, and he was curious about it. In the summer after he finished the seventh grade, Bart went into a toy-and-hobby shop in Danville, found the basic beginner's game, and talked his mother into buying it for him. He brought it home, read all the material, and taught his brother Emory to play it. He next brought his cousin Kenyatta into the game.

After classes resumed in the fall, he found more players in school friends. They usually played after school, sometimes by telephone. By the time Bart began ninth grade, he was bringing the game to school. Soon a group of students was playing at lunchtime each day in the school cafeteria. Others, curious about the game, began their own groups, called dungeons.

Weldon Slayton hadn't heard of the game until Bart got it going at school, and he took the time to find out how it was played. The game, he discovered, is a medieval fantasy in which the players assume various roles—thief, fighter, magic user—and set out upon adventures in which they face danger at nearly every turn. It is a game of castles and catacombs, of knights and assassins, elves and wizards, swords and daggers, truncheons and longbows, a game of gods and demons, of "lawful good" and "chaotic evil," of deformed beasts and horrid monsters. The object is to use basic abilities granted to each character in a point system to slay enemies, overcome monsters, and obtain treasure without taking "hit points," which not only sap strength and skills but can kill and end the game. Much of the action is determined by the throw of odd and many-sided dice, but the game is controlled by a godlike player, the dungeon master, who creates the often terrifying scenarios and settles disputes.

The game is immensely complicated, and can be played in brief adventures or in campaigns that go on for weeks, months, years, in which the characters move through many levels of development and gain immense powers.

Dungeons and Dragons, or D&D, as it is more often called by devoted players, was invented in the early '70s by an enthusiast of historical and war games, Gary Gygax, who started his own company to manufacture the game in 1973. Within six years, *Parade* magazine was calling D&D the hottest fad on college campuses since streaking. By the early '80s, the game had made millions for Gygax and had spread into high schools and junior high schools, even into isolated spots like Caswell County.

Slayton realized that the game was a genuine stimulus to imagination and creativity, and the students most interested in it clearly were among the brightest in the school. But he was concerned that some of them seemed to be getting too deeply involved. They played for many hours each week and talked about the characters they were playing as if they were real people. Were some of the students getting so wrapped up in the game that it became more real than reality? Slayton couldn't help but wonder, especially after some of the players' grades began to suffer.

What bothered him more was the nature of the game itself.

"The underpinnings seem to be without any moral base," he said. "The object in winning is not that the good guy has won and justice has been served but that you've used your power to outwit and outsmart and come out on top. Evil or good doesn't really matter as long as you win. D&D takes the accepted moral values and turns them on their ear."

But when he tried to caution students about his concerns, they showed little interest in listening. It was, they countered, just a game, and one in which they found not only escape from the isolation and boredom of Caswell County but great pleasure as well.

For Bart Upchurch, D&D apparently answered a need on an even deeper level. From the time he was small, he always wanted to be in charge. At first, there was only his younger brother to control, later his cousin, Kenyatta. Years later, Kenyatta would recall wonderful games that Bart created for them to play, but he always made up the rules, and she and Emory always had to follow them. Emory was easygoing and usually let Bart dictate their play. On the occasions when he balked, however, Bart would run to his parents, saying, "Emory won't play. Emory won't play."

"I'm tired of playing your game," Emory would protest.

Jim and Joanne would encourage Bart to leave Emory alone for a while. "Then he'd go off and play on his own and everything would be fine," Jim recalled later. "But when they played together, Bart had to be in charge. The game had to

140

be set up and run his way. Bart had to make the decisions. He was always the game master."

Bart and D&D were a perfect match. Since he had been the first to learn the game and had introduced it to his friends, he became the dungeon master. As the games he conducted became more complicated, his group more experienced, Bart's skills grew. And as other groups formed and the game spread, Bart gained a reputation as the master of dungeon masters.

That power and recognition filled a void in Bart's life, Weldon Slayton thought.

By the time Bart was in high school, most of his fellow students and teachers thought him weird, off the wall. He seemed determined to set himself apart from others, to be different. "He made his claim by being odd," said Slayton. "I think he just found it difficult to deal in the social area, especially where girls are concerned." He never dated and didn't even associate with girls. "He went around with guys who were loners," Slayton said. "I always thought James was very lonely and the only way he could connect was by being really weird and running with other weird kids."

Tall and thin, Bart often wore a camouflage military field jacket to school and carried a backpack filled with D&D paraphernalia. He had taken a strong interest in the military and martial arts, and in eleventh grade he began taking karate lessons after school in Danville. Rambo movies delighted him.

Despite Bart's determination to be unconventional, outrageous, and unconcerned with authority, Weldon Slayton, who kept a relaxed atmosphere in his classes, found him to be obedient and respectful.

"I took no foolishness," Slayton explained. "If I would say, 'James, sit down,' he would sit down. He never defied me. He never faced me down about anything. He didn't argue."

And there were times when Slayton found Bart to be uncommonly conventional. Whereas most of his other students simply called him Slayton, Bart always called him Mr. Slayton. Slayton was an instructor at the prestigious Governor's School to which top high school students from around the state were sent for six weeks of summer study and activities each year. Bart was chosen to attend after he completed the eleventh grade. Slayton, who encouraged informality as a means of making students feel comfortable and accepted, offered Bart an opening.

"Why don't you call me Weldon?" he said.

"I can't," said Bart, who went right on calling him Mr. Slayton, always keeping a formal distance between them.

The place where Bart felt most comfortable, creative, and accepted was where he was in control: in the D&D games over which he ruled.

By the time the regular players in Bart's dungeon were in high school, they were such experienced participants and had moved into such advanced stages of play that the game had taken on a different cast. No longer were their characters going out on adventures to face mere monsters. They now were competing against each other in long-running, multileveled campaigns, scheming and plotting and conniving to destroy one another and seize the other's treasure.

"Everybody's character disliked everybody else's," Bart recalled years later. "It gave a comedic edge to the game. We used to joke, 'You better shut your mouth or I'll kill your character.' 'Yeah, I'd like to see you try it.' We'd laugh when somebody was stepping in traps or falling in pits.

"You really want to win when you're competing against each other. It's a matter of prestige.

"It stimulated a lot of thought about the game, generated a lot of theory. It was hard to make it run smoothly. They would challenge every ruling I made."

Although Joanne sometimes complained that Bart was spending too much time playing D&D when he should be studying, neither she nor Jim really knew much about the game, nor were they especially concerned about Bart and Emory playing it. They were pleased that Bart had an activity he could enjoy that also stimulated his fertile and creative mind.

Yet concern about D&D was growing among other parents around the country. On June 9, 1982, Pat Pulling of Montpelier, Virginia, came home to find her sixteen-year-old son, Bink, a straight-A honor student, dead on the front lawn. He had shot himself through the heart with his father's handgun. Bink, an obsessed D&D player, left a note revealing that his soul no longer was his because another player had put the curse of a werewolf on him. Only four months later, Tony Gowin, an eighteen-year-old D&D zealot, walked into a hobby shop in Bardstown, Kentucky, to inquire about a D&D book he had ordered, got into an argument with the twenty-year-old clerk, and impaled her with a medieval broadsword, killing her.

So many teenage suicides and murders were being connected to D&D that Pat Pulling began a crusade against the game. She was joined by Dr. Thomas Radecki, an Illinois psychiatrist who headed the National Coalition on Television Violence and had studied several cases of teenage violence that he related to D&D.

By the fall of 1985, when Bart Upchurch, the most accomplished dungeon master in Caswell County, was beginning his senior year at Bartlett Yancey High, Pulling and Radecki had begun generating national attention. The popular TV show *60 Minutes* featured a segment on the dangers of D&D. An article appeared in *Newsweek*. Newspapers were writing about the possible perils of the game. Ministers were denouncing it as a doorway to the occult and Satanism. As many as fifty teenage murders and suicides had been tied to playing the game, and the number was growing monthly.

The company that was now producing the game, TSR Hobbies Inc., denied any proven links between the game and the rash of violence. Players who killed themselves or others had deeper problems from other causes, the company said. D&D, it claimed, was being made a scapegoat by parents seeking desperately to blame anything but themselves for their children's actions. Millions of teenagers played the game every week without harming themselves or anybody else, the company pointed out. Still, in 1983, the company had added to the games a warning about players becoming too closely identified with their characters.

None of this controversy affected the most ardent D&D players in Caswell County, those in the dungeon over which Bart Upchurch was master. But their game had begun to go in a different direction. A new player had been added to the group. All of the players had known him for years, even had played D&D with him on occasion. But he had spent a year away from the county at a special school, where he had been master of his own dungeons. Now he was back and playing in Bart's group. His name was Neal Henderson. He was smarter than Bart, and, to some minds, even weirder.

21

CASWELL COUNTY NEVER had seen the likes of Neal Henderson. He arrived in the county when he was nearly eight with his two-year-old sister, Heather, and his mother, Ann, who was fleeing a bad marriage. They moved into the small brick house of his maternal grandmother and step-grandfather, set far off the road on a sandy lane guarded by three green-sided tobacco barns, only a short distance from the spot where Abisha Slade's slave Stephen accidentally created Bright Leaf tobacco.

Neal had been born only a few miles across the state line in Danville, where his parents had met. But before Neal was a year old, his father, Jerry, moved the family to Richmond, where he went to work for a major construction company. By the time Neal was six, his parents' marriage was in trouble. Later, he still would carry vivid memories of their arguments.

"They didn't like doing it in front of me," he said. "I'd jump up, throw my hands in front of them, and try to stop them. I hated it."

Ann Henderson left her husband after Neal finished the first grade. The separation was wrenching for Neal. "That was my dad," he said years later. "I loved him to death and he loved me to death. I was always with my dad." His mother brought her children to North Carolina and moved in temporarily with her brother and his family in Chapel Hill. Neal missed his daddy and didn't understand why he couldn't be with him. "I remember being in Chapel Hill and Mom had to go to Richmond to see about the divorce and she wouldn't take me. All I understood was that Mom was going to see Dad and I couldn't go see him."

Neal completed the second grade in Chapel Hill, and by the time he entered the third grade at Bartlett Yancey Elementary School he already had left behind a string of amazed teachers and school officials who never knew what to do with him.

His kindergarten teacher thought he should be at least in the second grade. His first-grade teacher succeeded in having him sent to the second grade, but he had to repeat it again after he moved to Chapel Hill. There his teacher kept pulling him out of class to be tested.

In the third and fourth grades in Caswell County, he was stymied, so far ahead of his classmates that he didn't have to pay attention to any of the instruction and still could make perfect scores on any tests they took.

"I was bored," he said later. "I read constantly. I can't ever remember not reading. I think I was reading at three. I could just get a book, kick back, be happy."

His reading was eclectic. He loved comic books, especially those about superheroes, and read them until he had memorized them. He even created his own comic books about a character he called Solar Boy, who performed amazing feats with bursts of solar energy. He discovered science fiction and fantasy and read whole series of several authors.

One day, soon after Neal began the fifth grade, Weldon Slayton, then teaching at Dillard Junior High School, got a call from Steve Williamson, director of special education.

"He said, 'We've got this kid in the fifth grade and his mother is demanding we do something with him because he's knocking the top out of every test we give him,'" Slayton recalled. "'Do you think you could do anything with him?'"

Slayton, who was just beginning to teach gifted and talented students, was willing to try. Like the teachers who had encountered Neal before him, Slayton was amazed at the results of the tests Neal had taken. This fifth grader obviously was capable of high school work. His IQ had tested as high as 180, well into the range of genius. Slayton went to the elementary school and met with Neal and his mother.

"He was just a pudgy little kid who had a wonderful vocabulary and, I thought, found the world very amusing," Slayton recalled.

Ann Henderson was worried about her son's social development if he advanced into higher grades with older classmates, and Slayton worked out an arrangement in which Neal would spend mornings with him in his eighth-grade English and social studies classes, then return to the elementary school in the afternoon.

The other students in Slayton's class looked upon Neal as an oddity. "They liked me," he said. "But even in the GT class, I was still that smart kid. I'd run from the girls. They enjoyed chasing me. They thought I was just the cutest little thing. I enjoyed the attention."

Slayton discovered that Neal had a mischievous sense of humor. He came into class one day to find Neal missing and the other students grinning. Then he heard a giggle coming from a cabinet. He opened it to find that his star student had crawled into it to hide from him.

Neal found Slayton's classes to be different from anything he'd encountered. Slayton gave multiple assignments and left it to his students to figure out how to spend their time to accomplish them. For the first time, Neal was not bored in school.

"I enjoyed doing the work," he recalled. "I was sometimes late with it. I could never focus my interest on any one thing. If something else interested me, I would go and study it for a while. But I would get the work done."

"Neal procrastinated forever," Slayton said. Yet, astoundingly, it didn't seem to matter. Slayton recalled a time when he had scheduled a block of tests. Neal put off reading the material and still hadn't gotten to it when the time came for the tests to begin.

"Let me have the tests," Neal told him.

"Neal, you've got some time," Slayton said. "Why don't you take a couple today, then do the reading and take the others later."

"Give me the tests," Neal said.

He sat down and breezed through them. When he finished, he had scored higher than anybody in the class.

Slayton had never seen another student like him. "He just devoured books," Slayton said. "He loved learning anything and everything."

The following year, when Neal normally would have been in the sixth grade, Slayton went to teach at the high school. The decision was made to keep Neal in eighth-grade classes.

"I spent that year pretty well bored," Neal recalled. "Just played the entire year. I did try to help the new teacher with her course work."

The next year, when he was twelve, Neal went off to high school to again become one of Slayton's kids. That year Neal was allowed to take the SAT college entrance exams with the gifted and talented members of the senior class. He scored higher than any of them.

In the next year, however, his life would take a fateful turn, though he didn't realize it then. He'd heard two acquaintances his own age, Coy Odom and James Upchurch, talking about a new game they'd begun playing, Dungeons and Dragons. Intrigued, he got hold of the basic book and read it, then moved on to more advanced material.

The following year, when he normally would have been in the ninth grade, Neal was taking junior and senior courses but was assigned to a sophomore homeroom. "They really never could decide exactly what I was," he said.

But school officials recognized that he needed more than what was available at Bartlett Yancey High, and that year Neal was accepted at the prestigious North Carolina School of Science and Mathematics in Durham, a free-tuition boarding school for some of the state's best students, where he would be considered a junior.

Weldon Slayton had grown closer to Neal than he'd ever allowed himself to get with any student, and although he and Neal's mother realized that Neal needed to get away from Caswell County to live up to his academic potential, both were concerned about him going off at age fifteen to live on his own with older students. Neal never had close friends. He was still very immature, without social skills or self-discipline. Would he be able to function without close and caring supervision? Would sending him away help him or harm him?

Before Neal was accepted by the School of Science & Math, he wrote in Weldon Slayton's yearbook:

> All hail the mighty Slayton!
> You've always been the guiding force in my life.
> But who knows where you're guiding me! I hope that
> (if I'm here next year) I get you for English. I don't
> know why though, maybe I'm a masochist.
> Always your semi-willing Slave
> Neal

After his acceptance, Neal wrote again in Slayton's yearbook:

> Revenge of the Neali,
> Ha! I've remembered to write in your year book
> more (pitiful grammar). I suppose I'd better get

147

serious. I'm really sad that I'll have to leave prematurely. Your strange ways and speech patterns have become part of my existence. Going away will tear that out (albeit temporarily). I hope that you won't mind if I call, half-crazed with panic instead of completely crazed (as usual). You'd better come and visit me or I'll come and visit you! Just always be around and be my mentor/friend and everything should be alright.

Your devoted pupil,
Neal Henderson

Neal did call Slayton from Durham on a regular basis, and Slayton called him. Slayton also went to the campus to visit him, yet everything was not all right. Neal was doing more than procrastinating with his class work. Some of it he wasn't doing at all.

Soon after his arrival he had become involved in several groups playing Dungeons and Dragons and other role-playing games, and for the first time he began making some close friends among the players.

During a D&D game in his first week at school, he met a female student from Charlotte and they began seeing each other regularly. Neal never had dated before, and he was mesmerized by having a girlfriend. When they broke up after a month, Neal soon met another young woman. And with yet another girlfriend he had his first sexual experience. Girls and D&D were taking far more of his time than studies, and his grades soon showed it. He was placed on probation, the principal lamenting that he was among the school's top students in ability and among its lowest in using ability. Despite warnings from his mother and Slayton, Neal did little to improve his work, and although he passed all of his subjects with Cs and Bs, he was not invited to return the following year, a polite way of ejecting him.

He returned home to finish his final year of high school at Bartlett Yancey, still a year ahead of his classmates from elementary school, chagrined about letting down his mother and Slayton and others who had expected great things from him, but not at all sorry about leaving the School of Science and Math.

"It wasn't for me," he said. "I just couldn't handle the freedom. I didn't have the self-discipline to do my work."

Despite his lack of success, Neal returned to a campus where he was as well known as the captain of the football team and the head cheerleader.

"He was the Great Neal Henderson," said Kenyatta Up-church, who soon was to play a major role in his life. "He was a geek, but he was *the* real smart guy on campus."

Neal was keenly aware of his reputation, or, as he called it, his "celebrity for better or worse. They think I'm weird. Fine. I'm going to be weird. And I think I was remarkably successful in that endeavor."

He made friends with a few of the smarter male students and organized them into a group playing some of the fantasy and strategy games he'd learned at the School of Science and Math. He created a spy game and ran around the school hallways pretending to be Agent Double O Six and a Half. He was secretary for the band, in which he played tuba. He worked on the school yearbook. He sold candy to help the Junior Engineering and Technical Society raise money to buy a computer, then became the school's computer whiz, programming it even to play his fantasy games.

Weldon Slayton remained concerned about Neal and some of the habits he had gotten into during the year he was away. He spent too much time playing games and too little time at his schoolwork. And he was personally slovenly. Slayton had been shocked at the condition of Neal's basement room when he visited him at home.

The room, which had been partitioned off with plyboard paneling, was a scene of wild clutter. Somewhere beneath it all was a bed, a dresser, a bookcase, a chair rarely employed for sitting. A stereo and records filled a big shelf. Another shelf was lined with trophies and certificates. A big closet was packed with his grandparents' old clothing. Posters—the Beatles, characters from science fiction and fantasy tales—decorated the walls. Clothes were strewn with superhero comics, books, and Dungeons and Dragons materials.

"Neal, this is a pigsty," Slayton said. "You need to clean this place up."

If Slayton was concerned that Neal had become slovenly and lazy, paying too much attention to frivolous activities, before the school year was up, he would discover that Neal had found another reason to devote even less time to his studies.

Kenyatta Upchurch, first cousin of Bart and Emory, knew Neal only by reputation. She was in the eighth grade at Dillard Junior High, where she, too, was a gifted student. Resentful of her free-and-easy, back-to-the-land upbringing and embarrassed by her parents' continuing sixties-alternative lifestyle, she had begun spending much of her time with her grandmother Carolyn at her big house in Milton. Her life, as she saw it, had been independent and lonely. As a small child she had been shy and withdrawn, but that had changed. Now she was talkative and almost hyperactive, aggressive and outspoken about her feelings.

Kenyatta played flute in the junior high band, and in the spring of 1985, she was scheduled to take part in a concert at the high school auditorium. Friends who were supposed to pick her up failed to do so. Fearful that she was going to miss the concert, she rode her bicycle to her uncle's house in tears. Her cousin Bart drove her to the school. She arrived still upset. In the lobby of the auditorium, a friend beckoned to her.

"Kenyatta, come over here. I want to introduce you to Neal Henderson."

"I was crying," she recalled years later. "I thought, well, big deal. I didn't pay any attention to him."

Not long afterward, she was in the band room at the junior high when Neal came in to pick up some equipment to take back to the high school. "Something about him just clicked," she said.

She developed an immediate and immense crush, although she could never explain why.

"Neal looked like the Pillsbury Dough Boy," she said, "a real veg type. And he walked like a turtle with his head all stuck out. I would see him get off the bus and just watch him walk. I was just crazy about him. You know how eighth-grade crushes are. They're very embarrassing."

Her cousin Emory had become friends with Neal, and she pestered him to tell Neal that she had a crush on him until he did it. On Thursday, April 18, a date she never would forget, she got word that Neal wanted to meet her after school. She came on her ten-speed bike.

"He was standing at the road waiting for me by the stop sign," she said.

They went into the school and talked while Neal plunked away at a computer. Two hours later, they were still talking, and Neal had given her his class ring.

"He told me later that he was desperate to get a girlfriend at that point," she said.

By summertime, they had moved beyond going steady. A basement door led to Neal's room at his grandparents' house. Kenyatta began riding her bicycle several miles to the house, hiding her bike in the woods, and sneaking up to the basement door, where Neal would let her in. "I bet I spent half the summer in that basement," she said later.

By telling her parents that she was staying at her grandmother's and telling her grandmother that she was staying at home, she even was able to spend nights in Neal's room, and they reveled in the illicit excitement of knowing that they were getting away with something right under the feet of Neal's mother and grandparents. It was made all the more delicious by the knowledge that Neal's mother didn't like Kenyatta and didn't want him seeing her.

All of that came to an end soon after school started again late that summer. Neal was repeating the twelfth grade. After his poor performance at the School of Science and Math, his mother and Weldon Slayton thought it best that he hold back and go to college with classmates his own age. Another year of high school would allow him a chance to mature and think about the responsibilities of college. That fall he was to begin an independent study of calculus, a class of one, the first student ever to do such a thing in Caswell County.

But one school-day morning in September, Neal and Kenyatta were in bed in his basement room. Neal got up and went upstairs to bid his mother goodbye before she left for her job at J. C. Penney's in Danville. Kenyatta remained in bed.

"Next thing I knew," Kenyatta recalled years later, "I heard her high heels clicking down the stairs."

Neal's mother tried the door, but Neal had locked it from the inside as he left.

"Why is this door locked?" Kenyatta heard her demanding. "There's somebody in there, isn't there?"

"There's nobody in there, Mom."

"Open the door, Neal."

"I can't."

"O-pen the door," Neal's mother said with deliberateness and force.

"Open the door, Kenyatta," Neal said in resignation.

Kenyatta opened the door to find Ann Henderson in a hot fury.

"She called me everything in the book," Kenyatta recalled later. "Called me a homewrecker. She told Neal, 'I can't believe you would jeopardize this family like this.' She said if his grandfather knew this was going on, he would kick the whole family out.

"I just stood there. I'm like, 'Excuse me, Neal, would you like to step in here?' He never said a thing. He never took up for me. He just let me take the brunt of it.

"I just left. I got all my stuff together and split. Next day at school he told me, 'I think it would be better if we broke up for a while.' "

The breakup did not last long. It was only the first of many in what would be a long and tumultuous relationship. Once tapped, Neal's libido was boundless. "He was excited twenty-four hours a day," Kenyatta claimed. Three times during Neal's final year at Bartlett Yancey High, Kenyatta would discover that he had sex with other girls while going steady with her.

"He didn't think that sleeping with other girls should affect me, because he didn't love them and it was only satisfying a physical need, so it wasn't a big deal," Kenyatta said. "Of course, we argued about that. That was a big point of disagreement."

"Neal told me that girls were easy to use," Weldon Slayton said. "It was their fault if they got hurt."

As Slayton recalled it, he said, "Neal, you can't *use* people."

"But they're so easy to manipulate," Neal replied.

"Be more honest," Slayton said.

"Well, it's their fault if they can't figure it out."

Kenyatta discovered that year that her competition for Neal's attentions was not just the vulnerable girls he found so easy to manipulate, but his games and his male friends as well. Neal had joined Bart Upchurch's Dungeons and Dragons group and was becoming more and more involved in their long campaigns. Kenyatta thought that Bart and the other dungeon members resented her, thought that she was imposing herself on Neal and trying to take him away from the game. Neal balanced precariously between the two. The truth was, however, that he found D&D more mystifying and intriguing than Kenyatta or any other female.

"It was a kind of intellectual exercise," he said later of D&D. "I like the idea of having spell-casters and ladies to save."

When he first joined Bart's dungeon, Neal became a magic-user-fighter and created the Legion of Love, his own version of King Arthur's Knights of the Round Table. But the game soon took another turn.

"Neal was always scheming," Bart later remembered. "His character was always trying to get more powerful. He rarely went on adventures. He was just scheming to kill somebody's character and get his stuff. Neal controlled everybody, and they never knew they were being controlled. With Neal, if you didn't work for him, you worked against him. You were his enemy. It got to be everybody against Neal."

22

JOANNE KNEW THAT SOME-thing was troubling Bart. For several days, he had seemed nervous, distracted. She asked Emory if he knew what the problem was, but he didn't.

"Something's eating at Bart," she told Jim one afternoon in late February 1986, Bart's senior year in high school. But both knew that it would do no good to quiz him about it. He simply would deny any problems and retreat into himself as usual.

The answer to what was troubling Bart came with the ringing of the telephone after school on Thursday, February 26. It was for Bart. As her son talked quietly on the phone, Joanne knew that something bad had happened. His neck flushed, he looked frightened.

"Mom, I've got to go to the sheriff's department," he said after he'd hung up. "A friend has been arrested for something he didn't do and I can testify to where he was."

Joanne was not about to let him leave the house. "You're not taking the car and going up there by yourself," she said. "You sit down here and tell me what's going on. Something's wrong, Bart. Something's been wrong. What is it?"

His friend had been charged with breaking into the high school eleven days earlier and stealing a computer, Bart told her. It had happened the night Bart and three other boys had gone camping at the lake. The boy who had been arrested was one of the camping group, along with his brother, so Bart knew he couldn't have done it.

The fourth member of the camping group, Joanne discovered, was Gary Hampton*. She should have known. Gary was the one friend of Bart's whom Joanne distrusted and disliked. She really didn't want Bart to associate with him, but she'd been reluctant to forbid it.

She'd sensed that Hampton was trouble from the first time she saw him. He was older than Bart. He'd dropped out of high school, joined the navy, been kicked out after only a few months. He lived in a trailer beside another trailer in which his grandfather lived. Joanne had driven Bart there to play Dungeons and Dragons. Later, she'd heard that other high school boys went to Gary's trailer to drink beer.

Joanne had expressed her feelings about Gary to Jim and suggested that he needed to talk to Bart about it.

"He said, 'Leave him alone,' " she recalled later. " 'Let him make up his own mind. You can't choose your children's friends.' "

Now, as Bart told her about his friend's arrest, Joanne realized that Bart knew more about what had happened than he was telling. When she pressed him, he finally admitted that he had taken part in the break-in, too. Joanne broke into tears. Distress and anger burst from her. She was angry not only because Bart had participated in a burglary but also because he had been ready to lie to cover it up.

Jim came home from work to find Bart quiet and sheepish and Joanne "almost hysterical, ranting and raving and crying."

"It was the magnitude of the screwup that astounded her," Bart said later. "She was hopping mad. She told me that was what I got for hanging around with people like Gary."

"I was very upset," Joanne admitted later. "I knew with the company he was keeping something could happen, and it had. I felt responsible."

"Look, let me handle it," Jim told Joanne when he managed to get out of her what had happened.

"Did you do it?" he asked Bart.

Bart looked away from him and nodded. He clearly didn't intend to talk more about it.

"Bart can turn you off like a light," Jim said later. "The madder you get, the more he closes you out."

Jim called a friend, Osmond Smith, a lawyer who lived nearby, and told him what had happened. Smith advised Jim to take Bart to the sheriff's department, let him admit his part in the break-in, and tell what he knew about it. This was a serious matter, a felony, Smith pointed out. Although it was unlikely that a first offender would be sent to jail, it was possible.

Before Jim had a chance to take Bart to Yanceyville, the telephone rang again. A sheriff's department detective asked to speak to Jim. Jim knew the man. He knew everybody in the county government. In an apologetic tone, the detective told Jim that he had a warrant for Bart's arrest. He wanted to extend the courtesy of allowing Jim to bring in his son. They would be right there, Jim told him.

Jim was angry, too, although he tried not to show it. "Bart, the best thing to do when you've made a mistake is face up to it, pay the price," Jim told him. "Your mother and I'll support you. We'll get you a lawyer."

Everybody at the sheriff's department was obviously embarrassed for Jim as the warrant was served and his son was taken away to be fingerprinted.

Afterward, Bart was taken before a magistrate, another acquaintance of Jim, who released Bart to the custody of his father without bond. Nobody had any doubt that an Upchurch would appear for trial.

Bart was quieter than usual after his arrest. He went to school the next day seemingly untroubled about the prospect of facing his teachers and fellow students, who surely would know about the charges against him. Word spread quickly in Caswell County.

Later, Bart would admit to feeling embarrassed at the way teachers looked at him that day, although none said anything to him about it. From friends and classmates he took a lot of kidding. "Hey, man, know anybody who's got a computer they want to sell? You really fucked up this time." But the kidding was good-natured, and beneath its surface was a certain awe at Bart's nerve and daring.

That night, Jim Upchurch got another call from the sheriff's department. Another warrant for Bart. This one for burglarizing a lake house on the same night of the school break-in and stealing five cases of beer, four bottles of wine, a TV, a set of binoculars and two clocks.

"I thought, shit, what in the world's going on here?" Jim said later. "I was getting real mad."

Bart admitted this one, too. The reason he hadn't mentioned it the day before was simple: he wasn't sure the authorities had connected the two crimes. No sense in asking for more trouble.

For the second night in a row, Jim had to take his son to Yanceyville for another hearing before the magistrate. This time, Bart assured his seething father that there would be no more surprises.

Although Bart remained quiet about the details of the break-ins at the time, he later claimed that they were unplanned, merely a lark.

The camping trip was supposed to be an adventure, a test of endurance, sleeping out in the bitter cold in the middle of winter, cooking over an open fire. It was planned spur-of-the-moment, something to do on a Sunday night of President's Day weekend with no school on Monday.

Bart had picked up the other boys in his mother's beige Ford Escort station wagon. They burdened the small car with tents and sleeping bags and headed for a cove on Hyco Reservoir, not far from Bart's house, where his uncle, John Thomas, Jim's half-brother, had a lot and kept two canoes.

At the lake, the boys loaded the gear into the canoes and set out across the muddy red water in search of a campsite. Darkness was nearing, the wind was bracing, and the water was so cold that it had begun to form a skim of ice in spots sheltered from the wind. Although all the boys were bundled in heavy jackets, they began to shiver at the thought of spending the night on the cold ground in sleeping bags. Why should they do that, somebody asked, when right by the lake, unused, were so many summer cottages where they could build a fire and sleep in comfort?

They picked a likely house, set back in the trees, landed their canoes, and scouted out the place as darkness was settling. Nobody was anywhere around. They knocked out a downstairs window. One of the boys went inside and opened the door for the others. They found the power box and turned on the electricity, brought in wood, built a fire, turned on a small black-and-white TV. Meanwhile, a treasure trove had been discovered in the house: cases of beer and several bottles of wine and champagne. They started drinking beer, scavenged the cabinets for food, popped the cork on a bottle of champagne.

"At first, everybody was saying, 'Oh, hell, we're going to get in trouble for this,' " Bart recalled. "After everybody had a few beers, it was 'Hey, this is fun.' Out in the middle of Caswell County. Wasn't anything else to do. It was something we did. We just got a little adrenaline rush out of the whole deal."

The rush soon died, however, and somebody suggested that they go for a ride. Bart and Gary hiked back around the lake and got his mother's car. Then they ferried his uncle's canoes back one at a time, sticking out of the back of the station wagon. Finally, they loaded up the remaining cases of beer, the wine, and the easy-to-carry items that they found in the house, and set out whooping and hollering. They were talking about video games as they rode into Yanceyville.

"Somebody said, 'Well, hell, let's go get a computer while we're at it,' " Bart recalled. "I don't know whose idea it was."

Bart knew that a physics teacher at the high school always left a classroom window slightly open. They went through that window and snatched an Apple computer, complete with color monitor and keyboard, from a classroom. Bart dropped the keyboard and broke two keys on it as he was running back to the car.

The four boys then went to Gary's trailer, where they hooked up the computer and played with it while they polished off more of the beer. Lulled by alcohol, they finally slept for a few hours. After they awoke, Bart drove his two friends home, then went home himself to proclaim his camping trip a cold but satisfying success.

Bart was keenly aware of his parents' anger about his arrest. "They were mad for a good long while," he said. "At the time,

I couldn't say very much to them. I couldn't do anything but hang my head and be real meek and humble."

"He didn't show a lot of guilt," his father said later. "He was mainly concerned about the outcome."

A month after his arrest, Bart appeared before Recorder's Court Judge Peter McHugh in the old white courthouse in Yanceyville, where his great-grandfather once had been so prominent. Jim had again hired George Daniel, who had helped Joanne out of the wool business mess, and Daniel had worked out a plea bargain with the district attorney. The charges would be consolidated and reduced to misdemeanors in exchange for Bart's plea of guilty. Judge McHugh sentenced Bart to a year in prison, suspended on the following conditions: that he be on supervised probation for three years; that he remain in school in good standing or be employed full-time; that he not associate with Gary Hampton and the other two boys with whom he committed the break-ins; that he perform 150 hours of community service in the next six months; and that he pay court costs and restitution. That was a considerably lighter sentence than the maximum twenty years in prison.

"I don't think anybody wanted to prosecute Bart to the fullest extent of the law," his father said later. At the same time, he was concerned that he had been lax in disciplining Bart. He had left it to Joanne to be the disciplinarian in the family, and she often had been frustrated in reprimanding Bart.

"Bart was her match," Jim said later. "He was always a discipline problem, from the time he was real small. Tell him something, he wouldn't do it. He just didn't mind very well.

"He knew how to push you, knew how to get your temper up. He used to make Joanne terribly mad. She'd say, 'I'll be glad when he turns eighteen and leaves home.' It would just drive her bananas. Sometimes I think he just wanted to see how mad he could make you before he gave in. It was almost a game sometimes, I think. By the time he got to high school, it was more like an attitude problem, like he just resisted anything you wanted him to do."

Weldon Slayton thought that Bart had an attitude problem, too, and he was afraid that Bart had moved beyond the point where his behavior could be greatly influenced by parents or teachers. "James just had no moral compass to go by," he said later.

Slayton had regrets about Bart. Bart was so smart, so capable, yet he had no direction, no goals. His grades were barely above average. He rarely exerted himself to accomplish anything. Slayton could recall only one time that Bart had really thrown himself into a project, an oral presentation on Mark Twain, in the first semester of Bart's junior year.

"He talked about his life so convincingly," Slayton said, "as if he actually were living it."

"That's the type of thing I really wish you all had done," Slayton told his class after Bart had finished.

He gave Bart an A on the assignment and a 99 for the semester, the highest grade Bart ever got. It helped Bart to get appointed to the Governor's School for special students the next summer, after he was named a National Merit semifinalist. If Bart had applied himself more to his studies and less to Dungeons and Dragons, Slayton knew, he probably would have been chosen to attend the School of Science and Math. Science was his one genuine interest. He always watched the *National Geographic* specials and science-related shows on TV. He read a lot about astronomy. His mother knew that he really wanted to go to the School of Science and Math and that he was hurt when his friend and dungeon member James Long was chosen and he was not. Nobody other than his mother would know that he cared at all about whether he was chosen, though, because he never showed his disappointment.

Slayton couldn't help but wonder if Bart had applied himself and received more of the recognition he was so capable of achieving, if he still would have taken such great pleasure in thwarting the system to show he didn't care. He was always doing outlandish things to draw attention to himself, such as listing in the school yearbook all kinds of clubs to which he never belonged and activities in which he hadn't participated.

"I would ask him, 'Why, James, did you do such a thing?' " Slayton recalled. "He would just shrug his shoulders. He did things just to see if he could get away with it."

Slayton saw Bart's troubles with the law as a logical outgrowth of his earlier defiant behavior. But he did not ask Bart about his arrest and conviction. When students had problems, he left it to them to come to him if they wanted to talk about them. Bart didn't come.

"James thought it was stupid to believe what I did," he said. "He had developed the attitude that life is out there for you to get out of it what you want the easiest way you can get it. And it's just a game."

23

BART'S PROBLEMS WITH the law only added to the tumultuous mix of emotions that had been simmering in his family, and soon after his sentencing, those feelings boiled to the surface.

Joanne's job at Memorial Hospital in Danville regularly took her out of Caswell County and made her realize how much she resented its isolation and attitudes. "Caswell County is not the real world," she said later. "You're never accepted as an outsider. Unless you're going to talk about tobacco or the weather or the latest car wreck on the front page of the Caswell *Messenger*, there's nothing to talk about. I would walk into a country store and there would be dead silence."

Her resentment of Caswell County was nothing compared to her resentment of Jim's infidelity. The unforgiving nature that had caused her to shun her father's funeral and sever all ties with her mother would not allow her to forget. "I couldn't get over Judy Gold," she said. "It wasn't the same after that. I couldn't make it the same."

Although she loved Jim, she had concluded that they were too much unalike. "We were two people just existing in the same household. We didn't communicate, didn't even really know each other. There was no common ground except for the children. Jim had such a passion and love for the farm. I wanted more than I had there. I knew there was more out there. We couldn't make it together."

Jim knew that Joanne was unhappy, but he wasn't expecting what happened on Saturday, May 3, only five weeks after the trauma of Bart's court appearance. Joanne called him into their upstairs bedroom and told him that she was leaving. She had rented an apartment in Danville. She wanted to get away from everything and think.

"I tried to get her to stay," Jim said later. "She walked out. Just left."

And left all four children with him. Bart was seventeen, Emory fifteen, Carrie seven, Alex five. Joanne had taken them all upstairs to talk with them before she left. Bart and Emory had little to say afterward. Bart, as usual, showed no reaction. Emory was at first distraught, later grieved. The girls, especially Alex, were confused and worried. Alex kept asking when her mother was coming back.

Jim's mother, Carolyn, would never forget that day. After Joanne left, Jim came to her house with the children. Once again she had been left largely in the dark about what was going on in her son's family. She hadn't even known that Bart had been arrested until she read it in the newspaper. She had been shocked by that, and when she saw Jim this day, she knew she was in for another shock.

"He looked perfectly awful," she said. "Just ghastly. I said, 'What is it?' He said, 'Joanne's gone.' "

Carolyn couldn't believe that Joanne had left her children.

"I don't think anybody can understand why I did it," Joanne said later. "The only way it was going to work was for me to leave. I had no attachment to the farm and Jim did. I couldn't afford to take the children. And Jim needed to know his children. He never packed their lunches, never tucked them in, never disciplined them. He didn't know who liked what on their plates. He called me one time when Carrie was in the hospital and asked me how to wash Alex's hair. I had to leave. That was the only way it was going to work, the only way he was going to get to know his children."

A week after she left, Joanne returned to pick up the children for Mother's Day. They talked about almost everything but her leaving. Nobody but Alex wanted to bring that up.

"When are you coming home?" she asked.

Joanne had no answer.

Jim knew the answer already. He returned home that night to discover that she had taken all her clothes, the silver and china from their wedding. He knew she'd never come back.

Not long afterward, Jim discovered that if Joanne had left to think, it hadn't taken her long to decide what she wanted.

He learned that a coworker, Alan Ferguson,* was living in the apartment with her. Ferguson had just married for the second time a year earlier, to a woman who had two children from a previous marriage. Jim and Joanne had gone to their house for a Super Bowl party in January. Jim knew that Alan and Joanne were good friends. He just hadn't realized they were that close. Alan was the coach of the hospital's women's softball team. Joanne was on the team. They played on Thursday nights, and afterward the team members would go drink beer and eat pizza. Jim had seen it as a night out with the girls for Joanne. Now he realized it might have been something else.

He called Alan's wife, who had become suspicious of Alan and Joanne long before Jim. She had hired a private detective, who had come up with evidence of a tryst before Joanne and Alan left their spouses. She was going to use the evidence to obtain a divorce, she said, and Jim was welcome to use it, too.

Alan Ferguson, meanwhile, had begun looking for jobs outside of Danville. He landed one in another Virginia town and Joanne followed him there.

Back at the farm, Jim was coping with taking care of his children. Emory took most of the responsibility for the girls. Carolyn came to get the girls each morning and took them back to Milton so they could catch the school bus at her house. Then she waited for them in the afternoon and took care of them until Jim got home from work.

Alex continued to say that she wanted her mother and daddy together again, and Jim tried to make her understand that it probably wouldn't happen.

"It may be the best thing," he told her. "Your mother's happy. We'll be happy, too."

"I was trying to be a lot more optimistic than I was feeling," he said later. "Joanne leaving was like knocking a crutch out. I was so dependent on her. I really wanted her to come back."

Jim worried that Bart might think his troubles played a part in the breakup and blame himself for it.

"Well, how are you taking it?" he asked his son one day.

"Okay," Bart said with a shrug.

Actually, Bart was the least affected by the situation of anybody in the family.

"When it finally did happen," he said later, "I knew it was for good. At some point, I think there was always some kind of tension that I never consciously recognized. Mom had sort

162

of started complaining when I was in about the tenth or eleventh grade, but that was as far as it got. There was never a lot of arguing, never any violence or anything like that. When it happened, I said, Damn, this has been going on and I never noticed it.'

"When they finally did separate for good, it wasn't anything that was like some violent, emotionally wrenching thing for me. As far as these things go, it was as painless as something like that can get."

Joanne returned in June for Bart's graduation. The family gathered at the farm afterward. The happiness of the situation was underlaid by unspoken anger, resentment, and pain. The tension grew worse when Jim opened Bart's report card, which had been enclosed in his diploma. Although Bart had been graduated sixty-fourth in his class of 228, with a B average, he clearly had done almost nothing in his last semester. He'd flunked two subjects, and he slipped by in three other subjects with only a point or two to spare. A C was his highest grade, and he had only one of those—in Weldon Slayton's English class. Jim's anger uncharacteristically exploded.

"If you're not going to get serious about life and about going to school, there's no sense in you even going to college," he told his son. "You're not headed in any direction that's positive. You've got to get control of your life. You've got to take on some responsibilities. If you want to go to college, you're going to have to work for it."

Joanne was surprised. "He was getting all over Bart about it," she recalled, "really chilling him out."

She figured Jim's outburst was prompted more by Jim's distress over the breakup than by Bart's lackadaisical attitude toward school.

"I preached for thirty minutes," Jim said later. "I was really mad. Bart just couldn't care less about grades, or school, or anything else. I just felt like he was heading down the drain."

"I think you've said enough," Joanne finally told him, bringing the sermon to a halt.

Bart's future was still in doubt. He had no idea of what he wanted to do with his life. His strong interest in the military had led him at one point to consider applying to the U.S. Naval Academy, and he actually had begun the process before discovering that his chances were too slim to be realistic. Instead, he'd sent out applications to three or four colleges. One of those was N.C. State University in Raleigh. In the space allocated for an essay describing why he wanted to attend State, Bart had been succinct: "North Carolina State University has one of the better schools of engineering in the Southeast. My family can afford the tuition. It offers Army R.O.T.C. It is close to home." Bart wasn't even interested in engineering. He was applying to the School of Humanities and Social Sciences to study sociology and anthropology, courses that piqued his interest when he read the catalog descriptions. And in February, he had received notice that he had been accepted.

But another possibility still appealed to him. His long-standing interest in the military led him to think about joining the army. The year before, when his family had been at the state fair, Bart had stopped by the army recruiting exhibit and talked with the recruiters. They had given him a test and told him he scored highest of anybody who had taken it that day. He had talked with the local recruiter since.

Bart had decided to enlist for three years, save his money, and earn enough in credits from the army to pay for his college later, but a hitch turned up. Because of his conviction, he would have to get permission from his probation officer to join. Jim went to talk to the probation officer.

"He said, 'No, Bart needs to go to college. He has to have half a term before we can get him off probation.' I said, 'I don't think he's emotionally mature enough to do it.' He wouldn't budge. Let's just say the probation officer and I disagreed."

Bart was upset about that decision. But with the army out of the question, he saw no choice but to attend N.C. State. He certainly didn't want to stay in Caswell County.

Jim talked to his mother about it.

"If he wants to go to State, let's let him go." Carolyn said.

"He seemed to be positive about it," Jim said later.

Carolyn sent off the check for tuition and took Bart to buy new clothes for campus.

In July, Jim and Bart went to N.C. State for freshman orientation. Bart was a little awed by the campus. "It was just full of pavement and bricks," he said later. "I walked up on campus, looked at Lee dorm, got lost."

On campus that day, Jim and Bart ran into Neal Henderson and his mother and stopped to chat. Although they played

Dungeons and Dragons together, Bart and Neal never had been close, perhaps because each felt a little competitive with the other. Neal was very close, however, with Emory. Yet here were Bart and Neal, friends, both from Caswell County, both coming to State. One thing had seemed logical months earlier when both had learned of their acceptance at State.

"You want to room together?" Neal had asked in class one day.

"Sure," said Bart. "Why not?"

Now they began making plans about what they would bring to the dorm room they would be sharing.

24

IN AUGUST OF 1986, WHEN Bart and Neal moved into room 405B of a four-room suite on the fourth floor of Lee Residence Hall, a high-rise red-brick dorm on the West Campus, N.C. State University was only six months away from celebrating its centennial. In its hundred years, it had become the largest university in the state, with some 24,000 students on a campus of 623 acres on the edge of downtown Raleigh.

The university had strong programs in engineering, math, textiles, agriculture, forestry, veterinary medicine, design. It was a national center for research in science and technology. It also had a seething rivalry, especially on the basketball court, with the University of North Carolina, the nation's first state university, thirty miles away in Chapel Hill. Carolina students considered themselves far more erudite and sophisticated than State students. Cars of Carolina supporters sometimes bore bumper stickers that read: "Honk if you love Carolina; moo if you from State."

The N.C. State campus was split down the middle by a main-line railroad track and bordered on two sides by major thoroughfares, Hillsborough Street and Western Boulevard.

Hillsborough Street was lined with diversions: restaurants, bars, ice cream parlors, record shops, used book stores, and other businesses catering to students. Western Boulevard offered a shopping center with movie theaters, a motel, fast-food restaurants, Pullen Park, Central Prison, the TV station where Jesse Helms gained fame as a commentator before his election to the U.S. Senate, and Dorothea Dix Hospital, the state's primary mental institution.

Bart was immediately drawn to the diversions, both on and off campus. "It was real easy to get distracted," he recalled later. "So many people your age doing parties and raising hell in such a concentrated area." At one period, soon after his arrival at State, Bart was attending parties almost every night, often staggering back to his room in a stupor.

Neal, on the other hand, detested parties and sneered at Bart and his activities, much as he had done in high school. Neal felt uncomfortable in groups of more than three and thought of parties as noisy and senseless wastes of energy.

This difference in attitude was only one of many things that separated Bart and Neal. Soon after moving in together, both realized that they probably should have chosen other roommates. Bart, for one thing, was neat. Neal was incredibly sloppy. A demarcation line was soon drawn down the middle of the room—cleanliness and order on one side, clutter and filth on the other. Beyond that, neither really liked the other, nor did they like one another's friends.

"A lot of people didn't like Neal," Bart said. "Maybe because he was a real disgusting person. Anytime he got drunk, he got sick. He'd go throw up in anybody's room he happened to be in. If you had a girlfriend coming, you didn't want him around. He'd hit on her. Absolutely no shame. He just got on a lot of people's nerves. Everybody more or less avoided him."

Neal's friends were mainly his acquaintances from his year at the N.C. School of Science and Math. Bart's friends all were new acquaintances, people he had met during orientation and after moving into the dorm.

"Some of Neal's friends were real genius types," Bart said later. "Really bright but extremely eccentric."

While Bart went out partying, Neal preferred staying in his room playing Dungeons and Dragons, Champions, and other role-playing games with his friends. Bart never played with them, although he did play occasionally with others. Most of his time, however, was spent hitting bars and clubs where he could pass himself off as twenty-one, listening to rock and roll, and prowling the nearby campuses of Meredith and St. Mary's colleges, attempting without much success to pick up the well-to-do young women who attended those private schools.

"We never partied in my room, just because Neal was there," Bart said later. "Neal would bug everybody, drive everybody crazy, chase all the women away."

Another thing separating Neal and Bart was study. Neal later would claim that he never saw Bart pick up a book during their year of rooming together. Only a few weeks into the semester, Bart quit going to his math and English classes for the simple reason that they were scheduled too early in the morning.

Neal, on the other hand, felt obligated to study, at least perfunctorily. In his final year at Bartlett Yancey High, he not only won top honors in English and mathematics, he was captain of the Quiz Bowl team and president of the Junior Engineering and Technical Society. He scored 1500 on his SATs, only 100 points short of perfect, prompting his admitting officer at N.C. State to note that it was the highest score he'd ever seen. More than that, Neal had won a full scholarship to N.C. State, the Aubrey Lee Brooks Scholarship, granted each year to the top student in each county of an eleven-county area. It was renewable for four years on the condition that he maintain acceptable grades.

Neal did not have much spending money, however, and several weeks after classes began, he took a job at a Pizza Hut near campus, first working behind the counter, later delivering pizzas. When he told Bart about openings for delivery drivers, Bart applied and was accepted. Soon Bart was working long hours on weeknights to support his weekend partying, and his grades suffered even more.

On October 17, another warrant was issued for Bart's arrest, this one for probation violation, charging that he had failed to complete the 150 hours of community service he was ordered to render within six months of his sentencing for breaking into the lake house and his high school. His probation officer reported that he had completed only 49 hours and seemed indifferent about the rest. Bart was angry.

"It was mostly the fault of the guy assigning the community

service," he claimed later. "He didn't assign me enough work to do. I did everything I was told, but he didn't tell me to do enough stuff."

On October 29, Judge Peter McHugh gave Bart a choice: he could complete his remaining community service or spend a week in the Caswell County Jail. Bart chose jail, and the judge allowed him to serve the week during the fall break in classes.

"It wasn't a scary experience," he said later. "It was a real pain in the ass. It was boring. Nothing to do except sleep and read. I felt embarrassed. Neal went around and told everybody about it. I was just glad to get it over with and be done with it."

Soon after his week in jail, Bart had another brush with the law. He drove his pizza delivery truck in the wrong direction down a one-way street on campus to take a shortcut between dorms. A campus public safety officer stopped him and wrote a ticket. It was not his first.

Near the end of his junior year in high school, Bart got a warning ticket when he only slowed at a stop sign at a rural intersection in Caswell County. One week later, at the same spot, the same highway patrolman stopped him for the same violation and wrote him another ticket, this one no warning. Bart didn't tell his parents about it. He and Emory and his friend Coy Odom scratched together enough money to pay off the ticket.

When he got the ticket on campus, Bart intended to go to court and argue that it was unjustified, but the court appearance came just two days before Christmas, while he was home between semesters, and he didn't bother to return to Raleigh for it. When he came back to campus in early January, he received notice that his driver's license had been revoked. It was of little concern to him. He had given up his job at Pizza Hut because it was taking too much of his time (sometimes he didn't get back to his dorm room until 3 A.M.). He had no car and little opportunity to drive. Once again, he didn't tell his parents about his difficulties.

Throughout his first semester, Bart had told his father that he was doing okay in class, making Bs and Cs. Jim was understandably perturbed when a transcript of Bart's grades arrived showing mostly failures and incompletes. Bart blamed the bad grades on working too much and vowed to do better during his second semester. For a few weeks he did. He kept up his grades, didn't party as much on class nights. A friend in ROTC helped him get a part-time job that didn't interfere with his class schedule, writing parking tickets for the campus police.

Soon after the second semester began, Bart and Neal had a falling out.

"We need to get a stereo for this room," Bart told Neal one day and Neal went along with the suggestion. Bart called a rent-to-own place and found that he could get a top-grade stereo for one hundred dollars a month. He had money that he'd gotten as a gift at Christmas. Neal was awaiting the spending money that came with his scholarship. Bart said he would pay the first month's rent, Neal could pay the second.

"About the third week, Neal's money came in and I told him, 'Now don't forget, you've got to pay the stereo bill this month,'" Bart recalled later. "'No problem,' he said. Then came time the bill was due. I said, 'Have you paid it yet?' He said, 'I've spent all my money.' I said, 'What did you do with it? He said, 'I spent it.' Made me mad as hell. I said, 'Damn it, Neal, we agreed we were going to split the cost.' He said, 'Well, my name's not on the lease.' It was just tough luck. That's the kind of guy he is. He didn't want to do anything he had to do if he could figure out a way to get around it. I just said, 'The hell with you. I'll return the stereo.'"

Bart and Neal hardly spoke for several weeks after the stereo incident, and during that time Bart found himself uncomfortably confined to the room they shared. He started feeling sick and thought he was taking the flu. But after a trip to the campus dispensary, he was told that he had mononucleosis.

He spent two weeks in bed and fell so far behind in his classes that he knew he never could catch up. He had a legitimate medical excuse for dropping all of his classes and maintaining his status as a student. And he received permission to do so. But he failed to turn in the forms in time.

"The real reason was that I was lazy and didn't feel like walking all the way across campus and seeing three or four people," he said later.

By the time he got around to turning in the paperwork,

it was too late. "Flunked every single class second semester. I was pissed. I said, 'Damn, I screwed up first semester. Now second semester's gone to shit.' "

With no hope of passing any course, there was no need to continue going to class, but he had paid for room and board, and even though he had to live with Neal, he remained in the dorm.

Late in April, he was sitting around with a suitemate, Fred Benson*, who was called Opie* because of a character he resembled in his favorite TV program, *The Andy Griffith Show*. Bart and Opie had little in common other than a strong interest in the military. Bart was Army ROTC, Opie was Air Force. Their politics, however, were widely divergent. Bart considered himself liberal. Opie was so strongly right-wing that some of his fellow students called him "the Nazi." Opie was wanting to buy himself a Jeep, and he and Bart were looking through the want ads for likely prospects. Bart saw an ad for a Datsun 240Z, a snazzy sports car, for only $1,700. Intrigued, he and Opie went to look at it. Bart liked it so much that he called his father and asked about the possibility of borrowing money to buy a car. He soon would be going to work for the summer, he said, and would have no trouble paying it back.

Opie liked the car, too, and he had enough money to buy it. He made Bart a temporary loan to get the car and told him if his father wouldn't let him have the money, he would keep the car himself. Bart proudly drove the burgundy-and-gold sports car to his father's farm in Caswell County.

"I pulled up and the first thing Dad did was look to see if it was stolen," he said later.

Jim negotiated a loan so his son could have his first car. He was unaware that Bart's driver's license had been revoked and that Bart had twice ignored summonses to come to court to face the charge of driving the wrong direction on a one-way street. Bart was unconcerned about the lack of a license and had no intention of staying off the road.

"I was a good driver," he said later. "Never got stopped. I didn't see any reason for a license."

Soon after he got the car, Bart took another job delivering pizzas, this time using his own car. When he wasn't delivering pizzas, Bart and Opie would load a case of beer into the car from the restaurant Opie's mother operated next to campus and cruise around looking for girls to talk to.

When the semester ended in May, Bart and Opie had to move out of the dorm. They already had rented a two-bedroom, two-bath apartment near the campus that they planned to share with another friend, Chris Williams. Neal frequently accompanied Bart and Opie on their apartment-hunting forays, unaware that they had no intention of letting him move in with them.

"Neal just tagged along," Bart said later. "We would try to sneak out without him, but he just glued himself to our group."

Once they found an apartment that they liked, Bart and Opie signed the lease. Although Neal had thought all along that he would be moving into the apartment with them, Bart informed him before the semester ended that they didn't want him living with them. Neal's objection offered Bart a chance to deliver the retort he'd been waiting months to get off his chest.

"Hey, your name's not on the lease. Remember, you left me hanging on the stereo."

Before Bart and Opie could move into the apartment, however, Chris Williams decided to take summer classes at the University of North Carolina at Wilmington and wouldn't be staying in Raleigh for the summer. Needing a third roommate to help pay the rent, Bart and Opie had to seek out Neal and see if he still wanted to move in with them. He did, although he later would proclaim it a mistake from day one. The three suitemates moved in early in May.

Bart received official notice that because of his grades, he no longer was welcome as a regular student at N.C. State. He could have his student status reinstated, however, by enrolling in summer courses and making acceptable grades. His father's fears had come true, and Bart still seemed to be without a course in life and little interested in finding one. Bart said that he wanted to take a year off from college to work and save money so that he could pay for his education himself when he reenrolled. Perhaps that would be best, Jim thought. Maybe he would mature a little and become more responsible having to make his own way. Joanne's main concern was that he not drop out of school permanently. She, too, went along with his plan, but reluctantly.

After a poor showing in his first semester, Neal's grades had declined even more in the second. Weldon Slayton, who held such great hope for Neal, had become concerned. Neal still called his former teacher occasionally, but the calls came less frequently because Slayton always brought up the subject of study and grades and never failed to let his feelings be known. "I'd get angry," he recalled later. "I told him, 'I ought to come down there and kick your butt all over that campus. You've got to do the work, Neal. They don't care what you made on your SATs anymore. You've got to perform.' "

At the end of the second semester, Neal found himself on academic probation, his scholarship threatened. "I was still okay," he said later. "They just told me to get my act together. I didn't really worry about it because I knew I could pull out of it if I wanted to."

He made a show of good faith by enrolling in summer classes, taking math and German. He rarely went to class, however, and soon dropped math. After a few more weeks, he dropped his German class as well. He played D&D with some of his friends who'd remained on campus for the summer, but he spent much of his time sitting around the apartment with Bart and Opie, watching MTV and drinking wine coolers.

In June, Opie announced that his stepbrother, Hank Foster*, was coming to visit and needed a place to stay. Bart and Neal agreed to let him stay in the apartment. Opie and Bart were sharing the large bedroom; Neal had the small bedroom. A huge closet-storage room would be fixed up for Hank.

Hank and his stepbrother were almost as much unalike as two people can be. Hank's father had divorced Hank's mother and later married Opie's mother, the owner of a popular off-campus gathering spot for students. Hank wore long, lank hair, considered himself extremely liberal, collected *Creepy* magazines, prided himself not only on his dexterity with a skateboard but also on his remarkable ability to consume vast amounts of alcohol and drugs without apparent serious repercussions. Hank had attended college but dropped out "to live." He had ranged about the country, living a counterculture existence on the edges of campuses in several cities. He'd been living with his mother in Wisconsin until they had a falling out and he headed to Raleigh, where his father, stepmother, and stepbrother lived. His stepmother had promised him a job in her restaurant.

Bart liked Hank much more than he liked Opie, who often argued with him about politics and accused him of being "just a redneck from the country." In Hank, he found a figure to admire and emulate.

"Hank is very intelligent," he said later. "He's probably one of the most talented people I ever met. He could do anything, but he wasn't sure what he wanted to do. I guess that's the way I am. He had this whole wellspring of ability but it was just kind of going nowhere. You know, you sit at a crossroads trying to make up your mind, and you end up just sitting there. Just sitting around saying, 'Well, what are we going to do?'"

When Hank moved into the apartment with Bart, Opie, and Neal, so did drugs, primarily marijuana. Neal later would say that he didn't use marijuana that summer, but Bart began using it regularly.

Bart had first tried marijuana only a year earlier on a traditional postgraduation trip to Myrtle Beach with many of his classmates at Bartlett Yancey High.

"Bunch of people partying, somebody said, 'Here, you want to try this?'" Bart recalled. "I tried it. I figured if I was going to college, I ought to at least try marijuana before I go."

Somebody put the *Star Wars* soundtrack on the stereo Bart had carted to the beach, and the whole group sat back and smoked pot and grooved on the music.

"It really wasn't that big a thing," Bart said later. "I didn't enjoy it enough that I'd want to go buy any."

But marijuana's very illicitness appealed to the antiestablishment sensibilities that had been developing in Bart. Then too, Bart knew that his Uncle Bill had used marijuana regularly and he suspected that his father had used it, too.

By the time Bart had begun using marijuana regularly in the summer of 1987, all of Caswell County was about to learn of his uncle's use. On Monday, June 29, a team of heavily armed sheriff's deputies and SBI agents, accompanied by a helicopter with a TV news crew, had converged on Hickory Hill Farm and swept through the old house where Bill and Lydia Upchurch lived. The officers had found twenty-nine marijuana plants growing near the edge of the woods, twenty-six plants cut and drying, and eight pounds of bagged marijuana in the house. The officers estimated its worth at more than one hundred thousand dollars. Bill maintained that the marijuana was for his own use, but he and Lydia were handcuffed and taken to the Caswell County jail, charged with manufacturing marijuana and maintaining a dwelling for controlled substances, both felonies. Bill's half-brother, John, who had just completed law school, bailed them out later that day. Carolyn did not learn about it until she read it in the newspaper the following day. She was horrified and embarrassed to show her face in the county where her own family and the Upchurches always had been so prominent and law-abiding.

She would have been even more horrified had she known that her eldest grandchild, Bart, not only was using marijuana regularly but also had not learned much, if anything, from his previous encounter with the law for theft. Unbeknownst to her, word already had filtered back to Caswell County that both Bart and Neal were stealing their way through college.

Weldon Slayton had heard as much from several students. Two Bartlett Yancey students who had gone to visit Neal at State had returned with a tale of Neal taking them on a shoplifting mission to a bookstore. Slayton couldn't resist bringing it up when Neal came home on a visit.

"Picked up any good books lately, Neal?" he inquired sarcastically.

Neal had acknowledged his guilt and sat meekly through Slayton's outraged lecture. "Don't you realize how stupid and childish that kind of thing is? There's no sense to it."

"I know, I know," Neal said. "I was just trying to show off."

Later, Neal and Bart would disagree over who was the greater thief, each downplaying his own thievery and enhancing the other's. Bart stated that Neal regularly broke into apartments and that he shoplifted on assignment. "Somebody would say, 'Look, Neal, I need some CDs.' He'd say, 'Give me fifteen bucks and tell me what you want,' and he'd go out and come back with it. Neal was getting by on stealing and shoplifting and he was doing a pretty good business."

Later, Neal denied that he regularly broke into apartments. The only time he ever did was during the summer of 1987, he said, and that was at Bart's suggestion. He and a couple of friends were sitting around drinking one night, he said, and Bart came in and said, "Hey, there's a place over here with an open sliding door and nobody at home."

All four slipped into the apartment and stole tapes and stereo equipment, he said.

"It was like an exaggerated, drunken cartoon, everybody joking around. Imagine the Keystone Kops going in somewhere. It was that silly."

Shoplifting was another matter, Neal acknowledged, something that always gave him an adrenaline rush. He did it several times with Bart, he said, once with Opie, and another time to impress some friends from Caswell County, the ones who later told Weldon Slayton about it.

"Once I did it, I'd let people think I did it a whole lot more than I did to build up an image," Neal said of the shoplifting. "Sometimes I'd buy something and throw away the bag and claim I stole it so they'd think I was cool. It was just a little bit of stuff, really, but we talked about it a whole lot. Boy, we talked about it like we were hot stuff. That way I got more respect from them than I ever got any other way."

Bart stole more than anybody in the group, Neal claimed. "He would come and tell me a lot of stories about what he was doing, breaking into cars and things like that. I had seen him steal CDs and tapes to sell to the Record Exchange. I saw him come home two or three times with car stereos he would sell to friends on campus. One time he stole some speakers and was carrying them down Mission Valley Road and the police stopped him, but he talked his way out of it."

Bart later acknowledged stealing car stereos "a couple of times."

"Neal kept telling me how easy it was," he said. "I'd be coming back drunk from some party, go by a car that was unlocked, pull the thing out. Usually, I had to be really drunk because I couldn't get up the courage otherwise. I did it just because it was so easy and I was so drunk. I probably sold them to somebody on campus to get some gas, but I didn't steal for money. I did it because I was bored and it was something exciting to do for the time being. No greater or lesser reason than that."

Kenyatta, Bart's cousin and Neal's off-and-on girlfriend, knew that Neal and Bart both were thieves. She had seen both of them steal, and it made her furious. She and Neal revived their relationship late that spring, and that summer she came to spend several weekends in the apartment that Neal shared with Bart, Opie, and Hank.

Neal showed her a telephone that he said he had stolen from an apartment, she said, and she saw him shoplift on several occasions. "I was always mad at him," she said. "Stealing, he just didn't think anything about it. He said, 'A lot of people steal. What's the big deal?' "

She was soon to have firsthand experience of being ripped off. Kenyatta had been a bicycle rider most of her life, and she had two bikes. She noticed that Bart was collecting bicycles as well, bikes she was convinced that he was stealing. He kept them chained on the patio of the apartment to prevent other thieves from making off with them before he could sell them, she said. That summer, Kenyatta let Neal borrow one of her bikes while she was gone on a long-planned bicycling trip to the West. She made the trip with her uncle Jim, cousin Emory, and a group of other riders from Caswell County and Danville in mid-August. Emory had developed an interest in bicycle racing, and Jim had taken up bike riding so that he and his younger son would have an activity to share. In the spring, both had ridden in the "Assault on Mt. Mitchell," the highest mountain in the East, a 6,600-foot peak in western North Carolina. That was considered to the toughest bicycle race in the East, and both had been proud of finishing, Emory well ahead of his father. Now they were ready for higher mountains. For eight days in August, they undertook a 600-mile run from Albuquerque, New Mexico, to southern Colorado, staying in the mountains all the way. They even made a run up Mt. Evans, a 14,260-foot peak. Kenyatta went with them and had a wonderful time. She returned to find that the bike she had loaned to Neal was missing. He said it had been stolen. She was sure that it had been. She also was sure that she knew who had stolen it: Bart. She was convinced that he had sold her bike with the other bikes he had stolen to help pay his share of the apartment rent. He denied it, but she didn't believe him. She hardly believed anything he said anymore. And the theft of her bicycle was an offense she never would forgive.

25

WHEN FALL SEMESTER BE-
gan at N.C. State in August of 1987, Neal moved out of the
apartment and returned to a campus dorm. Bart was pleased
to have Neal not only out of the apartment but out of his life
as well. They would not see each other again for nearly a year.

No longer welcome as a student and always short of money,
Bart took a five-dollar-an-hour third-shift job at a convenience
mart on Western Boulevard, Fast Fare, just across the street
from the campus, within walking distance of his apartment.
The job left his afternoons and early evenings free, and he
and Hank often spent them in front of the TV, watching classic
movies and old situation comedies on cable, or listening to
heavy-metal rock music, drinking beer, smoking pot, and
talking.

"We spent a lot of time just sitting around shooting the
shit," Bart later recalled. "Hank is a weird type of guy. Nine
times out of ten, he's going to get ragingly drunk after work,
still get up, and go to work the next day. I sort of admired
that about him."

Bart felt that he had more common ground with Hank
than with anybody he ever had known. They agreed on almost
everything. Both saw themselves as being outside convention
and society. They believed in living for the moment and not
worrying about the future. Neither could picture themselves
old or settled or—especially—married.

"Hank looked at marriage as being right along the lines
of life imprisonment," Bart later said with a chuckle. "I used
to kid him, say, 'Yeah, you're going to end up married with a
houseful of kids and a station wagon.' Terrorize him with the
idea of a Ford station wagon."

Bart looked at women as objects to be desired and pursued
for the physical pleasures they could provide, but he shied
from relationships with them. Although he boasted of one-
night stands (his cousin Kenyatta later claimed that these were
with girls he met at parties who were too drunk to resist), he

never dated, never had a girlfriend, and was wary of any young women who showed an interest in him.

"I wasn't looking for a relationship," he said later. "I didn't like planning that far ahead. When you make long, drawn-out plans, something's going to come along and screw it up. I guess I had some sort of phobia toward relationships. I just didn't want to get involved."

Yet he was about to become involved in a relationship with a woman he had no desire to meet, a decidedly unromantic relationship that would prove to be long, tumultuous, and ultimately, at least for Bart, binding. In November, a file bearing Bart's name landed on the desk of Christy Newsom, an overworked probation officer for Wake County.

Christy Newsom was only four years older than Bart. She was five feet two and a half inches and 116 pounds of intensity and fierce determination that showed in her powerful, almost mesmerizing eyes. At times, she appeared to be all eyes, their color changing from green to topaz according to her moods, which often were dark when she had to deal with Bart.

Born in Sumter, South Carolina, she had moved with her family to Spring Hope, thirty miles east of Raleigh, when she was thirteen. Like Bart, she had been in gifted and talented classes in high school. Unlike him, her ideas were decidedly establishment, her politics conservative. Her father operated a Western Auto Store, served as an auxiliary police officer, and was strict with his three children. When his only daughter grew old enough to date, he insisted that the first date be spent in the living room in his presence—torture sessions, Christy came to think of them. He always took down the boys' car tag numbers and never failed to drop into the conversation that he liked guns.

Christy was nine when her father started teaching her to shoot, first with a twelve-gauge pump shotgun—"It almost knocked my arm off," she remembered—then moving on to handguns. When she started driving, he gave her a .38 revolver to carry in her car.

In high school, Christy worked part-time for a local attorney and did school papers on child abuse and sexual abuse. After her graduation from Southern Nash Senior High School in 1982, she, like Bart four years later, went off to Raleigh to college; she chose exclusive Meredith College, just up the street from State. Her intention was to go to law school, but after her graduation in 1986, she began having second thoughts.

"I just couldn't be a defense attorney," she said. "I saw too many deals going on." And she saw little future in becoming a prosecutor in Wake County, where the district attorney's office was a revolving door for young lawyers.

In college she had interned as a probation officer, enjoyed it, and thought she might like to work at it again, at least for a while. But those jobs were hard to come by, and she had to take an interim job with the clerk of court, processing arrest warrants for probation and parole violators until a job opened. One finally became available in May of 1987. She was just beginning to get a handle on the job when Bart was assigned to her already heavy caseload.

After reading Bart's file, she was amazed to discover that for all practical purposes he was not on probation at all. He had paid none of the monthly supervision fees he was supposed to be paying, and he was under no real supervision. Only a couple of times had anybody even bothered to check on his whereabouts. She decided to correct that situation. She found where he was living and began calling his apartment to have him come in for an office visit. But every time she called, she got one or another roommate who would not identify himself. They told her that Bart was not there and they didn't know when he would be back. She left messages for Bart to call her, but he never did.

Soon after Christy was assigned to supervise Bart's probation, unbeknownst to her, Bart was receiving another conviction for misdemeanor larceny in Wake County Recorder's Court, this time for stealing beer.

As he told the story later, he had gotten bombed at a party one night by drinking a six-pack of South African malt liquor called Elephant. He was staggering home to sleep it off when he wandered through the parking lot of the Mission Valley Inn on the edge of the campus. A racing team sponsored by a beer company was spending the night there, their sleek race car in a trailer pulled by a beer truck. Bart noticed that one of the sliding doors on the beer truck was unlocked. He pushed it up, peered inside, and saw cases of beer and a cooler loaded with chicken salad sandwiches. He tossed the sandwiches out of the cooler, reloaded it with beer, and started walking off with it. But one of the race team members spotted him from the motel, yelled, and came out chasing him, followed by other team members and a uniformed police officer on private duty at the motel, all of them yelling for him to stop.

"I wasn't about to stop," he said. "I knew I didn't want to get my shit stomped."

He was beginning to outdistance them when he heard a different yell: "Stop, or I'll shoot!" He looked back to see the police officer reaching for his pistol.

"Like a dumb ass, I stopped," he said.

He set down the cooler and held up his hands as his breathless pursuers surrounded him, the racing team members looking as if they wished the police officer weren't there.

"You dumb son-of-a-bitch, what did you stop for?" the police officer asked him with a grin. "Did you actually think I was going to shoot? You must go to State. All of you are alike."

When Christy got no response to her repeated calls to Bart's apartment on Avent Ferry Road, she went by and left a note on the door, which, she noticed, was covered with drawings of medieval-looking daggers. Still she got no response. Finally she wrote him a letter, telling him in no uncertain terms that if he didn't appear at her office she would issue a warrant for his arrest and attempt to get his probation revoked so that he would have to serve his full sentence in jail. This time Bart responded, showing up at her office as requested on January 4, 1988. He was wearing jeans and a sweatshirt and carrying a knapsack. A typical, clean-cut, all-American-boy college student, Christy thought. But he had a hollow look that made her wonder if he was using drugs.

Christy wanted this to be a get-acquainted session and they chatted at length. Bart was extremely polite, seemed to want to impress her, and she realized quickly that he was highly intelligent. She also thought that he was trying to play on her sympathies. He told her that he was a perpetual runner-up, always coming close but never quite achieving his goals. He'd been nominated for the School of Science and Math but wasn't accepted, he said. He'd been a National Merit semifinalist but hadn't won a scholarship.

When Christy asked why he had gotten into trouble in the first place, he told her that he'd done it for attention, to make up for never being recognized by his parents and schoolmates.

When Christy asked about his parents, Bart said that he

wasn't seeing them at all. His mother lived in Virginia, and his probation didn't allow him to travel out of state without permission. He wasn't close to his father, he said, and called him only when he needed something.

He told her that he wanted to be an anthropologist, planned to return to college, and intended to live a clean and trouble-free life. And that included paying his probation supervisory fees and keeping his monthly appointments with her. "I didn't trust him at all," she said later. "I had an eerie feeling about him and I even went to talk to my supervisor about him. He was one I knew I was going to have to watch. He was always thinking about what I was going to say so he could outsmart me. Bart derived self-satisfaction from knowing that he was smarter than anybody else around him."

In February, Bart decided that he wanted a new car. He sold his 240Z and found a 1983 Camaro T-top for $4,500. His father arranged a loan through the State Employees Credit Union with payments of $160 a month, and Bart picked up the car on the day he got the check and drove it to work that night at the Fast Fare.

He had just got out of bed the next afternoon when a friend and three acquaintances dropped by the apartment to see his new car. "Let's see what that Camaro will do," one of them said, and the five young men piled into the car and struck out on Avent Ferry Road for the expressway that encircled the city. Bart was driving fifteen miles over the speed limit when he pulled out to pass a BMW in a curve and lost control of his car. It went into a spin and the left rear smashed into a roadside power pole, snapping it in half. The rear window flew from the car, shattering on the pavement. Power lines fell, sparking on the ground.

"Get out! Get out!" somebody yelled. "It's going to blow up!" And five startled young men came piling out of the top of the car—none of them, miraculously, injured—and ran to the other side of the road, away from the wreckage.

"Damn," said Bart. "How did that happen?"

The car did not explode, but it was damaged beyond repair. The police officer who came to investigate was less than sympathetic when he discovered that Bart was driving with a revoked license. He arrested him on the spot and took him to jail, charged with driving without a license, careless and reckless driving, and driving without liability insurance. Opie came to the jail and bailed out Bart later that day.

Soon after the short trip that produced the accident, Bart had another trip: his first on LSD. Hank had been telling him for months that a lot of LSD was around. "I said, 'Might as well try it and see what it's all about,'" Bart said later. "I gave him some money and said, 'If you run into any, buy us some. One day he said, 'Hey, I got some. Want to try it?'"

Each did a whole hit while sitting in the apartment one evening, listening to Opie's stereo. For half an hour, nothing happened.

"I didn't feel anything at all," Bart said later. "I said, 'Let's make a joint and see what happens. Thirty minutes later, everything just went wild on me. I felt like I had to go do something but I didn't know what. I went to the refrigerator and just stood there and asked myself, 'Why did I come here? Oh, yeah, to get a beer.'"

A red neon Budweiser sign that decorated one wall of the apartment added an eerie glow to the scene, and suddenly, as Bart later put it, the walls seemed to be breathing. He and Hank drank a few more beers, relishing the hallucinogenic effects of the drug, while Bart tried to decide what it was that he had to do.

Opie was at a keg party at an Air Force ROTC fraternity house, and Bart and Hank finally decided that what they had to do was join him there. Hank had bleached his hair blond, and Bart had been allowing his hair to grow long in the back. Neither had shaved in days, and both felt immediately out of place at the party, "kids from hell" among the ROTC straights, as Bart later described himself and Hank.

"We started feeling real paranoid," he said.

They left the party on foot, beers in hand, staggering down Avent Ferry Road, back to their own apartment. Once there, they put Jimi Hendrix on the stereo and went out into the parking lot to sit on car hoods listening to the music and admiring the stars.

"Hank says, 'You got thirty dollars?'" Bart said, recalling the night several years later. "'I know where some hookers are if you want to go get laid.' I said, 'Are they worth a damn?' 'Yeah, they're young and good-looking.'"

As Bart told the story later, it sounded more like an

adolescent fantasy than an actual event. They walked to a nearby apartment, where they were greeted at the door by an attractive blonde young woman in black lace underwear who knew Hank and invited them in. Inside were more young women, "chicks," Bart called them, all beautiful, all college students, in various states of undress. A stereo was playing Top Forty tunes. A bar offered many brands of liquor in tiny bottles like those sold on airplanes. A black dude sat at the kitchen table with an array of drugs spread out before him. Everybody knew Hank.

"I was sort of enjoying the whole scene, saying, 'Wow!' " Bart remembered. "I said, 'How long has this been here?' Hank said, 'Since we've been living here. Hell, where do you think all my paychecks have been going to?' I said, 'And you didn't tell me!' "

They were just beginning to talk with the girls and enjoy themselves, Bart said, when a guy made a pass at Hank.

"He was a fag working at the whorehouse," Bart said. "Hank flew into a rage and knocked him down. The pimp comes out all mad. He was an Arab guy, had a gun. He's yelling. I said, 'Come on, Hank, let's go, let's get out of here.' Hank wanted to stay and beat up the fag, but I got him out of there. The whole evening had an alcoholic, dreamlike quality about it."

Later, Bart said, somebody asked him what it was like taking his first hit of acid. "He said, 'How was it?' I said, 'Neither me nor Hank has any words to properly express the experience.' "

On March 1, Christy Newsom was at the Wake County Courthouse, passing by a courtroom, when she looked inside and saw Bart standing before the bar. Bart was pleading guilty to the charges that resulted from his wreck. It was the first Christy knew that he had been arrested.

Bart received a six months' sentence, suspended for a year, and was placed on supervised probation. He was fined two hundred dollars, ordered to pay court costs, and instructed not to drive again until his license was properly restored.

Christy followed him out of the courtroom as he left.

"I said, 'Why didn't you tell me about this?' " she recalled. "He said, 'I was scared. I thought you would put me in jail.' I told him, 'If you would tell me things versus me finding them out on my own, it would be a whole lot easier on you.' I chewed him out and told him to come by my office the next day."

Bart didn't show up for his appointment, and Christy went looking for him, leaving a note on his apartment door to no effect. She didn't talk to him again until March 14, when she got him on the phone and demanded that he come to her office. He said he would be there that day, but he didn't appear until March 25, following several more threatening messages left with roommates.

Why was he not keeping his appointments?

"His answer to everything was that he was afraid of me," Christy said later. "He thought that was flattering to me, but it wasn't. He figured if I thought I was an authoritative figure to him that I would back off. I told him he wasn't afraid of the devil himself. He just looked at me and grinned."

She set his next appointment for April 11. When he failed to appear, she sent him another letter, instructing him to be in her office at 10 A.M. May 3. He didn't come. Fed up, she cited him to court, intent on revoking his probation.

On May 30, Bart appeared before District Court Judge George Greene. Christy had gotten to know Judge Greene during her internship in college. She liked him, had attended parties at his house, thought of him as a friend. But she had little respect for him as a judge. He was, she thought, too soft on criminals.

Christy presented her case against Bart, citing his failure to appear for meetings, the recent charges against him, the supervisory fees he hadn't paid. She made it clear that she thought Bart should be in prison, his probation revoked.

"I said, 'What else can the Probation Department do?' " she said later. " 'He's going to do what he wants to do. This judgment to him is nothing more than a piece of paper. He needs to learn that fire burns.' The judge told me, 'I'll decide who needs to go to jail.' "

Christy had to hand it to Bart, though. He handled himself well.

"He suckered the judge royally," she said later. "He presented himself as a college student trying to get his life together. He said with a probation officer like Mrs. Newsom, he thought he could do better if the judge would just give him another chance. George Greene ate that up."

The judge gave Bart another chance, continuing his probation without additional penalties, instructing him to catch up on his payments and heed his probation officer.

Christy was in a cold fury, struggling to control herself, especially when she saw Bart looking at her, as she later described it, with his "I got you again" look.

Christy was then handling 180 cases, and she thought that half of them probably should be in jail. Bart was her most difficult case, the one giving her bleeding ulcers. She knew that he should be in jail. He defied all the rules, yet he got the same treatment as probationers who obeyed them all. "My biggest problem with the courts," she said later, "is that if the law says this ought to happen, it ought to happen. Judges give these conditions of probation. Why do they give them if they're not going to enforce them?"

Christy did not control her fury when she met Bart outside the courtroom.

"I promised him he was going to jail," she said. "I said, 'One day you're going to jail, and I'm going to see to it.' "

Later, she even went to see Judge Greene to express her displeasure privately. "I didn't do it in a disrespectful way," she said. "I asked him, 'What am I supposed to do with these people?' He told me I was doing a good job, but he just couldn't put everybody in jail. He was nice about it."

When Christy next saw Bart, only two weeks later, she barely could believe her eyes. He had come on schedule for his appointment, but gone was the clean-cut college student who had so impressed Judge Greene. Bart had bleached his hair and shaved the sides of his head in patterns. He was wearing torn jeans, a tie-dyed T-shirt, and rawhide moccasin boots laced to the knee. And he arrived at her office by skateboard.

"It's the new me," Bart said with a grin.

"I liked you better the other way," she said.

Bart was indeed a student again when he appeared before Judge Greene. In April, he had left his job at the convenience mart after a dispute with the manager. He hadn't been able to save any money and he was tired of working. Things were about to change. As soon as the semester ended, Opie was going off to basic training with the Air Force. Hank was planning a long trip to visit his mother and friends. Both would be giving up the apartment, and Bart couldn't afford to keep it alone. He decided to enroll in summer school and try to reestablish his standing as a student at State. His parents were pleased and relieved about his decision, especially his father, who was in frequent contact with Christy Newsom and was worried about his son's activities and the company he had fallen into.

Bart returned again to Lee dorm, this time to the eighth floor, room 807B, in which he was alone for the first ten days. Almost everybody Bart knew had gone away for the summer, and without close friends or a job, he was at loose ends while he waited for classes to begin.

Soon after moving into the dorm, Bart bumped into Quincy Blackwell, a casual friend from Caswell County, who, he discovered, was living just three suites down from him, also waiting for summer school to begin. Quincy, a dedicated aficionado of Japanese cartoons, had played Dungeons and Dragons in Bart's group during high school. He also was a good friend of Neal and had been rooming with him in Burgaw Hall until the semester ended.

Bart suggested that they get a D&D group organized to help kill the time, and he asked Quincy where Neal was living. Quincy said that he had moved into an apartment on Ligon Street on the western edge of the campus, only a short walk from Lee dorm. Neal's apartment would be an apt spot to hold the game, Bart thought, and he and Quincy walked over to Ligon Street to propose that to Neal.

The past nine and a half months had been a downward spiral for Neal, and he was just beginning to try to pull out of it.

Neal had returned to classes the previous fall with a renewed determination to study hard, but personal problems soon intervened. With Kenyatta now at the School of Science and Math in Durham, less than thirty minutes away, he began seeing another old girlfriend, Jane Freeman*. They had remained close friends, and they went out for dinner on his birthday, September 21. They talked about their earlier breakup, decided that the reasons for it were stupid, and began to go out again. There was only one little catch. Jane also was seeing another guy. And she couldn't decide which one she liked better.

One of her criticisms of Neal was that he wouldn't express his feelings, that he kept his emotions bottled up. He knew

186

that she was right about that, and one night he opened up, telling her his deepest feelings, his innermost longings.

"I cried and made a mess of myself," he said later.

After that episode, Jane decided that she couldn't decide—and until she could, she wouldn't date Neal or the other guy.

Kenyatta also contributed to Neal's emotional turmoil that fall. Convinced that he was in love with Jane, Neal tried to break up with Kenyatta. Kenyatta later said that he came to see her one Sunday and told her that a girl he had been seeing had a sexual disease. On another occasion, she claimed, he invited her to Raleigh, had some of his friends take her off on a pretense, then staged a scene in which she returned to his room to find him on the bed with another girl. "I was supposed to see it, get mad, and go back to school."

Finally, Kenyatta came over for a long, volatile, heart-cleansing session with Neal. It went on for hours at the student union. When it ended well after midnight, they returned to Neal's dorm room to find his friends sprawled over the beds, leaving them no place to sleep. Kenyatta was crying and had a terrible headache.

"I said, 'Neal, why not wake them up and make them get off the bed?' He wouldn't make them leave. Instead, we went down to the lounge and pushed couches together at three or four o'clock in the morning and slept there. He had no respect for me or our relationship at all."

She left the next morning thinking that Neal probably was out of her life for good.

The emotional turmoil and his continuing dedication to Dungeons and Dragons and other role-playing games often kept Neal out of class and away from his books that fall, and his grades continued dropping.

At the beginning of the second semester, Neal learned that Jane had moved into a condo with the other guy she had been dating.

"I was already extremely upset that she didn't want to see me," he recalled. "She moved in with him and I went into a tailspin. I was crushed. Up to that point, I had never really applied myself fully to anything. That way, if I failed, I could say I didn't try. With her, I tried one hundred and ten per cent and fell on my face. There was no excuse other than that I wasn't good enough."

He quit going to classes and rarely even left his room. "I

said, 'I don't care anymore,' " he said later. " 'I refuse to work at this crap anymore.' " Soon he was spending most of his days in bed with his D&D books. The only time he ever left his room was when a close friend forced him to go. "He would drag me physically out of my room and make me go and do stuff," Neal said. But Neal still managed to show up every Sunday for his regular session of D&D.

Others worried about Neal. His mother. Weldon Slayton. Kenyatta.

Neal didn't want to face Slayton, didn't want to talk with him, or anybody else.

"I tried to get him to tell me what was wrong," Kenyatta said later. "He said, 'I can't explain it. I'm just depressed. I just don't feel like going to class.' "

His mother came on several occasions, but Neal couldn't bring himself to tell her what was bothering him and assured her that he would be all right. Finally, at her instigation, he went to talk with a campus counselor.

"The guy I got struck me as an idiot," he said later, "and I didn't talk to anybody after that."

The end of the semester brought the inevitable: the revocation of Neal's scholarship. "I already knew I'd lost it," he said. "I'd decided the whole college thing needs to take a break."

He had to move out of the dorm and he couldn't face going home. He knew that he had to find a place to live and get a job. A fellow D&D player, Butch Mitchell*, was looking for an apartment and suggested that they move in together. "I thought, what the heck, let's try it," Neal said later. "Boy, was that a mistake. Beats living on the street, but not much."

The apartment they found was in a rundown building on Ligon Street, close to the campus. Nearby on Western Boulevard was a big Sav-A-Center supermarket where Neal applied for a job and was hired as a third-shift stock clerk.

Soon after Neal and Butch moved in, Neal's two former roommates, Bart and Quincy, came calling.

Neal was amenable to the idea of starting a new D&D group. Quincy and Butch said they would play, too. Bart said he would put up some posters around the dorm to try to bring in more players.

"FREE BEER!" Bart scrawled in big letters on a page of

notebook paper. "Aha. Now that I've got your attention, if you're interested in playing D&D, come to room 807B."

He would remember signing his name to it. Not Bart, or James, but his new name, a nickname: Moog. "He and I were sitting around the room early that summer," Neal recalled. "He said, 'You know, I need a nickname.' One of us said, 'Moog, as in synthesizer.' He thought it was interesting. He picked up on it. After that, every time anybody asked him, 'Where'd you get that name, Moog?' he'd say, 'It's a long story. Ask Neal sometime. He knows it.' "

Soon after Bart put up several of his handmade posters in the dorm, he heard a knock on his dorm room door one evening.

"I open the door," he remembered later, "and there's this little guy, real flashy dude, real well dressed, blazer, dress slacks, silk tie, shades. It was like he was making an entrance. He comes into the room, throws his foot up on the bed, reaches down and pulls up the cuff of his pants, and says, 'Excuse me while I scratch the head of my dick.' I laughed. I thought he was high. I thought this is a peculiar fellow. He seemed to be pretty cool. He stuck out his hand and said, 'Hi, I'm Chris Pritchard.' "

26

LATER, WHEN HIS FRIENDS tried to describe Chris Pritchard, they called him "off-the-wall," "strange," "weird," "a character." He was smarter than average, and funny, if often in a loud and crude way. He was a show-off, frequently doing things to draw attention to himself. "He was the kind who was always trying to prove something," one friend said. He was a dreamer, too, filled with big plans for the future that regularly bubbled out of him. But some friends wondered how he would ever accomplish such grand schemes, for he was easily bored, impulsive, anxious. "He was always in a rush," said his mother, Bonnie Von Stein.

Two passions occupied most of Chris's time outside of school: cars and role-playing fantasy games, especially Dungeons and Dragons. He first had become interested in D&D while he was still in grammar school in Indiana. After his family moved to Washington, he began playing regularly with a small group of friends he met in school, a group that his other friends considered to be brainy but odd.

Chris's passion for cars led him to a different group of friends, less brainy, more outgoing and raucous. Among the teenage cruisers in Washington, Chris was well known both for his car and the way he drove it. His car was a classic '65 Mustang fastback. It was black with a gold stripe down each side when he got it, a sixteenth-birthday present from his mother and his stepfather, Lieth Von Stein. Later he had it repainted in its original color, Wimbledon white, with black stripes. Steve Outlaw, one of his closest friends, also had a Mustang, and they spent many hours together working on their cars. Chris loved the sense of power that the car gave him, and behind the wheel, he became a different person, forceful and reckless.

A good student in high school, Chris maintained a B average until his senior year, when personal problems got him off to a bad start. The summer before his senior year, he spent several weeks with his father, Stephen Pritchard, his first long stay with him since his father had left when Chris was three, barely old enough to remember. Chris rode with him on one of his long-distance trucking runs to the West, and his mother worried about the emotional effects of the visit. Soon after his return, Chris started dating one girl regularly, his first real love affair. When she broke off the relationship after only three weeks, he nearly went to pieces. His concentration faltered, his grades plummeted, and some friends thought that he began to develop an uncaring attitude.

His best scores in high school were in science and math, and at the end of October during his senior year, he applied to the engineering program at N.C. State University, the program Lieth Von Stein had flunked out of twenty years earlier.

Although his SAT scores were not exceptional, 1020, they were high enough to get Chris accepted as a nuclear engineering student at State only a month after he sent in his application, a matter of great pride to his stepfather. Although Chris had a troubled senior year in high school, nearly flunking English and college-preparatory math, he still was graduated sixty-eighth in his class of 266, with a 2.86 grade point average.

But once Chris got to State in August 1987, his study habits grew far worse. At the end of the first semester he had a grade point average of only 1.3, barely passing. And his grades became a matter of contention with his stepfather, who could see Chris going down the same path to failure that he had taken at State. Although Chris improved his grades slightly at the end of the second semester, he still was far from living up to his potential.

Drinking was a part of Chris's failure to study. He had begun drinking in high school, but once at college and away from the strictures of home, he began drinking more and more. In the first semester, he drank mostly on weekends, usually Canadian Mist, or vodka, sometimes spending Sundays and some Mondays nearly too sick to get out of bed. He never had liked beer, but by the second semester he had acquired a taste for it and began drinking it every day. When a friend pointed out that he was drinking too much, Chris became worried that he was an alcoholic. He quit drinking completely for a month, during which he brought up his grades to a low C, but at the end of the period he started drinking again, this time more than ever.

Chris was enjoying his liberty too much to return home to Washington at the end of his freshman year. Although his mother and stepfather thought that he needed a break from classes, Chris decided to go to summer school, which allowed him to keep his room on the sixth floor of Lee dorm. During the ten-day interim between spring semester and the beginning of the first session of summer school, Chris returned home and brought back to school his beloved Mustang, which had remained in Washington since the previous summer, because freshmen at State were not allowed cars. Now he had mobility with his liberty, and to supplement the $50 allowance his parents put into his account each week, he got a $4.50-an-hour job in the men's department at Miller & Rhoads, a clothing store in Crabtree Valley Mall, only a few miles from the campus. He had just gotten off work after one of his early days on the job when he saw a misleading notice on a dorm lobby bulletin board that said: "FREE BEER." When he saw that the notice actually was about Dungeons and Dragons, which appealed to him as strongly as beer, he went straight to the eighth floor and introduced himself to the dungeon master, James Bartlett Upchurch III, who by the summer of 1988 wanted friends to call him Moog.

Bart moved back onto campus that May with more money than he'd ever had. An insurance company had just paid him nearly $5,500 to replace the Camaro he had demolished on the day after he bought it in February. The money should have gone to the credit union, which held the lien on the car, but through a fluke Bart received the title to the car, and the check came to him. Rather than pay off the loan on the car, Bart decided to keep the money and continue making payments on the car, which now, unbeknownst to the credit union, rested in a junkyard. When the check came, Bart paid a bank to cash it and took the money in $100 bills. He called Opie, who was about to leave for basic training, and arranged to meet him to pay off a debt he owed for back rent. Bart climbed into Opie's Jeep, gleefully pulled out the big roll of bills, and began counting them off.

"If a damn cop comes by, he's going to know we're doing a drug deal," Opie said. "You better watch yourself. Somebody will kill you for that."

After flashing the money around to his friends, Bart put $2,000 in the bank, made several advance payments on the car loan, so he wouldn't have to worry about that for a while, and went on a spending spree with the rest. Among other purchases, he bought tickets to a Pink Floyd concert for himself and all of his friends, and on the night before the concert, he threw a big party and provided all the alcohol and drugs with his windfall money.

Bart wanted to use the $2,000 he put into the bank to buy a Jeep, but the one he and Opie found that was to his liking cost considerably more than he had. With his usual audaciousness, Bart asked the bank to make a loan on it. When the bank said no, he began to look for a lesser-priced vehicle. A want ad for a '67 Ford Galaxy convertible with a new paint job, new chrome, and a new top caught his eye. He went to look at the car. It was a big, hulking machine, dramatic, a sure attention getter, and Bart could picture himself and his friends charging wildly around in it, making all the girls take notice.

Bart bought the car, only to discover that it needed new brakes and other expensive repairs. He put it into a shop to have the work done, but the bill came to more than $1,000, and Bart realized that he wouldn't have the money to pay it and still get through summer school, even though his mother had given him the money for the first session's tuition. The shop owner agreed to hold the car until Bart finished summer school and could pay the bill.

Later, Chris would say that he met Neal Henderson on his first visit to Bart's dorm room, but Bart would say it actually was on his second visit, when they got together to plan around their class and work schedules to play D&D. Bart was taking two courses the first summer session, prehistoric archeology and anthropology. Chris was enrolled in a single course, calculus. Neal was working third shift at the Sav-A-Center, giving him time to play in the afternoon and early evening. They decided that they could play at least twice, possibly three times a week, and Bart began mapping a campaign.

During the first week of classes, both Bart and Chris attended faithfully and did their classwork. But soon after the session began, Chris met another student in his calculus class, Tim Parker. Soon after their meeting Parker asked Chris if he smoked pot. "Sure," Chris told him. Later, he would claim that he actually had smoked only a couple of joints during his entire freshman year. Parker was a heavy marijuana user, Chris later claimed, and he offered it to Chris without charge. Within a week after Parker first offered him pot, Chris said, he was smoking it every day.

During the second week of classes, Chris came to Bart's room to talk about D&D, but the conversation took another turn.

"Do you get high?" Chris asked.

"Yeah, man. Sure."

"Well, come on down later, if you want to. We got plenty of dope."

When Bart went downstairs to Chris's room, he heard loud rock music coming from within. He knocked and heard people shuffling around before the door cracked open and somebody peeked out.

"Ah, it's Moog," Bart heard Chris say. "Hey, man, he's cool."

And the door swung open to a smiling group of students and a haze of marijuana smoke.

Neal Henderson spent little time on campus with Bart, Chris, and Quincy. He came over for the D&D sessions, which, when not scheduled at his apartment, were played in Bart's room or the dorm's downstairs study room. But he rarely stayed for the partying, usually walking back to the apartment he shared with Butch Mitchell on Ligon Street. Part of the reason was that he was back with Kenyatta, who had finished her first year at the School of Science and Math and did not want to return home for the summer. Neal invited her to move in with him. Kenyatta saw this as an opportunity to revive and rebuild their relationship, and she resented the long hours that Neal spent playing D&D. Soon, she and Neal were bickering and yelling just as they had in their tumultuous past.

"I liked having her around. I liked her as a person," Neal later said of Kenyatta. "But when we stayed around each other too long, she got on my nerves. She's a very hyper person. She gets upset extremely easily. I go and play D&D twice a week and she magnifies that into never spending any time with her." Because Neal worked late at night and Kenyatta had taken a daytime job at McDonald's, they had opposite schedules and little time to be together. Kenyatta wanted to have that time alone with Neal. "I'd want to cook him dinner or go out somewhere," she said. "He wanted to spend all of his time doing D&D."

A couple of times she went with him to his games on campus, only to draw the ire of her cousin, Bart, whom she still called James, despite his preference for Moog. "He treated me really bad," she said of Bart. "It was like, why are you here? He picked on me. He knew my weaknesses and he would use my weaknesses against me. I would go over there and he would make me cry and I would start walking back to the apartment. After James abused me, Neal would ask me, 'Why did you leave?' I'd say, 'You saw how he treated me.' But he wouldn't say anything about it. I hated James. I hated him for letting my bike get stolen, but I really hated him for making me cry.

194

He didn't care about himself. He didn't care about anybody."

Although Kenyatta's relationship with Neal's roommate, Butch, started off okay, it, too, began to deteriorate and soon led to yelling. Neal also had begun to realize that moving in with Butch was a mistake. He hardly knew him, had only played D&D with him. Butch had a powerful temper, Neal discovered, and he never knew when his roommate might explode in anger. He was unaware that in the past Butch had been hospitalized for emotional problems and that Butch's mother worried that when he drank he might become violent and hurt somebody. Like Bart, Butch resented Neal's sloppiness and disorder. And although Butch was a regular member of D&D groups with Neal, he also resented Neal's form of play. "Neal was always trying to rule the world," he said later. "The boy was hungry for power, put it that way. I hated playing with him. Neal's philosophy is, if you've got it, I want it and I'll kill you for it. What he wants, he is gonna get it. He's calm. He's sneaky. He's not physical, but he's always thinking."

By the third week of the first summer school session, Chris had a smoking device called a bong in his room and was using marijuana daily—and paying Tim Parker for it. He also was drinking prodigious amounts of beer each day.

As Chris and Bart were smoking pot one day, Bart asked if he ever had used acid. Chris said no.

Later, Chris remembered Bart telling him, "You ought to try it. It's cheap. Only three dollars a hit. It gives a great high and it lasts a long time."

Soon after that, Chris, Bart, Neal, Butch, Quincy, and Brew were playing D&D in the dorm study room. Chris was sure that Bart was on acid. He thought that he could tell because Bart was "jumpy," as he described it, more hyperactive than usual, and his eyes "rolled and darted."

When the game ended, Bart told Chris and Neal that he had some acid and suggested that they try it. Both were willing. They went to Bart's room, and Bart sold two hits to Chris and one to Neal, suggesting that they take only half a hit to begin. Chris took half, but Neal decided to take the whole hit. Bart took a whole hit, too. Afterward, they went to Chris's room and smoked pot. When Chris reported feeling nothing from the acid, he took another hit, this time a whole one. Within thirty minutes, he later reported, he began seeing bursting colors and hearing the music to which he was listening much differently than he ever had heard it before. He felt euphoric, "on top of the world," bolder than he ever had felt. And he could not contain his energy. He had to go outside. It was after midnight, and the three went out and walked for hours around the campus. It was nearly five when Neal went home and Bart returned to his room. Chris was still too energetic to sleep, and he went to his room and listened to music for another hour before dozing off.

Hank had now returned from his travels, and Bart introduced him to Chris three days after Chris's first acid experience. Hank began coming frequently to Chris's room to join in the activities.

By the fourth week of the first summer session, both Bart and Chris were attending class less frequently. Chris decided to change his calculus course from credit to audit, thinking that would release him from having to turn in homework and take tests, but he was soon to learn different.

At the end of that week, Chris got his paycheck from Miller & Rhoads. He bought half a gram of cocaine and half an ounce of marijuana from Tim Parker and went up to Bart's room, where Bart, Hank, and two of their friends had gathered. Already high on marijuana, Chris bought ten hits of acid from Bart. He still had $150 in cash, and he held it aloft, along with the cocaine, the acid, the marijuana. "Fellows," he grandly announced, "now this is *power*."

He offered up his marijuana and cocaine to the others, and before the night was out, the drugs all had been used, and the campus police had been summoned after the group began throwing firecrackers from the balcony. Later, Chris reported that he was "really messed up," but again he was so energy-filled that he couldn't contain himself. Once more, he and Bart and the others walked off their high, this time off campus, covering five or six miles, Chris later estimated. It was on this walk that Bart told Chris about the tunnels.

Bart had learned about the tunnels as a freshman, and he already had made several forays there, exploring. The tunnels were concrete underground passages that crisscrossed the entire campus, carrying steam pipes and other utilities from building to building. Their entrances were barred and locked, but Bart and other students had discovered that many manholes about the campus offered access. Chris was excited about the

CLOCKWISE, FROM UPPER LEFT: Bart Upchurch when he was arrested on a drug charge in the spring of 1989. Bart at the age of five. (JIM UPCHURCH) Bart at the time of his arrest in high school. While in high school, Bart posed as a desperado in a gag photo made at the state fair. After going away to college, he became the real thing. (JIM UPCHURCH)

ABOVE, LEFT: Joanne Upchurch gave up a full scholarship and dropped out of college to marry Jim Upchurch and move to a farm. (JIM UPCHURCH) ABOVE, RIGHT: The farmhouse where Jim and Joanne moved with their young children. Although the family lived a near-primitive existence in this house, Jim found his greatest happiness here. (JIM UPCHURCH) RIGHT: Jim Upchurch, whose family was considered to be the "cornbread aristocracy" of Caswell County, North Carolina. (JIM UPCHURCH)

Neal Henderson's IQ qualified him as a genius, but he flunked out of North Carolina State University in the spring of 1988. (KENYATTA UPCHURCH)

Neal with Kenyatta Upchurch, Bart's cousin. (KENYATTA UPCHURCH)

Lieth von Stein, the executive who was murdered in his bed in July 1988.

Bonnie Von Stein could not believe that her son, Chris Pritchard, had anything to do with the murder of her husband and the attempted murder of herself. This photo was taken on the day Chris testified at Bart's trial in January 1990. Bonnie, her daughter Angela, who slept through the murder, and Chris were returning to court after lunch. (MICHAEL BARKLEY)

Washington is called Little Washington in the rest of North Carolina. But residents of the river town prefer to call it the original Washington, because it was the first town to be named for the country's first president. (JERRY BLEDSOE)

This burned, hand-drawn map, which miraculously escaped a fire set to destroy the evidence of Lieth Von Stein's murder, led detectives to the murder plotters.

Lieth Von Stein's murder in this house on Lawson Road brought fear to Washington's plushest subdivision and set off wild rumors and demands for a quick arrest. (JERRY BLEDSOE)

ABOVE: Bart Upchurch saw his trial as a game and was confident that he would be exonerated. His lawyers told him to bring his finger to his mouth to avoid the appearance of smirking. (MICHAEL BARKLEY) BELOW: Chris comforts his grandmother, Polly Bates, shortly before being taken away to prison for his role in the conspiracy. (MICHAEL BARKLEY)

ABOVE: Chris's voice choked and he wiped away tears when he testified that he conspired to have his mother murdered along with his stepfather so that he could inherit $2 million. (MICHAEL BARKLEY) BELOW: Neal Henderson, the first to reveal his role in the murder, points out the unusual markings on the baseball bat used in the attack on Lieth Von Stein. (MICHAEL BARKLEY)

CLOCKWISE, FROM UPPER LEFT: Christy Newsom, Bart's feisty probation officer, that Bart was mocking her and swore to have him sent to prison. (JERRY BLEDSOE) Wh John Crone became Washington's new police chief, he was given two directives: straigh out the police department and solve the Von Stein murder. (JERRY BLEDSOE) Attor Wayland Sermons, a member of one of Washington's privileged old families, had ne tried a capital murder case. He rarely had indigent clients with names like James Bar Upchurch III. (JERRY BLEDSOE) Melvin Hope, the first detective assigned to the Von St case, was a former marine who sometimes was called the John Wayne of the Washing Police Department. (JERRY BLEDSOE) John Taylor drove a pickup truck and wore blue je and cowboy boots to work as a Washington Police Department detective. He was just when he was handed the job of solving the town's biggest murder case. (JERRY BLEDSOE)

tunnels and wanted to go immediately. Nobody else was interested, but Bart agreed to take Chris to see them. It was about 4 A.M. when they lifted aside a heavy grate near the D. H. Hill Library and dropped into the darkness of N.C. State's underworld. Bart knew the locations of switches to turn on the fluorescent lights, and they wandered through the intricate network of pipes, pausing to smoke another joint and to read the graffiti that other student explorers had painted on the tunnel walls, giving them the look of a New York subway car. When they climbed back out of the manhole cover through which they had entered, Chris knew he had discovered a place he would want to revisit again and again.

A week after Chris's first venture into the tunnels, he, Tim Parker, Bart, and Brew were in Chris's room one afternoon, smoking pot. All of them were stoned, and they began discussing what they wanted to do after they got out of college. Chris and Brew had similar dreams: they wanted to be writers. Bart said he might like to run a restaurant and a club. They would be wealthy and popular.

Chris mentioned that it was just a matter of time before he would be wealthy anyway. His family, he said, had millions. Not to mention three houses and seven cars. This was the first time the others had heard anything about Chris's family being rich, although they knew they were well-to-do.

"I didn't know his parents had money," Bart said later. "I knew he'd call up his mom and ask for fifty or a hundred bucks and he'd get it. I said, 'Damn, I wish I could call my parents and do that.' But I didn't know they had that kind of money."

How did his old man get that money? somebody asked. Chris said he had inherited it.

"Hey, man, you ought to just off your parents and go ahead and get that money," somebody said, although later nobody would recall who.

"Yeah, I could buy a big house in the woods," Chris said.

"Up in north Raleigh," somebody said.

"Got to have a swimming pool," somebody else put in.

"And a Ferrari," Chris added.

"A satellite dish. And a big-screen TV."

"And a pool table."

They began fantasizing about the possibilities. They all

could live together, buy plenty of drugs and booze, play D&D whenever they wanted, attract fabulous babes. Chris said he would buy a "killer" stereo system, and two "serious" computers for him and Brew to write on. He might just buy the Swenson's ice cream parlor near the campus, too, and turn it into a restaurant and club for Bart to run.

Later, Chris called this session "bullshitting and day-dreaming."

"We were all joking," Bart said. "Just being ridiculous. We were wish-listing."

27

BY THE FIFTH AND FINAL week of the first session of summer school, Bart and Chris had stopped going to class.

Chris had been upset to learn that even though he had changed to auditing his calculus class, he still was expected to do homework and take exams. He had no intention of doing either. He explained to his mother that there had been a misunderstanding, and he was getting no credit for his class. That was fine with her, but she tried to talk him out of staying for the second summer session, telling him that he needed a break from classes and a chance to enjoy himself before starting his sophomore year. Chris was already enjoying himself almost more than he could stand, however, and he insisted on enrolling for the second session, this time taking chemistry and a political science course in American government.

Although Bart had paid little attention to his studies in the final weeks of the first summer session, he thought that he would slip by in cultural anthropology and get an incomplete in prehistoric archeology, and that was how it turned out. For the second summer session, he signed up for math and English, and his grandmother, Carolyn, whom he rarely saw anymore, ended up paying his tuition.

When the first summer session ended on June 28, Chris's closest friend from his freshman year, Chuck Jackson, moved into the dorm room with Chris. Like Chris, he was a Dungeons and Dragons player, but unlike Chris, he was a serious student who refused to neglect his studies. Chuck brought an air conditioner with him and installed it in the dorm window, ensuring that the room would be the gathering place for all of Chris's friends. After Chuck moved in, he and Chris completed the sleeping loft that Chris had been intending to erect but never had gotten around to, making even more room for friends to gather to party, and play D&D.

On Thursday, June 30, during the week-long break between summer sessions, Bart and Chris were finishing off a pitcher of beer at California Pizza*. Both had smoked pot and taken a hit of acid earlier and were waiting for the acid rush to hit.

California had become the chief gathering spot away from campus for Bart, Chris, and their friends. It seemed an unlikely choice, for it was a yuppie establishment in a suburban shopping center. Bart had worked there briefly, soon after the place opened. California's chief appeal to Bart, Chris, and their friends was that they could buy beer there without question, although they were under age. Chris usually drank at least a pitcher of beer at California every day, sometimes two or three. When friends from home visited, he loved to take them there and show off by buying beer. He spent so much time at California and depended so much upon it that he had begun to call it "the center of the universe," and for him and his friends that summer, it was.

On this day, Chris and Bart were bored. Chris hadn't gone to work at his clothing store job the day before and hadn't even bothered to call and explain why. He was tired of the job and ready to quit. It interfered with his drinking and pot smoking and kept him from playing Dungeons and Dragons.

With July 4 weekend looming, many of Chris's and Bart's friends had left town. Bart and Chris had made no plans.

"Hey, we can go to South Carolina," Chris said. "We can visit my aunt. She'll have a party waiting for us."

Bart was skeptical. Partying with an aunt?

"Hey, she's cool," Chris said. "She parties heavy. First time I ever got drunk was at a party at her house. I always have a good time down there."

Beyond that, Chris said, he knew a girl there, and his aunt, who was his mother's younger sister, had a daughter. "My cousin's good-looking. I'll set you up with her."

It was only a matter of a telephone call, Chris said. Bart was agreeable, and Chris called collect from the restaurant. He returned to the table to report that the party was on.

They went back to the dorm to pick up a few things, loaded a case of Michelob into Chris's Mustang, and headed for I-85 and South Carolina.

On the way, they drank most of the case of beer and were drunk but still frenetic from the acid when they stopped at a truck stop near the state line to call Chris's aunt in Inman. They arrived at her house to find numerous vehicles, including several pickup trucks with gun racks in the back window. A party was in full swing inside the small brick house, many of the participants members of a local volunteer fire department.

Later, neither Chris nor Bart would remember many details of the party. Bart would recall somebody showing off a .357 magnum and being offered his fill of moonshine liquor. He would recall somebody offering him what was called a "blueberry daiquiri," actually a mixture of moonshine and ipecac syrup, which he declined but Chris accepted to his dismay and the great amusement of the partygoers, as Bart later told it. Bart also would recall being called a "city boy" by the rural firefighters, a charge he found especially ironic when he thought of the wilds of Caswell County where he had spent most of his life.

Bart later remembered being distressingly hung over the following day, but by afternoon he and Chris had recovered sufficiently to accompany Chris's cousin on a visit to a nearby zoo. That night, Chris wanted to go to another party with a girl he had gone out with previously, a friend of his cousin. Bart declined and stayed behind with Chris's aunt, who changed the dressings on wounds on his elbow and shoulder that he had incurred from an earlier skateboarding fall.

Chris returned bragging of taking the girl to a motel room and of partying with big-time drug dealers who showed off Uzis, Bart said later.

On Saturday, Bart was loading his stuff into Chris's car when he saw wires dangling from the dashboard and an empty space where the expensive stereo radio and tape player that

Chris's mother and stepfather had given him for Christmas had been.

"Hey, man, somebody stole your stereo," Bart said.

Chris didn't believe it.

"Go look," Bart said.

Chris was angry and worried about what Bonnie and Lieth would say. They didn't even know where he was. His mother had called, asking her sister if she had seen or heard from Chris, but Chris had asked his aunt to say she hadn't heard from him, and she had covered for him. Now his aunt called the sheriff's department to report the theft. A deputy came and took a report, but Chris knew he would have to tell his parents that the theft occurred elsewhere.

On the trip back to Raleigh, Chris began to worry about what to tell his mother of his whereabouts for the past three days. His mother called him several times each week, sometimes daily, and he knew by the call she had made to his aunt's house on Friday that she was worried about him. He had no idea just how worried she was, however.

Bonnie and Lieth had planned to spend that weekend in Winston-Salem. Chris's sister, Angela, and her friend Donna Brady were going to leave on Thursday and spend the night with Chris in Raleigh, then drive on to Winston-Salem to join Bonnie and Lieth on Friday. Angela had called and arranged it all with Chris, who had forgotten about it. Angela and Donna arrived in Raleigh Thursday night, while Chris and Bart were just reaching South Carolina. Unable to find Chris, Angela and Donna later reported that they slept in Angela's car in a campus parking lot, before driving on to Winston-Salem.

When Angela told her mother about being unable to find Chris, Bonnie began calling all of Chris's friends and all of her relatives looking for him. When she still hadn't located him by Saturday morning, she called the campus police. The police seemed less than concerned after Bonnie had told her story, but she insisted that Chris was very good at remembering appointments and wouldn't have forgotten that his sister was coming. He always called in to work when he couldn't be there, she said, and he always called her if he was going someplace. She was certain that something terrible had happened to her son. The campus police told Bonnie that she would have to send a letter stating that she felt that Chris was missing involuntarily. But they could begin an investigation immediately if she made a recorded statement to that effect. Bonnie recorded the statement by telephone at 4:06 P.M., five hours after making her first call to the campus police. By that time, Chris and Bart were on their way back to Raleigh.

The campus police meanwhile were checking with the Raleigh police and with all area hospitals, including the nearby mental hospital, and a missing persons report went out to police agencies across the state.

"You either have to tell the truth or just make up something totally outlandish," Bart was telling Chris as they drove toward Raleigh. "If it's wild enough, they'll believe it."

Laughing, they made up the story that Chris later told his parents about going to see Bart's uncle, the car breaking down, an old lady feeding them goat's milk and baloney sandwiches that made them deathly sick.

"Don't worry about it," Bart assured Chris when they had finished concocting the tale. "They'll believe it."

When Chris and Bart arrived back at campus Saturday evening, friends told Chris, "Man, you better call your mama. She's got the cops and the National Guard out looking for you."

At ten-twenty-five that night, a campus police sergeant knocked on Chris's dorm room door. Chris assured him that he was in good health. He had been in Roanoke Rapids, a town near the Virginia border, visiting relatives, he said, and had forgotten to let his parents know that he was going. The officer told him to call his mother and Chris assured him that he would do it immediately.

Chris was apologetic when he called his mother. He had forgotten all about Angela coming, he said. Then he told her the story that he and Bart had dreamed up. Bonnie was so relieved that she was willing to accept any explanation. But when she told Lieth what Chris had said, Lieth said he didn't believe that story for a minute.

A day after their return from South Carolina, Bart and Chris were ready for another party. This was Sunday, July 3, and the campus was almost dead because of the holiday weekend. Few students were still in the dorm, and Bart set out through the building to see if he could round up some potential merrymakers. On the fifth floor, he encountered two young women and told them to come up to the sixth floor later for a party in Chris's room.

The young women were Sybil Cook*, and Sandra Goodman*. Sybil, who was from a nearby town, was a sophomore who wanted to work with children. She just had transferred from another university and knew almost nobody at State. Sandra Goodman was the first person she had met. Sandra, a day student who was commuting to summer classes, was visiting in Sybil's room when Bart came by, introducing himself as Moog. Sybil thought Bart was cute, and she and Sandra decided to go upstairs and see what was going on. Later, neither would recall anything special happening that night, but the party was significant because it allowed them to make the acquaintance of Bart and Chris and several others. They would remember it as the night that they were drawn into the circle of Bart's and Chris's friends. In coming weeks, they would see Bart and Chris almost every day.

Two days after meeting Bart and Chris, Sandra and Sybil joined them at California Pizza along with Chris's roommate, Chuck Jackson, Brew Simpson, and another student who occasionally played D&D with the group. All were sitting at a big round table, eating pizza and drinking beer, when Sandra and Sybil realized that the conversation had taken an unexpected turn. The others were talking about killing somebody. This person had too much power, they said, and they were plotting how they could slip up on him in his sleep and slay him with a sword.

"What in the world are they talking about?" Sandra later remembered asking herself.

"It seemed like something that they were really planning on doing," she said.

"I was getting real nervous because I didn't know these guys and I was thinking this was awfully strange," Sybil recalled of the conversation. "I was looking at Sandra kind of funny."

It took them a little while to realize that the guys were talking about a game. It was the first they knew that the circle they had fallen into was one betrothed to Dungeons and Dragons, a game that neither of them knew anything about.

Two days later, on Thursday, July 7, Bart, Chris and Hank were sitting again at California, downing more pitchers of beer, when they decided to take off on another trip, this time to the beach. They stopped to see friends of Chris's in Greenville, and Chris showed off the quarter-gram of cocaine and the ounce of Hawaiian pot that he had bought. Later, they drove through Washington with Bart and Hank urging Chris to roar down his street so they all could take a piss on his parents' front lawn.

"We were in that Hunter S. Thompson, drug-induced spirit of adventure," Bart said. "We figured, we've already fucked up so much, let's go and fuck up some more."

They got to the beach at three in the morning and headed back after a short frolic in the surf. At Havelock, Chris was stopped for speeding. The cops searched the car but didn't find the pot that Bart had hidden under the dashboard. Chris got away with nothing more than another speeding ticket.

Although both Bart and Chris still made efforts to go to class sporadically, their outside activities left them little time to study. Chris, who had quit his job at Miller & Rhoads after the trip to South Carolina, was playing in two D&D groups and keeping track of his games and his characters' powers on the computer in his room. After the long D&D sessions, which sometimes stretched far into the night and usually were enhanced by marijuana, alcohol, and acid, Chris often wanted to go adventuring in the tunnels beneath the campus. Usually, he and the others carried flashlights, but they sometimes made torches from sticks wrapped in toilet paper, and Chris usually carried a falchon, a bamboo martial arts sword.

"Chris was always saying, 'Let's go tunneling,' " Bart said later. "He liked going down there. He'd always take some pot, and we would walk around and smoke pot and read the graffiti."

Once, they took cans of spray paint and left behind their own graffiti, Chris spraying "Underground Guild" and "CWP, July 1988" on the walls.

They never attempted to play D&D in the tunnels, and the most exciting thing that ever happened there was unexpectedly hearing another group of students and chasing them, making them think the cops were after them. "After a while, it got boring," Bart said of their underground adventures. "It was hot and uncomfortable down there, but Chris never got enough of it."

Chris spent more time with Sandra and Sybil than Bart did, sometimes devoting evenings to playing a card game called spades with them in one dorm room or another. Sandra often spent nights in Sybil's room rather than driving back home.

Bart shied away from being alone with Sandra and Sybil after he realized that Sybil had a crush on him. He wanted nothing to do with her, and after she realized that he wasn't interested in her, she never pressed her attentions.

Sandra was engaged, but her fiancé had transferred to an out-of-state college in May, and they had since agreed to begin seeing others. She was dating somebody off campus and had no romantic interest in Chris or any of his friends.

Nonetheless, Chris tried hard to impress Sandra and Sybil. For one thing, he led them to believe that he kept important secrets in his computer. One was a "cool plan" that would bring him a lot of money, he boasted. Both Sandra and Sybil had heard Chris bragging about knowing big-time drug dealers, and they assumed that the plan had something to do with a drug deal.

Drugs were becoming more and more a part of Chris's life by then. He was smoking pot at least three times a day, often sleeping for a while afterward. He continued drinking at least a pitcher of beer a day at California. And he used acid two or three times a week, usually a hit and a half at a time. His fifty-dollar weekly allowance all went for drugs, and his credit card was at its limit. Sandra and Sybil later recalled Chris asking his mother for money to buy clothes and bragging when she sent it that it was all going for drugs. He stopped buying cocaine because it was too expensive and didn't offer a long-enough high. He continued to depend on Tim Parker and Parker's friends for marijuana. And he got his acid from Bart and Hank, he said, although Bart later denied that he and Hank were Chris's suppliers.

Chris made several more trips as the second summer school session wore on, twice going to Greenville to visit friends from high school. On one of those trips he took a friend named David, who was called Wasted White Skin, and a black friend of David's.

On another trip, he and Brew went to the beach, stopping first at Chris's house in Washington and visiting briefly with his mother. The real purpose of that trip was to go to the courthouse in New Bern and pay off the speeding ticket he had gotten on the earlier trip to the beach with Bart and Hank, but Chris was careful not to let his mother know that. He'd already had four previous traffic tickets and had lost his license once, and he knew what his parents' reaction would be if they found out about this one. He told his mother on the stopover that he and Brew might come back and spend the night, but they returned to Raleigh instead. Chris waited until he got back to the dorm to call his mother and tell her that he wouldn't be returning to spend the night, but he would come back soon for a longer visit, he promised.

He kept that promise on Friday, July 22, calling his mother first to let her know that he was coming. Before leaving, he tried to make a marijuana buy from a friend of Tim Parker, a high school student who took his money and a check, left him waiting three hours in a shopping center parking lot, and never returned.

Angry and frustrated, Chris drove on to Washington and spent that night at home. His visit took an unexpected turn on Saturday when the mother of the high school student from whom Chris had tried to make the drug buy called his house seeking an explanation for the check Chris had given to her son. Chris finally had to admit to his upset mother and stepfather that the check had been for marijuana and that he did smoke a little pot now and then. After that unpleasantness, Chris remained to grill hamburgers for his family. But despite his mother's plea that he stay another night, he returned to campus after supper, saying he had to get back to work on a report for his political science class that was due Monday morning.

But when he got back to Raleigh that Saturday night, Chris did not work on the unwritten report that had been nagging at him for days. Instead, he and Bart went to California Pizza and drank beer. He didn't work on his report the next day either. Sunday night, July 24, he, Sandra, and Sybil rode to the Sav-A-Center and Sandra went in and bought a case of beer. They brought it back to the dorm, put part of it in the refrigerator in Chris's room, and took the rest to Sybil's room, where they were joined by Chuck and Brew and began a game of spades. About eleven, Brew got upset at Chuck for helping the girls with the game, and they had words. Chuck left and went back to his room, but Chris and Brew remained, drinking and continuing the game.

The summer was not turning out as Kenyatta Upchurch hoped that it would. Instead of she and Neal rebuilding their relationship, they seemed to be growing further apart. Almost everything that he did irritated her and they argued constantly.

She hated that he remained so devoted to Dungeons and Dragons and focused most of his energies on the game, ignoring her. She hated that he continued stealing, slipping something into his clothing every night as he left his job at Sav-A-Center (later Neal would say that this was mostly food and he didn't really consider that stealing). She hated the stupid things he was doing, like playing in the tunnels and using drugs. She was particularly upset that Neal had started using acid.

"I hate drunk people," she said later. "I'm scared of drugs. I asked Neal, 'Why do you have to do this?' He said, 'I just want to try it.' Neal is big on this experimental stuff, thinks you should try everything. I said, 'Well, you're going to get addicted to it.' 'No, no,' he said, 'It's just experimental, it's not really addictive.' I said, 'Yeah, yeah, sure.'"

More than anything, Kenyatta hated the people Neal was associating with that summer, his roommate Butch, her cousin Bart, whom she still called James and despised ("He's scum," she told Neal), and Chris Pritchard.

"Every time I saw Chris, he was either coming off or going on a high," she said later. "Drugs or alcohol, every time he did it, he did it to excess. He was very skinny, very sick looking, black rings around his eyes, totally nasty looking, like he was right on the edge. He just looked real weird to me. Looked like he didn't care about anything. James and Chris both had that look: We don't care what happens."

Kenyatta worked a later shift than usual at McDonald's on Sunday night, July 24. She got off from that shift early and came back to the apartment thinking that she and Neal might do something together. As usual, she found Neal playing Dungeons and Dragons with Butch and another friend in the clutter of the living room.

"It just pissed me off," she said later.

She went into the bedroom she shared with Neal, slammed the door, changed clothes, went about furiously cleaning the room. Several times, she went out to the kitchen or the bathroom, each time giving cold scowls to Neal and his friends, who played right on. Each time, she returned to the bedroom, slamming the door.

After a while, the game broke up and Neal came in looking sheepish.

"Kenyatta, I just did acid," he said. "It's going to take effect in about twenty minutes."

"Well, thank you very much for telling me," she said. "You can leave now. I don't want you in this apartment."

"He stood in the doorway a long time," she recalled later. "He said, 'I can't believe you're throwing me out.' I said, 'Just go. And don't take your key. I'm not going to let you back in here. I don't want to see you on a trip.' He got his stuff and left."

"Where did Neal go?" Butch asked her later.

"He's doing acid," Kenyatta said with disgust. "I guess he's going to wander off somewhere in the tunnels."

When Sandra and Sybil tired of spades sometime after midnight, Chris suggested another game, Truth or Dare. They played it for an hour or so and then went back to spades. Sandra and Sybil were tired and sleepy from the effects of the beer, and they began yawning and giving other signs that they were ready for bed, but Chris was drunk and wanted to play more.

"Can we please quit playing this game?" Sybil said at one point, but Chris and Brew showed no signs of stopping.

Several more times, Sybil and Sandra mentioned how tired and sleepy they were. Still Chris and Brew didn't leave. Finally, Sybil insisted that they quit the game.

"What time is it?" Chris asked.

"It's nearly three-thirty," somebody said.

And much to the relief of Sandra and Sybil, Chris and Brew finally left. Brew headed for home. Chris went up one flight of stairs to his room, where Chuck had been long asleep, and climbed into his sleeping loft. In little more than an hour, the phone by Chuck's bed would ring, and he would awaken long enough to jog Chris from his brief sleep and hand him the receiver. Chris would hear his sister's voice telling him that his mother and stepfather had been stabbed and that he'd "better get his butt home."

28

Soon after dawn on
Monday, July 25, 1988, Kenyatta Upchurch was awakened by
a tapping noise at her bedroom window. Rousing herself, she
was momentarily startled to see a frightened and forlorn face
staring through the glass at her. It took only a second for her
to register that the face was Neal's.

"Let me in," he pleaded.

Kenyatta got up and opened the front door of the
apartment.

She never had seen Neal looking like this. His eyes,
normally as hooded as a tortoise's, were wide open.

"He was frightening looking," Kenyatta recalled. "He was
sweating like a dog. I'd never seen him so wired. I thought he
was coming off a bad trip."

Her impulse was to say, "I told you so" and lecture him
about drug use. But she felt sorry for him and took him into
the bedroom and comforted him.

"It took him a long time to calm down," she said later.

He hadn't slept. That was obvious. And Kenyatta knew
that he had an appointment later that morning with an officer
from the Army ROTC program at State. Neal had been hoping
somehow to get back in college, perhaps with help from ROTC.
Kenyatta urged him to go to bed and try to get some sleep
before the officer arrived.

Before he went to bed, Neal pulled two twenty-dollar bills
and a ten from his pocket and gave them to Kenyatta as a
peace offering. Where'd you get that? she wanted to know.
He'd found a wallet the night before, he said, and he had
taken the money from it and thrown the wallet and identification away. It was an unexpected bit of luck. They needed
the money.

Sandra and Sybil got up late Monday morning. After dressing,
they went looking for Chris. He'd asked them the night before
if they wanted to go to lunch the next day and maybe go

swimming that afternoon. It was the first time they could remember him making plans that far in advance. Sandra and Sybil thought they saw Chris's car in the parking lot. When they found nobody in his room, they thought he might be in class. But a suitemate appeared from an adjoining room and told them that he had heard that Chris had to go home because of an emergency. What kind of an emergency? And why would he have gone and left his car? Sandra and Sybil were left to wonder.

When they returned to the dorm from their lunch at California Pizza, Sybil got a call from Chuck Jackson. He asked if she and Sandra could come up to his room. He had something important to tell them, he said. Chuck met them at the door. Brew was in the room, and so was Bart, whom they called Moog. Sandra and Sybil had never seen these guys looking so serious.

"Somebody broke into Chris's house last night and attacked his parents," Chuck told them.

Chris's stepfather had been killed; his mother was in the hospital. Both had been stabbed and beaten. It apparently had happened in the early morning hours. Campus police had taken Chris home. Beyond that, not much else was known. A burglary of some sort. Shocked, Sandra and Sybil returned to Sybil's room. Poor Chris, they thought. Poor, poor Chris.

Neal got up when the ROTC officer came, but he begged off talking with him, saying that he was sick, making apologies and asking for a later appointment. Afterward, Neal went back to bed and didn't get up until well after lunch, when Bart and Brew showed up to tell Neal and Butch what had happened to Chris's parents. Neal seemed surprised at the news and asked questions, but Bart and Brew had few answers. Kenyatta couldn't remember the group being so sobered. Later, she recalled that they all agreed that what had happened was terrible, and they were sorry for Chris.

Sandra, Sybil, Brew, Bart, and Chuck gathered in Chuck's room late that afternoon to watch the TV news, hoping to learn more about what had happened at Chris's house, but the news offered no mention of a murder in Washington, and they were left to speculate. Nobody knew if there had been an arrest, or even if there were suspects. Who could have done

210

it? Somebody who knew that Chris's family had a lot of money, more than likely, they figured. Whoever did it, Sandra, Sybil, and Brew knew one thing for certain. It wasn't Chris. He was with them, playing cards.

Two days after his friends at State learned about the murder, Chris returned briefly to campus to pick up his car and some clothes. He came with his uncle, George Bates. Sandra, Sybil, and Bart all went to Chris's room to see him. Chris was not his usual self. Nobody expected him to be, but he seemed more than saddened: he seemed depressed. Nobody really knew what to say to him, except that they were sorry. Chris didn't talk much about the murder, and his friends were reluctant to ask. His mother was still in the hospital, he said, but she was going to be okay. Lieth's funeral would be tomorrow. He wouldn't be returning to finish summer school.

In the days that followed, Bart and Brew recalled the conversation in which they and Chris and Tim Parker had been laughing and joking about Chris "offing" his parents so that he could go ahead and collect the millions he would inherit while he was young and could enjoy it. Each expressed regret at having been part of that conversation. They also asked one another if perhaps Chris could have taken it seriously. Could Chris have been somehow involved in the murder? Both said they couldn't imagine it.

"Chris is a little crazy," Bart said, "but he's not *that* crazy."

On Friday, August 5, four days after his mother was released from the hospital, Chris and his sister, Angela, came back to State so that Chris could officially withdraw from summer school and pick up the remainder of his belongings. With Chris's approval, Bart had moved into Chris's room with Chuck for the more comfortable accommodations, and Chris called ahead to tell them that he was coming and wanted to have a party, a real blowout. He wanted all of his friends to be there, and he wanted plenty of liquor and beer. Bart and Chuck got the liquor—half a gallon of tequila, half a gallon of vodka—and two cases of Coors Light. But Bart was concerned about one thing.

"I got on the phone and called everybody I knew and told them, 'If Chris comes looking for acid, don't sell him any. He doesn't need that on his mind right now,'" Bart said later.

When Chris and Angela went to California Pizza that night with Sandra, Sybil, and several others, Sandra and Sybil later recalled that he told them he was giving up drugs. "My mother doesn't need me doing that," he said.

Somehow, though, neither Sandra nor Sybil was surprised at what happened at the party later that night. Chris was drunker and higher, wilder and bolder than any of his friends ever had seen him. He smoked pot, chased shots of Pepe Lopez with Coors Light, took one hit of acid, then another—and soared into hysteria. A bad trip, everybody called it later. But to Chris it was a nightmare.

"I can't breathe," he kept yelling. "I'm dying. I'm dying. Somebody call an ambulance."

First one, then another of his friends took him outside, walked him, and tried to calm him. Finally, they got him into his loft bed, where he eventually passed out.

"I knew he shouldn't have taken that acid in his state of mind," Bart said.

After that night, all of Chris's friends at State agreed on one thing about the murder of Chris's stepfather and the attack on his mother: Chris was taking it awfully hard.

By the time Chris returned for the party, Bart had not gone to class for more than a week. He knew that he was going to flunk both courses and that his attempt at reinstating himself as a student was doomed for now.

"I figured what the hell, it wasn't no big deal," he said later. "I'd just take the classes over."

But the end of summer school meant that Bart no longer had a place to live and had to make another decision. He had been talking with Brew and another friend about getting an apartment together. They finally decided to do it and found one at 2001-B Gorman Street in a different section of the complex in which Bart had lived with Hank and Opie, just off Avent Ferry Road.

Bart had not worked since April. He had been living off the insurance payment from his car wreck. In addition, he was helping to make ends meet by writing bad checks.

"I got into the habit of it," he said of the check writing. "I got a big kick out of it. I was buying beer under age with bad checks. We figured you had to have balls to do that. I figured I'd just pay the bad checks back if they caught up with me."

Many of the bad checks were to restaurants, often for food that was delivered. And a couple of times the recipients did catch up with him, sending big, stern guys who cornered him and said, "You gonna pay for those subs you got."

"Hey, man, no problem," Bart told them, although once he had to borrow quickly from friends to make good.

Others sought legal recompense, issuing warrants for his arrest. "I never wrote a bad check unless I was drunk," Bart said later. "It got completely out of hand. It all added up to a lot more than I figured."

Bart didn't have money to pay off the checks or to pay his share of the apartment rent and deposit, but he did still have the big '66 Ford convertible that he had bought in the spring. It still was at the shop where the brakes had been fixed. He'd left it because he couldn't afford to pay the repair bill. If he could find a buyer for the car, Bart reasoned, he would be able to pay the repair bill and still have enough to pay off his bad checks and ante up his share of the rent. True, he still would be left with a car payment and no car, but that really wasn't his problem. His father had cosigned the note and it would fall to him to take care of it.

A maintenance worker at State bought the car. Bart paid off his bills—his mother sent money to cover a couple of the bad checks—and he, Brew, and another friend moved into the apartment in mid-August.

Through June and early July, Bart had kept his regular appointments with his probation officer, Christy Newsom. But soon after moving off campus, he awoke after noon one day too hung over to make his 2 P.M. appointment. No problem, he figured. He'd just go next day. But the next day he was lying by the apartment pool when he realized that he had failed to go again. Oh well, he thought, if she wanted to see him bad enough she would find him. No need to worry about it.

That Bart failed to make his appointment came as no surprise to Christy. She had expected him to fall back into his old habits. But she had no intention of allowing him to get away with it.

Kenyatta was relieved that August was coming to an end. Her dream of a romantic summer with Neal had turned into a nightmare. August had brought the worst weeks. Clearly, Neal

213

was lapsing back into the depression that had had such a strong hold on him earlier in the year.

"I couldn't even communicate with him," she said later. "He never smiled. He was never happy. He wouldn't talk to me. He wouldn't do anything with me. I couldn't make him happy. I couldn't even make him smile."

She was relieved when the time came for her to move out of the misery of the apartment on Ligon Street and return to the campus of the N.C. School of Science and Math in Durham for her senior year of high school. She still loved Neal but she had begun to realize that they probably couldn't make it together.

Chris returned to campus for the beginning of the fall semester at the end of August. Bart saw him several times. "He was acting really paranoid," Bart recalled. "Really jumpy." He told friends that his mother was afraid that the killer might return and try to get her and other family members. He said his mother had hired former Green Berets as bodyguards. He was taking care of his own protection, however. He showed off a .22 semiautomatic pistol that he kept in his car.

The opening of fall semester is always a big party time on campus, and Chris still made the parties, still drank heavily. He confided to several friends that he was afraid that he might be an alcoholic. Once that fall, Bart later recalled, Chris got terribly drunk, whipped a long dagger out of the back of his pants, and began jumping around, slashing wildly at the night air.

Chris's worried mother kept a closer watch on him than ever, and as he began skipping classes again and acting more depressed and erratic, she encouraged him to seek counseling. Chris began seeing a college psychologist, who advised him that he should drop classes temporarily until he had more understanding of his problems and better control of his emotions.

Chris withdrew from classes at the end of September to go and live with his mother in Winston-Salem. He told friends that he was dropping out to look after his mother. After all, he said, he was the man of the family now.

Christy Newsom still had not found Bart. Early in September, she had called Student Information at State and discovered that Bart was not registered. Two days later, she went to the campus looking for him without success. The next day, she got his father's number at work in Raleigh. Jim had left his job at the Social Services Department in Caswell County and gone to work for the Department of Human Resources in Raleigh, each day commuting the fifty miles back and forth to Caswell County. Jim was surprised and upset to learn that Bart wasn't in school, and he didn't know his whereabouts. Jim tracked Bart down by calling Hank at his mother's restaurant. He then called Christy and gave her Bart's address at 2001-B Gorman Street. When Christy went by the apartment, nobody answered her knock. She sent Bart a letter telling him that he was again in violation of his probation and that she was going to have him arrested. Still, she heard nothing from him.

Bart and Brew had become very close and spent many hours talking about life, philosophy, and politics over beer. They had much in common. Both were smart. Both had been playing D&D since junior high. Neither knew what he wanted to do with his life.

"You're so smart and so capable of doing so many things that you're scared to do anything, because the minute you start doing one thing, all your options are closed," Brew said later, echoing words Bart had said earlier.

Unlike Bart, Brew did have one certainty in his future. He had a girlfriend, and he planned to marry her when he finished college.

"His girlfriend was a really private thing with him," Bart said later. "We didn't really know her."

In October, Bart came into the apartment one night and found Brew sitting in front of the TV with a half-empty bottle of vodka and an empty Valium bottle at his side. His girlfriend had found somebody else.

"Brew just went off the deep end," Bart said later. "His girlfriend was the one anchor of his life. It just threw his whole life into chaos."

Bart and his other roommate sat up late that night, trying to keep Brew awake and to get him to talk about his feelings. "He really wouldn't talk that much," Bart said. "He just wanted us to go get him some beer. We wouldn't do that. Finally, he just went in and crashed."

When Bart got up the next morning, he discovered that

Brew was gone. The next he heard about him, Brew was in the hospital.

"He went to his grandma's house, took every pill in the medicine cabinet, almost died," Bart said.

"I didn't try to kill myself," Brew said much later. "I was really hurt and I wanted to stop hurting."

Brew's mother came to the apartment while he was still in the hospital, packed up his belongings, and took them away. Brew would not be returning, she said.

To Bart, as he later put it, "everything seemed to be turning to shit" that fall. Chris and Brew had flaked out and gone away. Without Brew, he and his roommate couldn't afford to keep the apartment. He was broke, out of school, with no job. He soon would have no place to live, and he had no place to go. Well, there was one place to go: Christy Newsom was again threatening to send him to jail. She had issued a warrant for his arrest.

On October 21, Bart went to the probation office and said that he had come to turn himself in. Christy was not there. The person Bart spoke with told him that the paperwork had been turned over to the Wake County Sheriff's Department. He would have to go there.

Bart left, but he didn't show up at the sheriff's department. He'd made the effort, he figured, and if they didn't want him bad enough to keep him, that was their problem.

Christy was furious when she came back to the office and discovered what had happened. "Why didn't you hold him and have the deputies come here and arrest him?" she demanded, but she never got an acceptable answer. She knew that she likely wouldn't see Bart again for a long time.

Bart got a job at a sub shop, answered a roommate-wanted ad in the newspaper, and moved into an apartment at Parkwood Village on Gorman Street, not far from where he had been living with Brew. He told all of his friends that if Christy Newsom came looking for him, they were not to tell his whereabouts.

As Bart later recalled, not long after he moved into Parkwood Village with a stranger, Hank came by. "Hey, man, the cops are looking for you," Hank said.

"I know," Bart said. "It's that probation shit."

"Nah. This was SBI and some cop from Washington. They're investigating what happened to Chris's folks."

They probably were just trying to talk to all of Chris's friends, see if they thought Chris might have had something to do with it, Hank figured. Even among Chris's friends, the question had arisen: Could he have been involved? All thought it unlikely.

"If they come back, don't tell 'em anything about me," Bart told Hank. "They'll put me in jail on that probation shit."

PART THREE

CHASING MOOG

THE GODS VISIT THE SINS OF THE FATHERS
UPON THE CHILDREN.

—EURIPIDES

29

ONE NIGHT LATE IN 1988, Bruce Radford, the gangling city manager of Washington, North Carolina, received a call at his apartment. A man with a slightly northern accent identified himself. Radford didn't recognize the name. John Crone was one of nearly seventy people who had sent for applications for the job of Washington police chief. Crone happened to be passing through and wanted to drop off his application personally and introduce himself. It was 10 o'clock and he was at McDonald's on Highway 17. Radford drove out to meet him over cups of coffee.

Only a few weeks earlier, Crone, the deputy chief of police of Ocean City, Maryland, hadn't even known that Washington existed. The father of three children, he was engaged to be married for the third time. He and his fiancée, a North Carolina native, had driven to Myrtle Beach, South Carolina, to attend an annual gathering of her family so that he could meet his future in-laws. While he was there, he scanned the want ads in the Charlotte *Observer* and came across the ad Bruce Radford had placed for a police chief.

Crone's future wife, Cindy, who lived in Rehoboth Beach, Delaware, wanted to move back closer to her family. He wanted to be a police chief. He got out a highway map and discovered that the town of Washington was on his route back to Maryland. He and his fiancée drove through it on their way. Nothing much impressed them about the town, except for its location on the Pamlico River, but they thought that it seemed to be a pleasant enough place, just a five-hour drive from Cindy's family in Mooresville, in the western part of the state. When he got home, Crone wrote for an application.

John Crone had been a police officer for twenty years. The son of the one-time chief of ballistic missile defenses at the Pentagon, he had grown up in the affluent suburbs of Washington. Unable to decide what he wanted to do with his life as a young man, he had joined the Army and served in Korea while the Vietnam War was going on. He was nearing the end of his enlistment at the Redstone Arsenal in Huntsville,

Alabama, when he saw a bulletin board notice that he could be discharged up to five months early by joining the Washington, D.C., Metropolitan Police Department. He took the test and passed it.

Crone really wasn't much interested in becoming a police officer. He figured he would just go through the academy training and quit. But he finished in the top three in his class, an honor that not only accorded him a scholarship to study the administration of justice at American University on his off-duty hours, but that also got him assigned to an elite special operations team patrolling high-crime areas. Crone proved to be an able officer, but his spirited sense of humor soon got him into trouble. As a practical joke, he donned a gorilla mask while in his patrol car parked in front of the Vietnamese embassy during a demonstration. A nearby ABC-TV news crew taped him, and he made the evening news. He soon found himself summoned before a captain who was holding a photo enlargement of the D.C. gorilla cop and demanding to know, "Is this you?"

"Yes, sir," he replied, ending his career in special operations.

He rebounded quickly as a precinct cop in Georgetown, was named officer of the year in his third year on the force, and was promoted to sergeant in his fourth year, six years ahead of the normal schedule. In 1977, he got his degree from American University with one of the highest grade averages ever attained by a D.C. police officer. That same year, he married for a second time, this time to a fellow officer in the department, who always had dreamed of living in Colorado. They quit the department and moved to the town of Arvada, a Denver suburb, where Crone joined the police force while his wife tried to start a rental business. After a year, Crone was fed up with the petty jealousies and politics of a suburban police department, and he and his wife moved back to Washington. He soon joined the Ocean City Police Department as a lieutenant and began a ten-year climb through the ranks. But he knew that he wasn't likely to become chief there any time soon, and he had reached the point that he wanted to do things his way.

Crone was an amicable and amiable man with a quick and easy sense of humor and an ability to charm strangers. And his on-the-way-through encounter with Bruce Radford had the effect Crone hoped that it would.

"I liked him, which was what I was trying to avoid," Radford said later.

Radford had set up an elaborate system for choosing a police chief that would nullify his personal feelings: a panel of police chiefs and city managers from other North Carolina towns and cities would winnow down the applicants and settle on the best. The seventy applicants were cut to six, one of them being John Crone. The six were called before the panel for interviews. From those, the panel chose two, one being John Crone. Both men were sent to Cary, near Raleigh, for a full day of psychological testing. John Crone came out on top, and the town that liked to call itself the original Washington got a former police sergeant from the upstart Washington as its new chief of police.

Crone knew that he faced a challenge. He'd been told that the police department was a mess. His instructions were simple and twofold: Straighten out the department and solve the town's most glaring crime, the murder of Lieth Von Stein.

Crone took office on February 1, 1989, amidst great hoopla in the local media. "They made me into a hero before I ever got here," he said later. "Said I was going to solve the Von Stein case and all this crap. I thought, Good Lord, this is really wonderful, but what if I can't solve the Von Stein case?"

Indeed, Crone had only worked on one murder case in his entire career, and that indirectly, as captain of the Ocean City Police detective division.

But before he could think about murder, he first had to learn the personalities and problems of his twenty-five-person police department, so that he could begin improving it. After a few weeks, he had become familiar enough with the department that he felt free to begin looking at the second part of his directive, solving the Von Stein murder. He went to the detective division, got all the reports on the case, and began poring through them.

Crone quickly saw that the initial months of the investigation had passed without anything of substance happening, and nothing at all had been done since Bonnie and Angela had passed lie detector tests in early January. Clearly, the case had been left to languish until his arrival. After finishing the reports and having noted that Bonnie's son, Chris, had declined to take the polygraph test, Crone's impression of the case was the same as those of the officers who had worked it without success. He thought the murder was an inside job, a family affair. And Chris Pritchard was the most likely suspect.

Crone also thought the only way to bring new life to the case was to assign a new investigator. He'd had time now to evaluate his staff of four detectives, and he knew the one he wanted for the job.

Bruce Radford was still keeping close tabs on the police department and the progress of its new chief, and he was not surprised when Crone came to him and said he planned to put the department's youngest and most inexperienced detective on the cold trail of the town's biggest murder. Radford had been impressed with John Taylor, too. Taylor was just twenty-seven years old, a country boy with only four years in the department, but everybody connected with law enforcement in Beaufort County had taken note of him.

"He was and is the brightest star of the young people in the department," Radford said of Taylor after Radford had left the job of city manager. "Kind of lean. Kind of hungry. Very dedicated. Always wants to do a good job."

The only person surprised by the assignment was the one chosen.

John Taylor's early years had been the nomadic existence of an Air Force brat: Georgia, where he was born, South Carolina, England, France, California. But his father retired when John was twelve; he returned to Beaufort County, where he had grown up in a farm family of nine brothers and sisters, and settled into a job at the post office.

John Taylor spent his teenage years living in the country, playing baseball, and working part-time in a grocery store. After graduating from high school in Chocowinity, across the river from Washington, Taylor went to work for an electrical contractor doing industrial construction. He left that job to study electrical engineering at Beaufort Community College for two years. Following his graduation, he went to work for the region's biggest employer, Texas Gulf, at the company's huge phosphate mine in nearby Aurora, where he operated a drag line in the pit mine until he was laid off in company cutbacks.

While he was out of work, Taylor encountered a cousin who worked at the Beaufort County Sheriff's Department. There were openings for deputies, his cousin told him. Why not give it a try? Taylor was accepted and joined the department in October 1982 as a patrol deputy. Less than four months later, he got a taste of just how dangerous law enforcement work can be.

After answering a call to Terra Ciea, a Dutch flower-growing community in the county, he and other officers encountered a berserk armed man who had barricaded himself inside his house. The man had lost both feet and thought the Mafia was coming to take away his disability payments. While Taylor and other officers hunkered behind cars and other cover, a neighbor decided to try to talk the man into surrendering. When the neighbor stepped from behind a car to start toward the house, the man inside opened fire with a deer rifle. The neighbor fell from a shot that passed completely through him, side to side. He died gurgling and gasping on the ground, his eyes still open wide in disbelief. The man fell only a few feet from Taylor, but neither Taylor nor anybody else was able to help him. Taylor did reach out, however, and pull the neighbor's farm cap down over his open eyes.

After twenty months as a sheriff's deputy, Taylor joined the Washington Police Department as a patrol officer in June 1984. When a detective's job came open two years later, he applied and got it.

In many other places, Taylor might have been considered unconventional, but in Washington he fit right in. He drove an old Chevrolet pickup truck, wore tight blue jeans, western-cut shirts, and cowboy boots to work. He liked Jack Daniel's whiskey and the "outlaw" country music of Waylon Jennings, David Allen Coe, and Hank Williams, Jr. Tall and athletic in appearance, Taylor was the strong, silent type. His closely cropped hair lay in tight curls on his head, and his light blue eyes betrayed a sense of constant amusement. An impish grin gave him a boyish look that women found irresistible.

Early in March 1989, Taylor's captain, Danny Boyd, told Taylor that he needed to talk to him, but he couldn't do it in the close confines of the small detective office, where everybody's desks abutted. They got into the crime lab van, and as they rode aimlessly around town, Boyd laid it out for him. The new chief wanted Taylor assigned full-time to the Von Stein case, and he could follow it wherever it led. The chief wanted the case solved and he would work closely with Taylor on it himself.

"What about Melvin?" Taylor asked.

Melvin Hope, Taylor's sergeant, had been in charge of the Von Stein case.

Hope would not be working the case anymore, Boyd said.

Taylor was concerned about Hope's reaction. He was sure that Hope would resent having to hand over his case to a younger subordinate, even though Hope had not been able to find time to work the case.

He was not to worry about that, Boyd told him. Boyd and the chief would be talking with Hope.

Nonetheless, Taylor dreaded having to go to Hope to ask for his notes and files after Hope had been informed of the decision. "I hope you're not pissed at me," Taylor told Hope. "I didn't ask for this and I'm not sure I particularly want it."

"I'm not pissed," Hope said. "I understand. This is not a ballgame. We're trying to get something done here. Look, let me know how I can help you."

Much later, Hope would say, "It was time for somebody to come in with a fresh perspective, and John is a good investigator."

His concern about Hope had not been Taylor's only worry about taking the case. The greater burden was personal and more enduring. Could he find the killer? "Now everybody's eyes were on John Boy," he said later.

He realized that failure not only could affect his own reputation and career but the new chief's as well.

But underneath his worry was a growing sense of challenge and excitement. And he knew that now that he was committed, there was only one thing he could do.

"Just take it and go with it," he told himself.

30

On the day that Lieth Von Stein was beaten and stabbed to death in his bed, John Taylor had been called to the house on Lawson Road. He had photographed the body and the house, then had helped SBI Agent Lewis Young gather evidence at the scene, because no SBI crime lab was available. He also had videotaped Lieth's autopsy and helped to tag the evidence gathered at the roadside fire site in Pitt County where the map of Smallwood and the knife that apparently had killed Lieth had been found. Beyond that, he'd had no further role in the case, and had not kept up with the day-to-day details of the investigation. Now he had to undergo a crash course to determine what had, and, more important, what had not been done, so that he would know where to begin.

He immersed himself in the three fat casebooks of reports that already had been filed, and when he emerged, he, like every other officer who had become familiar with the case, felt that Chris Pritchard had to have had something to do with the murder. Chris was his obvious beginning point.

Taylor also saw that several avenues had to be explored further. If Chris had planned the murder, and if he actually had been at N.C. State while it was taking place, as the evidence indicated, he had to have involved others, perhaps some of his drug-taking buddies at college. Yet only a couple of those had been interviewed. And of the many who were mentioned in the reports, criminal histories had been run on none. Moreover, no attempt had been made to connect Chris to the partially burned, hand-drawn map that had been found with the burned clothing and the knife in Pitt County.

Taylor requested criminal histories on all of Chris's college acquaintances whose names were mentioned in the reports. And he began preparing a list of Chris's friends whom he wanted to interview.

One of those at the top of the list was Davida Cox, whose mother had mentioned the previous fall that Chris had given her daughter papers to read. Perhaps Davida still had some of those papers, Taylor thought, and if they were written in Chris's hand, he might be able to compare them to the writing on the map.

Davida had dated Chris a few times when they were in tenth grade, and although they had quit dating, they had remained close friends. Davida said that she hadn't seen Chris much since he had gone away to college, and she had not had a chance to be alone with him since the murder.

Chris was still coming to Washington to visit periodically. He had shown up at the Christmas parade with a four-foot-long pet boa constrictor he had named Elvis draped around his neck—typical Chris, always seeking attention. After the first of the year he had returned and given Davida a short story he had written. He had been giving her things that he had written for her to critique since they were in high school. She always returned them to him, but she still had this particular story. Taylor asked to see it and was disappointed to find that it was neatly printed out by computer and not in Chris's hand. Taylor read the story anyway, to see if it might hold some clue.

The story was two and a half pages long, in two parts. The first part told about a man driving home on the same stretch of road that he had ridden daily for years. He encountered a dead dog in the road, its entrails spread over the pavement, and he continued on, thinking about the dog. The second part told about a rabbit that lived along the same road. The rabbit called the road the Demon Track and thought of the vehicles passing on it as demons. He saw the dog killed by one of the demons but was unconcerned because the dog had eaten most of his family. The side of the road that he lived on had been burned, and he needed to get across the road for food. When he finally built up his courage to make the attempt, a car nipped him, but he made it across and survived. Taylor didn't bother to consider symbolism. The only thing the story told him was that Chris had an active and strange imagination.

Davida said she couldn't imagine Chris having anything to do with the murder. He always was so nice, she said, so eager to please. She'd never heard him say anything about hating Lieth, and she was close enough to Chris that if he had any problems with his stepfather she was certain he would have told her about them.

Taylor had requested criminal histories on Friday, March 10. When he came to work Monday morning, he had received a response. One of Chris's friends at college, James B. Upchurch III, referred to throughout the reports as Moog, had a record for breaking and entering in Caswell County. That caught Taylor's attention. A person who had broken into one house likely wouldn't have qualms about breaking into another. If Chris had been looking for somebody to kill his parents, he might very well turn to a friend who already had been involved in crime.

Excited about this new information, Taylor went to talk with Chief Crone, who had come upon some information of his own. In his youth, Crone had been fascinated by strategy games, especially military games that he played with his father. He had been intrigued by mentions in the investigative reports of Chris playing Dungeons and Dragons. He knew nothing about the game, and neither did anybody else in the department. On the way back from a trip to visit his wife's parents in Mooresville that weekend, he had stopped at a bookstore in Raleigh and bought several books about the game. His wife read one of the introductory books to him aloud as he drove on home. The more she read the more excited Crone became. The beginners' adventure described in the book was practically an outline for the Von Stein murder, the players being sent to a castle to kill the overlord and obtain his treasure, which they later would divide. The players carried weapons and supplies in a knapsack. There even was a young woman named Elena asleep in another room in the castle, and Crone couldn't help but think how close the names Elena and Angela were. Crone noted that players even got extra points for multiple hits, and Lieth certainly had been hit and stabbed many times.

Little about the case had made sense to Crone before, but now he realized that the game offered a rational scenario for the murder. Perhaps Chris and his friends had become so obsessed with the game that they were enacting it in real life.

"My mind was racing," Crone recalled later. "She'd read a paragraph and I'd say, 'Underline that right there.' I was so excited I didn't even remember driving back."

Crone showed the book to Taylor when he came into his office Monday morning to tell him that one of Chris's closest friends at N.C. State had a criminal record. Taylor thought the chief's theory of the murder as a Dungeons and Dragons game acted out was interesting and should be pursued, but he didn't share his enthusiasm. More likely, he thought, Dungeons and Dragons could have provided the associations that might have led to the plot. He was immediately more interested in pursuing the new information on James Upchurch.

He called the Caswell County Sheriff's Department and talked with a detective who told him about the break-ins in which Upchurch had been involved in high school. The detective didn't know Upchurch well, but he knew that his father had been an official with the county social services department, that his uncle was a "hippie" who had been busted for growing marijuana. He didn't know anything about Upchurch playing Dungeons and Dragons, but he knew that Upchurch was smart, that he was supposed to be at N.C. State, and that he was still on probation for the break-ins.

Taylor called the probation office in Wake County, learned that Christy Newsom was Upchurch's probation officer, and spoke with her. Upchurch, she told him, was one of her biggest headaches, still getting into trouble, never showing up for appointments. She hadn't seen him in months, she said, but she was looking for him. She had three outstanding warrants on him for probation violations.

Now Taylor was even more intrigued. He wanted to talk with James Upchurch, but he knew he would have to find him first. After talking with Newsom, he called back the detective in Caswell County to tell him about the warrants. "If he shows up over there," Taylor said, "nail him, and call me."

Taylor also called the FBI and arranged to have Upchurch's fingerprints compared to prints found in the Von Stein house. And he began trying by telephone to locate other of Chris's friends mentioned in the reports, some not fully identified, so that he could arrange to talk with them. Perhaps one of them could lead him to Upchurch.

He also made several calls to N.C. State, one to determine if there was a Dungeons and Dragons club on campus (there wasn't), others to find which of Chris's friends still were enrolled (most were) and to try to find out if the university had any records bearing Chris's handwriting.

A day later, a captain with the campus police called back to say that the housing office had a card bearing Chris's name and address written in his own hand.

Chief Crone was pleased when Taylor told him about this. With that card, the word "Lawson" could be compared with the same word on the map. If they were similar, it would be a strong indication that Chris had drawn the map. Taylor was wary of this as hard evidence. His experience with the SBI lab on handwriting analysis told him that the lab liked to see lots of samples before coming to conclusions. One word would hardly suffice, he thought.

Despite his misgivings, Taylor went to talk with District Attorney Mitchell Norton about getting a subpoena for the card, primarily to appease the chief, and Mitchell issued it.

But before Taylor could go to Raleigh to take a look at the card, he had to take care of another matter. He wanted to meet Bonnie Von Stein.

Taylor had found out the day before that Bonnie was in the area. He had gone to talk with Bonnie's close friend and across-the-street neighbor, Peggy Smith, primarily to see if she could remember anything more about Chris's actions following the murder. Peggy told him that Bonnie had been in Washington just the day before to take care of some personal business, had spent the afternoon in the Von Stein house. She and Bonnie had had a long talk.

Bonnie had tried to call Lewis Young recently, Peggy Smith said, but was told that he would be away for several weeks. Bonnie expected to be able to see the investigative file on the case the next time she came to Washington, Peggy said. Bonnie also had compiled a list of suspects. Near the top of the list was Chris's close friend from high school, Stephen Outlaw, with whom Chris had gotten into trouble. He was the only one of Chris's friends, Bonnie said, that she always felt leery about.

Peggy knew that the police were suspicious of Chris. She told Taylor that she was at the hospital when Chris arrived there on the morning of the murder. She met Chris in the hallway outside his mother's room, and he asked her to wait for him because he might need a ride. He went into his mother's room, she said, stayed a few minutes, and when he came out she went over and hugged him. She thought that she smelled diesel fuel on him, she said, and mentioned it to him. He told her that he'd had a rough morning and hadn't had time for a shower. Peggy gave him a ride to Smallwood. On the way, she said, he quizzed her about what his mother had said about the attack. Peggy told him everything Bonnie had told her. When she said Bonnie had described the shadowy attacker as young and strong, Chris responded, "You mean it could have been one of my best friends?"

Peggy thought that was a curious thing for him to say, and so did John Taylor.

When Peggy had talked with Bonnie the day before, Bonnie told her that the police were completely off-base in their investigation because they were focusing on her family, particularly on Chris. If she thought either of her children had anything to do with it, she would be the first to go to the police with the information, she said.

Taylor knew that Bonnie soon would know that he had come to talk with Peggy Smith. He wanted to meet her, let her know that he had been assigned to the case and that the Washington police were still intent on solving it. He drove to Greenville, where she was staying at a motel, to meet her and Angela. He had no intention of conducting an interview. This was just to be a get-acquainted session. He wanted to find out how he could reach her, and he wanted to leave his business card with her and let her know that she could call him at any time. He took no notes, but he did form some impressions.

"She seemed like a nice, sweet lady," he said later. "She seemed concerned. She seemed genuinely interested in finding out who killed her husband."

Taylor left the meeting with another question answered in his mind. "I just didn't think she was involved in it," he said.

On Thursday, March 16, Taylor drove to Raleigh armed with the subpoena to see the document bearing Chris's handwriting. He went first to the campus police department, and Captain Laura Reynolds took him to the Department of Housing and Residence Life. An official brought out the document. Taylor handed him the subpoena. The official handed him the card and turned to leave.

"Do I keep this?" Taylor asked. The subpoena only gave him authority to see it.

"Yes, if you've got a subpoena, keep it," the official told him.

Taylor took the card back to Capt. Reynolds's office and fetched the photograph of the burned map from his briefcase. He and Reynolds sat down to compare the two, and a smile began to spread across Taylor's face. "Lawson" on the card looked identical to "Lawson" on the map.

"Looks like you've got your man," Captain Reynolds said.

"The son-of-bitch drew the map," Taylor said to himself in amazement. "He drew the damn map."

It was after dark when Taylor did get back to Washington. He drove straight to the chief's house. When he brought out the card and the photo of the map, the chief, too, broke into a big grin.

Now their suspicions had been confirmed. Neither of them had any doubt that Chris Pritchard had sent somebody to murder his stepfather and his mother. And John Taylor had a good idea of who that might have been.

31

THE SBI HAD BEEN PART OF the Von Stein murder investigation from the beginning, and John Crone knew that he would have to involve the agency in the renewed effort. The district attorney's office would see to that. Crone's first few months in office had told him that the district attorney's office essentially viewed the Washington police "as a bunch of dummies," new chief or not, and had little confidence that the department could solve the case alone. So after conferring with City Manager Bruce Radford, who still was requiring regular reports on the case, Crone put in a request for help from the SBI.

The agency responded not only by freeing Lewis Young to work on the case again, but by assigning three agents from its special Murder Unsolved Team to help when needed. A strategy session was set between the agents and the Washington police for Monday morning, March 20.

Crone and Taylor filled in the agents on the progress of the case. Crone also brought up his Dungeons and Dragons theory. He could tell that the SBI agents were skeptical about it, but he let them know that he planned to pursue it anyway.

The primary purpose of the meeting was to plan an

immediate strategy. The almost identical handwriting on the map and Chris's housing card clearly made Chris and his friends the focus of the investigation, even if it wasn't solid evidence. More samples needed to be compared, but the officers didn't want to go to Chris or Bonnie asking for handwriting samples, because that would let Chris know that they had the map, one of the few key facts in the case that they had been able to keep secret. If, however, they could use some ruse to get Chris to draw a map of Smallwood, that would strengthen their hand.

Having new officers assigned to the case gave them a plausible reason to try that. A new officer could tell Bonnie and Chris that he wanted them to go over their entire stories once more so that he could become acquainted firsthand with the case. Not being familiar with Washington and the Smallwood subdivision, he could, presumably, ask Chris to draw a map of Smallwood without arousing suspicion.

SBI Agent Terry Newell, a member of the Murder Unsolved Team, was assigned that task. He called Bonnie and arranged the interviews for two days later. Chris worked at a tire store until 7 P.M., and Newell and Agent Tom Sturgill arranged to meet him at the sheriff's department at eight-fifteen, after he'd had a chance to clean up and have supper.

Chris repeated the story he earlier had told Hope and Young, this time adding a bit more detail. He told of going home on the weekend of the murder and returning to campus the following day. On Sunday, the day before the murder, he said, he and his roommate, Chuck Jackson, his friends Moog and Brew, and two girls named Sandra and Sybil (he didn't know their last names) went out to eat and drink beer. After they returned to the dorm, he said, Chuck and Moog went off to study and he and Brew went to Sybil's room to play cards.

Asked how Chuck and Moog could study after drinking beer, Chris said that they didn't drink that much, but he noted that this was one of the few times he could recall Moog studying.

He and Brew didn't leave Sybil's room until after three, he said, when he went to his own room and to bed. When his sister called about five, he tried to find his car keys but couldn't. He went to his car, thinking he might have left his keys inside, but found the car locked. The car only could be locked with the key, so he knew that the keys weren't inside. He returned to his room to search some more, he said, but still couldn't find them. He then went for a walk to try to decide what to do, saw the call box, and summoned the campus police. Chuck later found his keys in a chair in the room, Chris said.

Sandra Goodman and Sybil Cook had told John Taylor that when they had returned to the campus with beer they had bought on the night before the murder, Chris had done something that he hadn't done before. He parked in an isolated lot about a quarter of a mile from the dorm, when plenty of spaces were available in the dorm lot where he usually parked.

Why did he do that? Newell wanted to know.

Because there was a big light there, Chris replied, and his car had been broken into and his radio stolen on a trip to South Carolina a few weeks earlier.

This didn't make sense. Why would he suddenly begin parking in a different spot three weeks after his radio was stolen? But Newell chose not to press Chris on it and risk alienating him.

Chris said that after the campus police took him to Washington, he ran into his mother's neighbor, Peggy Smith, at the hospital, and she had given him a ride to Donna Brady's house in Smallwood.

This gave Newell a chance to ask about the comment Chris had made to Peggy Smith that morning about the possible identity of the killer: "Do you mean it could have been one of my best friends?"

Did he say it?

Chris acknowledged that he did.

What did he mean by that?

He only meant that whoever did it must have been familiar with the inside of the house, he said, and the only people he could think of who fit the description and would have known the layout of the house were his friends in Washington.

Had any of his friends from State been inside his house?

Yes, Chuck Jackson had been once or twice. And Brew Simpson once.

How about Moog? Newell asked.

Never.

What was Smallwood like? Newell wanted to know. Chris said that it was a "real nice" section. All the houses were nice, and every house had a lot of about an acre. But the houses were bigger and nicer in the back part of the subdivision, where the rich people lived. His family lived in the front part.

Would Chris mind drawing a map of the subdivision, so the detectives could see just where his house was situated? Chris said he'd be happy to. The detectives tried not to smile as Chris sketched out the map, twice scribbling "Lawson" on the line representing the street where he drew the little block indicating his house.

The mission accomplished, the detectives still had to ask the obligatory questions. How did he get along with Lieth? No real problems. Was there any trouble between his real father and Lieth? None that Chris knew about. What if his mother had died and Chris and Angela had ended up inheriting Lieth's money and his real father had come to him asking for money, would Chris have given it to him? Probably so. Who did he think might have killed Lieth? Maybe somebody in the trust department at the bank.

Asked about his current situation, Chris said that he had a new car, an '87 Volkswagen GTI that he was paying for himself, that he had met a girl from High Point who was a student at Appalachian State University in Boone, and he drove there to see her most weekends. He had no intention of returning to N.C. State, he said, but he might go to Appalachian in the fall.

"They've got a great business school," he said, "and I'm planning on getting an M.B.A."

Brew Simpson was still in his underwear when he answered the knock at his mother's apartment door on Thursday, March 23, and found John Taylor and Lewis Young standing there. They were investigating the murder of the stepfather of his friend, Chris Pritchard, they told him, and wanted to ask a few questions. Brew appeared nervous as he invited them in.

He'd known Chris since the first semester of Chris's freshman year, he said. He'd met him through Chuck Jackson, who had become a friend of one of his high school friends who had gone to State. They'd all played D&D together. Brew said that he'd been playing D&D since he was in seventh grade and all of his friends had started playing before they got to college. They'd started playing more regularly during the summer session, he said, after they met a guy named Moog, who posted a notice on the bulletin board for D&D players.

Then they'd played maybe every other day for four or five hours at a time.

Brew named the other players, some of whose last names he didn't know, but he was closest he said to Chris and Moog. All three had become good friends. And he even had roomed with Moog for about a month the previous fall. He described Chris as "a sweetheart, a real nice guy, but easily led." He said that Chris could be led by Moog, whom he described as "real friendly" and "a near genius."

"All Moog is interested in is partying," he said.

Both Chris and Moog used acid and other drugs, he said. Chris had started using marijuana and acid heavily last summer, he said, and he'd tried to get him to stop on several occasions, but without success. "Moog is worse about drugs than Chris is, though," he added.

He couldn't picture Chris being involved in the murder. He never spoke badly of his parents, Brew said, and he had the impression that Chris loved his parents very much. He'd heard him tell his mother and Lieth that he loved them when he talked with them on the telephone.

Asked about the weekend of the murder, Brew said he'd gone to Chris's room on Sunday night after he got off work, arriving about nine-thirty. Chuck, Chris, Sandra, and Sybil were there, he said, and they went to Sybil's room to play cards and drink beer.

"What about Moog?" Taylor asked.

He didn't remember seeing him, Brew said, but that wasn't unusual.

Taylor made special note of that. When he had talked with Sandra and Sybil separately the week before, neither had remembered seeing Moog that night. He thought that he knew where Moog was: on his way to Washington.

On the other hand, Brew didn't remember Sybil asking several times that night that they stop playing cards, as she had told Taylor, but he did recall that they played much later than usual, leaving after three. He went home and to bed, only to have Chuck call him about seven to tell him that something awful had happened to Chris's parents. Chris didn't talk much about the murder afterward, he said, but Chris did tell him that the campus police had taken him home that morning because he couldn't find his car keys.

"Sounds kind of suspicious, doesn't it?" he added, as if the thought had just occurred to him for the first time.

Taylor and Young climbed three flights up the rusty steel steps at the back of an old red brick apartment building on Hillsborough Street near the campus of N.C. State. A young woman answered their knock and left them standing in the rain while she went to fetch Hank. They waited several minutes before Hank peered around the edge of the door, looking extremely edgy, his long, bleached hair unkempt.

"You mind if we come in?" Young asked.

"We can talk here," Hank said.

The detectives' patience was wearing thin. "Look, man, it's raining," Taylor said. "We're not going to cause you any trouble. We're not going to search your house. We just want to ask you a few questions about Chris Pritchard."

Hank grudgingly let them inside the door, but not far beyond it. Taylor and Young stood in the kitchen to ask their questions, which Hank clearly didn't want to answer.

He'd met Chris at the restaurant where he worked, Hank said, and they had gotten drunk together a lot. He hadn't seen Chris since the previous fall, however.

Had Chris ever talked to him about the murder of his stepfather?

"He keeps switching his stories about it," Hank said. Once he'd told him that his parents came home and surprised a burglar. Another time, Chris told him that a burglar had broken in, raped his mother, and killed his stepfather.

Had Chris ever spoken ill of his family? Not to him, Hank said. He always spoke about his mother and stepfather as if he loved them.

Did Chris ever talk about his family having money?

He once had said that his family owned thirty-five percent of all of R. J. Reynolds stock, Hank said, but Angela had told him that it actually was only thirty-two percent.

Chris always took care of his friends, Hank noted, always bought expensive beer for them.

Did he know Chuck, Brew, and Moog?

"Yeah," Hank acknowledged.

Had he seen them recently?

Yes, he said, but only in passing on the street.

Did he know where Moog might be?

He'd heard that he was working somewhere on campus, maybe in microfilm. He wasn't sure.

The detectives couldn't resist letting Hank know one bit of information in their possession.

"We told him that we had information that he was supplying the acid for Chris and his friends," Taylor recalled later with a laugh. "He was just flabbergasted. He didn't do that type of thing and had never heard of Chris being involved with acid."

Taylor and Young still had lots of questions that they wanted to ask Moog, but they realized that their chances of finding him on their own were slim. Their best hope lay in Christy Newsom, Moog's spunky probation officer, who knew his friends, his habits, his hangouts, even if she hadn't been able to find him herself in months. Earlier that day, they had gone to her office to meet her for the first time.

Everybody had been formal and businesslike. Christy told them that Moog had last been seen at the restaurant where Hank worked, a place he went often. She offered his last address, where he had lived with Brew months earlier, his parents' addresses and phone numbers, some of his mother's telephone records showing calls he had charged to her number.

When Taylor first had called Christy, he had told her only that he wanted to talk with Moog because he was a friend of a suspect in a murder case. Now Christy suspected that it was more than that. Her suspicions were confirmed when Young asked, "Do you think he's capable of murder?"

Without hesitation she answered, "Yes." It was something she had thought for a long time. After her third meeting with Bart she had gone to her supervisor and told him that she had an eerie feeling about him. "He just looked like the type who could kill somebody and laugh while he was doing it," she recalled later. "He just had that look in his eye."

Now she was wondering if he had, indeed, killed somebody. She also was wondering about the two detectives who wanted to talk to him.

Taylor remained silent throughout their meeting, and she couldn't help but wonder if the silence was a mask to disguise that he was just another less-than-bright country boy cop, feeling squirmish in his Sunday clothes. Young had been smooth and professional, as SBI agents usually were (she was married to an ex-SBI agent), but she could tell that he was the kind of person who would wear a suit to a tractor pull or a pig picking. "He had 'cop' written all over him," she said later. How these two would be able to infiltrate the underground around N.C. State and pluck out a long-haired, acid-dropping, D&D-playing character called Moog, she couldn't imagine.

"When they left," she recalled later, "I said to myself, 'That boy will never be caught.' "

32

ON THURSDAY, MARCH 30, John Taylor called the FBI lab in Washington, D.C., to find out how the map that SBI agent Terry Newell had gotten Chris to draw compared to the map found in the fire. The handwriting analyst who had examined both declared them a match. He was certain that both had been drawn by the same person.

Flush with excitement, Taylor took the news to the chief and called Lewis Young to tell him about it. They finally had solid evidence that could be used to put Chris behind bars. All they needed now was to find who had used the map to locate the house at 110 Lawson Road and kill Lieth Von Stein.

And they were all but certain that it was James Bartlett Upchurch III, otherwise known as Moog.

They knew that Moog was among Chris's closest friends. They also knew that the two were bound by drugs and Dungeons and Dragons, an unholy alliance, and that they influenced one another. Of Chris's closest friends at college, Moog was the only one with a criminal record, making him, in their eyes, the one to whom Chris most likely would turn for a partner in murder. Moreover, Moog had never been to Chris's house. Chuck had been there. Brew had been there. But Moog would need a map.

When Crone, Taylor, and Young next sat down for a

strategy session, their plan was simple: find Moog and see what he had to say. If he refused to talk, that would at least be an indication that they were on the right track. Even if he lied, they still would have something to work with, a framework that could be used to trap him.

Christy Newsom was seething about Bart. A perfectionist who could not abide things out of order, she took it personally when any of her probationers absconded. But Bart galled her more deeply than any other, because she knew how much he enjoyed outsmarting her. "He was driving me crazy," she said. She blamed him partly for the ulcers in her stomach. But she was determined to find Bart and keep her promise of sending him to jail. She had spent so much time looking for him that her supervisor had suggested that she needed to back off, but she couldn't.

"I've never done anything in moderation," she said. "I can't do it."

Her chance to go all-out in her hunt came in early April when John Taylor called, officially requesting her assistance in finding Moog.

"John couldn't believe I was so willing to help," she said later.

But before she agreed, she put pressure on Taylor to tell her exactly what she was getting into. Taylor and Young had been chary with information, telling her only that they wanted to talk with Moog because he was a friend of Chris's, their primary suspect.

"Listen," she said. "Y'all are not after him just because he's a friend of a possible suspect. What's going on? Y'all want me to take my time, at least let me know what we're dealing with here."

Taylor filled her in on the details of the case, confirming what she already suspected: that the detectives thought that Moog may have been the actual killer. The information gave Christy an even greater sense of mission in her search for him.

Christy oversaw a group of more than 180 probationers, many of whom moved through the underworld of drug dealers, bikers, punk rockers, satanists, street poets, and assorted other characters who congregated in the cafes, fast-food joints, bars, and dives that nestled around the campus of N.C. State. Among them Christy had developed informers, several of whom regularly fed her information about Bart and other miscreant probationers.

Several times her informers' information about Bart had been correct. She had missed him only by minutes on a couple of occasions. In recent weeks, though, she had been told first that Bart had dyed his hair pink, then that he had dyed it black and wrapped it into a spike on top. She didn't know what to believe, and she and Taylor had no idea how he might look.

Probably not like the photo that Taylor had had printed up in large quantity.

Two weeks earlier, he had driven to Caswell County to get the mug shot that had been taken of Bart when he had been arrested in high school. Taylor planned to pass the mug shots around to cops and others who might be inclined to help in the search.

Christy was certain that one place that Bart still went regularly was the restaurant where Hank worked, although she never had been able to catch him there. On an earlier trip to Raleigh, Taylor and Lewis Young had staked out the place—two guys in suits in a conspicuous SBI car—but within fifteen minutes, customers had started pointing at them and smiling and they had given up and moved on.

Now the restaurant was the first place that Christy took Taylor. They were still calling one another Detective Taylor and Mrs. Newsom at this point, but by the end of the day they not only would be calling one another John and Christy, they would be arguing, as Christy later put it, "like brother and sister."

Both were still in their twenties, young enough to pass as college students, and that was what they hoped to do. They were dressed accordingly, in jeans and sweatshirts, but they were riding in a dark blue, '87 Chevrolet Caprice unmarked Washington police cruiser that had been wrecked four times, John's favorite car.

"You've got to get rid of this police car," Christy said.

"Yeah, it's pretty dumb, uh?" John replied with a little grin.

They spent a slow couple of hours parked at the back of the restaurant, chatting, trying to pass themselves off as a couple, keeping a close eye out for Moog. When they had been there long enough for people to begin to get suspicious, they slipped into a nearby building and found a viewing spot at a second-floor window where they could watch all entrances of the restaurant. There they remained until after dark without ever getting a glimpse of Moog.

Christy's informants had supplied her with the names of several bars where Moog was supposed to hang out. One was on Hillsborough Street, a place that attracted bikers. A sign at the front door proclaimed: "No violence; no weapons; no drugs; no dogs; no bad attitudes." The bar had a big plate-glass window in front, and John and Christy had driven by several times, but they couldn't see inside well enough to pick out faces in the crowd.

Christy wanted to go in. John was reluctant. Raleigh police officers had warned him about the place: Don't go in alone. No matter how he was dressed, he knew he never could be inconspicuous amidst a swarm of grungy guys with long hair, beards, tattoos, leather jackets, and motorcycle gang colors.

"Are you crazy?" he said. "I'll get my ass stomped."

"Don't worry about it," she replied. "I've got the bartender's husband on probation."

They pulled up to the back of the place, where a squadron of Harley-Davidsons stood in formation. John parked the cruiser behind a dumpster, hoping to keep it out of sight.

"Now, Christy, I'm going to go in here with you," John said, "but you're going to go straight to the bar, and you're going to find this woman you're talking about. You're going to show her the picture and ask her right quick if she knows him. Right?"

"Okay."

"Now, listen," John persisted. "I'm not staying in there any half-hour. I ain't shooting any pool or none of this other shit. We're going in there and coming right back out, right?"

"Right."

The sea of black leather jackets at the back door parted as John followed Christy through it. Later, John would recall feeling that he was in a scene from a movie. Wherever he and Christy moved, silence fell, pool balls quit clacking. All eyes turned to the intruders.

A giant loomed ahead of them, nearly seven feet tall, weighing more than 350 pounds. Suddenly, John heard his companion, five-feet-two and 116 pounds, barking, "Hey, I want to talk to you."

"I'm thinking, shit, I reckon," John recalled later.

The giant turned and smiled. "Yes, ma'am," he said, as sweetly as a teddy bear.

In following days, John and Christy made the rounds again and again, driving back and forth on Hillsborough Street, day and night, checking the bars, the fast-food joints, the record stores, the game shop where Dungeons and Dragons materials were sold. They prowled the N.C. State campus, passed out photos of Moog to campus police, as well as to Raleigh police who patrolled in the area. They stopped people on the street and showed them the photo. Time and again, they called on Moog's friends, just to let them know that they were around and weren't going to quit until they found him, sometimes separating to make these calls.

John went so many times to see Chuck Jackson that Jackson developed an "Oh, it's you again" look. Jackson had been cooperative, but his memory had been poor. He couldn't remember much about the weekend of the murder. Taylor had the feeling that he didn't want to remember much, probably to keep from getting his friends in trouble.

On one occasion, when Christy climbed the rickety staircase to Hank's third-floor apartment, a young woman answered the door and let her inside, saying she didn't know whether Hank was in or not. The door to his room was closed. Christy noted that a mural had been painted on the living room wall, a wizard on a dark blue background with a quarter moon and gold stars. On the door to Hank's bedroom was a note, on paper ripped from a spiral notebook, stuck to the door with a nail inserted in the narrow crack between the door and the facing.

> Hank,
> Just stopped for a second. Headed towards the
> Cellar for a while.
> The Killer

Little medieval-looking daggers were drawn on the note. Christy had seen drawings of daggers like these before—on the front door of one of Bart's apartments. Christy took down the note.

"Can I have this?" she asked the young woman who had let her in.

"It's Hank's note."

244

"Who left it?"

"I don't know. It was here when I got here."

Uncertain about taking it, Christy put the note back on the door.

After leaving the apartment, she hurried to a phone to page John. Both rushed to the Cellar, only to find no sign of Moog. When they returned to Hank's apartment, nobody answered the door.

Had Moog written the note? Did the signature mean that he was indeed the murderer they thought he might be? Did it indicate he had told Hank about his role in the murder?

When they accosted Hank about it later, he didn't know anything about a note.

Two nights after their first venture into the bikers' bar, John and Christy were driving past the place again when Christy spotted somebody inside that she thought she recognized, a young man in a punk hairdo.

"Stop," she said. "I want to talk to him."

"I'm not going to let you go in there by yourself," John said.

"What do you mean *let?*" she asked with a smile, hopping from the car.

"Is your insurance paid up?" John called after her. He parked across the street, where he sat fretting and watching through the bar's front window for signs of trouble.

"What took you so long?" he asked when she finally returned.

"I was winning at pool," she said, grinning.

John and Christy made the rounds until well after midnight before giving up each day. On some days they were joined by SBI agents. On a couple of nights, Christy recruited her closest friend to help, the two going to bars as if they were two young women on the town, hoping to spot Moog or find an acquaintance who might innocently betray his whereabouts to flirtatious questions. John waited outside in the car.

Nothing seemed to help in the search. Christy had a friend at the Employment Security Commission run a check on his social security card to see if he was working somewhere, but that proved unsuccessful. In searching for a more recent photo to show around, Christy checked on an off-chance with the City-County Bureau of Identification, where mug shots and fingerprints of area felons were kept, and discovered a photo only a few weeks old. On March 11, Bart had been arrested at Triangle Correctional Institute adjacent to Central Prison for passing marijuana to an inmate through a fence and for possession. The nameplate that he was holding in the mug shot did not say James Bartlett Upchurch III, however, but James Alan McIntyre, the name he had given upon his arrest. Before his real identity had been established, he had been released on the promise to show up for trial, a promise he didn't keep, not to Christy's surprise.

The arrest was confirmation of one thing that Christy and John suspected: that Bart was supporting himself by selling drugs.

They also knew that he still was around. One of Chuck's suitemates reported one day that Moog had been by the dorm just the day before. Confronted at the restaurant one afternoon, Hank said that he had seen Moog on the street only a few hours earlier. Both said that Moog hadn't changed his appearance. His hair was still long, still bleached. He had a scraggly beard. If other people could spot him, John and Christy kept asking themselves, why couldn't they?

Once, when an informer told Christy that Moog was staying at a certain apartment, John kept an all-night vigil outside: no Moog. Later, Christy talked the young man who lived in the apartment into letting her search inside, but she found no evidence that Moog ever had been there.

John and Christy began checking every rooming house near the campus, showing Moog's picture without success. They got a list of homeless shelters and began checking those. At the Salvation Army shelter one night they encountered a group of gay men in the parking lot who immediately recognized them as cops, despite their casual attire.

John approached the group to ask if any of them recognized Moog's photo. None did, but one smiling young man recognized the opportunity to needle a cop.

"Why don't you take her in there and come back and talk to me," he said, touching John's arm in an exaggerated, feminine gesture.

"Man, don't touch me," John muttered, walking briskly away.

"You don't like gay men?" the man asked, following along.

"Look, man," John said sternly, "don't give me any trouble. Just leave me alone."

"I don't have AIDS," the man called after him, as his friends laughed.

Christy was enjoying the scene immensely.

"He thinks you're cute, John."

"Shut up," John muttered.

The taunting gay in the parking lot was almost symbolic of the helplessness and frustration that John and Christy were beginning to feel. Both had devoted untold hours to the search for Moog, including most of their off-duty hours. Christy's supervisors had begun to complain that she was obsessed with the search and spending too little time with her other probationers. She recognized that their complaints were more than a subtle hint that she should leave Moog to the police.

Christy had applied for a job in the probation office with the new house arrest program. On April 20, she learned that she had gotten it and called John to tell him about it. The hunt for Moog had forged a close and comfortable friendship between them, and each had come to respect the other's professional abilities immensely, despite their inability to find Moog. Christy would assume her new duties in May and no longer be able to devote working hours to the hunt for Moog. But she still could work with John until then, perhaps on a curtailed basis, and afterward she would be willing to devote her off-duty hours to the hunt.

April passed, and neither John nor Christy, nor the SBI, nor the campus police, nor the Raleigh police had been able to find Moog. He had become a phantom, seemingly appearing and disappearing at will. Christy knew that he hadn't fled. She sensed that he was watching them, enjoying their frustration, laughing, mocking and taunting. For her, the capture of Moog had become a personal quest, and she vowed that she never would quit until she had kept her promise to put him in jail.

33

ON MAY 1, THE OFFICERS
involved in the Von Stein case held another strategy session.
The SBI's Murder Unsolved Team and Agent Lewis Young
had worked on the case full-time for about a week in March,
then had been pulled away by other investigations. They still
helped on the case now and then as their duties allowed, and
most were present for the strategy meeting.

John Taylor, the only detective working the case full-time,
brought the other officers up to date on his activities in recent
weeks, relating at length the frustrations of his futile search
for Moog.

The inability to locate Moog caused the group to decide
on a new strategy. They would confront Chris directly, let him
know they had evidence that he was involved in the planning
of the murder, face him down, and try to provoke a confession.

The following day, Taylor, Washington Police Chief John
Crone, SBI agents Lewis Young and Terry Newell, and Assistant District Attorney Keith Mason drove to Winston-Salem
and met SBI Agent Tom Sturgill at the Holiday Inn.

The group was in high spirits, everybody certain that Chris
would break under pressure. He would tell them who else was
involved—they had no doubt that he would be mentioning the
name Moog—and with murder warrants in hand, an all-out
manhunt for his accomplices could be launched. The case soon
would be over.

But when Young called Bonnie to try to arrange separate
interviews, the high spirits dissolved. Bonnie said that she
would be happy to come for an interview, but Chris would not.
She had retained William Osteen, a Greensboro lawyer, to
represent Chris, and he had advised Chris not to talk with any
police officers.

The officers did not have to ask who William Osteen was.
A former U.S. attorney and one-time legislative leader and
congressional candidate, he was one of North Carolina's most
esteemed criminal lawyers. Bonnie earlier had retained another
of the state's top criminal lawyers, Wade Smith, to represent

248

herself and Angela. The officers knew that no better defense team could have been assembled in North Carolina, and likely few better anywhere. Clearly, Bonnie was willing to spend the money Lieth had inherited to keep any member of her family from being connected to his murder.

The officers' spirits plummeted with the news that they would not have the opportunity to confront Chris and get the confession they expected. But Bonnie had agreed to meet with them, even though her son would not. And the officers clung to some hope that she might be swayed to their side. That hope was faint, however.

When Bonnie came to talk with the officers at seven, Young told her that they had evidence proving that Chris had taken part in planning the murder. They felt obligated to tell her that they thought she could be in danger from within her own household.

Bonnie listened coolly and politely. When she spoke it was in a calm voice. The officers simply were wrong, she said. She had no concern at all that she might be in any danger from Chris. "I *know* my son's not involved," she said. "I *know* he didn't have anything to do with it."

She said it with such conviction that Terry Newell suddenly realized what had given her such confidence.

"I know what you're talking about," he told her. "Just remember this. You get what you pay for when you buy a polygraph test."

After Bonnie left, Newell told the others, "That little son-of-a-bitch took a polygraph and passed it, and she's banking everything she's got on it."

Later, the officers discovered that was exactly the case.

The jubilant celebration the officers had expected to follow Chris's confession turned into a glum motel-room gathering in which the officers drank beer and told stories about cases with happier outcomes.

John Crone had never seen Chris, and before he left Winston-Salem, he was determined to at least get a glimpse of him, perhaps introduce himself, look him in the eye, and let him know that another master gamesman was at play, this one on the side of the law. Next morning, he drove by the tire place where Chris worked, only to discover that Chris had called to say he would be late coming in that day.

On the way back to Washington, Crone and Taylor stopped

in Raleigh to see Brew Simpson. They wanted to get the word out that they knew Chris had planned the murder and they figured that Brew would spread it.

Brew appeared surprised when told about Chris, and became noticeably edgy afterwards.

"What we want to know," Crone said, "is who Chris would have gone to to help him with the plan?"

Brew said nothing for a few moments. Finally, he spoke. "Moog would be the only one."

"Would you help us find Moog?" Crone asked.

Brew nodded.

Two days later, on Friday, Taylor drove to Raleigh again with David Sparrow, one of the first officers at the murder scene, who just had been made a detective. They photographed the steam tunnels where Chris had wandered and went to talk again with Brew, who told them about the dorm-room conversation the summer before in which somebody had suggested to Chris, "You ought to off your parents and inherit that money." Brew said he'd heard that Moog was saving up money to leave town, and he told Taylor and Sparrow the name of an apartment complex near campus where he'd heard that Moog was living.

Taylor and Sparrow checked the apartment complex without finding anybody who had heard of Moog or recognized his photograph. When they met Christy Newsom for lunch at Rock-Ola Cafe near the campus, she gave them two new criminal summonses for Moog, both for passing bad checks to a deli delivery man.

Later that afternoon, the deli owner told the detectives that Moog had written the checks for sandwiches delivered to room 235 in Tucker dorm on campus the previous semester. He had put off filing charges for about six months, but in March, when another order for subs came from that room, the delivery man recognized the young man who again wanted to pay by check and asked for identification. When the young man handed him a Virginia driver's license, he kept it and told him that he would get it back when he paid off the earlier checks. When the young man didn't come to get the license, he filed charges.

The deli owner still had the license, issued to James B.

Upchurch III at his mother's Virginia Beach address, and he gave it to Taylor.

Taylor and Sparrow went to room 235 in Tucker dorm only to find it unoccupied. Classes for the spring semester were just ending and many students already had left for the summer.

As Taylor and Sparrow were knocking at the door, one of the dorm's resident advisers recognized them as police officers and said, "If it has to do with drugs, you've got the right room."

Shown a photo of Moog, the RA recognized him and said he'd seen him going into the room as recently as a couple of weeks ago.

Taylor got the names and addresses of the two students who had occupied the room, and on Monday morning, he and Terry Newell drove to their hometowns of Benson and Four Oaks, east of Raleigh, to interview them. Each denied knowing Moog and claimed that he'd never been in their room.

Taylor was spending so much time in Raleigh that he had emptied the police department's travel budget. City Manager Bruce Radford had to raid other funds to keep the investigation going, but Radford was determined to do what it took to break the case.

Taylor was back in Raleigh the following day. He had obtained a list of the names and addresses of all students who were in Lee dorm in the summer of 1988, and Christy was going to help him check out each one, to see if anybody knew anything that could help them.

Taylor also called Brew, who told him that he'd heard Moog was now working for a painting company, but he didn't know the name of it. Moog had found out about the job from a notice on a dorm bulletin board, Brew said. Taylor went to the campus to check bulletin boards, only to find all of them had been cleaned off at semester's end.

Taylor had begun to expect that kind of thing. Nothing he did seemed to work when it came to finding Moog. He was back where he had been weeks earlier, he and Christy still riding the streets around campus, searching the now familiar spots were Moog was believed to go, checking out reported sightings and tips from informers, talking with police officers, tracking down everybody who had any association with Moog and Chris in the summer of 1988. Taylor found himself visiting with a self-proclaimed witch who was supposed to be advising

Moog but claimed she'd never heard of him, and sitting alone through another all-night stakeout outside an apartment, only to discover next morning a case of mistaken identity. In the search for Moog, frustration was proving to be the only reward.

34

Bᴀʀᴛ ᴡᴀs ᴡᴇʟʟ ᴀᴡᴀʀᴇ that the police were searching for him. He kept getting reports from friends and acquaintances who had been interviewed by John Taylor, Christy Newsom, and the SBI agents who joined the search whenever possible.

Hank told him that cops were regularly watching the restaurant where he worked, and Bart quit going there early in April. He still moved freely around the N.C. State campus and surrounding area, however, usually on foot, often by skateboard. He still had not acquired another car or gotten back his North Carolina driver's license, which had been revoked. He had become adroit at avoiding detection, always checking from windows and doors before leaving buildings to make certain nobody was watching, always fading into crowds or shadows, stepping into shrubbery or into doorways or behind buildings at the approach of police cars or other official-looking vehicles.

At the beginning of March, Bart had moved out of the apartment he had been sharing. He had not gotten along with the guy with whom he was living. The guy was a "Dead Head," a fanatical follower of a rock group called the Grateful Dead, and he frequently let other Dead Heads stay at the apartment. Bart had had disputes with them. At the same time, he had to give up the job he'd held for only a few weeks at a bar on Hillsborough Street because Christy had discovered he was working there. He had moved into a boardinghouse near Dorothea Dix Hospital but he didn't like it. It was a little too far from campus and Hillsborough Street.

Soon after Bart had moved, he had encountered Neal on the street unexpectedly. It was the first time they had seen each other since the previous summer, and they chatted for only a couple of minutes. Bart said that he might soon be looking for another place to live. He was lying low, he said, because Christy was after him again for parole violations, and this time, if she caught him, he almost certainly would have to go to jail.

By early April, when John and Christy were heating up their search for him, Bart had moved back onto campus, staying with friends in Burgaw dorm who let him sleep on the floor. As he continued to hear reports from friends who had been interviewed by police, it became apparent that they were talking to Chris's entire circle of friends, but he thought their interest in him was greater than that. If the police were suspicious of Chris, Bart figured, his friendship with Chris and his criminal history also likely made him suspect, and he was sure that the police knew about his high school break-ins and other troubles.

"You ought to think about leaving town," Hank told him, and Bart agreed, but, as usual, he was nearly broke, and he was afraid to call his parents for money, for fear that might lead the police to him.

Late in April, Bart went looking for Neal. He stopped by the apartment Neal had shared with Butch Mitchell on Ligon Street, only to discover that Neal no longer lived there. He had moved the previous fall, and Neal's and Bart's old high school friend and fellow D&D player, Quincy Blackwell, had moved in with Butch, with whom Neal had had trouble getting along. Quincy told Bart where Neal was living with two new friends in Sylvan Park Apartments on Marcom Street, only about half a mile away.

Neal had left his job at Sav-A-Center the previous fall and gone to work at Hardee's. He remained there only a couple of months before leaving after Christmas to work at Wendy's on Western Boulevard, near the campus. After breaking up with Kenyatta at the end of the summer, Neal had started seeing her again in the fall. She was finishing her senior year at the School of Science and Math in Durham, and she often came to Raleigh on weekends to be with him.

Neal's depression from the previous summer had contin-

253

ued, and Kenyatta remained concerned about it. She questioned him about it repeatedly.

"Neal, what is the matter? Why aren't you happy?"

"It's something I can't explain," he would tell her, to her immense frustration. "I can't put it in words."

Neal's mother was deeply worried about him as well. He was not going to see her or anybody else in the family. She had come at Christmastime and found him in the clutter and filth of his apartment, his skin broken out in psoriasis.

"She kept asking me, 'What's wrong?'" he recalled later. "'Nothing,' I said. 'I'm fine. Doing just great.' We had a talk about school. I tried to let her think that was what was bothering me. I may have cried a little bit. At all times, I was trying to put her mind at ease. I didn't want Mom to have to worry about me. She had enough to worry about."

Kenyatta kept trying to get Neal to talk with Weldon Slayton, but he refused. He had let Slayton and his family down, he said, and he just couldn't face them until he could prove himself worthy again.

Kenyatta had talked with Slayton about the problem. Slayton said that if Neal wanted his help, he would have to ask for it. It was not his place to interfere uninvited.

"I told Slayton, 'He's not going to come and talk to you until he's got something to show you,'" Kenyatta recalled later.

If he made manager at Wendy's, Neal told Kenyatta, he might go and see Slayton.

By the end of April, when Bart again showed up in Neal's life, that prospect seemed close at hand. Neal had worked hard at Wendy's. He was willing to work long hours and those hours that others didn't want. His coworkers liked him, his bosses liked him.

"I was finding my own sense of self-worth in the opinions of coworkers," Neal said later.

Bart told Neal that he needed a place to stay. Would Neal mind if he moved in with him for a few weeks, just until he could get a little money stored away? Neal said he would have to check with his roommates. They didn't object. Others were always sleeping on the floor amidst the clutter anyway. Neal always seemed to have a group over playing Dungeons and Dragons and other role-playing games. Neal said it would be okay, and Bart brought his few belongings and settled in shortly after the first of May. A week later, he took a job with AAA Student Painters.

Three weeks after moving in with Neal, Bart was in the kitchen making iced tea shortly after noon when he heard a knock at the front door. He went to the peephole and looked out but saw nobody. Must be the cops, he thought. Only cops would stand back where they couldn't be seen. But cops were not unusual at the door of this apartment. Officers had been brought there often by calls from neighbors complaining about the loud music that came from the stereo. Bart went to the window, peeked through the blinds, and saw a police car.

"I thought, well, they've found me," he recalled later. "Let's see if I can bluff this one out."

He opened the door.

"James Upchurch?" asked one of the two officers who were standing back from the door with hands on their holstered weapons.

"Who?" Bart asked.

"Are you James Upchurch?"

"We're looking for James Upchurch. Do you have any ID?"

A friend who had left campus early in the past semester had given Bart his meal card so that he could eat free in the campus dining hall. The photo on the card had only a slight resemblance to Bart. He went to get that and gave it to the officer.

"This your ID, Mr. Upchurch?" asked the officer.

"I'm not Upchurch," Bart quickly responded.

"Mind if we come in and have a look around?" the officer asked.

"No problem," said Bart. "Help yourself. I'm making some tea. Just go ahead and look all you want."

Bart went back to the kitchen and nonchalantly went about making tea while the officers poked around the apartment. They soon thanked him and left.

"Man, that was a close one," Bart said to one of Neal's roommates, the only other person in the apartment.

"You played it just right."

"They were snowed, weren't they," said Bart. "Wonder how they found out I was here?"

"I don't know," said the roommate.

Bart got on the phone and called Neal at Wendy's. "The police just came by to arrest me."

"Really? What happened?"

Bart described the entire incident. "I think I'm going to have to pack my bags and get down to the bus station."

"Wait until I get there," Neal said. "We'll talk about it."

As soon as Bart put the receiver back onto the telephone, another knock came at the door, this one loud and certain. When Bart opened the door this time, there was not one police car but three, not two officers but six. This time there was no question of bluffing his way out. The officers put in their reports that Bart tried to run, but he claimed later that two officers grabbed his arms and he had no chance to try to get away. They wouldn't even allow him to put on his shoes, he said. They snapped on handcuffs and led him barefoot to the backseat of one of the cars. Over the police radio, Bart heard one of the officers reporting that the subject had been apprehended, that he was wanted as a suspect in a homicide in Little Washington. All the way to the jail, Bart kept insisting that he was not James Upchurch.

John Taylor had just come back from lunch when the phone rang in the detective division of the Washington police department and a Raleigh police officer told him that James Upchurch was in the Wake County Jail, being held on probation violations. Without hanging up the receiver, Taylor dialed Christy Newsom's number in Raleigh. She knew already. The Raleigh police had called her, too. Both were laughing in jubilation. The great frustration was behind them.

"There's not any chance that he might get out before we can get up there, is there?" Taylor asked.

"I'll see that there isn't," Christy said.

Grinning broadly, Taylor went to the chief's office.

"Raleigh PD just picked up Moog," he told John Crone.

Taylor had Lewis Young paged. Young called from Kinston, where he was working on another case, and agreed to meet him in Raleigh.

Taylor arrived at the Raleigh police department headquarters at five to find Young and a Raleigh police department detective waiting for him. They drove to the jail and waited for Bart to be brought down. A court order had been arranged that would allow the officers to take Bart back to a police department interrogation room, where he could be interviewed more comfortably. Bart was wearing the orange coveralls issued to all the jail's guests.

"Man, we've been looking for you for a long time," John Taylor said.

"Yeah, I heard you wanted to talk with me," Bart said with a little grin.

Would he be willing to talk with them?

That depended, Bart said. He didn't want to talk about anything that could affect his probation. He might want to talk with a lawyer before answering certain questions, if the answers might get his probation revoked.

The officers assured him that they didn't want to hang him on probation violations. The contents of his interview would not be passed on to his probation officer. They were investigating the murder of Lieth Von Stein, they said. They wanted only to ask him about Chris.

Fine, Bart said.

Both officers were impressed at how cordial and relaxed Bart appeared to be, showing no sign of anxiety or nervousness, although he appeared thin and a bit drawn, as if he had been using a lot of drugs or under a lot of strain. They were surprised at how talkative he turned out to be.

He told of meeting Chris through the bulletin board notice and of finding Chris's room filled with marijuana smoke the first time he went there. He said that he was with Chris when Chris took his first hits of acid and cocaine and that Chris's drug use had grown progressively heavier.

"Chris was obsessed with drugs," Bart said.

He described Chris as "strange" and "eccentric," a "show-off." Chris especially loved to show off with drugs, he said. Chris would boast about having drugs and take them out in front of strangers. When he got a fresh batch of acid, he would run through the dorm telling everybody that he had it and asking if anybody wanted any.

Bart told about the trips he and Chris had made together, going into detail about their visit to Chris's relatives in South Carolina, whom he described as "real rednecks." He claimed that he spent most of his time in a motel room with a girl on that trip, while Chris went out with another girl and associated with some bad characters. Chris later told him that he'd met

257

some people that weekend "who could supply him with anything that any man could ever want," and that he was thinking about going into business with them.

Did Bart think these people Chris told him about could be capable of murder?

Probably so.

Bart told about Chris taking a group of his friends to the Golden Corral, a popular steak house near the campus, and paying for everybody's dinner, the bill coming to more than one hundred dollars. Somebody mentioned that Chris didn't make enough at his job to pick up such a tab, Bart said, and somebody else said, "Why don't you off your parents and inherit all their money?" To that, Bart said, Chris replied, "Yeah, I've thought about that a few times." Afterward, Bart said, he heard others mentioning "offing" Chris's parents to him on several occasions, but always in a joking manner.

Asked about Chris's relationship with his parents, Bart said that Chris loved his mother and liked his natural father. He didn't think Chris loved his stepfather, but they got along okay.

Did Bart think it conceivable that Chris might have hired someone to kill his parents?

"Yeah," Bart said. "It's conceivable."

He and Brew Simpson had talked about that possibility in depth after the murder, Bart said. They had agreed that Chris didn't kill his parents himself because he liked them and didn't have the guts. The only motivation they could think of for Chris to have had it done was money, but they figured Chris's stepfather was smart enough that he would have put his money into some kind of trusts so Chris wouldn't have been able to get any of it. Their theory, he said, was that Chris's real father might have had something to do with it.

Bart said that Brew had had a conversation with Angela about the murder, and Brew had come away from it saying he thought that Angela was evil, because she'd showed no emotion when talking about it.

A friend who had talked with Sandra about the night before the murder had told him that Sandra said Chris had kept looking at his watch as that night wore on, Bart said, as if Chris were concerned about staying until a certain time.

What was he doing that weekend? Young wanted to know.

Bart said he really couldn't remember. He'd been into

drugs so bad that summer that it was difficult to recall details about specific days and times. He thought he probably was in his dorm room on the eighth floor studying English the night of the murder. He thought he remembered Chris calling and asking him to come down and play spades. Sybil might have called, too—he wasn't sure—but he knew he didn't go. He didn't like spades.

Bart went on to tell about trying to keep Chris from getting acid after the murder, and about Chris's bad trip. He said that Chris had acted crazy that fall before dropping out of college, brandishing a pistol and a big knife. "He was really paranoid," Bart said. He saw Chris only a few times before Chris dropped out and hadn't seen him at all since January when Chris came back to show off his new Volkswagen. They'd talked for only a few minutes then, he said, and the murder didn't come up at all.

In talking with the man whose house Bart and his friend had broken into in high school, Taylor had learned that the group had left something behind in the house: a clublike weapon. The owner had kept it because he thought it a handy thing to have around. Taylor had asked the man to take a snapshot of it, and the man had sent it to him from California where he now was living.

Taylor showed the snapshot to Bart and asked if he recognized the weapon. He said that he didn't.

Taylor also produced an enlarged photograph of the burned knife that had been used to kill Lieth Von Stein, and asked Bart if he'd ever seen it.

"Is this lifesize?" Bart asked.

"Yes."

"No," Bart said. "I don't think I've ever seen it."

The interview had taken about two hours, and it had not accomplished what Taylor and Lewis had hoped. They hadn't expected a confession, but they had hoped to get something more solid to work with. They had been a little taken aback by Bart's openness, and they had let him go on without pressing him on certain matters out of concern that he might clam up. They thought that he was lying about some things. For example, no one in the group that gathered at the dorm with Chris on the night of the murder remembered seeing Bart that night, and no one had mentioned anybody calling him to come down. But Taylor and Young wanted Bart to say as much as he wanted to say. Maybe he would slip up and say more than he intended. That hadn't happened, but at least they now knew his position. They also knew that they weren't apt to get much out of him that would help them, and as they drove him back to the jail that night, they realized that they would have to find somebody else to give them the break that they needed in this case.

35

Bart SPENT TEN DAYS IN the Wake County Jail before being brought to district court to face charges for probation violations that Christy Newsom had filed against him.

Christy did not attend the hearing. She was now working with the house arrest program, and Bart had a new probation officer, Brian Strickland. Christy had thoroughly briefed Strickland about Bart's long record of violations and defiance so that he could plead for a prison sentence from Judge James R. Fullwood.

But the judge thought that Bart deserved another chance to straighten out his life and sentenced him to six months of house arrest. Bart would have to wear a waterproof electronic band around his ankle that would set off an alarm if he wandered more than two hundred feet from his monitor. He would have to remain at his residence—for now, Neal's apartment—whenever he was not at work or in class. A computer would randomly call the telephone at the apartment whenever Bart was supposed to be there, and he would have to answer it to confirm his presence. His voice would be recorded for the computer, which would be able to tell his voice from that of any person pretending to be him. The computer also supposedly could tell from his voice patterns whether he had been drinking or using drugs, two things he was prohibited from doing.

When Christy came to work that afternoon, she was greeted by a colleague who told her, "You're going to be in a bad mood today."

She had been certain that Bart would go to jail this time, and she was incensed about the judge's decision. Once again Bart had outsmarted her and defied her promise to put him in prison. She could just feel him smirking at her. She thought that the judge was putting herself and others in danger by giving Bart any opportunity at freedom. So angry that she could not let the matter rest, she went to see Fullwood that afternoon to try to get him to change his mind.

"If he hasn't already killed somebody, he will," she warned him.

"I can't judge him on intention," Fullwood told her. "I have to go by the facts."

He made it clear that he had no intention of reconsidering and that he didn't want to talk anymore about it. "He told me I was too spunky, but not to worry about it. When I got older, I'd calm down," Christy recalled later. "He said I'd realize I couldn't change the world. I told him, 'I'm not trying to change the world. I'm just trying to put the people in prison who need to be there.' "

To make matters worse, now that Bart was in the house arrest program, Christy once again had the frustrating and personally infuriating job of supervising him.

After Taylor and Young interviewed him in jail, Bart was certain that they were trying to entangle him in the murder of Lieth Von Stein. "I knew I was in serious shit," he recalled later. He talked to other inmates about it.

"Man, you need to leave town," said one who once had been charged with murder. "Murder trial ain't no joke."

Several others agreed.

"I decided if I ever get out, I'm going to split," Bart said. "I ain't going to let 'em pin a murder on me."

Surprisingly, after his court appearance, he was turned loose without restriction until he could be outfitted the following day with his electronic band. His inclination was to leave immediately, but he had an old problem: no money. He was due a paycheck from the painting company, but it would be a while coming. Also he wanted to see his friends, maybe even throw a big good-bye party before he took off. And he knew the cops didn't have evidence to charge him with murder or they already would have done it.

After leaving court, feeling really free for the first time in months, knowing that for now no cops were searching for him, he went first to the restaurant where Hank worked, a place he had been avoiding for more than two months. The place fell silent when he walked in.

"It was like watching a cowboy movie where the bad guy walks into the bar, everybody gets quiet, the piano quits playing," he recalled. "People's mouths dropped open. It looked like Jesus Christ had strolled through the door."

Hank wasn't working, but his stepmother was behind the counter. Bart knew her well, was always joking with her. He greeted her with a smile, sat on a stool, ordered iced tea, started making small talk, but he could tell that she was uncomfortable. She leaned over and began whispering to him.

"What are you doing here? Don't you know the police are looking for you all over? The SBI has been in here I don't know how many times."

Bart tried to assure her that he had taken care of everything, but he could tell that she wasn't sure whether to believe him and that she didn't appreciate him bringing the cops down on her place.

He took his tea and left, strolling across the campus that he had first come to not quite three years earlier for freshman orientation, letting his mind wander back over all that had happened since that innocent day.

"I was asking myself, 'Man, how did things get so fucked up?'" he later recalled. "I was telling myself, 'It's a bit more serious than I've been thinking. I've got to do something.'"

That morning, Thursday, June 1, John Crone had driven to Raleigh to meet John Taylor at the motel where he had stayed the night before. Crone and Taylor still were trying to find something to connect Moog to the murder, but they also had to follow up other possibilities.

The Negroid hair that had been found in the burned Reebok tennis shoe at the fire site where evidence had been destroyed led them to believe that Moog might have had a black accomplice. They had learned that he had one black friend, Quincy Blackwell, a high school classmate who had sometimes played Dungeons and Dragons in his group back in Caswell County. Blackwell also had come to State but had dropped out recently and was rooming with another black acquaintance of Moog's, Butch Mitchell, Neal Henderson's former roommate. Mitchell, the officers had been told, could be volatile when drinking. Moog might have turned to either for help, they thought.

Taylor had spent much of the previous day in Caswell County asking questions about Moog and Quincy. He had talked with a county detective, with Quincy's father, and with Bart's companion in his high school night of crime, Gary Hampton, but he had come away with little that was helpful. From what he had learned, Quincy was harmless. And he turned up nothing damning about Bart.

One of his purposes in talking to Hampton was to show him a photo of the knife used to kill Lieth Von Stein. The owner of the lake house that Bart, Hampton, and their friends had broken into had reported a hunting knife missing. Taylor had sent a photo of the murder knife to the house owner, who responded that it looked similar to the one taken from his house. Hampton, however, said that he didn't know a knife had been taken that night. And he'd never seen James, as he called Bart, with a knife like that. Furthermore, he said he couldn't imagine James hurting anybody. He'd never known him to have any violent tendencies.

Crone wanted to get a feel for Moog himself, and shortly before noon, he and Taylor drove to the Marcom Street apartment where Bart was now staying with Neal. Their knock was answered by Neal, who allowed them to step inside the apartment, where Bart, just freed from jail, was seated on the sofa. Another young man, a roommate who never spoke in the officers' presence, was also in the living room. All three looked as if they had just gotten up.

Crone and Taylor were taken aback by the incredible clutter. There was little furniture: the sofa, a chair, a stereo, a TV. A monstrous inflatable dinosaur occupied one section of the room. The floor appeared to be the place where most activities took place. It was littered with dozens of Dungeons and Dragons books, scores of figurines of monsters and warriors. Sleeping mats were spread about. Shed clothing lay amidst empty pizza boxes and beer cans. A computer with a keyboard and joysticks used for playing games also were on the floor.

Crone and Taylor didn't want to talk to Moog in the presence of others, and they asked if he would mind stepping outside to their car. Bart got into the front seat with Taylor. Crone sat in the back.

Taylor showed Bart the photo of the burned knife that was used to kill Lieth, telling him he thought it was the knife that had been taken from the break-in in Caswell County. Bart remembered a knife being taken but said this one wasn't it. The knife they'd taken was bigger. He hadn't kept it, he said, and didn't know who ended up with it. He already had a hunting knife and didn't need one.

The officers wanted to know more about the discussions Chris and his friends had about "offing" Chris's parents, but Bart said Chris never got serious about that and never talked about how it might actually be done.

Did he know the names of any blacks with whom Chris would have associated?

Only Quincy Blackwell and Butch Mitchell.

Were either violent?

Not Quincy, for sure. But Butch had been in fights.

Asked about Brew Simpson, Bart said he hadn't talked to him in a couple of months. Brew was "unbalanced mentally," Bart said, a former "cokehead." He believed Brew was now using cocaine again and selling it to support his habit.

As the questions continued, Bart's sometimes flippant answers and smirking smile irritated Crone and Taylor, leading them to believe that he wasn't really taking this seriously.

"You think this is a game?" Taylor asked him. "You think this is funny?"

"Have you still got those pictures, John?" Crone asked from the backseat.

"Yeah, they're in the trunk," said Taylor.

"Get 'em," Crone said.

Taylor went to the trunk. When he returned, he was carrying an eight-by-ten color photograph of Lieth Von Stein's bludgeoned and bloody body, which he held out to Bart.

"Does this look like we're playing?" Taylor asked.

Bart flinched and turned his head away.

"Man, I don't want to look at that," he said. "That ain't my business."

"Little son-of-a-bitch was about to puke," said Crone as he

and Taylor drove away a short time later, leaving Bart with what they hoped was an indelible image.

After leaving Moog, Crone and Taylor met SBI agents Lewis Young and Terry Newell and Assistant DA Keith Mason at the Rock-Ola at Mission Valley for lunch. Young, Newell, and Mason had been on another mission that morning. They had taken all of their evidence against Chris to Bonnie's Raleigh lawyer, Wade Smith. Their objective was not to try to get Smith to convince Bonnie that her son had tried to have her killed. They had given up any hope of that. They wanted to go through Smith to get word to Chris's lawyer, Bill Osteen, that they had a strong case. If Osteen knew the evidence, they reasoned, he might get the truth from Chris, and once broken, Chris might want to make a deal, come forth with his story, and reveal his accomplices. Smith had been cordial and heard them out, and Young, Newell, and Mason had no doubt that he understood their purpose.

After lunch, Taylor and Crone drove to Ligon Street to call on Quincy Blackwell and Butch Mitchell. Quincy was not there, but Butch invited them in. The apartment was much neater than the one the officers had been in earlier that day, but they took note of all the violent Japanese comic books lying around. Those, Butch said, were Quincy's. He always had his nose in one.

A blocky young man of medium height, with a broad face and thin mustache, Butch boasted that he was himself a practitioner of martial arts, particularly kung fu, and considered himself to be a good fighter. Indeed, he said, he was such a good fighter that he had to watch himself. That was why he couldn't drink or take drugs.

"When I do that I get mad and like to hurt people," he said.

Asked about his background, Butch said that his father died when he was eleven and his mother had supported the family afterward. He described his mother, an employee of a manufacturing company, as "amazingly perfect."

"She keeps me from doing bad things," he said.

Butch said that he knew Chris and Moog, although he knew Moog better. He'd played Dungeons and Dragons with both. Neal, his former roommate, also played with them, along with others now and then. He and Neal didn't get along so well anymore, he said, adding that Neal had "a mind control problem with power."

"Neal is great with strategy," he said, "but he wants money and power and there lies his problem."

Had he heard about the murder of Chris's stepfather?

He had. He'd also heard that Chris was going to get some money because of his death. Moog, he believed, had told him that.

Did he have any idea who could have been involved in the murder?

No.

How about Quincy?

"Quincy couldn't do it," he said. "Quincy doesn't have the guts." Besides, Quincy was not in the least prone to violence.

Did Butch remember any of the D&D players carrying an army knapsack?

Yes. One guy carried his D&D books in an old army bag. Butch described it as worn and faded. But he didn't know the name of the player. White boy. Had long straight hair. Parted it down the middle.

Did any of the players have a knife?

Not that Butch knew about. He wouldn't have stayed around if anybody had brandished a knife. He didn't like knives. Or guns either.

Crone wanted to know about D&D. How did Butch see the game?

"The object of D&D is to look out for number one," Butch said. "If somebody is in your way, you get them out of your way by whatever means necessary."

Did he remember being involved in any specific D&D games with Chris and Moog about the time of the murder back in July? Butch did. He was a cleric. Moog was dungeon master, as usual. Neal, as always, was a magic user. Chris was a thief, his favorite role, with a hireling fighter as a bodyguard. Another player, a resident adviser in the dorm, whose name Butch did not know, played a barbarian.

Butch said he was told that he was the lord of a castle with a great treasure that had been taken over by raiders. He was to reclaim his castle and his treasure, but the castle was well guarded and he could not take it alone. He had to hire the other players' characters to help him, promising to pay each a thousand-dollar gold piece if they were successful in their quest.

As dungeon master, Moog drew a map to the castle and sent them on their way. They went on horseback and stopped in a woods near the castle, where they found a small building covering a secret underground passage into the bedroom of the evil overlord who had seized the place. They had to pass through a trap door into the bedroom, and once there, they found the overlord asleep in bed.

Butch posted the barbarian at one side of the bed, and Chris's thief and fighter companion on the other side and gave them instructions to kill the overlord, beating and stabbing him until there could be no doubt about his death.

Crone and Taylor sat listening with growing excitement. In effect, Butch was describing the murder of Lieth Von Stein. They hardly could believe this was happening. Was this Butch's way of confessing?

With the evil overlord dead, the dungeon master told Butch that he had to cleanse the castle of all evil before he could reclaim his treasure. But in the next room, Butch and his hirelings encountered a skilled fighter of such great powers that no matter what Butch threw on the die, he and the other players could not subdue this character. They had to retreat and returned to town, where they split up the loot they had seized: only a few dollars each.

Crone and Taylor were well aware that only a small amount of money, no more than eighty dollars, had been taken from the Von Stein house.

Butch had grown more vocal and agitated as he told the story. He had been angry at Moog, he said, for creating a character of such brilliance that he couldn't be overwhelmed. And he had hated his character in the first place. He didn't believe a cleric was suited to his personality. He'd have been much better as a fighter.

Crone began questioning Butch closely about this game, getting him to go through it again, then once again. The apartment was stiflingly hot, with no air conditioner, no fan, little air stirring, the temperature well into the nineties. Butch grew more agitated as he went through the story again. His voice rose. He got up, paced the floor, gestured dramatically.

Essentially, he told the story the same each time, but on a

couple of occasions he mentioned "the folks" in the bed at the castle.

"How many were in the bed?" Crone asked on the second mention.

"Just one."

"Just the evil overlord?"

"That's it."

At another point, telling how they had left the castle after their retreat, Butch said, "We just got in the car . . . uh . . . on the horses . . . and came on back to town."

As Crone led Butch through the story a fourth time, Taylor quit taking notes. "I felt we were playing to his ego, and he would keep telling us stuff he thought we wanted to hear," Taylor said later.

As the chief kept Butch talking, Taylor grew more and more impatient. He was thirsty. He was sweating heavily. He was concerned that sweat might be staining the armpits of his good suit. He wanted out of that miserable apartment. He wanted away from Butch Mitchell and his eerie story.

Sensing Taylor's discomfort, Crone didn't take Butch through the story another time. He simply thanked him and said that they might have to come back and talk with him more later.

But when Crone and Taylor got back to the car, Crone couldn't contain his excitement. "He told us exactly what happened," he said.

If Butch were telling the truth about the D&D game, one of three things seemed evident: either Butch was at the Von Stein house on the night of the murder, or Moog had taken his dungeon members through a rehearsal of the crime, or the game was an amazing coincidence.

The chief thought that Butch must have taken part in the murder. Taylor thought it possible, but he had doubts. Chris didn't know Butch very well, and Taylor couldn't see Chris putting his trust in somebody as unstable as Butch appeared to be. Yet, he acknowledged, it was also possible that Moog had engaged Butch for the mission without Chris's knowledge.

After they had gotten cold drinks and had a chance to cool down, Crone and Taylor went back to Neal's apartment to question Moog about the D&D game Butch just had told them about.

Bart was alone at the apartment this time, and he didn't appear surprised to see them again.

Asked about Butch, Bart described him as "pigheaded and quick-tempered," violent when he was drinking, but he had stopped drinking now. Of those who had played D&D in his groups, Bart said, Butch and Chris were most fanatical about it.

He recalled the game Butch had told the officers about. It was one adventure in a high-level campaign, he said. Butch was playing a "chaotic good" character, and Chris's and Neal's characters were neutral. He liked for the characters to be on the good side, he said, because it made for a more interesting game.

He didn't remember anybody being stabbed or beaten in this particular adventure, he said. And the evil overlord wasn't in bed either. He had heard the invaders coming and had gotten up and assembled his fighters to repel them.

Having nailed down Bart's version of the game, Crone asked if any of the players carried their D&D materials in a book bag. The only one Moog recalled was Neal. He described his bag as cream-colored and old.

Did he know any acquaintances of Chris, other than Butch, who might have weapons or violent tendencies? Bart told about one friend who kept a club in his car and boasted of beating people in high school. He remembered a friend of Butch's who, he said, was crazy and liked to dress up in ninja outfits. This guy had rappelled off one of the top floors of Lee dorm and had climbed through the ductwork to get into a girl's dorm room. He also once had his girlfriend do a striptease for Bart in a dorm room, then threatened to kill him if he ever told anybody about it. Bart also gave the officers the name of a student who he claimed had sold cocaine to Chris. This student, Bart said, kept an AK-47 assault rifle, a compound crossbow, and a crossbow pistol in his dorm room.

Crone and Taylor left wondering if many parents had any idea of what their children were doing when they sent them off to college these days.

They had one more stop that they wanted to make before they called it quits this Friday night and had to face the long drive back to Washington. They wanted to have another chat with Brew Simpson. But this proved to be a bust. He couldn't recall anybody having a green army book bag, didn't remember anything about Butch's adventure in the D&D game, although he did recall Butch's character being killed at some point. And he didn't think he'd ever discussed with anybody the possibility of Chris being involved in his stepfather's murder.

Crone and Taylor discussed the day's events as they drove home that night. Both thought they had made a lot of progress. Because of the D&D adventure he had told them about, Butch had to be considered a suspect. Moog's confirmation made them certain that such an adventure had taken place, and they figured that Butch was more apt to be telling the truth about it than Moog, who made a point of denying that a beating and stabbing in a bed had taken place. Crone was more convinced than ever that his original theory was sound. The murder of Lieth Von Stein was a Dungeons and Dragons adventure come true.

36

THE GREEN ARMY KNAP-sack that had been found on the enclosed back porch of the Von Stein house on the morning of the murder was John Taylor's next thread of hope for a solution to his perplexing case.

On Friday, June 2, he and David Sparrow, the newly appointed detective, drove to Raleigh with the bag, hoping to find somebody who recognized it. Their plan was to confront every person who knew Chris and Moog, tell them where the bag was found and when, let them know that whoever owned it likely was a murderer. Maybe somebody would remember it and connect it to the owner.

Butch Mitchell, the first person to be shown the bag, was pretty sure that he recognized it. It belonged either to Chris or to the white guy with straight blond hair he had mentioned earlier. Whichever had it kept D&D books in it. He recalled the bag because he remembered asking where he could get one like it.

Bart and Neal claimed they'd never seen the bag, as did Brew, who was concerned about the tone of Chief John Crone's questions to him the night before. He thought the questions implied the chief's belief that he was a drug user. He was willing to take a urine test to prove otherwise, he said. Not necessary, Taylor told him. Don't worry about it. By the way, did he have a picture of himself that Taylor might borrow? Brew gave him an expired driver's license.

Sandra Goodman and Sybil Cook didn't remember the bag. Neither did Quincy Blackwell, who said that he just couldn't believe that James or Neal could have had anything to do with a murder. While talking with Quincy, Taylor showed his roommate, Butch, the expired license Brew had given him earlier. Was he the person who might have owned the bag? No, said Butch, not him.

Before leaving Raleigh, Taylor and Sparrow dropped by Neal's apartment to question Neal and Moog again about the bag. Were they certain they'd never seen it? Both were. When Taylor told them that Butch remembered the bag, Neal said that Butch was not to be trusted.

"He's a psychotic son-of-a-bitch," Neal said.

Taylor wanted to make sure that he had impressed the importance of the bag on Moog. If Moog was involved in the murder, he would have to be concerned that somebody might recognize the bag and tie it either to Chris or himself. As he drove home that night, however, Taylor found it strange that the only person who claimed to recognize the bag was Butch, who had made himself one of the suspects with his strange tale of the D&D game. Surely if Butch had been involved, he wouldn't have wanted the police to know that he knew anybody connected with the bag.

When he arrived at home late that night, Taylor found a message on his answering machine from Sandra Goodman, asking that he call. Because it was late, he waited until the next day to call. She and Sybil had talked after he'd shown them the knapsack, she said, and their memories had been jogged. Both were fairly certain that they had seen the bag in Chris and Chuck's room, filled with D&D books.

Taylor returned to Raleigh alone with the bag on Monday to show it to any student he could find who had been in Lee dorm during the previous summer sessions. A couple thought they might have seen it before but didn't know to whom it belonged.

When Taylor took Brew's driver's license back to him, Brew now said that he, too, had been thinking about the bag and it did seem familiar, but he just couldn't recall who might have had a bag like that.

Sandra Goodman took Taylor to the isolated lot where Chris had parked his car when he, Sandra, Sybil, and Chuck returned from buying beer on the night of the murder. She had thought it strange that he had parked so far from the dorm that night, and Chris wouldn't tell them why.

Taylor thought he knew why Chris had parked in this spot: so it would be easier for whoever was to drive his car to Washington that night to get to it without being seen. He knew from all of his interviews with Chris's friends that Chris was highly particular about his car and that it took an unusual circumstance for him to let anybody else drive it. But murder, he knew, was among the most unusual of circumstances.

Christy Newsom was on her way out of the office to lunch on Tuesday, June 6, when the computer began making one of its random calls to a detainee under the house arrest program. She immediately recognized the case number of James Upchurch, her most troublesome client, when it popped onto the screen. Always wary when it came to Bart, she paused to listen to the call. Nobody answered. She knew that that likely meant only one thing: Bart had run, just as she knew he would.

Forgetting lunch, she called for a colleague, and the pair rushed to Neal's apartment.

Neal answered the door looking bleary-eyed, wearing red running shorts with an N.C. State Wolfpack emblem on the side. He seemed nervous.

"Where's James?" Christy demanded.

"I don't know," Neal replied. "He just left. He didn't say anything to any of us."

"I want to come in and have a look," Christy said, and Neal stood back and invited her in.

The apartment was dark, all the blinds pulled at midday. At least four people were asleep on the apartment floors, one with the mattress on top of him. None bothered to stir as Christy threaded her way through bodies and garbage and debris. She found Bart's leg band, neatly severed, lying atop the receiver, where it was still busy confirming that he had not strayed.

"I know you know where he is," Christy told Neal.

"No, I don't."

"You know I can have you charged with obstruction of justice if I find out you're lying to me."

"I don't know, honest," Neal persisted.

Despite her limited experience with Neal, Christy knew that he would cover for Bart. He would try to protect anybody who befriended him, she thought, but more than likely he was afraid of Bart. She realized, too, that Neal was weak and that she could pressure him. Her intensity prompted Neal to suggest that perhaps Bart had gone to Virginia, where his mother lived. He'd found two unused Greyhound bus tickets in the apartment, he said, and he was sure that they belonged to Bart.

Neal fetched the tickets for Christy. One, bought on May 13, was one-way from Richmond to Williamsburg. The other, bought the following day, was one-way from Raleigh to Richmond.

Why would Bart buy a ticket from Richmond to Williamsburg before buying one from Raleigh to Richmond? And why didn't he take them when he fled? Neal had no answers.

Christy and her colleague cut through the campus of N.C. State, searching everywhere. No sign of Moog. They went to the sandwich shop where Hank worked. Hank was off. Nobody had seen Moog. They went to Hank's apartment. No answer. Finally, they returned, dejected, to the office, where Christy notified her superiors and the police—and called John Taylor in Washington.

"Guess what?" she said, remembering all those long hours she and Taylor had searched vainly for Moog.

"Don't tell me."

"You got it."

"Son-of-a-bitch," Taylor exclaimed.

Taylor went immediately to tell Crone of this not altogether unexpected development. In one way, it was discouraging. Moog was once again out of their reach, perhaps already hundreds of miles away. But in another way, it was a cinching factor. No doubt about it, Moog was their man. Earlier, he could claim that he had been on the lam because of fears of prison from his probation violations. But the probation violations had been cleared, allowing him to avoid prison. Now the situation was different.

"The only thing he could have been running from," Taylor said later, "was us."

Although he made fun of it, calling his friends and telling them to come and see how he had been banded like some lumbering creature on the old TV show *Wild Kingdom*, the five days that he had been under house arrest had been miserable ones for Bart.

"House arrest was a lot worse than being in jail," he said later. "It's a lot more annoying. You're still locked up, but you're sitting out there in the world with all the temptations. Unless you've got a steady girlfriend coming by to see you, it's just horrible."

It was primarily the temptations of freedom, he later claimed, that prompted him to cut his band and leave, but he acknowledged other reasons, too. He knew that John Taylor was not coming by so frequently without purpose. He knew that he was as suspect as Chris in the murder. Hank came by regularly to see him and they had talks about that.

"I don't see how you can stand it," Bart later recalled Hank telling him. "This thing's going to drive you crazy before it's over. SBI and these guys, they've come too far on this. They're too stubborn to think they're investigating the wrong guy. They're going to try to hang your ass. If I was you, I'd skip town. You ought to leave."

"Yeah, I know," Bart said. "You're right. I know."

But Bart also was aware that running would be a tacit admission of guilt. "SBI's going to say, 'He must've had a guilty conscience.' They're going to arrest me for sure. Up to this point, I've been like a guy walking up a hill seeing an avalanche coming and saying, 'It ain't going to hit me. It ain't going to hit me.'"

Now, however, he realized that the avalanche was certain to envelop him unless he ran and dodged.

On the night before he made his decision, a party was going on in an apartment across the street. Bart sat on his doorstep with one of Neal's roommates, talking about girls, sipping rum and Coke and watching the merriment. Several young women were drinking beer in the parking lot and one called an invitation to join them. The realization that he couldn't do that was the final frustrating factor in his decision, Bart later claimed.

He waited until the computer made its final call of the day to check on him, sometime around midnight, then he cut his band, left it atop the receiver, joined the party, and had a good time smoking pot, drinking and laughing until the early morning hours. When he returned to Neal's apartment, everybody had gone to sleep, sprawled about the floors. He packed all of his belongings into a single suitcase and a nylon backpack, waited for the computer to make its first check of the new day, and left on foot.

Later in the morning, he called a friend who lived in a suburban apartment.

"Hey, man, let's get some liquor and go camping," he said.

Despite Bart's fears, he was in no danger of being arrested for the murder of Lieth Von Stein. Nobody in the investigation had any evidence to connect him to the case. Now Taylor, Crone, and Young decided they would have to leave Bart to Christy and the Raleigh police until they could find some solid reason to join the search for him. They had to concentrate on finding somebody else to connect Chris and Moog to the killing.

John Crone still thought that Butch Mitchell was their best prospect. His story of the D&D game and the hair found in the burned shoe indicated that he could have taken part. On Friday morning, June 9, Crone and Taylor drove to a county near Raleigh to talk with Butch's mother.

She was concerned about their reasons for wanting to talk with her and tried to put them off, but they finally persuaded her to tell them about Butch.

Butch, she said, was the eldest of her four sons. Their father had died of diseases related to alcoholism. Butch, she said, had a lot of anger in him. His biggest problem was losing his temper. She'd never known him to do it with anybody outside the family, but when it blew, it really blew.

"I don't know what makes that boy go off like that," she said.

She worried about her son, she said, and once she had sent him to the county's mental health center because he wouldn't communicate with her and had so many problems with his brothers.

He was smart but lazy, with a vivid and extravagant

imagination that tended toward fantasy. Sometimes he had trouble separating fantasy and reality, she noted.

She thought that her son was just bragging when he claimed to be such a good fighter. But he had studied karate, and she thought that he was capable of hurting somebody with his hands. She didn't think that he would ever shoot anybody, but he had practiced, she acknowledged, with a knife.

Crone left the meeting with Butch's mother more convinced than ever that Butch could be their killer, but Taylor still couldn't picture Chris putting his trust in a braggart with obvious emotional problems. He thought that Butch couldn't resist telling about it if he'd been involved. As they talked about it on the drive to Raleigh, Crone and Taylor decided to talk with Neal about Butch. Neal had been his roommate. Maybe he knew something. They called Neal, but he said that he had to go to work at Wendy's. He was working a split shift and would be back at his apartment after two-thirty.

The detectives arrived to find that Neal had left a message. He had to stay over at work, but he could take a few minutes to talk with them there. Only a few customers were in Wendy's at midafternoon. Neal, still wearing his Wendy's smock, joined the officers in the empty sun room on the western side of the building, where nobody could overhear their conversation. Neal sat at a table with his back to the window. Crone and Taylor sat facing him.

Crone began by asking about the Dungeons and Dragons game Butch had described to the officers. Neal recalled the game but said his character hadn't been hired to go on the adventure. Butch would never do that, because he was jealous that Neal's character was so much more powerful than his own. Indeed, Neal said, immediately after that adventure, Butch had made such a fuss about hating his own character that Neal killed off the character to accommodate him, which also made Butch angry.

Butch, said Neal, as he had told the officers before, was psychotic.

"What's your definition of psychotic?" Taylor asked.

In this case, Neal said, it was someone who could keep his temper at times, then go berserk for no reason. That was Butch.

Had he ever known Butch to hurt anybody?

No, but he thought that Butch might have gotten drunk and hurt somebody in the past. He wasn't sure. He really didn't know about Butch's past.

Did he think Butch could beat someone to death?

No.

Did Butch ever confuse D&D games with reality?

Not that Neal had ever seen.

Did he think that Butch could have murdered Chris's stepfather?

It was possible, Neal said, but he really doubted it.

How about Moog, James? Had Neal noticed any change in his attitude and personality since the murder?

Not really, but he knew that James was worried about something more than his probation violations. He had talked about being tired of house arrest and tired of the murder investigation before he cut his band and took off. He had tried to impress people by talking about the large scale of the investigation, Neal said.

Did James know anybody he could have gotten to commit the murder?

"He knows some pretty shady people," Neal said.

Did he think that James could be involved?

"It would be an uncharacteristic risk, if he was."

"What would you think if we told you that Chris was involved?" Crone asked.

"I don't know," Neal responded.

Neal appeared to be completely in control, not in the least nervous or uncertain about his answers. Both Crone and Taylor thought that he was telling the truth.

At this point, Crone remembered his wife, Cindy. They were supposed to meet in Raleigh, then go on together to Mooresville for a weekend visit with her parents. She was to call Lewis Young at SBI headquarters in Raleigh to find out where her husband was so that they could meet. Young was unaware that she was to call. Crone asked Taylor if he would mind stepping out to the pay phone in the parking lot to give Young a call and let him know about the situation.

When Taylor left, Crone looked at Neal, sitting diagonally across from him and thought that he saw vulnerability.

"I thought, what the hell," he said later. "Might as well give this thing a shot."

"Look," he said. "We know Chris is involved. We know that for a fact. This whole thing is about to go down. Anybody who's involved could get the gas chamber."

The SBI already had talked to Chris's attorneys to let them know they'd be willing to listen if Chris wanted to come clean and work out a plea bargain deal, Crone said. The first person to come forth would find the going a lot easier than for any others. Chris might come over at any time.

"I think you know something," Crone said, looking Neal straight in the eye. "If you do, it would be better for you to tell us now while we still can help you."

Neal looked away but he said nothing. For a few moments he sat silent. Crone felt a sudden chill run down his back.

"What if I just kind of gave them some advice?" Neal said softly.

Crone's pulse quickened, but he tried not to show it.

"It depends," he said. "What do you mean by advice? A lot of it depends on how much you're involved. If you know something, you can clear that up by just telling us. But if you're involved in this thing, then I need to get the DA up here."

"Well," Neal said. "I guess you'd better get the DA."

"Look," Crone said, "it's a two-hour drive up here from Washington. If he comes up here, are you going to have enough information to make his trip worthwhile?"

"Let's put it this way," Neal said. "I can lay the whole thing out for you."

37

JOHN TAYLOR HAD TO WAIT nearly ten minutes at the outdoor phone for Lewis Young to answer his page and call him back. He told Young to expect the call from Crone's wife and let him know that they were at Wendy's, near the campus, talking with one of Moog's friends.

Young said he would meet them there and they all could go out for dinner and discuss the case.

As Taylor started through the doorway back into Wendy's, he met Crone coming out.

"Come back out here a minute," Crone said.

Taylor stepped outside, waiting to hear what the chief had to say.

"Neal wants to talk."

"Chief, don't mess with me," Taylor said, looking at him skeptically. "What the hell you talking about?"

Crone was smiling broadly. "He says he's going to lay the whole thing out for us."

Both Crone and Taylor were dying to know what Neal had to tell them. Did he just know something about the murder? Had he taken part? Neither could picture this lumpish, lethargic boy killing somebody. But they wanted to be especially cautious about doing everything just right so that the case wouldn't later be lost on some technicality. They didn't want Neal to say anything about the case until they had further instructions from the DA.

Neal checked out of work and joined the two officers outside, where they stood by picnic tables awaiting Young's arrival.

"I can't wait to hear what you've got to say," Taylor told Neal, whose own curiosity also was aroused.

"How did you know that Chris was involved?" he asked.

"We can't talk about that right now," Crone said.

Young arrived, expecting only to have to make a decision about where to have dinner, discovering instead that the case he'd been working on for nearly a year was on the brink of solution. He called to Washington to let the district attorney know that he was needed.

Crone and Taylor drove Neal to his apartment so that he could change clothes, then took him to a seafood restaurant, where they met Young. The situation was awkward for the officers. The only thing that they had in common with Neal was the murder, and that was the one thing they couldn't talk about. They talked about anything else instead, TV, sports, music, the weather. Minutes ticked by with agonizing slowness.

Shortly after six, just as they were getting ready to leave the restaurant for SBI headquarters, Young's pager beeped. He went to find a telephone and returned looking dejected.

The district attorney, Mitchell Norton, was just leaving Washington.

Here was the biggest case Beaufort County had had in years. Crone, Taylor, and Young were waiting with a solution within their grasp. The officers had assumed that the DA would drop everything to come to their assistance. Now they would have to nursemaid Neal for another two hours or more while he pondered whether or not he was making a mistake, two more hours during which he could change his mind, tell them that he didn't know a thing and walk away. They would be helpless to stop him.

It was after nine when Norton finally arrived with his assistant, Keith Mason. They strode into SBI headquarters and walked straight up to Young.

"What does the boy want to do?" Norton asked.

"You need to talk to the chief," said Young.

"What does he know?" Norton persisted, ignoring Crone, who stood by silently, miffed that the DA would assume that only the SBI could have broken the case, never the dummies in the Washington Police Department.

"I haven't talked to him," Young said. "He talked to the chief."

Crone finally stepped in and told the two DAs what had taken place.

"We can't make any deals," Norton said abruptly. "We're not going to talk to him."

The officers had been waiting five hours with a young man willing to tell them about a murder and the DA wasn't going to talk to him? He reminded the DA that they had gone to Bonnie's attorney with the evidence against Chris, certainly offering the implication of a deal.

That was different, the DA said. If he or Mason talked with Neal, they could become witnesses and be required to testify. If they offered a deal in advance, then any evidence that came from Neal would be tainted, perhaps conceived as being contrived for the promise of reward.

"Well, at least go tell him that you can't talk to him," Crone finally said in exasperation.

Neal could see the officers talking with the DAs, and as the conversation dragged on, he became more and more nervous.

"What are they talking about?" he asked Taylor.

"Oh, they're just filling them in on what has happened so far," Taylor said, trying to calm him.

Finally, Norton agreed to let Mason explain the situation to Neal. The two gathered with the three officers in a conference room. Mason said that no deals could be made. There would be no offer of leniency. If Neal had been involved, he would be charged with murder. If he wanted to talk, he had to understand that.

Taylor and Young could see their case slipping away. They began scrambling to convince Neal that he should talk anyway.

"You have to trust us," Taylor said. "I know you've only just met us, you don't know us, but you have to believe that we'll look out for you. We'll do what we can."

As the officers pleaded, Neal grew more solemn and dejected. Before the arrival of the DAs, he had seemed hopeful, optimistic. At one point he'd even mentioned to Crone that he'd heard about a reward and asked if he might have some chance at claiming it. "Don't press your luck," the chief had told him. Now Neal was slumping in his chair, visibly depressed.

Crone quietly interrupted. "Why don't you guys all go out for a minute," he said to Taylor, Young, and Mason.

They looked at him as if asking, "Are you sure you know what you're doing?"

He nodded and they left.

After the door was closed, Crone turned to Neal and said, "Do you understand why we can't make any deals, any promises?"

"Yeah, I understand," he said.

"You told me at Wendy's that you wanted to get this off your back. There's only one way you're going to do that, and you know what that is."

"I know."

Crone knew that Neal had to be considering the direness of the consequences if he chose to talk.

"I've got a son about your age," Crone said. "If you were my son, I'd tell you to do the right thing."

"Well, I guess there's still some hope," Neal said, making an attempt at a smile.

"Are you going to give us a statement?"

"Yeah."

"Do you want to talk with me, or with one of the other officers, or with all of us?"

"I'd rather just talk with you."

"Would you mind if John Taylor came in and took some notes?"

"No, I guess not."

"He's going to talk to us," Crone said when he went back out to the others, "but right now he only wants to talk with me and John."

As eager as he was to hear what Neal had to say, Crone was still anxious about his wife. He was supposed to meet her in Raleigh hours earlier. She hadn't called recently, and he had no idea where she was now. He needed to call his in-laws to find out if they had heard from her, but first he had to hear Neal out.

After waiving his rights, Neal told Crone that Chris and James had come to him a few days before the murder with a plan for Chris to get his inheritance early by killing his parents. He thought the idea was incredible, but he went along with it because his only role was to drive James to Washington to commit the murders. Chris drew a map directing them to his house. Neal said that he drove James there, let him out near the house, and waited nearby until James reappeared, saying he'd done it. James was supposed to steal jewelry to make it look like a robbery, but he only had taken a little money. They drove back to Raleigh, stopping along a deserted road on the way so that James could pile up the clothes he'd been wearing and burn them.

The story fit the evidence. It was highly unlikely that Neal could have learned about the fire and the map without being part of the plot. Crone had no doubt that he was telling the truth, but he felt a strange sort of letdown.

"Is that it?" he asked, a little incredulously, when Neal had finished.

"That's it," Neal said with a shrug.

"It didn't have anything to do with Dungeons and Dragons?"

Nothing, said Neal.

After their long investigation, all the plodding hours of searching and questioning, all their elaborate theorizing, it all was so simple. Motive and method were as ancient as murder. The motive: greed. The method: a key, a club, a blade.

Crone wanted to hear more, but his wife came first. He

had to go find her. Would Neal mind if Lewis Young, who'd worked the case from the beginning, came in to get the details? Fine, said Neal, and for the next five hours he told Young and Taylor everything that he could remember about the murder.

A week or so before the murder, Neal said, Chris and James had gone to Washington together to kill Chris's parents. He'd heard them talking about it, but he knew no details. They had talked of putting Chris's family to sleep with sleeping pills before killing them, but they had chickened out because Chris decided it would be better for him not to be at home when the murders occurred.

At some point before the weekend of the actual murder—Neal couldn't remember the date—Chris and James had come by the apartment on Ligon Street that he shared with Butch Mitchell. They came about noon. Only the three of them were there. At first they chatted about things in general. Then James said that they had come up with a plan for Chris to get his inheritance early, a plan for murder. Was Neal interested? Neal did not want his friends to think that he was too timid or cowardly for such a bold adventure. Sure, he said.

James did most of the talking. He would carry out the actual killing. Neal's job would be to drive Chris's car. James had no license and didn't want to take a chance on blowing the whole mission by being stopped for a traffic violation. Neal would be paid for driving, but he wasn't sure whether the amount was to be $2,000 or $20,000.

Only Chris's parents were to be slain. No mention was made of killing Chris's sister, Angela. Chris said that he would be willing to share the inheritance with her. That inheritance, Neal believed, was about $10 million. He had been told that earlier, although he wasn't sure whether it was Chris or James who had told him. He had no idea how much James was to receive for the killing.

Chris sketched two maps on a white legal pad. One showed how to skirt the northern edge of Washington to reach his neighborhood. The other was a map of Smallwood that identified the Von Stein house, showed where James was to be let out at a wooded lot behind the house, marked a spot where Neal could park near a utility substation, even pointed out the locations of nearby dogs that might bark and cause alarm.

Once in Smallwood, Neal was to drive only on back streets, because neighbors might recognize the sound of the loud mufflers on Chris's car.

James was to enter the Von Stein house through the back door with a key that Chris would provide. He was to take jewelry from a kitchen cabinet and make the killings appear to be related to a burglary.

Chris was to stay in Raleigh while the murders were taking place, making certain that he was seen by others, so he would have an alibi. If Chris received a call about the murders before Neal and James got back to Raleigh with his car, he would claim to have lost his car keys as an excuse for not being able to drive immediately to Washington.

Before leaving that day, Neal said, Chris told him that his parents were about to disinherit him because he was fucking up and flunking out of school. They were on the verge of cutting off his funds for school, Chris said, and if this plan didn't come off, he might have to find a job and go to work.

A couple of days later, Neal said, he went by James's dorm room. Chris was there and they again talked about the plan, although no mention still was made about how the killing would be done. Chris said that after the murders, he would have to appear distraught and depressed. The way he would come out of his depression, he said, was to go to the beach and buy cars for all of his friends.

Three or four days after that chance encounter, Neal said, he again stopped by James's room. He couldn't remember exactly, but he thought that it was on this occasion that he found James putting black paste shoe polish on a pair of white batting gloves and on a wooden baseball bat that he had seen previously in James's room. The bat had a line of triangles drawn around it in ink, just above the trademark. The question-mark-like symbol of a rock group called the Blue Oyster Cult had been sketched on the fat end of the bat. The handle was wrapped with black friction tape. James also showed him a new hunting knife. He and Chris had bought it for the job, James told him, but Neal couldn't remember whether he said they'd bought it at Kmart or the flea market. The knife was only for backup, James said. He planned to "take out" Chris's parents with the bat.

"One good blow on each ought to do it," James said, taking a hearty swing.

It was on this visit that James asked about his work schedule, Neal said, and he thought they may have set a date for the mission then.

Anyway, no more than three days later, James came to his apartment in the morning, gave him the keys to Chris's car, and told him to meet him in the fringe parking lot on Sullivan Drive behind Lee dorm that night between 11:30 and 12:30.

Questioned by Young, Neal recalled that James was wearing blue jeans with holes in the knees, a dark, button-up shirt over a white T-shirt, and the moccasin boots that he wore so often. He had brought along a black sweater, a ski mask, dark trousers, and black tennis shoes to wear when he went into the house. Over his shoulder, said Neal, James had slung an army knapsack that he usually used for carrying Dungeons and Dragons materials. Now it held a knife, a flashlight, and other items. The handle of the baseball bat protruded from it, throwing it out of kilter.

Months after telling the officers about this night, Neal would recall that James was excited and hyperactive as they left for Washington.

"He was grinning a lot," Neal said. "He didn't seem at all concerned at what he was going to be doing. He seemed fairly happy about the whole world. I was happy just to be driving him down there."

On the night that Young and Taylor questioned him, Neal said that he never dreamed anybody actually would be killed, despite all the planning. He thought that James simply would go into the house, steal the jewelry, and slip away. About that, he said later, he had no qualms.

"On one level I knew that breaking into that place, stealing from those people was wrong. I was contrasting that with these are my friends and they would really respect me if I went through with this kind of daring thing. I told myself that these people are rich. They aren't really going to miss this kind of piddly stuff. Besides, they were going to disinherit Chris.

"What I was doing, I didn't really see it as hurting anybody. Hurt somebody? That was too crazy. It didn't fit. Killing people was so far outside of anything that I knew James to be like that I didn't dream it was possible.

"I thought, we're going to go down there, somebody else is going to go in and steal something, so I wasn't even doing that myself, and when it was over, we would just drive off. We would be laughing and joking about how killing somebody could never happen.

"I didn't expect to be paid anything. I was just driving down for the fun of it. And it *was* fun, I don't care what anybody says. Driving off in the middle of the night. It was exciting."

On the way, he said, they didn't talk about what lay ahead. They talked about Dungeons and Dragons. They talked about music. After passing a store dealing in baseball cards, they talked for a long time about collecting cards and comics.

Somewhere near the town of Wilson, they stopped on the side of the road to take a leak. As they neared Washington, James began changing clothes as they drove, putting on the dark trousers, black sweater, black tennis shoes.

They followed Chris's map to Smallwood but drove past it and had to turn around and go back. They located the house, the wooded lot where James was to get out, the utility substation where Chris suggested that Neal park to wait. They cased the neighborhood, including the darker and more isolated nearby roads to the fairgrounds and airport. They rejected Chris's suggested waiting spot because a new house was under construction there and they were afraid that the car might arouse suspicion if anybody saw it. Instead, Neal would wait in the darkness of the dead-end road to the fairgrounds.

James smeared black shoe polish around his mouth and eyes and pulled a purple ski mask over his head as Neal coasted slowly down Marsh Street and came to a stop at the wooded lot. Neal paused only long enough for James to hop out of the car, slinging his army knapsack across his shoulder. Later, Neal wouldn't remember either of them saying anything. He didn't look back as James slipped into the trees as quickly and silently as a ninja warrior.

Neal grew increasingly anxious and fearful as he waited in darkness for James to return. As the minutes ticked agonizingly on amidst the loud and eerie insect sounds of a coastal summer night, he began first to worry that something had gone wrong, then to worry, as he later put it, that "something was going right," exactly according to the plan.

When he could stand the anxiety no longer, he started the car, pulled up to Market Street Extension, turned left toward town, and drove slowly past Smallwood, looking for James. Seeing no sign of him, he turned around and drove past again, this time going on to the airport road, where he pulled in and stopped a short distance from the main road. Another fifteen minutes passed before he heard the sound of running feet slapping against the pavement and turned to see a tall, dark figure loping toward him out of the blackness.

He'd never seen James as excited as he was when he opened the passenger door and climbed quickly into the car, he told the officers.

"I actually did it!" he said James exclaimed. "I don't ever want to see anything like that again. I never saw so much blood in my life."

Neal told the officers that he saw blood on James's hands and clothing, but later he claimed that he really hadn't seen any blood, that if he had he might have panicked more than he did.

"My first thought when James said, 'I did it,' was one long scream," he said later. "I kept thinking, they were serious. They really were serious. He really meant to go in and kill people. My God, what has he done? What have *I* done?"

Instinctively, he started the car.

"James said, 'Go, go.' I went. I just pointed the car and kept it in the road."

He turned north on Market, away from town, going back by the same route they had come. He didn't ask questions, he said later. He couldn't even speak.

"What do you say to a man who's just killed someone? I was afraid to be in the same car with him. He tried to tell me what happened, but he didn't tell a coherent story. He said something about how he had broken something he shouldn't have broken, left something unlocked that should have been locked. I remember him mentioning someone made a lot of noise and he didn't understand why the whole neighborhood wasn't awakened."

For Taylor and Young, Neal recalled James telling him that he had to keep beating Chris's stepfather with the bat, had to use the knife on him, too, several times. He also had beaten Chris's mother.

"Part of me was saying, 'No, no, this can't be happening,' " Neal recalled later. "I just didn't treat it as reality."

Was James carrying the bat when he got back to the car? Neal didn't remember.

He wanted only to get away from Washington, back to

Raleigh. He missed his turn but was unaware of it. He took the next road to the left, which led back to U.S. 17, just as did the road he had missed. Soon after making the turn, he told the officers, James instructed him to turn into a rutted lane by a farm field, stop, and cut the lights. James got out, changed clothes, and asked Neal to open the trunk. There James placed the clothes he had been wearing.

The lane turned out to be muddy from the earlier thunderstorm, and the sides of the car were covered with mud when they got back on the road. In his eagerness to get away from the area, Neal kept speeding and James kept reminding him to slow down.

Somewhere west of Washington, James told him to turn onto a side road to the right so that he could dispose of the clothing and knife. But too many houses, too many outdoor lights lined this road, prompting Neal to turn around and drive back to the highway.

Another road soon loomed, this one to the left. About a quarter of a mile along the road, they came to a patch of woods on a curve, and James said that this would do. Once again, Neal opened the trunk. James piled the clothing on the road's shoulder, tossing in the shoes, the knife, the wadded maps. He doused it all with gasoline from a two-gallon can in the trunk.

Neal was urinating, his back to James, when he heard a whoosh, he said later, and saw the night light up behind him.

"Come on, quick, let's go," James yelled, and Neal hurried toward the car, zipping his pants as he went.

When they came into a town (Neal wasn't sure of the town, but the officers figured it had to be Greenville), James told him to stop for gas at an all-night convenience store, an Amoco Mart, he remembered. James pumped. Neal went in to pay. While he was buying a soft drink and candy bar, James came in and got a bottle of Gatorade and a stick of beef jerky.

Had James wiped the shoe polish from his face? How and when did he do that? Neal couldn't remember.

James decided that they had to run the car through an automatic car wash adjacent to the convenience store. They couldn't take it back with all that mud on it. That might cause questions to be raised.

At the store, Neal later said, James handed him three folded twenty-dollar bills, loot from the raid, and said, "Here, keep this." (Neal had told the officers that James had given him the money soon after he got in the car.) He put it into his pocket and later gave what was left of it after paying for the gas to Kenyatta.

Daylight was breaking, Neal remembered, when they arrived back in Raleigh. Neither had said anything more about the night's activities after leaving the car wash. They had ridden mostly in silence.

"I was trying to pretend it didn't happen," Neal said later. "Maybe if I didn't talk about it, it didn't happen. Talking about it made it seem more real."

Neal drove back to the parking lot where he had picked up Chris's car and left it in the same area. James told him to take the keys to Chris's suite and leave them on a high shelf in the utility closet in the bathroom that was shared by the occupants of the four rooms in the suite. Neal protested.

"Why do I have to do this? I want to go home."

James, he pointed out, would be going right past Chris's floor on his way to his room. Why couldn't he take the keys?

"I can't risk being seen anywhere near Chris," James said, and Neal reluctantly trudged to the dorm and left the keys. Chris's room door was closed, he said, and he heard no sounds coming from within.

Exhausted, frightened, and emotionally drained, Neal walked the quarter-mile to his apartment and pecked on the window to awaken Kenyatta.

The following day, Monday, July 25, Neal recalled later, James came to the apartment and told Butch, Kenyatta, and himself about the attack on Chris's parents. A burglary of some sort, he said. That was when Neal learned that Chris's mother had survived. A 50 percent success for their mission was a total failure for their goal. Chris wouldn't be inheriting anything. He and James never would be paid for their efforts.

Did James consider going back to finish the job?

Neal didn't think so.

A day later, Neal went by James's dorm room. James was alone, he said, and they talked about the murder. James kept assuring him that he needn't worry. He was certain that he had succeeded in making it look like a burglary.

"The police don't have anything to go on," Neal recalled James telling him. "If they did, they would have already been up here. Chris is going to keep me posted. Don't worry. Forget it ever happened."

Neal told the officers that he never talked with Chris about the murder after it happened and only saw him a couple of times briefly in the company of others after Chris returned to college that fall. He talked with James about it only a couple of times. James told him about Chris leaving school that fall and reassured him that nobody was going to talk.

"You're in no danger," he recalled James telling him. "Even if Chris should decide to say something, it would be his word against yours and they'd never take his word. Don't worry about it. Forget it."

But Neal couldn't forget. The memory kept gnawing at him, pushing him back into a depression from which he couldn't escape. He thought about telling somebody, anybody, even going to the police, he said, but the longer he waited, the more difficult it became. He was terrified at the prospect of prison, scared of retribution from James or Chris, worried about what people would think about him.

"I tried throwing myself into my work," he recalled later, "just trying to forget about it. If I don't think about it, it will go away. But I couldn't work twenty-four hours a day. There were inevitably quiet periods and my thoughts would bring it back. I didn't mean for it to happen. I never thought it would happen. But no matter what I told myself, I knew that if I had acted differently, I could have saved a man's life."

He realized that he had to atone for that, and the only way he could do it was by coming forth with what he knew. Still fear held him back.

He did not see James from the fall of 1988 until the spring of 1989. He was concerned and wary, he said, when James came to him asking for a place to stay. Was James worried that the police might come to him and he might break? Did he want to be close at hand to stop it if he saw it coming? Still, he thought it would be better to have James where he could keep an eye on him, and he agreed to let him stay.

James didn't talk about the murder investigation until after he got out of jail, Neal told the officers. Then he told him about Taylor and Young questioning him at the jail. He and Chris were under a lot of pressure, James said, but there was no need for concern because he had given the investigators a lot of false leads that would take them in the wrong direction. "You really didn't do anything," James told him. "Don't worry about it." But James himself had become worried, Neal said, after the officers started bringing the knapsack around, fearful that somebody would associate him with it.

Neal had recognized the bag immediately. Until then he hadn't realized that James had left the bag at the scene. Soon after the detectives brought the bag by, Neal said, James began talking about leaving town. Then he cut his band and disappeared.

Neal said that he didn't know where James was, but he knew that he hadn't left Raleigh. He had talked to James by telephone just that day. James wanted money to get out of town, and Neal told him he would see what he could do. James was supposed to call him at work again in a few days about the money.

The officers questioned Neal until three-thirty Saturday morning, and when they had finished, they did not arrest him, as he had expected. To arrest him would be premature. News of an arrest would tip off James and Chris, and the officers might never again see either of them. They needed Neal's help and cooperation to make certain that everybody involved was brought to justice.

Their first objective was to find James. After arresting him, they would pick up Chris. Only then would Neal be charged.

Before taking Neal back to his apartment, Young and Taylor arranged to pick him up on Sunday morning to take him to Washington and have him retrace the route he had taken on the murder night and identify all the landmarks. They warned him to say nothing to anybody about talking with them. If James or Chris found out, he could be in danger.

Despite his promise not to tell anybody about his confession, Neal knew that there was one person he had to tell: his mother. He caught a ride home with a friend from Caswell County Saturday. He got out at the convenience mart in Milton, just down the street from Carolyn Thomas's house, where Kenyatta was spending the summer with her grandmother while working at a department store in nearby Danville.

Neal and Kenyatta still were seeing each other. He had taken her to the senior prom at the School of Science and Math in May. When she stopped in Raleigh on her way back from a graduation trip to the beach only a week earlier, she visited Neal's apartment, bought James a cheeseburger, and spent the night with Neal at an inexpensive motel.

In her first week on her summer job, she had come down

with chicken pox, and Neal had promised to come to see her. When he didn't show up as promised, she wrote it off as being typically Neal.

Now he called, finding her at a friend's house, apologizing for not coming because the police had interviewed him for twelve hours, he claimed. She met him at her grandmother's big gray house on the hilltop. He had flowers, jewelry, and a sheepish grin for her. He looked drained, and she knew immediately that something was terribly wrong. He was extremely nervous. They sat in the living room to talk, while her grandmother busied herself in the back of the house. Within minutes, Kenyatta had pulled the whole story out of him.

"That night you told me you'd done acid, was that the night?" she asked.

"Yeah, but you'd best forget that," he said.

"He wanted me to say I didn't remember anything about it," she said later. "I said, 'I am not lying for you, Neal. I'm not going to jail for you.'"

Kenyatta was stunned nearly to disbelief by the story Neal had told her. "I was in shock," she said later. "I kept saying, 'Why would you do something so stupid?' I felt sorry for him. He was really scared. He was crying."

Neal still had hope that he might not have to go to prison, that he might get probation for cooperating, but Kenyatta thought that was being unrealistic. This was murder. *Murder.* And Neal Henderson, of all people, a genius, a person she expected to become an innovative scientist or a brilliant professor, the man she had once wanted to marry, was involved in it. How could a person so smart be so stupid? It was simply beyond her comprehension.

Yet she could not abandon Neal. "I felt like he'd been pulled into this," she said later. The real blame, she felt, lay with her scummy cousin, James, and that scuzball, Chris. Her support would go to Neal.

Neal felt relief after telling Kenyatta, but the worst was yet to come: telling his mother. Later, he said it was the hardest thing he ever went through, worse even than the ordeal his conscience had been putting him through since the murder.

"She knew something was wrong. I told her I was in pretty big trouble this time. She was distraught when I told her what it was. She kept saying she just couldn't believe this was happening. Every other sentence, I was saying, 'Don't worry. Don't worry. Everything's going to be all right.' "

38

ON THE DAY BART WALKED away from house arrest, he later said, he called two friends whom he would identify only by first names, Bill* and Tim.* They came to fetch him, and all three spent the night camped by a lake on university land used for agricultural research not far from the main campus. They shot BB guns and slingshots, got drunk, smoked pot, and slept on the ground in sleeping bags.

The next two days he spent at his friends' apartment in Raleigh's southern suburbs, watching TV and listening to the stereo. That proved boring, however, and he got his friends to bring him back to the campus.

He lurked on campus that day until he saw Hank going to work and called him over to get a feel for the situation.

"It's ten times as bad as it's ever been," Hank told him. "Man, you better not be hanging around here."

It was not only because Bart didn't have money that he didn't flee, he later said. Indeed, he was thinking of going to Myrtle Beach to join hordes of other college-age young people in a summer job serving the annual throngs of vacationers. More than anything, he said, his decision to stay was not a decision at all, only a lackadaisical attitude.

Although he knew that the SBI and the Washington police were trying to connect him to the Von Stein murder, he was confident that they had no evidence against him and couldn't arrest him. Sure, Christy Newsom and the Raleigh police were after him, but even if they caught him for breaking house arrest, he figured the worst that could happen would be having to spend six or eight months in jail.

He was confident that they would not catch him, however. In the past year he had grown so expert at eluding the authorities that it was almost like a game, one at which he had decided he was more masterful than they.

"To be perfectly honest," he said later, "I got a real kick out of it. It was fun. I had this job painting houses, the most boring job in the world, which I couldn't do anymore because of them. All of a sudden, this great adventure just fell into my life. I was this desperado, on the lam. I got a great thrill out of it. I was playing cat and mouse with the police, skateboarding right under their noses."

Soon after he returned to campus, Bart later claimed, he went into the Burger King at Mission Valley Shopping Center on Western Boulevard—the BK Lounge, he and his friends called it—where he encountered a casual acquaintance, a girl he had met at a keg party one night. Her name was Angela, but he didn't know her last name. She was a student at State but now was co-oping, working between studies at the nearby Research Triangle.

"What's up?" she said, as he later told the story.

"Police are after me," Bart said with a smile.

"What's this about?"

"It's a long story."

"Where are you staying?"

"I don't have any place."

"Well, if you need someplace to hide out, you can stay at my place. My roommate's gone for the summer."

Her apartment was in the same complex where Bart had lived when he first moved off campus. She gave him a key, and he fetched his suitcase and a plastic laundry bag full of clothes from hiding and moved in that night.

The days that followed, he said later, were "like a whole string of Saturdays off." His hiding out was done mostly in the open, much of it spent sprawled reading under trees in out-of-the-way campus spots or by various apartment complex swimming pools. He spent a lot of time in the campus library. He even checked out *Moby Dick* because of an incident from high school.

When he was supposed to have read the book and reported on it in Weldon Slayton's class, he had read the Classics Comics version instead. Slayton had been immediately aware of it and had chastised him. "You're not getting away with something," he told Bart, "you're missing something." Now Bart finished the book as a tribute to Slayton and realized that his teacher had been right. He enjoyed it immensely.

He even began writing himself, keeping a diary of sorts in a spiral-bound notebook that he kept in his backpack. His first entry was on Thursday, June 8, two days after he broke house arrest.

There are times when I wonder if there is any hope for mankind, and then I slap myself for being so silly; of course, there's no hope for mankind.

If you assume that ⅓ of all the people in the world give a damn, and ⅓ of the people know they are contributing to the downfall of society, then what are the other ⅓ doing?

I would assume they are sitting on their butts not giving a damn and waiting to be influenced by somebody with a motive for swaying the masses, ulterior or otherwise.

If a small group of wealthy individuals with enough cash to cover their asses want to do something, they can do just about anything. Look at Exxon, after doing nearly irreparable damage to 520 miles of coastline they blamed the captain (it was his fault) and told the government and public that they would take care of it.

This don't-worry-be-happy attitude was exactly what the public wanted to hear. After 3 months nobody really cared that much, it was old news. Exxon, one of the largest corporations in the world, managed to get out of their basic responsibility by selectively influencing the ⅓ of society who don't give a damn. As for the government, whoever said that government wasn't big business was a total loon. Ask Ollie North; he became a millionaire and a hero by selling Stinger missiles to Iranian fanatics. Ignorant bedouin camel jockeys with high tech weaponry is a tactical mistake of the caliber of the Maginot line. After, say, 5 years of arms dealing, the Ayatollah would've been another Col. Khadafy.

North came out of the whole fiasco smelling like roses, even better than Reagan. That's the problem with the American public; the ⅓ that don't give a damn are easily swayed by appearances and aren't bothered by facts.

Thus, I deem society doomed because eventually the ⅔s that are getting pissed on will become pissed off.

I plan to try my hand at fiction, I think I may have a knack for it.

By the following day, his mood had grown melancholy, his writing more personal.

I have nothing now. No money, no material wealth, no civil rights. I do have a few good friends and the clothes on my back, and even though that's enough to keep me alive it's not enough to keep me happy.

It has been a long time since I was happy. I don't remember the last time I was. For too long merely being satisfied with my existence was enough for me, but being satisfied isn't being happy.

There were times when I was happy and not satisfied and vice versa, but it has been a long time since I've had both. That is what I want now.

I'm sitting on top of some type of transformer on the intramural field, watching late middle-aged men run around the track. I guess they must be feeling fairly mortal to put themselves through this in the middle of June.

At the time Bart was writing those words, unbeknownst to him, his friend Neal already had told John Crone that he wanted to talk and was waiting to tell a story that would bring drastic change to Bart's life.

By the following day, while Neal was in Milton at Bart's grandmother's house, telling his shocking story to Kenyatta, Bart's writing had grown introspective and morose.

I'm sitting on the top level of the parking deck next to Reynolds Coliseum. Earlier this year, most of the slabs of concrete on the south side of the building's top (where I'm sitting) fell off 4 stories to the pavement below. N.C. State is an engineering and agricultural school and they can't even build a building right.

The humidity is so high that you can see what looks like a fog up under the streetlamps.

The Smothers Bros. are playing Reynolds tonight; judging by the turnout, they aren't making much money.

I remember the very first time I came to N.C. State on a high school field trip. It was open house and I must have been in the 9th grade. That would've been in '82.

Back then, when "Fast Times at Ridgemont High" was a fairly recent movie, I thought a lot differently about the university than I do now. Back then, it was all so new and amazing and big. Now it's small and tiresome.

It's taken almost 3 whole years, but its gotten old quick. If I had not led my life so foolishly, the things I could have now would stagger the mind. I mean it. The procrastination did me in, in the end.

I love my family now more than ever. I think that I can tell my dad I love him now, I could never have done this before. We never got along well, mostly because he never encouraged me to work hard, only to punish me if I failed. And though he has done more for me than anyone else, ever, I am more saddened and grieved to think that nearly all he has done for me has now come to naught.

My father grows older each year, I think he's 46, and my deepest, most sincere wish, is to make him happy in his old age.

If I continue writing this, I'm liable to get suicidal. More so than I am already.

Neal Henderson returned to Raleigh after telling his mother that he had taken part in a murder, and on Sunday morning, June 11, John Taylor and Lewis Young drove to Raleigh to pick him up. They took him back to Washington and had him direct them, as best he could, over the route he had followed to Smallwood. He went through his actions on the night of the murder step by step, showing the officers exactly where everything had taken place. Although there were things he didn't remember, the officers had no doubt that he was telling the truth, for all that he told them fit their evidence.

Neal was expecting Bart to call him the following day at work about a loan to help him get out of town, and the officers persuaded Neal to arrange a meeting with Bart at Wendy's. Neal was to wear a hidden microphone and transmitter and try to steer Bart into an incriminating conversation.

When Neal went to work at Wendy's at six-thirty Monday morning, June 12, a squadron of SBI agents surrounded the restaurant. Taylor, Crone, and Melvin Hope, who had conducted the first stages of the investigation, also were there. A sophisticated SBI electronics van waited nearby, with technicians at the ready. As soon as Bart called, Neal was to step outside and give the officers a sign.

The officers watched the breakfast crowds come and go, then the lunch crowds, but Neal never emerged to give them the sign they were hoping for. When Neal's shift ended at two-thirty, the bored and disappointed officers gave up their stakeout. Could James have gotten money somewhere else and already be far from their grasp?

They doubted it, and they fanned out over the area around the campus searching for him until midnight. Christy Newsom joined them in the hunt.

"I can't believe we're doing this again," she said to John Taylor. If she'd had her way, Bart would have been in prison and no officer would have had any trouble finding him to serve him with a murder warrant. That was what peeved her most.

The officers spent the following day in another frustrating search of the campus area. Still no Moog. Late that afternoon, Taylor, Crone, and Hope drove back to Washington for a conference with the DA.

Washington City Manager Bruce Radford was overjoyed about the break in the case. But he was fearful that Moog might never be caught, that he might already have fled the state. He suspected that Bart's family knew his whereabouts.

During a meeting with Crone, Radford, who sometimes couldn't resist playing detective, picked up the phone and called Bart's father in Caswell County. He identified himself as a friend of Bart's from college.

"I'm going to be getting married in Myrtle Beach in a couple of weeks and we're going to have the biggest throw-down bachelor party the world has ever seen," he said. "I wanted to make sure Moog could come, but I don't know how to get in touch with him. Can you tell me where to find him?"

"To be honest with you, I don't know where he is," Jim told him. "I haven't heard from him in a good while."

The missing baseball bat that had been used to beat Lieth and Bonnie was still puzzling the officers. Neal simply couldn't remember whether Bart had the bat when he got back to the car. At one point, he said Bart might have thrown it into a creek that they crossed on the main highway after leaving town, or he could have tossed it away when he set the fire on the deserted roadside.

Police had thoroughly combed Smallwood at the time of the murder without finding any kind of a weapon that could have been used as a club. After Neal told the officers where he had parked to wait for Bart, they realized that one area never had been searched, a stretch of woods that lined Market Street Extension across from the front edge of Smallwood. If James ran back to the car as Neal said, then he had to pass those woods.

On Wednesday morning, as Taylor was getting ready to leave for Raleigh, intending to stay until he found Moog, Crone and Hope were about to begin a systematic search for the baseball bat, going to every location mentioned by Neal. Their first site would be the unsearched woods on the edge of Smallwood.

Not wanting to attract attention and stir up fresh rumors among Smallwood residents, Crone borrowed a city maintenance truck to use in the hunt. He and Hope wore street crew coveralls.

Before they set out, the chief made a friendly bet with Taylor. "Case of beer says we find the baseball bat before you catch Moog," he said.

"You're on," said Taylor.

Fields also lined part of the route along which Bart supposedly had run, now planted in corn, shoulder-high. If he had tossed the bat into the fields, it might have been plowed under. Part of the quarter-mile route was lined in high grass and weeds, part in thick undergrowth along the wood's edge. The search clearly would be difficult, and the sun, already growing blisteringly hot, wouldn't make it any easier. Crone and Hope began at opposite ends of the route, working toward each other, and both were sweating heavily by the time they got started.

When Crone came to the large stretch of woods, he decided to go back into the trees about the distance a person could toss a baseball bat, fifty feet or so, where he could walk with fewer obstructions from undergrowth and with more protection from the sun. He had gone only a few hundred feet when he came upon a little depression in the ground. An opening in the undergrowth made a path from the street to the depression. There, lying in last year's leaf fall, amidst decaying tree branches, was a baseball bat weathered gray, its handle wrapped with black tape, cracked and worn. Just above the bat's trademark, a faded circle of small triangles drawn in ink was still visible.

Crone walked out to the street and summoned Hope with his hand radio. Hope came puffing up to find the chief grinning broadly.

"Melvin, how many baseball bats do you think would be in these woods," Crone asked.

"Probably just one, Chief."

Crone gleefully called the dispatcher to see if Taylor had left yet for Raleigh.

"No," she said, "he's still here."

Have him detour by Smallwood, Crone said.

"You put that damn thing out there," Taylor said when he walked out and saw the bat.

"You're not getting out of this bet that easy," Crone said.

Taylor delayed leaving for Raleigh to photograph the bat from every angle, collect it (termites had begun devouring it on the side that lay next to the ground), and process it as evidence. He took the film with him to drop off at the SBI lab in Raleigh when he finally left at midafternoon. Early that evening, he met Christy for supper at California Pizza. When Lewis Young came to join Taylor to begin the evening's search, Young hadn't eaten, so they returned to California, thinking it a place that Moog might appear. This time, Taylor took a photo of Bart and showed it to the waitress, who'd been working there only three days.

"Ever seen him?" Taylor asked.

"Oh, yeah, he comes in every day about five-thirty to have a beer," she said.

But that day, he hadn't come.

At that moment, Bart was indeed having supper, only a mile away, at the Burger King at Mission Valley Shopping Center, where he was writing in his diary.

> The wonder of it all sometimes amazes me. In the past 12 hours I've run from the law, been asked for doses from a black guy I haven't seen since last September, checked the new freshmen girls and cold-busted an incredible babe doing likewise to me in a Burger King (B.K. Lounge). Incidentally, she had the most beautiful smile when I caught her. It came naturally to her which doesn't follow for everyone. Actually, she's sitting 20 ft. away and if I wasn't the most wanted man this side of D.B. Cooper I would endeavor to make her acquaintance.
>
> We keep looking at each other, and in truth this is getting ridiculous. If she's not in business, she damn well could be. Oh my misspent youth.

It would be his final entry.

Bart already had had several close calls with both the campus and the Raleigh police. The first came soon after he returned to campus from his friends' apartment. He had been to Sullivan dorm looking for other friends. He had left the dorm and was walking along the trail between the soccer field and the tennis courts when two campus police cars went by with emergency lights flashing and stopped at the dorm. He went back to see what was going on and saw the officers emerging from the building. He heard one say, "Where did he go?"

"I said, 'Man, I don't like this,'" Bart recalled later. "'I think they're looking for me.'"

One thing that he learned was that the officers didn't like to get far from their cars, and by avoiding their cars he usually could avoid them.

On a second occasion, Bart was on his way to campus, wearing swim trunks, a T-shirt, and tennis shoes, when he was distracted by several attractive young women in bikinis sunning by the pool at an apartment complex across from the campus. He decided to take the sun near them, hoping to strike up a conversation, he said.

301

After taking a dip, Bart went to a soft drink machine inside the clubhouse, where he left wet footprints across the floor and a small puddle in front of the machine. He had returned to poolside and was pouring rum into the Coke from a bottle in his pack, when a maintenance man approached, angry about the puddle he'd left inside.

"I have to clean that up," the maintenance man said.

"Hey, man, it's no big deal," Bart told him.

"Do you live here?" the irritated man asked, now suddenly suspicious.

"Yeah."

"What's your apartment number?"

"Four-twelve."

"You don't live here," the man said. "You stay right here." And he stalked off to the clubhouse.

Bart put on his shoes and was leaving by the pool gate when the man returned and tried to grab him.

"You're not going anywhere," he said.

"I'll be damned, if I'm not."

"You don't live here. You're trespassing. You're coming with me. I've called the law."

"Man, you're crazy as hell," Bart said, breaking free.

He tried to walk away calmly, without attracting any more attention than had already been drawn to him, but before he got far, he saw a police car approaching. He ducked into some bushes, pulled himself over a low fence, cut across a parking lot, and crossed into some woods where he hid and waited, listening as two police officers nearby talked about his whereabouts on their handheld radios.

On a third occasion, Bart lurked near the campus library, waiting for Hank to go by on his way to work. After they had talked, standing by the sidewalk, Bart went into the library. A few minutes later, he looked out a window from the sixth floor and saw two police cars pull up at the spot where he and Hank had been talking. One car peeled away. The other pulled into a bank parking lot across the street and backed into a space from which the officer could watch the street and the library. Bart hurried downstairs and exited on the opposite side of the building, slipping away amidst the students.

One rainy afternoon, Bart walked into a bakery near the campus where one of his former roommates worked.

"Man, what are you doing here?" his friend said. "Police are crawling all over the place looking for you."

"No kidding," said Bart. "Man, that's wild."

"Yeah, the SBI said the net is out. They're going to get you."

His friend offered him a cinnamon bun, but Bart took a soft drink and a five-dollar loan instead.

Later, he remembered calling Neal once during this period, but didn't recall asking for money. "I might have tried to get him to let me eat a free Super Bar," he said. "I didn't call him back. I thought he was acting funny."

John Taylor and Lewis Young spent another fruitless night searching for Moog after leaving California Pizza on the night of Wednesday, June 14.

The following day they met with officials of the campus and Raleigh police to make sure that all officers on all shifts were alerted to be on the lookout.

At 4 P.M. they began a stakeout of California Pizza. SBI agents were parked out of sight near the restaurant. Taylor sat near the entrance in a sporty Mazda RX7 that he had borrowed from one of Christy's friends to make him less likely to be spotted.

Once again the stakeout failed. The discouraged officers drove to an Applebee's Restaurant near the Howard Johnson's where they were staying. While they were eating, a vicious thunderstorm rolled in with roiling black clouds, sharp lightning, window-rattling thunder, and pelting rain.

"I'll tell you, boys," Taylor announced, "my ass ain't going out in this mess tonight. Moog ain't going to be out in this rain. I'm going to stay at the motel and man the phone. You fools can go out in this."

And he ordered himself a beer, then another one. It was going to be his night to kick back and relax a little. Moog could wait another day for John Taylor to catch him.

Bart had gone to campus about noon that day, leaving his skateboard behind because he was carrying heavy books in his backpack and they would throw him off balance. He went by Sullivan dorm to call on friends and find out what they were planning for that night. He was wearing a boxerlike aquamarine

303

swimsuit, and he went to the soccer field behind Lee dorm and lay in the sun, reading and listening to his GE stereo radio through headphones.

When he had endured all the sun that he could stand, he walked to a used book store on Hillsborough Street, Reader's Corner, and browsed through the music tapes. Beginning to get hungry, he went back to campus, intending to eat at the campus dining hall with a meal card a friend had given to him, but the dining hall was closed. He thought about eating at a campus snack bar, but decided he would splurge on the $3.99 buffet at the Village Inn Pizza on Western Boulevard, not far from the campus.

First, he wanted to go by the library. He dropped off *Moby Dick* and picked up *The Decline and Fall of the Roman Empire* and *The Complete Works of William Shakespeare.*

He walked back across campus, went west on Sullivan Street, behind Lee dorm, turned left on Gorman Street. At an intersection one block from Western Boulevard, a car pulled up to the stop sign. A young man was driving, a young woman riding with him.

"Hey, Moog," the young man called through his open car window. "How you doin'? Where's your skateboard?"

Bart didn't recognize him, but he called a greeting anyway.

He took a shortcut through the parking lot of the Sav-A-Center. Two female students that he knew were coming out of the store, and he paused to chat with them.

"So what are you doing?" one asked.

"Just going to eat," Bart replied.

He took a table in the back of the pizza place, ordered iced tea, made several trips to the buffet bar, making sure he got his money's worth, stuffing himself with pizza and salad. A terrible thunderstorm came up while he was eating, and he decided to wait it out. A big-screen TV was playing near his table. A movie came on, *Helter Skelter,* about the Manson Family murders in California, but Bart paid it little attention. He was sipping tea and reading *The Decline and Fall of the Roman Empire.*

When a break came in the rain, Bart decided to try to make it back to campus. He went back by the same route he had come, but after he had crossed through the Sav-A-Center parking lot and cut through King Village, a campus housing area for married graduate students, the rain started coming down hard again. He took shelter under an apartment entrance.

304

During his wait, he struck up a conversation with a Korean student who lived in the apartment. The student had a small garden plot nearby, lush with vegetables, and the two chatted about gardening, Bart telling how he had grown up on a farm.

When it began to seem apparent that the rain was not going to end, Bart said to hell with it. He took off his shoes and the Cornell University sweatshirt he was wearing, stuffed them into his backpack, and struck out, walking barefoot in the rain. Soon after he turned onto Sullivan Drive, he saw a campus police car coming toward him, moving slowly.

At 7:06 P.M., Patrolman Terry Wright of the N.C. State Public Safety Department had been driving west on Faucette Drive, a campus street paralleling Western Boulevard, when he spotted a tall, thin young man with long, blondish-brown hair dressed in what he took to be green shorts and a dark blue sweatshirt, carrying a blue backpack, walking in the same direction. Wright had been alerted to be on the lookout for a former N.C. State student named James Bartlett Upchurch, wanted by the SBI for questioning about a murder. He had a photograph of Upchurch in his car, as did all patrol officers. This young man fit the description, but by the time Wright had turned his car around, the young man had disappeared. Wright figured he had slipped into nearby woods. He called for help. Several officers showed up, and they thoroughly searched the area without finding any sign of the young man. It was as if he had evaporated.

Now it was nine-thirty. A severe thunderstorm had swept over the campus and was rumbling on to the east. Thunderstorms always set off alarms in campus buildings, and Terry Wright was headed west on Sullivan Drive to check on an alarm. Rain was still falling hard, and he wasn't expecting to see any pedestrians in the darkness. But in the glow of the fluorescent street light near West Dunn Avenue, Wright saw a figure approaching. It was the same young man he'd seen two and a half hours earlier, still carrying the blue backpack, but without his shirt and shoes. He was strolling along nonchalantly, a small, portable radio and earphones in his hand. This time Wright took no chances. He radioed immediately for assistance, and keeping his eye on the young man, he turned around and sped back toward him.

At first, Bart started to run, a technique that had saved

him several times already, but he was barefoot, which would make running harder, and the cop was already on him. He decided to rely instead on a snow job.

Wright called to Bart from the open window of his patrol car. Bart stepped over to the car, the picture of innocence. What was the trouble?

Just looking for somebody, Wright said. Did he have any ID?

No, Bart said, he didn't have any with him.

"What's your name?" Wright asked.

"Edward Michael Owens," Bart replied.

He went on to say that he was from Tennessee, born on October, 17, 1970, and that he had a Tennessee driver's license but wasn't carrying it because he didn't have a car in Raleigh.

As they were talking, another campus police car pulled up, and Sergeant Lenora Mitchell got out. Yet another car quickly arrived.

Bart gave the same false name to Sergeant Mitchell, who seemed not to believe him. She asked if she could look inside his backpack.

"Sure," Bart said with a shrug.

As she began unzipping it, Bart added, "You won't find anything in there but a knife."

The knife, snuggled amidst clothing, toiletries, books, cassette tapes, a baseball, Bart's diary, and other items, was a kitchen knife with a seven-inch blade in a homemade cardboard sheath.

"What do you use this for?" Mitchell asked, examining the knife.

"I don't carry a pocketknife and I just use it for things you need a knife for," he said.

Sergeant Mitchell and Officer Wright were certain that this was James Upchurch. Mitchell asked if he would mind coming to the public safety office until his identity could be established. With all the officers surrounding him, Bart realized that he had no choice. He had to play this one out.

At the public safety office, Bart again repeated his false identity. He said that he lived in apartment 203 in the Kensington Apartments on Avent Ferry Road with his girlfriend, Justin Anastanoff, but he'd rather that they didn't involve her in this. They didn't have a phone, he said.

He was asked to wait in the upstairs conference room while

his identity was established. Couldn't he just wait at his apartment? Bart asked. The answer was no. How long did they think this would take? Bart wanted to know. He had to get some books back to the library before it closed at eleven. Couldn't he just run over there while they were doing this?

It only would take a little while, he was assured.

Indeed, Sergeant Mitchell already had called Captain Laura Reynolds, who had long been assisting John Taylor and Christy Newsom in their search for Moog. Reynolds immediately called the number for Lewis Young's pager.

Young and Terry Newell had left Howard Johnson's at a little after nine. They were on Western Boulevard alongside the campus, just beginning the evening's search when Young's pager began to beep. He went straight to a telephone and soon was talking with Reynolds, who said that their officers were fairly certain that they had Moog in custody. Young and Newell were at the public safety office in minutes.

"Hey, Moog," Young said when he walked into the conference room. "Do you remember me?"

Bart's head dropped. "Yeah," he said with resignation. "I remember."

Bart was given his socks, tennis shoes, and sweatshirt and was allowed to put them back on. Young told him that he was under arrest and would have to come with him. They went down the stairs and out the door into a tunnel-like opening in the building's ground floor. The building once had been an athletic fieldhouse, and the opening was a passageway leading to a tunnel beneath the railroad tracks that students used to get from one side of the campus to the other.

Bart was neither handcuffed nor shackled. Both agents had come away without handcuffs that night. Rain was still falling.

"You're not going to make me get out in the rain are you?" Bart said.

Newell said he'd go get the car, an SBI undercover Ford Mustang.

"We'll wait right here," Young said.

Newell pulled the car out of its parking space and began backing toward the breezeway. Suddenly, Bart spun to the left and bolted.

Young had kept a hold on the back of Bart's sweatshirt with his left hand and he clung to it as Bart began to run, pulling Young off balance. Young, who stood six feet tall and weighed just over two hundred pounds, was not about to be dragged far. He recovered after a few awkward steps, grabbed Bart's shoulder with his right hand, yanked him back, and slammed him against the breezeway wall, thrusting an elbow against his throat.

"Listen," Young said angrily, his face in Bart's, "you can go easy or you can go hard, but you're going one way or the other."

"Hey, man, no problem, no problem," Bart said, straining to talk. "I'll be cool."

Bart was taken to a suite of rooms on the third floor of the Holiday Inn, where he was handcuffed to a chair. Several SBI agents attempted to get him to talk. Neal had told them everything, they said. They even had found the bat. They knew that Chris had put him up to it. They wanted him to tell them about Chris. One agent tried to get him to sign a waiver of his rights.

"I told them, 'I think I'd better talk to a lawyer,'" Bart recalled later. "They said, 'That's the worst thing you can do. We'll work with you but you've got to help us.' I said, 'I want to talk with a lawyer.' This one said, 'Okay, if that's the way you want it.' Threw the paper down like he was all pissed off."

Soon afterward, Lewis Young came into the room, carrying a sheaf of papers. "I'm serving a warrant on you for first-degree murder," he said somberly.

"Right then, the guillotine dropped," Bart said later. "I said, 'I didn't have anything to do with this. I think you've got the wrong guy.' That was when I knew I should've left town a long time ago. Before, it all had seemed like a game. For the first time it was deadly serious."

Bart was taken before a magistrate at the Wake County Jail, then returned to the Howard Johnson's, where the officers who had searched so hard for him were celebrating with beer and takeout fast food. Christy Newsom had come by, although she couldn't have a beer because she was on duty. The only thing she was unhappy about was that John Taylor hadn't actually captured Moog. She knew how hard he had worked to break this case. Some uniformed officers who had assisted in the search dropped by with congratulations. Bart sat alone in an adjoining room, handcuffed to a chair, looking glum, watching a movie about an American mercenary in Nicaragua. He declined offers of pizza and hamburgers, but accepted a Coke.

John Crone had been the first person Taylor called with the good news. Crone wanted Melvin Hope to be in on this moment, and he dispatched him and Detective David Sparrow to Raleigh to pick up Moog and bring him back. It was about 2:00 A.M. before Hope and Sparrow got to Raleigh to hear the story of the capture. A short time later, as Moog shuffled to their patrol car, manacled, Hope said, "I hear you've got rabbit blood."

Bart didn't respond.

"Well," Hope went on, "I'm too fat and too old to chase you, but if you try to run, I guarantee you that when I do catch you, you won't want to run again."

Hope got into the backseat beside Bart. On the two-hour drive back to Washington, Sparrow kept the car radio on an oldies station. When one Elvis tune came on, Sparrow couldn't resist looking back over his shoulder grinning and singing a few verses of "Jailhouse Rock."

39

WAYLAND SERMONS learned of the murder of Lieth Von Stein when he got to the Beaufort County Courthouse on the morning it happened and overheard talk about it. His wife, Penny, called later, upset and worried, as most people were in Washington that day, concerned that a maniac might be on the loose in their pleasant little town.

Sermons hadn't heard of Von Stein before that day, which was unusual, because he knew most of the town's prominent citizens. He had grown up in Washington's privileged class, and it was, for the most part, a small and tight circle.

Sermons was just thirty-four, and he still lived in the

rambling, well-crafted house in which he had grown up in a private waterfront enclave in east Washington. His father, a state legislator for a dozen years, owned a chain of tobacco warehouses in North Carolina, Georgia, and Florida. His father also built the Carolinian, for decades a popular oceanfront resort hotel at Nags Head on North Carolina's famed Outer Banks. Wayland had spent all of his boyhood summers at the hotel, working as a lifeguard during his years at a private high school in Washington.

After high school, Sermons entered the University of North Carolina at Chapel Hill with no idea of what he wanted to do with his life. He soon got caught up in the good times of the fraternity scene, causing his classroom performance to be less than impressive. In his junior year, at the urging of a family friend, he dropped out to work as a political aide for a candidate for lieutenant governor.

When his candidate failed, Sermons returned to the university, this time with more resolve. He won a degree in business administration, married soon afterward, and enrolled in the prestigious law school at Wake Forest University in Winston-Salem. His marriage ended in the second year of law school, but he got his degree and passed the bar exam. He had several job offers, including one with the civil rights division of the U.S. Department of Justice in Washington. He chose instead to return home, working briefly for an older lawyer, another family friend, before opening his own practice in a storefront at the corner of Market and Main streets, just a block from the courthouse.

Now remarried and the father of two children, Sermons was getting ready to go off to Myrtle Beach for a weekend of fun with two old law school chums on Friday, June 15, 1989, when he got a call asking him to come immediately to the district courtroom. He arrived to discover that he had just been appointed the attorney for an indigent client charged with one of the biggest murders in Washington's history.

Like almost everybody else in Washington, Sermons had heard all the rumors about the Von Stein case: that it was an inside job, a family matter. He had heard courthouse scuttlebutt that an arrest might be imminent, and he had assumed that if that were true, the defendant likely would be Von Stein's stepson. He was not expecting the glum young man who turned out to be his client. Clearly, this was not the type of person he

310

usually represented in court. Indigent murder defendants rarely had names like James Bartlett Upchurch III.

Bart had arrived in Washington in the predawn hours. He was taken first to the police department, where he was photographed and fingerprinted, then whisked over to the jail in the basement of the courthouse, where he was told to shower and issued a set of orange coveralls. Both the police and the district attorney wanted to keep his arrest a secret, so as not to tip off Chris, and without any sleep, Bart was hurried into a district courtroom, where he could be quickly arraigned and have a lawyer appointed without reporters learning about it. He was charged not only with first-degree murder, but with conspiracy to murder, with assault with a deadly weapon with intent to kill, with first-degree burglary and felonious larceny. He was immediately taken back to the jail, where Wayland Sermons first talked with him in a small interview cell.

Sermons could tell that Bart was scared and obviously depressed, but he was immediately talkative. He knew nothing about any murder, he said, and he certainly hadn't committed one. He felt sure that Chris was involved—the police had said as much—and a guy he had lived with before his arrest, Neal Henderson, might be as well.

Bart told how he had gotten to know Chris and said he'd only been to Washington once, when he and Hank and Chris had passed through on their way to the beach.

On the night of the murder, he said, he was in his dorm room alone, studying. Chris was downstairs playing cards with his roommate, Chuck, and two girls, Sandra and Sybil. Chris had called about 12:30 A.M. and asked him to come and play spades, but he said he had to study. A little later, about one, Neal came by his room, high on acid, but he only stayed for a while and left alone. The next morning, Chuck called and told him that Chris's parents had been attacked.

He told about Chris's extensive drug use and how he had acted crazy after the murder. He said that the police and the SBI had talked to him on several occasions and gave a rundown of what he had told them. He went through all the events of his arrest the night before. Sermons warned him not to talk to anybody, not to jailers, not to other inmates, and certainly not to any police officers about any aspect of the case.

Bart was especially concerned about one thing. Would this

be on TV? Would it be in the newspapers? He didn't want his family to know that he had been arrested.

Sermons was certain that the news soon would be carried by local newspapers and TV stations, but he didn't know how widespread it might be. Although the murder had been big news in Washington, it hadn't been reported in most of the state's major cities. Unless Bart's arrest made the wire services, his family likely wouldn't hear about it in the news. But they would have to know about it eventually, Sermons reminded him. There was no way to avoid it.

After sleeping late Friday morning, John Taylor and SBI agents Lewis Young and Terry Newell drove to Winston-Salem. They arrived about 1:00 P.M. and met Agent Tom Sturgill at the Forsyth County Sheriff's Department. Before Melvin Hope and David Sparrow had driven to Raleigh to pick up Bart the night before, they had met with District Attorney Mitchell Norton, who drew a warrant for Chris's arrest. Young now had that warrant, and at midafternoon the four officers drove to the modest Von Stein house on Konnoak Drive.

Bonnie answered the door. She was expecting them. Despite all the efforts of the district attorney and the police to keep Bart's arrest a secret, a friend from Washington had called that morning to tell her that a friend of Chris's had been arrested for murdering Lieth (a young woman who had dated Chris was a receptionist in the town hall, her mother was secretary to a local attorney). Chris had spent the previous night at a friend's house and Bonnie had called him there.

"Chris, you need to come home and sit with me, because things are happening," she later recalled telling him. Chris was on the phone to his attorney, Bill Osteen in Greensboro, when Bonnie invited the officers in. Bonnie was polite and businesslike as usual, unemotional, but she did not hesitate to let the officers know of her irritation. She simply couldn't understand why they were doing this, she said. They were making a big mistake, and they would have to answer for this injustice that they were inflicting upon her son and her family.

Chris was wearing Bermuda shorts and an N.C. State Wolfpack T-shirt. He seemed nervous but compliant when Young served the warrant and placed him in handcuffs. The officers told Bonnie that they would take Chris to a magistrate's office at the courthouse, where they would remain for about thirty minutes, before going on to Washington. She told Chris that she would follow and see him there. No tears came from either. Chris asked to get some cigarettes from his car before leaving, and the officers got them for him.

At the sheriff's department, Chris was allowed to use the telephone in a detective's office to make several private calls to friends, before the magistrate found probable cause for his arrest and left him in the custody of Young. Bonnie and the officers missed one another at the magistrate's office, and Chris was put into an SBI car without seeing his mother again. Young and Newell drove him back to Raleigh, where Newell was to pick up his own car. Taylor followed.

Chris was talkative along the way, although he didn't bring up the charges against him. He chatted about the tornadoes that recently had wreaked havoc in Winston-Salem. He said that he'd quit his job at the tire company about a month earlier and had enrolled in summer school at Wake Forest University in anticipation of attending either Appalachian State University, where his girlfriend was a student, or Guilford College, where his stepfather had gotten his degree, in the fall semester. He seemed to have no doubt that he would be free to return to school. He was taking chemistry, he said, but that was a mistake. What he really needed was some easy credit hours, and chemistry was far from that.

Despite the attempt to keep Bart's arrest a temporary secret, word of a break in the case had swirled swiftly through Washington. City Manager Bruce Radford got a call from a TV reporter saying he had heard that an arrest was about to be made. Could Radford help him? Radford suggested that he talk with Chief Crone.

"I've already talked to Crone," the reporter said. "He won't tell me anything."

At 5 P.M., Radford went to the police department to find out if Chris actually had been arrested. Crone wasn't there. Instead, Radford found a note that Crone had left for John Taylor, saying that he would be at the district attorney's office. Radford went there. As he was approaching the office's open door, he heard Norton saying, "Radford is our leak. He called the TV station and told them."

Radford knocked at the door, and stepped into the office. A hush fell over the room.

"Mitchell, I heard you say I was your leak," Radford said. "Let me tell you, I'm not. If you've got a leak it's somewhere else."

Radford was aware that his involvement in the case had been resented by many, but he was not about to step aside now that the case was coming to flower. He joined the planning for Chris's arrival. It was decided that Chris would be taken directly to the jail to try to avoid reporters and photographers. Chief Crone would call a press conference at the police station to divert their attention.

Nevertheless, TV camera crews and newspaper photographers were waiting at the back of the courthouse when Young pulled up to the jail entrance and hurried Chris inside.

At the police department, Crone announced the two arrests and said that a third suspect was yet to be picked up. The police knew where he was, Crone said, and bringing him in would be no problem. He could not go into the details of the case, but a witness, he said, had "told us exactly what happened." After offering details of the arrests, he was careful to point out that neither Bonnie nor Angela was implicated in the murder.

Bruce Radford stepped forward to commend Melvin Hope, John Taylor and especially Chief Crone, who, he said, brought "new angles of approach" to the investigation.

"This should allow the citizens of Washington to rest easier knowing arrests have been made in the case and that police department efforts led to the arrests," Radford said.

Wayland Sermons had tried only one murder case before. His client had pleaded self-defense and been convicted of second-degree murder. Bart's case would be much different. Sermons had no doubt that Norton would seek the death penalty.

Before he left for Myrtle Beach on Friday evening, Sermons learned that Norton would be going to the grand jury on Monday, seeking indictments against Bart and Chris and one other person, presumably Neal Henderson. When he got to the beach, he discussed what he knew about the case with his friends, Davis North and Wayland Cooke, both experienced trial attorneys in Greensboro, who were well acquainted with Chris's lawyer, Bill Osteen. Then Sermons realized that the reason Norton was seeking grand jury indictments was to avoid a probable cause hearing during which the state would have to make known the basis of its case. "It was deliberate," he said later. "It was to avoid having to reveal anything, to keep me from finding out what was going on."

Bart slept for a long time Friday. On Saturday, he had little appetite. He thought idly of suicide, although he knew that would be difficult and would require more thought and energy than he felt capable of mustering at the moment. Other thoughts preoccupied him, thoughts about his family. Yet when he was allowed access to a phone on Saturday, the first call he made was to Hank at the restaurant where he worked in Raleigh.

"Hey, man, where you at?" Bart recalled Hank saying after accepting the collect call.

"I'm in Little Washington."

"Man, what you doing there?"

"I got arrested for murder."

"No way, no way."

"Yeah, it's true."

"Look, Neal came by here, said he wanted to give you some money to get out of town, said he was going to come by here and bring it tonight."

"I think Neal may be working for the police. If he does come by there, he might be wearing a wire."

A little later in the conversation, talking about the seriousness of his situation, Bart's voice broke. "They're going for the death penalty," he said.

"Can't be good, man."

"They're going to kill me for this."

Now Bart couldn't control himself any longer. He started to cry. "Throw me a good wake," he said. "Make sure there's a lot of beer and a lot of pizza there. Make it a good party."

Afterward, Bart steeled himself to make the call he had been dreading, the call he had been putting off for more than a day. He dialed his mother's number in Virginia.

Joanne had remarried and had a fifth child, another son, but things had not been going so well for her in recent months. In December, her husband, Alan Ferguson, had undergone surgery for a knee injury and almost died from a pulmonary embolism that developed from the operation. Joanne herself had been hospitalized numerous times since April for tachycardia, a rapid and uncontrollable heartbeat. Several medications had been tried without success, including one potent drug that produced toxic side effects. She was scheduled to check into the University of Virginia Hospital in Charlottesville on Sunday, June 18, for a series of tests. She was packed and ready to leave when her telephone rang shortly before dinner Saturday evening.

A collect call from Bart. Yes, she would accept. Was he calling to wish her well at the hospital?

"Hi, honey, how are you doing?" she said brightly.

"Hi, Mom."

She thought she detected a quiver in his voice, something unusual for Bart. "Are you all right?"

"No," he said in a sudden gush of tears. "I've been arrested."

"Arrested? For what?"

She had been through this before. What had he gotten himself into now?

"For murder," he said, crying as she had never heard him before. "Mom, they want the death penalty."

Joanne could not believe her ears. Murder? The death penalty? This couldn't be happening. She wasn't even aware that she had begun to scream. "No, Bart, no."

"I didn't do it, Mom," Bart kept saying. "I didn't do it. Please don't cry. Please don't cry."

Later, Bart would recall his mother being hysterical. "She said, 'How many times have I told you you've got to watch the type of people you're hanging out with? You can't hang out with white trash.' I said, 'Mom, I wasn't hanging out with white trash. The people who got me into this trouble were rich white kids.'"

A year after their separation, Jim and Joanne had agreed that their children really should be with their mother, and they had gone to live with her in Virginia. A week before Bart's call, Joanne had sent her two daughters, Carrie and Alex, to North Carolina to spend several weeks with their father and grandmother. Their father had taken them camping along the Blue Ridge Parkway, and they had returned on Saturday. Jim had dropped his daughters off at his mother's house in Milton, then gone on home to the farm.

Carolyn was happy to have her granddaughters with her,

and when the phone rang Saturday evening and she heard Joanne's voice on the line, she assumed that she was calling to check on the girls.

Instead, Joanne said, "You'd better sit down. I've got something terrible to tell you."

"What on earth?" Carolyn said.

"Bart has been arrested for murder."

Carolyn immediately called Jim.

"Jim, I've got something to tell you. Bart is in jail in Beaufort County."

"What for this time?" he asked, not in the least surprised that Bart was again in jail.

"For murder," Carolyn said aghast.

A long silence came from the other end of the line.

"I was numb," Jim recalled later. "Disappointed. Let down. Defeated and helpless. Here was the culmination of all my worries. You've talked and talked and begged and tried to get him to do what he needed to do, and here he goes again, back into another mess, but this time far worse than anything before."

Wayland Sermons returned home from the beach Sunday night and had a conference with the district attorney on Monday morning. "Mitchell Norton says no way to bond hearing in district court," Sermons wrote in a memo to himself. "Case's going to grand jury today."

Lewis Young spent more than an hour outlining the case against Chris, Bart, and Neal for the grand jurors that morning before they returned all of the indictments requested by the district attorney.

Bonnie and Angela had driven to Washington after Chris's arrest, and on Saturday Bonnie had met with James Vosburgh, the Washington lawyer who had represented Chris when he got into trouble in high school and had handled other legal problems for the Von Steins. Vosburgh, whose own son had graduated from high school with Chris, met with Chris for more than an hour in the jail Friday night. He accompanied Bonnie on a visit to Chris on Saturday. On Monday Vosburgh told a reporter for the Washington *Daily News*, Mike Voss, that Chris was frightened by the murder charge.

317

"His reaction is one of shock, amazement, and disbelief," Vosburgh said.

Bart's cousin, Kenyatta, went to Raleigh on Monday to comfort Neal on the night before he was arrested. He called and asked her to be there with him. "He was scared," she said. "He cried that night. I hemmed his pants. We washed his clothes. He didn't have any good shoes except for the ones that went with his Wendy's outfit. We polished those."

John Taylor and Lewis Young left Washington for Raleigh before seven Tuesday morning. Neal was ready when they got there, and they were back in Washington before noon. Reporters and photographers were waiting to get a look at this third suspect. At a little before five that afternoon, Neal was brought into Superior Court wearing shackles and the standard orange jumpsuit. Judge Herbert Small questioned him about his ability to hire an attorney.

Speaking in a voice so soft that it was barely audible a few benches back, Neal said that he couldn't afford a lawyer. He had only $10 in the bank and $40 in his pocket when he was arrested, he said. His job paid him $4.15 per hour. He was to have received a raise the following Monday, he noted, when he was to have been promoted to shift manager. Although he didn't mention it to the judge, that was the promotion that would have given him the courage, as he had promised Kenyatta, to go and face his former teacher, Weldon Slayton, again.

While Neal was in the courtroom, Jim Upchurch was talking for the first time with Bart's lawyer. Jim had been so dispirited after receiving the call about Bart's arrest, so resentful about being sucked into another morass of misery into which his son had wandered, that he had put off calling. Now Sermons told him that Bart appeared to be in shock over his arrest and that he kept adamantly insisting that he had had no part in any murder.

Until talking with Sermons, Jim had thought that Bart must be involved in some peripheral way. He would not have been surprised, he told Sermons, if he had learned that Bart had been arrested for any number of other things, but to be accused of actually killing somebody, sneaking up on a sleeping innocent and beating and hacking him to death was beyond his comprehension.

"I just can't believe that Bart could do anything like that," he said. "He's not an aggressive or violent person. I've never even seen him get into a fight or hit or shove anybody."

Sermons was reluctant to talk about details over the phone. The case was a big one, he said, with local political implications, and he was wary that his phone might be tapped. Jim told him that he would drive to Washington on Saturday.

Bart looked completely different when he was brought into the tiny cell where Jim was allowed to meet with him in the Beaufort County Jail that Saturday, nearly nine days after his arrest. His long, bleached hair had just been shorn, the locks still lying in a jail corridor where they had been swept. He looked pale and thinner than when Jim last had seen him a few months earlier. The atmosphere was less tense than Jim anticipated, almost casual.

"How you doing?" Jim asked.

"Okay, I guess."

"So what's going on?"

The story came from Bart in a gush. It was all about Neal. Neal had framed him. Neal was lying. Neal must've been the one who did it. Neal was going to the gas chamber for sure.

"He was a little cocky," Jim recalled later. "Bart can get cocky when he feels like he's in trouble."

"Where were you when the murder happened?" Jim asked.

"I was at the dorm that night," Bart said.

"Did anybody see you?"

It was hard to remember, he said, but he thought that a couple of people did. Hank. And a girl maybe.

Would they be willing to testify?

Bart was sure that they would.

Jim felt better after talking with Bart. If he had an alibi and witnesses, he at least had hope.

But mainly Jim felt better just because he had come.

"I think he was glad to see me," Jim said later, "I was glad I was there. I felt guilty about waiting that long."

40

By THE FIRST OF JULY, the Beaufort County Courthouse was swamped with lawyers filing motions on behalf of the three defendants in the Von Stein murder case.

Two Washington lawyers, Michael Paul and Chris Mc-Lendon, who would be running for a judgeship soon, had been appointed to represent Neal. He had done fine, they told him, but now it was time for him to quit talking and let them take care of matters, their first priority being to get him out of jail on reasonable bail.

Frank Johnston, a Washington native and Wake Forest University law graduate who had been practicing in the town for more than seventeen years, had been appointed to work with Wayland Sermons on Bart's behalf. Their major problem was finding out just what evidence the state had against their client, who proclaimed complete innocence and said the police had come after him only because he was the only one of Chris's friends who had been in trouble before.

Chris's attorneys, Bill Osteen, his son, Bill Jr., and James Vosburgh, who was assisting the Osteens in Washington, were having similar problems.

During the last week in June, all of the lawyers filed detailed discovery motions seeking to know all of the evidence that the state had accumulated about their clients.

The state had by no means finished gathering evidence. For John Taylor and Lewis Young, the case was ongoing.

Two days after arresting Neal, Taylor and Young were back in Raleigh, calling once again upon the friends of Bart, Chris, and Neal, telling about the arrests, warning that lawyers and private investigators might be calling, trying to decide who would make good witnesses and who would not, attempting to tie up loose ends. Quincy Blackwell looked at photos of the bat John Crone had found and said that it looked like one Moog had in his dorm room the previous summer. The markings on it were familiar, he said; Moog liked to diagram stuff like that.

Sandra Goodman told them that she'd recently had a long

talk with Brew and he was frightened that the police might be trying to implicate him and Chuck in the murder. He assured her that he knew nothing about the attack on Chris's parents either before or after it happened, and he was positive that Chuck didn't know anything either.

A week after Neal's arrest, Taylor dropped by the jail to visit with him. Neal, Chris, and Bart were kept in separate cell blocks and couldn't communicate with one another. Taylor wasn't on business. He had come to like Neal and he had gone to a used book store and bought a stack of science fiction for him. He just wanted to drop off the books and reassure Neal that things would work out for the best.

A week later, Taylor and Young returned to Winston-Salem to interview Chuck Jackson at his summer job. As before, the officers got the impression that Chuck wanted them to leave him alone, that he'd answered all the questions he wanted to answer about Chris and Moog. They showed him the bat, the knapsack, the knife. He claimed he'd never seen any of them.

Did he remember seeing Neal on the day before the murder?

A private detective had asked him the same thing a few days earlier, Chuck said.

Taylor and Young were surprised that a private eye was already making rounds. He had to be representing Chris. Obviously, Bill Osteen didn't intend to waste any time in preparing Chris's defense.

Chuck said he told the detective that he thought Neal had come by his and Chris's room that night, but he really didn't remember whether Neal had come by or not. The private eye had asked him repeatedly about whether or not he had found Chris's car keys after Chris left on the morning of the murder, he said, and he'd told him that he did. Actually, he said, he couldn't remember whether he did or not, which was what he had told Taylor earlier.

Chuck did remember one thing. Shortly after noon on the day of the murder, he had looked out and seen Chris's car parked where he usually left it, between Sullivan and Burgaw dorms. He was certain about that.

Both Sandra Goodman and Sybil Cook had told the detectives the same thing. Yet Neal maintained that he had left the car in the fringe parking lot that morning when he and James returned. And Neal claimed that he had hidden the keys in a bathroom closet in Chris's suite. Had somebody driven the car later that morning?

Nearly a month after the arrests, the Von Stein murder was still big news in Washington. On Wednesday, July 12, the residents of Beaufort County got their first indication of motive when a story appeared on the front page of the Washington *Daily News* under a big headline that said "Murdered Von Stein left $2-million." Until then, Von Stein's newly acquired wealth hadn't been made public. Quoting probate documents, the newspaper set the value of his estate at $1,940,206.92, including life insurance of $770,000, all of which was left to his widow. The report went on to note that if Bonnie had died in the attack, her children would have inherited the entire amount. In Washington that day, many people were commenting that now they could understand why Chris had been charged. Many also were noting that Bonnie would be coming out of this ordeal well fixed.

That night, Bonnie called John Taylor at home and asked if he would mind having lunch with her the following day. She wanted to talk about the case, but she didn't want it to be an official meeting. They agreed in advance, Taylor later said, that it would be personal and private. Neither would take notes. Taylor accepted because he wanted one more chance to try to persuade Bonnie that they were only prosecuting, not persecuting, her son. Bonnie suggested the King & Queen Restaurant in Greenville, and Taylor agreed to meet her there at noon.

He called the district attorney after talking with Bonnie to make certain that he wasn't doing something wrong. Norton didn't object, nor did he instruct him as to what he could say.

Taylor was nervous about the meeting. He wanted to do everything right, and he especially didn't want to make any faux pas. The King & Queen was not the type of place where he normally dined. He knew that it was very expensive, and he was uncertain whether he should try to pick up the check, since Bonnie had invited him. He called his close friend and confidante, Lila Howard, the city personnel director, to ask for tips on etiquette. She told him to let Bonnie pay if she attempted to do so and assured him that he would do fine.

Taylor arrived at the King and Queen to find Bonnie waiting and the restaurant closed for lunch. She was wearing

Bermuda shorts and a blouse. He had forsaken his blue jeans and cowboy boots for dress slacks, a tie, and short-sleeve shirt. Bonnie suggested Sweet Caroline's, the restaurant where she and Lieth had their last meal together, and Taylor followed her there.

Taylor felt awkward, and he sensed that Bonnie did, too. After all, it was his efforts that had put her son in jail, awaiting trial for his life.

In the next hour, Taylor revealed all the basic facts he and the other officers had uncovered about the case, answered all of Bonnie's questions, but even as he did it, he knew that Bonnie was not accepting his vision of the truth.

When he told her that the FBI had verified Chris's handwriting on the map, Bonnie maintained that wasn't concrete evidence. Somebody could have tricked him into drawing it, she said. He might have drawn it for some other purpose at some point in the past and somebody had come upon it and taken it.

The waiter brought the check while they talked and left it by Taylor's plate. As their conversation was drawing to a close, Bonnie discreetly reached over and retrieved the check. The meeting ended amicably with Taylor assuring her that he would continue looking into the case, Bonnie thanking him for telling her much that she had not known before. Taylor's only disappointment was that once more he had failed to sway Bonnie to the state's view.

"Bonnie just couldn't accept it," he said later. "Her boy couldn't have done that, and that's all there was to it. She was a very stubborn woman when it came to that."

Later, Taylor was surprised and disappointed to learn that despite their agreement that the lunch was to be personal and private, without note taking, as soon as they parted, Bonnie wrote down everything she could remember that he had told her and took it straight to her lawyer in Washington, James Vosburgh.

On Friday, July 21, Neal was taken from the Beaufort County Jail and whisked twenty-five miles north to Williamston in Martin County, where Superior Court Judge Thomas Watts was holding court. With no reporters present, Judge Watts set a bond of $200,000, $50,000 of it to be secured by money or property owned by an assortment of relatives and family friends of Neal's mother. The arrangements had been worked out previously. Neal was released on condition that he not associate with Chris or Bart, that he reside with his mother, who had moved into a small house in Danville, Virginia, and that he report weekly to the court or to his lawyer in Washington, Michael Paul. Neal's former employers already had arranged for him to have another job at a Wendy's in Danville.

On the day of Neal's release, James Vosburgh filed a motion at the Beaufort County Courthouse to have Chris released on a bond of $100,000 so that he could assist his lawyers in preparing his case and continue the psychiatric care that he had been receiving before his arrest. The motion noted that Chris "has suffered severe depression over the loss of his stepfather and the near fatal injuries inflicted to his mother."

Not until the next week did the people of Beaufort County learn of Neal's release. Even then, the district attorney declined to comment about it.

That week brought another flurry of motions from lawyers on all sides.

Wayland Sermons was furious when he learned that James Vosburgh had received crime scene photos and FBI evidence reports from John Taylor the week before, but he had yet to receive anything from the state. Although he was certain that Neal was to be the state's chief witness, he still had no idea what Neal had told the police about Bart's involvement. He prepared a volley of motions asking that Bart be released under a $150,000 bond, that money be provided to hire private investigators to help him prepare his case, and that the state be compelled to turn over evidence against Bart so that his lawyers could fight the charges.

Chris's lawyers also filed several motions, asking that police officers be required to preserve all the rough notes from their investigation, that all court proceedings be fully recorded, and that his eventual trial be removed from Beaufort County because of adverse news coverage.

The state, meanwhile, filed a motion asking that Chris's attorneys be required to turn over the evidence they intended to use at his trial.

Neal's attorneys also requested evidence from the state and filed a preliminary indication that they, too, would seek money for private investigators.

Lawyers anticipated that many of these motions would be

heard when the regular session of Superior Court opened in Washington on Monday, July 31.

Neal was required to be in court that morning to hear motions in his case and answered when the calendar was called. He left and returned a couple of times that morning, at one point sitting in the same row as Bonnie and Angela, who had come to court hoping that Chris's bond motion would be heard.

When the normally calm Bonnie caught her first sight of Neal, she became so upset that she fled the courtroom and had to be taken to her lawyer's office nearby to be calmed. Later, she told John Taylor that Neal gave her an eerie feeling and she thought that he was the person who had been in her bedroom the night of the murder. The shadowy figure that attacked her and her husband, she said, resembled Neal's thick and blocky body more than Bart's long and lanky frame.

Chris's motion for bond was heard the following morning. He was brought into the courtroom, where he hugged his mother and sister and sat attentively through the proceedings. Judge Watts set his bond at $300,000, half of which had to be secured. When Watts learned that Bonnie intended to use two certificates of deposit to meet the secured bond, he noted that he had "problems" with property that belonged to the victim being used to secure bond for the accused, but he allowed the certificates to be used anyway.

Chris was released at two-thirty. Dressed in dark gray slacks, an expensive sport jacket, a purple print tie, his mother on his arm, she wearing sunglasses, her long hair tied into a pony tail, Chris hurried from the courthouse behind his lawyer, all three ignoring questions from a reporter who trailed along.

Bart was the only defendant in the case now left in jail, and his chance at freedom came two days later, when he was ushered into court for his bond hearing. Judge Watts set the total bond at half a million dollars, all of it to be secured. Not even Bart's grandmother, who always had come to her family's financial rescue in the past, could afford such risk, and Bart was returned to jail to await his trial, the date of which remained unknown.

Bart actually had believed that he might be able to get out on bond—a pipe dream, his father had called it—and the judge's ruling sent him back into depression.

His father came again to see him. Carolyn came with his Uncle John, who just had become an assistant prosecutor in

Alamance County. His mother was not able to visit. After undergoing an elaborate series of medical tests during the week following Bart's arrest, doctors determined that she needed a pacemaker implanted in her heart. Complications followed the surgery and she had to be rehospitalized several times. It would be September before she was finally recovered enough to visit Bart.

The person Bart was most frequently in contact with was Hank. Bart regularly called him collect at his mother's restaurant. Sometimes Hank would even hold the receiver up to a speaker so Bart could hear a favorite song on the jukebox.

But it was Bart's inability to find out what was happening to himself that was more responsible than anything else for pulling him out of his depression.

"I didn't know what was going on, who was saying what. It was really a strange position to be in. I had a hard time understanding it and coping with it. Wayland would come by. He didn't know what was going on. He told me, 'You've got to help me. If we're going to fight this, you've got to work with me.' What happened was I started getting mad. The SBI and the Washington Police Department were fucking me over, setting me up, doing shit to my family. I just got more and more pissed off, started getting involved, started working. Eventually, I started using a line on myself: might not be as bad as it seems, might be able to get out on bail. I said, 'Hell, I ain't going to give up the ghost yet.' "

The bond hearing burst that bubble of hope temporarily, but it didn't squelch Bart's will to fight.

"I started looking at the situation," he said later. "As far as I could tell, there was no evidence that I did anything. I had been arrested on Neal's word, I figured. I just started gathering all the information I could get about what Neal had been saying to people."

Others were trying to find out what Neal had said, too, including Bart's father. Sermons had urged him to find out anything he could about Neal from his niece, Kenyatta, who was living that summer at her grandmother's house in Milton. That proved to be more difficult than Jim expected. Although Kenyatta liked Jim, her loyalty clearly was to Neal, not to Bart, her own blood, whom she openly detested.

That made the summer particularly difficult for her grandmother, with whom she was living. Her own grandson, Bart, her first grandchild, whom she deeply loved despite his problems, was in jail facing the possibility of the death penalty, and her granddaughter was loyal to her grandson's accuser.

"It was the most difficult situation you've ever seen in your life," Carolyn said later. "She was living here, hating her cousin. Everybody was just handling her with care. It was like walking on eggs all day long, every day."

During the days when Neal was in jail, he called Carolyn's house regularly, collect, sometimes twice a day, talking long periods with Kenyatta. Before his arrest, Neal made one request of Kenyatta. He wanted her to make peace with his mother, so that they could support one another during this difficult period.

Kenyatta had made an effort. She called Ann Henderson at Penney's, where she worked, and arranged to meet her for dinner. Neal's mother was not able to go out when Kenyatta arrived, because she had to be home with her daughter. Instead, they ordered a pizza and sat in the living room at Ann Henderson's house, chatting.

"She was being really nice to me," Kenyatta said later, but Kenyatta could tell that it was a strain for her. Kenyatta was wary and soon became skeptical about Ann Henderson's motivation.

"The only reason she wanted to talk with me was to get information to get her son out of jail," Kenyatta said later. "I really tried with Ann Henderson for Neal's sake. I spent the whole summer trying to be friends, but that wasn't possible. She hated me. Oh, God, she hated me.

"As the summer progressed, I got angrier and angrier at Neal. I got so fed up with the whole thing, I said, 'I don't care what happens.' I was so mad I didn't care what happened to Neal or to James or to anybody."

Despite her anger, at her grandmother's request, Kenyatta agreed to talk with Bart's attorneys, Wayland Sermons and Frank Johnston, who drove to Milton on August 16, and met her at Carolyn's big gray ghost of a house.

She told them about the night Neal claimed to have taken LSD, when he stayed out all night, returned agitated the next morning, and gave her fifty dollars. She told them how he had been preoccupied and depressed after that. She said that after the police began questioning Neal, he told her that he had been involved in the murder of Chris's stepfather and that he and Bart had done it. Neal wouldn't give her any details, she told the lawyers, although, in fact, he had. She said Neal told her that he had talked with the police because he thought it would help him. She had not been approached by anybody else about the case, she said, but Neal had warned her about Chris's investigator who was "a bad FBI type."

Kenyatta hadn't wanted to tell the lawyers anything, especially if it might help Bart, who deserved whatever was coming to him, in her opinion. She had taken an immediate dislike to Sermons. "He was just covered in syrup," she said later. "Biggest politician I ever saw in my life. I couldn't stand him."

Carolyn was relieved at the end of August when Kenyatta left to begin her freshman year at the University of North Carolina at Chapel Hill. No longer did she have to worry about saying something about Bart or Neal, whom she'd always liked, that might provoke Kenyatta's volatile nature.

41

LAWYERS ON ALL SIDES OF the Von Stein case scrimmaged throughout September and into October, filing dozens of motions, arguing in court over technicalities and procedures, the defense lawyers seeking separate trials for each defendant, trying to get those trials moved from Beaufort County, asking for rulings that would relieve their clients of the possibility of the death penalty.

In October, Judge Watts authorized the hiring of private detectives on Bart's behalf, and Sermons called on Bill Sirgenson of Greenville, who had provided bodyguards for Bonnie immediately after the murder.

Early in October Bart was taken from the Beaufort County Jail without notice and driven to Raleigh, where he was placed in the Wake County Jail, more than a two-hour-drive away from his lawyers. The ostensible reason was to have Bart tried for probation violations.

Bill Sirgenson and another detective who worked with him, Paul Davis, went to Raleigh to talk with Bart about the case. He asked if Bart recalled anything unusual happening about the time of the murder.

"Unusual?" said Bart, thinking. "Well, the night of the murder, I guess, Henderson came by and he said that he had an outfit that he wanted to go rob. He told me he had an outfit he wanted to hit, that there was a house that he wanted to rob."

"Who was that?"

"Henderson."

"Was that the night of the murder?"

"That was the night of the murder. I told him that I was through doing that."

"What time of night?"

"Around twelve or twelve-thirty, one o'clock, somewhere along in there. The next day, of course, Chris Pritchard's roommate called and told me about the murder happening."

Later in the interview, Sirgenson quizzed Bart about the investigation, why the police had begun looking at him, why they had talked to Neal. Bart said that he figured they came after him because he had a prior record and was hiding out because of his probation problems.

"Not long after I dropped out of sight, they talked to Henderson. I don't know if they had some evidence on Henderson or whether Henderson decided to come clean, but apparently Henderson told them that I was the actual hit man in this murder and he was the get-away-car driver and Chris Pritchard was the mastermind behind it all.

"Okay. That does not really follow. For one, Chris is not really that smart. Two, I don't see why they needed a get-away-car driver. In the first place, why would he want to bring in a whole bunch of people on something like this? Now I can drive as well as anybody else. I guess the main-line reason we are going on now is that Henderson is faced with the possibility of a lot of time, and to do something to cover his ass, I guess he decided to implicate me."

A few minutes later, Sirgenson said, "Let me ask you this. Did you, and I want you to answer truthfully, did you have anything to do with this murder, either planning it, doing it, or knowing about it right after it happened? Or before it happened?"

"After it happened, like a couple of weeks after it happened, everybody sort of got the details, knew what was going on. Every once in a while, when we were sitting around drinking beer, we would sort of start discussing what went on, you know, and what did we think really happened, and all of this. Like having a bull session. It was then I reflected back to what Neal was talking about, that he had a house he could hit and that he could make a lot of money on it, and you know, he said it was going to be a big one. He was expecting to make several thousand dollars."

"I'm going to ask you the question again," Sirgenson said. "Did you have anything to do with it?"

"Oh, no sir. Not at all. Not at all. No hesitation about that. No sir."

"Did you know about any of this beforehand?"

"No sir." Bart rambled on about Chuck calling to tell him about the murder afterward.

"All right, I want you to look me in the eye. Did you have any knowledge beforehand? Was there any discussion of doing this around you before the murder?"

Bart, who had a habit of holding his head down and glancing away from people while talking with them, looked him in the eye. "There was never any discussion of anything like this. There were people would occasionally make jokes along the line of, you know, 'Well, Chris, when are you going to off your folks?' Chris knew about it. Everybody knew about it. It was like the common joke."

Later, Sirgenson said, "I want to ask you another question before we leave. Who did the killing, do you think?"

"Probably, if Neal didn't actually do it himself, I would think maybe Butch or Quincy, one of his roommates, because Butch told the SBI that he would kill someone if he was paid enough. I know Butch had a history of being violent when drunk, or whatever. There was one time he and Neal almost got into a fight."

Bart knew that when the police detectives first came around, they asked many questions about Butch and Quincy, especially about Butch; he would have known that had to be for some purpose.

A few days after the private detectives interviewed Bart at

the Wake County Jail, Paul Davis questioned Butch Mitchell at his apartment on Ligon Street and came away with some startling information that Butch had not told the police.

"Were you involved in that murder in any way?" Davis asked Butch.

"No, not deliberately, if that's what you're trying to say."

"Well, then, what way?"

"Well, they know that I'm hurting people, and like, we usually play these D&D games. They ask me, like pertaining to the game, what would I do, what would you do to kill somebody?"

"Yes."

"And I told them—I didn't think nothing of it—I told them and that was it."

"What did you tell them?"

"I told them that, like in the game, when you go kill someone to make sure. Kill them fast and don't make noise. What you would do is wait till they're asleep, the person be laying there, you get the easy side, I don't know how many people you got, you get the easy side, and then you all attack at the same time. That way you get as much damage as can be done. There's no way for them to scream or yell out."

"Okay."

"And you do something else to make it look like it was a robbery. You just happen to go in there to rob them and surprise them. And make sure you have somewhere to corroborate an alibi. Because the alibi is the main thing. Show up someplace so people can see you. At a party, you gonna see somebody for a few minutes and then leave. You can leave and come back and nobody knows the difference."

"How about this particular murder? Did you advise anybody on this particular murder, how they could do it? Was this particular murder discussed? That's what I want to know."

"No."

"Did they ever sit around and talk about how they could get rid of Chris's father?"

"Not that I heard."

A couple of minutes later, Davis asked, "Who do you think committed the murder?"

"You mean the actually stabbing and stuff like that? I think they all did it."

331

"When you say 'they all,' you're referring to Chris Pritchard?

"Yes, Chris Pritchard."

"Neal Henderson?"

"Neal, you know, may have done it."

"James Upchurch?"

"Yes, Moog."

"Do you think James Upchurch was there the night the murder was committed?"

"He was with them. He said he was with them."

"Did you hear him say that he was with them that night?"

"Yes."

"You heard Moog say he was with them when the murder was committed?"

"Yes, because he say, I asked him, 'If you all went and came to pick up Neal, why didn't you let me go?' He say, 'You don't go there because there was, like, a lot of dope and stuff like that there.'"

"Were they doing acid at that time?"

"They said they had some drugs there."

A little later Davis asked, "Do you think anybody else was involved in this besides the three you told me?"

"I understand there was two more guys."

"Who do you understand there were?"

"I don't know. It had to be somebody that I don't know."

"You never heard names?"

"No. They ain't said. If they were doing something, they never told me about it."

"But you think there were five involved?"

"Yes."

"Do you think Chris actually went down there with them?"

"Yes. His car was there. He ain't gonna let nobody go with his car."

Just as John Taylor had done, the private detectives and Bart's attorney's discounted Butch's version. But Wayland Sermons knew one thing for certain: He wouldn't be putting Butch Mitchell on the stand.

By the end of October, Judge Tom Watts had sorted through the sea of motions and settled most of the major issues in the Von Stein cases. There would be two trials, one for Neal, a combined trial for Bart and Chris, who would be tried for their lives. Judge Watts also ordered that the trials be moved from Beaufort County to Elizabeth City in Pasquotank County, one hundred miles northeast of Washington, where there had been little news about the case. The first trial, that of Bart and Chris, was set to begin January 2, 1990.

Bart's attorneys were distressed that they did not win a separate trial. That might have allowed them to keep out some evidence, such as the map, which had been tied only to Chris. Also Chris's trial undoubtedly would have been first and they could have used it to learn the state's entire case. As it was, they knew very little about the state's evidence. Despite all their motions for discovery, they still didn't even know exactly what Neal had told the police, their only knowledge coming from the bits and pieces that had been disclosed in the state's own motions.

By early November, after spending three weeks in the Wake County Jail, Bart was back in Beaufort County, his family friend, George Daniel, now a state senator, having succeeded in getting any hearing of his probation violations postponed until after his murder trial. He was now taking an active role in his own defense, placing calls to feel out potential witnesses, keeping notes for Wayland Sermons.

On Wednesday, November 7, he called Kenyatta at her dorm room at the university. He was pleased with the conversation and made these notes after they had talked:

*She's dating Phillip Thompson.
*No shoe ID from her.
*Said Neal expects to be free.
*Said she knew Neal was stealing for sure.
*Got along real good w/her, she'll be glad to testify at trial.
*She's talked to Neal about once a month until a couple of months ago when she pissed him off by telling him about other guys she's seeing.

His notes about his conversation with his cousin were indicative of Bart's ability to delude himself. Kenyatta's view of the conversation was decidedly different.

"He called me up from jail, talking just as sweet and nice. 'How you doing? How's Carolyn?' I'm thinking, bull, bull, bull. Then he says, 'So what did Neal tell you?' It really pissed me off. He thought he was going to use family influence to tell his lawyer stuff to get him off. I felt totally harassed. I told my grandmother, 'I have no loyalty to James at all. There's a lot you don't know and a lot you don't want to hear.' I hated him. I thought he was total pond-scum. I thought he was the worst person in the world. I wouldn't do anything to help him. I got sick of my family protecting him. I just got sick of it."

Further evidence of Bart's ability to delude himself lay in notes he made about a conversation with a fellow inmate, a former military policeman turned drug dealer, jailed on child molesting charges. "Fairly smart," Bart noted.

The inmate claimed that he had met Neal on a bus in Williamston in 1987 and later had seen him several times in Washington "down around the block," a drug-dealing area in a black neighborhood near downtown. At one point, the inmate said, he had talked with Neal for twenty minutes, each remembering the other from the meeting on the bus. The inmate said that at least three people who worked selling drugs for him had seen Neal and sold drugs to him at various times in the past year and a half. Bart noted that this inmate might be willing to testify.

"Is he lying?" Bart wrote. "He has nothing to gain."

Five days after calling Kenyatta, Bart telephoned Weldon Slayton, the first time he had talked with him in more than two years. Slayton was surprised to hear from him and told him that a Caswell County detective had checked with him the week before to find out if Bart ever had been on the baseball team. Bart was pleased with the call and was certain that Slayton would make a good witness in his behalf.

"What could he testify to at trial?" Bart wrote for Sermons.

"1. Was I ever aggressive in high school during four years he knew me? *No.*

2. Was I greedy? *No.*

3. Was I ever ambitious? *No.*

4. Did Neal and I appear to be very close friends, anywhere near close enough to conspire together for murder? *No.*"

Bart continued making notes about who could testify in his behalf.

"Hank and Opie can testify to Neal's criminal activities and his fascination with throwing stars, knives, Book of Poisons . . . etc. Who could testify towards my apathy towards assassin in D&D? Chuck? Coy? Butch? All of the above can testify that

334

me and Neal never did anything together. . . . Brew, Chris and Hank, etc., can all testify to do acid by oneself can lead to bad trips, i.e., poor association with reality, inability to distinguish fact from fantasy, a feeling of being alone. Being in a group lends a calming effect because any action is talked out as to whether it would be safe, i.e., climbing into trees, crossing streets, playing with guns, etc."

Two letters that Bart wrote to Hank in November revealed how much he had become divorced from the reality of his own situation. In the first letter, he enclosed a collection of newspaper articles about the case that Hank had been asking to see. After an introductory paragraph about the clippings, he got to a more important point: drugs, acid.

> If you send any doses, put them under a stamp on a letter and mail them to Wayland Sermons office. He's handling my mail to ensure I get it fairly untampered with. Don't send them on a package because sometimes they throw the wrapping away before I can get it.
>
> I'm getting Wayland to send this out so I don't have to worry about it being screwed with. . . .

Sermons was unaware that Bart was attempting to use him as a courier for drug deliveries and wouldn't learn about it for several weeks.

After giving the drug instructions, Bart revealed where some of his hope had been coming from: jailhouse scuttlebutt.

> Would you believe that we've fairly reliable reports from at least 2 and probably 5 different people placing Neal in Washington between fall of '87 up till the murder? All from dealers on one of the local drug streets.
>
> Drop me a note and tell me about your Halloween exploits and tell me how everyone is doing.

He closed by telling Hank to tell his stepmother that if he won, he was going to buy her restaurant "and turn it into a shoe store for transvestites."

A couple of weeks later, Bart wrote again to Hank, addressing the envelope to "Compadre de Postas" Foster. On the back of the envelope he drew a Kilroy face looking out from between bars and added "Happy Damn Thanksgiving."

> Hey Hank,
>
> What's up in the Real world? How 'bout that Berlin Wall coming down? Is that some shit or what? The single biggest problem except for nuclear weaponry erased overnight. Maybe there's some hope for the world after all. . . . Nah, must be a commie trick.
>
> Good news down here. The DA's gotten a court order to see my bank records between May 23, '88, and July 25th, '88, because Neal said I bought a knife at Kmart or flea market by check. Not only have I never written a check at Kmart, but I don't think I went there all summer. Flea markets don't take checks, and the last time I'd been to the flea market since I owned my 240Z was when you, me and Wolf and Jessica went last fall.
>
> This may not sound like much but it's damned important. It's the first bit of Henderson's statements we've gotten and it contains a provable lie. The more we can prove Henderson is full of shit, the less a jury will believe anything he says. His statement also said he never left the get-away car the night of the murder. On June 14th of this year, he took the police to the baseball bat, which was hidden in dense woods near the Von Stein house. How will a man be able to explain in court how he knew where a murder weapon was hidden near the house if he'd never left the car?
>
> His statements contain a few other things that don't make any sense at all. We expect he'll crack up on the stand in January. Don't let any of the specifics I mentioned about the knife or bat get out to the general public. We're trying to appear ignorant to the D.A. Just don't tell anybody who'll spread anything other than Henderson's full of shit and we can prove it.
>
> You know, I've been thinking about all of this shit the last week or so, and I've come to the conclusion that I'm actually sort of getting a kick out of it. I mean, it's like the ultimate game of me against THEM and winner take all. Win millions of dollars or lose

your life for a crime you didn't commit. I guess somebody will say it's perverse but that's what it boils down to. To me none of this is real, it's just a part of THE GAME OF LIFE and somebody upped the stakes. At least that's how I've come to think of it.

It looks like (from the way things are going) I'm going to be a very rich guy a year from now. I don't think being a millionaire will suit me much. I've decided I'll probably give a lot of it away to my close friends and family (but keep the Lion's share for myself, of course!)

Peace
James B. Upchurch III

Later, Bart said that the millions he mentioned in this letter were the proceeds he planned to win from the state when he sued for malicious prosecution after his innocence was confirmed in court. And by this time, he had managed to convince himself beyond doubt that he was going to be exonerated.

Bart had no way of knowing that neither of these letters ever reached Hank. He sent them to the wrong address. The recipient opened them and took them to the police. A few weeks later, they made their way into the hands of Mitchell Norton.

On December 5, Neal walked into the superior courtroom of the Beaufort County Courthouse shortly after 5 P.M., as court was ending for the day. He was wearing a gray suit and was accompanied by his lawyers, Michael Paul and Chris McLendon. Mitchell Norton asked Judge Thomas Watts for permission to bring up a case that was not on the court calendar. Neal Henderson stood ready to plead guilty to two felonies in the Von Stein case: aiding and abetting second-degree murder and aiding and abetting assault with a deadly weapon with intent to kill inflicting serious injury. Norton agreed to drop all other charges against Neal.

Judge Watts read questions to Neal from a standard form, including, "Do you understand that upon your plea you could be imprisoned for a possible maximum sentence of life plus twenty years?"

"Yes," Neal responded.

A plea bargain had been worked out with the district

attorney. Under its terms, Neal was to testify truthfully against Bart and Chris. Failure to do so would nullify the agreement. Sentencing would be left to the discretion of the judge.

His lawyers had approved the agreement, Neal said, in response to questions from Judge Watts, and he had discussed it with his family, who also approved.

Judge Watts accepted the plea, postponed sentencing until after the trials of Bart and Chris, and allowed Neal to continue to remain free under the bond that had been previously posted.

Neal remained in Washington for two days after his guilty plea, talking for hours with John Taylor, Lewis Young, and prosecutors, going over his story again in minute detail, checking for contradictions and other problems. Before he left, he agreed to return to Washington on December 19, so that he could be put to a trial before the trial, a mock court session that would give him a taste of what was to come.

John Taylor, who had been promoted to detective sergeant in August, still wasn't finished with his investigation, and in mid-December, he was back on the road once more, talking again to people in Raleigh, traveling to Caswell County to learn more about Bart.

On December 14, he met Kenyatta at the public safety office at the University of North Carolina at Chapel Hill. She told him what had happened on the night of the murder, the night Neal told her he'd taken acid and she ordered him to leave.

When Taylor asked if Neal had told her about the murder and his role in it, she said, "I'm not going to lie to you about it, because there's no love lost between me and Neal, and there's no love lost between me and my cousin, and I'm not going to lie to you to save either one of them."

"All I want you to do is tell me the truth," Taylor said.

"Yeah, the truth is that Neal did tell me about pretty much everything."

Had she talked with her cousin?

Yes, he'd called twice in recent weeks, she said, asking questions.

About what?

"Picky stuff, like he's trying to set up a case against Neal. He's trying to help out his lawyers." He wanted to know if

Neal had a pair of black Reeboks, and if she and Neal had gone shopping at Kmart and what they bought.

Had they shopped at Kmart that summer? Taylor asked.

Several times, she said, but she'd never seen Neal buy a hunting knife.

Bart had been a totally changed person when he called, Kenyatta said. Previously, he had abused her or totally ignored her, but now he was different. "He was really interested in everything I was doing, like he was really trying to butter me up, like he really wanted to get something out of me."

Neal had asked her to lie for him when he first told her about his involvement, she said. He wanted her to say she couldn't recall things, particularly the night of the murder, but she had told him she wouldn't do it.

"Has Neal asked you to lie for him since his arrest?" Taylor asked.

"No. I haven't been in his life to have to lie for him or do anything like that. I just call him up and talk to him to make sure he's doing okay."

Taylor said that he wanted to ask her opinion on some things.

"Do you think Neal has the guts to kill anybody?"

"Hell no!" she said. "I have never seen him violent. He won't even stick up for me. I've almost gotten beaten up by his roommate."

Taylor sketched out the scenario of the murder as told to him by Neal. "Does that sound like something he could be led into doing?"

"Yeah," she said. "If it's his friends, he'll do anything to get respect."

Had she ever seen Neal hit anybody?

"He's only hit me like maybe once, and that's because I was being spastic."

"Was he trying to calm you down?"

"Like, would you shut up, please, trying to calm me down, because I have a very bad temper."

What was the maddest she'd ever seen him?

The time she told him that she liked his best friend. He stormed out of the room and "creamed his fist through a wall."

Taylor asked her opinion of Bart (she'd never known him to be violent either) and of Chris.

"He sat bug-eyed in the corner all the time," she said.

When Taylor asked what she meant, she perched on the edge of her chair, making a face at him, wide-eyed.

"Are you trying to portray a paranoid-type person?"

"A very drugged-out paranoid person. He just sort of looked very dangerous to me. It was like I would not like to be left in a room with him by myself. He just looked like he was getting ready to blow up all the time."

"You don't have a stake in this do you?" Taylor asked. "There's not some great Upchurch fortune there in Caswell County?"

Kenyatta laughed. "I wish I knew about it."

Kenyatta had a question for Taylor. "Are my grandmother and I going to be on the stand at the same time, not the same time, but the same day?"

Taylor had realized from his interview that Bart's lawyers certainly couldn't risk putting Kenyatta on the stand. If she testified, it would be as a prosecution witness. Her grandmother surely would be only a character witness for her grandson. They wouldn't likely be testifying on the same day. Kenyatta seemed relieved. She didn't want to have to ride home with her grandmother after "blowing away" her cousin on the stand, she said.

Taylor couldn't resist a personal question before he left. "Do you still love Neal?"

"Nah," Kenyatta said. "I mean, I love him in a kind of admiring way, you know, like he was once a great guy." She chuckled. "I'm past the . . . no, we'll never get back together or anything like that."

The following day, Taylor was back in Caswell County, talking with Weldon Slayton and George Bush, teachers of Bart and Neal. Slayton said that Bart had called him recently from jail and told him that when he got out in February "there were going to be lawsuits."

Taylor came away from these interviews with the impression that Bart had grown up "without a moral structure," that he had been imbued with an attitude that told him: "You're smarter than other people; take advantage of it, gain from it; stuff's there for the taking; people are stupid; if you can con 'em, con 'em."

On December 19, Neal rode from Washington to the court-house in Williamston, twenty-five miles north, with John Taylor. There they met Mitchell Norton and Assistant District Attorney Rob Johnson. In an empty courtroom, the lawyers put Neal on the stand and led him through a scenario similar to the one he would be facing two weeks later.

The lawyers thought that Neal was not taking this whole thing as seriously as he should, that he had no idea of the stress that he might come under in court.

Norton assumed the role of DA. Johnson played the "bad guy" defense lawyer.

As they got into the proceedings, the lawyers grew more concerned about Neal. He wanted to joust intellectually with his questioners. He seemed cold, inhuman, almost robotlike in some of his responses.

Later, Neal admitted that he wasn't taking the mock court seriously. Several times he got the giggles when one side or the other would raise objections and the other would overrule or sustain.

While trying to answer one question, Neal forgot Lieth Von Stein's name and called him "something Von Stein."

Rob Johnson suddenly threw down his pen and leaped from his chair, ripping off his glasses. "At least you could address the man by his true name," he said angrily, launching into a tirade that Neal never would forget.

"He yelled at me for quite a while," Neal said later.

"He laid into Neal's ass," is how John Taylor later put it.

"You are going to have to get serious about this," Johnson told him hotly. "You may think this seems funny now, but there's nothing funny about it. You killed a man and you're going to have to accept responsibility for that. You are a murderer. You're just as guilty as James Upchurch, whether you did the actual killing or not."

Neal sat silently, his face paling as if he had just been kicked in the gut, while Johnson went on and on. When he finally had finished, Johnson turned and stalked out of the courtroom in disgust.

Saying nothing, Neal got up and walked quickly back to a jury room, closing the door behind him.

Taylor and Norton sat looking at one another. "You think you ought to go back there and check on him, John?" Norton asked.

"He'll be all right," Taylor said. "Let him get it out of his system."

Several minutes later, Neal returned to the courtroom. He was composed, but his eyes were red from crying.

The prosecutors felt better knowing that Neal could break. Perhaps he could look human and sympathetic on the stand, after all.

Bart's mother, Joanne, always grew sentimental at Christmas. Each year, she took a treasured collection of ornaments from storage when time came to decorate the tree. From the time Bart was a year old, she had made a special ornament each year for each of her children, matching ornaments to personality. For the first time, Bart would not be with her for Christmas; indeed, he might never be able to spend Christmas with her again. She cried when she brought out the ornament collection this year and saw all of the ornaments she had made for Bart over the years: the clown, the teddy bear, the egg from first grade, and the first one she ever made for him, the one celebrating Woodstock. Just as she had in the past, she hung all of them proudly on her tree.

Two days after Christmas, six days before the trial of Bart and Chris was to begin, the phone rang in Wayland Sermons' house shortly after 10:30 P.M. Sermons was in bed and already had nodded off to sleep. He answered the call groggily but immediately recognized the district attorney's voice.

"Wayland, Mitchell Norton. I just wanted to let you know that Christopher Pritchard has decided to plead guilty."

PART FOUR

AN EYE FOR AN EYE

DIOGENES STRUCK THE FATHER
WHEN THE SON SWORE.
—ROBERT BURTON

42

In AUGUST 1989, JIM UP-church had taken a job with the North Carolina Department of Human Resources, inspecting nursing homes in a wide area of North Carolina's mountains. He worked out of Black Mountain, near Asheville, but he still drove the 230 miles home to Caswell County every weekend. He had spent Christmas Day, Monday, with his mother, and had driven back to Black Mountain the day afterward. He was planning to spend New Year's Day in Caswell County, and already had arranged time off from work to be with Bart at his trial in Elizabeth City, starting on January 2.

He was at his desk at work on Thursday, December 28, when the telephone rang. His former wife was on the line.

"We've got a problem," Joanne said.

Wayland Sermons had just called to tell her that Chris Pritchard was pleading guilty and would be testifying against Bart. Sermons said that Bart still was denying any role in the murder, but Jim knew that this was a devastating development. It instantly devoured the glimmer of hope that he had been able to muster about Bart's chances.

Sermons wanted both of them to come to Washington immediately, Joanne said, and Jim arranged to meet her there shortly after noon the following day. He left at 4:30 A.M. for the eight-hour drive.

Sermons was at the jail with Bart when Jim and Joanne were ushered into the private cell where they had been allowed to talk out of the hearing of jailers and other inmates.

Two days earlier, Chris had spent nearly nine hours telling his story to John Taylor, Lewis Young, Mitchell Norton, Keith Mason, and his own attorney, Bill Osteen. Osteen had let Sermons have his handwritten notes of the marathon interview, and Sermons was grim when he revealed the essence of their contents to Jim and Joanne. Although there were some inconsistencies, Chris was backing up Neal's story that Bart was the murderer.

The day before, Sermons and Frank Johnston had come

345

to the jail to tell Bart about the situation. It came as no surprise to him. "I said, 'Well, I've known he was going to do this all along,'" Bart recalled later. "It wasn't a shock, but it was a tremendous, depressing letdown."

With two witnesses ready to testify against him, his lawyers told him, he stood a good chance of getting the death penalty. He should think about pleading guilty and letting them go to the district attorney to try to save his life.

"Bart didn't flinch," Sermons recalled later. "He said, 'I am not going to take a plea bargain. I'm going to trial.'"

Sermons and Johnston felt that Bart hadn't thought about the situation, that he didn't realize how real it was. Now Sermons explained that to Bart's parents, hoping they could get him to change his mind. He went outside to give Jim and Joanne a chance to talk with their son alone.

In the beginning, Bart had told Sermons and his father that Hank could give him an alibi for the night of the murder. When Sermons had called Hank soon after Bart's arrest, Hank told him that he wanted to help if he could, but he couldn't really remember where he or Bart or any of his friends were on the night of the murder. Later, he told Sermons that he thought he had gone to Bart's room between two and three that night and Bart was there. Still later, he became wary and began backing away from that statement. He had dodged the private detectives who tried to talk with him, just as he had attempted to dodge John Taylor, Lewis Young, and Christy Newsom when they came to question him. Sermons realized that he would be of no use as a witness.

Now Bart was telling his parents that he possibly was with a girl that night. But what girl? And where was she? And would she be willing to stand behind him? Bart was vague.

Sermons had brought to the jail the evidence against Bart that had been provided by the state to this point. It included copies from the pages of the journal Bart had been keeping just before his arrest. Joanne had been going through the material and she began crying as she read the journal entries. She handed one page to Jim, but he saw that some of it was about him and put it down, unread. That, he thought, was private, and he would read it only if Bart asked him to.

Jim left Joanne talking with Bart and went outside where Sermons was waiting.

346

"What do you think?" Jim asked.

"I don't know," Sermons said.

"It doesn't sound too good," Jim offered, hoping to draw Sermons out.

Sermons agreed.

"What's your gut feeling?"

"I'll go with whatever Bart says," Sermons said. "If he wants to go to trial, I'll go to trial."

Bart had turned twenty-one in the Beaufort County Jail. He was legally responsible for his own decisions. His parents could advise him, but they could not direct his defense. His attorneys were in the same position.

Sermons returned to the cell with Jim to explain what likely would happen if Bart did plead guilty. He'd probably get life plus twenty years for murder. Maybe a little more, depending on what they were able to work out on the other charges.

"What does that mean in terms of active sentence?" Jim asked.

"Could be thirty years."

"I'd rather die than spend thirty years in prison," Bart said.

Was there any chance for a lesser sentence? Jim asked.

The DA would ask for the maximum, Sermons said, and the judge no doubt would go along with it. The time for bargaining clearly was past. The only hope that a guilty plea offered now was to save Bart's life.

"Bart, do you know of anything that you could tell us?" his father pleaded. "Is there anything you're hiding? Are you protecting somebody? Now's the time to speak. This is your life at stake."

There was nothing he was hiding, Bart said, nobody he was protecting.

"We'll go with whatever you say," his father told him. "Just make sure you know what you're doing."

"I can't live with myself if I plead guilty to something I didn't do," Bart said, and for a moment the only thing that could be heard in the room was his mother's sobbing.

"I knew you were going to say that," she said.

Everybody in the room realized that Bart understood what he was doing. It had been spelled out to him as clearly as possible, and he had made the decision. He would play out the ultimate game, win or lose, his life the treasure at stake. But this time Bart would not be the dungeon master.

43

ELIZABETH CITY WAS IN many ways like Washington. Although larger by a few thousand people, it, too, was a river town, the river in this case being the Pasquotank, named for Indians who once lived in the area. The Pasquotank emptied into Albemarle Sound, giving Elizabeth City access to the sea, and the town had sprung up as a site for shipbuilding.

Like Washington, Elizabeth City was proud of its history, which dated back more than three hundred years. The town could claim many firsts: the first land deed in the state, the first General Assembly, the first public school. The first soybeans grown in this country were planted at a plantation near Elizabeth City.

In another important way, the town was very much like Washington. Its people were largely conservative, many of them fundamentalist Christians, strong supporters of U.S. Senator Jesse Helms. They believed fervently in Old Testament edicts of justice: an eye for an eye.

If Bart had any concern about that, he did not show it on the day his trial opened in an austere second-floor courtroom at the brick colonial-style Pasquotank County Courthouse. Judge Thomas Watts, a short middle-aged man with a balding head and heavy-rimmed glasses, asked Bart to stand so that the courtroom full of potential jurors might identify him. Bart rose, smiling, pointed at his red tie, and bowed slightly, tugging at the back of the blue blazer that his mother had brought for him to wear during the trial. It was not an auspicious beginning. Throughout the trial, observers would be talking of the bow he took at the beginning, as if he were an actor savoring his role.

The tedious process of jury selection was speeded somewhat because potential jurors had filled out information sheets about themselves, but it still went on all week. Joanne came to the courtroom every day, driving back and forth from her home in Virginia. Jim stayed for the first day of jury selection, then drove back to work in Black Mountain until testimony began. Bonnie came to court every day and sometimes took notes. She had told friends that she planned to write a book about the case and had hired a photographer to take pictures of the trial participants.

The jury that would try Bart for his life was made up of eight women and four men, nine of them white, three black, ranging in age from twenty-two to fifty. Half had attended college, but only one had received a degree. Both alternates, a man and woman, were white. All had said that they could in good conscience sentence Bart to death if they determined that circumstances warranted such a penalty.

As Bart was being led manacled into the courthouse for the opening day of testimony in his trial on a blustery, rainy Monday morning, January 8, the news media was waiting. Reporters and photographers had come from newspapers in Washington, Raleigh, Norfolk, from TV stations in Washington and Greenville. Bart smiled and answered their questions.

"You innocent?" one asked.

"Yes sir," he said.

"Are you sorry it all happened?" another called as he reached the door.

"I'm sorry I'm where I'm at now," he said over his shoulder.

Despite the pessimistic outlook of his lawyers and his parents, Bart still had hope. He thought that the jury would see Chris and Neal as liars and he was certain that he could convince them of that if he got onto the stand. His mood appeared to be one of jaunty confidence.

The appearance Bart was giving was of concern to his lawyers. His natural facial expression made him look as if he were smirking. When he smiled, which was frequently, that appearance was amplified. Added to his natural cockiness, that could lead jurors to think that he held the entire process in contempt. And although that was indeed the case, Bart's lawyers saw no point in letting the judge and jury know it. If such an attitude were perceived, it could only lessen whatever slim chances Bart might have. Throughout the trial, Bart would be reminded not to smile and to put a finger to his mouth to keep from giving the appearance of smirking. His lawyers gave him a legal pad when he sat at the defense table beside them and encouraged him to take notes to keep him occupied.

Before opening arguments and testimony could begin, another matter had to be decided. News organizations had petitioned to have the trial opened to photography from both still and TV cameras. Judge Watts overruled objections from both the state and defense to allow that for the first time in the First Judicial District.

In his opening argument, Mitchell Norton detailed how the state would show that three bright boys from good families entered into a conspiracy to kill Lieth Von Stein so that Chris Pritchard could come into an early inheritance. These boys, he said, had been brought together by Dungeons and Dragons, which he described as "a medieval game of clubs, daggers, knives, and sticks."

"But this is not the story of a game gone crazy," he said. "The game simply influenced the way they thought and lived. It accustomed them to thoughts of 'me.'"

Norton promised evidence that would be "unusual and bizarre," and warned the jurors that they could expect to hear some discrepancies in testimony—which was quite normal, he pointed out. But in the end, he said, the state would prove that Bart alone had done the "cold, calculated killing."

"The state doesn't have any absolute evidence that shows Bart Upchurch did this," Frank Johnston responded in his opening statement, which revealed the defense strategy—to cast doubt on the word of Neal and Chris.

Why, he asked, had it taken Neal eleven months to have "this great conscience breakdown"? And why had Chris waited until days before the trial to admit his part? "By the evidence from his own mouth, we know that he conspired to carry out this dastardly act. He thought of this and pursued it."

Norton began his case by calling to the stand Michelle Sparrow, the Beaufort County dispatcher who had taken Bonnie's call on the night of the murder and had kept her on the line until officers could get to her. Michelle had been so nervous with anticipation about the trial that her digestive tract had been in turmoil for days.

It was not just the prospect of testifying that had upset her. Her experience that night had affected her deeply. She knew that it would be painful to go through it again. Also she still had not met Bonnie and she knew that finally meeting her would be an emotional moment.

Michelle's husband, David, who was to testify after her, had pointed out Bonnie when they arrived at the courtroom that morning, and Michelle had been struck by how tiny and fragile she seemed. How, she wondered, had she ever survived so brutal an attack?

Michelle tried to avoid looking at Bonnie when she took the stand. She was determined to be professional and not break down in tears. As she sat down after being sworn, her eye caught her husband's and he winked. Everything would be all right.

When the district attorney tried to introduce the tape recording of Bonnie's call that night, Sermons objected. Sermons and Johnston didn't want the jurors affected by the raw emotion of the tape if they could avoid it. The jurors were asked to leave the room while the lawyers wrangled, and court was recessed for lunch without the matter being settled.

When Michelle and David got back to the courtroom after lunch, before court reconvened, two of Bonnie's friends came up to Michelle and thanked her for saving Bonnie's life. Then, suddenly, Bonnie was standing there.

"She just kind of eased up to me," Michelle recalled later. "She said, 'I'm Bonnie.' I said, 'I know, and you don't know how bad I've wanted to meet you.' We hugged. She said, 'I just wanted to tell you thank you for all you did. If it hadn't been for you, I might be dead.' When somebody tells you something like that, it makes the whole job worth it, low pay and all."

After hearing the tape, some of which was nearly inaudible, the judge ruled it admissible, and Bonnie and Michelle had to listen to it again, Michelle still maintaining her professional demeanor.

After David Sparrow came off the stand from telling what he had seen at the house that morning, Mitchell Norton called Bonnie to the stand. It was 4:45 P.M., not long until normal stopping time, and everybody in the courtroom knew that she would only begin to tell her story this day. Bonnie had asked that her testimony not be taped for TV, and the judge had ordered the camera shut off to preserve her privacy.

She wore a short-sleeved black dress with a capelike white linen collar, and her long dark hair, flecked now with gray, was pulled together at the back and held by a wide white barrette. She was composed, and her face looked thin and haunted. She spoke so softly that after a few questions, the judge interrupted to make certain the jurors could hear her.

Mitchell led her through an abbreviated story of her life from the time she met Lieth until they settled in Washington. He had her identify a photograph of Lieth and another of their house in Smallwood. He questioned her about the difficult year in which Lieth's parents died and about the inheritance. He took her through Chris's relationship with Lieth, including the outburst that nearly caused a fistfight between them. Bonnie acknowledged that both Chris and Angela occasionally called Lieth an "asshole" before the judge interrupted to declare a recess for the day.

The second day of testimony was Bonnie's. She took the stand shortly after court opened at nine and did not step down, except for breaks, until nearly three-thirty. Norton took her carefully through the events of the weekend of the murder, right up to the attack, when Lieth awoke screaming.

"And can you describe Lieth's scream to us, please."

"It was short. It sounded piercing right in my ears, just a series of short screams like—ah, ah, ah—very loud to me."

"And as best you can, can you duplicate for us here in the courtroom, you say it was very loud, can you duplicate the scream for us that awakened you?"

"Objection," said Sermons.

"Overruled."

Bonnie tried, but the sound was soft and feeble, hardly a scream.

"And with the volume that Lieth used that you heard that night?"

"I don't know if I can or not."

"Can you try?"

"Objection," said Sermons.

"Well, sustained," said the judge.

"Is there some reason that you feel like that you can't do it, Mrs. Von Stein?"

"Yes," said Bonnie after the objection had been overruled. "That's one thing that I've not been able to face for myself."

Bonnie went on to describe the attack in detail. "Everything looked dark, black. Everything looked black to me. It was just dark."

Of her attacker, she said, "He looked bulky, big through this area," indicating the shoulders and chest. "It looked like he didn't have a neck. It looked like the head just sat right on top of his shoulders."

Later, after asking her to describe the injuries she received, Norton said, "Can you pull up your bangs—I guess that's what they call them—and show us where those . . ."

"Well," said Bonnie pulling back her hair, "I've had plastic surgery on two occasions since the injuries, but you'll always be able to see it if you look closely." She pointed to the scars, which were hardly visible from the jury box.

A little later, Norton asked if she had suffered any permanent effects from her injuries.

"I've had some seizure-type activity and had testing done because of that."

What kind of seizures?

"I would be in the shower or driving down the highway and all of a sudden it was like I was standing on the outside watching somebody else doing something totally different. And it was explained to me as a daydream-type seizure."

"Did you ever have those prior to being beaten?"

"No."

After telling how she had summoned help and the police had arrived, shining a light into the room—"Everything—everything was red. The whole room looked red to me"—Bonnie remembered somebody telling her that nothing could be done for Lieth and she recalled asking about Angela.

"I didn't want Angela to see what I saw in the room," she said. "I heard her voice and that was a beautiful sound."

"All right. Now you say that you saw Lieth?"

"Yes."

"I show you what's marked for identification as State's Exhibit No. 9, Mrs. Von Stein, and ask you to take a look at that," Norton said, handing her a color photograph of Lieth's bloodied body. "Do you recognize that state's exhibit?"

"Yes," said Bonnie, breaking into tears.

"Who is that individual?"

"That was my husband, Lieth," she said, struggling to control herself.

"Does that photograph fairly and accurately show and depict the way he was that night in bed?"

"That morning, yes."

Did she know who had been arrested for doing that to Lieth? She did, naming her son as one of the three. At first, she didn't believe Chris had anything to do with it, she said. Initially he denied knowing anything about it, but he finally had told her everything two days after Christmas, just before he made his long confession to the police.

"And up until that time in December, did you believe or want to believe that your son could not and would not do such a thing?" Norton asked.

"Yes."

Cross-examination was to begin immediately after lunch, but it was put off for more than an hour because the prosecution did not deliver copies of Bonnie's statements to Sermons and Johnston until 1:00 P.M., leaving them no time for lunch and insufficient time to read the reports before court reconvened. Judge Watts made it clear to Norton that he would not tolerate any more such delays.

During the lunch break, Bonnie had stopped behind the rail where Bart's parents were seated. They never had met. Now they did. Jim stood and took her hand.

"I'm sorry all of this is happening," Bonnie said.

"I'm sorry, too," said Jim.

For a few moments they stood patting one another's hand, uncertain what else to say, parents drawn together by their children in tragedy, their lives forever changed.

Sermons was to conduct Bonnie's cross-examination. He knew that it would be a delicate matter. No jury would take kindly to a lawyer who was hard on a woman whose husband had been murdered in bed beside her, who had been beaten and stabbed herself and who had to face the sorrow of learning that her own son had tried to have her killed.

When court resumed at midafternoon, he took Bonnie back over her testimony, touching on the fight with Chris— "Did that cause any animosity or split feelings between you and Lieth?" "No."—the children calling Lieth "asshole"—"Did either of these children say that to his face?" "Occasionally."

On one point, Sermons did zero in: Bonnie's description of her attacker.

"Now you have described this person that you saw as appearing that he had very broad shoulders and no neck, is that correct?"

"Yes."

He handed her a photograph of Neal.

"Can you tell us when the very first time is you saw Mr. Henderson?"

"I saw him in the courtroom in Beaufort County when I was there for some motions to be heard."

"Mrs. Von Stein, can you describe to us whether or not you had any feelings of recognition of Mr. Henderson at that time?"

The judge allowed her to answer over Norton's objection.

"I didn't recognize Mr. Henderson. I recognized, you know, that he had a shape that frightened me."

"Can you describe to us how frightened you were?"

"I was upset to the point that when we broke, I left the courtroom and did not return until after the lunch break."

"Now, did you have an occasion to see Mr. Upchurch in court after that?"

"Yes."

"You did not feel frightened?"

"No."

"Does the defendant, James Upchurch's physical features match the silhouette you saw in the bedroom?"

"In the conditions I've seen him, no."

Sermons continued driving home the point that Bonnie had not seen any identifying features of the person who had attacked her and Lieth except for being big, broad-shouldered, strong, neckless.

All in the courtroom could clearly see that Bart was tall and thin with a long neck and shoulders that were hardly broad.

Norton was squirming with impatience as he waited to counter that point. When his turn came, he began a long series of vivid, repetitive questions designed to show that Bonnie's comparisons had been made under different circumstances, one in a brightly lighted courtroom, the other under the conditions in her bedroom the night of the attack.

"You've said that the individual that you saw appeared to be broad shouldered and appeared to have no neck. If you were laying on the floor, looking up, having been struck in the head several times, bleeding from the chest, hearing your husband scream at the top of his voice, and awoken from a deep sleep, saw an individual dressed in dark clothing head to toe, something over his face, drapes drawn, dark light filtering through a side door, a bat or stick somewhere in his hands with his hands raised over his head . . ." Norton rose from his seat raising his hands threateningly over his head. ". . . in this manner . . ."

"Objection," called Sermons.

"Sit down, Counsel," ordered the judge.

Norton sat even as he continued speaking ". . . hands raised over the head in this manner with the bat, as you've described it, what happens to the shoulders and to the neck?"

"Yours appeared to blend together," Bonnie said over another objection from Sermons.

Sermons came back with questions reconfirming that it was Neal whose physical appearance had frightened her.

"You have never seen Mr. Henderson dressed in black clothing with a baseball bat standing over your body?"

"Not to my knowledge."

"Would you say the circumstances under which you saw Mr. Upchurch and Mr. Henderson in the courtroom were pretty much identical?"

"Yes."

"And again, Mr. Upchurch did not cause you to feel frightened in any way, did he?"

"No."

John Taylor was the first witness on the third day of testimony. He spent hours on the stand as the state slowly worked in dozens of pieces of physical evidence picturing the scene at the Von Stein house on the morning of the murder.

The significance of it all, however, was summed up in a single question from Frank Johnston during cross-examination.

"In all the tests that were submitted regarding fingerprints, fibers, any other identification procedures that were done, is there any evidence to connect James Bartlett Upchurch with ever having been in that house?"

"No, sir," said Taylor.

The highlight of the trial on Wednesday was the appearance of Dr. Page Hudson, the highly acclaimed medical examiner who had performed the autopsy on Lieth. His testimony raised intriguing questions at odds with the evidence.

In describing the scrapes on Lieth's shins and the front of his ankles, Dr. Hudson said that in his opinion the injuries occurred at the time of death.

"Sir," asked Norton, "do you have an opinion satisfactory to yourself as to what type of object could or might have caused those injuries?"

"Yes, sir."

"What is that opinion?"

"They are not specific injuries, but they were quite consistent with and identical to injuries I have seen by the heel of a shoe."

"Do you have an opinion satisfactory to yourself as to whether or not they could or might have been caused by the swing of a wooden bat?"

"Yes, sir, I do. And my opinion is they were probably not caused by the swinging of a wooden bat."

Bonnie had told police that Lieth simply had tried to sit up when he was being attacked but never had gotten off the bed to face his attacker.

Asked to describe the stab wound that killed Lieth, Dr. Hudson said, "The track was through the skin, through the chest wall rib area and into and through the heart."

"When you say through the heart, do you mean literally completely through the heart?"

"I mean at least this point of the blade penetrated into the heart and through the tissue therein, and really came a little ways out of the backside of the heart."

All of Lieth's wounds had occurred within a short period of time, Dr. Hudson said.

"Do you have an opinion, assuming the wounds were inflicted within a short period of time, how long it would have taken him to have died from the combination of his wounds?"

"I would have expected death to have occurred within a very few minutes."

"What did you find in the stomach?" Norton asked a short time later.

"I found a rather large quantity of food, rather undigested rice and meat, which I thought was most likely chicken."

Stress might have caused that food to remain undigested for six or seven hours, Dr. Hudson said, but only severe stress. Financial and family worries likely wouldn't cause it.

Under cross-examination from Frank Johnston, Dr. Hudson said that it should have taken no more than an hour or two for the food to have cleared Lieth's stomach and the appearance of the food, if eaten at 8 P.M., or so, as Bonnie had testified, was inconsistent with a death at 3:00 or 4:00 A.M. Of the more than four thousand cases with which he had dealt, Dr. Hudson said, he had seen a few in which trauma had slowed digestion. "But I don't recall any at all where it stopped to the point that even some simply digested material like rice didn't get changed any more than this was."

The questions raised by Dr. Hudson's testimony—Did Lieth in fact die much earlier than Bonnie said? Did something happen that Sunday other than the pleasant evening of love-making and dinner out that Bonnie had described?—were left to hang. Nobody ever had confronted Bonnie about them, and now that she had completed her testimony, nobody would.

44

DESPITE WIDE MEDIA COV-
erage, the Upchurch trial was not attracting many spectators, probably because the people of Elizabeth City had taken little notice of the Von Stein murder. On most days the courtroom was largely empty, populated only by those who felt an obligation to be there: the participants, their friends and family, and, of course, the small cadre of out-of-town reporters, photographers, and TV technicians.

Among those who had an interest in the trial, nobody wanted to be late when court reconvened from lunch recess Thursday, January 11. The state was about to call its star witness, Chris Pritchard. He took the stand wearing a double-breasted blazer, a wide, patterned luminescent tie, and a grave and shell-shocked expression. His face seemed pale and lined, his eyes hollow and deeply set. He looked older than his twenty-one years.

"Very dark hair that's short and spikey on top," Martha Quillen, a reporter for the Raleigh *News & Observer* wrote in her notebook. "Has a widow's peak which makes him look much like Eddie on the Munsters."

The first portion of his testimony was all background: his mother's marriage to Lieth, his relationship to his stepfather, his Dungeons and Dragons playing, his troubles during high school, his bad grades after he went off to college, his meeting Bart and Neal, his drug use and drinking during the weeks preceding the murder, the charges against him, his plea bargain with the state.

It was midafternoon before Norton began getting to the subject that everybody was waiting eagerly to hear about: the details of the murder plot, which never had been made public.

"Now, when did you first meet with James Upchurch to begin talking with him about the murder of your parents?"

"The Wednesday prior to July 25."

The meeting, Chris said, was at the Golden Corral, a steak house on Western Boulevard near the campus of N.C. State, but he couldn't remember whether it took place during daytime or at night. His roommate, Chuck Jackson, and his friend Brew Simpson were there, but they had left the table to go to the potato bar.

"And I looked straight at James and said, 'What do you think about patricide?' He said, 'Well, you better not believe in God.'"

"What occurred next?" Norton asked.

"Well, Chuck and Brew came back and the conversation was dropped."

Norton led Chris through the conversations that he and his friends had had about his family's wealth and his potential inheritance, although Chris couldn't remember many specifics about it. He recalled boasting that his parents had about $5 million, plus houses and cars, and if something happened to them, he would have plenty of money and would set his friends up in business and they all would live together and have a big time.

"It was just daydreaming," Chris said.

After this rambling digression, Norton brought his witness

back to the plot. He and his friends left the restaurant that night and returned to the dorm, Chris said.

"James and I were alone. And he said, 'Chris'—you know, this is a general idea; I don't know specifically what was said. James said to me what was I talking about earlier in the restaurant. And I said, 'Well, you know, killing my parents.' And I don't remember—we did discuss it further, but I don't remember exactly what was said or even close to what was said after that point. But the conversation did continue for a little period of time . . . maybe fifteen minutes."

"Did you develop any plan at that time?"

"I don't remember."

The next day, Chris said, they talked again, but again he couldn't remember specifics.

"There was talk about finding some way to get rid of my parents without looking suspicious. There was talk of starting a fire with the fuse box, switch box in the house. And I told James I was going home that weekend. And I asked him did he want to go. And he said, no, he didn't want to go with me, but if I would pick him up behind Sav-A-Center in Raleigh at one o'clock Saturday, he would come back with me and we would proceed to burn the house by using the fuse box, switch box, whatever."

"How were you going to use the fuse box or the switch box to burn the house, Chris?"

"We were going to attempt to get a fuse to blow or make it look like a fuse blew and then throw gasoline on the switch box and, you know, start an electrical fire that way."

"What about your parents? Would you state whether or not you discussed them waking up when you set the fire?"

"Yes, sir, we did."

Again, Chris said that he couldn't remember specifics, but he was going to make supper for his family on Saturday night.

"In making supper, I was to slip some crushed sleeping pills into the food so that everyone in the house would be asleep."

Chris said that he came home that Friday night, went out to see friends, returned to the house to sleep. When he got up Saturday morning, he said, he told his parents that he was going to visit friends and would return to cook supper. He left about eleven, drove to Raleigh and picked up Bart behind the Sav-A-Center. On the way back to Washington, Bart gave him a cigarette box with blue powder in it that he said was eight crushed Sominex sleeping tablets. Chris was to mix this into the hamburgers that he made for his family that night.

When they got to Washington, Chris said, he left Bart at "a little metal shack" about a mile from his house, where he was to wait until he returned for him in a few hours, after cooking supper.

Back at home, Chris said, he set up the grill for cooking hamburgers, poured the blue powder into the meat, put ketchup over it, and kneaded it in. He made ten hamburgers, he said. His father ate two and he, his mother, his sister and his sister's friend, Donna Brady, all ate one.

Norton interrupted his questions about supper to ask about another matter. "Had you and James talked either that day or any prior time about what would happen to your sister, Angela?"

"We had discussed it. It was—I don't remember what day it was. But James said something to the effect of, 'Well what about your sister?' And I said, 'Well, if she is there, then I guess her too; but if she is not, that's fine too.' "

Angela was seated beside her mother behind the prosecution table and most eyes in the courtroom turned to her, but she showed no change of expression.

"So there was no specific intent at that time to kill Angela?"

"No, sir."

"Unless she happened to be there?"

"Yes, that's correct, sir."

After supper, Chris said, he bade farewell and said that he was returning to campus. Instead he drove to the shack where he had left James, arriving "between seven o'clock and nine o'clock."

"And can you describe for us what you did and what was said when you drove up?" Norton said.

"Well, he came out and asked if I had cooked supper. I said that I had. I then brought out a marijuana cigarette. And we smoked that and tried to figure out a way to break this fuse open."

They had picked up a glass fuse that day, Chris had testified earlier, although he couldn't recall where or when, with the intention of breaking it and putting it into the fuse box at the house to make it look as if a fuse had blown, starting the fire.

"We opened the hood of my car and tried slamming the hood on it and that didn't work. I put the fuse over a pin hole where the pin that keeps my hood closed goes, and when I brought the hood down, it broke the fuse and shoved it so far down the hole that we couldn't get it out."

The more Chris talked, the more this murder plot sounded like some Buster Keaton farce. It was all so farfetched, so juvenile, so utterly ridiculous. These were college students with high IQs. Were they actually so naive as to believe that they could put a whole family to sleep with a few over-the-counter sleeping pills crushed into their hamburgers? That they could start a fire with a fuse in a house in which there was no fuse box, something they hadn't even bothered to check? Did they really believe that a gasoline-fueled fire would not attract immediate attention or be detectable afterward?

As Chris discussed driving the fuse down the latch hole, some in the courtroom had to suppress their laughter. Would this movie end with the bungling plotters fleeing, their car hood flapping in the wind because the latch would no longer catch?

The fuse in the latch hole was no joke, however. After interviewing Chris, John Taylor had discovered that it was still there. He took a photo of it, and Norton now introduced it as evidence.

"Now, after you got the fuse stuck in there," Norton said, "what was going on?"

"James said, 'Well, this isn't going to work, because you don't have an alibi. And arson is pretty suspicious looking. So what do we do? Now what?' 'A burglary?' He said, 'Yes, that sounds like a good idea.' At this point we left and proceeded back to Raleigh."

"During the course of the trip, what was discussed?"

"The burglary basically. He said that when we got back to Raleigh that we should go to an army surplus store so that he could get a machete so that he could just chop my parents' heads off so it would be quick and painless."

"What was your reaction to that talk about going to get a machete?"

"I said, 'Aren't the army surplus stores closed?' First of all, you know, I wanted it to be painless. But the army surplus stores were closed when we got back to Raleigh."

"Did you go looking for an army surplus store?"

"Yes, sir. James said he knew where one was. We went by there and it was closed."

"After you found that the store was closed, what was the next thing that you did?"

"We went back to the room and I said, 'Well, how are you going to get back down there? You don't have a car.' He said, 'Well, I could borrow yours.' I said no way because he had lost his license. 'You've got to find somebody to drive you there or use somebody else's car because you're not using mine.'"

Bart suggested, Chris said, that they talk to Neal.

"And did you do that?"

"We did talk to Neal Henderson. It was on Sunday, the next day. I had taken James to Kmart to buy a hunting knife. And then we went to see Neal. We—I don't remember specifically what was said—but we talked to Neal about driving James to Washington. Neal was receptive to the idea, and they said they were going to discuss it between themselves further."

"What was the plan that you and James had talked about?"

"James was to go into the house, steal some small items, some valuables. I told him where my mother's purse was, underneath the microwave. And I told him that there was money lying about the bedroom, my parents' bedroom. I also drew them two maps—one of the neighborhood and one was floor plans of the house and directions on how to get to Little Washington."

"Did you talk about how he was to get into the house, what weapon was to be used?"

"He was supposed to use the key to get into the house. He was supposed to take some items. At that time, he was supposed to murder my parents."

"What type of weapon?"

"The knife, the hunting knife."

"Was any other weapon ever discussed?"

"No, sir, just the knife."

"What was to occur after the killing?"

"James was to come back to Raleigh. He was to leave the key in my car and then he was to come back later that day and see if the car was still there."

"What was the purpose of killing your parents? What were you going to get out of it?"

"A large inheritance."

"And had you talked with James about that?"

"Yes, sir, I did."

"What did you tell him that you were going to do with this inheritance?"

"I told him that I would give him a car and $50,000. More to the point, a Porsche and $50,000."

"The initial plan to kill your parents, whose thought was that?"

"I brought up the idea."

"After that initial statement, what part did James Upchurch play in the thought process?"

"He was equal in the planning in that he came up with some ideas, I came up with some ideas."

"Had you discussed what your alibi was going to be?"

"Not in any great detail. I was to either go out and stay up late with Chuck or with Sandra and Sybil."

"Whose idea was that?"

"The alibi itself was James's idea. What I was going to do was up to me entirely so long as I was seen in Raleigh."

"And was there any timetable set for you being seen in Raleigh?"

"I needed to be up until around three o'clock in the morning."

"Why was the time three o'clock important?"

"Because they were to have left around midnight."

"And was this plan laid out for Neal Henderson?"

"Yes, sir."

"Was Neal to get some reward, some payoff?"

"Yes, sir. He was to get $50,000 and a Ferrari."

Following the afternoon recess, during which time Chris chatted and laughed with his mother and sister, Norton led Chris through other details of the plan.

When Bart and Neal returned, Chris said, they were to leave the car at the same spot where they had picked it up. They were to leave the keys inside. Bart was to check back by the car later Monday. If the car was gone, it meant that Chris had taken it after receiving word about the murder. If it was still there, it meant that the call had come before Bart and Neal got back and he had to find some other means to get home. In that case, Bart was to take the keys out of the car, carry them to Chris's room, and leave them in a chair.

Asked about Neal's duties, Chris said that he simply was

to drive James to Washington, let him out at a predetermined spot, go to another isolated spot to wait for him, then drive him back to Raleigh. Neal, he said, had never been to Washington, which was the reason for drawing a map.

"I drew a layout of my neighborhood. And I wrote down directions on how to get to that neighborhood."

Norton handed him the partially burned map that had been found at the fire site in Pitt County following the murder. The jurors had heard testimony about the map the day before from Noel Lee, the farmer who found it, and from Lewis Young.

"I ask you to take a look at that and see if you can identify that for us, please."

"This is the map of my neighborhood that I drew for Neal and James."

The blocks he had drawn along the line indicating Lawson Street represented houses, Chris testified. The four-legged symbols were neighbors' dogs that were to be avoided to keep them from barking and alerting somebody, the rectangle behind the block representing the fifth house on the street was the six-foot fence behind his house, the shaded spot on the street directly behind Lawson was a wooded lot without a house where Neal was to let Bart out so that he could slip up to the fence without being seen.

Chris said that he also had drawn a floor plan of his house and had written directions to Washington on the back of it. On the floor plan, he said, he drew in the bedroom where his parents slept and noted who slept on each side of the bed.

After he drew the maps at Neal's apartment on Sunday, July 24, the afternoon before the murder, Chris said, Neal and Bart accompanied him back to the dorm, where he gave Neal the keys to his car.

"When I gave him the keys, I had not intended on going back out that evening, but I did go back out. And when I did, I went out with Chuck Jackson and Sandra Goodman and Sybil and James. And I sent James to Neal's apartment to get my keys while Chuck, Sandra and Sybil and myself waited at the car for him to return."

When he did return, Chris said, they all went to California Pizza to eat and drink beer and stayed a couple of hours. On the way back to the dorm, they stopped at a grocery store for

Sandra to buy beer, and when they returned to the campus after dark, Chris parked under a street light in a fringe lot distant from the dorm.

"Why was it that you parked away from your dormitory?" Norton asked.

"So it would be easy for James and Neal to find and so that it would be—I told the girls it was because I had got my stereo stolen recently and I didn't want any vandals coming to my car without being able to be seen."

Chris locked his car, he later told the jurors, but dropped his keys back inside through a window vent, through which they could be retrieved later by Bart and Neal.

After the group returned to the dorm, Chris said that he last saw Bart about 11:00 P.M. in the room Chris shared with Chuck Jackson. Only the three of them were there, he said. Sandra and Sybil were in Sybil's room.

"And what was discussed between you and James at that time?" Norton asked.

"He said that he was going to go do some homework. I said, 'Well, good luck.' And that was it."

Afterward, Chris said, he went to Sybil's room to drink beer and play cards. Brew was there, and they stayed until about three, when he returned to his room, undressed, and went to sleep, only to be awakened about five by a call from his sister telling him that their parents had been beaten and stabbed.

Norton wanted to know why Chris had initially thought about murdering his parents. "Why was it? Why did you do it?"

"I honestly don't know the answer to that question," Chris said. "There were many reasons that went through my mind, but I honestly don't know why I came up with this idea."

"What reasons were going through your mind?"

"Well, money."

"What about money?"

"I would have inherited a lot of money. I wouldn't have had to do anything else. I wouldn't have had to go back to school or anything. I could sit around, buy a house, and do drugs all the time. I could play D&D all I wanted to. I had a term paper due that Monday that I hadn't even started on."

Norton led Chris through his drug use prior to the murder,

366

smoking pot three times a day, drinking as much as three pitchers of beer a day, using LSD at least once a week.

"What effect did the LSD have on you?"

"I saw colors. I felt invincible. My mind raced. And I had incredible amounts of energy for about six or seven hours straight."

"What about the marijuana?"

"When I was smoking it three times a day, after each time I smoked it, I would fall asleep for a little while. I listened to music. It seemed to make music better. It seemed to make TV more interesting, commercials especially."

And the drug called ecstasy that Chris also used?

"I was very mellow. I felt very mellow. I had a lot of energy still, though. And I just wanted to sit down and contemplate life."

"Were thoughts of money part of your life at that time?"

"No. It was generally politics. That was what I was contemplating, world politics."

"You also said that . . . you had a term paper. Surely you don't mean that you killed your father because of a term paper?"

"What I mean is that was a thought that went through my mind as one of the reasons because I was very upset over the fact that I hadn't done it. I was very upset over the fact that my parents would be upset about it."

"Why did you feel your parents would be upset?"

"It would have directly affected my grades."

"And what caused you to be concerned about your grades?"

"I had already had two talks with my father and mother about my grades. I knew a third would mean that I probably wouldn't go back to school."

Norton took Chris through his actions after receiving the call from his sister on the morning of the murder. Chris emotionally told of wandering around for a time before picking up the public safety phone.

"What was going on at that time?"

"I was in shock," Chris said, tears showing in his eyes.

"Why were you in shock? This was something you had planned."

"On one level I did not really believe this would happen."

"But you had provided an automobile. You had provided

keys to the house. You had purchased a knife, supplied the knife for the killing."

"Yes, sir. But it was just like the game. In the game you sit down and you plan out things. And you get your ducks in a row. And I knew that this would happen. But at a deeper level, I didn't believe that it would happen."

"When you got the telephone call from your sister, did you believe that it had happened then?"

"Yes, sir, I did."

"What was going through your mind at that time?"

"The only thing that was on my mind was to stick to the plan."

Chris described how the public safety officers had taken him to Washington and how Melvin Hope had told him what had happened.

"You found out at that time that your mother was alive?"

"Yes, sir."

"Where did you go then?"

"I don't know how I got there, but I went straight to the hospital and straight up to the intensive care unit to see my mother."

"What occurred when you were talking to your mother?"

"I don't remember. I was just happy that she was alive."

"Did you go to the funeral?" Norton asked a short time later.

"Yes, sir."

"Have any feeling about it at that time, about the killing?"

"Yes, sir, I did, very strong feelings," Chris said after the judge had overruled Sermons' objection.

"What kind?"

"Incredible remorse."

"But did you also have other feelings at that time, Chris?"

"Yes, sir," again over Sermons' objection. "I was thoroughly disgusted."

"Did you think about the police?"

"Yes, sir. I thought about the police. I thought about keeping myself away from them. I didn't want to be arrested, thrown in jail. I didn't want my mama to know."

His voice choked when he spoke about his mother and tears welled again.

Asked what he had done to keep his mother from knowing, Chris said, "I deceived the police as best I could. I lied to my family and to my friends. When she asked me did I know what had happened or did I know who was involved or any of that, I told her no, I did not."

"Stuck with the plan?"

"Yes, sir. I stuck with the plan."

Chris said that he never had any contact with Neal after the murder, only with Bart. When he called his roommate from Washington to ask about his car keys, Bart was there and expressed condolences. He saw Bart again when he returned to N.C. State, he said, but not on a regular basis.

"What was the reason that you didn't see James on a regular basis?"

"I was afraid of him and I was disgusted with him."

Bart, who had been writing regularly on his legal pad during Chris's testimony, was scribbling away for his lawyers at this comment: "This is simply not true. Ask Brew or any of Chris's friends if he seemed to be scared of me."

Chris said that he had talked with Bart once about the murder, at a party in his old dorm room before the fall semester began.

"We went to a room—I don't remember where it was. It was in the dorm. And he said, 'You didn't tell me that the window on the back door was Plexiglas.' He said he had to cut the screen and break the glass on the side window to get the door. And then before I could say anything, he said there was blood everywhere. At that point I told him to shut his mouth. I didn't want to hear another word. I told him to forget it and make sure that Neal forgot it. And that was the end of the conversation. I walked out of the room."

"Why did you tell him to shut up?"

"Because I was disgusted with the whole thing. And I didn't want to hear anything about it. I did not want to hear a word about it. I was afraid of the boy, you know, and I didn't want to hear anything else come out of his mouth about how he killed my father."

Sermons objected and moved that the remarks be stricken from the record, but Judge Watts allowed them to stand. A few minutes later, at five-eighteen, the judge recessed court for the day.

Soon after court was dismissed, Toni Whitt, a reporter for the *Virginian-Pilot* of Norfolk, approached Wayland Sermons to ask about Chris's testimony.

"He obviously has reason to lie," Sermons said. "It's not the first time someone has testified to save his own life. I think the jury will see through his testimony. In four days of testimony, the only evidence the state has is from someone who did seventeen hits of acid in thirty days saying, 'I, along with the defendant, planned it.'"

Bart was "incredulous" at the testimony, Sermons said. "He can't believe the things that came out of Pritchard's mouth."

When Whitt returned to her office across the street from the courthouse to write her story, she began it with this paragraph: "Bonnie Von Stein showed little emotion as her only son, Christopher Pritchard, calmly told jurors Thursday about three plots to kill her and her husband, including setting them afire, cutting their heads off with a machete and stabbing them to death."

Friday, January 12, was a special day for lawyers on both sides of the case. It was Wayland Sermons' anniversary. And it was the second birthday for Assistant District Attorney Keith Mason's only son. Both lawyers had been away from home for two weeks and wanted to spend part of this day with their families. Judge Watts noted the occasions at the opening of court and said that he would try to cut the day short, pushing on until perhaps one, then stopping for the week. Monday would be the Martin Luther King holiday, so this would be a long weekend for everybody, a break from the strain of the trial.

Chris again took the stand and identified the transcript of his grades at N.C. State and several photos, including one of his car, another of the parking lot where he had left the car on the night of the murder.

"Mr. Pritchard," Norton said after the evidence all had been received, "you had stated, I believe yesterday, that in your initial plan with Mr. Upchurch, the fire plan, that you did not talk specifically about Angela, is that correct?"

"Yes, sir."

"How about in the burglary plan?"

"Yes, sir, we did."

"What was discussed at that time?"

"She was to be murdered also."

"And is there any reason for that?"

"Not any particular reason, no, sir."

"What, if anything, did you stand to gain by Angela's death?"

"The entire insurance."

"All right. Now, would you state whether or not you have ever seen or heard or read Neal Henderson's statement to the police."

"No, sir, I have not."

"And since the time of the murder, your initial conversations with Neal Henderson, have you ever at any time talked with him?"

"No, sir."

"All right, sir. If you will answer Mr. Sermons' and Mr. Johnston's questions."

"Mr. Pritchard," Sermons began, "you stated yesterday that during your high school days you had broken up with a girlfriend and that had caused you great stress. Is that correct?"

"Yes, sir."

"And how long had you dated this person?"

"Three weeks."

"And breaking up with her caused you what type of stress?"

"I couldn't concentrate on schoolwork, family, friends."

"Did you seek professional treatment for that?"

"No, sir, I did not."

"Did you receive any counseling from school counselors, any ministers, people like that?"

"No, sir."

"Did you discuss it with your parents?"

"Yes, sir, I did."

"And did they help you through it?"

"Yes, sir, they did."

Sermons took Chris carefully back over his testimony, an easygoing, gentle questioning in the beginning, as if Sermons only wanted to make sure of all that Chris had said. But when he came to the murder plot, he began zeroing in on inconsistencies. After questioning him about the conversation at the Golden Corral, Sermons asked, "And then you had another conversation later on in James's room that night?"

"Yes, sir."

"Do you recall whether James lived in a dorm or lived in an apartment?"

"I do not remember where he lived at that time."

"So you don't remember whether or not when you left the Golden Corral you went back into James's apartment or back to his room, do you?"

"No, sir."

"And then you say the next day, the Thursday the 21st, you either went to his room or his apartment, am I correct?"

"Yes, sir."

"But you can't recall which one?"

"No, sir."

"And isn't it true that you were the one that stood to gain if all three of your family members were killed, two million dollars?"

"Yes, sir."

In questioning him about the weekend of the murder, Sermons kept bringing out that Chris actually remembered very little. After asking about picking up Bart and taking him to Washington that weekend, Sermons asked, "Where did you go when you got back to Raleigh?"

"To Mr. Upchurch's room—apartment."

"I'll ask you, if you haven't previously stated and specifically on the 27th of December that you went back to California and drank beer and got drunk?"

"That's possible."

"So you could have stated that on the 27th?"

"Yes, sir, I could have stated that."

"And so that would be inconsistent with what you are telling us now, is that correct?"

The objection was sustained.

"Do you remember which one it was, Mr. Pritchard?"

"As I said, my best recollection is that we went back to Mr. Upchurch's room or apartment."

"And the next night, or the next day—pardon me—what time did you wake up?"

"Approximately eleven, twelve, something around there."

"And did you go to Mr. Upchurch's room or apartment?"

"Yes, sir, I did."

"And you still don't recall which one, do you?"

"No, sir."

"Then you said you went to a Kmart store. Do you remember where the Kmart store was?"

"No, sir, I do not."

"Just some Kmart in Raleigh?"

"Yes, sir."

"And then you drove to Mr. Henderson's apartment, is that correct?"

"Yes, sir."

"You knew where Mr. Henderson lived, did you not?"

"Yes, sir, I did."

"Had no trouble finding his apartment?"

"No, sir."

"While you were in Neal Henderson's apartment, you drew two maps, is that correct?"

"Yes, sir."

"And according to you, James had already been to Washington the day before, isn't that also correct?"

"Yes, sir."

"And according to your information, Mr. Henderson had not been to Washington previously, is that correct?"

"Not to my knowledge, no sir."

"So you drew the two maps in Mr. Henderson's apartment and you stated that you gave them to James Upchurch?"

"Yes, sir."

"Could you have given them to Neal Henderson?"

"That's possible, yes, sir."

Sermons launched into a series of questions to show that in every incriminating statement Chris had made against Bart, no other person was there to verify it except Neal and he in only a few instances. He followed that with another series of questions hammering home that Chris had lied repeatedly to the police, his parents, and others about many things.

Finally, Sermons came to Chris's statement to the police in the week before the trial was to begin. Chris acknowledged that he knew his trial was imminent when he made his confession.

"I'll ask you did you not know and have in either your possession or your attorney's possession a copy of the map that you previously identified you drew?"

"Yes, sir."

"Isn't it true that you knew that you had written that map in Neal Henderson's apartment on July 24, 1988?"

"Yes, sir."

"Isn't it true that you knew that Neal Henderson was scheduled for trial in two weeks?"

"Yes, sir."

"And I'll ask you if you knew that Neal Henderson was prepared to testify that you asked him to drive your car down there?"

"Yes, sir."

"Down to Washington."

"Yes, sir."

"And I will ask you at that time, if you did not know that Mr. Henderson was contending that Mr. Upchurch actually did the killing?"

"Yes, sir."

"You knew all of those things, did you not?"

"Yes, sir."

"I'll ask you if paragraph four of your plea bargain, your *deal*"—the word came out with disdain—"with the state of North Carolina does not read, 'Christopher Wayne Pritchard understands that if he fails to abide by this agreement then the agreement shall be null and void and he will face trial on the original charges?' Did you not know what it said?"

"Yes, sir."

"And did you know that that's what it said before you talked to Mr. Norton and Mr. Mason and Officer Taylor and Special Agent Young on the night of the 27th of December, 1988?"

"Yes, sir."

"Mr. Pritchard, isn't it true that you knew that if you were convicted of first-degree murder that you stood a chance of being put to death in the gas chamber of North Carolina?"

"Yes, sir."

"I will ask you isn't it true that by your plea bargain you no longer face that possibility?"

"There was a chance if I did not complete my agreement."

"And you knew at the time that you made the deal that that was saving your life, did you not?"

"Yes, sir."

Norton attempted to counter any damage that Sermons might have inflicted by taking Chris through the reasons for many of the lies he had admitted telling.

"You were asked by Mr. Sermons about whether or not you were the only person to have something to gain by the murders. Was there anything that James Upchurch was to gain?"

"Yes, sir, fifty thousand dollars and a Porsche."

374

"You were also asked about your knowledge of Mr. Henderson being prepared to testify, not only against yourself, but also James Upchurch. Did you learn about that in the courtroom at the various hearings that have been held in this case?"

"I sort of heard about it through the grapevine."

"But had you seen the statement, heard his statement, read or knew anything specifically about what Neal Henderson was going to say?"

"I had no idea what he was going to say from anything that anyone had told me."

"You were also asked by Mr. Sermons about whether you had discussed any other weapons than the knife. Had you, on the occasions in which you went to James Upchurch's room, seen any sporting equipment, any bats?"

"Yes, sir. I had seen the baseball bat."

"Where was the baseball bat when you saw it?"

"Generally it was leaning up against the heater by the window."

"But you never actually discussed with James the use of the bat in the death?"

"No, sir."

After a brief recess, Sermons had a few more questions for Chris.

"You were asked about a baseball bat that you saw in Mr. Upchurch's room. Now where was this room?"

"On campus, sir."

"So it was in a dorm?"

"Yes, sir."

"Okay, so you can remember now that it was in a room in a dorm that you saw the bat, but you can't remember during the week of twenty through the twenty-fifth whether he lived in a room or an apartment?"

"That's correct. I saw the bat when we played the games."

"And certainly everybody that you have testified to playing the game had access to the room and was in and out of the room?"

"Yes, sir."

Sermons established that there were two people per room, four rooms per suite in the dorm.

"Is it fair to say that suitemates are visiting each other from time to time?"

"Yes, sir."

"In and out of each other's rooms quite frequently?"

"Yes, sir."

"Do all kinds of things in each other's rooms?"

"Yes, sir."

"And you certainly don't know whose bat that was, do you?"

"No, sir."

"All right. That's all the questions I have."

"All right," said the judge. "Anything else, Mr. Norton?"

"No, sir."

"Thank you, Mr. Pritchard, you may step down."

Sandra Goodman was the next witness. She spoke in a soft voice, and the judge had to ask her to remove her gum and remind her repeatedly to speak up.

She told of meeting Chris and Bart and their friends in summer school and of drinking and smoking pot and going to California Pizza together. Her version of events on the night of the murder varied from Chris's on several points that were summed up in the final exchange of questions and answers between her and the district attorney.

"Let me see if I understand you correctly," Norton said. "On the twenty-fourth of July, you are saying that you did not go to California Pizza with Mr. Pritchard that night?"

"I do not remember doing that."

"But you do recall buying the beer at the Sav-A-Center?"

"Yes, I do."

"And you recall playing cards until three-thirty that morning?"

"Yes, I do."

"Do you recall seeing James Upchurch that night?"

"No, I do not."

Frank Johnston asked questions showing that Sandra remembered many other events of the day before the murder—that she had spent the night before with a friend, that she had come to campus to work on a computer program, that she had gone to Sybil's room afterward—all designed to cast doubt on Chris's story.

In response to another question, she said that she had visited in Bart's dorm room.

"Ever see any kind of baseball bat in his room?"

"No."

"Do you recall ever seeing James Upchurch wearing black Reebok tennis shoes?"

"No."

Johnston then brought out the knapsack that had been found on the back porch of the Von Stein house on the morning of the murder. Sandra recalled John Taylor showing it to her, and she recalled calling him at home to tell him that after thinking about it, she had remembered seeing it earlier.

"And where did you tell him you had seen that bag?"

"On the floor in Chris's room."

"Do you recall telling him that you had seen it with Dungeons and Dragons material in it?"

"Yes."

Norton leaped on this when his turn came, seizing an opportunity he had been waiting for.

"When you say Dungeons and Dragons books, what do you mean by that?" he asked. "What was the purpose of those?"

"I am not sure," Sandra said, "except they had different books that they had about the game. I never really looked at them."

"Just Dungeons and Dragons books?"

"Yes."

"Chris, of course, you said Chris Pritchard was a player?"

"Yes."

"James Upchurch was a player?"

"Yes."

"Now, do you know what role in the game James Upchurch played?"

"Objection," said Johnston.

"Overruled, if she knows."

"I know that he was the one that—well, I saw them play once or twice. And he was the one that called out the plays. He's the one that made up the stories, and then they had to choose what they were going to do to get out of their situations."

"Do you recall hearing the phrase that he was the 'dungeon master'?"

The objection was quickly sustained, but Norton knew that the image of control and manipulation would remain in the jurors' minds regardless.

45

THE SECOND WEEK OF TES-
timony began on Tuesday with problems. A juror had an eye
infection and had to go to a doctor. Another juror had to be
dismissed for reading news accounts of the trial, and an
alternate took his place.

It was midafternoon before Mitchell Norton was able to
call his feature witness of the day.

"Gerald Neal Henderson."

Neal took the stand wearing the same gray suit he had
worn in earlier court appearances, his dark hair neatly coiffed,
his expression humble.

After Neal acknowledged his identity, Judge Watts asked
him to speak louder. "It's obviously important that all these
folks hear what you have to say. It's important that I hear what
you have to say. And I have a terrible cold."

Norton took Neal through his years of school, his fast
advancement, his year at the School of Science and Math, his
two years as a senior at Bartlett Yancey. Neal answered in a
monotone, sounding rehearsed to some in the courtroom.

Why had he remained a senior for two years after all of
that acceleration in earlier grades? Norton asked.

"My parents and myself decided that I wasn't ready to go
to college at that point, so I wanted to stay around another
year to, well, catch up on some aging."

"Catch up on some aging?"

"Yes, sir. Academically I was ready to go, but I wasn't
mature enough at that time to deal with college."

Neal went on to tell about meeting Bart, about his first
two years in college, about moving off campus. He told about
getting together with Bart in the spring of '88 to start another
Dungeons and Dragons campaign. He described meeting Chris
and went on to tell about the D&D games that they played.
Norton asked if there had been any discussion of Chris's family.

"James and I discussed it once, after a trip he had made
with Chris; he mentioned that Chris's parents were quite

wealthy. That's the only time Chris's parents were mentioned up until the conspiracy."

Frank Johnston objected.

"Well, sustained to the use of the word *conspiracy*, members of the jury. That's for you ultimately to determine. Strike it from your mind."

Had Bart told him exactly how much money Chris's parents had?

"He said millions, perhaps as much as ten million."

A short time later, Norton got to the meeting at Neal's apartment when Chris and Bart first brought up the plan to kill Chris's parents, which took place two or three weeks before the murder, according to Neal, not the day before, as Chris had testified.

"Describe for us what happened."

"James and Chris came in. We chatted for a couple of minutes about Dungeons and Dragons. Then James said that he and Chris had an idea, a plan for Chris to come into his inheritance early. I remarked to them, 'Oh, you are going to rob the place?' And James shook his head and said, 'No, we are going to murder his parents so that he inherits.' "

"What did you say?"

"My exact words were, 'Isn't that a little extreme?' Chris laughed. James said, 'No, no. We are serious. Here, let me show you.' And they started outlining a plan. Most of the talking was being done by James."

Neal described the plan and explained why he was needed as driver.

"Now at the time that you agreed to do this, what were you to get out of it, Neal?"

"I remember it was either two thousand or twenty thousand. To this day, I am not sure exactly which it was."

"Was anything said about fifty thousand dollars and a Ferrari?"

"No sir, I don't remember that."

Later, Norton asked about the second time that Neal talked with Chris and Bart about the murder. That came two or three days later, Neal said, when he stopped by Bart's dorm room in the afternoon and Chris was there.

"I just dropped by," Neal said. "They were sitting around talking. When I got there, the conversation turned toward the plan. Not much was discussed about the actual plan at that point. More it was discussed about what would happen afterwards."

He told about Chris saying he would have to be depressed after the murders and that he would go to the beach to cheer himself up and buy cars for all of his friends.

"How did the business about buying everybody cars come up?"

"James was concerned that if only he received a car people would wonder why he was getting a car. Well, Chris said that was no problem, he would go ahead and buy everybody cars."

Neal said that he left that day with no timetable set for the murder and no plan for another meeting. Three or four days later, he went by Bart's room again. This time Bart was alone, and he pulled a baseball bat from the closet, Neal said.

"He laid the bat on one of the beds in the room. He said that he thought about how he was going to do it and the bat as the primary weapon. He said that he wanted something that would at least knock someone out in one hit. He was not at all sure that he could use a knife and quickly do anything. He said one good hit from a bat should do what he wanted done."

"Was that the first time that you had ever seen that bat?"

"No, sir. For about as long as I've known him, he's always had a bat like that."

"That's bullshit," Bart scrawled on his legal pad.

Neal continued, saying that Bart showed him a hunting knife that he planned to use, then pulled out a pair of black-and-white batting gloves and began putting black shoe polish on the white parts.

"He said that we were going to try for a day in the upcoming week," Neal said. "I think this meeting was on a Thursday or Friday. He said that Chris had either already left to go home or was going to go home the next day to find out the family's plans for the upcoming week, I think to get a house key. I am not sure whether he had one with him at State or not. He asked me what my schedule was for the coming week, and I told him that I had Sunday night off. He told me to keep it open, that that would probably be the night we were going to go."

On Sunday morning, Neal said, Bart came to his apartment, gave him the map and told him to meet him at the parking lot about midnight. And that was what he did.

380

"Now, did he have anything with him at that time?"

"Yes, sir. He had a green book bag or backpack and the baseball bat."

"And what, if anything, did he say to you when you arrived?"

" 'Let's go.' That's about it."

Norton retrieved the knapsack that had been introduced as evidence, handed it to Neal, and asked if he recognized it.

"Yes, sir. This is James's book bag."

Neal went on to describe how Bart had the bat stuffed into the bag along with the knife and clothing. Always before, Neal said, Bart had used the bag to carry school books or Dungeons and Dragons books.

Norton got Neal to describe the Dungeons and Dragons books and asked, over Frank Johnston's objections, why Bart would need them.

"He would have to have access to the books frequently as he was the games master."

"Is that what it was called, the 'games master'?"

"Its technical term would be dungeon master."

Despite all of the defense efforts to keep it out, Bart, the dungeon master, with all of its sinister connotations, was finally and formally in evidence.

Neal went on to describe the route he took to Washington and how Bart had changed clothes—shirt and pants—in the car as they neared the town. "I believe he changed shoes. I think he was wearing boots when he arrived at the car, and he changed into tennis shoes."

"Do you recall anything about the tennis shoes he put on?"

"I think they were black."

Jim Upchurch shook his head. To him, all of Neal's testimony sounded planned and practiced.

Neal carefully described the route he took to Smallwood, pausing to identify photographs of landmarks that the district attorney submitted into evidence. They arrived about two-thirty, he said, and drove past the subdivision without noticing it at first, then turned and went back.

"James asked me to pull into Lawson Road. He wanted to see the area in front of the house. So I pulled in. You know, we went by Chris's house from the front. I didn't identify it. James kind of counted down five houses and said, 'That's the place.' "

They drove on around the block and found the wooded lot that Chris had marked as the spot for James to get out, Neal said.

"We didn't stop. We kept on going. He wasn't ready. We were just looking around and seeing what things looked like."

The judge, however, was ready to stop. It was well after five, and he called the attorneys to the bench and declared a recess.

Neal returned to the stand Wednesday morning to finish his story of the murder mission, telling it just as he first had told it to the police months earlier. He identified the baseball bat as being the one Bart had carried that night (he had been present when Bart drew the black triangles on it with a Magic Marker, he said), identified the burned remnants of clothing as being the sweater and jeans Bart had worn that night. He told of talking with Bart about the murder in the weeks after it happened, then not seeing him again for months until Bart came asking for a place to stay the previous spring. He described Bart's reaction after John Taylor brought the knapsack around to ask if they'd ever seen it.

"He admitted to me that he had forgotten the bag and left it in the house," Neal said. "He then said that the police were closing in on him and he was heading out of town. He told me that I didn't have anything to worry about. His exact words were, 'Look, you just drove the car. If worse comes to worst, and Chris confesses, it's your word against his. And no one's going to believe Chris over you. So don't worry about it. But I'm getting out of town.' "

After leaving the apartment, Bart called him at work rather than at home, Neal said. "He was afraid of the phones being tapped. He asked me to get together as much money as I could and to get it to him as fast as possible, that he was going to get out of town."

Neal went on to describe his confession and to explain that no deal was offered beforehand. He told of making his plea bargain with the state in December.

Norton asked specifically if Bonnie Von Stein, Angela Pritchard, Butch Mitchell, or Quincy Blackwell had anything to do with the plot to murder Lieth and rob the house. Neal answered no in each case. Only he, Bart, and Chris were involved, he said.

Norton handed him a color photograph of Lieth's bloody body.

"I want you to look at that photograph. Did you do that?"

Tears came to Neal's eyes. He choked on his answer.

"No, sir."

"You participated in seeing that it was done though, did you not?"

"Yes, sir," he said, still fighting to regain composure.

"Neal, why? Why did you get involved in the murder of Lieth Von Stein?"

Judge Watts overruled the objection.

"At that time, I really didn't feel very good about myself and I needed friends," Neal said. "James Upchurch and Christopher Pritchard were my friends. What they proposed to me, it seemed like an adventure, just to go off in the middle of the night and come back. Yeah, the plan was there for somebody to get hurt, but up until he actually got out of the car with the weapons, I really didn't fully believe that he would do it. I kept telling myself, yeah, he's just going to go in and come back out and it will all be a big joke and we would all go back and joke about it for years to come. Only he didn't come back and say it was a big joke. He came back and said he had killed somebody."

"Did the money have anything to do with you agreeing to participate in driving the car?"

"Not really."

"If you didn't do it for the money, Neal, why did you do it?"

"It's like I said, my friends wanted me to help them out. I didn't really think anybody would get hurt, so I helped them out."

"Cross-examination?" asked the judge.

Just as Wayland Sermons had done with Chris, Frank Johnston began with gentle questions for Neal, asking about his years in school. But Neal had been warned about a sharp and a vigorous cross-examination, and he was braced for it. The hard questions were not long in coming. Johnston quickly zeroed in on the discrepancies in Neal's and Chris's testimony.

Johnston handed Neal a calendar for July 1988 along with a red pen and asked him to mark the day that Bart and Chris came to him with the plan.

"Objection, if Your Honor please," Norton interjected. "He said he wasn't sure of what the date was."

"Overruled," said Watts. "If you can do so, if you know."

"I'm willing to try," Neal said. "Looks like somewhere in the second week."

He was only able to mark the week, though, not the day, but that served Johnston's purpose. He mainly wanted to demonstrate to the jurors that Neal was right-handed.

After determining that it was sometime during the week before the murder that Neal met the second time with Bart, when Bart supposedly brought out the bat and gloves, Johnston questioned him about that.

"You indicated that you had seen James put shoe polish on these gloves—batting gloves, you call them?"

"Yes, sir."

"Are you familiar with batting gloves?"

"Yes, sir."

"You've played baseball, used batting gloves?"

"No, sir. But James had had those gloves for a long time. I was with him when he got them."

"Now you've told us too that on this occasion you saw a knife."

"Yes, sir."

"And have you seen the knife that was burned?"

"Yes, I have."

"Now, isn't it true, Mr. Henderson, that there's no way for you to say that the knife that you saw that was burned was the same knife that you say you saw in Mr. Upchurch's room?"

"It looks like the knife that I saw in his room would look like if it had been burned."

"Had you ever burned the knife that was in his room?"

"No, sir, but this was a burned knife and it looked about the same size and shape."

"And when you observed the knife in his room, was it by itself?"

"No, sir. It had a sheath."

"Have you seen that sheath since then?"

"Not that I remember."

"Did you see that sheath on the night of July 24th?"

"I don't remember seeing it."

Later, Johnston returned to the fire scene, confirming that Neal had taken the officers there.

"And the reason that you were able to identify the area is because you drove there, isn't it?"

"I had been to it before, yes."

"And the reason you were able to identify what was burned in the fire and the sound of the fire is because you were there and you did it, isn't that true?"

"No," Neal said firmly. "I was there and I heard it. I did not do it."

Johnston went on to bring out other discrepancies, that Neal had identified Chris's car as black instead of white, that he originally told the police that he and Bart said little on the way back to Raleigh, that they just turned up the music on the radio and listened to it.

"Isn't it true that Chris Pritchard's car didn't have a radio in it?"

"I don't know."

"Isn't it true that his radio had been stolen the weekend of July 4, 1988?"

"I don't know."

"Isn't it true that when you made your statement to the officers on June 9th that you had been told that someone had told the officers that you were involved in this matter? And that it would be better for you to go ahead and tell what happened rather than to remain silent?"

"No, sir. That's not what happened."

"Now you have told us that you were accelerated through school, skipped several grades, that you were recommended to the School of Math and Science because of your academic abilities. Isn't it true, Mr. Henderson, that you were termed by many as a genius?"

"Some might say that. Some might not. It depends on who you ask."

"And isn't it true that you had from the time that this incident occurred until June the 9th, approximately eleven months, before you ever made any statement to any officers that you now say is the truth about this matter?"

"Eleven months sounds about right."

"And before you made that statement you, in fact, had several denials of any involvement in this matter."

"No, sir. I said once that I did not recognize a book bag."

"And isn't it true that there has been an additional period

385

of six or seven months since you say you first came forward to the police with this information?"

"Yes, sir."

"And during all this period you have certainly had ample opportunity to think about your situation and what would be in your best interest, have you not?"

"Yes, sir."

"In recognition of your plea, is it not true that the state reduced charges against you and has agreed not to prosecute other charges?"

"That was the plea bargain, yes, sir."

"And isn't it true that by your plea, you are not facing the death penalty?"

"Yes, sir."

"And how you did in court and what you said may have a significant impact on what type of sentence you might receive, isn't that true?"

"I was told that it would be entirely up to Judge Watts."

"Weren't you told, Mr. Henderson, if you got on that stand and verified the facts that the state wanted you to verify that it may help you in sentencing?"

"No, sir. I was told to give truthful testimony. It says so on my piece of paper. And that's all I am doing."

"And isn't it true that in order for you to testify in this case, that you came down to Elizabeth City on Monday and spent some time with the district attorney's office going over your testimony and reviewing the maps and other pieces of evidence?"

"Yes, we have talked."

"And you've talked for several hours, didn't you?"

"A couple hours, probably."

After receiving permission from the judge, Johnston rose from the defense table and handed Neal the photograph of Lieth's bloody body that Norton had showed Neal earlier.

"Isn't it true that the last time that you saw Mr. Von Stein was that you saw him in that condition, or put him in that condition on July 25, 1988?"

"No, sir. That is not true. I did not do that and I could not do that."

"And isn't it true that none of these occasions that you've testified to that James Upchurch was with you?"

"No, sir. That is not true. He was with me and he did do what I said he did."

"I don't have any further questions."

Norton Mitchell did have more questions. Did Neal have any plea agreement when he made his statement to the police? A lawyer? No to both questions. Did he tell the truth? Yes. Was he concerned about the color of the car? Not at all. Had he described the bat to the police before they found it? "I think so. I can't remember exactly." Any doubt that it was Bart's bat? None. Was the bathroom in Chris's suite in Lee dorm where Neal put the car keys after returning to Raleigh actually in Chris's room? No.

"That's all I have," Norton said.

"Anything else, Mr. Johnston?" asked the judge.

"Just one question. Mr. Henderson, isn't it true that you had no reason to be in Lee dorm the morning of July 25th, 1988?"

"No, sir. I had to take the keys back up there."

"Didn't James have to go right up there within two floors of Chris's room?"

"He told me to put the keys there. I put the keys there."

"No further questions."

Bart had grown increasingly upset as Johnston's cross-examination had gone on. He had wanted Sermons to cross-examine Neal, but the lawyers had planned and prepared for Sermons to take Chris, Johnston to take Neal. Bart thought that he could have done a better job than Johnston. "Neal handled Frank more than Frank handled Neal," he said later.

After Neal's testimony, all in the courtroom were aware that the state had finished the essence of its case; the rest would be anticlimactic.

The big remaining question of the trial was whether Bart would take the stand to defend himself against his two former friends.

46

JIM UPCHURCH WAS THE
first witness in his son's behalf on Friday morning. He testified
that on Tuesday, July 19, 1988, the day before Chris, according
to his testimony, first brought up the subject of murder with
Bart at the Golden Corral, he picked his son up on Hillsborough
Street at about 5:30 P.M. and took him home to Caswell County.
Joanne's grandfather had died in Gaston County and Joanne
wanted Bart to attend the funeral. Jim said that he and Bart
drove to Gastonia Wednesday morning.

"And was your son present at the funeral?" Wayland
Sermons asked.

"Yes. He was there with his sisters and brother and
mother."

Jim said that he attended a business meeting in Charlotte
after the funeral, then drove back to his job in Raleigh, leaving
Bart with his mother in Gastonia. Joanne dropped Bart off at
Carolyn's house on Thursday, and Jim said that he picked him
up there after work and took him to the farm, where Bart
spent the night with him. He dropped Bart off on the campus
on his way into work Friday morning, Jim said. But from
Tuesday night until Friday morning, the time during which
Chris maintained they were planning the murder, Bart had
not even been in Raleigh.

Sermons asked if Bart ever had a baseball bat.

"No," Jim said.

"Did you ever see one around the house?"

"No, sir, not to my knowledge."

"Did your son ever have a green knapsack?"

"No, sir."

"Did you go by his room in Raleigh on occasions?"

"Yes, sir, a number of times."

"Did you ever see a wooden baseball bat in the room?"

"No, sir."

Under cross-examination, Norton showed that Jim knew
little about what Bart did in Raleigh. Jim had heard of Hank
and Chuck but didn't know their last names or anything about

them. He'd never heard of Chris until after Bart was charged with murder. He hadn't seen Bart much at all after dropping him off at the campus after the funeral.

"I talked to him on the telephone occasionally from my office. And I know he was home Thanksgiving. I don't recall exact times that I may have seen him during that time."

"Of course, you don't know where he was or what he did on the weekend of the 24th, 25th, do you?"

"No, sir."

"Do you know a person by the name of Christy Newsom?"

"Yes, sir."

"Do you recall telling Mrs. Newsom that you didn't know where your son was, didn't know how to contact him or get up with him?"

"Yes, sir, I told her that."

"In fact, Mrs. Newsom contacted you on several occasions, did she not?"

"Yes, sir."

"Trying to locate your son, wasn't she?"

"Yes."

"And do you recall over what period of time Mrs. Newsom or others were contacting you trying to find your son?"

"I spoke with Mrs. Newsom several times. I don't recall the exact time frame, but it was in the spring of 1989."

"How long a period of time was it that you lost track of your son?"

"I made contact with him by telephone from time to time, you know. I don't recall the exact—I may have spoken with him one time and then it may have been several weeks before I spoke to him again, usually by telephone. Sometimes he would call me and ask to borrow five dollars, he was running short. His job, he didn't pick up a paycheck or something. And I would drop off five dollars or ten dollars on Hillsborough Street. We would meet up there."

"Was that during the same period of time that you told Mrs. Newsom that you didn't know where he was or how to contact him?"

"Off and on, yes, sir."

"Did he play ball when he was a young man, child?"

"Played basketball with his friends."

"Never played baseball?"

"He wasn't that athletic."

389

"Never played baseball?"

"Not to my knowledge."

"Where was he supposed to be living in June of 1989?"

"He was staying with friends. I don't know where in Raleigh exactly."

"Did you know that he was supposed to be living with Neal Henderson in June of '89?"

"At one point he called me and said he was moving in with Neal."

"But you never went around then?"

"No, sir. I didn't know where Neal lived."

"And this was the same period of time where you lost track of him, couldn't find him?"

"Up until that point, I had lost track of him."

"After that point, when Mrs. Newsom called you, you didn't know where he was, did you?"

"No. She called during the spring a couple of times. I told her at the time I really didn't know where he was living."

"Specifically, after the 9th of June during 1989, didn't Mrs. Newsom contact you on several occasions then trying to find out where your son was?"

"She called me a number of times, but I don't recall what the dates of those calls were."

"Do you know when the last time was that you had contact with your son prior to his arrest?"

"It was sometime early June, but I don't recall the date. I honestly don't."

"All right, sir."

An uncle of Joanne's followed Jim to the stand, confirming Bart's presence at his great-grandfather's funeral, offering photographs as evidence.

Bart's high school friend, Coy Odom, who had introduced Bart to Neal years earlier, was next to testify.

He described himself as being close to both Bart and Neal, but closer to Bart. "Me and Bart has pretty much been brothers, you know, pretty much."

"And do you recall throughout high school Bart having a wooden baseball bat?"

"No, sir."

"And do you ever recall Bart having a green army knapsack?"

"No, sir."

Coy testified that he had visited Bart's dorm room at N.C. State three or four times and had twice spent the night there with him, but he'd never seen a bat or a green army bag in the room.

Coy said that he hadn't talked with Neal since the arrests, but he had talked with Bart three times.

"Did he suggest anything for you to testify to or say?"

"No, sir."

"Did you ever play baseball?" Norton asked after Sermons had finished.

"No, sir—or have *I* ever played baseball?"

"Yes."

"Yes. I've played baseball."

"Have you ever been convicted of any criminal offense, Mr. Odom?"

"No, sir."

Norton asked if he'd seen martial arts weapons in Bart's dorm room. He hadn't.

"Did you look in his closet?"

"No, sir."

"Look in his drawers while you were there?"

"No, sir."

"So what you are saying is you don't know what was in the closets or in the drawers or other things in the room, do you?"

"I don't really think he had much of anything. He had a bicycle that I knew of. And I think he had a sofa that, you know, he pretty much carried around with him."

"A sofa that he carried with him?"

"You know. Different places that he traveled. I ain't for sure, but it seems like to me two or three places."

"You don't know what he had other than the bicycle, do you, Mr. Odom? Isn't that the truth of the matter?"

"No, sir. I don't really think he owned much of anything besides the clothes on his back."

The next witness was a window glass manufacturer who had been sent to the Von Stein house to examine the glass in the door to the back porch after Chris's testimony. It was not Plexiglas, he said, but standard double-paned window glass.

Sermons offered a photograph of Butch Mitchell into evidence so the jurors could see that he was black and it was passed to them.

"Any other evidence for the defendant?" asked Judge Watts.

"Your Honor, that's the evidence for the defendant," Sermons said.

Reporters in the audience were surprised. They had expected, certainly had hoped, that Bart would testify in his own behalf. It was not that he didn't want to, for he did. He was certain that he could convince the jurors that he had nothing to do with any murder, but in this instance his lawyers had prevailed. Bart could testify to nothing that his plea didn't already say, his lawyers told him. Also if he got on the stand, his entire record would be bared for the jurors. They would know that he was under house arrest and had cut his leg band and fled after John Taylor came showing the army knapsack. He couldn't risk that, his lawyers warned. What they didn't tell him was that his cockiness, his eagerness to argue with the district attorney, his smirking expression surely would alienate the jurors beyond hope. Silent, with his parents and grandmother behind him, he at least maintained the appearance of the "clean-cut, quintessential upper-class college student," as one newspaper report had described him, an image the jurors might find sympathetic. It would be on that image, combined with the discrepancies in testimony and an appeal to reasonable doubt, that Bart's fate would rest.

Bart had been busying himself working on final arguments for his attorneys to present.

"Ladies and gentlemen of the jury," he had written on his legal pad, "the state has introduced 117 pieces of evidence, all of which have been linked to Chris Pritchard and Neal Henderson, and none of which have been linked to the defendant, except through the testimony of Neal Henderson and Chris Pritchard. These two gentlemen developed and followed through on a plan to get rich by murdering an entire family and now the state would ask you to believe them when they testify against a third party to avoid going to death row.

"Acting in their own self interest, C.P. and N.H. have caused the death of one man. Don't let them succeed in doing it to another.

"There is as much evidence that each of you committed this crime as did the defendant.

"The defendant gave an alias when questioned by a campus

police officer. Is this a strange thing for college students to do?

"When the SBI came and told the defendant he was under arrest for murder, he ran. Damn right, he ran. If he had gotten away maybe he wouldn't be here accused of murdering somebody he'd never even met. The defendant did not run when questioned by campus police. He did not even run when brought to the station house. He ran when he was told he was being charged with murder.

"If the defendant was the brutal murderer the DA says him to be, why didn't he strike or fight against Agent Young when he was dragging him off balance for about ten feet?

"If you were charged with murder and knowing you're innocent, would you come along peacefully and be in the defendant's shoes right now?

"Neal's plea bargain was to testify against me and Chris. Chris's plea bargain was to testify against me. Chris could've testified that I didn't have anything to do with it, but the DA would've said he was just covering for me. The DA thinks Neal's testimony is 'truthful,' even though there's no evidence to support it. Chris made a bargain to save his life. Of course, he's going to yes-man Neal.

"Do you have enough faith in the testimony of C.P. and N.H. to send Bart Upchurch to the gas chamber?

"ALL THE FACTS, EVIDENCE, TESTIMONY, MEDICAL TESTIMONY SAYS THAT C.P. AND N.H. ARE LYING."

The judge decided there would not be time for final arguments this day, however, and recessed court for the weekend.

Frank Johnston, who had announced before the trial that he was running against Mitchell Norton for the office of district attorney, argued first in Bart's behalf on Monday morning.

He suggested that the case was so confusing as to fall into the realm of the supernatural.

"I've listened to all the witnesses, looked at all the evidence, and I still don't know what happened," he said.

He went on to point out all the discrepancies in the testimony. "Inconsistencies, ladies and gentlemen, deficiencies, weaknesses. What's happening here? What's going on? What does your good common sense tell you? It's like a game of Clue. That's what the state wants you to believe. Draw cards, the ones you can't use, just throw 'em away, don't worry about 'em." Among the discrepancies that Johnston pointed to was the testimony of Dr. Page Hudson, the medical examiner, about the food in Lieth's stomach, which raised questions about the time of death.

"I think it tells us something about this case," Johnston said. "We aren't getting the truth."

Hands in the pockets of his gray suit coat, pacing in front of the bench, Johnston, a short man wearing glasses, described the evidence taken from the Von Stein house.

"There is not one shred of physical evidence that ties anything that happened to the defendant, James Upchurch."

Johnston spoke scathingly of Chris, calling him "cold, callous, bloodthirsty." In his descriptions, Chris "slithered" into meetings and "slithered" back out. But the person Chris had hired to kill his parents wasn't Bart, Johnston indicated; it was Neal.

"You've got to remember ol' Neal is the crucial figure in all of this. Have you ever seen anybody testify who looked more like a robot?"

Johnston recalled the negroid hair found in the tennis shoe.

"Neal Henderson roomed with Butch Mitchell, black male. What does your common sense tell you?"

He reminded the jurors that Bonnie had fled the courtroom in fear after first seeing Neal. And he used the baseball bat to take yet another verbal swing at Neal.

"Who is the only person who has indicated that this bat was at the Von Stein residence? Neal Henderson."

Even after the jurors made their decision, Johnston reminded them before closing his hour-and-a-half argument, they still couldn't know for certain what had happened in this case.

"I don't know what the truth is, but we haven't heard it in this courtroom. There's got to be reasonable doubt."

Wayland Sermons' wealthy elderly father, a former legislator, came to court this day to hear his son argue his first capital murder case. He sat beside reporters, occasionally nodding agreement as his son made an impassioned plea, his voice often rising.

"Lieth Von Stein suffered a horrible death," Sermons

acknowledged at the beginning. "There's no question about that. As horrible as that death was, equally as horrible is the thought that an innocent man may be found guilty upon the uncorroborated testimony of two confessed murderers."

Sermons went on to assault the evidence, noting that Lieth's head injuries indicated that they had been inflicted by a bat being swung by a right-handed person. Bart, as the jurors could see by watching him writing on the legal pad at the defense table, was left-handed. But as Sermons pointed out, when Johnston asked Neal to mark dates on a calendar, he had done it with his right hand.

Referring to Neal sneeringly as "the genius," Sermons noted that it was Neal who'd ended up with all the money taken at the Von Stein house, Neal who took the car keys back to Chris's room despite Bart living only two floors above Chris.

Sermons reminded the jurors of Chris's description of the effects of LSD—"You see colors; it makes you feel invincible; it gives you incredible energy"—and pointed out that Neal had told Kenyatta that he had taken LSD so that she would throw him out and give him an excuse to go on the murder mission.

"I contend to you that Mr. Henderson was telling you the truth when he said, 'I took LSD,' and he was telling Kenyatta the truth, and after taking LSD, he went and did this murder."

Sermons repeatedly called Chris a liar and argued that his stories defied "all logic and reason."

"He never formed a conspiracy with Upchurch," Sermons said. "He formed a conspiracy with Neal Henderson and fingered Upchurch because, one, he knew he lived alone, and number two, he knew he was an easy mark, a good guy."

Chris and Neal were simply lying to protect one another's stories and to save their lives, Sermons said.

"What other than them saying it's so do you have?" Sermons asked. "What other than their testimony? If you throw out all the evidence by somebody who has an interest in the case, you'll come to the conclusion that the state has failed to prove its case beyond a reasonable doubt. I contend the evidence shows Mrs. Von Stein's woman's intuition was correct that day in court when she became so frightened of Neal Henderson that she had to leave the courtroom and go to her attorney's office."

In closing, Sermons quoted John Locke, the seventeenth-century English philosopher: "One unerring mark of the love of truth is not entertaining any proposition with greater assurance than the truths it is built upon will warrant."

"That's a fancy way of saying don't believe anything that doesn't have proof that establishes it. I think that's what this case is about: not letting the state's 117 exhibits and 27 witnesses make you think that the guilt of Bart Upchurch should be embraced with any greater assurance than what it actually proves."

Mitchell Norton had been the district attorney for the Second Judicial District for five years, an assistant district attorney for ten years before that. He was of medium height, with a slight paunch. His hair was thinning dramatically on the right side, where he parted it, but longish in the back. He wore a drooping mustache to distract attention from his receding chin.

It had become clear during the trial that more than the normal courtroom tensions separated him from the defense attorneys. They did not move in the same social circles, as lawyers so often did in small towns. Despite having spent fifteen years in Washington, Norton still was not accepted by the old families of the establishment. Although a native of eastern North Carolina, from Sampson County, he had not attended prestigious universities, as had Sermons and Johnston. He was graduated from East Carolina, in nearby Greenville, which had a widespread image as the redneck branch of the state's university system. His law degree was from a little-known university in Birmingham, Alabama.

Norton had a slow, methodical, almost country manner about him, and he played it to great effect before the juries of his district, often saying "ain't," using sentences that weren't quite grammatical, now and then employing the eastern North Carolina colloquialism *wont* for *wasn't*. "It wont something they sent invitations to," he would say in explaining why Neal and Chris didn't have other witnesses to verify their nefarious activities with Bart.

"The question you have to face," he told the jury, "is who done it?"

But Norton left no reason for doubt about why it was done.

"The motive in this case is not strange. It's not supernatural, it's not Dungeons and Dragons gone crazy. The reason for this is age old. The motive in this case is greed, fast money, fast cars, easy living."

Chris, he said, was "caught in a world of pizza and beer and drugs and Dungeons and Dragons with no responsibility whatsoever, a world centered around me and self-gratification."

His answer to his problems: "Kill 'em and get the money. Yes, it's cold. Yes, it's heartless. Yes, it's cruel. Instant gratification."

Norton acknowledged the inconsistencies in testimony.

"These cases do not come tied in nice little neat packages," he said. "They come turned and twisted sometimes by time and faulty memories. But when tested and sifted by the rules of reason and common sense, the evidence in this case does point unerringly to the fact"—he walked to the defense table and pointed at Bart—"that the man who accompanied Neal Henderson to Washington, North Carolina, sits right here at this table."

Among the problems with the case that Norton recognized was one that Frank Johnston had touched on in his closing argument: the mystery of the undigested dinner in Lieth's stomach, which the medical examiner had testified was consistent with a much earlier death.

Norton suggested that the stress caused by the death of Lieth's parents, his inheritance, his problems with Chris was the cause of the disruption in digestion.

"If you believe, as they contend, that the rice had to be gone in two hours, if he was not under enough stress, then Lieth Von Stein was dead at eleven o'clock. And if Lieth was dead at eleven, Bonnie had to know about it. She had to be part of it. Neal Henderson and Chris Pritchard have admitted their part in this, but after an investigation of over a year and a half, there is not one shred of evidence, not one statement anywhere, that it didn't happen just like she said. And if he was dead at eleven o'clock—this is what they would have you believe, create a case out of air, not reason—if he was dead at eleven o'clock, what in the world was Neal Henderson doing, coming down here from Raleigh for five and a half hours, with the body lying in the bed and him sitting there and wait until four-thirty to go out and dispose of the clothes?"

The contention that Bart was being framed was specious, Norton suggested.

"Why frame James Upchurch? Why say something about James Upchurch that isn't so?"

It was Bart and Chris who were close friends, Norton reminded the jurors. Neal only played Dungeons and Dragons with Chris and had nothing else to do with him socially. "Socially, Neal Henderson was a nonentity," Norton said. Wouldn't it follow, Norton asked, that if Chris wanted help in killing his parents, he would turn to his good friend Bart, who had gone on trips with him and used drugs with him, not to Neal? And if they wanted to make up something to frame Bart, Norton said, "Don't you know they could have made it fit a lot better than they did?"

The defense, he said, was "grabbing at straws."

As he neared the conclusion of his argument, which had gone on for more than two hours, Norton picked up the burned map that had confirmed Chris's role in the murder.

"I don't know what saved it from the fire," he said, holding it up. "Something kept it. Was it luck? Was it fate? Or was it some other power that kept it from being consumed by the fire and being chopped up by the bushhog? They want to talk to you about supernatural things. Supernatural things have nothing to do in this courthouse. But look at the map closely. Look at the burn marks on the map."

He held it up to his face, the two holes burned near the center of the paper became eye holes, creating a mask.

"Are you looking at the face of death?"

He paused, slowly turning the map upside down.

"Or when you reverse it, are you looking at something more sinister?"

Now the mask seemed to have horns, a face of evil.

"I submit to you when you look at the evidence in this case it points unerringly to the fact that James Bartlett Upchurch III was a part and parcel of the conspiracy to commit murder and did, in fact, carry it out."

47

BART HAD BUOYED HIM-
self with so much hope before the trial that he could not see
the damage that had been inflicted by Chris's and Neal's
testimony. Although some of his family had become increasingly dismayed after hearing Chris's and Neal's stories, Bart
had grown more hopeful, despite his disappointment in the
cross-examination of Neal. He thought that Chris had seemed
"loopy" on the stand and Neal robotic and coached. He looked
at the differences in the testimony, not at the similarities, and
persuaded himself that the jurors would see that both were
lying, trying, as Bart later put it, "to cleanse their souls" with
deception.

He was especially encouraged that Bonnie had admitted
being frightened by her first sight of Neal and not by seeing
him. He thought that the medical examiner's testimony would
raise serious questions in the jurors' minds about the whole
scenario of the murder.

Now, on Tuesday, January 23, as Bart paced the floor of
a secured room on the east side of the courthouse, smoking
one cigarette after another—a habit he'd picked up in jail—he
was certain that it would be only a matter of hours, if not
minutes, before his innocence would be proclaimed and he
would walk out of the courthouse to the congratulations of
family and friends and go on about his life.

Mitchell Norton had concluded his final argument so late
the day before that the judge had put off final instructions to
the jury until Tuesday morning.

Before sending the jurors out to deliberate at 10:00 A.M.,
Judge Watts had one more thing to say.

"These are not my words. I can't claim credit for them. I
wish I could. Someone far wiser than I first put these words
on paper. I think that he probably summarized in about three
sentences your duties and responsibility. 'The highest aim of
every legal contest is the ascertainment of the truth. Somewhere, somewhere within the facts of every single case the
truth abides.'

"You are sworn jurors with the duty to perform. That duty is to take the evidence as it came to you from that witness stand, to take the law as it has been given to you by the court, sift through the evidence and determine the true facts of the case, apply the law which I've given you to those facts, and thereby render a verdict which will speak the ever lasting and abiding truth about these alleged incidents on the morning of July 25, 1988. You twelve ladies and gentlemen may retire, deliberate, and see how you find in these matters."

Bart had not been impressed by the judge's words and did not believe them.

"Justice is a pretty gray concept," he said later. "The truth didn't matter one damn bit. They didn't care for the truth. What they wanted was facts. Seemed to me it was like one big game of who was going to paint the best picture, but the game had a pretty large pot."

Now, as Bart waited to see who had painted the best picture, who would claim the pot—his life—he kept trying to figure out what the jury was thinking.

His father, who had asked his attorneys what they thought after the evidence was complete, summed it up succinctly for him. "Bart, if they believe those two boys, they're going to find you guilty," Jim said.

Joanne gave him a hard look. "Don't be so pessimistic," she said.

The trial had brought Jim and Joanne together in a public display of harmony and support for their son, but the situation had been strange and strained for both, and as the jury deliberated, the differences between them surfaced.

"Somebody's got to point out the goddamned facts," Jim said.

Joanne was encouraging Bart's hopefulness, but Jim thought it wild, wishful thinking.

"He was fantasizing, grabbing at straws," he said later. "I wanted to bring him back down to earth so that he could face the reality of this thing."

The jury was sent to lunch in a group and returned to continue deliberating. As the afternoon wore on, Bart's nervousness and tension increased. The long deliberation no doubt meant dissension within the jury. That was hopeful in that it meant that at least somebody thought him innocent, discouraging in that it also meant that somebody must think him guilty. His optimism flagged only to the extent that he began talking of a hung jury, which surely would mean the ordeal of another trial.

At five, Bart, his parents, and attorneys were summoned back to the courtroom. The judge had decided to call a halt to deliberations for the day. The agony of waiting would continue into Wednesday. Before leaving for the day, the foreman asked the judge if he would start the next day's session by instructing the jury again in the law on the charges of conspiracy and first-degree burglary. If they were still struggling with conspiracy and burglary, acts which had to occur before the murder, then perhaps there still was hope for acquittal.

After receiving those instructions the next morning, the jury began deliberating again at nine-thirty-seven, and Bart and his parents continued their strained and anxious wait. At twelve-twenty-five, they were called back to court again for the second lunch break since deliberations had begun.

This time the judge had questions for the jury. Had they reached a unanimous verdict on any of the charges? They had, said the foreman. On the charges that had not been decided, was the numerical division the same on all the charges? It was different from the day before, the foreman said.

"Do you feel that you are making some progress?" asked the judge.

"Yes," said the foreman.

This could not be good, Bart's attorneys realized. If the jury had reached a verdict of not guilty on any of the charges, they likely would have quickly voted not guilty on the others as well. But they did not convey this gloomy prospect to Bart.

During his lunch break at the jail, Bart was handed a letter marked "urgent," addressed to him. Bart recognized the name on the return address, a young man he had met in the Beaufort County Jail who claimed that he had gone to high school with Chris, now an inmate at a youthful offenders' institution in Raleigh.

The young man wrote that he had been in the same cell with Chris at the Beaufort County Jail and Chris had told him that Bart knew nothing about the plot to kill his parents, but he might have to place the blame on Bart if things got tough for him.

Bart gave the letter to Sermons, who knew the young man who had sent it as a chronic liar. He'd had dealings with him in other cases. Sermons checked with Keith Mason and discovered that the state would easily be able to refute the letter. If he tried to reopen the case with it, he would end up looking foolish. Sermons told the judge about the letter but offered no motion with it. The letter was accepted as a court's exhibit, ordered sealed by the judge, not to be opened.

At 4:05 P.M., Bart and his parents were again summoned to the courtroom. The jury was coming back.

"I don't even know that they have a verdict," the judge said. "They may simply be coming to ask some question, but assuming that they do have a verdict, let me say this, that I will not tolerate any outburst."

The jury filed in to take their seats at 4:09. Jim Upchurch noticed that none would look at Bart, who sat impassively in his brown tweed sportcoat and brown paisley tie. That, Jim thought, was a very bad sign.

"All right, ladies and gentlemen, and Mr. Foreman in particular, let me ask you this question, and please answer it with just a simple yes-or-no answer, sir. First of all, have you agreed upon your verdicts in this case, sir?"

"Yes."

Had they filled out their verdict forms? They had. The judge asked the bailiff to hand him the forms.

"Members of the jury, I don't know what your verdict forms are. In just a moment I'm going to read them aloud. Following the reading of each, I will ask you a question: Is this your verdict, so say you all? And if you agree you should answer yes. If you did not agree, then you will have a chance to hold your hand up. Everyone understand that? You must answer one way or the other.

"Members of the jury, with regard to File No. 89-CRS-3448, which was a charge relating to the offense alleged to be conspiracy to commit murder, your foreman has returned a verdict which reads as follows: 'We, the jury, unanimously find the defendant James Bartlett Upchurch, III, to be guilty of felonious conspiracy as charged.' Was this your verdict, so say you all?"

Bart's right hand went to his mouth at the word *guilty*. He paled noticeably. His head dropped. Behind him, his mother began sobbing and reached to touch him. Tears welled in Bart's eyes and the judge droned on, charge to charge, each time saying the dreaded word, *guilty*. And each time it was said, Bart's head dropped lower, lower, until it almost rested on his chest. He braced himself and sat upright as his mother reached to hug him. He patted the back of her head with his hand.

When the last charge had been read, that of first-degree murder, Frank Johnston requested that the jurors be polled on that charge. Each answered yes, that was their verdict, each still unwilling to look toward Bart.

As Joanne cried softly and Bart fought back his own tears to regain his composure, the business of the court was briskly carried forth. The attorneys were summoned to the bench for a brief conference. Afterward, the judge explained that the jurors, under North Carolina law, must next ascertain Bart's punishment, life in prison, or death in the gas chamber.

Another hearing would be held before the jurors decided punishment, and a problem had arisen that would prevent them from considering the matter the following day. A psychologist who had examined Bart was on vacation in the Caribbean and could not get back to testify until sometime Thursday. The hearing would have to be put off until Friday, an extra day for Bart and his family to wonder if the jurors would allow him life.

Two extra guards had been assigned to the courtroom this day, and they came close around Bart as he was led from the courtroom to the holding cell, trailed by his family and reporters. His grandmother, Carolyn, made her way to the room and hugged him. "I love you," she told him. A reporter crowded in to tell Bart's family that she was sorry about the outcome.

Later, Joanne would say that this was the most horrible day of her life.

"It's the most helpless I have ever been in my whole life. I'll do anything I can for my kids, I don't care what it is. You always respond to your children's needs. But there was nothing I could do for him. It was the most helpless, uncontrolled feeling. I wanted to hold him. I wanted to hug him. I wanted to see his face. I didn't want him to cry."

The officers allowed her to hug him for a few minutes and she clung to him, unwilling to let go, crying uncontrollably.

"He kept saying, 'Mom, please don't cry. Everything will be all right.'"

But it wouldn't be all right, not ever again, and she knew it.

Finally, the officers stepped in and led Bart away, leaving his family huddled, helpless, watching him go.

Joanne wouldn't leave until she had the clothes that Bart was wearing that day, some little piece of him to hold onto. Jim and Carolyn went with her to the jail to get the clothes, and afterward they walked her to her car, Joanne crying all the way, she and Carolyn holding to one another in support. Carolyn was worried about Joanne facing that long drive home to Virginia alone, but Joanne insisted that she would be all right, that she would compose herself before she got home to the children.

This was Joanne's birthday, but she had put it out of mind. She arrived home to find that Emory, Carrie, and Alex had baked a cake, bought her presents, and inflated balloons.

"I just broke down," she said later.

Jim and his mother drove back to Caswell County that night. Along the way, they stopped at a McDonald's for hamburgers and coffee. While they ate, Carolyn had the strange feeling that everybody was looking at them. Could they have been on the TV news that night, she wondered, or was it just that she felt that everybody who came into contact with them now could sense the shame that had been visited upon her family?

48

THE FIRST WITNESS AT THE sentencing hearing Friday morning was Weldon Slayton, Bart's high school English teacher. Slayton never had been as close to Bart as he had to Neal, or as close as he had been to Emory, Bart's younger brother. It was Emory who had called him the day before and asked him to testify for Bart, and Slayton had made the long drive to Elizabeth City. Wayland Sermons put him on as the first witness so that he still would have time to get back to school for a few classes after testifying.

Slayton told of getting to know Bart through his classes for the gifted and talented.

"Was he a capable student?" Sermons asked.

"Oh, yes, very capable."

"And did he achieve well in your class?"

"Yes."

"Did he ever exhibit any violent or aggressive behavior?"

"Never."

Slayton went on to recite Bart's activities, grades, and accomplishments in school, his school records being entered into evidence.

Sermons also asked him about Dungeons and Dragons. Slayton said that he knew that Bart and several other students played the game during high school.

Mitchell Norton seized on Dungeons and Dragons in his cross-examination.

"Isn't the game set in a medieval time period?"

"In some versions, yes."

"Use of clubs and swords and daggers and things of this nature?"

"Yes."

"And one of the objects of the game is to gain treasure, isn't it?"

"Yes."

"And in the course of pursuing this goal, isn't it true that the characters use swords and weapons to attack and slay either dragons or other people?"

"As far as I know, yes."

"And of course, Mr. Upchurch was a frequent player of the game, was he not?"

"Yes."

"Did you ever hear him referred to as the 'dungeon master'?"

"Well, when students play the game, one is selected as the dungeon master who makes the decisions for the others and directs the game. And he was at times the dungeon master, yes."

"And wouldn't you say then, Mr. Slayton, that the game helps to develop aggressive and violent tendencies?"

"I am not expert on that psychological evaluation, so I don't know."

Next to take the stand was Brad Fisher of Chapel Hill, a

forensic psychologist. He had first examined Bart in November, and had talked with him again the night before, after flying in from his vacation. A Harvard graduate, Fisher had evaluated thousands of people charged with crimes and had testified in criminal trials in forty states.

Fisher said that he had administered several tests to Bart, including tests for intelligence, brain damage, neurological problems, and personality disorders, in addition to interviewing him in jail for several hours about his family and his past.

"I did not find any evidence of what is called psychotic thinking or behavior, which would be a person who is not in touch with reality. I did not find any evidence of neurological brain deficit or organic brain damage. In other words, there's not a brain tumor, brain damage of any sort. There's no major mood disorder, such as manic depression or anything of that sort. So in those major categories—and I think I've covered the primary mood or thinking disorders—he didn't have any."

Neither did he find any violent tendencies or any history of violence prior to the crime or after it, he said. Nor was there any sign of repressed rage or any other psychological problem that might hold down aggression.

His analysis of Bart's method of dealing with his current situation was simple: "At the moment everything is pushed down. He has a lot of denial going on. It made the interview particularly hard both last night and before because he, to some extent, is aware that he will be dealing with this, but the thinking and feelings are powerful to the point that he ensures his survival by not thinking about it. He holds it at bay. He can intellectually talk about it, but he doesn't. There's some other projectoral material that starts speaking to the deep anxiety he has about how this will affect his family and the shame on his family and the like, but his basic procedure at the moment is to keep that at bay. And he is not capable of dealing with it. And so that's what he's doing."

Norton reiterated Fisher's findings on cross-examination.

"Dr. Fisher, as I understand, you found nothing organically wrong with him, no brain tumor, no brain damage?"

"That's correct."

"No psychotic thinking, nothing wrong with him from that standpoint, no brain damage, you said, no psychosis, I think was your answer."

"Right. His intelligence is normal. And he doesn't have what's called mood disorder, manic depression. He does have a lot of depression, but nothing that was qualified—"

Norton cut him off. "Certainly knows the difference between right and wrong?"

"He does."

"He knew it was wrong to kill Lieth Von Stein?"

Johnston objected, and Watts overruled him.

"Didn't he?"

"Yes."

"And he knows that it's wrong to kill, period. He knows that now, knew it then, didn't he?"

"Yes."

Joanne took the stand to tell about Bart being an acolyte, about his close relationship with his brother and sisters, his lack of violent behavior.

"As far as I can tell, he's always been happy, good-natured," she said.

When Joanne had come off the stand, the judge asked the jury to step back to the jury room so that some business could be attended outside their hearing. Sermons wanted to call a witness to which the prosecution objected: Bonnie Von Stein.

During the trial, Bonnie had been staying at the same motel as Jim and his girlfriend, Kathy, and they had chatted several times. During one conversation Bonnie had said something that Jim found of particular interest, and he had told Sermons about it. Sermons had asked Bonnie if she would mind saying the same thing from the stand and she had agreed. The judge wanted to hear what Sermons intended to ask her, as well as her answers, before he allowed her to appear before the jury.

Sermons got right to the point.

"Mrs. Von Stein, is it your desire to see the defendant James Bartlett Upchurch put to death?"

"No."

"You have a general objection to the death penalty, is that correct?"

"Yes."

"I believe you've previously indicated to me that there's a reason. It will not change anything, is that correct?"

"Yes."

"By that, what do you mean?"

"I mean that I just simply don't believe that taking another life could make amends to the loss of Lieth."

"Thank you very much, ma'am."

Norton asked her, "You are opposed to the death penalty under any circumstances?"

"Yes, sir."

"And that's a feeling that you've had for, I take it, for a long time, Mrs. Von Stein."

"Yes."

"Of course, you understand what the law is in the State of North Carolina, do you not?"

"Yes."

"And you understand that those laws have to be obeyed?"

"Yes."

The lawyers argued long and tediously after Bonnie's testimony about whether it should be allowed. In the end, the judge ruled that it would be constitutionally unacceptable to allow the testimony, saying that it would "invite the jury to use passion and emotion" in determining the sentence. Later, Jim thanked Bonnie for her effort. "I thought it took guts," he said.

There would not be time for final arguments and a jury charge on Friday, and Judge Watts recessed court for the weekend, sending the trial into a fifth week.

Mitchell Norton was first to argue before the jury Monday morning.

"What I am about to talk with you about this morning is not a pleasant task. It's not a task that I take lightly. I know that it's not a pleasant task for you. It's a question of law, a question of duty, a question of responsibility. It's a question in some respects of conscience. It's something that has to be done."

He pointed out that there were but two possibilities.

"One is the ultimate punishment of death. The other is life imprisonment, whatever that means. And who knows?"

"Objection," said Sermons.

"Sustained."

The jury would have to choose between aggravating factors and mitigating factors in determining their sentence, Norton reminded them, and he maintained that the aggravating factors were clearly there.

One was that the murder was committed in the course of a burglary. No question of that one, he said. Another was the crime was committed for pecuniary gain.

"Here, again, the evidence is uncontradicted. James Upchurch didn't even know Lieth Von Stein. He entered into this plan for the expectation of money and fast cars and quick fixes and easy living. It wasn't a situation where Von Stein had done anything to him, had wronged him in any way. A cold, calculated, pitiless, conscienceless act for money."

A third aggravating factor was whether the murder was part of a course of conduct of other crimes of violence. The beating of Bonnie was clear evidence of that, Norton said.

"What the evidence on these three factors shows is a cold, calculated, diabolical plan without pity, without conscience, without remorse whatsoever. This was not somebody that came from a slum neighborhood, somebody who was mentally defective, somebody who was poor and never had opportunity, never had a chance in life. Here was a young man, and I say man, 19 years of age, one month shy of 20, in the 97th percentile—he scored higher on his test scores than 97 percent of all the people in the country—smart, intelligent, bright, a student at one of the finest schools in the country, a man with ability, opportunity, a man of promise, not somebody that had to do this. He had been given everything, the opportunity to work like you and I, carry responsibility on his shoulders like you and I. But he doesn't want that. Quick money, easy money, to take it any way he could. That ought to shock the conscience of Pasquotank County. That ought to shock the conscience of the people of North Carolina, because this was not a case of some deprived person—depraved maybe, but not deprived."

Among the mitigating factors that the defense would be arguing would be Bart's age, Norton said.

"Is Lieth Von Stein any less dead because the bat and the knife were wielded by a nineteen-year-old?"

The defense also would be bringing up Dungeons and Dragons, he said.

"I told you from the very beginning that the evidence shows that Dungeons and Dragons didn't cause this. It was a game that helped develop the mindset, got them accustomed to thinking of killing, brought them together, but that's the only connection Dungeons and Dragons has with this case, no matter how people want to look at it."

The jurors, Norton said, were faced with grave responsibility in a time when nobody wants to take any responsibility.

"Over the last twenty years or so, society has become one of excuses, quick fixes on drugs and alcohol, and instant gratification in a me-centered world. Society is pervaded by a lack of responsibility. But I say to you that you ought to hold him responsible for what he did. He made the decision to bring himself here, not you, not I, not Lewis Young, and certainly not Lieth Von Stein and Bonnie Bates Von Stein."

Norton was careful to bring up a subject that he knew the defense would argue strongly: the far lesser penalty that Chris would receive for his role in the murder. But in bringing it up, he distracted attention from it by deftly weaving in the horror that lay at the base of the case, the fear that touched almost everybody in Beaufort County and even caused veteran police officers to lose sleep.

"Yes, Christopher Pritchard is morally responsible, guilty, perhaps, greater than any others because he planned the execution not only of his stepfather, but his own mother. But we are looking at the case of James Upchurch, and when Chris Pritchard was in Raleigh, that right there is the man with the bat in his hand, a knife in his bag, covered in dark clothing head to foot while Lieth Peter Von Stein was asleep in his bed, away from the world and tribulations of what was going on, in his own home just like you or I when you leave this courtroom and go home to wherever you live, whether it's an apartment, a mobile home, or a tent, the most important place on the face of this earth, where you ought to be able to feel safe and secure . . ."

Johnston had objected twice during this speech and been overruled each time.

"And to be awakened in the nighttime by the swish of a bat and the slap of it crushing the skull, and the knife as it came down through the rib cage and penetrated the heart . . ."

Norton kept going with his vivid description over yet another objection from Johnston.

"Yes, Neal Henderson is going to pay a price. Yes, Chris Pritchard is going to pay a price."

But without their testimony, he maintained, "the killer,

the one who had nerve to go in the house and carry out this killing," could have gone free.

Norton kept appealing to the jurors to use their "plain old ordinary everyday common sense" in sentencing Bart to death.

"It's the only way that you can be assured that he won't do it again. I say to you that you are required to do it as a matter of conscience, because it's right.

"The lawyers will tell you, 'Well, it won't bring Lieth back.' They may talk to you about biblical passages and say vengeance is mine, saith the Lord. They may quote to you the Sixth Commandment, 'Thou shalt not kill,' but if they do that, I submit to you that they haven't read far enough, haven't read the passages in the Old Testament, and even in the New Testament, when it comes to talk about the Sixth Commandment, as it was written in the original Greek is, 'Thou shalt not murder,' thou shalt not kill another with malice, with an evil heart. If you do read further, you will see that, not only is the penalty of death enacted by the state, but in biblical terms and in our spiritual existence, it's commanded. The eye for an eye and a tooth for a tooth. But I am not here to ask you to seek vengeance on James Upchurch. It's a question of what we, as a society, are going to tolerate in our community. You are the conscience of the community. Are you strong enough to speak the conscience?"

"Objection," said Johnston.

"Sustained. Don't consider that, members of the jury."

"Look at all the factors, be fair, be impartial, but focus on the case for what it is, what he did, and what we as a society have a right to expect from the people that live among us."

Norton's argument had carried past noon, and the judge declared a recess for lunch.

Wayland Sermons spoke first in Bart's behalf when court resumed at 1:15 P.M.

"Your duty," he told the jurors, "is not as Mr. Norton would have you believe, to put him to death because society requires it. Your duty is to do justice. You are going to have to have your conscience in it. And ask yourself, is it fair for Bart Upchurch to die?"

Sermons pleaded with the jurors to consider Bart's age, his immaturity and impressionability, the drug and alcohol use, the effects of his parents' divorce, the lack of violence in his past, the effect of Dungeons and Dragons.

"From the evidence, you can reasonably infer that this powerful, fantasy role-playing game goes a long way toward explaining how these three intelligent young men would find themselves in such a sinister affair."

Sermons hit hardest on the differences in penalties being faced by Bart and Chris.

" 'The deal.' Those are Mr. Norton's words. He told you he made a deal. Well, you are entitled to consider all the circumstances surrounding this case to decide whether it's just and appropriate that Bart Upchurch be given the death penalty. Is it just and appropriate that Chris Pritchard only face life plus twenty? Is that fair? I contend to you that were it not for Chris Pritchard, we would not be here today. Bart Upchurch would never have done what you have convicted him of. Is it fair for Chris Pritchard to enter into this arrangement December 27, 1989, five days before trial, when he was the one that started this whole mess and is not facing the death penalty? Is that fair?"

"Objection, if Your Honor please," said Norton.

"Overruled."

"You know," Sermons continued, "the biblical passages can probably be interpreted in different ways, but there are two circumstances from the Bible that I would ask you to consider when you consider the fate of Bart Upchurch. And one is that although Cain slay his brother Abel, the Lord did not see fit to punish him by death. He merely banished him for life. And although the Old Testament that Mr. Norton has harped on contained the adage, 'an eye for an eye,' the New Testament contained a much different message. I would ask you to return a verdict which banishes Mr. Upchurch."

Frank Johnston used his turn to touch on a question that was in many minds.

"The thing that impresses me most about this case is when you look back at these three young men in college, very intelligent, you say, 'How, how could this happen?' How do you explain it? How do you take this young man, place him in that house? How do you place him committing this crime?"

Nothing in his background suggested that he would do any such thing, Johnston said.

"There has got to be an explanation. And I don't know what it is. But I will submit to you that the use of drugs, his use of alcohol, playing Dungeons and Dragons, to mention the most obvious, should have a mitigating effect on the question of his life and death because nothing else makes any sense.

"If it's a case of greed, where is all the discussion and the bickering and the fighting afterwards of where is my money, I want a portion of it, because I did the act, I want my money? There's never any mention of money again. Never any question about cars or money or any kind of payment. In fact, the evidence is to the contrary. He got sixty dollars in the Von Stein residence and gave that to Mr. Henderson. So it's not money.

"What effect did their lifestyle have? What does the culmination of using drugs, using alcohol, playing Dungeons and Dragons have upon a young person's mental stability and being? I don't know. But is there any other answer to this unexplainable situation?

"You know, it's strange to me that Mr. Norton says to you that this is not a case of Dungeons and Dragons going wild. And yet, as Mr. Sermons has vividly pointed out, Mr. Norton also says it's a case where Dungeons and Dragons teaches people how to kill and use swords and talk about sorcerers. So obviously Mr. Norton thinks that Dungeons and Dragons had some effect upon these young men. And I think that it did.

"I was thinking yesterday when I was sitting in church about the map that Mr. Norton presented to you in his final argument. He put it up to his face to imply a mask or some type of a cult symbol and suggested to you that it was of some supernatural nature, or divine nature, that the map was not burnt up in the fire. And the fact that the only way that this investigation continued was because they were able to find this map and link Pritchard to it because of the word Lawson, Lawson Road. And as I thought of that in the minister's sermon yesterday on mercy, I could only think that I hope that God's mercy will be with you in your decision."

The judge declared a ten-minute recess, then brought the jurors back and gave them an hour of instructions. Shortly after three-thirty, the jury began its deliberations about Bart's life.

49

WHEN THE JURY HAD NOT
reached a decision by 5 P.M. Monday, Judge Watts sent them
home for the day to begin anew on Tuesday morning.

Bart had been more subdued since his conviction, no
longer hopeful and optimistic. From the moment he was found
guilty, he felt that he also would be sentenced to death. His
lawyers, on the other hand, were more hopeful than they had
been before the verdicts. Clearly the long deliberations on guilt
or innocence were evidence that some jurors had had doubts
about Bart's guilt and they would be less likely to sentence him
to death. Many of the jurors were mothers, and they might be
reluctant to send another mother's child to death.

On Tuesday morning, the jurors asked for renewed instructions on aggravating and mitigating factors, and the judge
read them before sending the jury out again at nine-forty-five.
Bart was returned to the holding cell, but this time his parents
were not allowed to remain with him because other prisoners
were there, awaiting trial in another courtroom.

To keep matters moving, Judge Watts wanted to go forth
with the sentencing hearings of Neal and Chris while the jurors
were deliberating Bart's fate, although he announced that he
would not sentence either until a decision had been reached
on Bart. Chris's attorney was on his way from Greensboro and
would not arrive until after noon, but Neal and his attorneys,
Chris McLendon and Michael Paul, were present, as were
Neal's mother, Ann, his aunt and uncle, and several witnesses
who were going to testify in Neal's behalf, and the judge
allowed them to proceed.

The first witness was Weldon Slayton. Questioned by Chris
McLendon, Slayton told of how he had first met Neal when he
was asked to help create a program for him when Neal was in
fifth grade. He went into detail about his abilities and academic
accomplishments.

"He was like a sponge," Slayton said. "He simply absorbed
information. He did not always work as hard as he could have,

but he was certainly the most gifted student I've ever dealt with."

Slayton told how Neal always had been thrown with older students, how they had looked at him as an oddity, how he had lived in an isolated spot with no playmates, how he had been stunted socially as a result.

Asked about Neal's father, Slayton recalled how Neal had attempted to establish a relationship with him late in high school and had spent a few weeks with him during the summer before his last year at Bartlett Yancey High.

"The one thing that sticks in my mind is that his father did not attend his high school graduation," Slayton said. "And he said something about, or at least it was related to me by another teacher, that he had said that it was okay, that I was there, so it made it better, but he wished his father had been there."

Asked about Neal's maturity, Slayton said, "Intellectually, Neal has always been mature. And I believe that was one of the problems that he experienced. He knew how bright he was. He knew how adults looked at him and other students looked at him. And he felt he had to react as an adult in a very organized and logical way. Socially and emotionally, he was always out of place. He often was laughed at, usually not in a mean or cruel way, but because he was odd in the groups he was with."

McLendon asked what he thought of Neal's future when Neal went off to N.C. State.

"Well, I was concerned about his maturity. But I felt if he would apply himself and get into his studies, I had every anticipation of him getting his Ph.D. and one day I would be saying, I taught that genius, that person that did thus and so, that is with NASA, or that discovered this, or that is teaching somewhere and making a big name. I had no question that he would do wonderful things."

As Slayton spoke those words, Neal sat at the defense table, head down, clearly embarrassed and shamed.

Doc Sawyer, one of Neal's former band teachers, testified to Neal's honesty. Neal handled all the money raised for the band's programs, Sawyer said, thousands of dollars. "And we were never a penny short."

Michael Paul called John Taylor and Lewis Young as

witnesses to say that Neal had come forward on his own without promise of reward.

Judge Watts had some questions of his own for John Taylor.

"Did he ever tell you why he made a statement, offer any explanation for his purpose in talking to you?"

"He never come right out and stated he had done this for such and such a reason. I got the impression it was a conscience clearing effort on his part."

"Did you get the impression that he had analyzed the situation and decided if I don't come forward now somebody else might and it might be better for me to do it now even though no promises are made?"

"Somewhat."

"In other words, cut your losses so to speak?"

"Well, we never came right out and discussed that. Any opinions I have of how he felt was stuff I picked up just by being around him."

Lewis Young backed up Taylor's impressions of Neal's motives. "I got strong impressions that this had been weighing heavily on him for months, for the whole year. And I also got a strong impression that he was tired of it."

Judge Watts also had questions for Young. In reading Young's investigative notes, he said, he saw many instances in which Neal's answers to the detectives' questions had been vague.

"I found him to be very vague in areas concerning certain details that night," Young said. One area was the bat, he said, another the car. "In talking to him, I immediately realized that I was talking to someone of superior intelligence, but at the same time I felt maybe he did not have the greatest common sense, that the mundane, the ordinary, the everyday did not seem to register with him. I noticed that he had problems with dates, and with things that maybe I would have thought I would remember that he didn't."

"It was not your impression that he was at all deceiving or being intentionally vague?"

"No, sir. I think when he would throw out a date or some fact that he was trying to be helpful."

If Neal hadn't come forward, would the case still be unsolved? the judge asked.

"I think it very easily could be still in the ongoing stage."

Two other witnesses would speak for Neal, his lawyers told the judge, but they would not be available until the next day. The hearing would resume then, the judge ruled. But one other matter had to be attended. With the hearing begun, Neal's bond was no longer effective. Despite appeals from Neal's lawyers, Judge Watts ordered Neal taken into custody.

"If ever he was going to try to flee," the judge said, "this would be the time to do it, because it's all been prologue until now. We are near about at the final curtain of this drama, tragic tale that it is."

Neal was led away by a Beaufort County bailiff, who would take him back to Washington for the night so that he would not be in the same jail with Bart.

50

THE STATE HAD STIPULATED that the testimony of six character witnesses could be summed up by Chris's attorney from Washington, Jim Vosburgh, so that the witnesses would not have to make the long drive to Elizabeth City to be questioned.

Those witnesses included a young woman from Washington who had dated Chris during the summer of 1988. Chris always deported himself as a gentleman, she said, and he never used drugs or alcohol in her presence. Another of the witnesses was Carl Smith, an industrial arts teacher at Washington High School, who, according to Vosburgh, "was influential in helping keep Chris on a pretty fairly straight path while he was in high school." Still another was Chris's close friend and fellow Dungeons and Dragons player Jonathan Wagner. All said that Chris was of good character when they knew him, and that his involvement in the murder was foreign to everything they had known about him.

With that out of the way, Chris's Greensboro attorney, Bill Osteen, a silver-haired man with a patrician face and an athletic build, called Dr. Billy W. Royal to the stand. Dr. Royal was a forensic psychiatrist who had a private practice in Chapel Hill and also worked at the Dorothea Dix Hospital for mental patients in Raleigh. A big, gray-bearded man with unruly hair, he had testified in hundreds of trials.

He had first met Chris Pritchard in August 1989, shortly after Chris was released from jail on bond, he said, as a result of a call from Osteen.

"You had a conference with Chris that day," Royal said, "and he was very disturbed. You were very concerned about his mental stability."

The situation was an emergency, Royal said, and he agreed to see Chris immediately. Chris was driven to Chapel Hill, where the doctor found him to be "acutely depressed" and "suicidal" and had him admitted to the psychiatric wing of the University of North Carolina Hospital that night.

Since that time, Royal said, he'd had more than thirty-five interviews with Chris, had done complete psychological testing of him, and had talked on several occasions with Chris's mother and sister.

Asked about his diagnoses, Royal said, "One was depression with suicidal ideation intermittent, meaning that at times he's been quite depressed and had suicidal thoughts with lots of plans at different times of how he would carry that out.

"Interestingly, early, these involved a great deal of use of an automobile. Chris is a person that's an automobile addict in a sense—drives a lot and a lot of his activities and fantasies have to do with those. And he had thoughts of going up in the mountains and having an accident and killing himself by automobile, or there were several variations on that. He at one point, when I thought he was quite disturbed and distressed, had possession of a gun that was part of his thinking. And his mother was able to object to the possession of that.

"Another diagnosis is chronic anxiety, which has been a problem, I think, since his youth, of just never being able to relax, always looking behind to see if something were gaining on him, never quite being comfortable in whatever circumstances he's in."

A third diagnosis, the doctor said, was drug and alcohol abuse. After he got to college, Chris's use of drugs and alcohol accelerated until it was out of control.

On the day that Chris was admitted to the hospital, he had

told his lawyers for the first time about his involvement in his stepfather's murder. He also told the doctor that night. But one important person had not been told: his mother.

"Was there a concern of Chris as to how his mother was going to accept this situation, or what her reaction was going to be?" Osteen asked.

"That was probably almost the foremost concern."

"At that time, his attorney, and in this case it was I, told you that Chris could not discuss what actually had happened with his mother, didn't I?"

"Yes."

"Were you having some problem dealing with the mother and the son on a basis of that Catch-22 situation?"

"Absolutely. My initial impression was that the suicide and the depression could not be resolved without resolution of the issue between he and his mother, resolution that allowed him to tell her what he had done, which was something that he wanted to do. I thought that ought to occur during hospitalization so that the issue could be dealt with in a therapeutic setting for him and for his mother."

"Now, you even explained that, I believe, to his lawyers, that you thought that ought to be done at that time?"

"That's correct."

"And what response did you get from his lawyers?"

"His lawyers did not feel that should be done if there was any way around that."

"Did his lawyer explain to you why that was necessary at that time not to be done?"

"Yes."

"Why was that?"

"Because the fact that if he had told his mother and it came to trial, that she would have to relate that and that, as I understood the contract that you had with his mother, that she had told you to do what you could to protect Chris."

"Now, Dr. Royal, let's move back. What is there in Chris's background that may shed some light on where he sits today?"

Two basic things determine how everybody develops, the doctor said: genetics and environment.

"Chris had several things going on with his background in terms of environment. His mother was married and had two children within a few years. Her husband was younger than she, and I gather, immature in some ways. When Chris was less than three, the father reportedly abandoned the family. Mrs. Pritchard was working trying to support the family, and the information that I've gotten from her is that economic conditions were quite distressful. Stressful, I guess, in terms of requiring assistance from her family not only in the financial economy, but in looking after the kids.

"The abandonment by the father, which resulted in little contact for a number of years, according to all information, affected Chris very much in terms of anxieties, behaviors. And in my view, it's been an insult to his psyche that he has never compensated for, because you can't go back and compensate for something like that at that age. He has therefore been insecure, anxious, depressed throughout his life.

"And his psyche has always been engaged in an attempt to deal with that, to deny that, to cover that over. I think as a result of that, he developed certain personality activities, enough so that I have made a diagnosis of borderline personality disorder, because I think he's got a significant number of personality problems. Even so, he was able to survive, cope with some difficulties until he went away to school.

"Unfortunately, at that time his stepfather's parents and uncle all became ill and died in a sequential period over thirteen months that removed the stepfather and, in some degree, his mother from contact with him, for the support of the relationship. As young people do going away to college—and this is not uncommon regardless of any other consideration—they get in a different environment, and Chris did not do well academically. He got involved gradually in drugs, alcohol. Significantly, he became more involved with a game that he was familiar with, Dungeons and Dragons, and became obsessed with that so that he and this group then began to play this game, at times almost consistently neglecting schoolwork and other activities."

Osteen interrupted to ask Royal what he knew about Dungeons and Dragons.

"Well, it has received notoriety in the last few years. There has been a great deal in the press about it. It's a game that involves skill, daring, a lot of intellectual kind of things, adventure, and there have been a number of tragedies with people that are involved in this game. Not infrequently meaning some people get hurt or killed through the use of the game or playing the game."

420

"Dr. Royal, specifically referring to Chris's participation in the game, are you familiar with the effect that in the playing of Dungeons and Dragons, people fantasize and create by allusion to themselves their own characteristics for the characters they play?"

"Yes. In my understanding, there are certain base kinds of games. They also have a dragon master who can create the game, assign people to have different characters, which are at times quite bizarre. And these people carry out certain activities. And they often involve aggression, war, things of that nature."

Combined with drugs and alcohol, the game became "a kind of modus operandi" for Chris and his friends, Dr. Royal said. "And to some degree this group became a family that was together a lot and involved a lot with each other. And that this game, with the alcohol and drugs, created for Chris a situation in which there was a separation from life, from his ordinary functioning, from what's going on in reality, into this fantasy world. And in my view then, the plans that were developed and carried out regarding Chris's stepfather were a direct result of this kind of activity coupled with the past history of all of these people that were involved."

Did he see any significance in the testimony that Chris was going to take his inheritance and buy a house where he and his friends could live and take drugs and play all the Dungeons and Dragons that they wanted?

"Chris was trying to find a solution that he was not going to be abandoned, that he was going to live a life that he didn't have to depend on other people in a sense, that he was not going to be hurt. And that he would create a nirvana where you wouldn't have to tolerate those potentials."

"Dr. Royal, I don't believe we've talked about this before, so forgive me for asking you this question. But do you have any knowledge of the results that are obtained by a person from the use of such drugs as LSD?"

"Well, all of these affect your brain chemicals and your thinking, how you perceive, how you look at things. Some people become only psychotic, have hallucinations, delusions. They alter the brain. They alter your thinking. If you use them very long, they permanently make alterations in how you function, how you perceive, so that people lose their initial personality totally and become another person, because of chronic brain damage from the drug.

"I might point out one other thing that we haven't mentioned regarding Chris and activities that have to do with his psychological state. It has to do with the fact that this so-called plan to get immediate money and satisfaction, that not long prior to this, Chris and his mother and father had a discussion regarding the wills the family had written. He, in fact, observed them writing wills, being involved in that, and asked them why they were doing that. His mother discussed with him what was in the will, and that he basically would not receive any benefit, even with their death, until he was age thirty-five, fifteen years from now. In his state of mind preparing for this activity, those conversations were totally ignored, totally repressed. He had no concept because, obviously, the other plans to utilize this money, as they were discussing at the time, were not possible, which he well knew. But psychologically that got totally erased."

Could anything be done to help Chris in the future?

"Chris, throughout his life, has developed a lifestyle of denial, of compartmentalizing things, pigeonholing things, and not dealing with them. Otherwise, he would become acutely anxious, acutely depressed. He's had periods of acute depression when he's got close to his feelings with dealing with this issue. He's also been aware and discussed that he is knowledgeable about his psychological makeup of not dealing with his real feelings and has requested that he wants therapy so that he can learn how to deal with himself so that his feelings and his intellect are on the same wavelength, which has not been the case.

"In attempts to deal with how his mother would accept his behaviors and how she would deal with what he did, this brought up some of the suicidal ideation that at some point, if his mother did not accept this, that he had plans that he would go commit suicide. Part of his activity during the time that I saw him, which created some anxiety on my part, and I think on your part when I relayed this to you, was that Chris would tell other people about his participation and his responsibility."

This was something that had amazed John Taylor and Lewis Young when they learned about it. While Chris was in the hospital for two and a half weeks, he told three young women patients about his part in the murder. Later, he told his closest friend in Winston-Salem and the young woman from Appalachian State University whom he had been dating.

Yet not one of these people had gone to the police to report that Chris had told them about his role in the murder.

"He did this," Dr. Royal now said, "as an attempt to see how they would accept him, as if somehow if they accepted him, maybe his mother would accept him."

Royal went on to say that he had talked to both Chris and his mother after Chris had finally told his mother of his role on December 27, the day the plea agreement was worked out.

"Chris was greatly relieved that he was able to tell not only his mother but his sister and other people that were important to him," Royal said. "He described it as having a great weight lifted off his shoulders. And he felt much better about himself that he could function."

Had therapy helped Chris so far? Osteen asked.

"It's been beneficial," Royal said. In addition to the therapy, Chris was taking some medication and had returned to work to keep himself busy. "I think a primary cause of his feeling better has been his being able to discuss this and resolve this with his family, primarily his mother. I think he needs continued treatment. He's got a lot that needs to be worked on."

Could Chris ultimately contribute to society?

"Yes. Chris and I have talked about this a lot. I think he's a good candidate and has motivation to continue his education, which I think he can do in prison. He's got a lot of interests. I think he's got some insight into what's going on with him."

On cross-examination, Mitchell Norton ascertained that Chris had no organic brain damage, that he knew the difference between right and wrong, both now and at the time the murder was committed.

"Nothing unusual about anyone in his situation charged with murder being depressed or being anxious, was there, Dr. Royal?"

"No."

The judge wanted to know if Chris's LSD use had caused him to lose his former personality.

"I did not come to find any basis that he had."

The judge declared a fifteen-minute recess after Royal's testimony, and when it was over, Osteen called to the stand Chris's grandmother, Polly Bates, a tiny, white-haired, sweet-faced woman whose husband had been killed in a woodcutting accident only a few weeks earlier. Now she was about to lose her grandson to prison.

"Were you close to Chris when he was growing up?" Osteen asked.

"Oh, yes. He spent a lot of time at the house with me and his grandfather, he and Angela both, while his mother worked and other times too."

"Did you and Chris's grandfather help Chris as he was growing up after his father left?"

"Yes, sir. We kept him while his mother worked, and we fed them, and sometimes her job would take her out of town, and we would keep them with us overnight. And we just loved them like they were our own children."

"Mrs. Bates, I assume that up until this incident occurred, everything was fine with you and Chris, that it was a grandson-grandmother relationship?"

"Yes, we've always been close."

"Knowing what the situation is with Chris now, how do you feel about your relationship with him now and what you expect it to be while he is in prison?"

"Well, that hasn't changed. We love Chris. He's a big part of our life and we'll stand behind him one hundred percent and do anything we can to help him."

"And you will stand behind him with your love as a grandmother?"

"Yes, I will. I want to see our family reunited some day."

Just as Mrs. Bates was leaving the stand, a bailiff came into the courtroom and caught Judge Watts's attention.

"Gentlemen, let me ask you to step aside, please," the judge said to Osteen, Vosburgh, and Chris. "The jury is ready."

51

BART WAS LED BACK INTO the courtroom by sheriff's deputies. His parents quickly took seats behind him at the defense table. The judge called the attorneys to the bench as the somber jurors filed back in.

Wayland Sermons cast an eye toward the jurors as they began to take their seats. Throughout the trial he had been watching one woman for reactions, his bellwether for what the jury might be thinking. His heart sank when he saw that she was looking at the floor and wouldn't even glance toward Bart and his family. Jim Upchurch saw that two of the women jurors appeared to have been crying and he knew that his hope that Bart's life might be spared would not be fulfilled.

When the attorneys had gone back to their stations, the judge turned to the foreman.

"Have you agreed upon your verdict as to the issues and recommendation as to punishment, sir?"

"Yes, sir."

The forms had been completed, the foreman said, and he handed them to the bailiff, who delivered them to the judge.

The judge told the jury that he would read the forms on each of the four issues and after each ask if that was their verdict, as he had done the week before. Each must answer yes or raise a hand to disagree.

On issue number one, whether any aggravating factor had been found, the judge intoned, "Your foreman has returned a verdict of yes. Was this your verdict, so say you all?" The jury agreed that all three aggravating factors were present.

On issue number two, mitigating factors, the jury agreed that Bart's age, his drug and alcohol usage, his Dungeons and Dragons playing, and the fact that he had two fellow conspirators all were mitigating factors. His high intelligence, his parents' divorce, his relationship with his family, his church experience, his lack of violent tendencies before and after the murder, and his adjustment to incarceration were found not to be mitigating circumstances.

On the crucial third issue, whether the mitigating factors were insufficient to outweigh the aggravating factors, the vote was yes.

Bart's hand again went to his mouth but in a pensive manner, not in the way he had grabbed his mouth when the guilty verdict was announced, as if he were holding back a scream.

On the fourth issue, whether the aggravating circumstances were sufficient for imposition of the death penalty, the answer again was yes.

"With regard to your recommendation as to punishment,

your foreman has returned a verdict which reads as follows," the judge said. " 'We the jury unanimously recommend that the defendant, James Bartlett Upchurch III, be sentenced to death.' Was this your verdict, so say you all?"

All agreed, but some women on the jury seemed to be holding back tears.

Fighting back her own tears, Joanne reached for her son, who seemed unsurprised by the verdict. "I love you," she said. "I love you, too," he replied. "I've got to go check on the girls," she said, and suddenly she was gone, hurriedly leaving the courtroom. Her daughters were home alone and she was afraid that reporters might call the house. She didn't want them learning about their brother's fate that way.

As the judge had read the final verdict, Wayland Sermons' head had sunk to the defense table, his forehead resting on his hands. He looked grief-stricken when he raised his head a few moments later and turned to Bart. "I'm sorry," he said.

By law, Judge Watts was required to poll the jury. Each rose when his or her name was called to answer yes, their verdict was death.

"Members of the jury," the judge said, "I am not permitted by law to comment upon your verdict. I do not presume to do so. I am permitted, however, to thank you for your consideration. And I'm satisfied it was careful and prayerful consideration that you gave this case. This is not a pleasant matter for anyone. It's not a pleasant matter for you, for me, for anyone in this courtroom, but we appreciate your conscientiousness in this matter."

The judge proposed to delay sentencing another day, but Johnston and Sermons requested that he go ahead with it, despite the late hour.

After the jury had gone, Sermons filed several motions for dismissal, which were quickly denied. Keith Mason submitted copies of Bart's criminal record for consideration. Lawyers for both sides took up several other sentencing matters before Judge Watts turned to Bart.

"Prior to imposing punishment against you, Mr. Upchurch, I'm required to give you a chance to speak in your own behalf, sir. You are not required to say anything. I can't compel you to say anything. I will not hold it against you certainly if you elect not to say anything. Neither will I hold it against you if you elect to say something. It's your decision. At this time I should be happy to hear from you."

"Yes, Your Honor," Bart said. He had been thinking for a long time about what he would do and say should this moment come, but he had mentioned it to nobody.

"All right, sir, if you will stand, I will be happy to hear anything you want to tell me about this matter."

"Well, first off," Bart said, sticking his hands in his pockets, "I want to thank my attorneys. They have done a remarkable job. And that's got my utmost respect. I want to thank you, Your Honor. You obviously have gone a long ways to keep this trial from becoming any more of a circus than it already is. You know, I respect the trouble that the jury has gone through to deliver their verdict. However, I am appalled and shocked at their verdict.

"I find it utterly amazing that the testimony of two confessed murderers would be enough to convict anybody to death. I am forced to believe that I am merely being convicted simply by the assumption of guilt by association. I think the state's withholding Mr. Henderson's statement has substantially impaired our ability to prepare a defense. Forty-eight hours' notice is simply not enough time to prepare to cross-examine somebody.

"I am innocent. You know, it may be that nobody will believe me, or will ever believe me now, but due to the burden that has been imposed upon my family by this trial and due to the fact that I don't believe that Lieth Von Stein's life was another person's for the taking, I do not believe that my life is another person's for the taking.

"I intend to take my own life by fasting. I am not going to eat. My life is not somebody else's to take. I am an innocent man. And maybe by doing this, I remove some of the burden from my family. Even if I got off of Death Row, the rest of my life in prison is not something I want to face up to. I am choosing to take my life in this manner to prove that I am not doing this out of depression or despair.

"It's just a decision I am making in lieu of the horrible things I've seen done to my family and friends over this. I think that this has been a terrible miscarriage of justice. And if justice is surely blind, I think that Mr. Henderson and Mr. Pritchard gave her a set of loaded scales in this one. I would hope that maybe the state would, or somebody would, at least honor my request and not hook me up to an IV and force-feed me to keep me alive until such time as the state sees fit to kill me. I am not a cow to be fattened for slaughter. I am innocent. And I would like to die innocent with as much honor and dignity as I can scrape together, Your Honor."

"Thank you, sir," said the judge.

Later, Bart said that he felt a sense of release and satisfaction as he sat down after making his statement. He had thrown the dice and lost, but he would allow no one else to take him out of the adventure.

"I didn't want to be a toy of the justice system," he said. "I just didn't want to play the game anymore, that's what it boiled down to."

On the charge of assault against Bonnie, Judge Watts gave Bart twenty years, on the larceny charge six years more, on the burglary an additional fifteen years.

"Stand up, Mr. Upchurch," the judge ordered, and Bart complied.

"Beaufort County File No. 89-CRS-3348, entitled State of North Carolina vs. James Bartlett Upchurch III, present is James B. Upchurch III, having been convicted of murder in the first degree by unanimous verdict of the jury duly returned at the January 24, 1990, session of the Superior Court of Pasquotank County, North Carolina, and the jury having this day unanimously recommended the punishment of death, it is therefore ordered, adjudged, and decreed that James Bartlett Upchurch III be and he is hereby sentenced to death by the administration of lethal gas, unless otherwise elected, pursuant to North Carolina General Statute 15-187.

"And it is further ordered that the sheriff of Beaufort County, North Carolina, in whose custody the defendant is now, is to forthwith deliver the said prisoner James Bartlett Upchurch III to the warden of the state's penitentiary at Raleigh, North Carolina, where the said warden on the sixth day of April, the year of our Lord, 1990, shall cause the said prisoner James Bartlett Upchurch III to be put to death as by law provided, and may God have mercy on your soul. He's in your custody, Mr. Sheriff. You gentlemen want to give notice of appeal?"

"Yes, sir," said Frank Johnston.

When the court had recessed, sheriff's deputies moved to

surround Bart and escorted him back to the holding cell. His father remained to talk with the attorneys.

"I thought you did a good job," he told them.

Sermons looked defeated and distraught when a reporter approached and asked for a comment. "You ought to ask Mitchell Norton how it feels to kill one and let one live," Sermons told him.

Jim was allowed into the holding cell where Bart had been taken. "Well, you certainly got the press's attention," he told his son. "I could see them all scurrying out the door."

Bart smiled.

"Did you mean it?" Jim asked.

"I don't know if I did or not."

"You might get hungry."

"Yeah," Bart agreed with another little smile. "I probably will."

"I was proud of how you handled yourself out there," Jim said.

Both were surprised that despite the outcome, they felt a sense of relief. At least it was over now. The torture of waiting for the jury's decision, the intense anxiety and tension were past. They were able to chat with ease.

Bart said that he was not surprised. He had expected the decision. Jim told his son not to worry, the chances of him being put to death were slim; this was just the beginning of a long process. He should maintain hope.

"And you'll be in Raleigh. At least I'll be closer to you. I can see you more often."

Jim left for the jail to pick up Bart's belongings while the lawyers remained to talk to Bart about the appeals process. As he walked to his car, Jim saw Bonnie and her Washington lawyer, James Vosburgh, standing in the parking lot. Both came over and told him they were sorry about the outcome. For a few moments, they chatted about how the case had similarities to some of the Dungeons and Dragons scenarios. They all wished one another well, and Jim got into his car to drive to the jail, then begin the long ride back to Caswell County, alone with his thoughts.

52

C HRIS'S SENTENCING HEAR-
ing resumed when court opened Thursday morning with a
large group of Chris's family and friends present. The first
witness was his sister, Angela, now a student at Virginia
Intermont College in Bristol, where she was fulfilling her love
for horseback riding.

Angela agreed that the family story as told in the courtroom
was as she saw it.

"For a long time after this tragic event, I believe you and
your mother believed that Chris had nothing to do with it,"
Bill Osteen said to her.

"Yes, sir."

"And there did come a time when Chris sat down and
talked to you about it, is that correct?"

"Yes, sir."

"Since that time, you obviously have had time to think
about your relationship with Chris. And you know he's going
to prison. Just tell the court what you expect your relationship
to be with your brother from this day forward."

"I expect to stay as close as we ever were, keep in contact
with letters or however. And I expect to be there to pick him
up when he gets out."

Angela said that she thought that Chris could contribute
to society and she would help him in every way possible.

"As a result of what has happened," Osteen said, "do you
have any fear of Chris?"

"No fear at all."

After the questioning of her daughter, Bonnie walked to
the stand one final time. Osteen began by asking if her view
of Chris's early background differed from that presented by
the psychiatrist the day before.

"No. Dr. Royal basically had the overall picture pretty well
covered. I struggled very hard to maintain the home that we
were living in when my husband and I separated so that the
children wouldn't have to be uprooted and moved out. And
we suffered in other ways by not having, I guess, balanced

430

meals on a lot of occasions. I just tried to maintain Chris's and Angela's environment as well as I could under the circumstances and continue with my job so that we could move forward at some point in our lives.

"My sisters kept the children on many occasions. My mother and father kept Chris and Angela a lot. At the time I was traveling some for the company. And on many occasions I would be out of town for as much as a week at a time. And during that period they helped a great deal with the children."

Osteen brought her next to the events on the morning of July 25.

"Was it your opinion that no one in your family had anything to do with the tragedy of that night?"

"Absolutely."

After the murder, Bonnie said, she had been greatly concerned about Chris and Angela. "Both of them were in somewhat of a panic as to how are we going to live. Do we need to quit school and go out and get a job? Things of that nature."

To quell that concern, Bonnie said, she began working on a new estate plan. She also set up two fifty-thousand-dollar certificates of deposit, one jointly in her name and Chris's, the other in her name and Angela's, "so that if anything happened to me, they could have fifty percent of that CD without having to wait for it to go through an estate or anything of that nature. And at any point, they could simply walk into the bank and withdraw that."

Did either take advantage of that? Osteen asked.

"No."

"Mrs. Von Stein, sometime after Chris was released from custody on bond, you became aware of the fact that things may not be exactly as you thought they were, is that an accurate statement?"

"Yes."

"But for a period of time, you did not know from anybody what the exact facts were in this case, did you?"

"I did not."

Soon after his release on bond, Bonnie said, Chris had gone to Greensboro to see Osteen and she got a call that evening telling her that Chris had been hospitalized in Chapel Hill. When she went to see Chris at the hospital he had seemed less tense. Dr. Royal told her that Chris wanted to talk to her but that that couldn't be allowed. Osteen had asked her not to discuss anything about the murder with Chris after that, and they had avoided the subject until Chris confessed in December.

"Did you notice any change in Chris after he was able to tell you what the facts of the case were?"

"Oh, yes. Complete relief. He just had a totally different attitude, like he didn't have anything to hide anymore."

Bonnie said that to her knowledge Chris had not used any drugs since he was released from jail and had drunk only an occasional beer in her presence.

"Mrs. Von Stein, you have heard what Chris had to say about this matter, and of course you were a victim of the matter. You are a mother and a victim. Would you, please, relate to the court what your feeling is about Chris presently, as he is getting ready to serve his time for what he's done."

"Chris indicated to me in every way and every action and everything that he says that he is looking forward to serving his time to pay for the things that he really can't explain to me, the things that he did. It's totally foreign to everything that he was brought up to believe in. It's totally foreign to his personality. Chris has always been the kind of person—he's a lot like me in that respect—that instead of stepping on a cricket in the house, he'll pick it up and carry it outside and turn it loose. And he's always been like that. And that's one of the reasons that I was absolutely sure that Chris had no involvement in this when the investigation started going in that direction."

"Mrs. Von Stein, do you remember meeting at my office where Chris was present, you were present, Mr. Vosburgh and the other Bill Osteen and I were present to discuss how we evaluated the chances in this case, if there was to be a trial, or what Chris should do."

"Yes."

"And after the attorneys had discussed the pros and cons of the case, do you recall what Chris said he wanted to do in the matter?"

"Yes. He said that he wanted you to move forward with trying to arrange a plea bargain agreement."

"And did he say that he felt that he was ready and should be punished for that matter?"

"Yes."

"Mrs. Von Stein, during the time that Chris is going to be serving time, what plans do you have about Chris?"

"I plan to do everything that I can working within the system to see if he can get whatever psychiatric and drug rehabilitation help that he might need. And I am going to stand by and be there for my son. I will love him as I've always loved him. I don't agree with and I don't approve of the things that happened, but it can't be undone. And I know in my heart that without the drug situation it never could have happened."

"What's your feeling about Chris's future?"

"Well, if he's out in my lifetime, I will do everything that I can to help him get on his feet and start a new life for himself. He has my support. I will also make arrangements that if he's not out during my lifetime those things will still be possible for him when he does come out of the prison system."

"Thank you. That's all the questions I have."

About Bonnie's absolute certainty that Chris hadn't been involved before his confession, Mitchell Norton asked if that had been based on Chris denying involvement.

"Yes."

"So you trusted your son?"

"Yes."

"Placed a lot of confidence in what he said and what he did?"

"Yes. And I couldn't be shown otherwise."

"And you also said that Lieth was proud of Chris?"

"Yes."

"So Lieth himself trusted and placed a lot of confidence in Chris?"

"Yes."

"I take it that you were not at all aware of his drug use during the summer of 1988?"

"No, not at that time. In early July, Lieth and I began to suspect that there could be some drugs involved in Chris's life."

"But you never saw any direct evidence of that?"

"Never."

"Even on Friday, the 22nd of July, when Chris came home from State, and also on Saturday, was there any indication at all that he was on drugs?"

"I didn't pick up anything. I don't know what a person on drugs acts like. Chris was always in a hurry, you know, to do whatever he was going to do. He was always in a rush."

"So you didn't notice anything unusual or different at all about him when he was home that weekend?"

"I did not."

"Of course, you know now that at that time he was planning your death and the death of your husband?"

"Yes."

Judge Watts had some questions of his own. Was it before Chris confessed to her on December 27 that she was present for the discussion between Chris and his lawyers about Chris's options? That was earlier, Bonnie said.

"I could not help Chris make a decision in any way because I didn't know what he was dealing with or what the circumstances were. And it's something that I had to pass on and leave entirely up to him."

Still, it was clear that Bonnie had to have realized soon after Chris's arrest that he had some involvement in the murder.

The judge also was concerned about another matter, the trust that had been set up by Lieth for Angela and Chris. He questioned Bonnie closely about it, recalling it being six hundred thousand dollars.

"It was at that time," Bonnie said. "It's grown considerably since then."

It was still at the same bank, she said, and it was irrevocable. Bonnie could draw from it as she saw fit, but it would pass to Chris and Angela only upon her death. The judge's purpose behind the questions was quickly made clear.

"It's a general principle of law of North Carolina that one can't gain in the form of a testamentary matter as a result of a death that one takes part in." He wondered if the bank had been notified. And Bonnie said that the bank was aware of Chris's involvement.

"I am the executrix on the estate," she said.

"You have counsel who are assisting you with that?"

"Yes."

Even if Chris could not receive the trust directly upon his mother's death, she still could remove the money, however, and after that, nothing would prevent Chris from eventually inheriting from the estate of his mother, who was a millionaire as a result of her husband's death. Eventually, Chris still could profit handsomely from his stepfather's murder.

The lawyers now were left to argue about Chris's sentence.

"It's been stated in court that the considerations of taking the pleas on Mr. Pritchard and Mr. Henderson were done capriciously and arbitrarily," Mitchell Norton noted in his argument. "It's not so. If Your Honor please, there was a lot of deliberation and careful consultation with us, the members of the investigative team, members of my own staff. We felt that it was the right thing to do, but it does not diminish, I don't think, from the brutality of the case.

"Chris Pritchard, I think, perhaps from a moral standpoint, is more guilty than any of the other two. I would ask the court to look at that maximum sentence."

"The argument of one person being more guilty than another, I don't think that's proper," Vosburgh told the judge during his turn. "And I don't think it should be considered. These three are equally guilty."

During his argument, Bill Osteen shed a little more light on the meeting in which Chris and his lawyers talked about his prospects with his mother present. As the state's case stood at the time, with only Neal as a witness against Chris and Bart, Osteen said, the lawyers had told Chris that he and Bart had a good chance of being acquitted by a jury. They also told him, Osteen said, that if he chose to go to trial, they doubted that he "could walk out of our office that day, or after a trial in which he may be found not guilty, and ever feel good about himself again. And his lawyers would not have felt good about it. And Chris sat there and said to us, 'I participated and I understand I am responsible for it, and I don't want to walk out on that matter.' And we attempted to work out something with the state.

"There are a few things that I want to call to your attention that I thought were bizarre in this case. Chris Pritchard had a record in his community of being an honorable person as he grew up. And it's just almost inconceivable as to where things could have gone wrong as they did. But it's not a unique situation, when coupled, as Dr. Royal indicated the other day, with his youth and the difficulties he encountered then."

Osteen said that he recently had been reading about "New Age" thinking, "which has moved away from some of the things that many people were taught in their youth and clung to, still cling to, as being the thing that perhaps makes people act in a better manner." He quoted from an article in the Los Angeles *Times* that called Dungeons and Dragons "a doorway to the occult."

"And it goes on to discuss Dungeons and Dragons further, saying that it's laced with references to magic, occult wisdom, violence, and power. What we are saying is that the hallucinogenic drugs, the Dungeons and Dragons game, the mind-altering games, is an attempt to harness a segment of society that's never had much religion to create an alternate religious view. In my view . . . the more fascinated a person gets with it, the more likely it is that they can become mentally imbalanced by the process itself. I submit that what we see there is essentially what we see in Chris Pritchard's case.

"I am also sure there are people who can play Dungeons and Dragons and never have any lasting results. There are people who unfortunately can use drugs and not have any lasting results. And there are people who can grow up in deprived homes and do wonderfully well. But once in a while those categories come together and create what has been created here.

"We don't contend that this man is incapable mentally of a defense, or was incapable mentally at the time this dastardly act happened, but he was changed.

"And through it all," Osteen said, gesturing toward Bonnie, "there is a mother who has gone through pure hell not knowing what was out there, but knowing something was, from the belief that my son was not involved to the understanding that something is not as I believe it is, to fully understanding. And a mother who sits and says I am going to help him. I am going to give him my love and I am going to work with him. And a sister who says, I will work with him and I love him and I will stay with him.

"And you know from this man's standpoint to hear people say that after what he's done has got to have a powerful effect. Dr. Royal says this man can come back sometime and serve, and probably Chris will be of benefit to society. I hope Your Honor will take those matters into consideration."

Judge Watts asked Chris if he had anything to say.

"Yes, sir," Chris said, standing. "I would like to speak. Thank you, Your Honor. I just want to say, first of all, that I believe Mr. Norton was extremely fair in allowing me to take this plea bargain agreement. I know that I am guilty and I do deserve to spend time in prison. And I think it was fair of him to allow me to have that opportunity.

"I want to speak with my family because I really haven't had a chance. You don't know the type of mental anguish that I have gone through," he said, as tears flowed. "As Dr. Royal has said, and it's generally true, I seem to deny my feelings. I don't know why, but I do. And they build up like a pressure in a cookpot. And they overflow as right now." His voice continued, choked. "I just want you to know that I love all of you. And I thank you all for being here and supporting me.

"I honestly feel that I do not deserve this. But the Lord has given me the strength to stand here today and do what I know is right. And I ask that he give you all the strength and support in the coming years, for I will not be here to do that myself.

"I can't hold anything against James Upchurch or Neal Henderson for what they did. The Lord asked me to forgive them and I have. Just as he has asked me to forgive myself, which I have not quite been able to do just yet. That's all that I have to say, thank you."

After Chris's emotional outpouring, the judge declared a ten-minute recess.

When court resumed, Judge Watts again noted the difficulty of the situation in which Chris's lawyers found themselves. "But if there's anybody in this courtroom that I personally have the deepest sympathy for, it is Bonnie Von Stein, a lady who lost her husband, the light of her life, a lady who is about to lose her son, at least in a physical sense of separation. I hope, Mrs. Von Stein, based upon what Dr. Royal has done, what you believe, that you may have in fact regained a son that had been lost previously. And my heart goes out to you, ma'am."

The judge recalled a hearing attended by Chris's lawyers in December, during which he had found a Bible lying open on the judge's bench.

"I had not placed it there. I don't know who did. But as you gentlemen were getting ready to speak, I glanced down and the book was open to Proverbs 28:24. I made a note of it at that time that I've carried with me since.

" 'Whoso robbeth his father or his mother and sayeth it is not transgression, the same is the company of the destroyer.' That's old law, but that's still good law."

Judge Watts also recalled that when Bart was arrested, he

437

was carrying the collected works of Shakespeare in his backpack.

"King Lear," he said. "Act I, Scene IV: 'How sharper than a serpent's tooth it is to have a thankless child.'

"I believe that you are now remorseful, Mr. Pritchard. I believe if you had it to do over again, if you could go back and undo that which you have wronged, you would do so, but you can't. And you must pay the consequences of those events which you put into motion. The genesis was Christopher Pritchard. The midwife may have been Dungeons and Dragons and drugs, and I would not argue with that, but the genesis was Christopher Pritchard. How sharper than a serpent's tooth.

"I don't speak to the plea arrangement. That was made. I don't criticize or condone that which has been done by either the defendant or by the state. I have to work with that which he gave me. That's all I can do."

That said, he sentenced Chris to twenty years for the assault on his mother, to life for the murder of his stepfather. With good behavior, Chris would be eligible for parole in nineteen years.

His family gathered around to give him hugs before sheriff's deputies manacled him and led him to a car to be taken to the Polk Youth Center in Raleigh. Chris left carrying a small white Bible he had been given as a child.

After her son was taken away, Bonnie, who had declined to answer questions from the media throughout the trial, handed reporters a written statement. She agreed to read it on camera for a TV reporter, but only if her face were obscured.

"The events of the past eighteen months have been tragic for me and my family," she read. "We have endured sorrows beyond any I have known before. I loved my husband Lieth and loved our quiet life together. On the night he died I almost died from wounds I suffered during the assault. I do not understand why I survived.

"Now my son Chris and two of his companions have been sentenced for participating in this tragedy. I love Chris as I am sure Neal's and James's parents love them. I hope and pray that these three young men can someday find peace within themselves.

"We now face the difficult talk of picking up our lives and trying to move forward. With the continuing support of our family and friends we will succeed."

53

ONLY ONE ACT REMAINED
in the drama that was the Von Stein murder case: the sentencing
of Neal.

That hearing resumed twenty minutes after Chris had
embraced his family and been taken away to be transported to
a youth center in Raleigh for eventual assignment to a state
prison.

Neal's lawyers called two more witnesses. The first was
Charles R. Sechrist, owner of three Wendy's restaurants, including the one in Danville where Neal had worked after being
released from jail. Neal had been promoted to assistant manager, he said, and was a good and trusted employee.

"He worked, strived real hard, real dedicated. He always
would come in to work early, stayed late, whatever it took. He
was always ambitious to learn more and be a better manager
for us. He's the type of person that I've always looked for in a
good manager."

He would not hesitate to hire Neal again, he said.

Ron Amos, another of Neal's band teachers from high
school, testified to his trustworthiness.

"I found him to be somebody I could place responsibility
on and have it carried out. It didn't matter what I needed
done, I could call on Neal. Neal was probably one of only four
students in all my tenure of teaching of fifteen years that I
allowed to have a key to my personal office so that he could
keep records and help me."

Asked whether Neal was an active or passive person, Amos
said, "Neal was active with things that he was motivated to do.
He was active with the band. You couldn't keep him out of the
band room. He was always there. He was active with a few
other things, maybe the chess club, some other clubs. But in
terms of aggression, he was a passive-type person. If he saw
trouble brewing, Neal would come to me and say, 'I think you
better check into this, Mr. Amos.' "

Asked if he wanted to be heard about the sentencing,

Mitchell Norton sounded more like a defense attorney than a prosecutor, noting that if not for Neal, this case might still be open. "He's done a terrible thing," Norton said. "He's going to have to be punished for that. But the court has seen his testimony in the trial. Frankly, I thought Neal made a good witness. And he was always ready at any time that we called or had some question."

Neal's attorneys, Michael Paul and Chris McLendon, made impassioned appeals for a short sentence and an alternative to prison. They pointed to Neal's vulnerability, his remorse, his assistance to the state, his tremendous potential.

"He is a young man who has a conscience, who wanted to do the right thing," said Paul. "This is a tragedy when you have a young man who has so much potential."

If Neal hadn't confessed, Chris McLendon said, nobody knows what might have happened later with Chris and Bart.

"But with the patterns, heavy LSD use, had they gotten away with a tragic murder like this, it can only set the scene for a real history of some potential violence. And with the brain power involved here, there may have been other crimes that may never have been solved. So, Judge, thank God for Neal Henderson's conscience. Thank God for his morality.

"To be quite honest with you, Your Honor, I am not used to having a client who tells me that he's fond of the district attorney. But in this case, I asked him one day what he thought of Mr. Norton. And his answer was that he thought he was a real good guy. And that, Your Honor, I think somewhat typifies this young man.

"He's got a bright future. Obviously, he can't do some things. He will never be a lawyer, probably never be a doctor. There's a lot of things this plea will keep him from doing. But he's going to be all right. He's going to do fine in life. He's going to finish school. He's going to co-own a Wendy's, or he's going to be with NASA. He's going to be in a role to help society. I know that. I feel that. I think that the district attorneys and the law enforcement people do, too."

"Do you have anything you want to say?" Judge Watts asked Neal when his attorney had finished.

"Your Honor," Neal said, looking sheepish and humbled, "I have heard a lot of my friends, my family, tell me they still have faith in me even after what I did. All I want is a chance to prove to them they are right."

"Mr. McLendon said you have an awful lot to offer this world," the judge said after Neal sat back down. "Indeed you do. You also have an awful lot to live down."

He went on to commend the law enforcement officers who did not let this case die, who kept looking for a solution.

"They did not quit. They were still out there digging, probing, still doing their jobs. And after panning in that stream and finding a lot of sand, they came upon the gold nugget that made their case, because without this young man, there was no case. And I absolutely agree with that, gentlemen.

"Quite to the contrary of what Mr. Upchurch said in this courtroom yesterday afternoon, Mr. Henderson, there was no motive for you to be untruthful in that initial statement. And there was absolutely no reason on the face of this earth that I can figure out for you to unload on James Upchurch, except that you told the truth.

"I am equally convinced that he, indeed, did invade the Von Stein house in the middle of the night, using the key that Chris supplied, and that he did indeed perform those terribly brutal and savage acts.

"But each, in the eyes of the law of North Carolina, is guilty. Your culpability at law is as great as the murderer's. Your moral culpability may be considered by some to be less. It was not your plan. You were not the killer. And if that makes you less culpable in a moral sense, then so be it.

"But you were an active participant. You could have stopped it at any time. And you didn't.

"So yours was more than a minor role. But yours was also the brightest star. And that's your tragedy.

"As nice as it would be to roll back the clock and see that little fifth-grader with the shiny face—and I can see it there—my duty to society won't allow me. But you can continue to grow, mature, and develop even in the circumstances in which you are about to be placed. And I hope you will do so. I pray you will do so."

For the assault on Bonnie, Judge Watts sentenced Neal to six years. For the murder of Lieth, he gave a sentence of forty years, the two sentences to run concurrently. Neal would be eligible for parole in five years.

Since noon, Neal had been expectantly watching the doors at the back of the courtroom. The night before, he had talked by telephone with his father in Virginia. His father had told him that he would be there for the sentencing, arriving after the lunch break. But he never came. Once again his father had not been there when he needed him. Neal was not surprised, but the disappointment and hurt were no less for it.

After bidding farewell to his mother and other family members, Neal was led, manacled, to a waiting sheriff's car, where he paused to answer a TV reporter's question.

"I still have a future," he said with a pained little smile. "It'll take a while, but I still have one."

EPILOGUE

CENTRAL PRISON IS A squat, tan fortress of sharp angles surrounded by high fences topped with razor wire on Western Boulevard near downtown Raleigh, just down the street from the campus of N.C. State University. In the predawn hours of January, 31, 1990, Beaufort County Sheriff Nelson Sheppard delivered Bart Upchurch to its sterile confines, so close to the inviting haunts of Bart's recent past, now impossibly out of sight and reach.

Bart was taken to the prison hospital, where he slept for a couple of hours on a wooden bench before being put into a tiny cell in the psychiatric ward that had a mattress on the floor and dung smears on the walls. If he caused trouble, he was told, he would be put into a straitjacket. He caused no trouble but refused food, and on the following day, after testing and processing, he was taken to Death Row, where he became the eighty-sixth resident. He was put in Block 15, an area of stainless steel and concrete, with fifteen other prisoners. His cell contained a bunk, a stainless-steel sink and toilet, a shelf and storage cabinet. It opened onto a dayroom with stainless-steel tables and stools and a black-and-white TV, where all on the block were free to venture from 8 A.M. until 10:30 P.M.

On the day Bart arrived on Death Row, an assistant warden came to talk with him. He offered hopeful words. The legal struggle for Bart's life was just beginning, he pointed out. It would take a long time and Bart should not give up so quickly. He also brought a pointed message. If Bart persisted in his fast for a week, prison officials would have no option but to return him to the psychiatric ward, strap him to a gurney, keep him docile with Thorazine, and feed him intravenously. The State of North Carolina would not allow him to starve.

When reporters called to inquire that day, they were told by prison officials that Bart had passed through the breakfast line. Later, he said that wasn't true. He did not eat until the third day, he said, when he went to the mess hall with the others on his block for lunch. Chicken livers were on the menu that day. He hated chicken livers, but he ate them anyway.

443

Bart knew that by eating he was giving victory to the legal system that he despised, but by that time he felt that he had won a bigger, inner victory of his own.

His decision to choose death on his own terms was genuine, he said later, and the very act of making it made it possible for him to live on death row.

"Accepting death that way, not out of depression or guilt or remorse, is freeing," he said. "All the toughest decisions I can ever make have been made. Everybody lives their lives always wondering if they can accept their own deaths. I already made that decision. I made that decision when I was twenty-one years old. When the time comes, I know I can deal with it. I can accept it.

"The realization comes to everybody on Death Row that one way or another, you'll get out of here. They'll either carry you out in a body bag, or you'll walk out and eventually be a free man. Like it or not, one way or another, I'm going to have to make it through to that point, whatever it is. It's a matter of sitting here and weathering the storm."

On the day after Bart arrived at Central Prison, Neal and Chris were delivered separately to Polk Youth Center on the western edge of Raleigh for processing. They were supposed to be kept apart but they ended up in bunks next to each other by mistake.

"Chris said, 'I don't hold anything against you for my arrest, that was all my own doing,'" Neal recalled later. "He wanted to get over it and be friends if that was possible. I wanted to believe him."

They didn't talk about the case, Neal said, because they didn't want other inmates to know why they were there. When the mistake was discovered, Chris was put into a segregation cell. Later, Neal got a note passed from Chris saying that he wished Neal would get himself moved quickly to a permanent camp so that he could get out of solitary.

Neal was eventually assigned to a prison camp at Lillington in the southeastern part of the state. Chris was sent to a camp at Asheville in the mountains, a three-hour drive from his mother's house in Winston-Salem.

Weldon Slayton was a dedicated Pentecostal Christian, although he never made an issue of it and never tried to force his religious views on others, especially his students. After testifying at Neal's sentencing hearing, he drove back to Caswell County praying that Bart's life would be spared. He arrived at school after classes had ended for the day and encountered Bill Bush, another teacher who had been close to Bart, who told him of the death sentence. Feeling numb, Slayton drove to his small country house, arriving to find the phone ringing. Another teacher was on the line, calling to ask if he'd heard the verdict. After that call, he took the receiver off the hook and went to bed, seeking relief from his sorrow and depression in sleep.

A week later, he wrote to Bart, trying to encourage him, telling him that he still cared for him, that he was still his friend, that he was praying for him. He let him know that he always had found comfort, hope, and assurance in his religious faith, implying that Bart might want to explore that for himself. Bart did not reply. The letter angered him because he thought that Slayton assumed his guilt.

Bart was right about that. Slayton did not think him innocent. It seemed clear to him that either Bart or Neal had killed Lieth Von Stein. That being the case, it had to be Bart. Neal would not have the nerve or the physical strength and dexterity to do it, Slayton thought. Neal was too much a wimp. And Slayton had never doubted Bart's nerve.

What he couldn't understand was how either of them could have gotten into this situation. It was so senseless that he simply couldn't fathom it. The more he thought about it, the more improbable and insane it seemed.

When Bart and Neal were his students, Slayton would have bet his life that neither ever would have become involved in such a heinous crime. How had he misjudged them so?

That question had caused him to doubt his effectiveness as a teacher. He always had struggled to instill values in his students, a moral sense and purpose. It troubled him deeply that so many of them seemed to value money, cars, popularity, fads, even games, over anything truly meaningful.

"Our whole society offers so little to young people in the way of anchors to hold onto," he said. "We're just telling them that there's no rhyme or reason to anything. No wonder they cling to magic."

Only the influence of the magic and moral baselessness of Dungeons and Dragons could offer any explanation to Slayton of how Bart and Neal could have become so embroiled in evil that they could commit murder. But how could that be more

445

powerful than the years-long ministrations of a moral and loving teacher?

For the first time, Slayton could feel stirrings within himself of something he always had fought to keep out: cynicism. Did he ever truly know his students? Could he really make a difference in their lives? Could he ever trust them?

It was, of course, Neal more than Bart who caused those cynical feelings, Neal, the student to whom he'd allowed himself to become closest, the brightest promise he'd ever known. He wanted to believe that it was a stricken conscience that had caused Neal to tell the police, but he never had known Neal to respond to any situation in any but an intellectual manner. In a situation in which he felt threatened, Slayton knew, Neal always would see the logical and reasonable way out and take it. It bothered him that Neal had waited so long to confess, and it made him wary, even when Neal wrote from the youth center in Raleigh to tell him, "You'll be interested to know that I am studying the Bible."

In the future he would be cautious, but he would not turn his back on Neal or Bart.

"I still love them," he said months after they had gone to prison. "I don't make any excuses for them."

Still, Slayton was touched when on Father's Day, Neal sent him a card and poems he had written. Later, he went to visit Neal with Neal's mother. And he was proud when Neal started taking college courses through a prison program, maintaining a perfect grade-point average, and tutoring other prisoners.

Strangely, though, it was to Bart, who always kept his distance, and who now was not responding to him at all, to whom Slayton found himself most drawn.

"I believe with all my heart that James is hurting and scared, terrified and wounded beyond anything I can understand," Slayton said. "I still believe there is that frightened child down in that being somewhere who wants so much for someone to love him. The only way he can deal with all that has happened is to keep up that bravura front.

"I have a very difficult time visualizing this child that I knew being executed. The thing I keep wondering is what's going on in his head? I have this terrible urge to help him, to somehow touch his mind and heart, to help him find some kind of peace. Of course, he would say that he doesn't need any peace, that I've just been duped into believing these people who have persecuted him."

Yet, at Christmas, after Slayton sent Bart a card, Bart wrote back, saying there were things that needed to be made right between them, asking if Slayton would like to be added to his visitor list.

Slayton responded promptly and positively, but by the spring of 1991, Bart still hadn't added his name to the visitor list.

Bart's trial greatly disturbed his grandmother, Carolyn. "I wanted to believe with all my heart and soul that Bart didn't have any part in it, that what he said was so," she said later, "but I was just horrified at what I was hearing at the trial."

After Bart was found guilty and sentenced to death, she found herself staying in her big gray house most of the time, unable to face her friends, unable to join her regular group for bridge.

"You spend your day wondering how it happened and why it happened and then you cry," she said.

Over and over she recalled the sweet moments of Bart's childhood: the concern he had shown when she seriously burned herself popping corn for him and Kenyatta, his loving response when she tended him in sickness.

"I loved him," she said, starting to cry. "We love him now. We don't love what he does. We don't love his problems. We love him. To me, something about him has always caught my heart. There's a vulnerability about Bart, a little boy in there, a gentle little fellow who has done some terrible things. We've died a thousand deaths about this. It's everybody's horror. I think of it as a family horror, and we can't do a thing about it. We'll have to live with it the rest of our lives."

Months after he arrived in prison, Neal still had trouble understanding the chain of events that brought him there, still had trouble accepting the reality of what had happened.

"Murder isn't part of anything I understand," he said. "Even after being involved in it, it doesn't seem like something that really happens. It happened. I can't change that it happened. If I keep trying to deny that it happened, I'll just go crazy. But I don't feel like a murderer. I don't feel like I helped kill a man. I feel awful that a man was killed and I could have stopped it. Maybe I should feel more remorse for helping kill a man, but I just don't see that I should feel badly for helping kill a man when I didn't think a man would be killed."

Did the harsh reality of prison make him regret talking to the police?

He smiled.

"I have to admit, some days I think I'm a total nut for doing what I did. But no, I can sleep now. I can face my mother and smile and know I'm not holding any terrible secret back. My friends, my family know all about me and they still love me. That makes it all worthwhile, no matter what happens."

After Neal arrived at prison, Kenyatta wrote to him, apologizing for the way she had treated him in the months after he got out of jail following his confession, enclosing a photo of herself. The letter got sent to several places before reaching Neal, and he was late responding.

"Ah, lass," he wrote, "hearing from you 'tis good for my soul."

He would be delighted to keep in touch, he said, and would like her to visit sometime, perhaps in the summer.

But he did not add her to his visitor list and did not answer later letters. Finally, Kenyatta went to Neal's mother to ask her help in arranging a visit, and the two adversaries for Neal's attentions went together to visit him at Christmas.

Joanne got angry at the cards that came from friends and family after Bart's conviction.

"Why don't they just go get a sympathy card?" she said when the "thinking of you" cards began to arrive.

Of course, Hallmark didn't make cards of condolence for mothers of sons who had been sent to Death Row, and Joanne knew that people were well-intentioned and simply didn't know how else to respond to such a situation.

For Joanne, what had happened to Bart was worse than death. Death at least was final. A death sentence was torment, death and sorrow dragged out interminably, unbearably.

"We all feel helpless now," she said. "We feel guilty sitting here watching TV, or drinking a beer, or walking on the beach and knowing that Bart can't do that. To know that Bart may never put his feet under my table again . . ."

448

She began to cry, unable to finish the sentence.

"Christmas and Thanksgiving his chair is there empty. I think of the Christmas decorations I made for all the kids. They always loved putting their own ornaments on the tree. Bart's not ever going to get to do that again, to be part of that. He's not ever going to get to take them and put them on his own tree with his own children."

While Joanne had questions about her failures with Bart ("I can't help but think there's something I didn't do, something I should have done differently, or could have done. I guess every parent would feel that way, but they can't understand how I feel"), Jim was agonizing about his own guilt in the months after Bart was sent to death row.

He kept going back over the years, trying to figure out what had gone wrong and when, asking himself what he had done or not done, said or not said, that might have made a difference in his son's life.

"At some time, there was a turning point," he said. "Was there an opening where I could have reached through and got him? Where did I lose him? I feel like there was some point that I lost him.

"Why he's done the things he's done, I don't know if I'll ever get a good answer. But I feel responsible that I didn't reach him, that I didn't try harder to get to him.

"I think I just closed my eyes to things I should have been concerned about. I can see now that there were warning signs. Now, with twenty-twenty hindsight, I feel like there were needs I didn't meet. Whether I could have reached him or not, I don't know. Bart retreats back into himself and it's hard to get through to him. But I have these nagging questions that I can't shake loose. I didn't have a father either. This father-son relationship, I didn't have any experience to go back to."

Wayland Sermons had been so upset by Bart's death sentence that he told Judge Watts he didn't want to handle Bart's case on appeal. The judge did not want the overworked appellate defender's office to have to deal with so complex a case and asked several prominent lawyers in the state to consider taking it. All declined. When Judge Watts called Sermons to ask him to reconsider, Sermons reluctantly accepted.

Only a few weeks later, Sermons was heartened by a five-four decision of the U.S. Supreme Court in the case of a North Carolina man charged with killing a sheriff's deputy. The court ruled that state law made it too difficult for jurors to consider mitigating factors in capital cases and granted the man a new sentencing hearing. The ruling meant that almost all Death Row inmates would get new sentencing hearings when that time came in their appeals processes, and Sermons was certain that included Bart. Later in the year, a new murder trial and Sermons's inexperience as an appeals lawyer caused him to withdraw from conducting Bart's appeals, but he still intended to represent Bart at the new sentencing hearing when it was ordered.

On April 6, 1990, the date originally set for Bart's execution, Sermons visited him to talk about the case. Bart arrived at the visitor cubicle wearing small, round John-Lennon-style sunglasses, ironically, the same type of glasses that Lieth Von Stein wore in his long-haired, pot-smoking college days, although Bart couldn't have known that. He had bought the glasses from another inmate.

"Helps me not see so much," he said. "The less I see of this place, the better."

In the spring of 1991, a teacher at Bartlett-Yancey High School sent a videotape to John Taylor. During his investigation, Taylor had shown the teacher the green army knapsack found on the back porch of the Von Stein house, hoping that she could identify it as Bart's, but the teacher couldn't remember the kind of book bag Bart had carried in high school. However, while watching a videotape that she had made in one of her classes while Bart was a senior, she realized that Bart was in it—and she saw something she thought that Taylor might find interesting. On Bart's desktop was his book bag: a green army knapsack.

In his first months on Death Row, Bart often tried to think back to what he was doing on the same day a year earlier when he was free on the streets outside the prison walls. His first anniversary on the block caught him by surprise. He saw the big stock car race at Daytona on TV and remembered that he'd watched it in this same place the year before.

Much had changed in that time. He had become resigned

to his existence, miserable though it was. Weathering the storm. He read a lot. He was keeping a journal. He had begun writing a novel. He still fiercely maintained his innocence, and he did not like to speculate about what might happen to him, but his prospects for a new sentencing hearing gave him hope.

"I like to think that maybe I'll get off Death Row and spend fifteen or twenty years in prison and get out," he said. "All it is is hope. You can only hope for the best and expect the worst."

All of his friends from his earlier days in Raleigh had drifted away. He didn't hear from any of them anymore. Hank had returned to Wisconsin to be with his mother, who was dying of cancer.

Bart had one new friend, a rock station DJ who'd become intrigued by him and visited regularly. But his most frequent visitor was his father.

Jim had sold the farm where he had been so happy in Caswell County and bought an antebellum house down the street from his mother in Milton that he and his girlfriend, Kathy, were restoring. He'd been transferred back to Raleigh in his job and worked only a short distance from the prison.

He enjoyed his visits with his son and Bart looked forward to them, too. They never discussed the case or Bart's situation.

"I'm not a preacher or a counselor," Jim said. "I'm just his dad. We talk about things. I think I understand Bart better than I did before. I feel closer to him, I don't know why. In some ways, I feel like I'm one of his only friends. He needs me and I'm there."